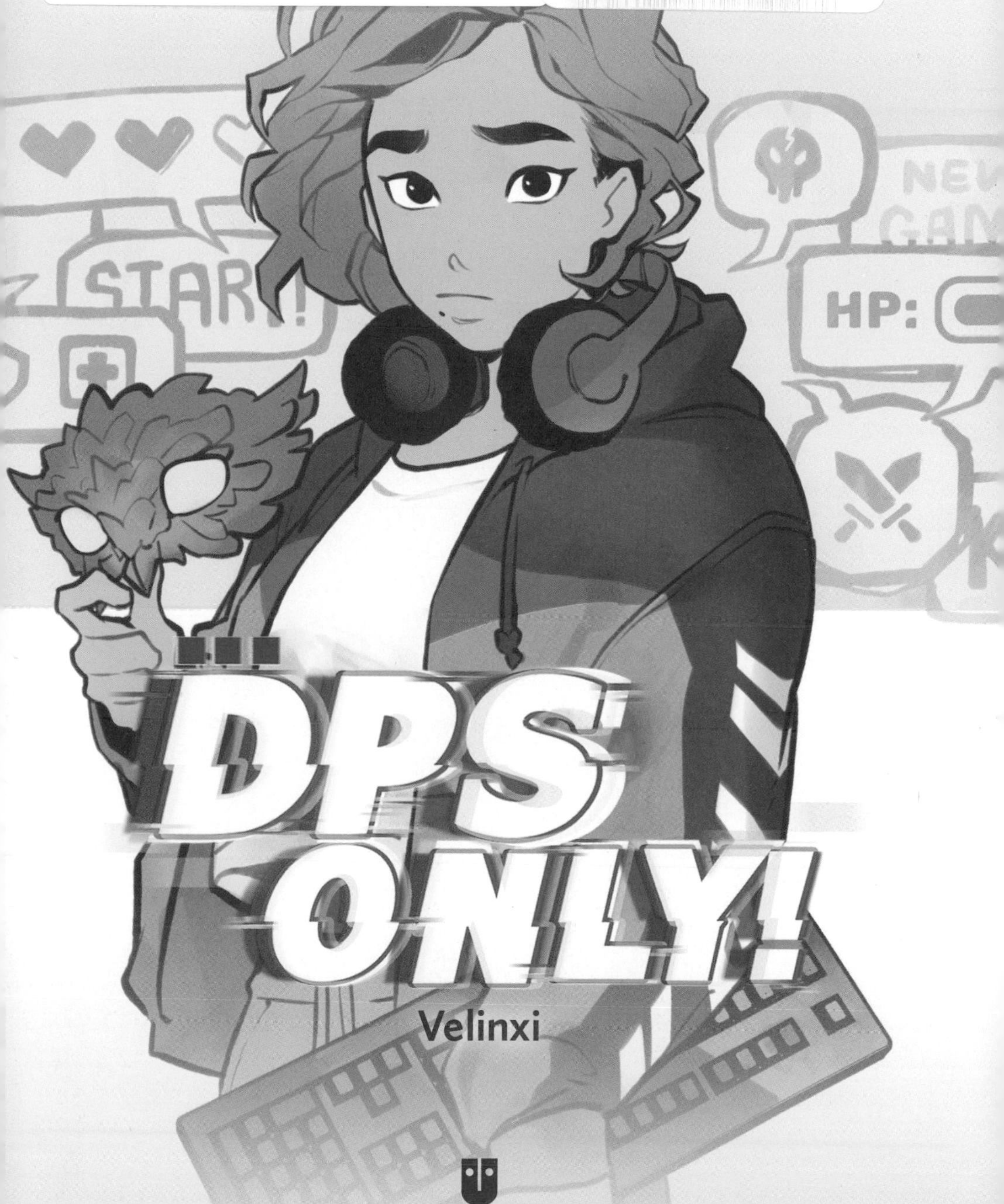
START!
HP:
NEW GAM

DPS ONLY!

Velinxi

Andrews McMeel PUBLISHING®

DPS Only! created by Xiao Tong "Velinxi" Kong

Andrews McMeel Publishing
a division of Andrews McMeel Universal
1130 Walnut Street, Kansas City, Missouri 64106

www.andrewsmcmeel.com

22 23 24 25 26 TEN 10 9 8 7 6 5 4 3 2 1

ISBN: 978-1-5248-7649-4

Library of Congress Control Number: 2022938110

Book Editor: Betty Wong
Book Designer: Sierra S. Stanton
Production Editor: Dave Shaw
Production Manager: Tamara Haus

Studio Tapas
Colorist: Dojo Gubser
Colorist Assistant: Selena Ahmed
Letterer: Claire Alacapa
Editor: Gabrielle Luu
Editor-in-Chief: Jamie S. Rich

ATTENTION: SCHOOLS AND BUSINESSES

Andrews McMeel books are available at quantity discounts with bulk purchase for educational, business, or sales promotional use. For information, please e-mail the Andrews McMeel Publishing Special Sales Department: specialsales@amuniversal.com.

CONTENTS

CHAPTER 1: IN THE CROWD

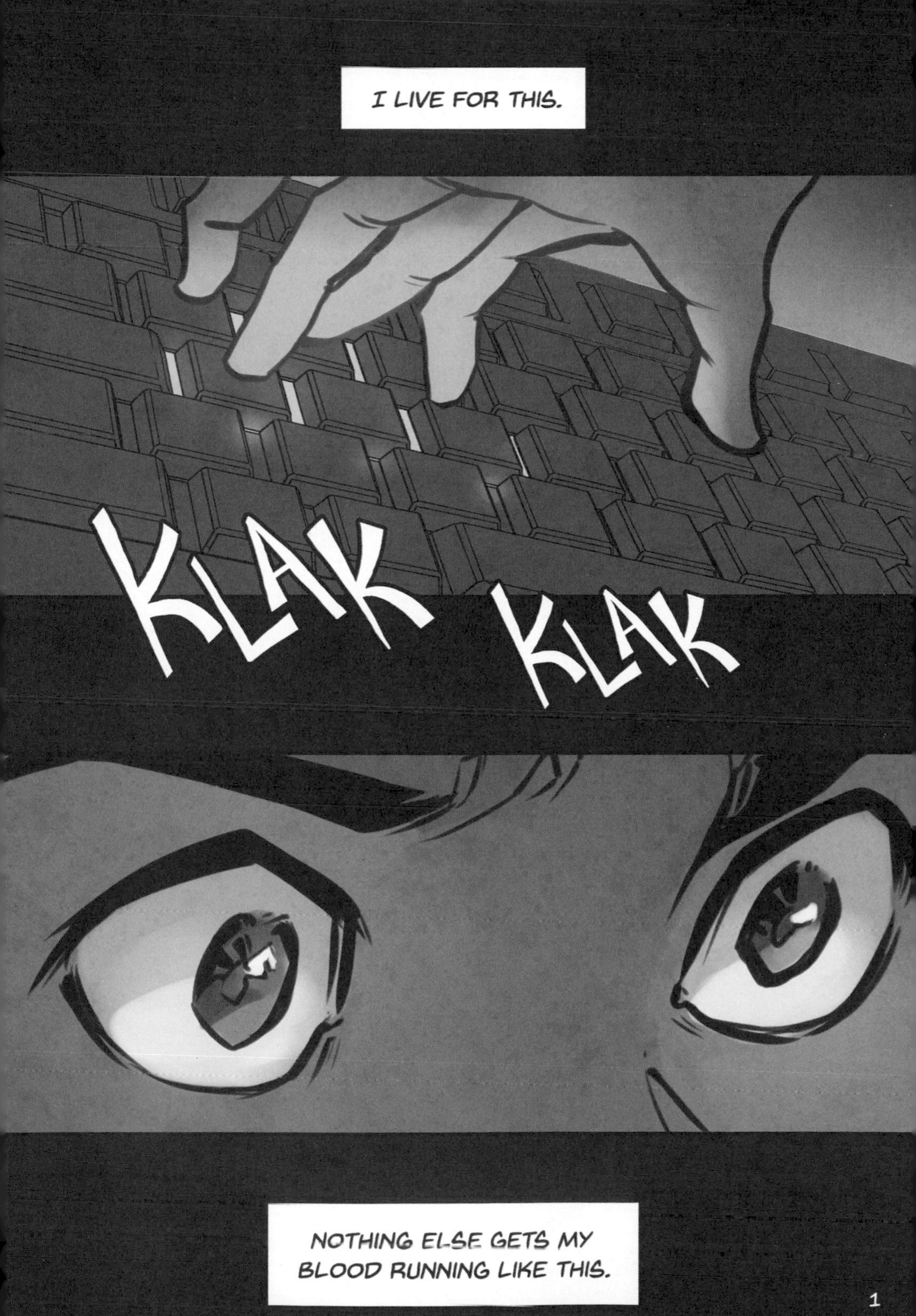
I LIVE FOR THIS.
KLAK KLAK
NOTHING ELSE GETS MY BLOOD RUNNING LIKE THIS.

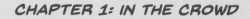

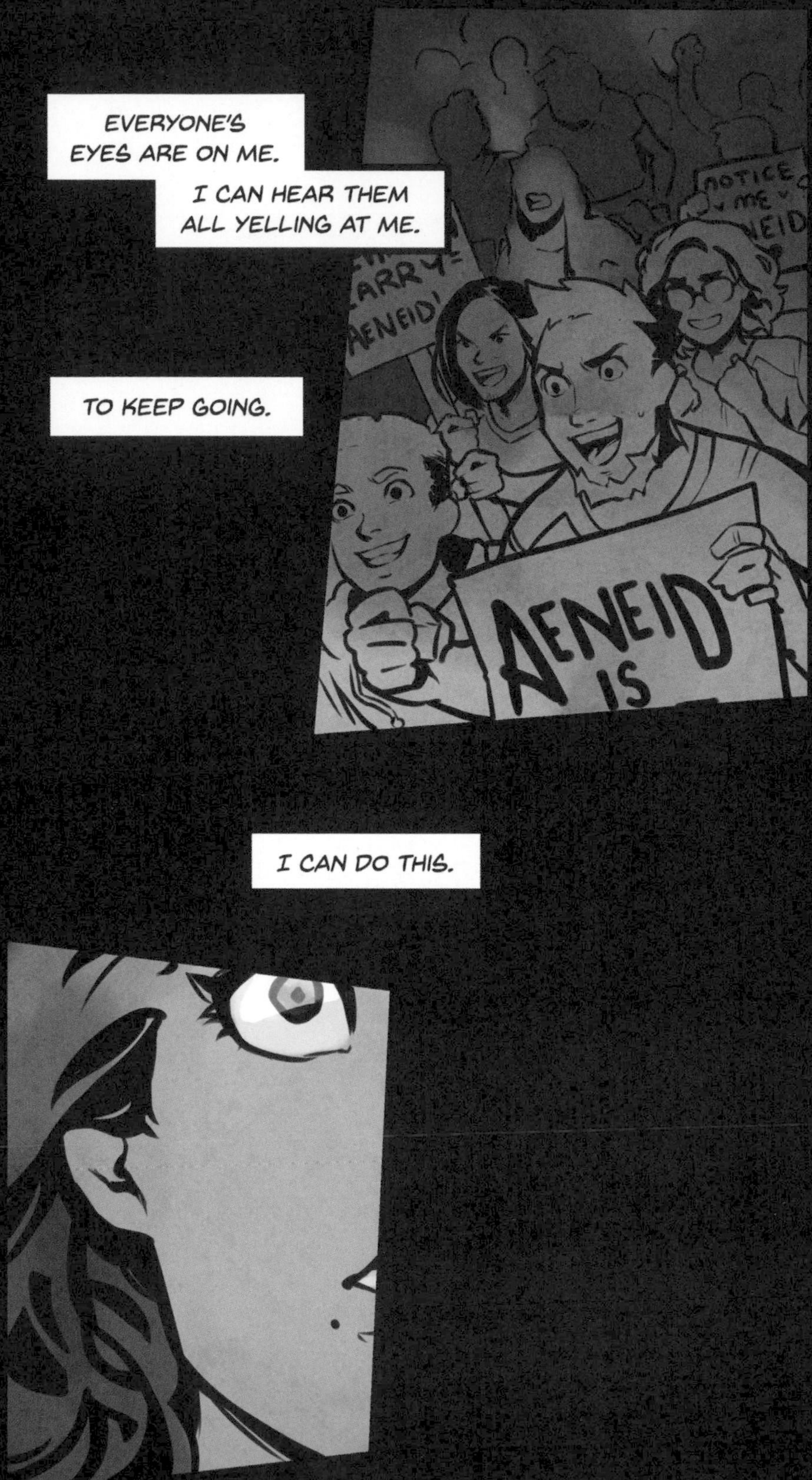
EVERYONE'S EYES ARE ON ME.
I CAN HEAR THEM ALL YELLING AT ME.
TO KEEP GOING.
AENEID IS
I CAN DO THIS.

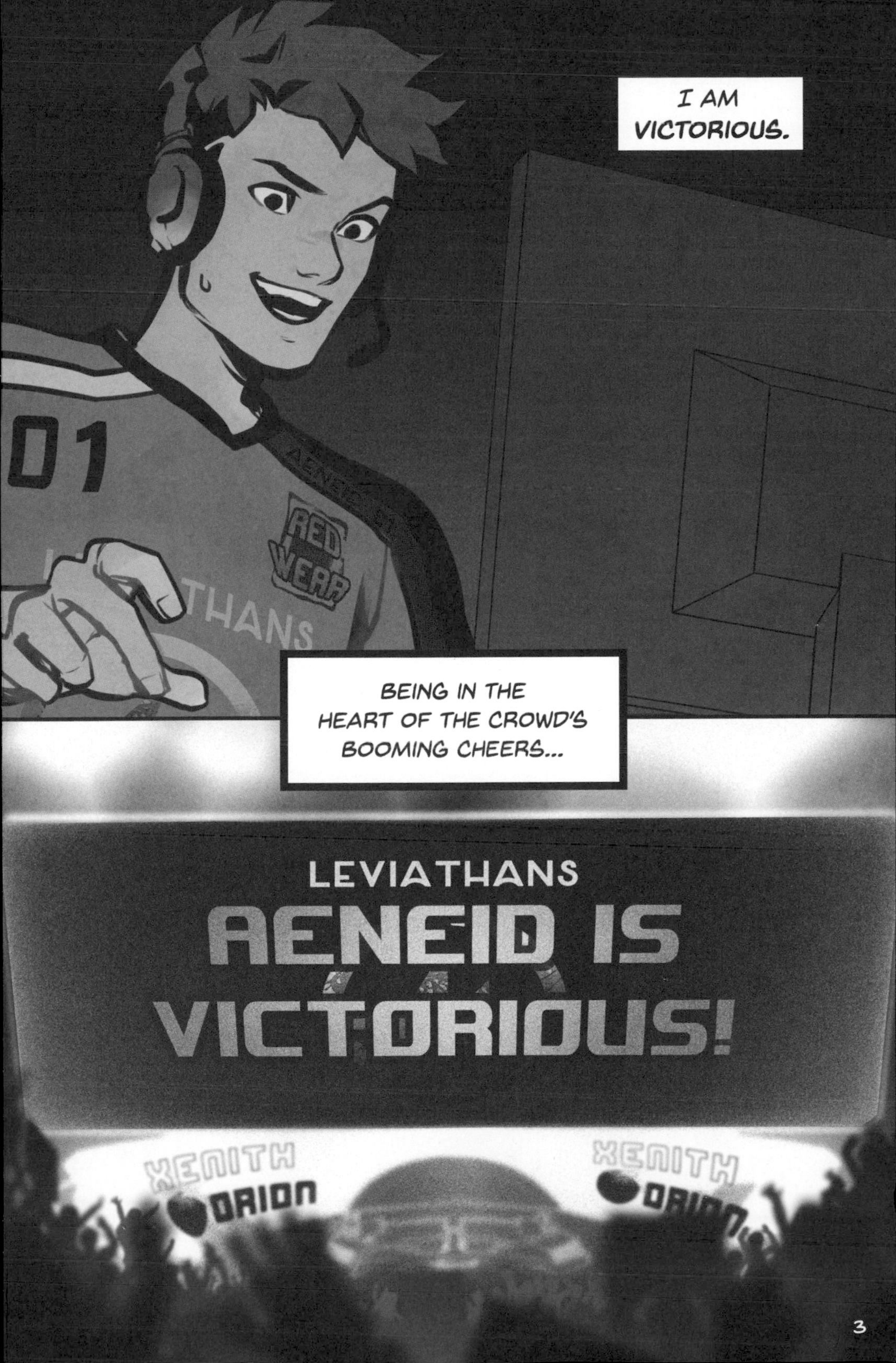
I AM VICTORIOUS.
01
RED WEAR
BEING IN THE HEART OF THE CROWD'S BOOMING CHEERS...
LEVIATHANS
AENEID IS VICTORIOUS!
XENITH ORION
XENITH ORION

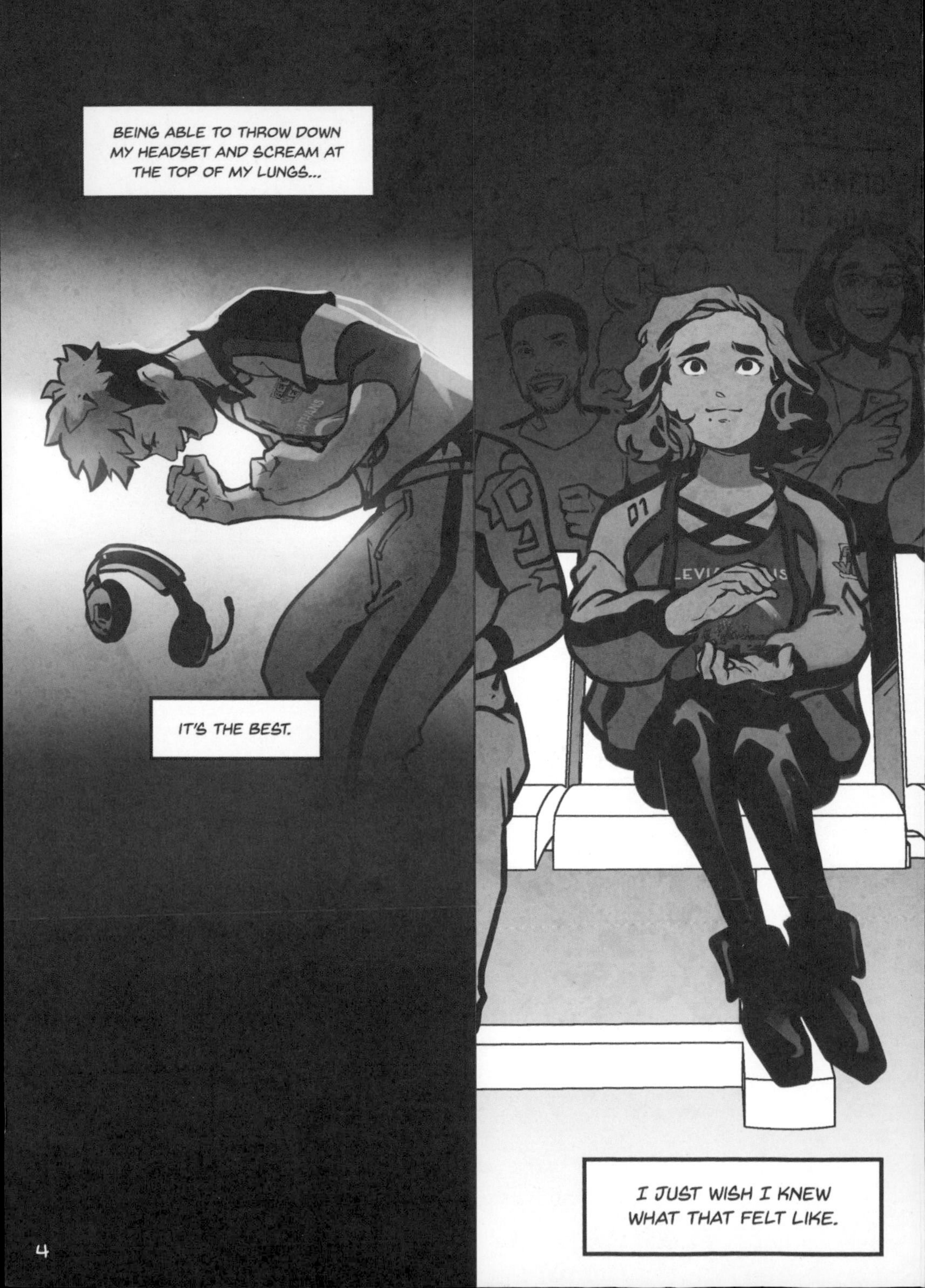
BEING ABLE TO THROW DOWN MY HEADSET AND SCREAM AT THE TOP OF MY LUNGS...
IT'S THE BEST.
I JUST WISH I KNEW WHAT THAT FELT LIKE.

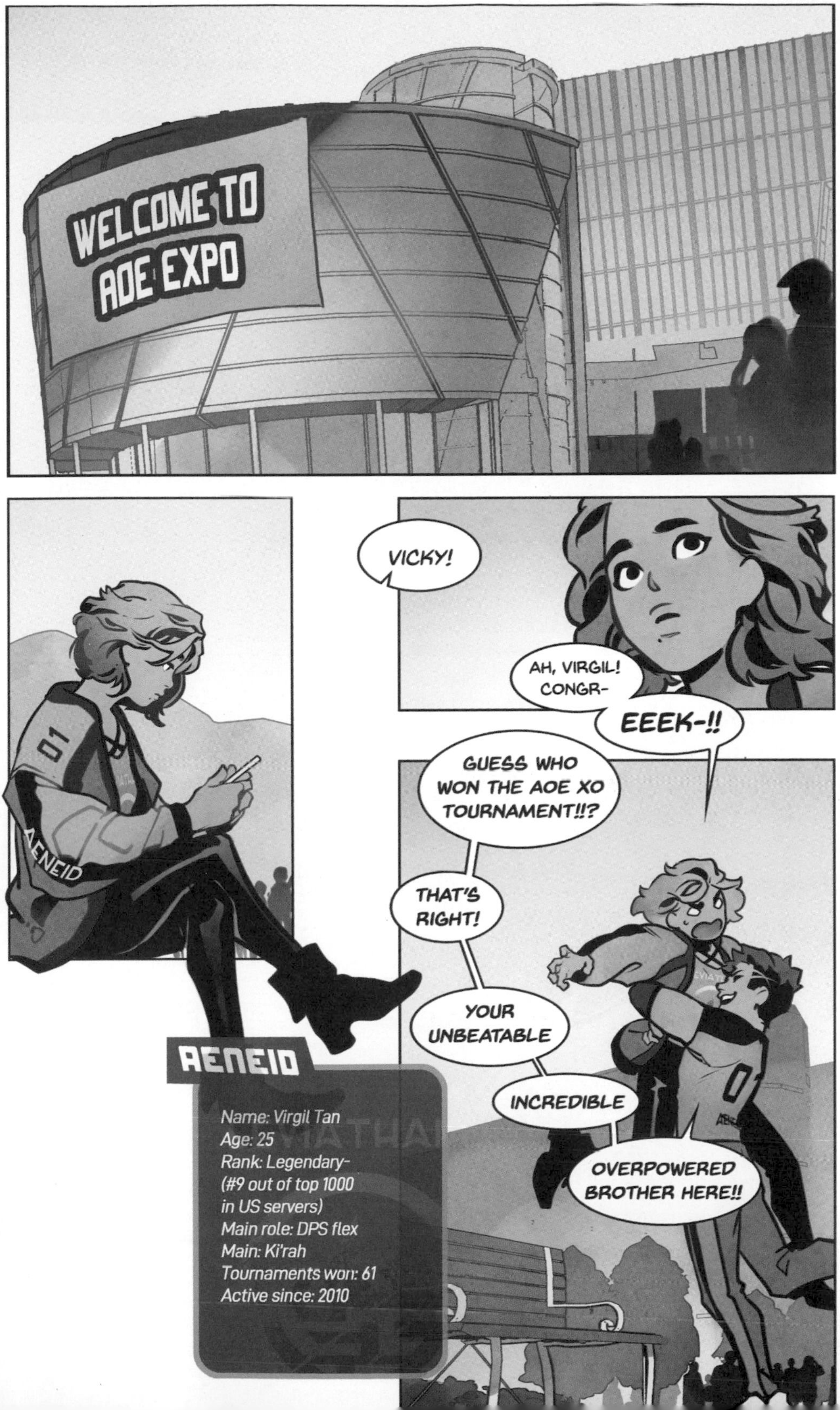
WELCOME TO AOE EXPO
AENEID
Name: Virgil Tan
Age: 25
Rank: Legendary-
(#9 out of top 1000
in US servers)
Main role: DPS flex
Main: Ki'rah
Tournaments won: 61
Active since: 2010
VICKY!
AH, VIRGIL! CONGR-
EEEK-!!
GUESS WHO WON THE AOE XO TOURNAMENT!!?
THAT'S RIGHT!
YOUR UNBEATABLE
INCREDIBLE
OVERPOWERED BROTHER HERE!!

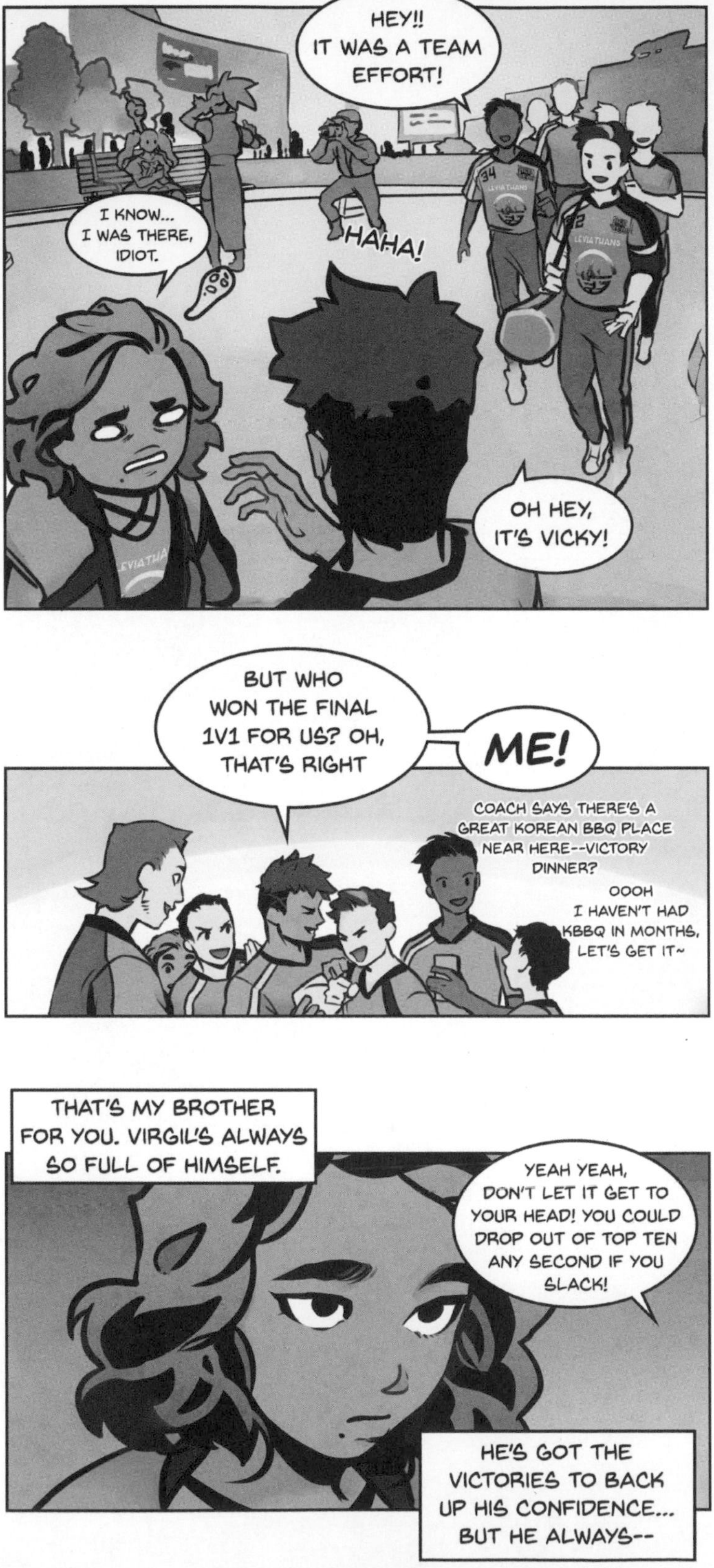
HEY!! IT WAS A TEAM EFFORT!
I KNOW... I WAS THERE, IDIOT.
HAHA!
OH HEY, IT'S VICKY!
BUT WHO WON THE FINAL 1V1 FOR US? OH, THAT'S RIGHT
ME!
COACH SAYS THERE'S A GREAT KOREAN BBQ PLACE NEAR HERE--VICTORY DINNER?
OOOH I HAVEN'T HAD KBBQ IN MONTHS, LET'S GET IT~
THAT'S MY BROTHER FOR YOU. VIRGIL'S ALWAYS SO FULL OF HIMSELF.
YEAH YEAH, DON'T LET IT GET TO YOUR HEAD! YOU COULD DROP OUT OF TOP TEN ANY SECOND IF YOU SLACK!
HE'S GOT THE VICTORIES TO BACK UP HIS CONFIDENCE... BUT HE ALWAYS--

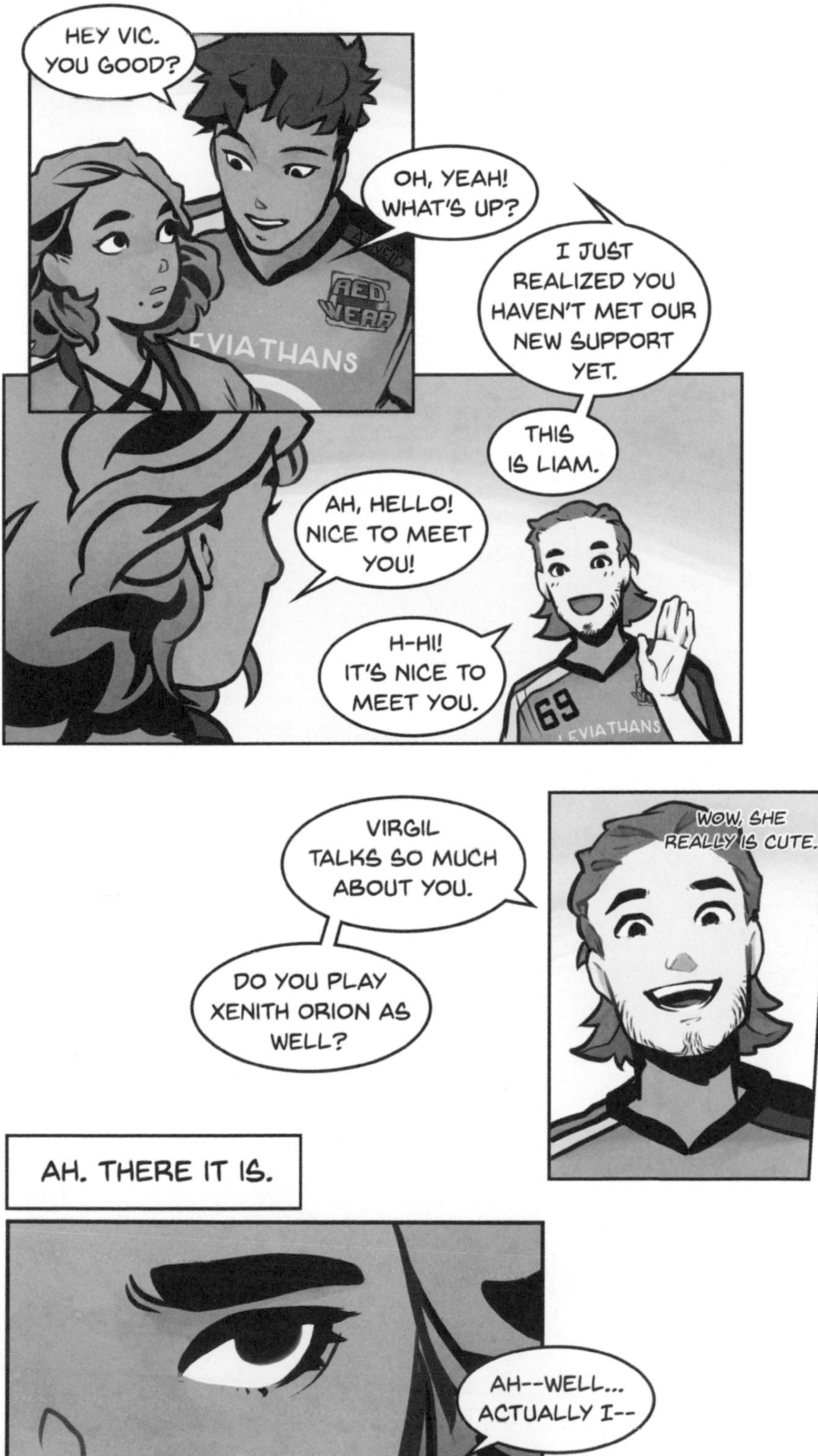
HEY VIC. YOU GOOD?
OH, YEAH! WHAT'S UP?
I JUST REALIZED YOU HAVEN'T MET OUR NEW SUPPORT YET.
THIS IS LIAM.
AH, HELLO! NICE TO MEET YOU!
H-HI! IT'S NICE TO MEET YOU.
VIRGIL TALKS SO MUCH ABOUT YOU.
DO YOU PLAY XENITH ORION AS WELL?
WOW, SHE REALLY IS CUTE.
AH. THERE IT IS.
AH--WELL... ACTUALLY I--

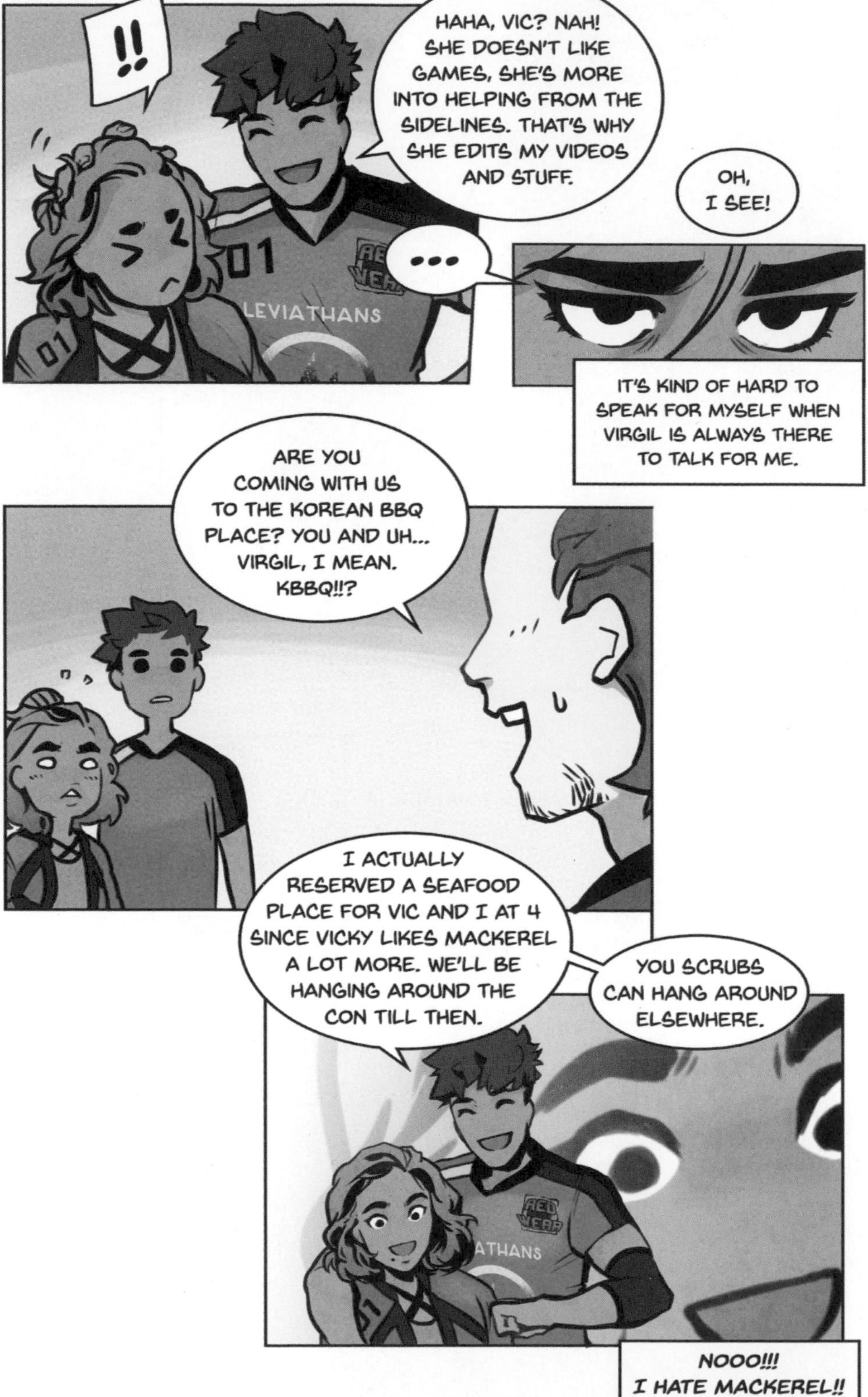
!!
HAHA, VIC? NAH! SHE DOESN'T LIKE GAMES, SHE'S MORE INTO HELPING FROM THE SIDELINES. THAT'S WHY SHE EDITS MY VIDEOS AND STUFF.
01
LEVIATHANS
OH, I SEE!
...
IT'S KIND OF HARD TO SPEAK FOR MYSELF WHEN VIRGIL IS ALWAYS THERE TO TALK FOR ME.
ARE YOU COMING WITH US TO THE KOREAN BBQ PLACE? YOU AND UH... VIRGIL, I MEAN. KBBQ!!?
I ACTUALLY RESERVED A SEAFOOD PLACE FOR VIC AND I AT 4 SINCE VICKY LIKES MACKEREL A LOT MORE. WE'LL BE HANGING AROUND THE CON TILL THEN.
YOU SCRUBS CAN HANG AROUND ELSEWHERE.
ATHANS
NOOO!!! I HATE MACKEREL!! I WANT PORK!!

AW C'MON DUDE, YOU COULDN'T EVEN RESERVE SPOTS FOR US? WE'RE A TEAM!

NONE OF YOU GUYS EVEN LIKE SEAFOOD! I'M JUST TREATING MY LIL' SIS WITH MY HARD EARNED PAYCHECK HERE.

HE MEANS WELL. BUT SOMETIMES I FEEL LIKE IT'S IMPOSSIBLE TO COMMUNICATE WITH HIM, ESPECIALLY WHEN HE GETS THIS EXCITED.

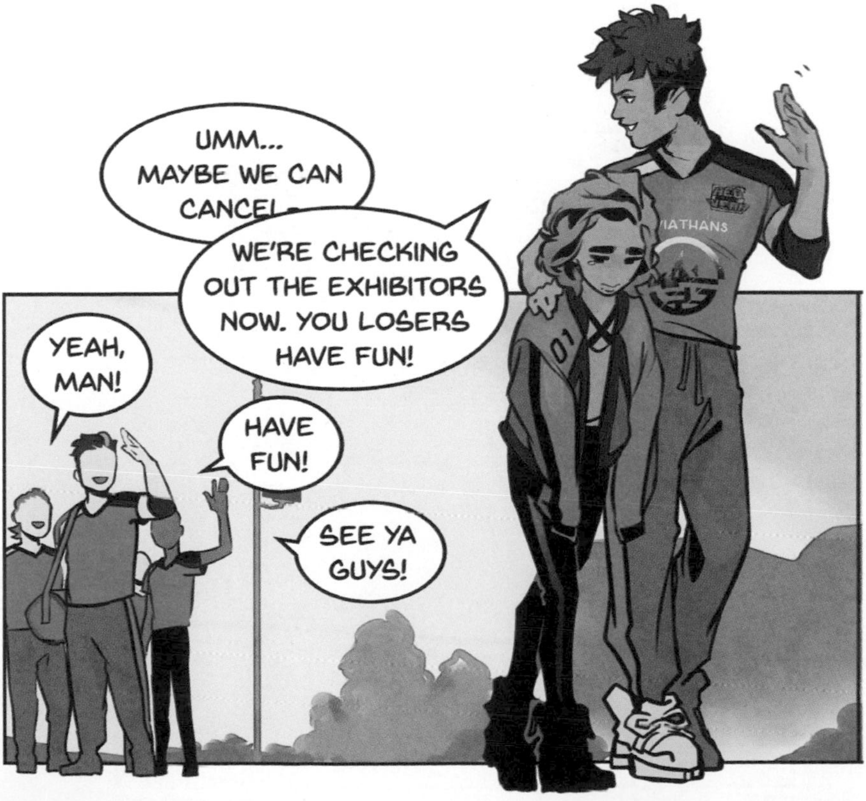
UMM... MAYBE WE CAN CANCEL–
WE'RE CHECKING OUT THE EXHIBITORS NOW. YOU LOSERS HAVE FUN!
YEAH, MAN!
HAVE FUN!
SEE YA GUYS!

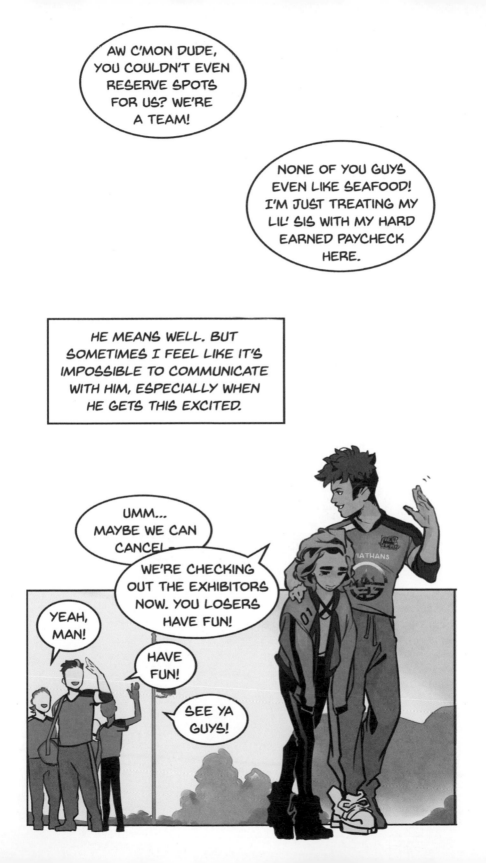

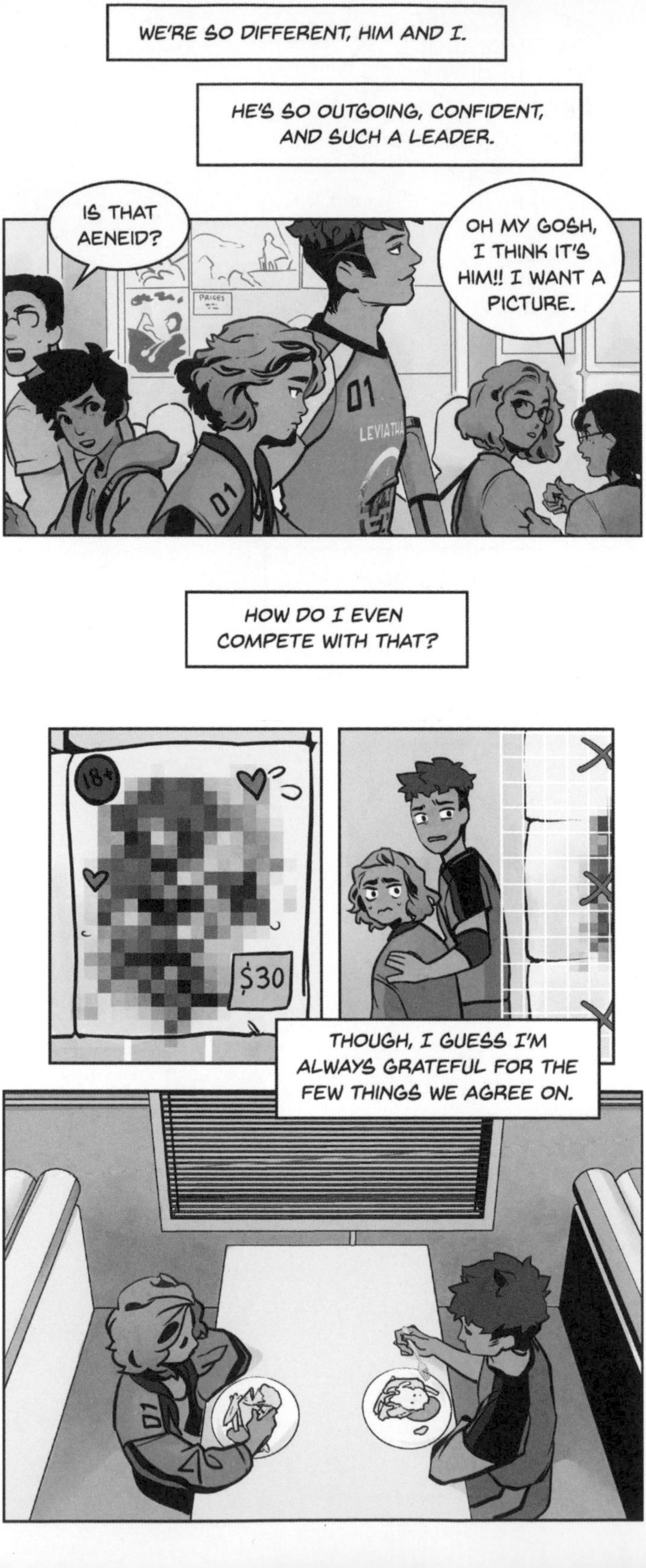
WE'RE SO DIFFERENT, HIM AND I.
HE'S SO OUTGOING, CONFIDENT, AND SUCH A LEADER.
IS THAT AENEID?
OH MY GOSH, I THINK IT'S HIM!! I WANT A PICTURE.
01
PRICES
HOW DO I EVEN COMPETE WITH THAT?
18+
$30
THOUGH, I GUESS I'M ALWAYS GRATEFUL FOR THE FEW THINGS WE AGREE ON.

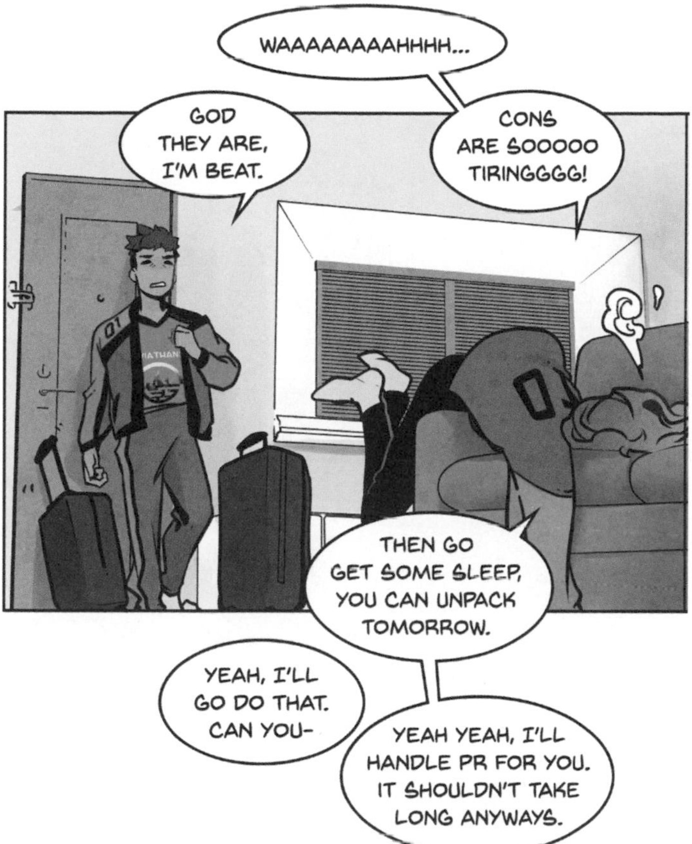
WAAAAAAAAHHHH...
GOD THEY ARE, I'M BEAT.
CONS ARE SOOOOO TIRINGGGG!
THEN GO GET SOME SLEEP, YOU CAN UNPACK TOMORROW.
YEAH, I'LL GO DO THAT. CAN YOU-
YEAH YEAH, I'LL HANDLE PR FOR YOU. IT SHOULDN'T TAKE LONG ANYWAYS.

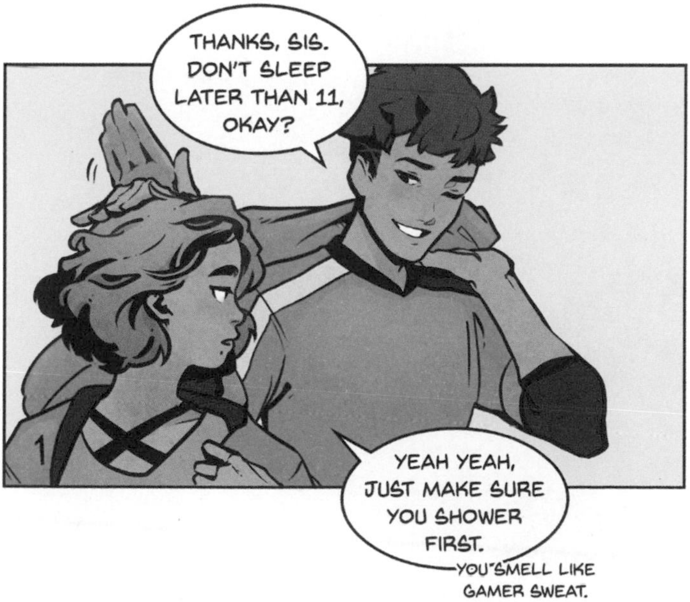
THANKS, SIS. DON'T SLEEP LATER THAN 11, OKAY?
YEAH YEAH, JUST MAKE SURE YOU SHOWER FIRST.
YOU SMELL LIKE GAMER SWEAT.

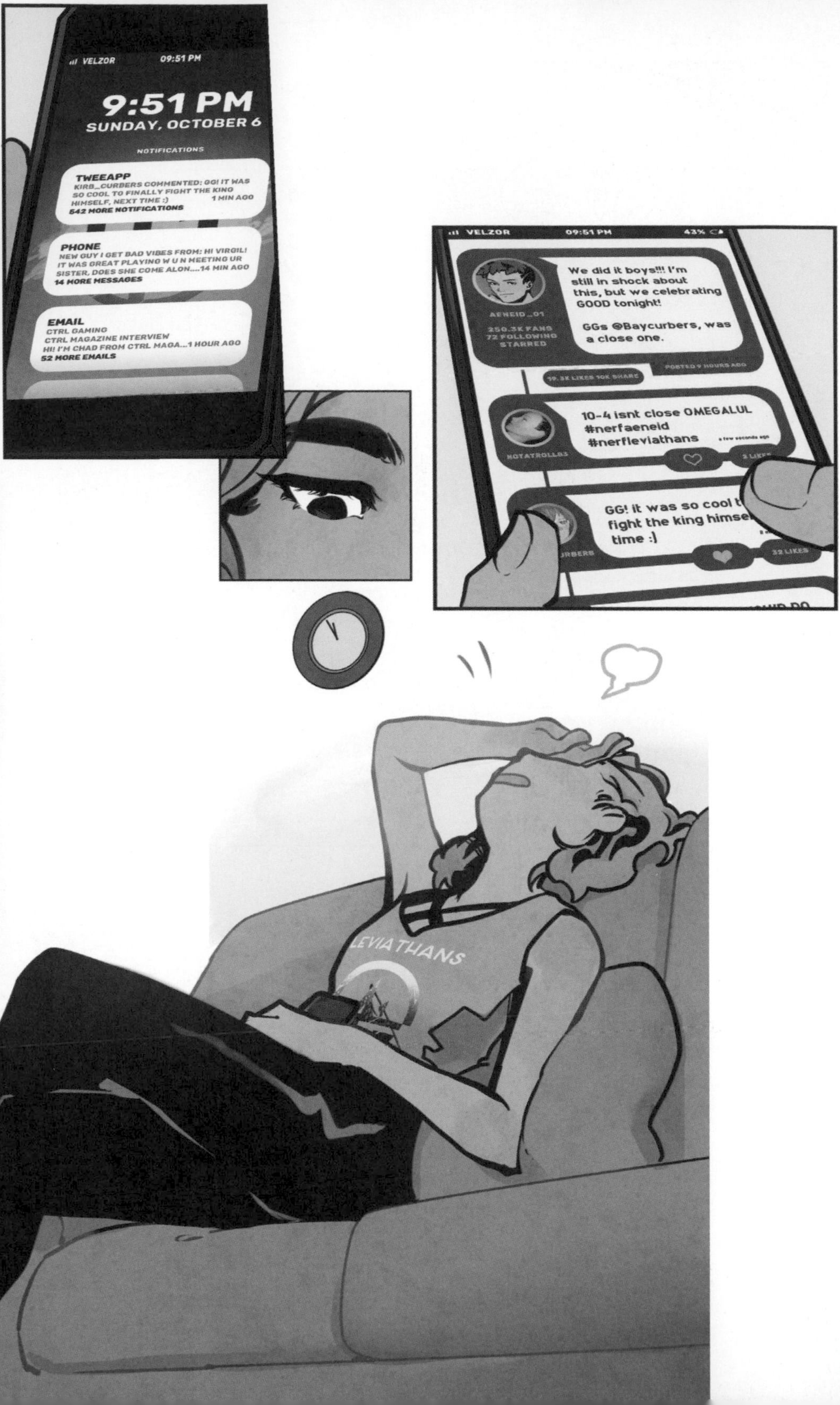

VELZOR 09:51 PM
9:51 PM
SUNDAY, OCTOBER 6
NOTIFICATIONS
TWEEAPP
KIRB_CURBERS COMMENTED: GG! IT WAS SO COOL TO FINALLY FIGHT THE KING HIMSELF, NEXT TIME :) 1 MIN AGO
542 MORE NOTIFICATIONS
PHONE
NEW GUY I GET BAD VIBES FROM: HI VIRGIL! IT WAS GREAT PLAYING W U N MEETING UR SISTER, DOES SHE COME ALON....14 MIN AGO
14 MORE MESSAGES
EMAIL
CTRL GAMING
CTRL MAGAZINE INTERVIEW
HI! I'M CHAD FROM CTRL MAGA...1 HOUR AGO
52 MORE EMAILS
VELZOR 09:51 PM 43%
We did it boys!!! I'm still in shock about this, but we celebrating GOOD tonight!
GGs @Baycurbers, was a close one.
AENEID_01
250.3K FANS
72 FOLLOWING
STARRED
POSTED 9 HOURS AGO
10-4 isnt close OMEGALUL
#nerfaeneid
#nerfleviathans
a few seconds ago
NOTATROLL83
GG! it was so cool t
fight the king himse
time :)
32 LIKES
LEVIATHANS

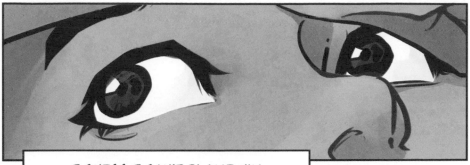

I GUESS I CAN'T BLAME HIM.
HE'S BEEN DRAGGING ME ALONG
EVERYWHERE SINCE WE WERE KIDS.

WE WORK WELL TOGETHER.

THERE'S NO REASON
TO DISRUPT OUR PEACE.

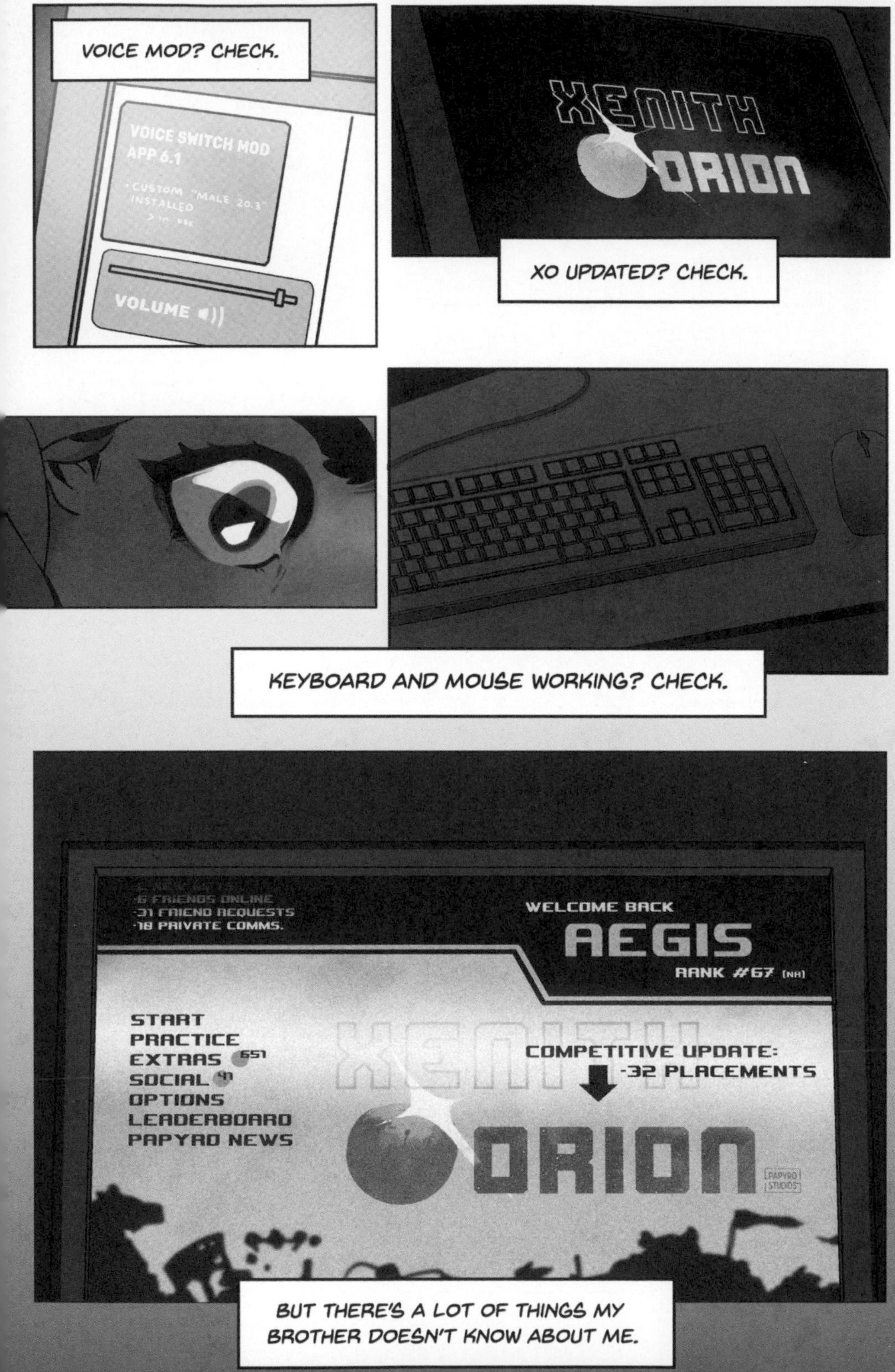
VOICE MOD? CHECK.
VOICE SWITCH MOD APP 6.1
•CUSTOM "MALE 20.3" INSTALLED
> in use
VOLUME
XENITH ORION
XO UPDATED? CHECK.
KEYBOARD AND MOUSE WORKING? CHECK.
-6 FRIENDS ONLINE
-31 FRIEND REQUESTS
-18 PRIVATE COMMS.
WELCOME BACK
AEGIS
RANK #67 [NA]
START
PRACTICE
EXTRAS 651
SOCIAL 47
OPTIONS
LEADERBOARD
PAPYRO NEWS
COMPETITIVE UPDATE:
-32 PLACEMENTS
XENITH ORION
PAPYRO STUDIOS
BUT THERE'S A LOT OF THINGS MY BROTHER DOESN'T KNOW ABOUT ME.

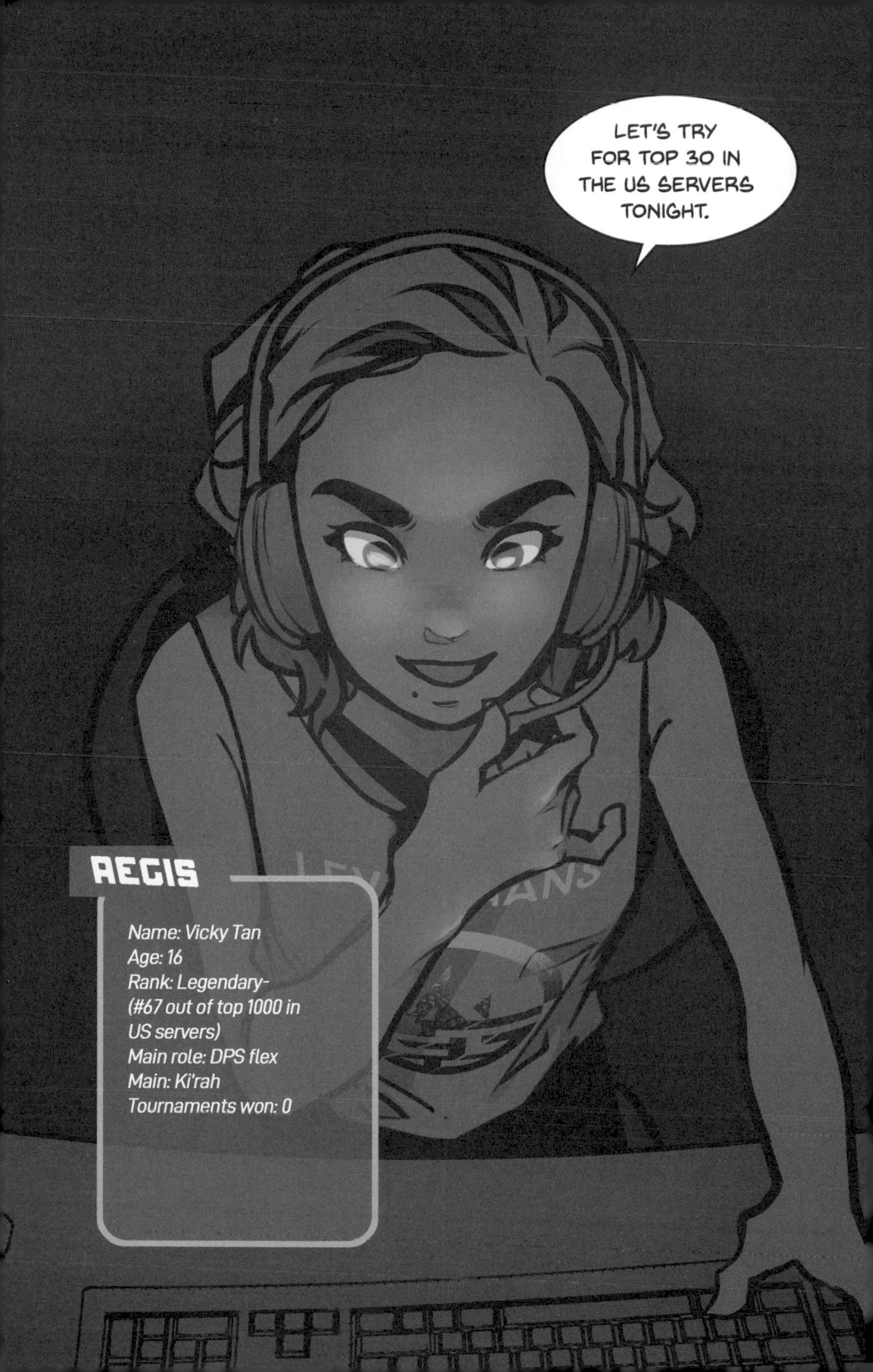
LET'S TRY FOR TOP 30 IN THE US SERVERS TONIGHT.
AEGIS
Name: Vicky Tan
Age: 16
Rank: Legendary-
(#67 out of top 1000 in US servers)
Main role: DPS flex
Main: Ki'rah
Tournaments won: 0

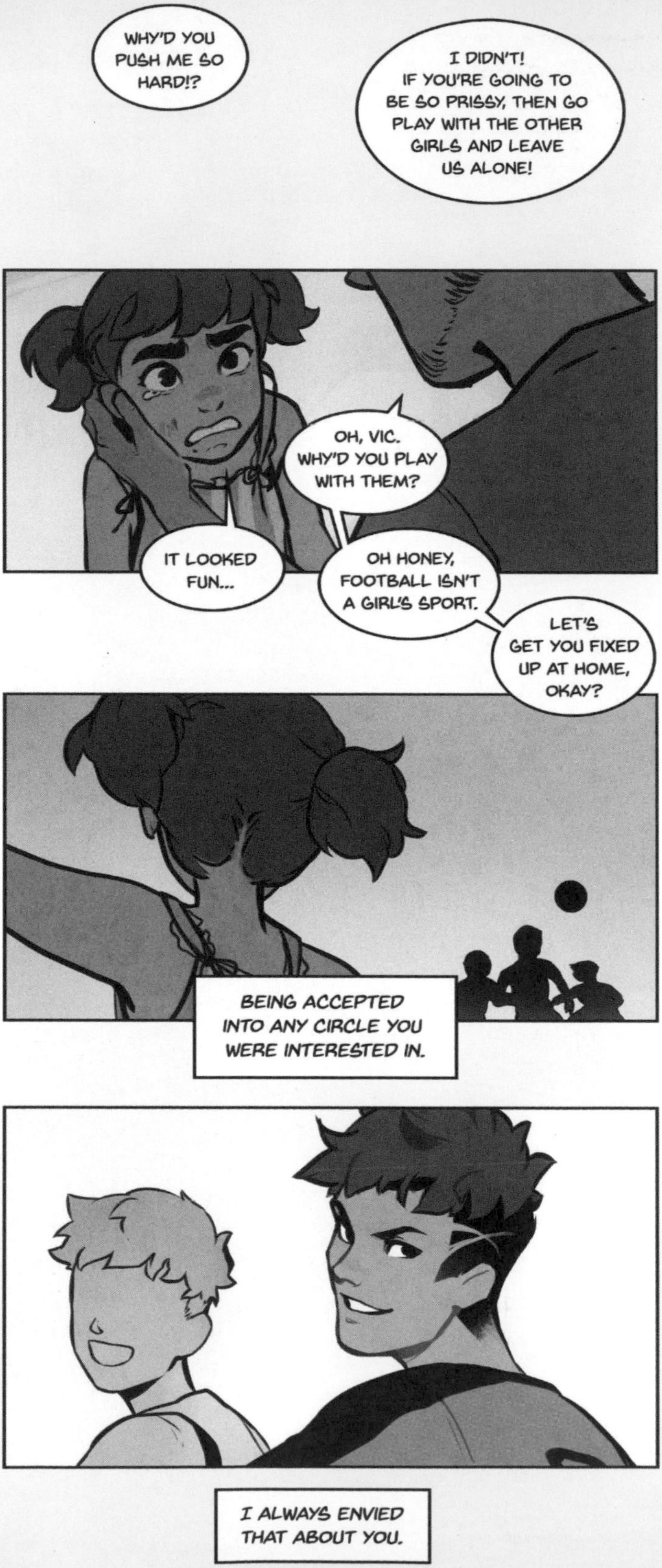
WHY'D YOU PUSH ME SO HARD!?
I DIDN'T! IF YOU'RE GOING TO BE SO PRISSY, THEN GO PLAY WITH THE OTHER GIRLS AND LEAVE US ALONE!
OH, VIC. WHY'D YOU PLAY WITH THEM?
IT LOOKED FUN...
OH HONEY, FOOTBALL ISN'T A GIRL'S SPORT.
LET'S GET YOU FIXED UP AT HOME, OKAY?
BEING ACCEPTED INTO ANY CIRCLE YOU WERE INTERESTED IN.
I ALWAYS ENVIED THAT ABOUT YOU.

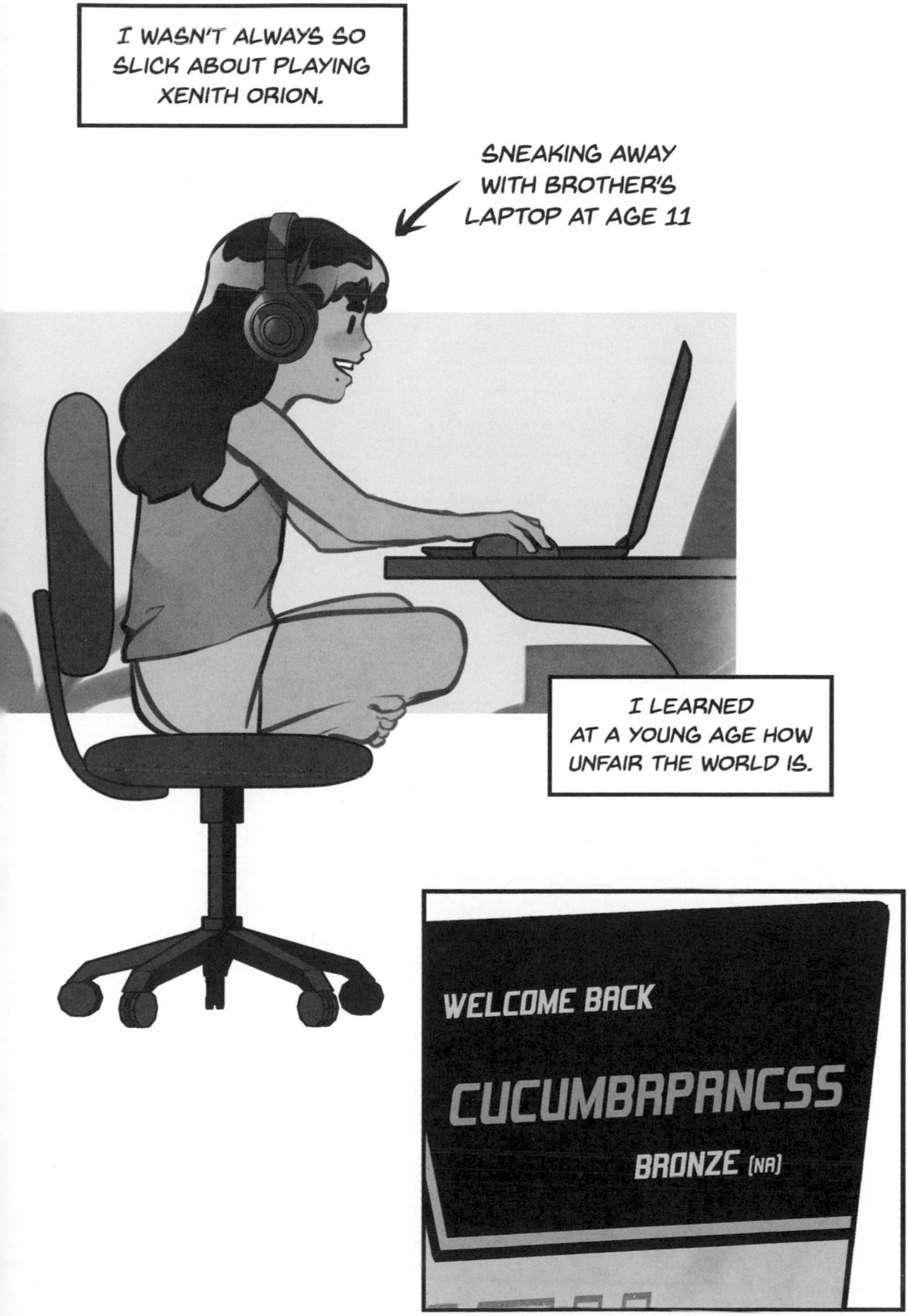
I WASN'T ALWAYS SO SLICK ABOUT PLAYING XENITH ORION.
SNEAKING AWAY WITH BROTHER'S LAPTOP AT AGE 11
I LEARNED AT A YOUNG AGE HOW UNFAIR THE WORLD IS.
WELCOME BACK
CUCUMBRPRNCSS
BRONZE (NA)

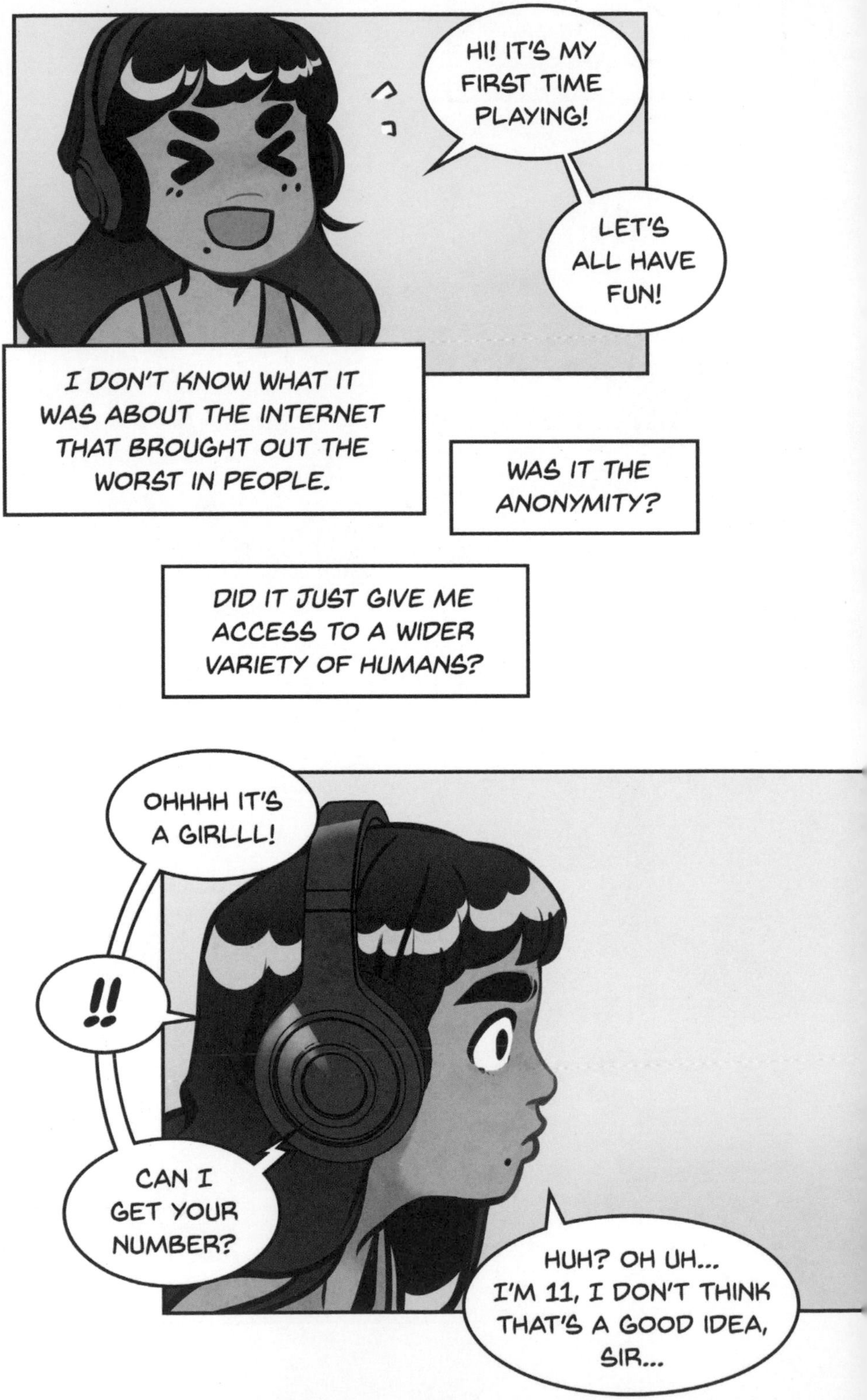
HI! IT'S MY FIRST TIME PLAYING!
LET'S ALL HAVE FUN!
I DON'T KNOW WHAT IT WAS ABOUT THE INTERNET THAT BROUGHT OUT THE WORST IN PEOPLE.
WAS IT THE ANONYMITY?
DID IT JUST GIVE ME ACCESS TO A WIDER VARIETY OF HUMANS?
OHHHH IT'S A GIRLLL!
!!
CAN I GET YOUR NUMBER?
HUH? OH UH... I'M 11, I DON'T THINK THAT'S A GOOD IDEA, SIR...

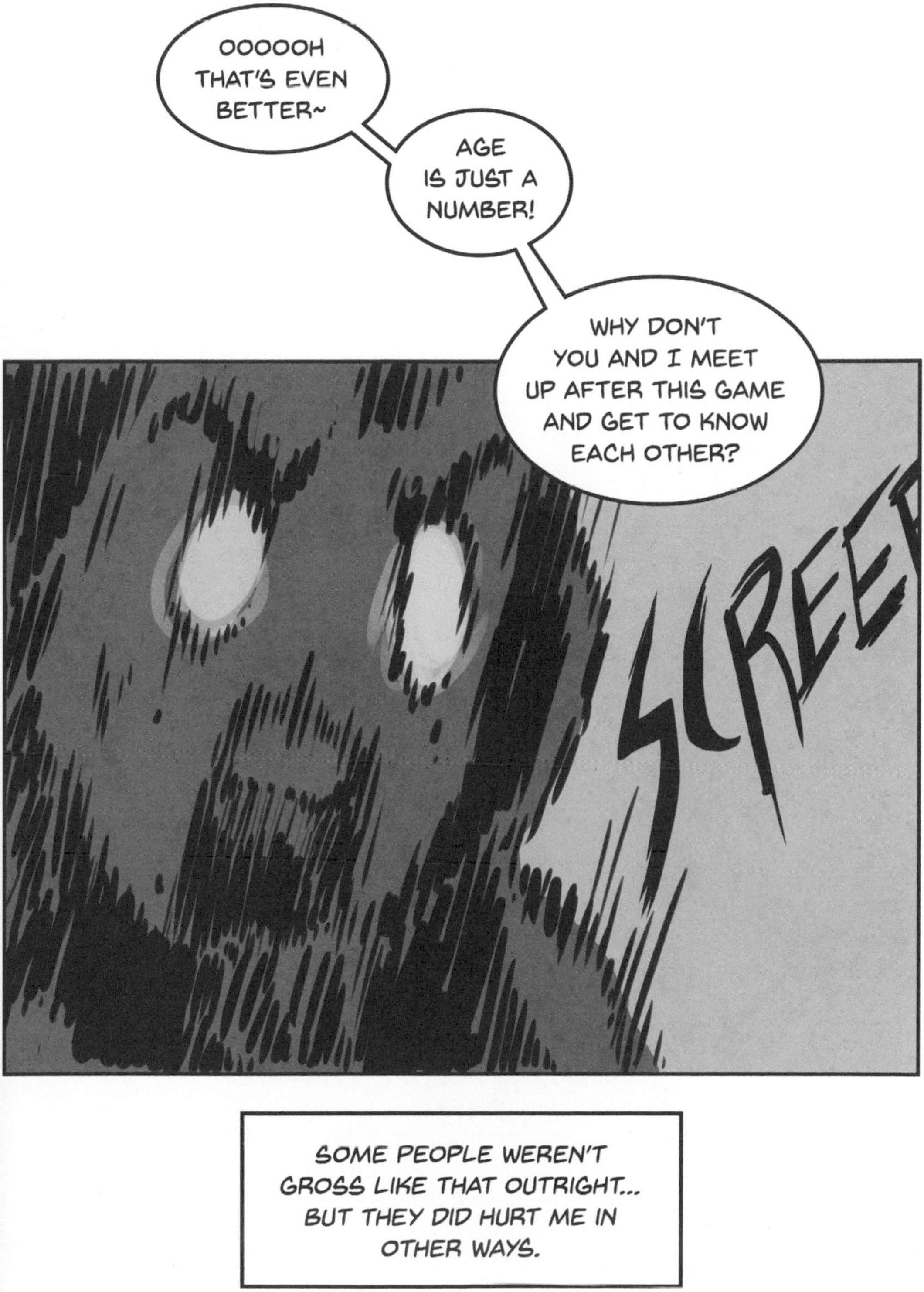
OOOOOH THAT'S EVEN BETTER~
AGE IS JUST A NUMBER!
WHY DON'T YOU AND I MEET UP AFTER THIS GAME AND GET TO KNOW EACH OTHER?
SCREE
SOME PEOPLE WEREN'T GROSS LIKE THAT OUTRIGHT... BUT THEY DID HURT ME IN OTHER WAYS.

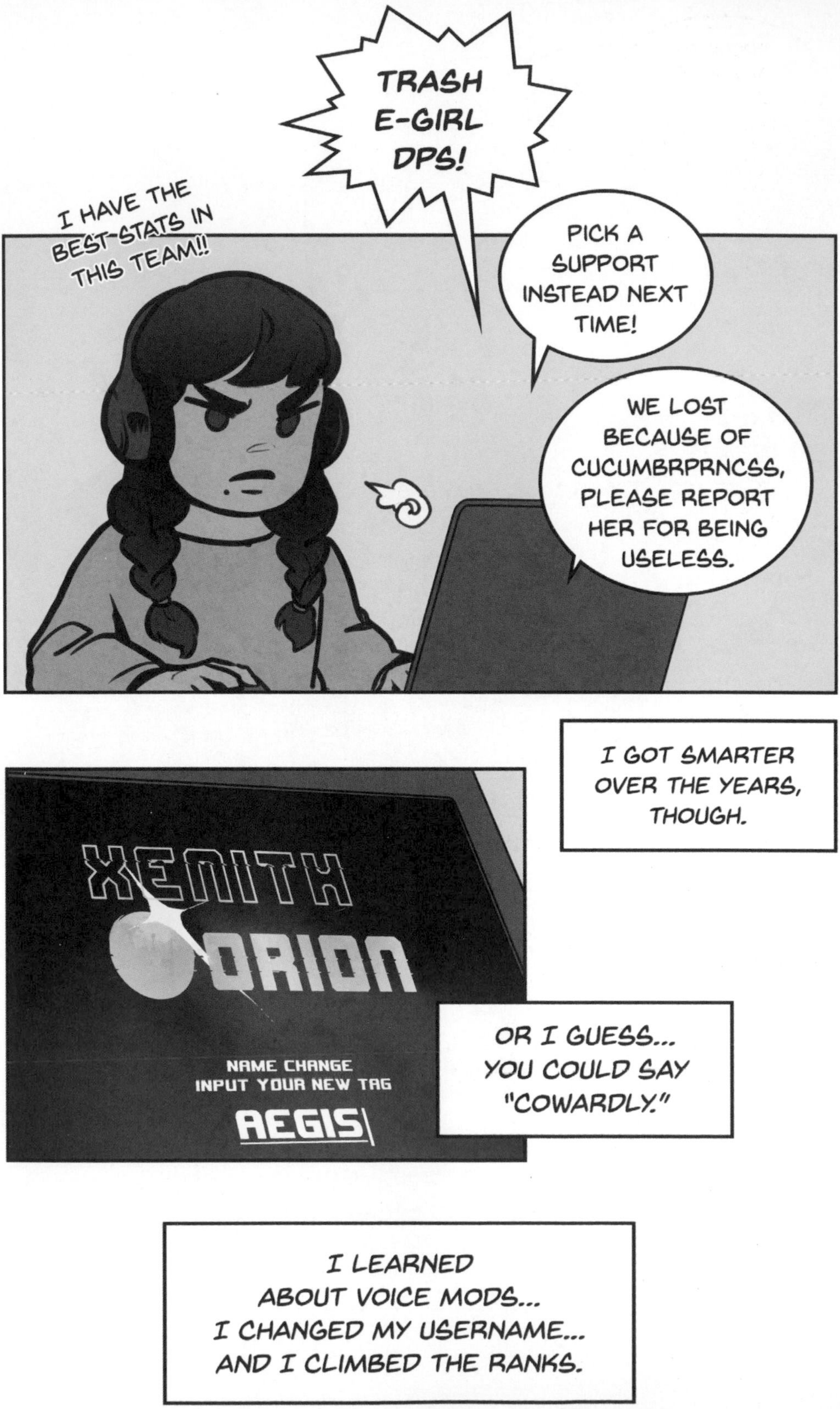
I HAVE THE BEST-STATS IN THIS TEAM!!
TRASH E-GIRL DPS!
PICK A SUPPORT INSTEAD NEXT TIME!
WE LOST BECAUSE OF CUCUMBRPRNCSS, PLEASE REPORT HER FOR BEING USELESS.
I GOT SMARTER OVER THE YEARS, THOUGH.
XENITH ORION
NAME CHANGE
INPUT YOUR NEW TAG
AEGIS
OR I GUESS... YOU COULD SAY "COWARDLY."
I LEARNED ABOUT VOICE MODS... I CHANGED MY USERNAME... AND I CLIMBED THE RANKS.

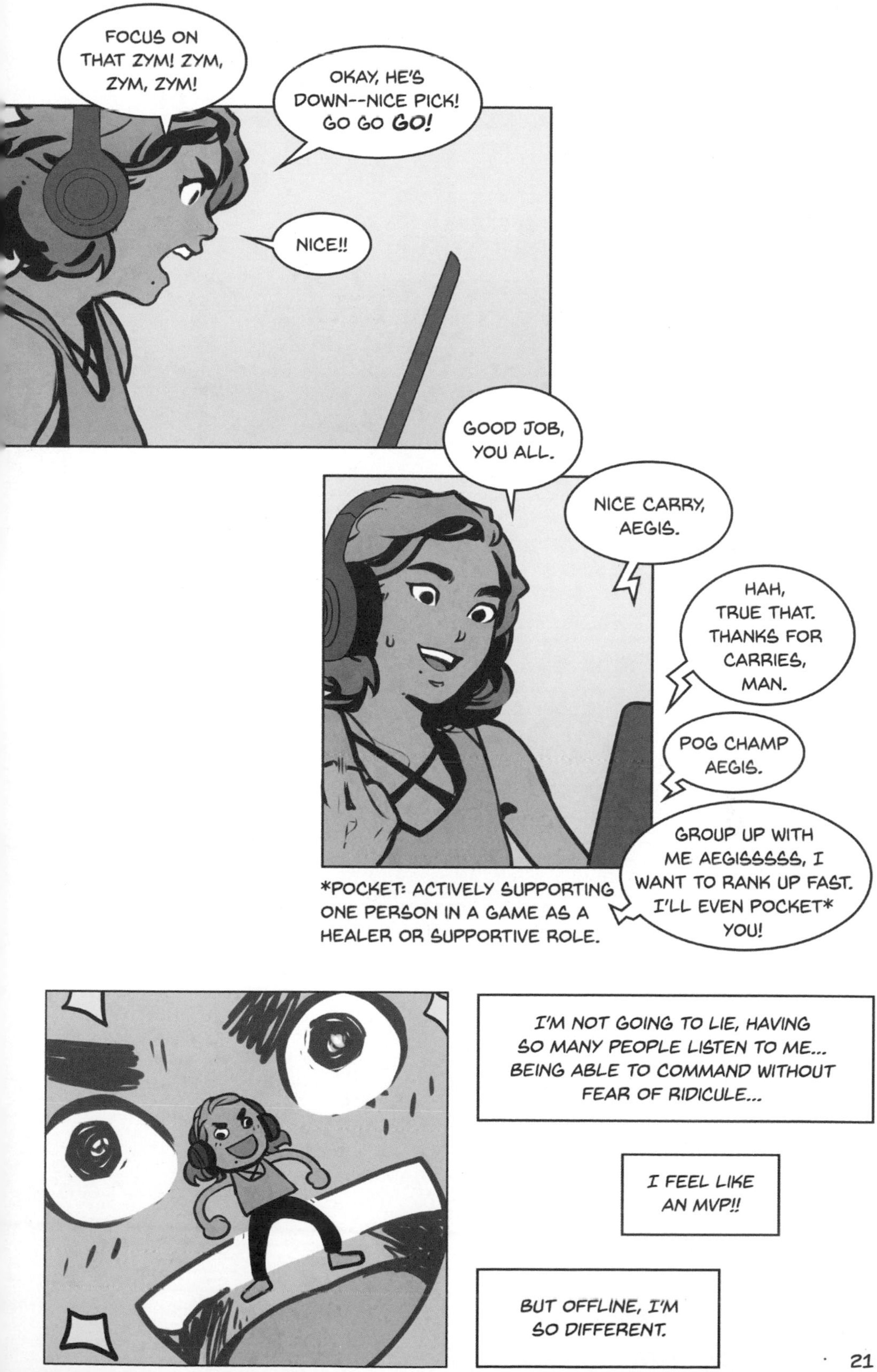
FOCUS ON THAT ZYM! ZYM, ZYM, ZYM!
OKAY, HE'S DOWN--NICE PICK! GO GO GO!
NICE!!
GOOD JOB, YOU ALL.
NICE CARRY, AEGIS.
HAH, TRUE THAT. THANKS FOR CARRIES, MAN.
POG CHAMP AEGIS.
GROUP UP WITH ME AEGISSSSS, I WANT TO RANK UP FAST. I'LL EVEN POCKET* YOU!
*POCKET: ACTIVELY SUPPORTING ONE PERSON IN A GAME AS A HEALER OR SUPPORTIVE ROLE.
I'M NOT GOING TO LIE, HAVING SO MANY PEOPLE LISTEN TO ME... BEING ABLE TO COMMAND WITHOUT FEAR OF RIDICULE...
I FEEL LIKE AN MVP!!
BUT OFFLINE, I'M SO DIFFERENT.

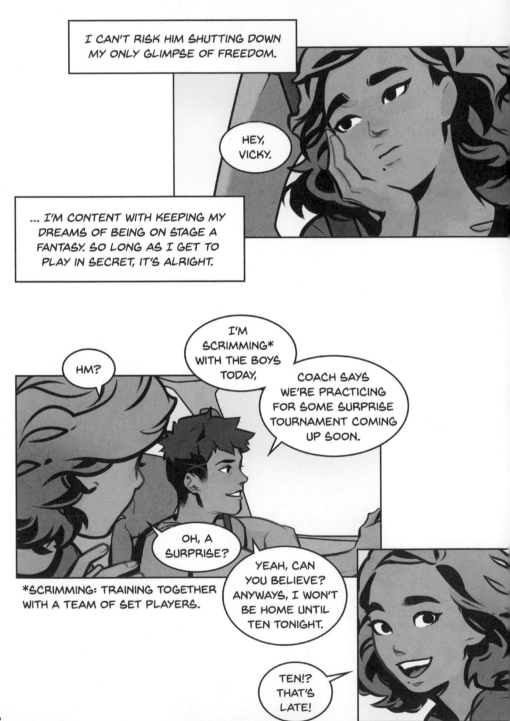

I COULD NEVER LET VIRGIL KNOW WHO AEGIS REALLY IS. HE THINKS HE KNOWS EVERYTHING ABOUT ME, WHO KNOWS HOW HE'D REACT?

I CAN'T RISK HIM SHUTTING DOWN MY ONLY GLIMPSE OF FREEDOM.

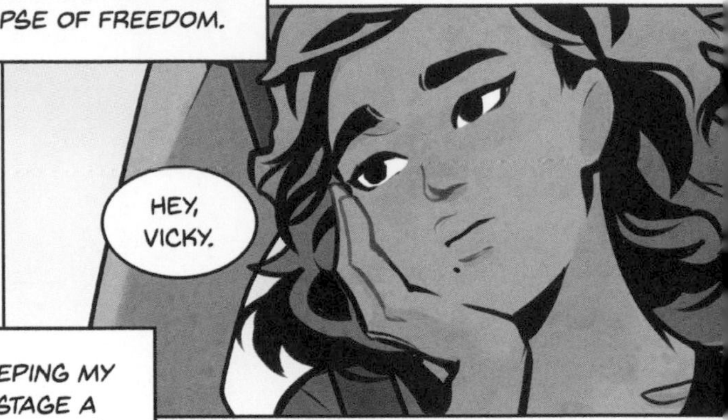
HEY, VICKY.

... I'M CONTENT WITH KEEPING MY DREAMS OF BEING ON STAGE A FANTASY. SO LONG AS I GET TO PLAY IN SECRET, IT'S ALRIGHT.

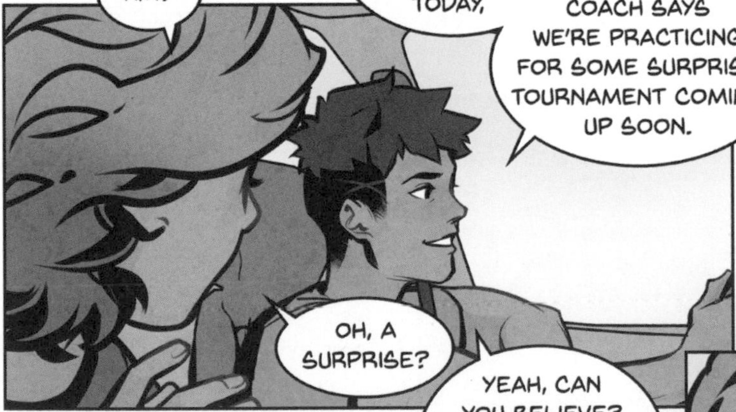
HM?
I'M SCRIMMING* WITH THE BOYS TODAY,
COACH SAYS WE'RE PRACTICING FOR SOME SURPRISE TOURNAMENT COMING UP SOON.
OH, A SURPRISE?

*SCRIMMING: TRAINING TOGETHER WITH A TEAM OF SET PLAYERS.

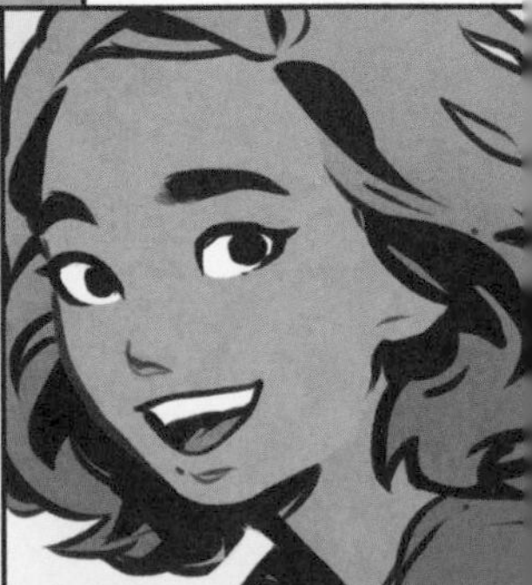
YEAH, CAN YOU BELIEVE? ANYWAYS, I WON'T BE HOME UNTIL TEN TONIGHT.
TEN!? THAT'S LATE!

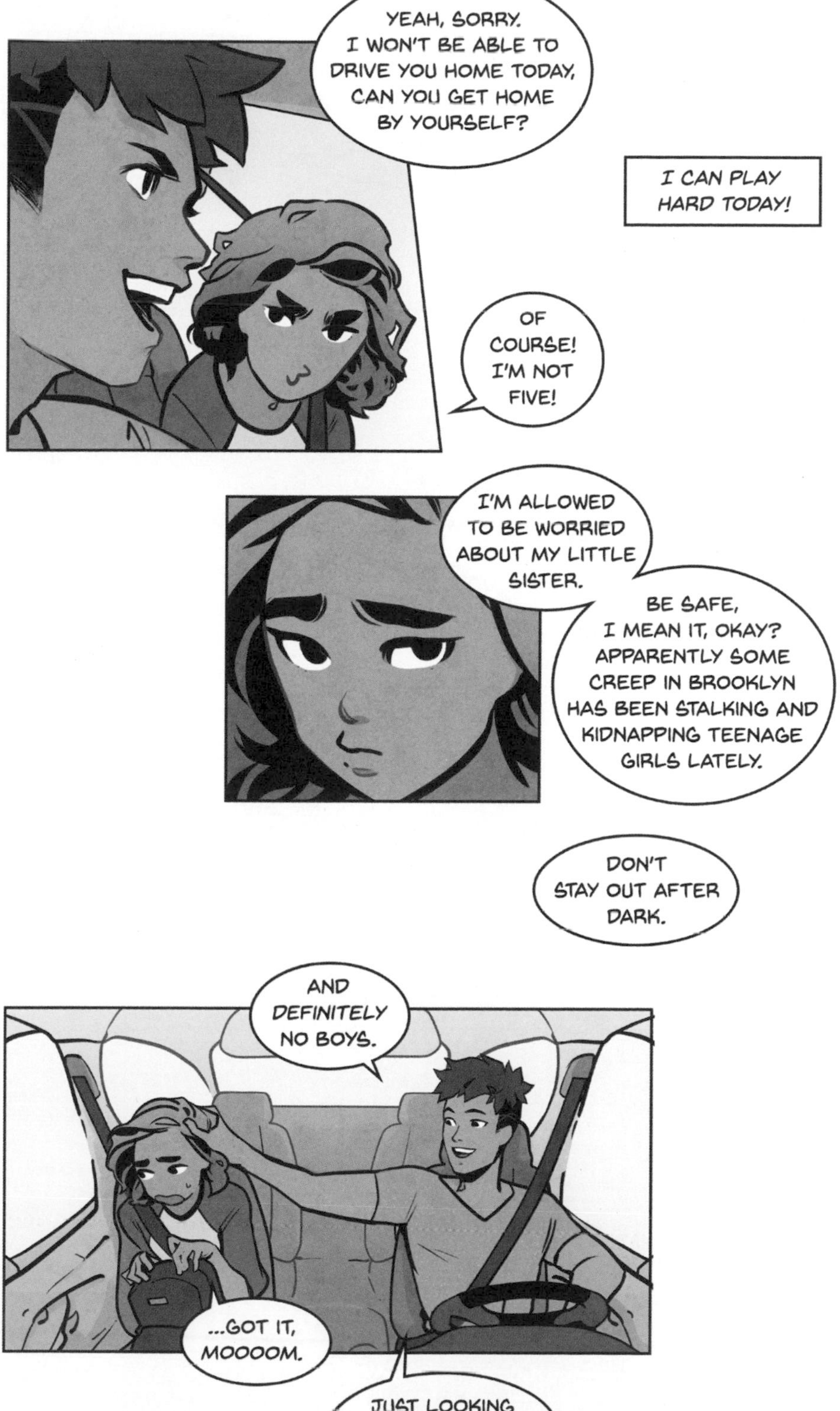
YEAH, SORRY. I WON'T BE ABLE TO DRIVE YOU HOME TODAY, CAN YOU GET HOME BY YOURSELF?
I CAN PLAY HARD TODAY!
OF COURSE! I'M NOT FIVE!
I'M ALLOWED TO BE WORRIED ABOUT MY LITTLE SISTER.
BE SAFE, I MEAN IT, OKAY? APPARENTLY SOME CREEP IN BROOKLYN HAS BEEN STALKING AND KIDNAPPING TEENAGE GIRLS LATELY.
DON'T STAY OUT AFTER DARK.
AND DEFINITELY NO BOYS.
...GOT IT, MOOOOM.
JUST LOOKING OUT FOR YOU, DAUGHTEEER.

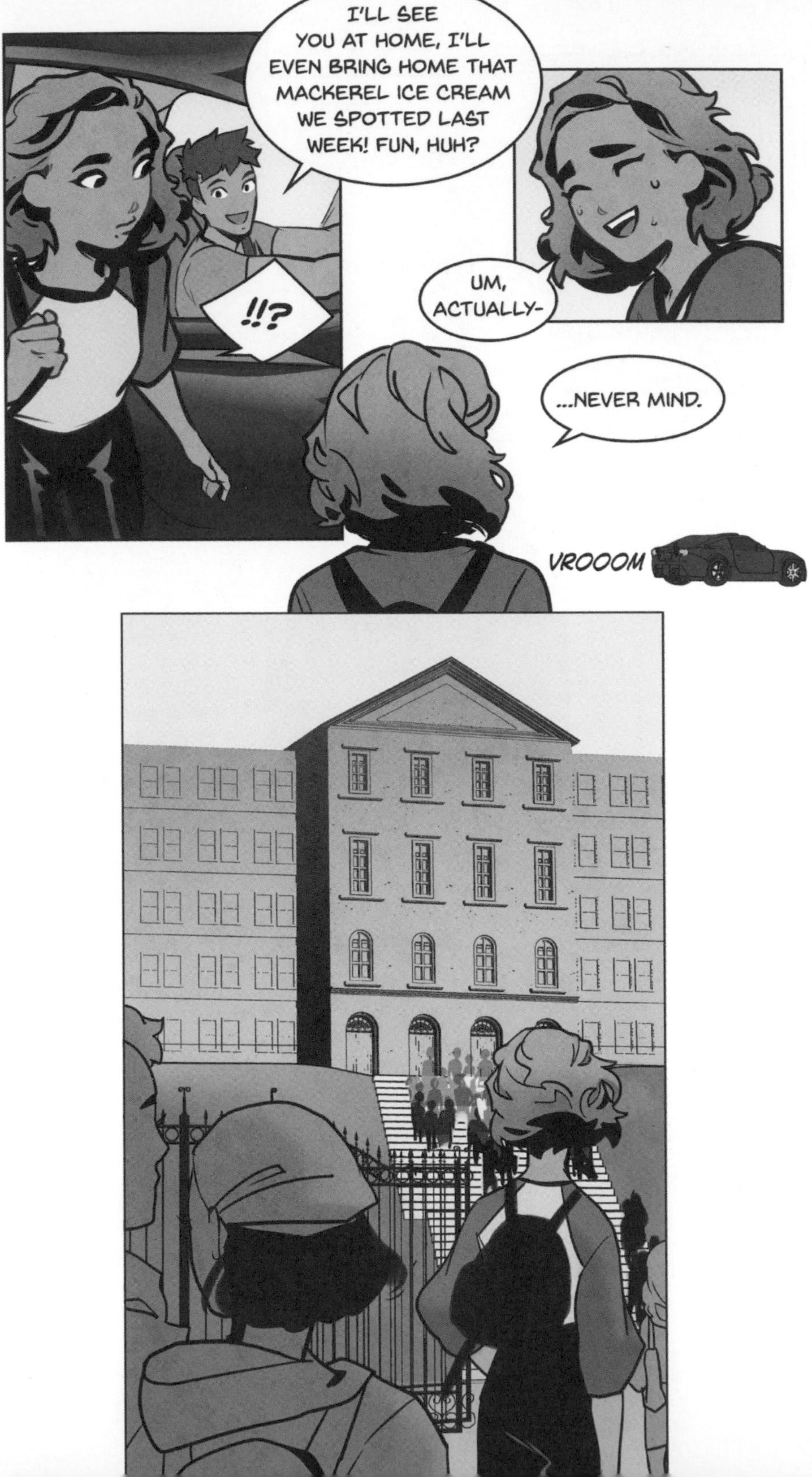
I'LL SEE YOU AT HOME, I'LL EVEN BRING HOME THAT MACKEREL ICE CREAM WE SPOTTED LAST WEEK! FUN, HUH?
!!?
UM, ACTUALLY-
...NEVER MIND.
VROOOM

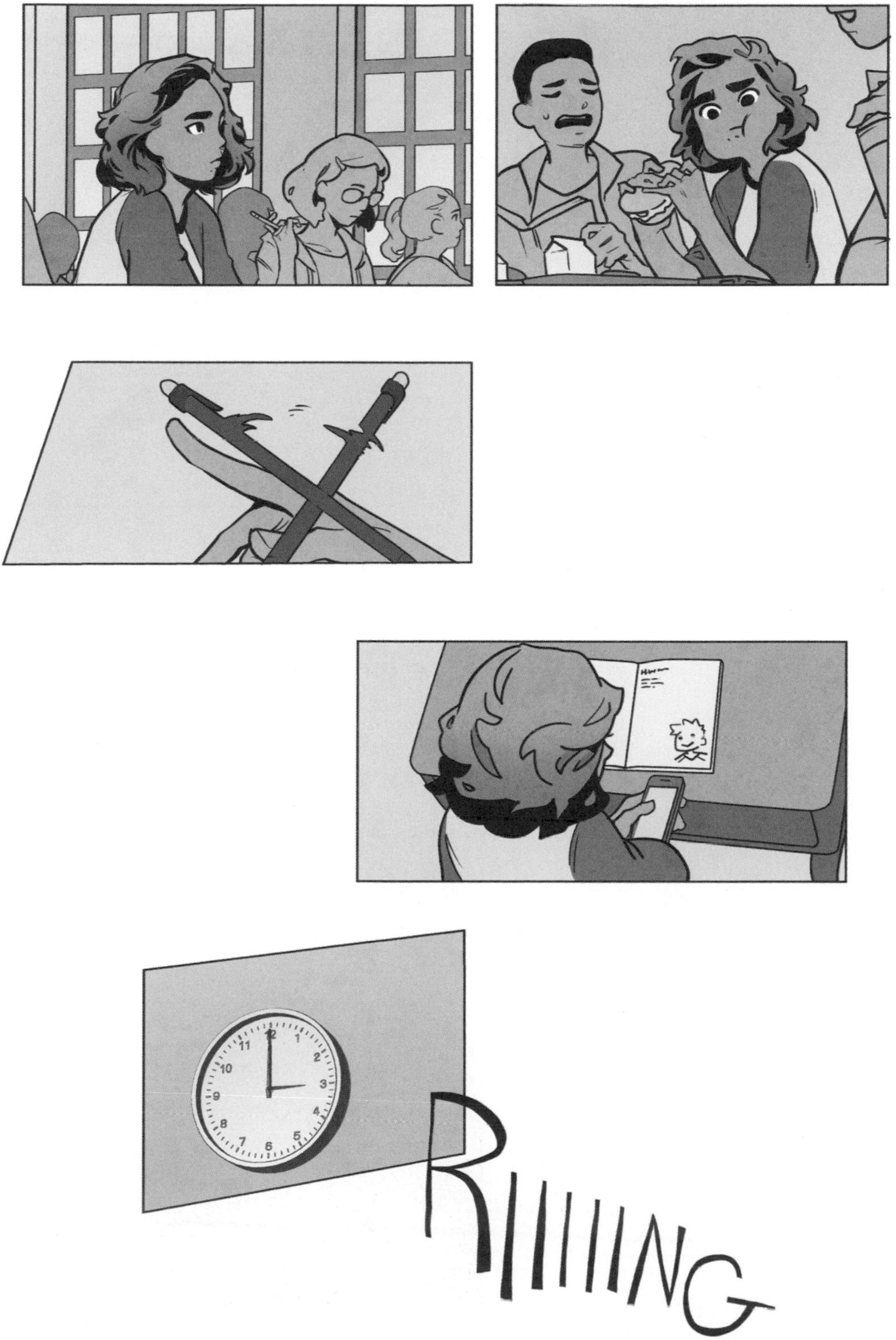
RIIIIING

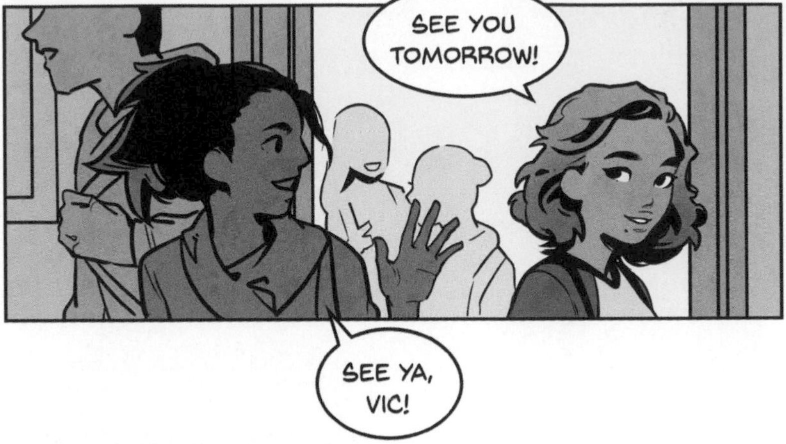
SEE YOU TOMORROW!
SEE YA, VIC!

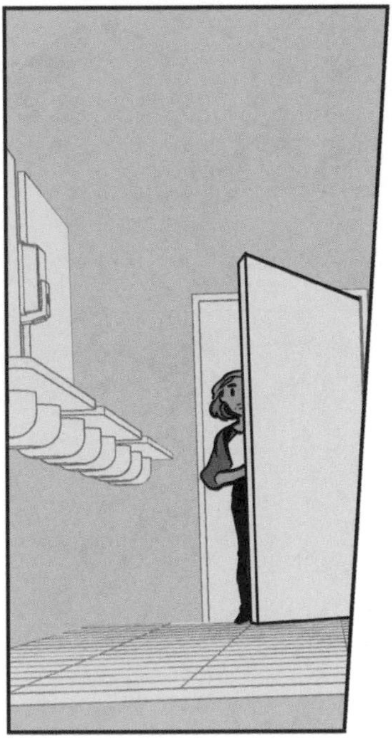

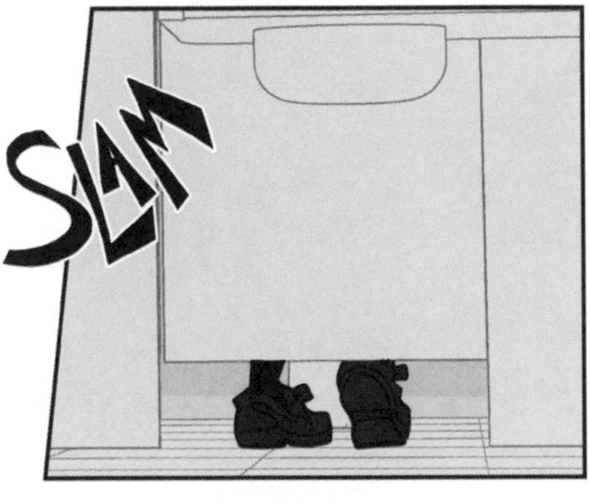
SLAM

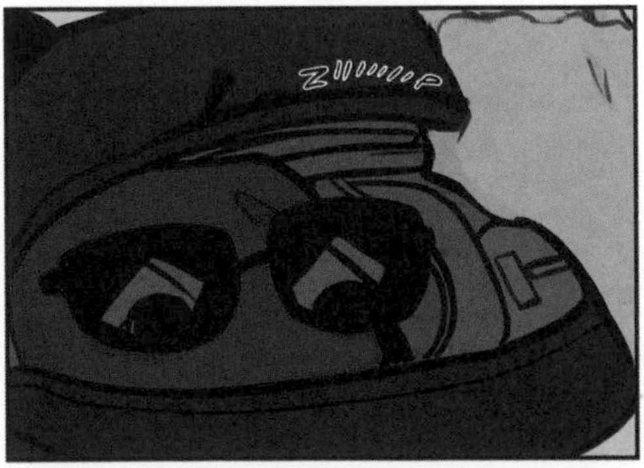
ZIIIIIIIIP

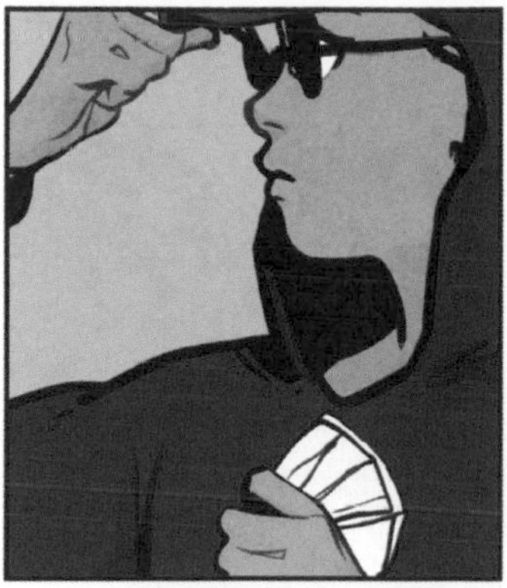

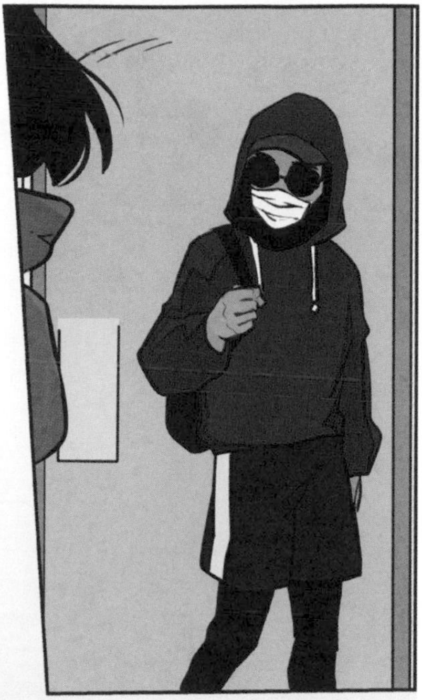

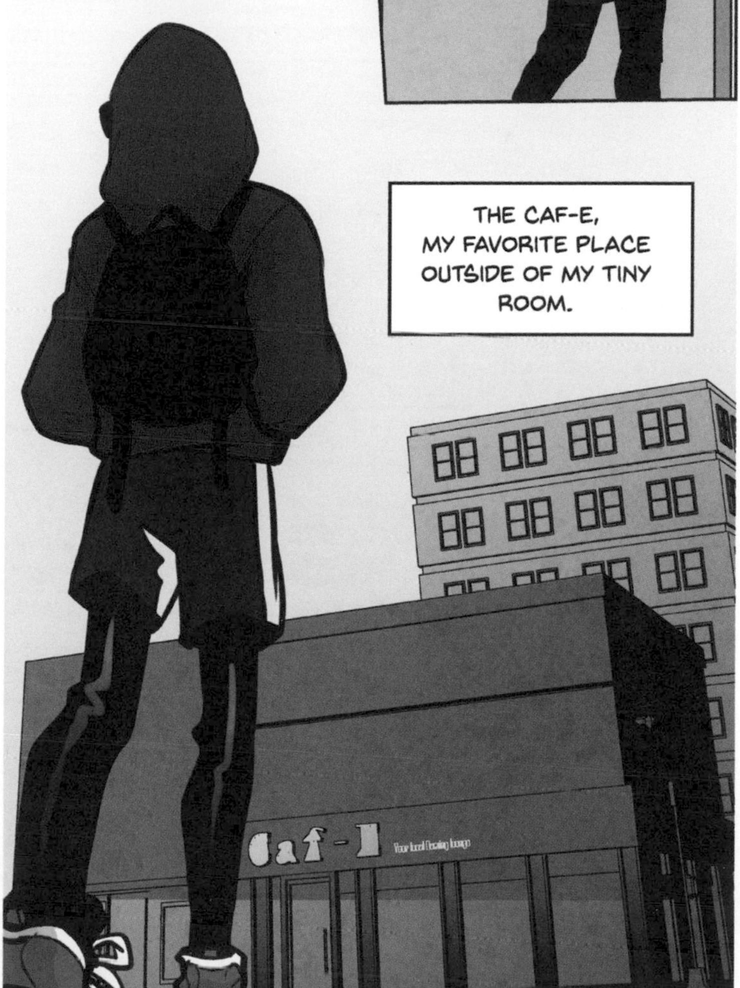
THE CAF-E, MY FAVORITE PLACE OUTSIDE OF MY TINY ROOM.

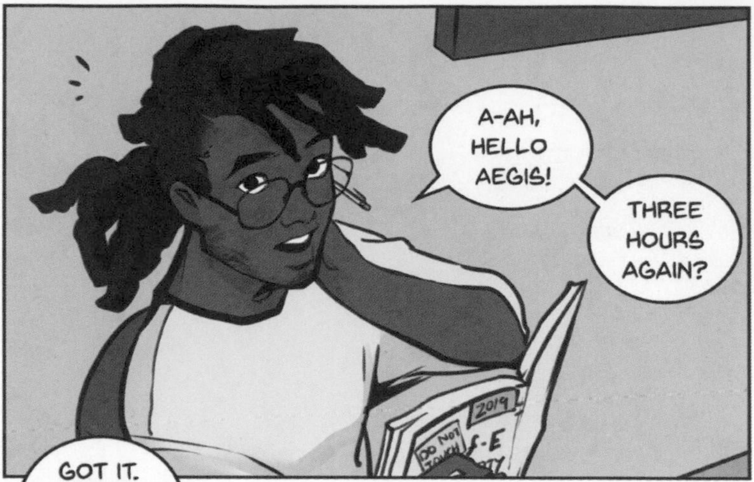
A-AH, HELLO AEGIS!
THREE HOURS AGAIN?

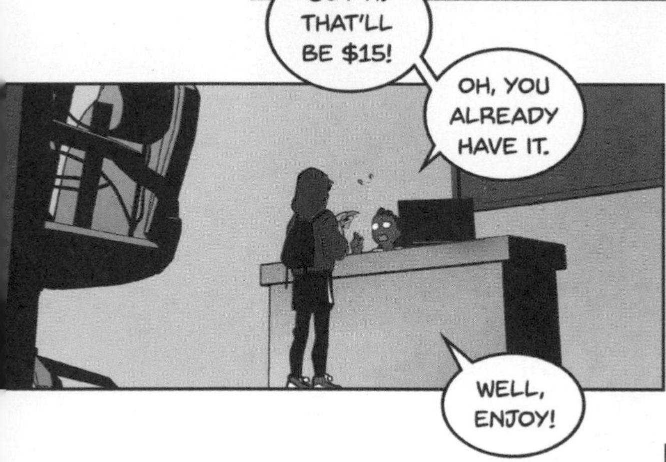
GOT IT. THAT'LL BE $15!
OH, YOU ALREADY HAVE IT.
WELL, ENJOY!

IT FEELS GOOD.

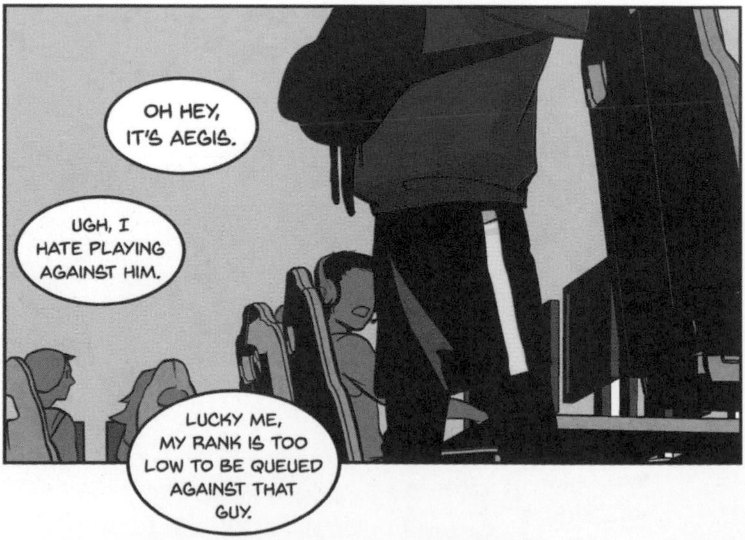
OH HEY, IT'S AEGIS.
UGH, I HATE PLAYING AGAINST HIM.
LUCKY ME, MY RANK IS TOO LOW TO BE QUEUED AGAINST THAT GUY.

I WONDER IF THIS IS WHAT VIRGIL FEELS LIKE ALL THE TIME?

BEING STARED AT IN RESPECT AND FEAR.

IT'S THE BEST.

NO WONDER HE ACTS THE WAY HE ACTS.

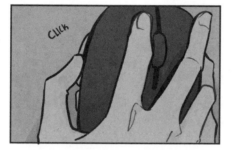

CLICK

BUT FOR ME, IT'S A TEMPORARY PLEASURE.

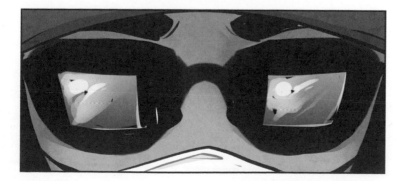

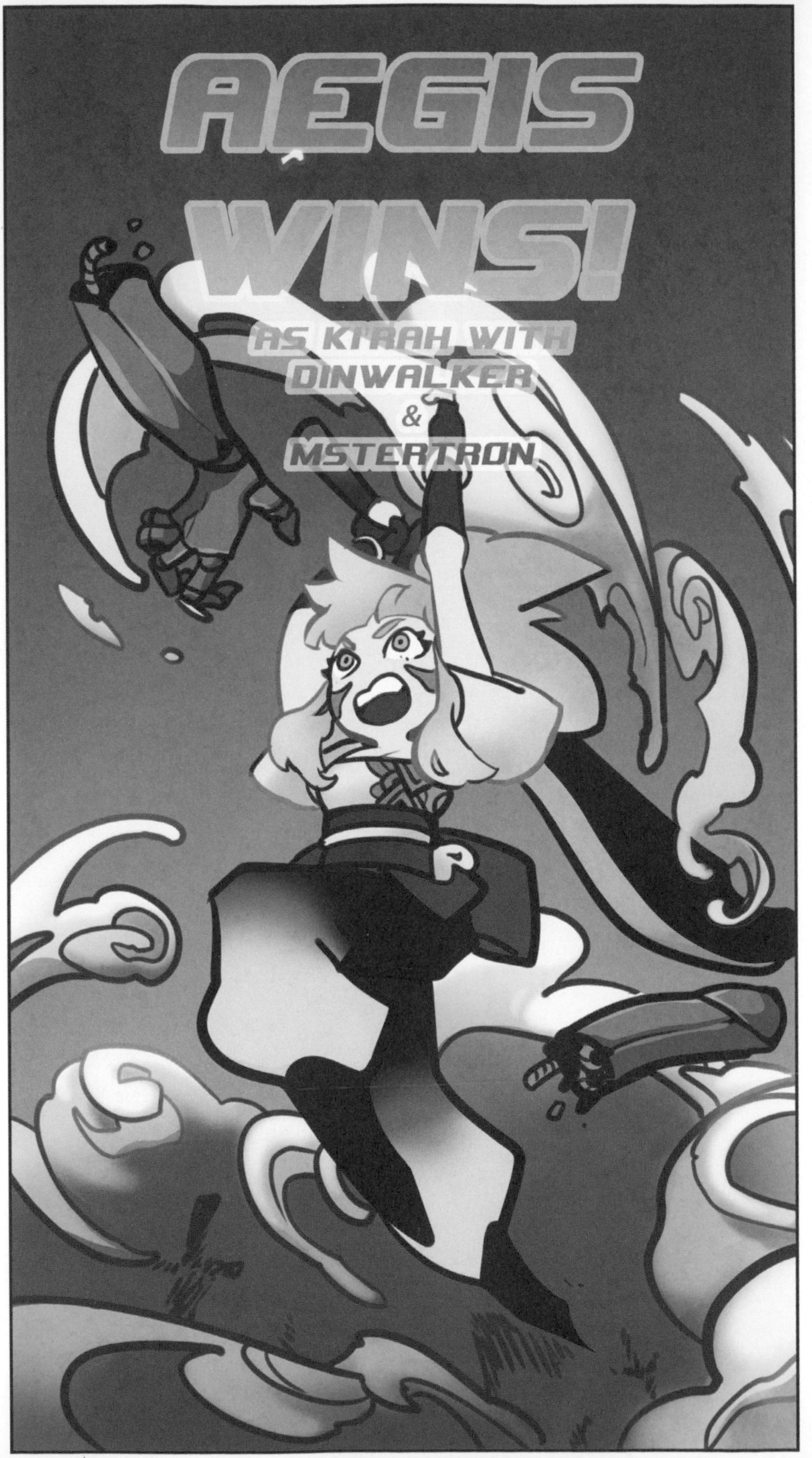
AEGIS WINS!
AS KI'RAH WITH DINWALKER & MSTERTRON

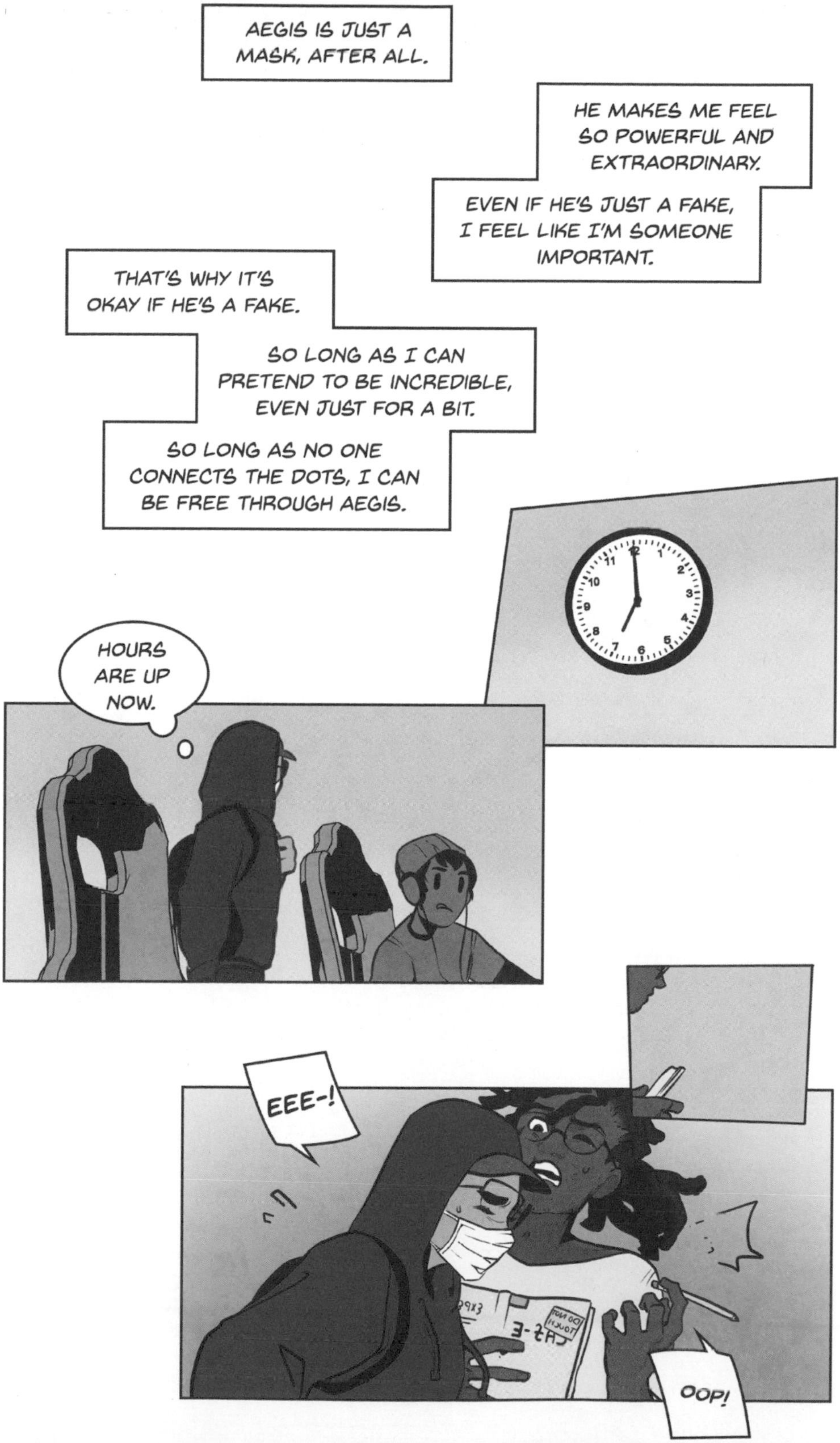
AEGIS IS JUST A MASK, AFTER ALL.
HE MAKES ME FEEL SO POWERFUL AND EXTRAORDINARY.
EVEN IF HE'S JUST A FAKE, I FEEL LIKE I'M SOMEONE IMPORTANT.
THAT'S WHY IT'S OKAY IF HE'S A FAKE.
SO LONG AS I CAN PRETEND TO BE INCREDIBLE, EVEN JUST FOR A BIT.
SO LONG AS NO ONE CONNECTS THE DOTS, I CAN BE FREE THROUGH AEGIS.
HOURS ARE UP NOW.
EEE-!
OOP!

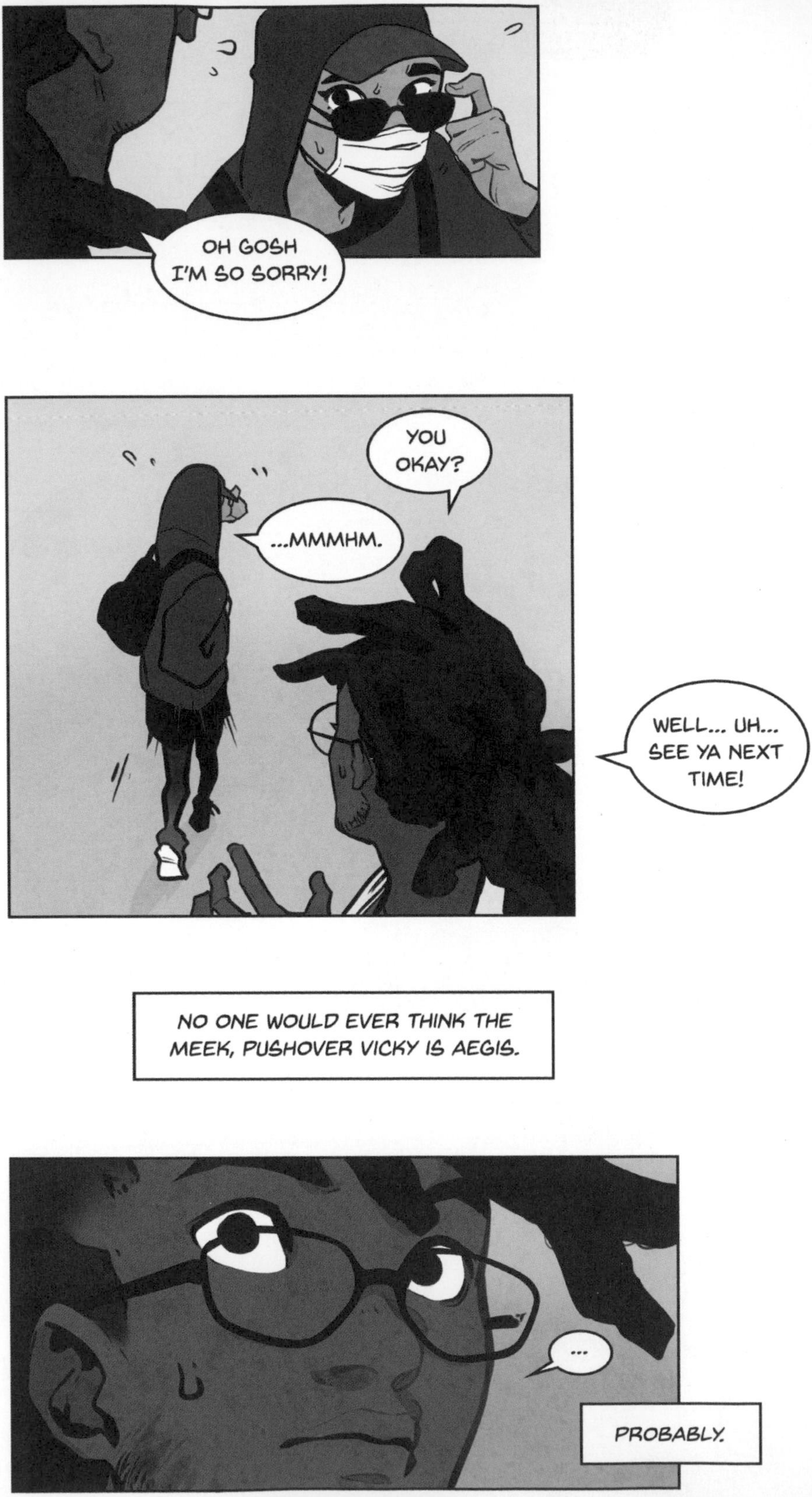
OH GOSH I'M SO SORRY!
YOU OKAY?
...MMMHM.
WELL... UH... SEE YA NEXT TIME!
NO ONE WOULD EVER THINK THE MEEK, PUSHOVER VICKY IS AEGIS.
...
PROBABLY.

CHAPTER 2: CONFIDENCE

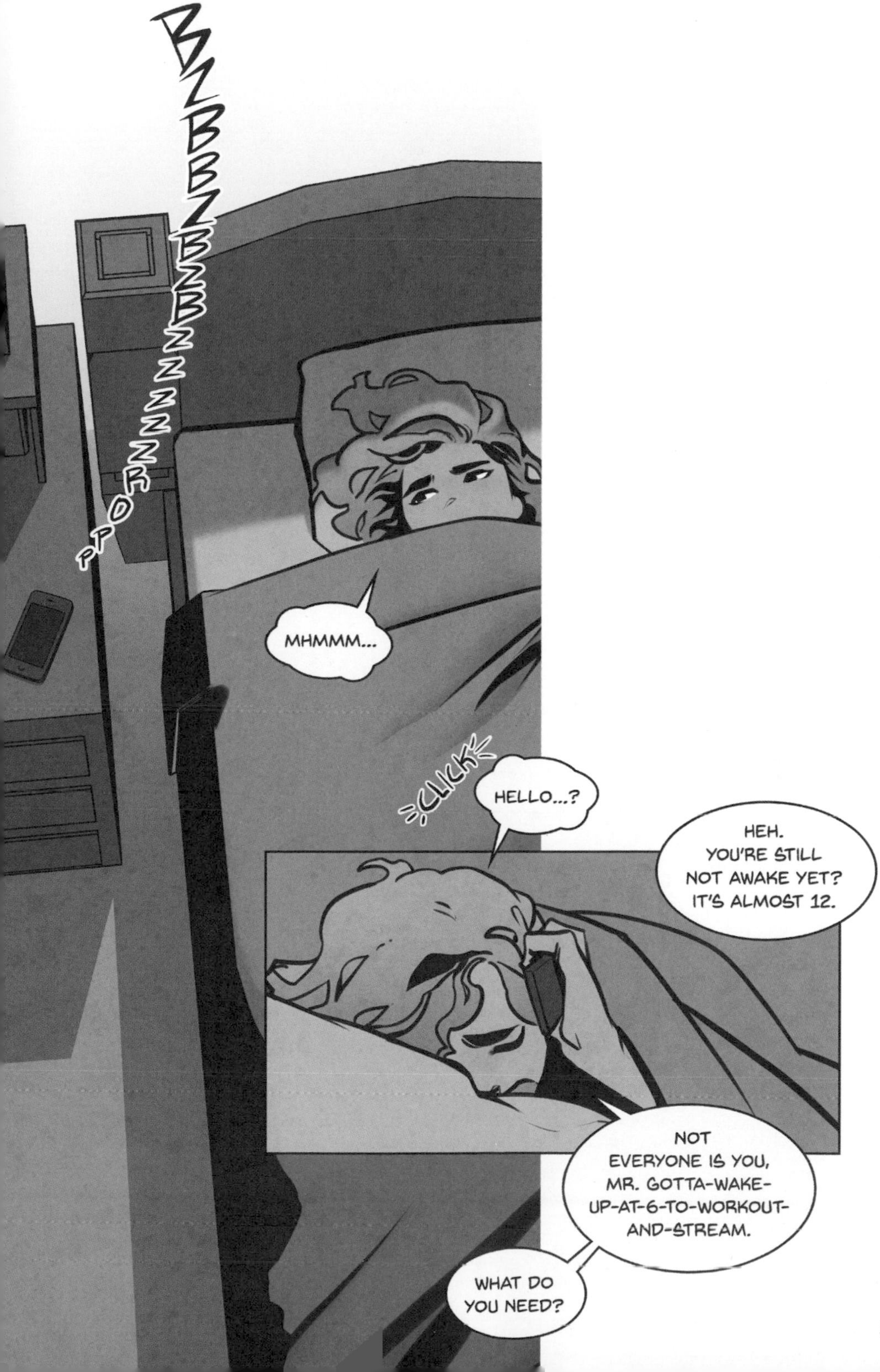
MHMMM...
CLICK
HELLO...?
HEH. YOU'RE STILL NOT AWAKE YET? IT'S ALMOST 12.
NOT EVERYONE IS YOU, MR. GOTTA-WAKE-UP-AT-6-TO-WORKOUT-AND-STREAM.
WHAT DO YOU NEED?

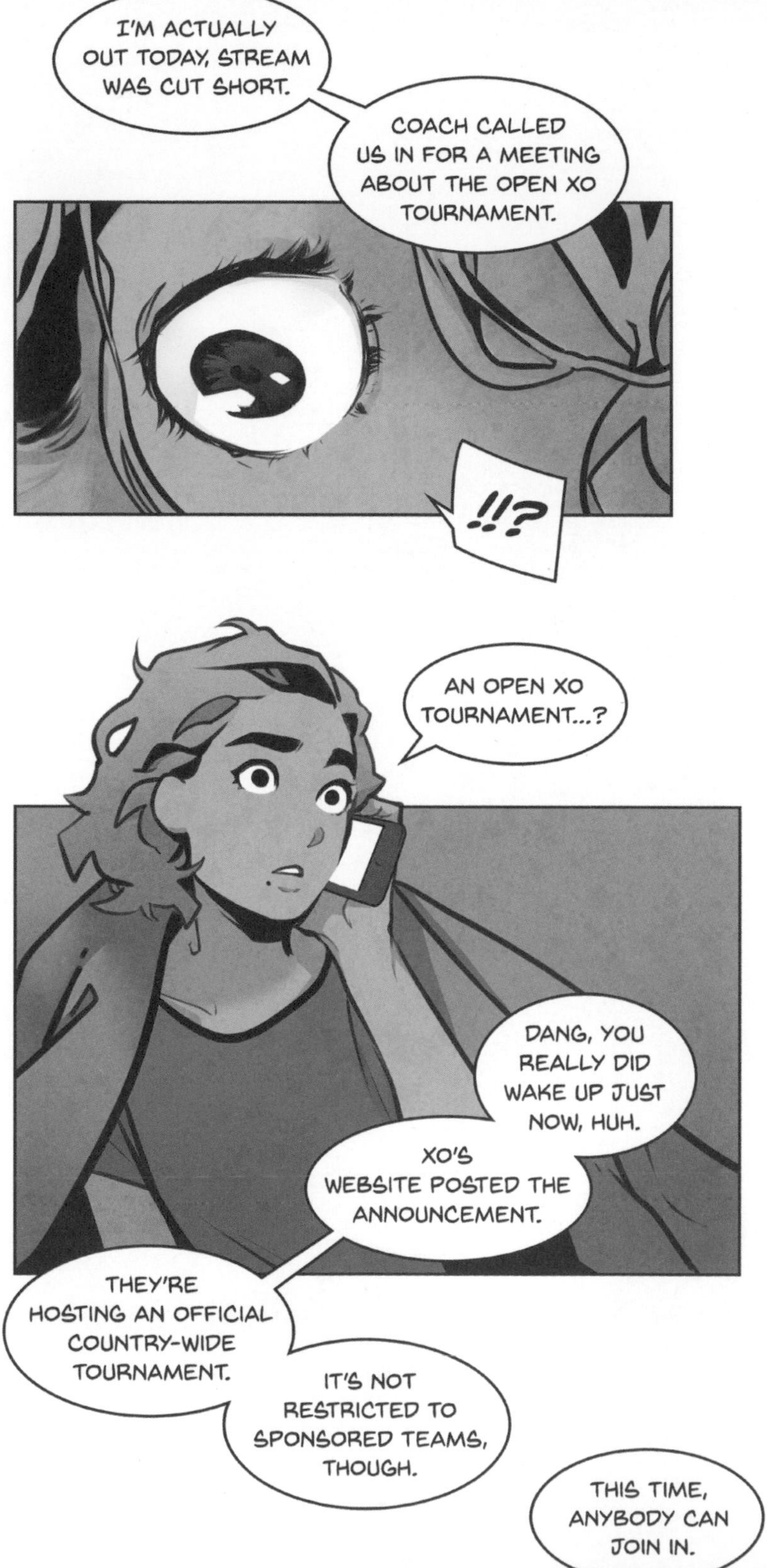
I'M ACTUALLY OUT TODAY, STREAM WAS CUT SHORT.
COACH CALLED US IN FOR A MEETING ABOUT THE OPEN XO TOURNAMENT.
!!?
AN OPEN XO TOURNAMENT...?
DANG, YOU REALLY DID WAKE UP JUST NOW, HUH.
XO'S WEBSITE POSTED THE ANNOUNCEMENT.
THEY'RE HOSTING AN OFFICIAL COUNTRY-WIDE TOURNAMENT.
IT'S NOT RESTRICTED TO SPONSORED TEAMS, THOUGH.
THIS TIME, ANYBODY CAN JOIN IN.

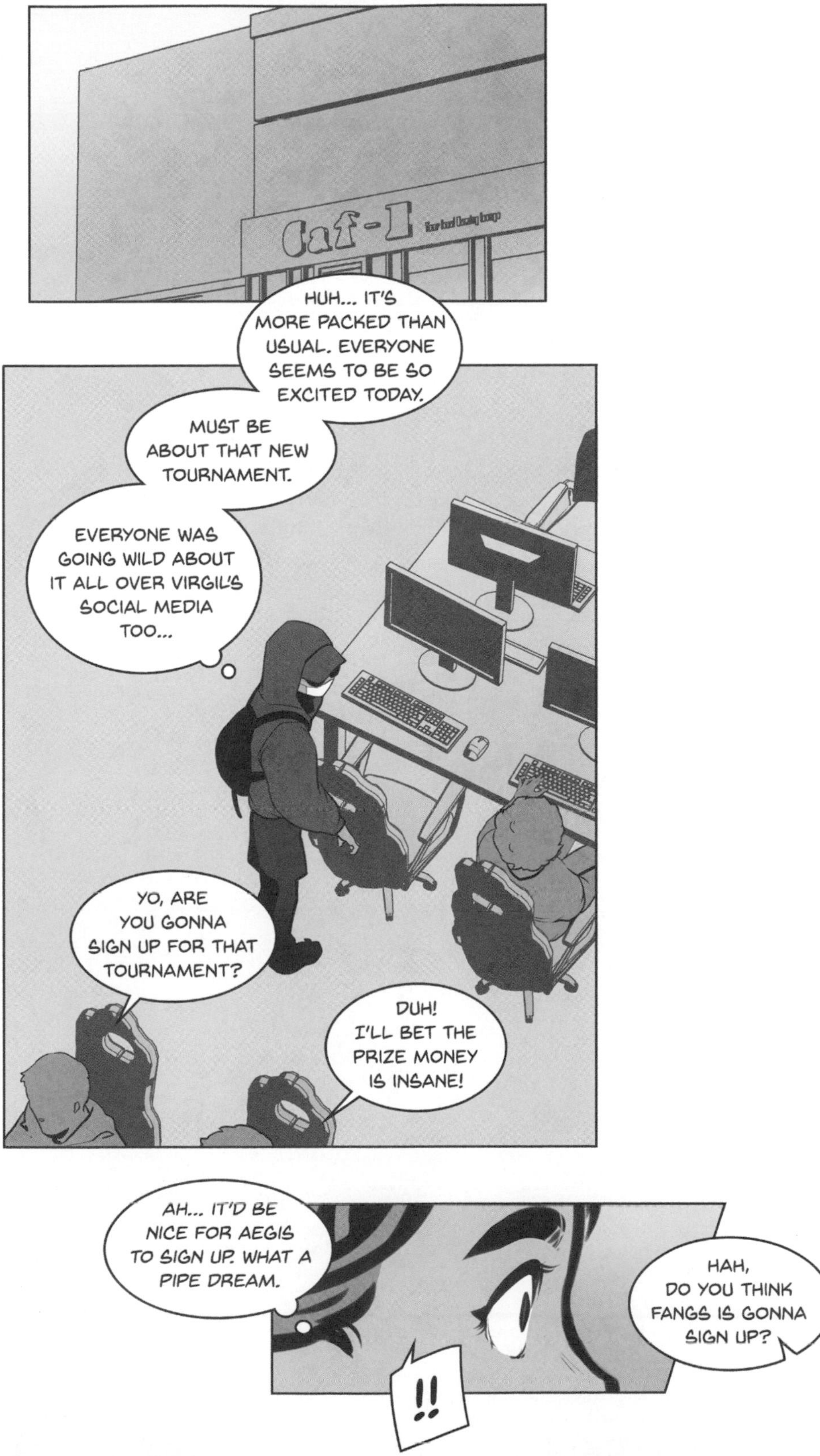
Caf-1
HUH... IT'S MORE PACKED THAN USUAL. EVERYONE SEEMS TO BE SO EXCITED TODAY.
MUST BE ABOUT THAT NEW TOURNAMENT.
EVERYONE WAS GOING WILD ABOUT IT ALL OVER VIRGIL'S SOCIAL MEDIA TOO...
YO, ARE YOU GONNA SIGN UP FOR THAT TOURNAMENT?
DUH! I'LL BET THE PRIZE MONEY IS INSANE!
AH... IT'D BE NICE FOR AEGIS TO SIGN UP. WHAT A PIPE DREAM.
HAH, DO YOU THINK FANGS IS GONNA SIGN UP?
!!

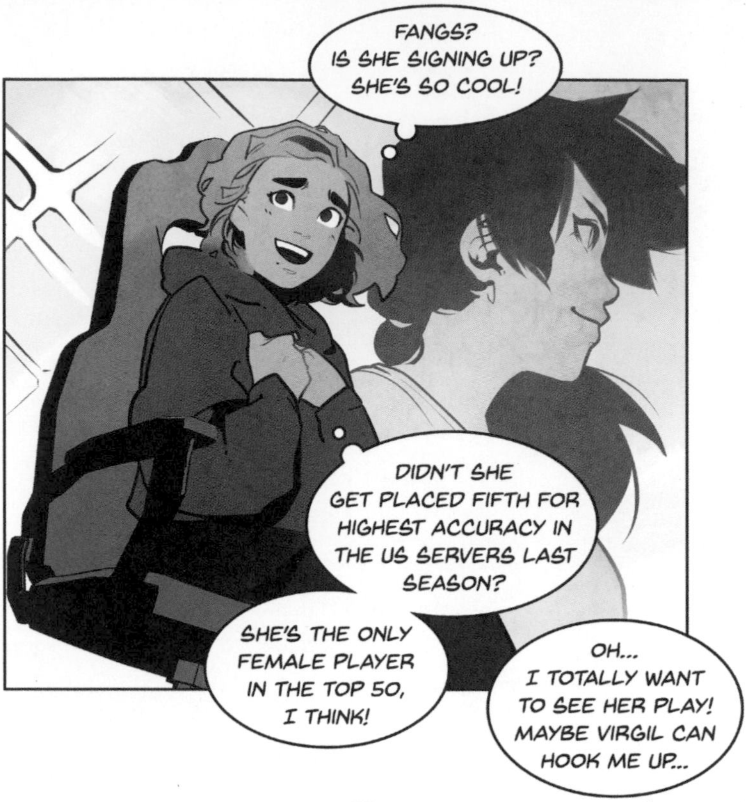
FANGS? IS SHE SIGNING UP? SHE'S SO COOL!
DIDN'T SHE GET PLACED FIFTH FOR HIGHEST ACCURACY IN THE US SERVERS LAST SEASON?
SHE'S THE ONLY FEMALE PLAYER IN THE TOP 50, I THINK!
OH... I TOTALLY WANT TO SEE HER PLAY! MAYBE VIRGIL CAN HOOK ME UP...

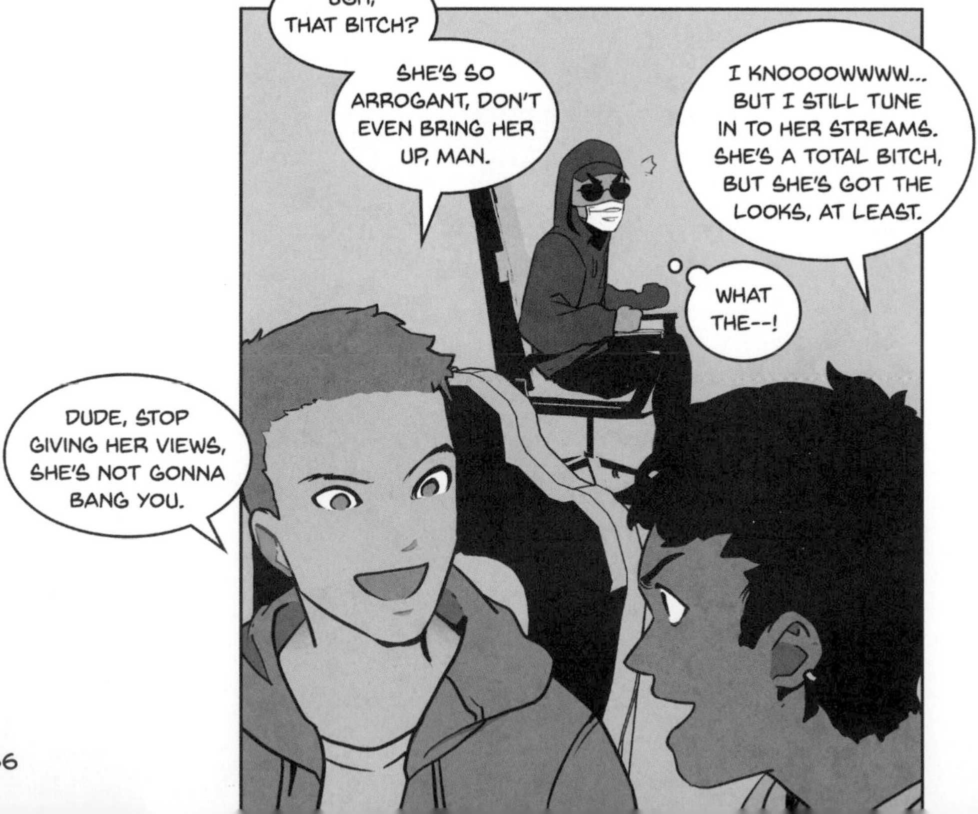
UGH, THAT BITCH?
SHE'S SO ARROGANT, DON'T EVEN BRING HER UP, MAN.
I KNOOOOWWWW... BUT I STILL TUNE IN TO HER STREAMS. SHE'S A TOTAL BITCH, BUT SHE'S GOT THE LOOKS, AT LEAST.
WHAT THE--!
DUDE, STOP GIVING HER VIEWS, SHE'S NOT GONNA BANG YOU.

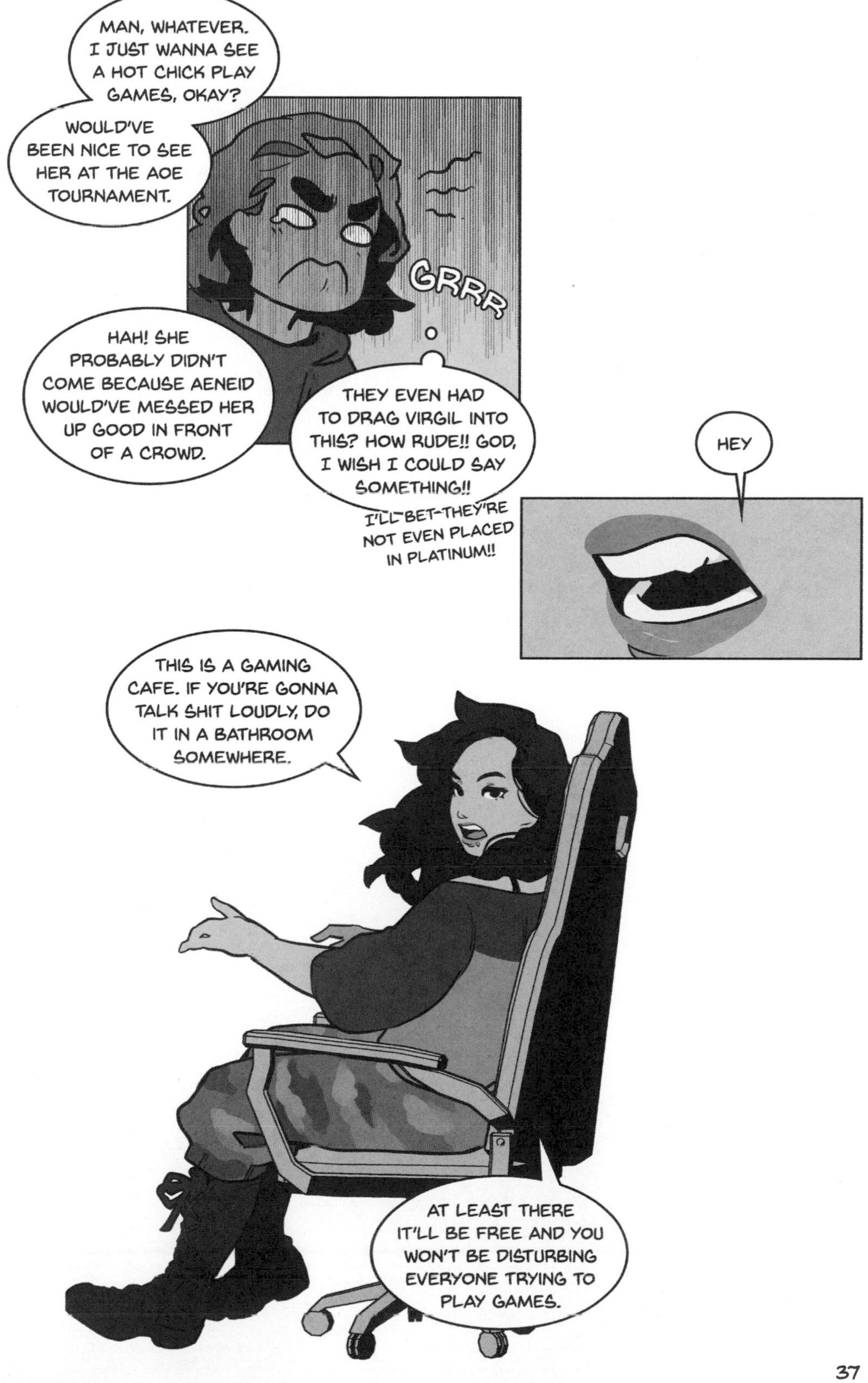
MAN, WHATEVER. I JUST WANNA SEE A HOT CHICK PLAY GAMES, OKAY?
WOULD'VE BEEN NICE TO SEE HER AT THE AOE TOURNAMENT.
GRRR
HAH! SHE PROBABLY DIDN'T COME BECAUSE AENEID WOULD'VE MESSED HER UP GOOD IN FRONT OF A CROWD.
THEY EVEN HAD TO DRAG VIRGIL INTO THIS? HOW RUDE!! GOD, I WISH I COULD SAY SOMETHING!!
I'LL BET THEY'RE NOT EVEN PLACED IN PLATINUM!!
HEY
THIS IS A GAMING CAFE. IF YOU'RE GONNA TALK SHIT LOUDLY, DO IT IN A BATHROOM SOMEWHERE.
AT LEAST THERE IT'LL BE FREE AND YOU WON'T BE DISTURBING EVERYONE TRYING TO PLAY GAMES.

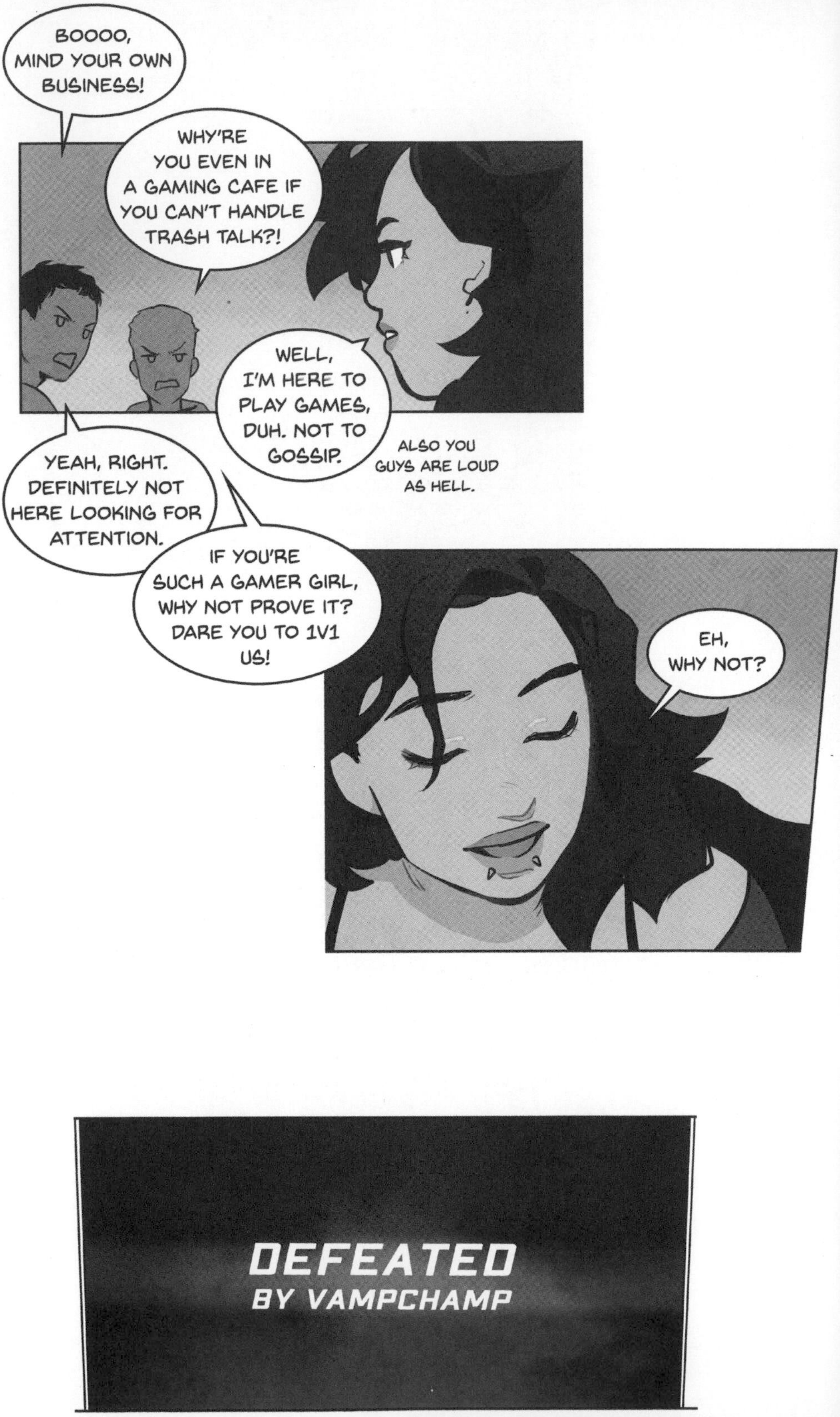
BOOOO, MIND YOUR OWN BUSINESS!
WHY'RE YOU EVEN IN A GAMING CAFE IF YOU CAN'T HANDLE TRASH TALK?!
WELL, I'M HERE TO PLAY GAMES, DUH. NOT TO GOSSIP.
ALSO YOU GUYS ARE LOUD AS HELL.
YEAH, RIGHT. DEFINITELY NOT HERE LOOKING FOR ATTENTION.
IF YOU'RE SUCH A GAMER GIRL, WHY NOT PROVE IT? DARE YOU TO 1V1 US!
EH, WHY NOT?
DEFEATED
BY VAMPCHAMP

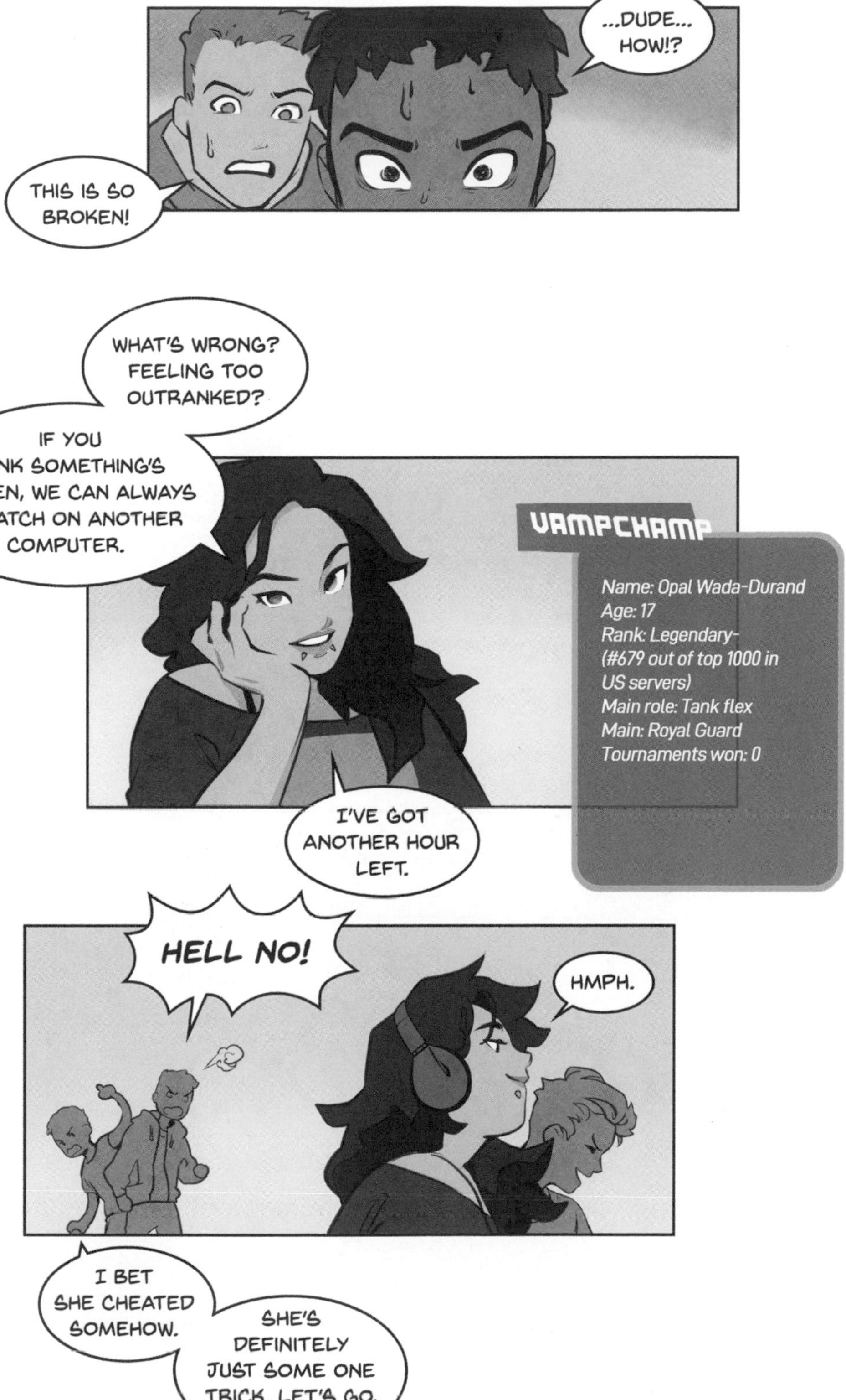
...DUDE... HOW!?
THIS IS SO BROKEN!
WHAT'S WRONG? FEELING TOO OUTRANKED?
IF YOU THINK SOMETHING'S BROKEN, WE CAN ALWAYS REMATCH ON ANOTHER COMPUTER.
VAMPCHAMP
Name: Opal Wada-Durand
Age: 17
Rank: Legendary-
(#679 out of top 1000 in
US servers)
Main role: Tank flex
Main: Royal Guard
Tournaments won: 0
I'VE GOT ANOTHER HOUR LEFT.
HELL NO!
HMPH.
I BET SHE CHEATED SOMEHOW.
SHE'S DEFINITELY JUST SOME ONE TRICK. LET'S GO, C'MON.

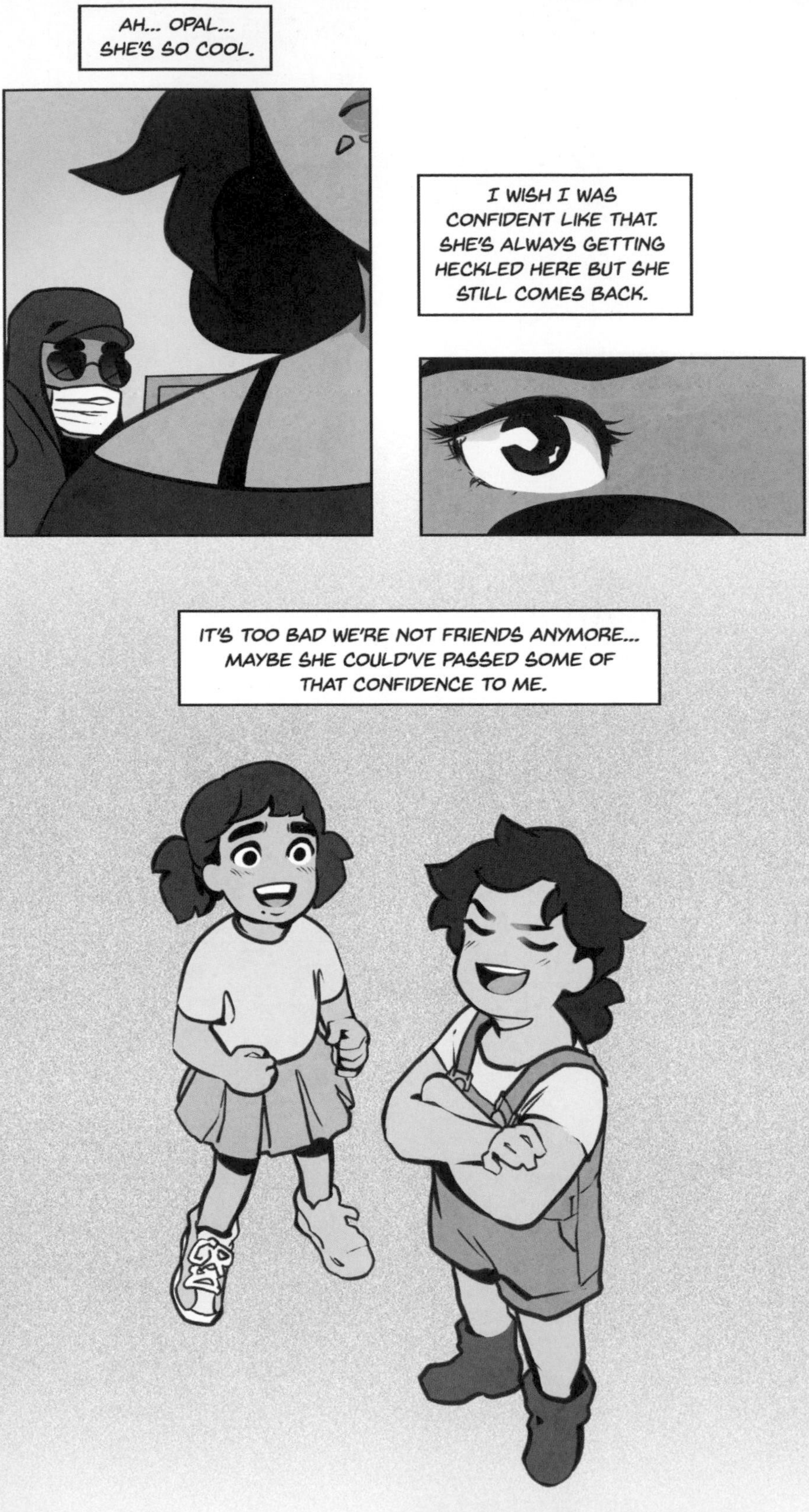
AH... OPAL... SHE'S SO COOL.
I WISH I WAS CONFIDENT LIKE THAT. SHE'S ALWAYS GETTING HECKLED HERE BUT SHE STILL COMES BACK.
IT'S TOO BAD WE'RE NOT FRIENDS ANYMORE... MAYBE SHE COULD'VE PASSED SOME OF THAT CONFIDENCE TO ME.

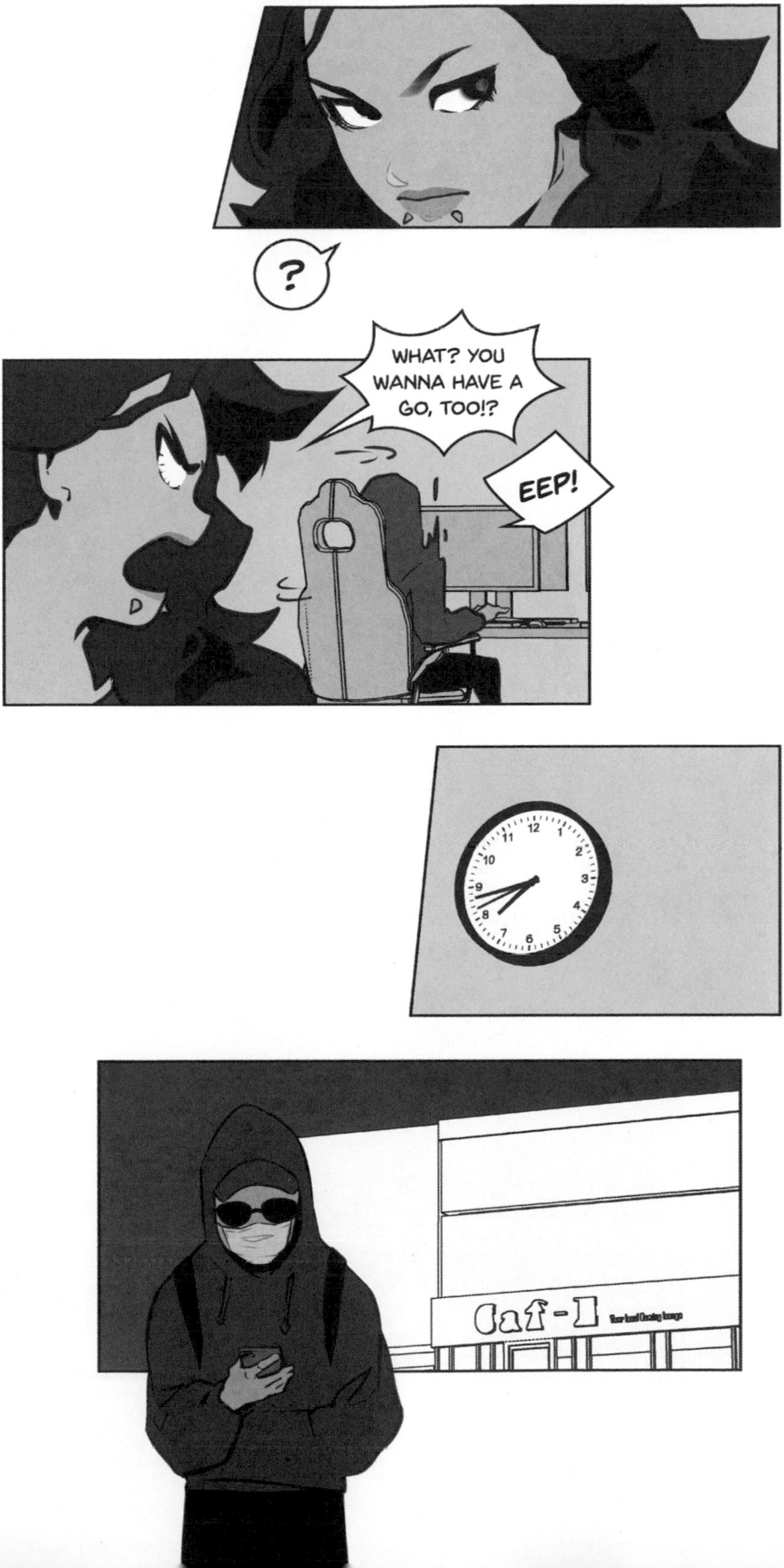
?
WHAT? YOU WANNA HAVE A GO, TOO!?
EEP!

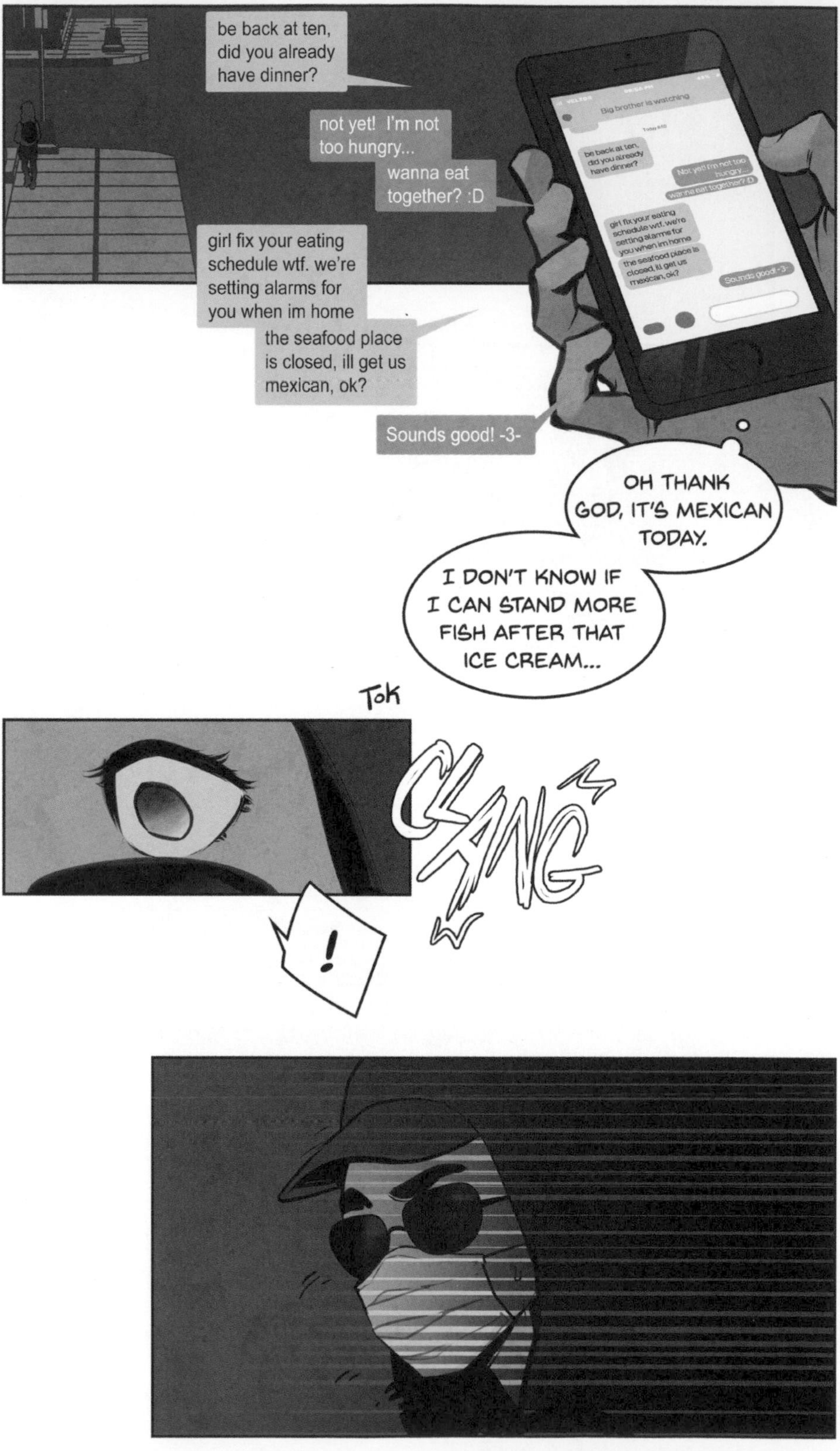
be back at ten, did you already have dinner?
not yet! I'm not too hungry...
wanna eat together? :D
girl fix your eating schedule wtf. we're setting alarms for you when im home
the seafood place is closed, ill get us mexican, ok?
Sounds good! -3-
OH THANK GOD, IT'S MEXICAN TODAY.
I DON'T KNOW IF I CAN STAND MORE FISH AFTER THAT ICE CREAM...
TOK
CLANG
!

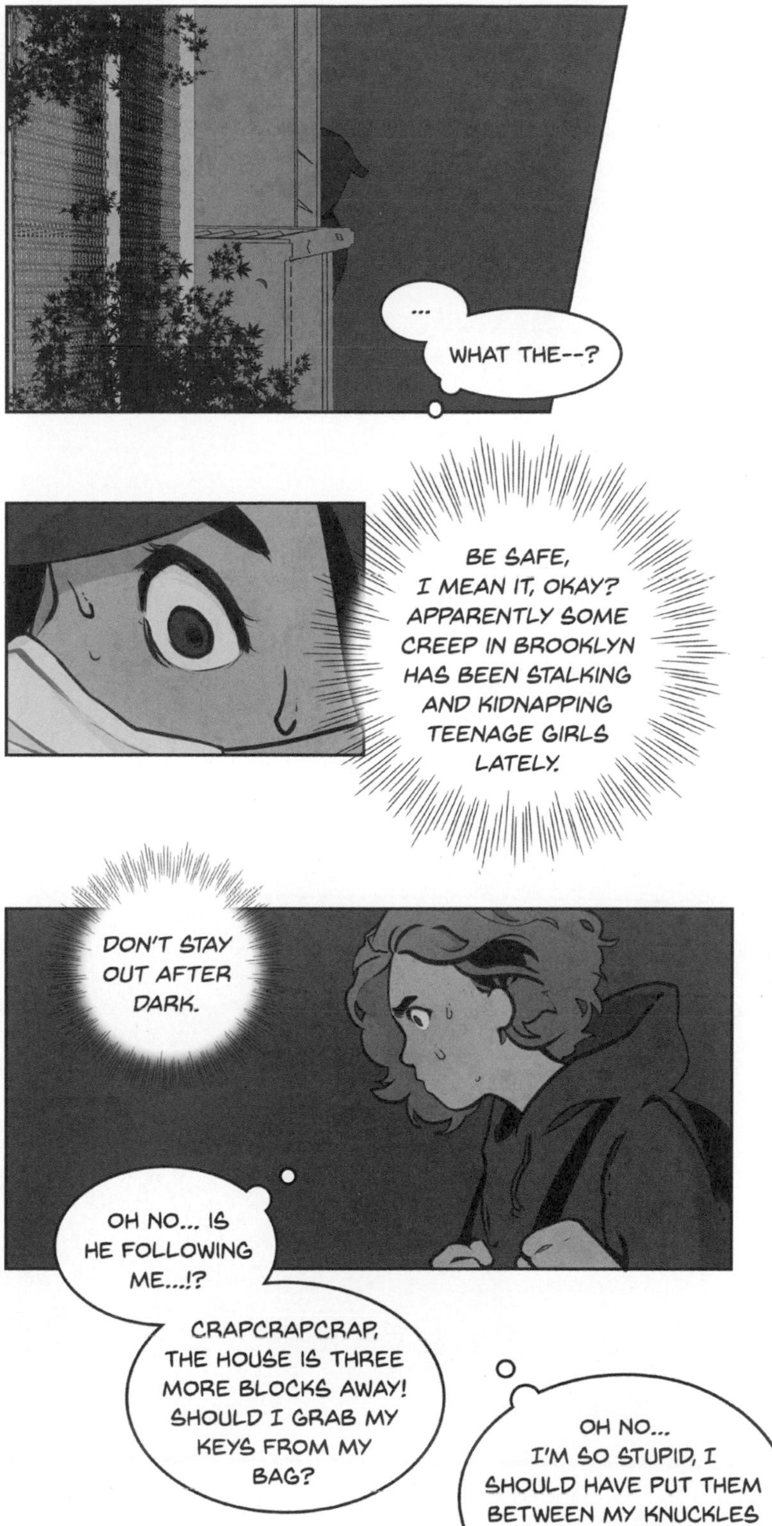
...
WHAT THE--?
BE SAFE, I MEAN IT, OKAY? APPARENTLY SOME CREEP IN BROOKLYN HAS BEEN STALKING AND KIDNAPPING TEENAGE GIRLS LATELY.
DON'T STAY OUT AFTER DARK.
OH NO... IS HE FOLLOWING ME...!?
CRAPCRAPCRAP, THE HOUSE IS THREE MORE BLOCKS AWAY! SHOULD I GRAB MY KEYS FROM MY BAG?
OH NO... I'M SO STUPID, I SHOULD HAVE PUT THEM BETWEEN MY KNUCKLES SINCE I STARTED WALKING!

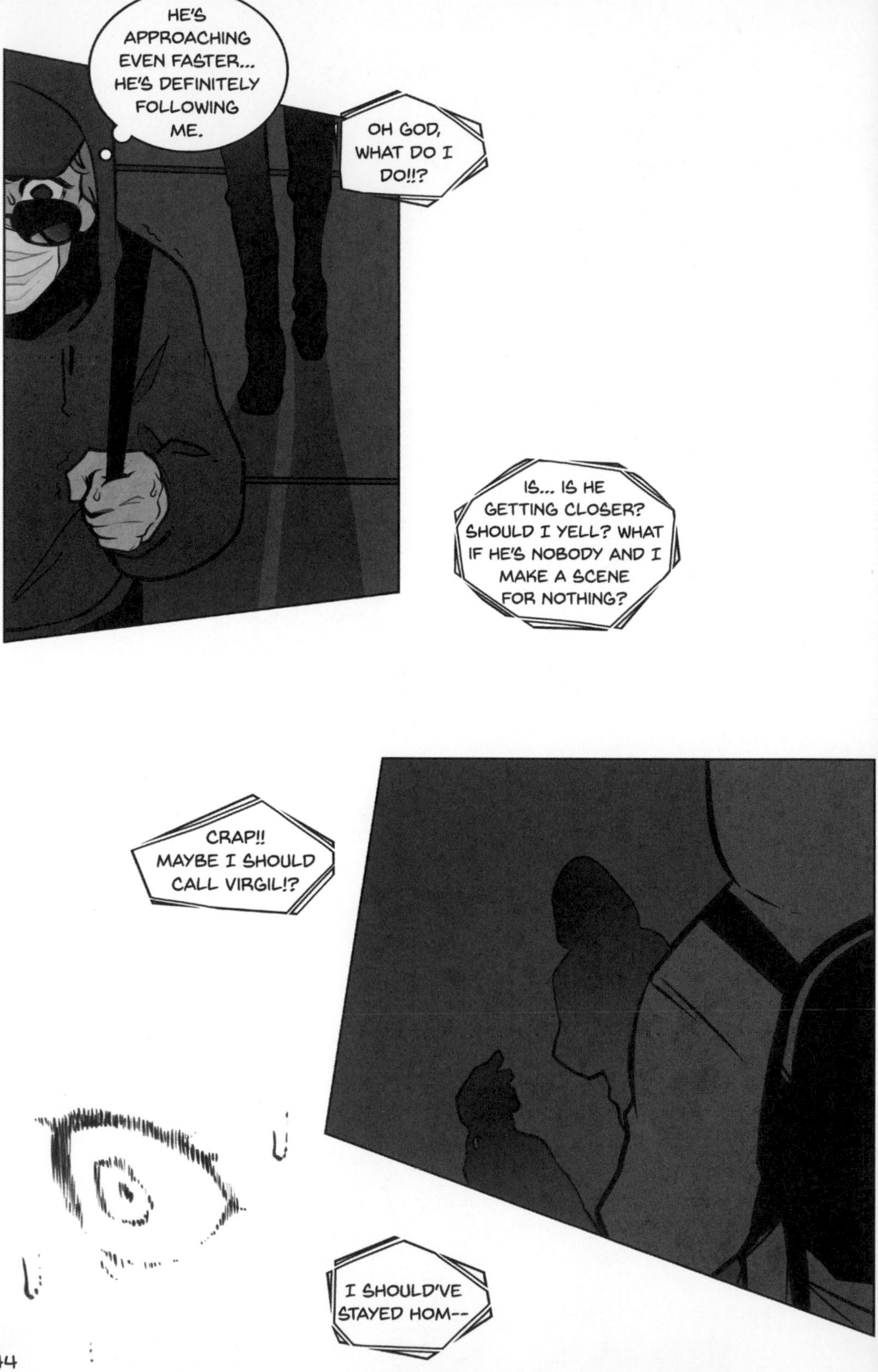
HE'S APPROACHING EVEN FASTER... HE'S DEFINITELY FOLLOWING ME.
OH GOD, WHAT DO I DO!!?
IS... IS HE GETTING CLOSER? SHOULD I YELL? WHAT IF HE'S NOBODY AND I MAKE A SCENE FOR NOTHING?
CRAP!! MAYBE I SHOULD CALL VIRGIL!?
I SHOULD'VE STAYED HOM--

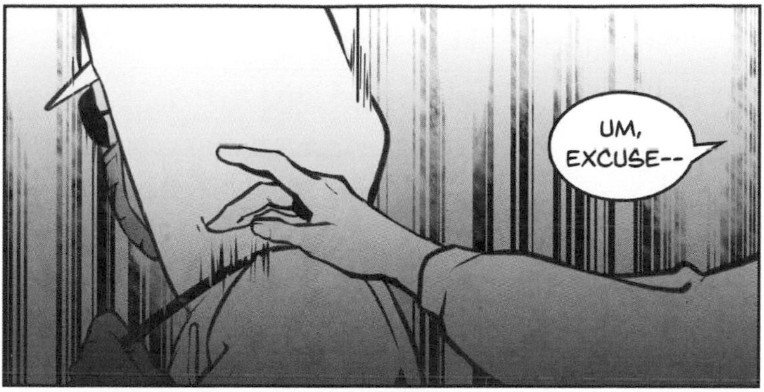
UM, EXCUSE--

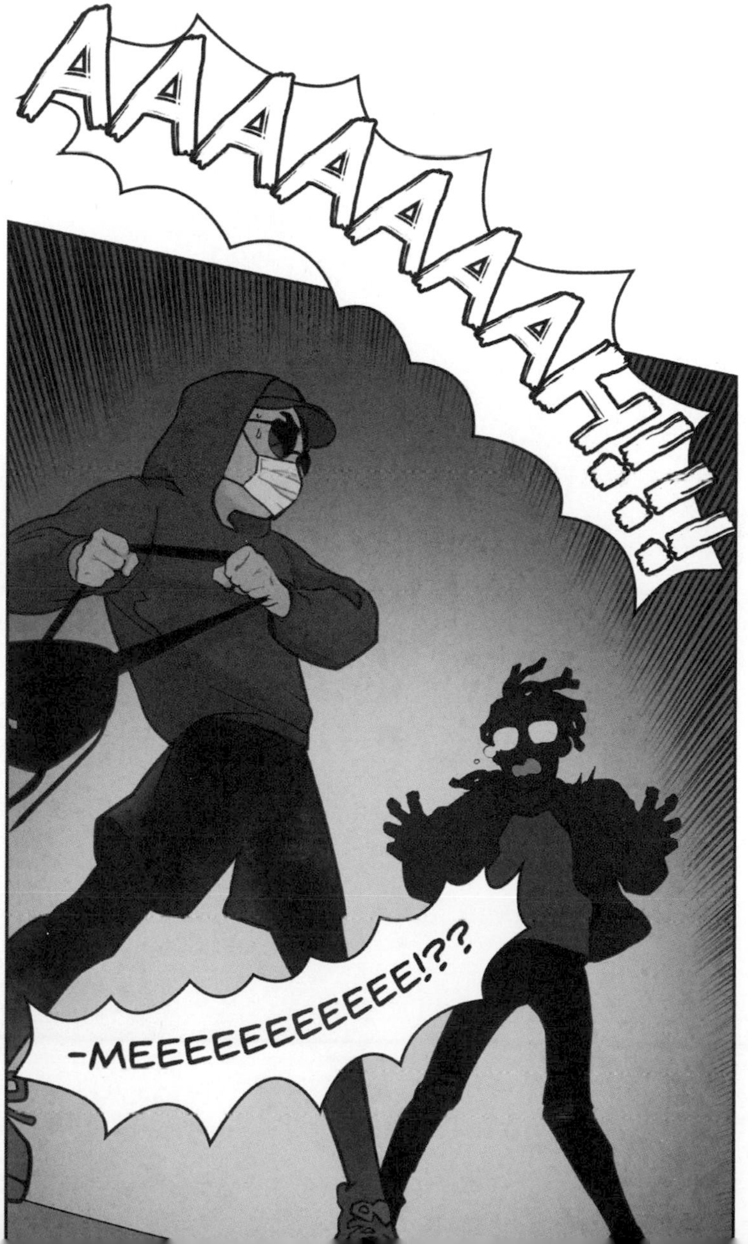
AAAAAAAAAAAH!!!!
-MEEEEEEEEEEEE!??

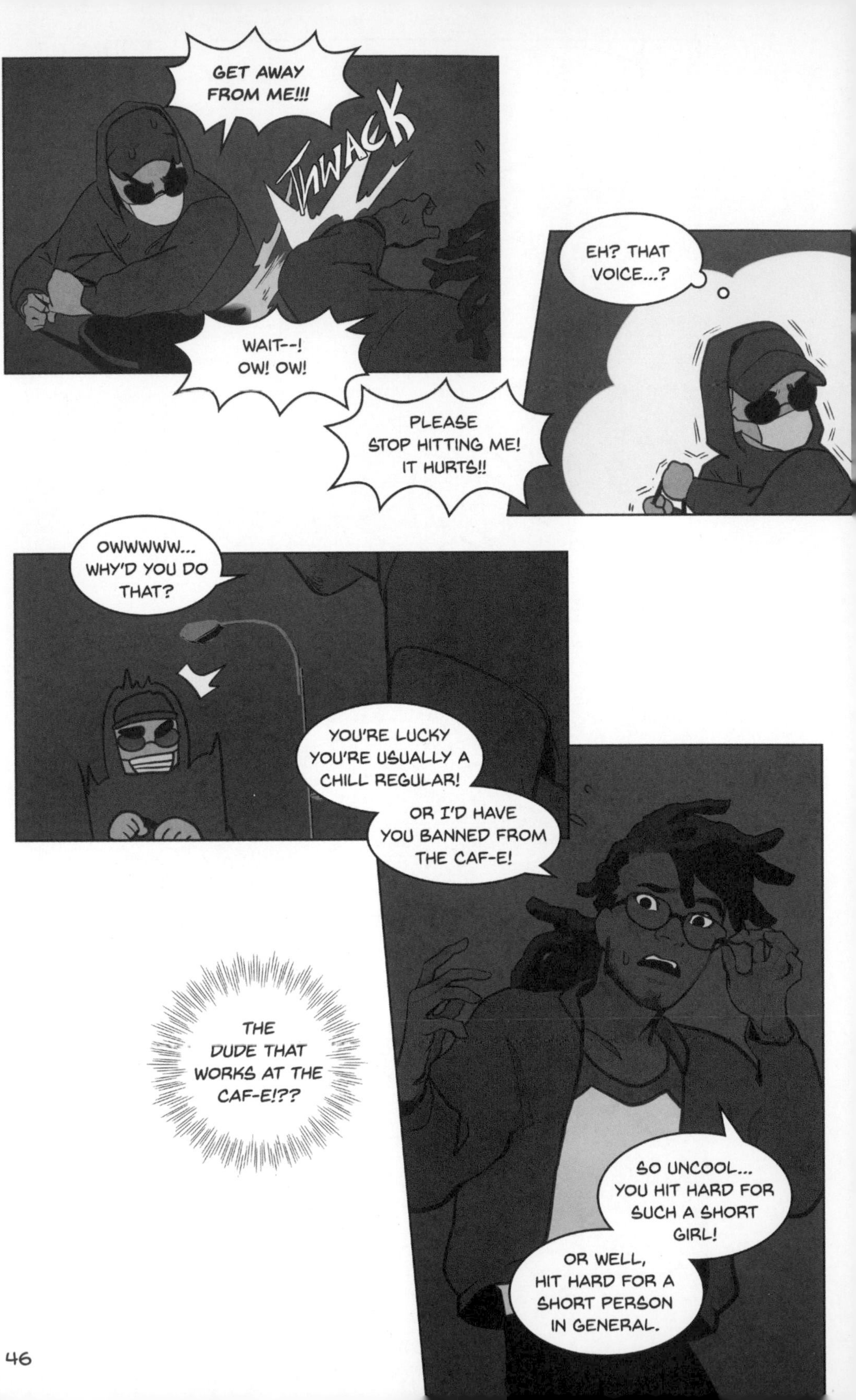
GET AWAY FROM ME!!!
THWACK
WAIT--! OW! OW!
PLEASE STOP HITTING ME! IT HURTS!!
EH? THAT VOICE...?
OWWWWW... WHY'D YOU DO THAT?
YOU'RE LUCKY YOU'RE USUALLY A CHILL REGULAR!
OR I'D HAVE YOU BANNED FROM THE CAF-E!
THE DUDE THAT WORKS AT THE CAF-E!??
SO UNCOOL... YOU HIT HARD FOR SUCH A SHORT GIRL!
OR WELL, HIT HARD FOR A SHORT PERSON IN GENERAL.

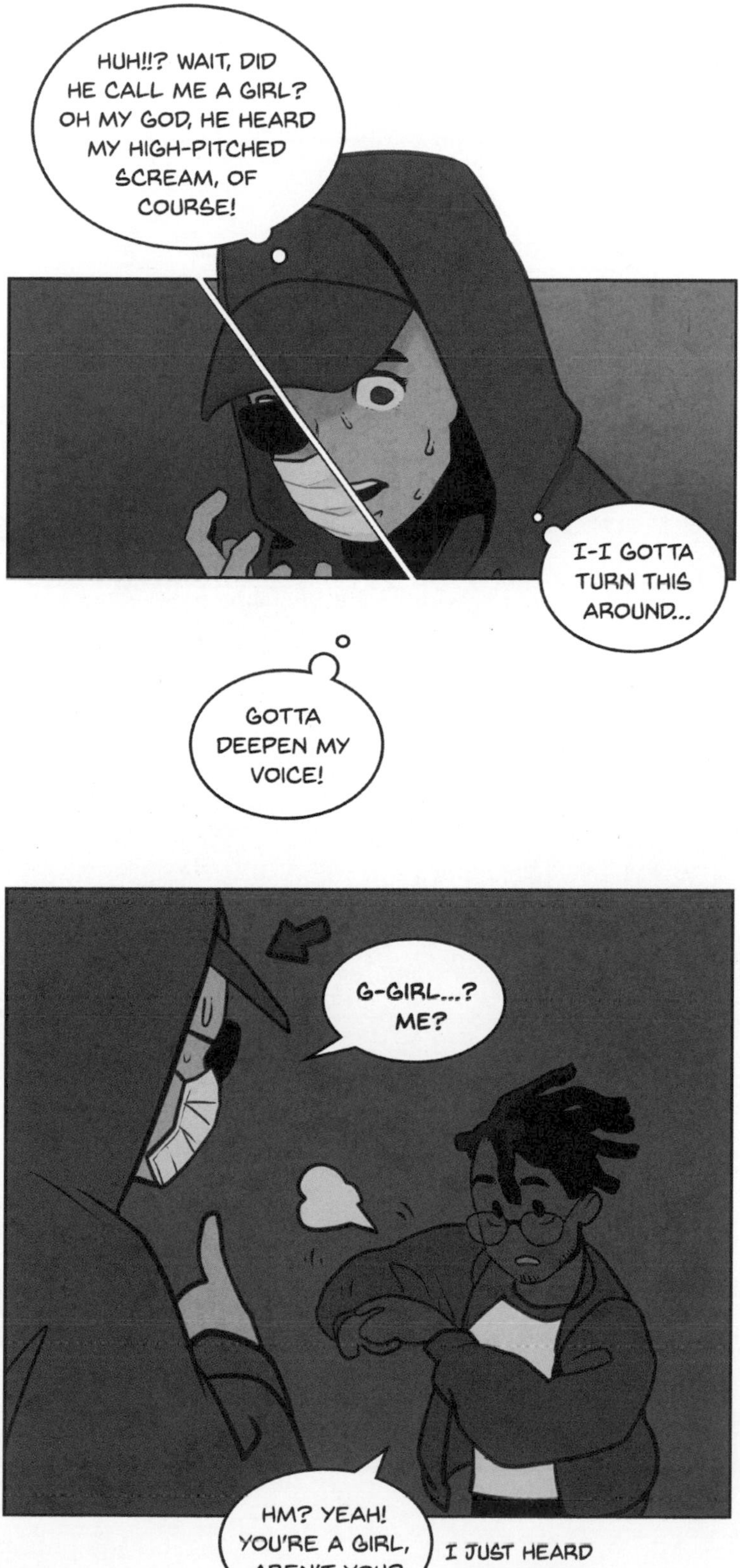
HUH!!? WAIT, DID HE CALL ME A GIRL? OH MY GOD, HE HEARD MY HIGH-PITCHED SCREAM, OF COURSE!
I-I GOTTA TURN THIS AROUND...
GOTTA DEEPEN MY VOICE!
G-GIRL...? ME?
HM? YEAH! YOU'RE A GIRL, AREN'T YOU?
I JUST HEARD YOU SCREAM LIKE ONE?

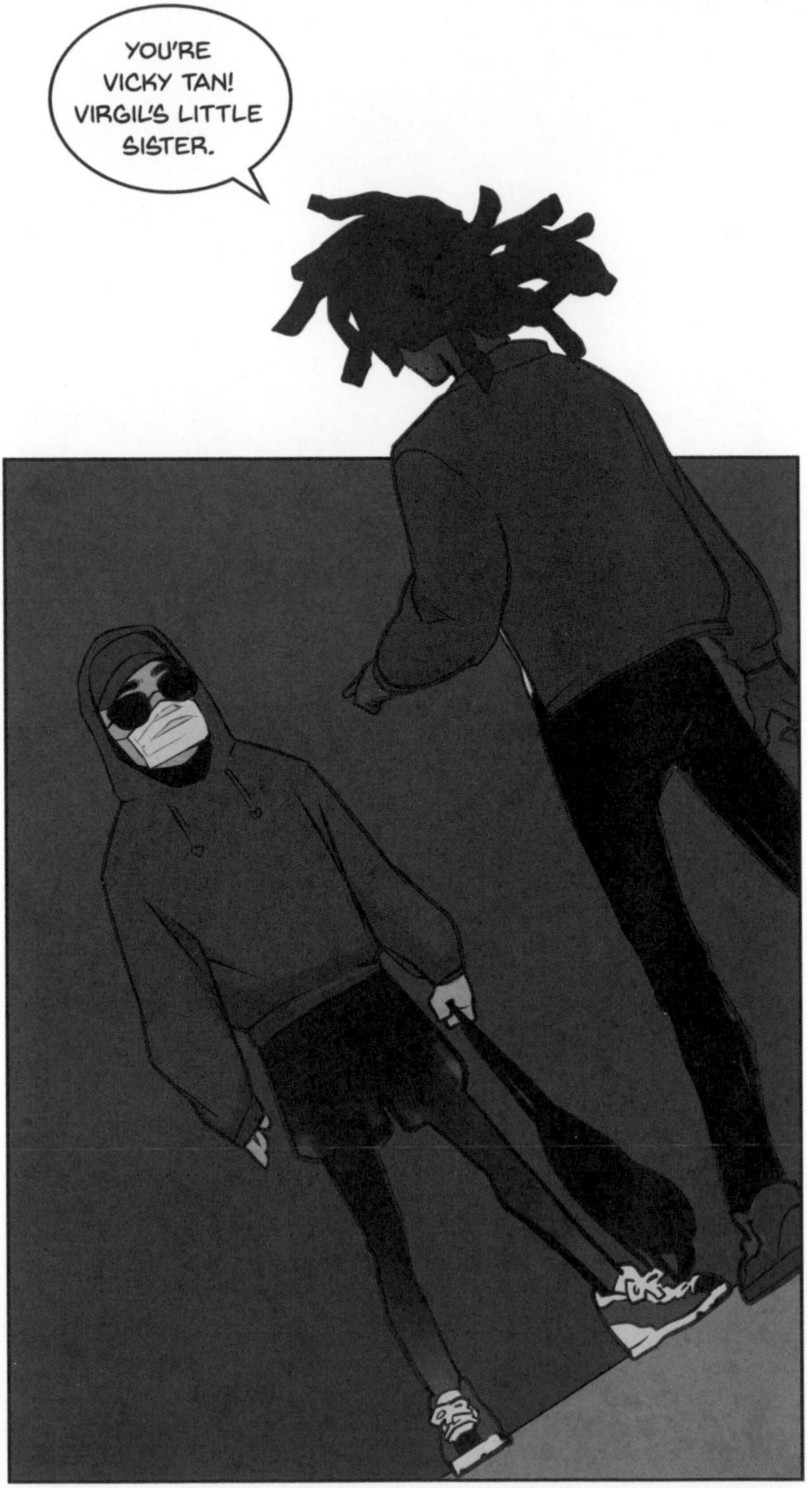
YOU'RE VICKY TAN! VIRGIL'S LITTLE SISTER.

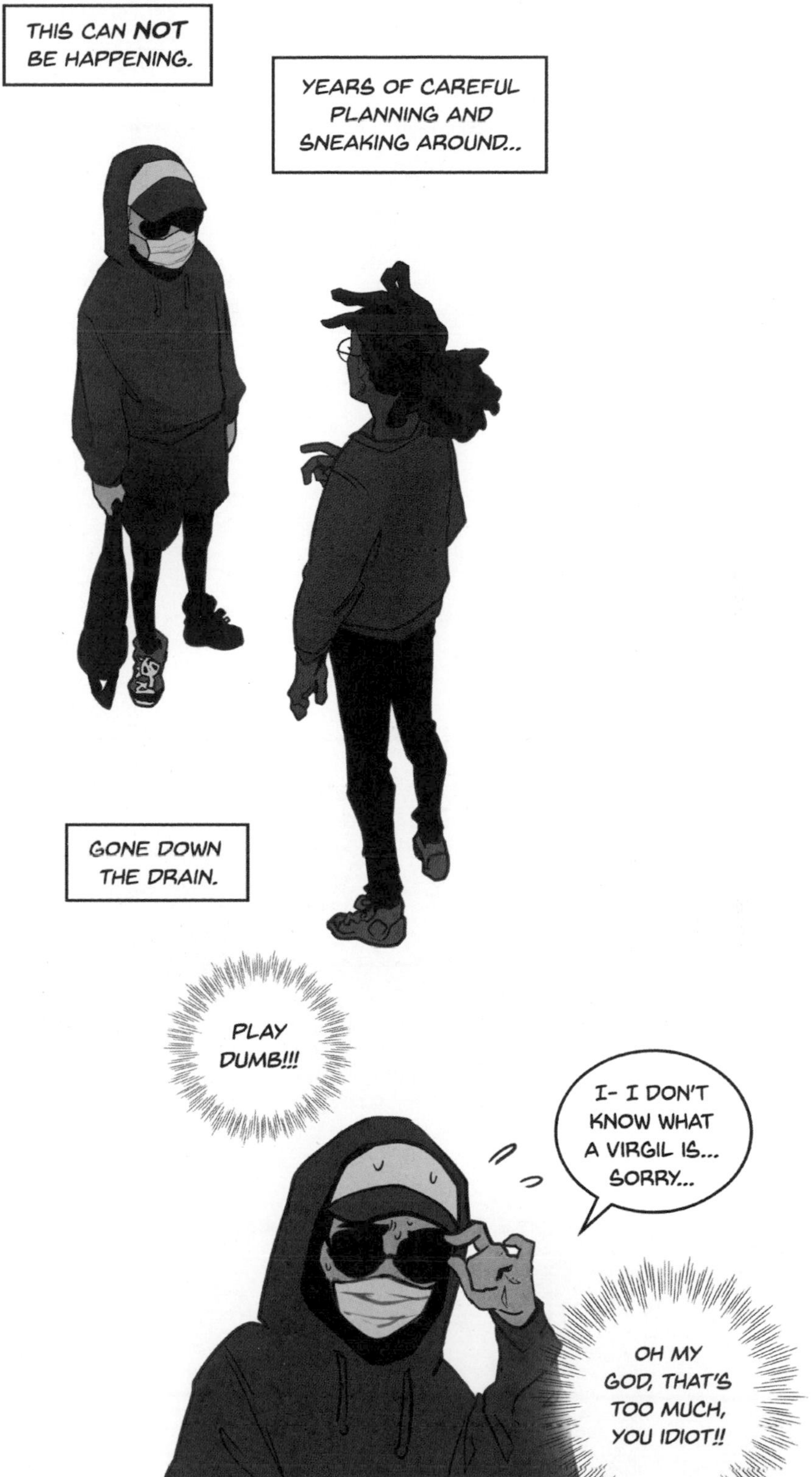
THIS CAN **NOT** BE HAPPENING.
YEARS OF CAREFUL PLANNING AND SNEAKING AROUND...
GONE DOWN THE DRAIN.
PLAY DUMB!!!
I- I DON'T KNOW WHAT A VIRGIL IS... SORRY...
OH MY GOD, THAT'S TOO MUCH, YOU IDIOT!!

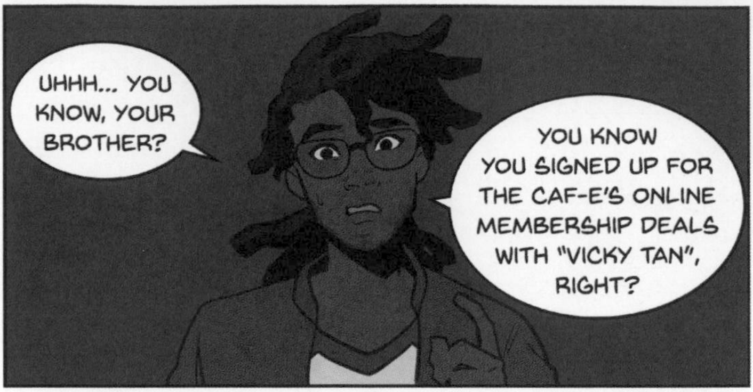
UHHH... YOU KNOW, YOUR BROTHER?
YOU KNOW YOU SIGNED UP FOR THE CAF-E'S ONLINE MEMBERSHIP DEALS WITH "VICKY TAN", RIGHT?

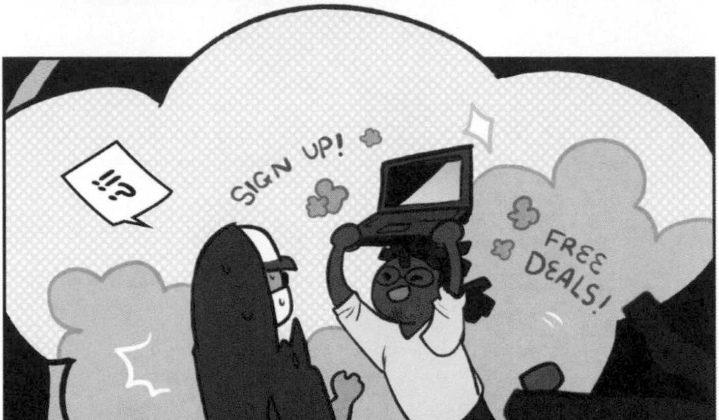
!!?
SIGN UP!
FREE DEALS!
WHAT!? I DID!? WHEN DID THAT HAPPEN!?

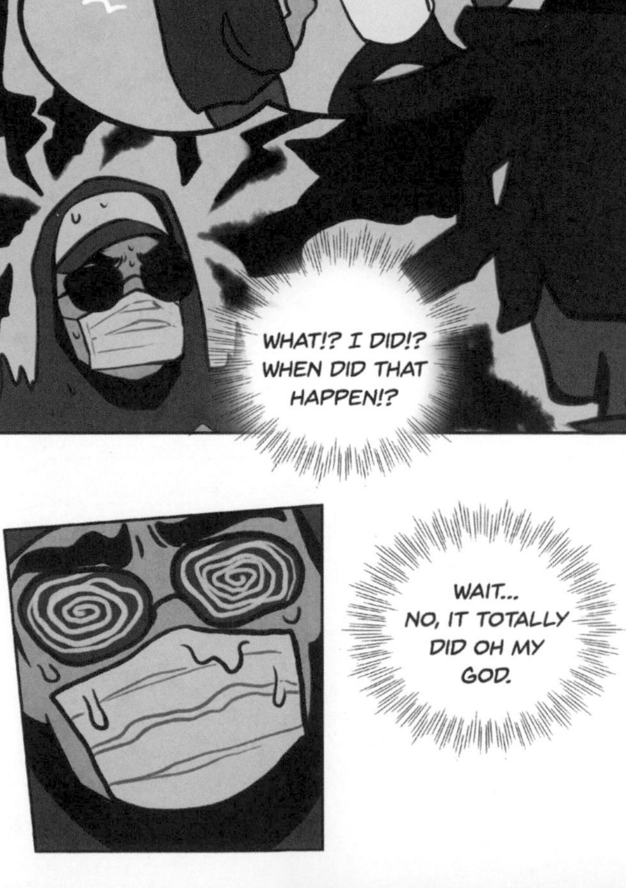
WAIT... NO, IT TOTALLY DID OH MY GOD.

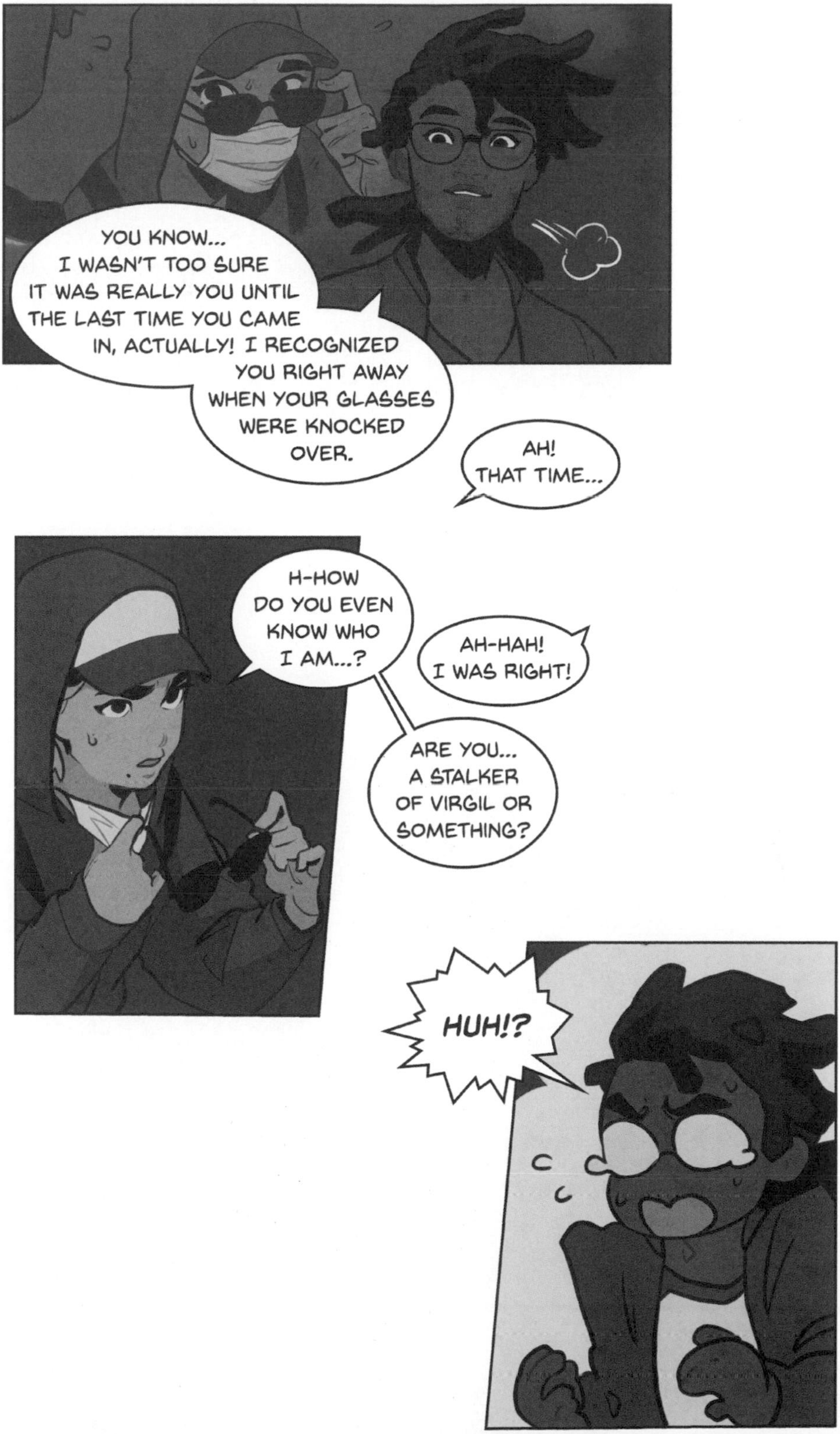
YOU KNOW... I WASN'T TOO SURE IT WAS REALLY YOU UNTIL THE LAST TIME YOU CAME IN, ACTUALLY! I RECOGNIZED YOU RIGHT AWAY WHEN YOUR GLASSES WERE KNOCKED OVER.
AH! THAT TIME...
H-HOW DO YOU EVEN KNOW WHO I AM...?
ARE YOU... A STALKER OF VIRGIL OR SOMETHING?
AH-HAH! I WAS RIGHT!
HUH!?

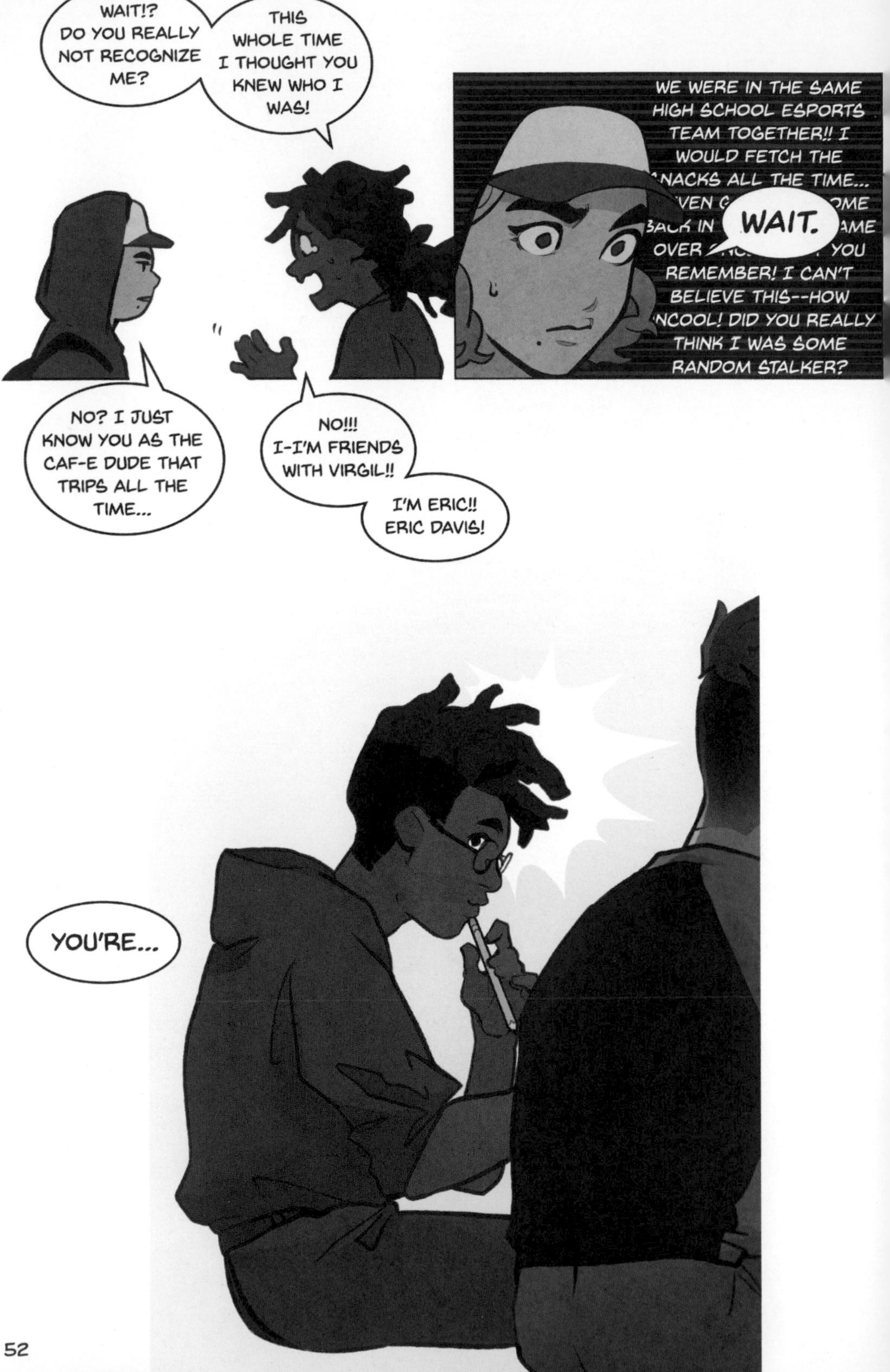
WAIT!? DO YOU REALLY NOT RECOGNIZE ME?
THIS WHOLE TIME I THOUGHT YOU KNEW WHO I WAS!
NO? I JUST KNOW YOU AS THE CAF-E DUDE THAT TRIPS ALL THE TIME...
NO!!! I-I'M FRIENDS WITH VIRGIL!!
I'M ERIC!! ERIC DAVIS!
WE WERE IN THE SAME HIGH SCHOOL ESPORTS TEAM TOGETHER!! I WOULD FETCH THE NACKS ALL THE TIME...
YOU REMEMBER! I CAN'T BELIEVE THIS--HOW NCOOL! DID YOU REALLY THINK I WAS SOME RANDOM STALKER?
WAIT.
YOU'RE...

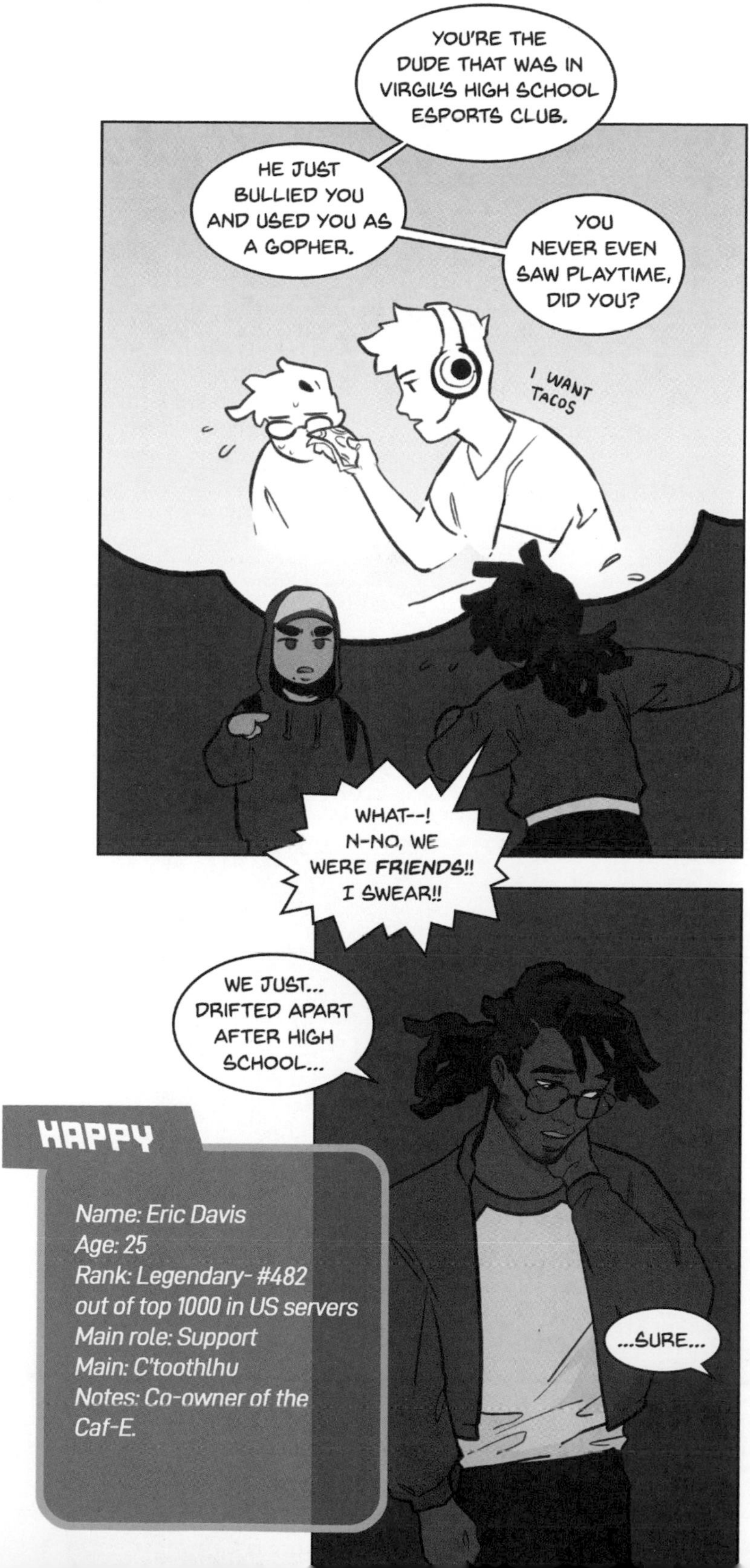
YOU'RE THE DUDE THAT WAS IN VIRGIL'S HIGH SCHOOL ESPORTS CLUB.
HE JUST BULLIED YOU AND USED YOU AS A GOPHER.
YOU NEVER EVEN SAW PLAYTIME, DID YOU?
I WANT TACOS
WHAT--! N-NO, WE WERE FRIENDS!! I SWEAR!!
WE JUST... DRIFTED APART AFTER HIGH SCHOOL...
HAPPY
Name: Eric Davis
Age: 25
Rank: Legendary- #482 out of top 1000 in US servers
Main role: Support
Main: C'toothlhu
Notes: Co-owner of the Caf-E.
...SURE...

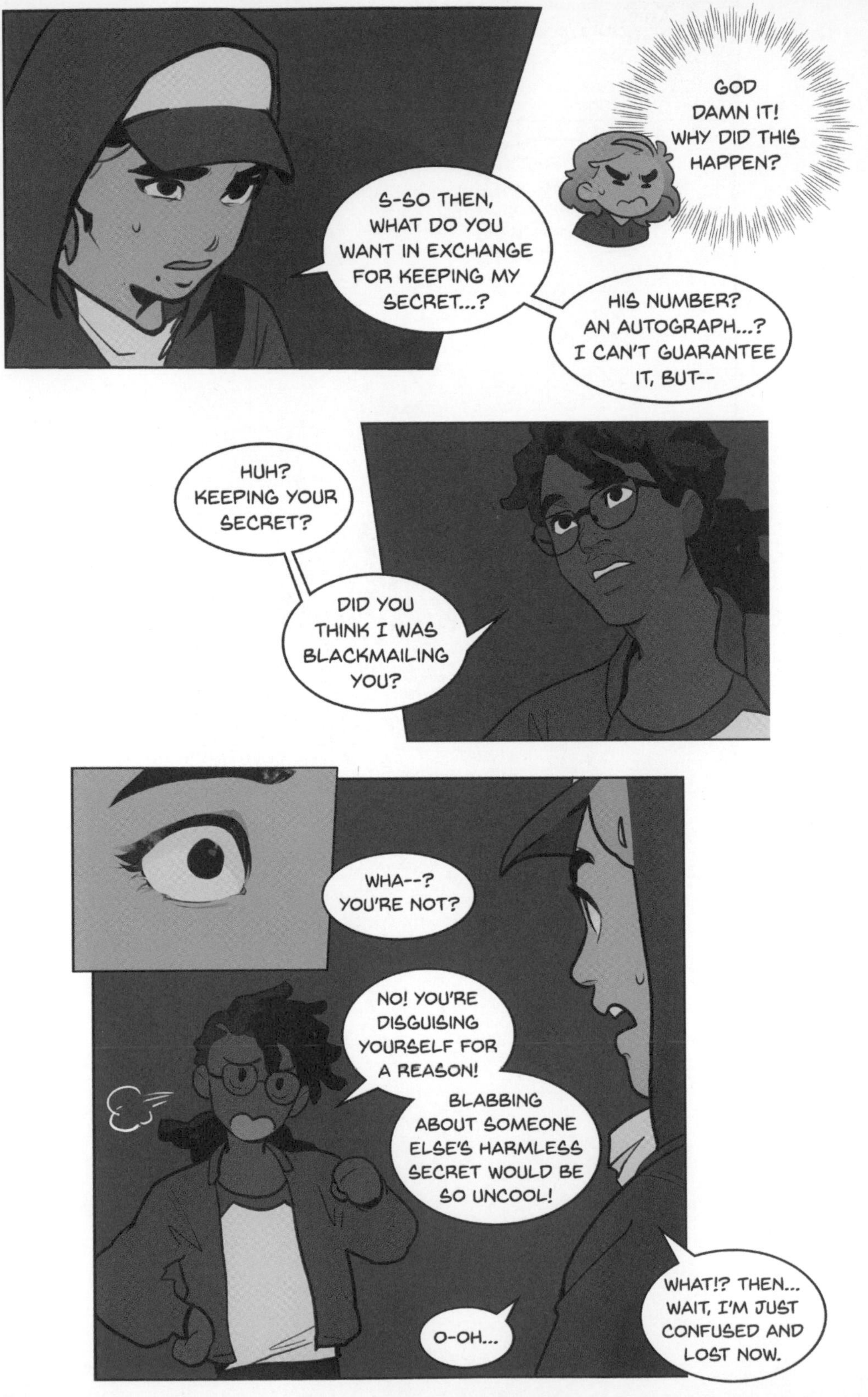
S-SO THEN, WHAT DO YOU WANT IN EXCHANGE FOR KEEPING MY SECRET...?
HIS NUMBER? AN AUTOGRAPH...? I CAN'T GUARANTEE IT, BUT--
GOD DAMN IT! WHY DID THIS HAPPEN?
HUH? KEEPING YOUR SECRET?
DID YOU THINK I WAS BLACKMAILING YOU?
WHA--? YOU'RE NOT?
NO! YOU'RE DISGUISING YOURSELF FOR A REASON!
BLABBING ABOUT SOMEONE ELSE'S HARMLESS SECRET WOULD BE SO UNCOOL!
O-OH...
WHAT!? THEN... WAIT, I'M JUST CONFUSED AND LOST NOW.

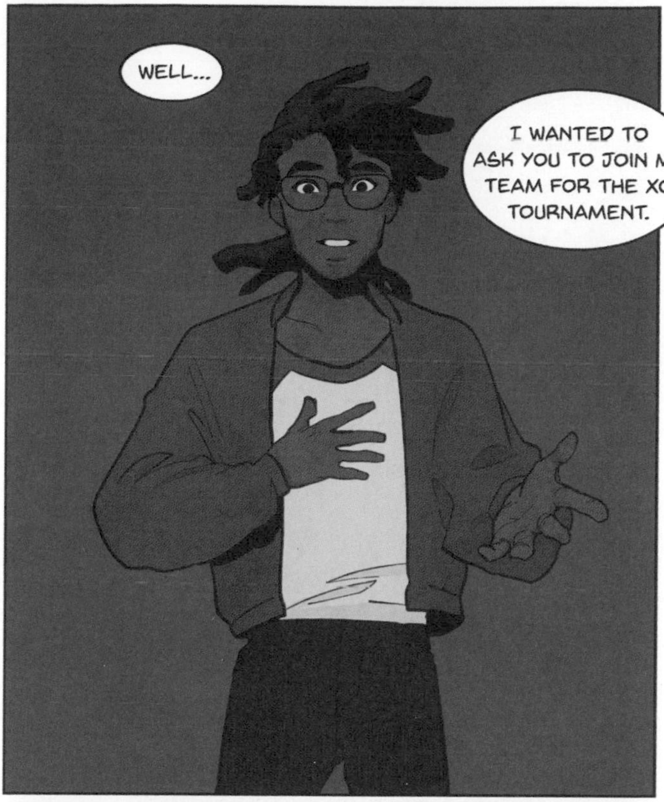
WELL...
I WANTED TO ASK YOU TO JOIN MY TEAM FOR THE XO TOURNAMENT.

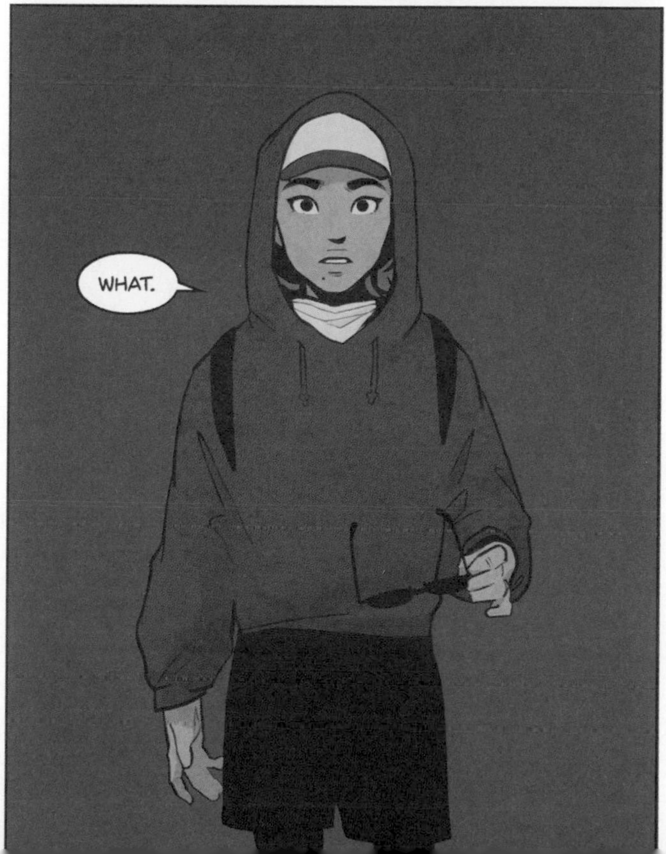
WHAT.

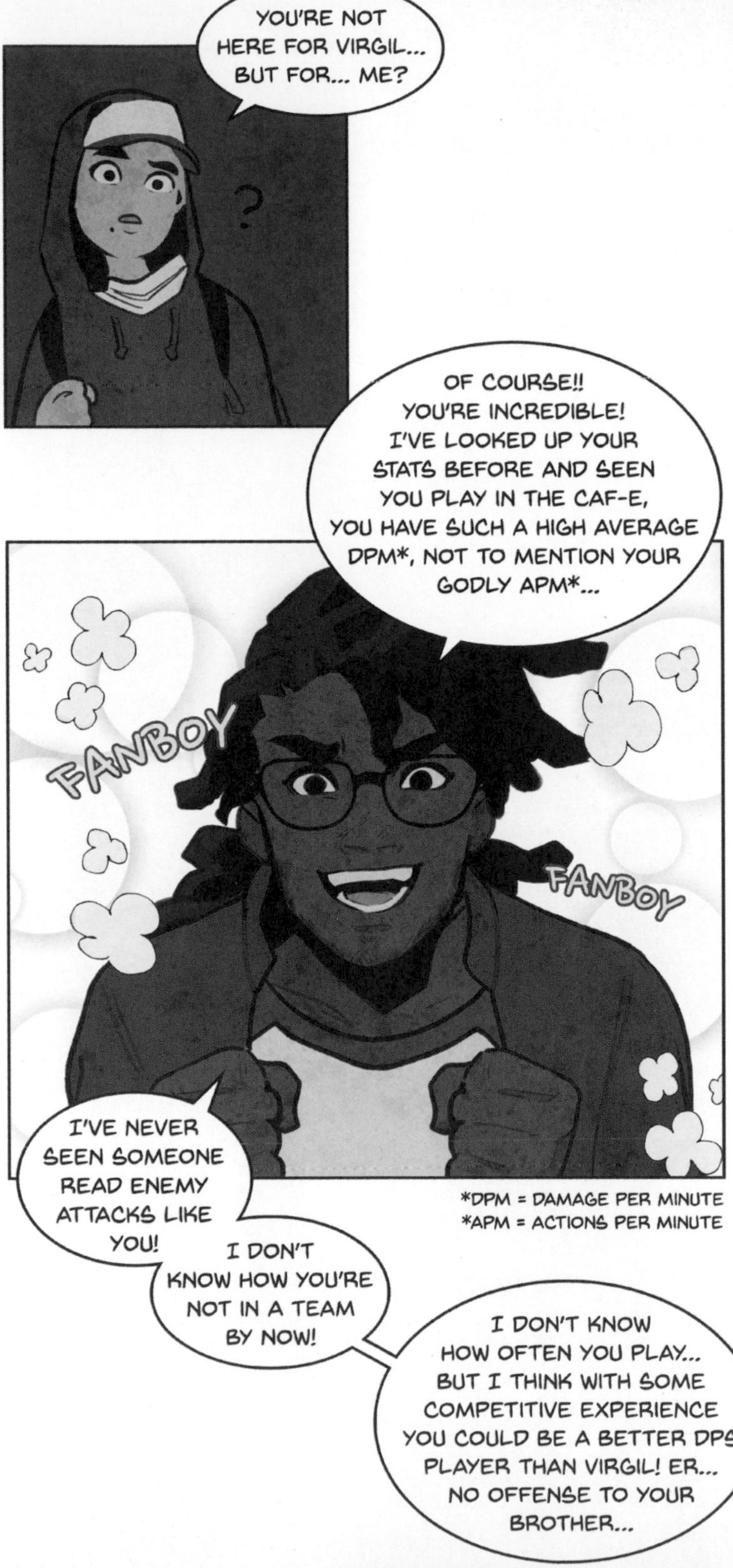
YOU'RE NOT HERE FOR VIRGIL... BUT FOR... ME?
?
OF COURSE!! YOU'RE INCREDIBLE! I'VE LOOKED UP YOUR STATS BEFORE AND SEEN YOU PLAY IN THE CAF-E, YOU HAVE SUCH A HIGH AVERAGE DPM*, NOT TO MENTION YOUR GODLY APM*...
FANBOY
FANBOY
I'VE NEVER SEEN SOMEONE READ ENEMY ATTACKS LIKE YOU!
I DON'T KNOW HOW YOU'RE NOT IN A TEAM BY NOW!
I DON'T KNOW HOW OFTEN YOU PLAY... BUT I THINK WITH SOME COMPETITIVE EXPERIENCE YOU COULD BE A BETTER DPS PLAYER THAN VIRGIL! ER... NO OFFENSE TO YOUR BROTHER...

*DPM = DAMAGE PER MINUTE
*APM = ACTIONS PER MINUTE

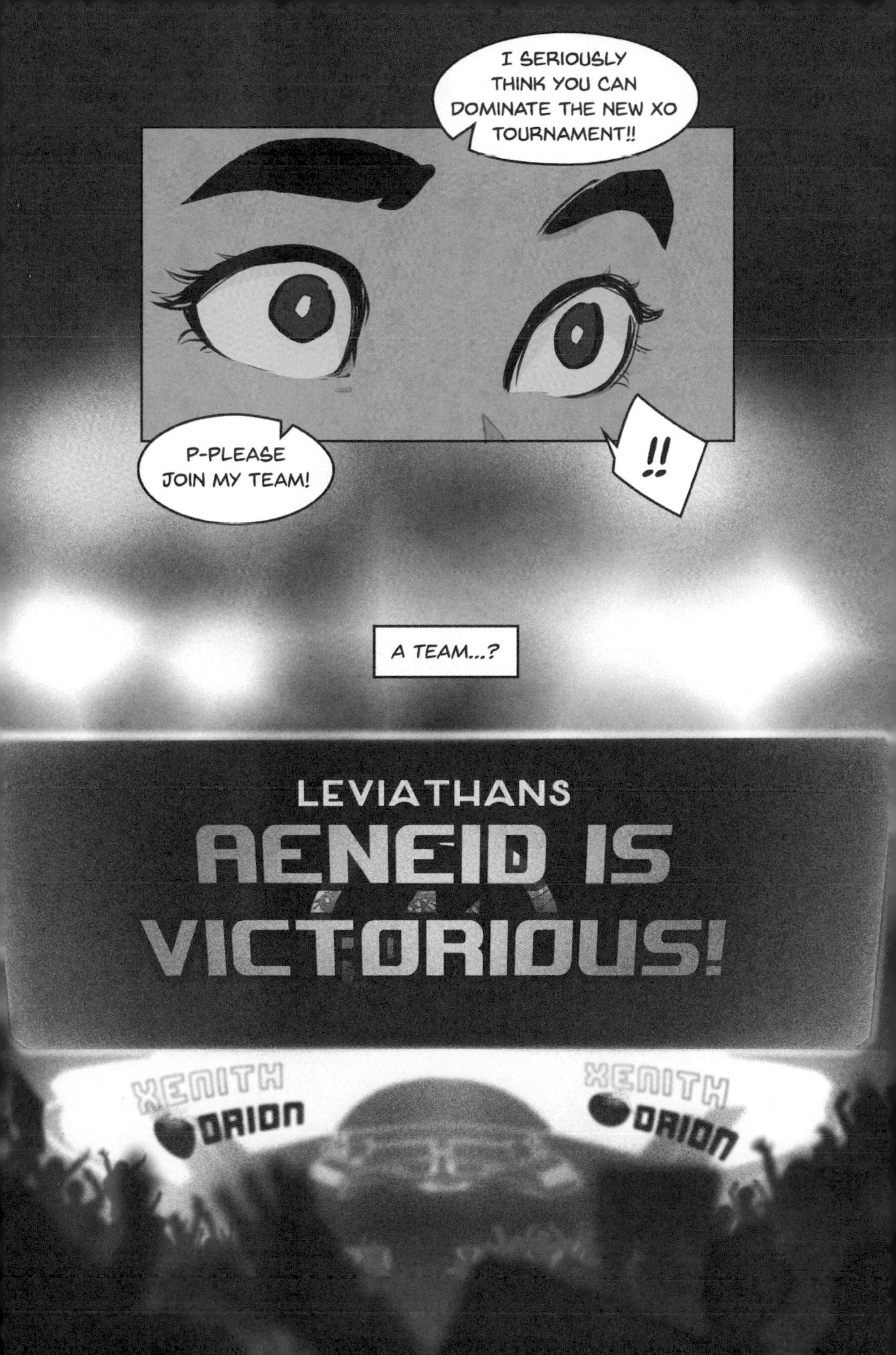
I SERIOUSLY THINK YOU CAN DOMINATE THE NEW XO TOURNAMENT!!
P-PLEASE JOIN MY TEAM!
!!
A TEAM...?
LEVIATHANS
AENEID IS VICTORIOUS!
XENITH
ORION
XENITH
ORION

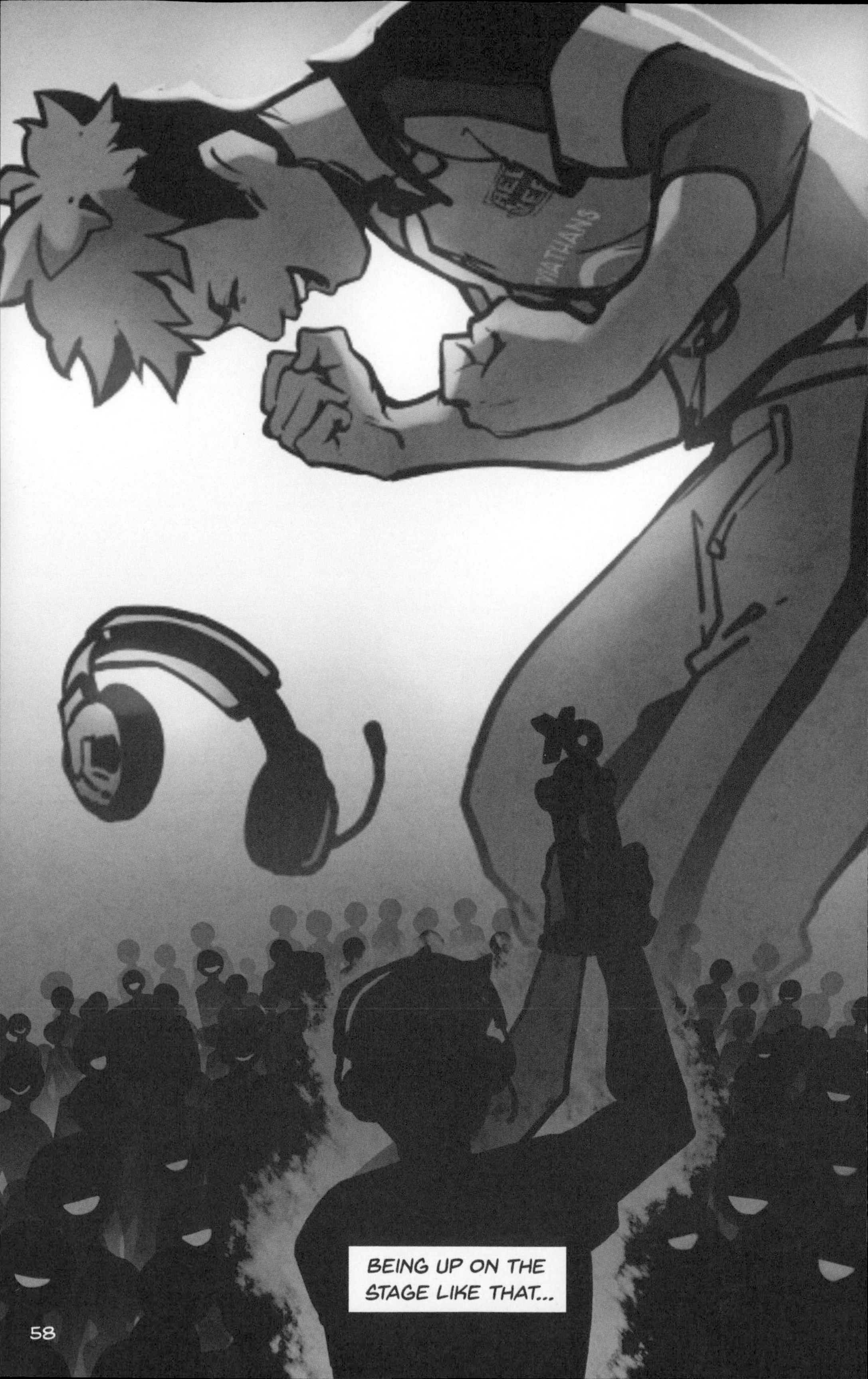
BEING UP ON THE
STAGE LIKE THAT...

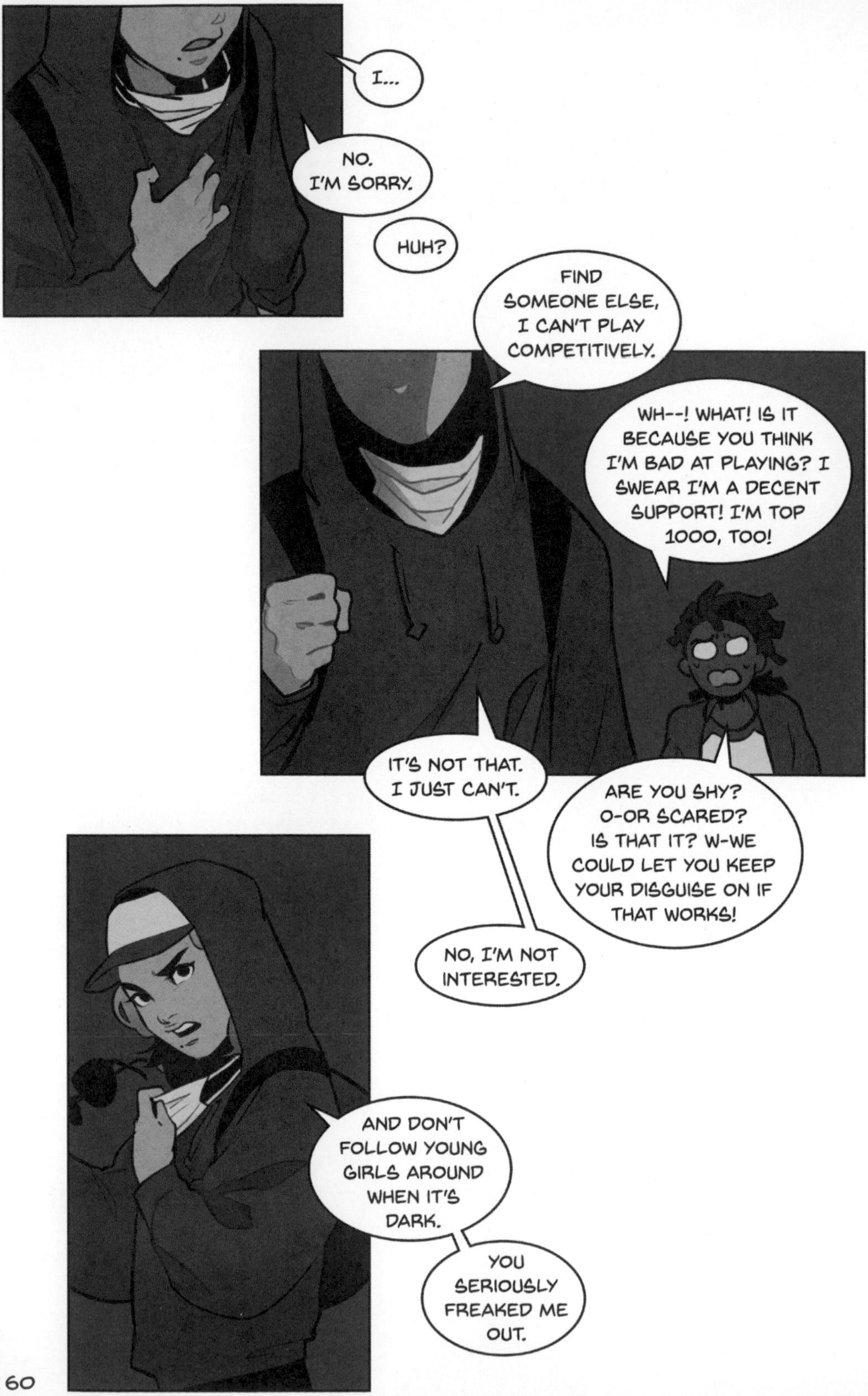
I...
NO. I'M SORRY.
HUH?
FIND SOMEONE ELSE, I CAN'T PLAY COMPETITIVELY.
WH--! WHAT! IS IT BECAUSE YOU THINK I'M BAD AT PLAYING? I SWEAR I'M A DECENT SUPPORT! I'M TOP 1000, TOO!
IT'S NOT THAT. I JUST CAN'T.
ARE YOU SHY? O-OR SCARED? IS THAT IT? W-WE COULD LET YOU KEEP YOUR DISGUISE ON IF THAT WORKS!
NO, I'M NOT INTERESTED.
AND DON'T FOLLOW YOUNG GIRLS AROUND WHEN IT'S DARK.
YOU SERIOUSLY FREAKED ME OUT.

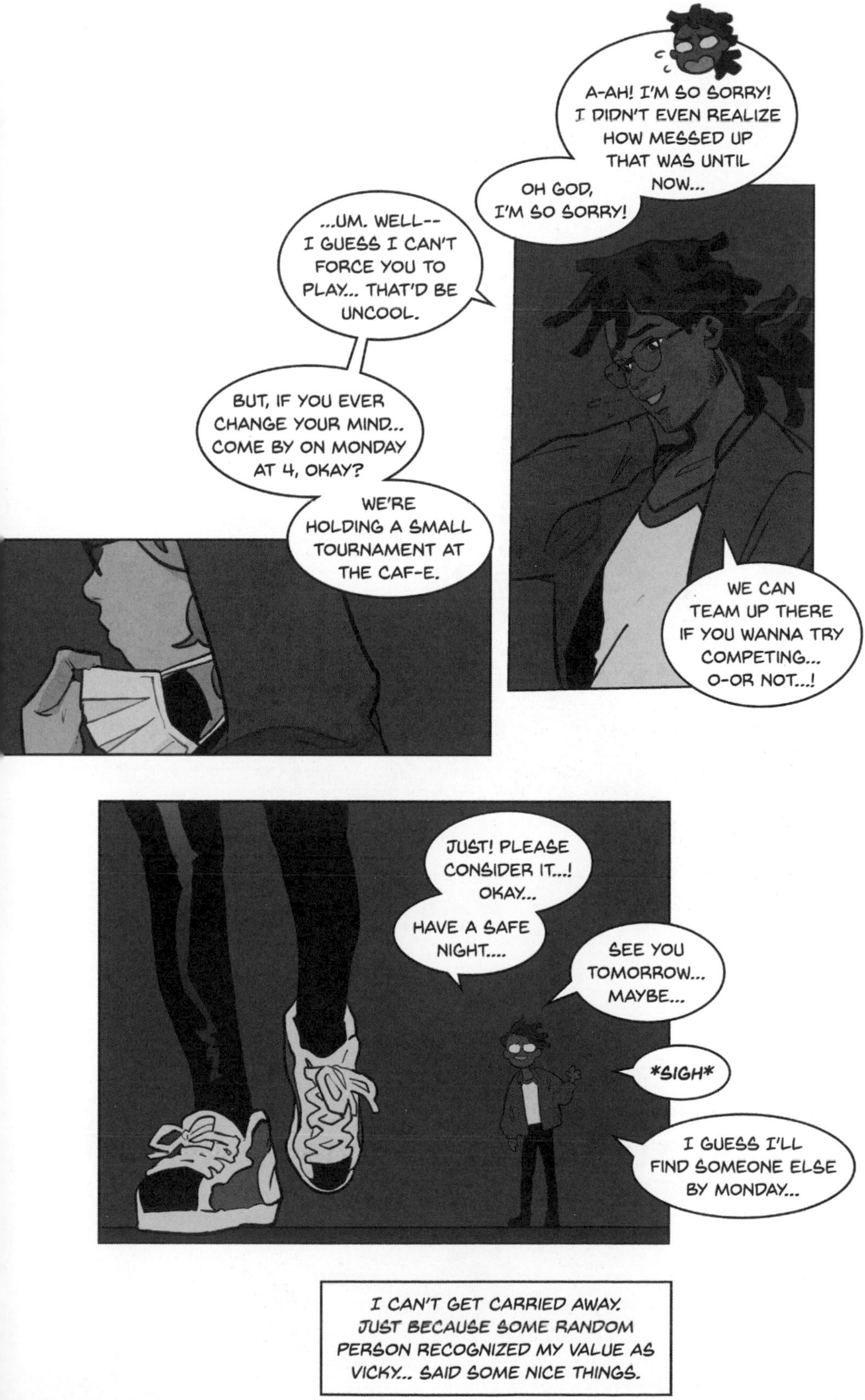
A-AH! I'M SO SORRY! I DIDN'T EVEN REALIZE HOW MESSED UP THAT WAS UNTIL NOW...
OH GOD, I'M SO SORRY!
...UM. WELL-- I GUESS I CAN'T FORCE YOU TO PLAY... THAT'D BE UNCOOL.
BUT, IF YOU EVER CHANGE YOUR MIND... COME BY ON MONDAY AT 4, OKAY?
WE'RE HOLDING A SMALL TOURNAMENT AT THE CAF-E.
WE CAN TEAM UP THERE IF YOU WANNA TRY COMPETING... O-OR NOT...!
JUST! PLEASE CONSIDER IT...! OKAY...
HAVE A SAFE NIGHT....
SEE YOU TOMORROW... MAYBE...
SIGH
I GUESS I'LL FIND SOMEONE ELSE BY MONDAY...
I CAN'T GET CARRIED AWAY. JUST BECAUSE SOME RANDOM PERSON RECOGNIZED MY VALUE AS VICKY... SAID SOME NICE THINGS.

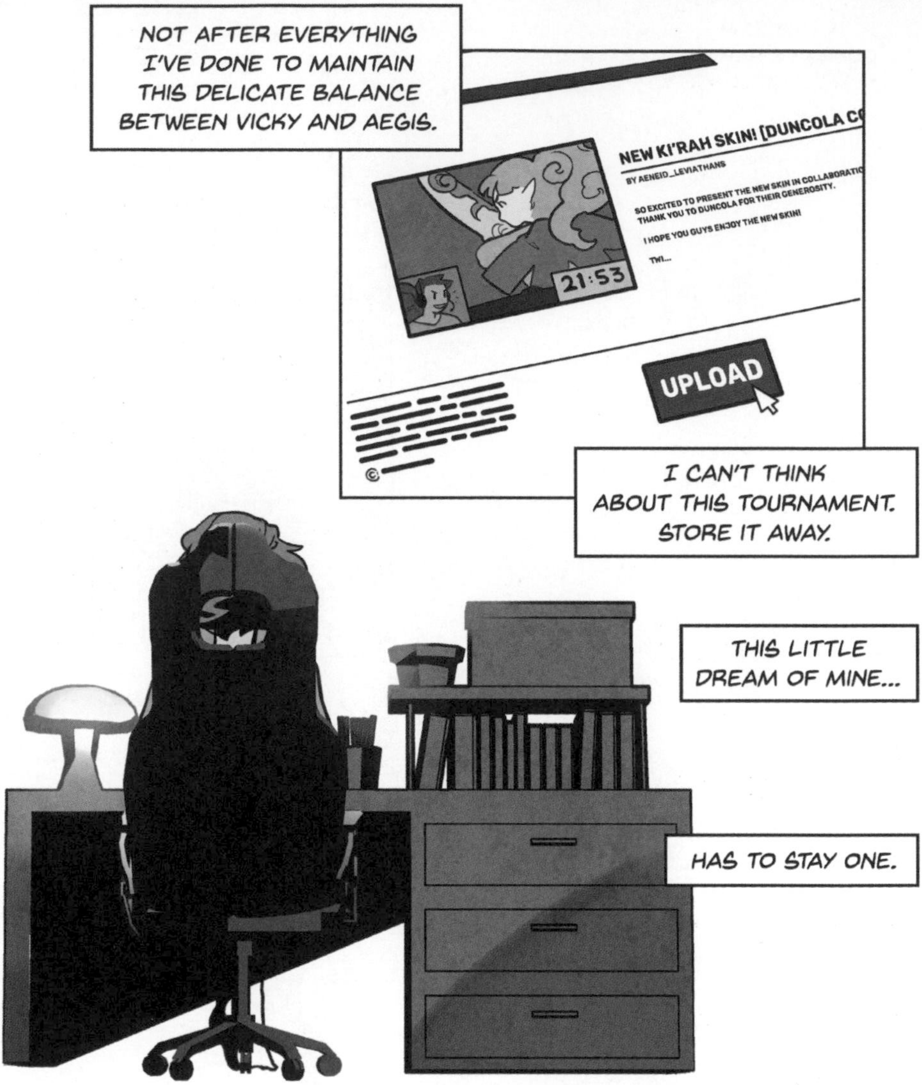
NOT AFTER EVERYTHING I'VE DONE TO MAINTAIN THIS DELICATE BALANCE BETWEEN VICKY AND AEGIS.
NEW KI'RAH SKIN! [DUNCOLA
BY AENEID_LEVIATHANS
SO EXCITED TO PRESENT THE NEW SKIN IN
THANK YOU TO DUNCOLA FOR THEIR GENEROSITY.
I HOPE YOU GUYS ENJOY THE NEW SKIN!
TWI...
21:53
UPLOAD
I CAN'T THINK ABOUT THIS TOURNAMENT. STORE IT AWAY.
THIS LITTLE DREAM OF MINE...
HAS TO STAY ONE.

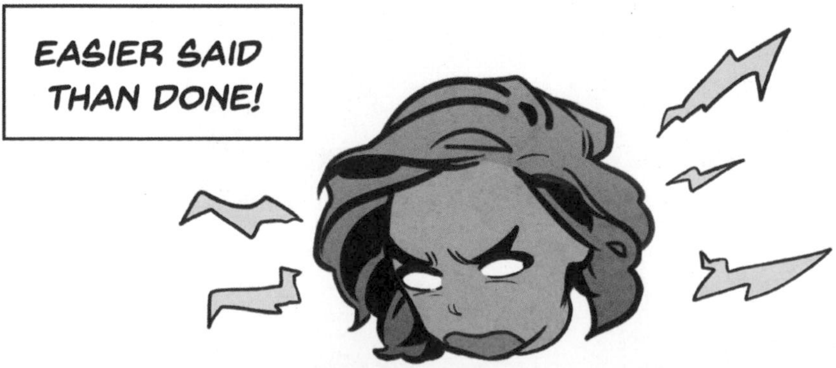
EASIER SAID THAN DONE!

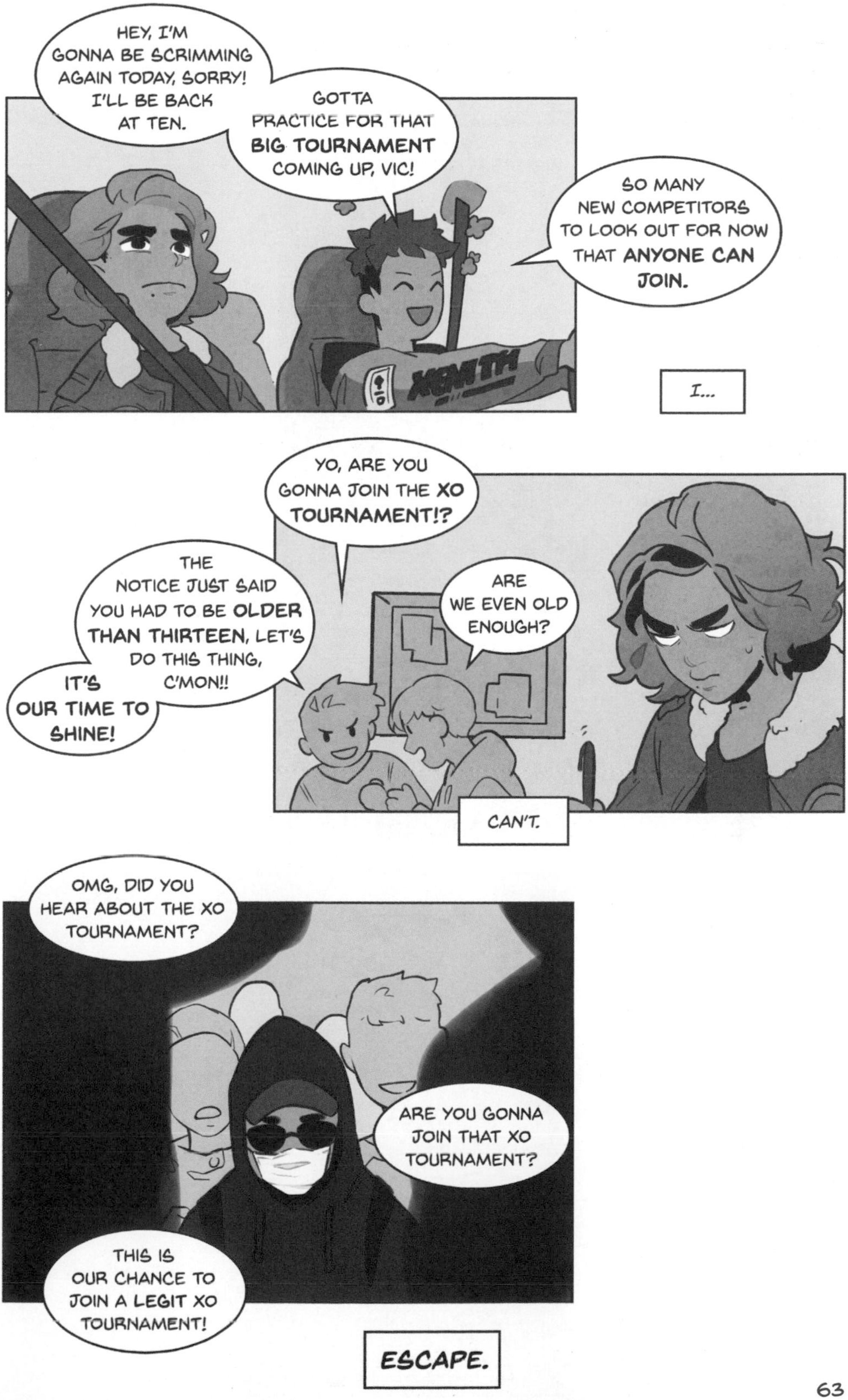
HEY, I'M GONNA BE SCRIMMING AGAIN TODAY, SORRY! I'LL BE BACK AT TEN.
GOTTA PRACTICE FOR THAT BIG TOURNAMENT COMING UP, VIC!
SO MANY NEW COMPETITORS TO LOOK OUT FOR NOW THAT ANYONE CAN JOIN.
I...
YO, ARE YOU GONNA JOIN THE XO TOURNAMENT!?
THE NOTICE JUST SAID YOU HAD TO BE OLDER THAN THIRTEEN, LET'S DO THIS THING, C'MON!!
ARE WE EVEN OLD ENOUGH?
IT'S OUR TIME TO SHINE!
CAN'T.
OMG, DID YOU HEAR ABOUT THE XO TOURNAMENT?
ARE YOU GONNA JOIN THAT XO TOURNAMENT?
THIS IS OUR CHANCE TO JOIN A LEGIT XO TOURNAMENT!
ESCAPE.

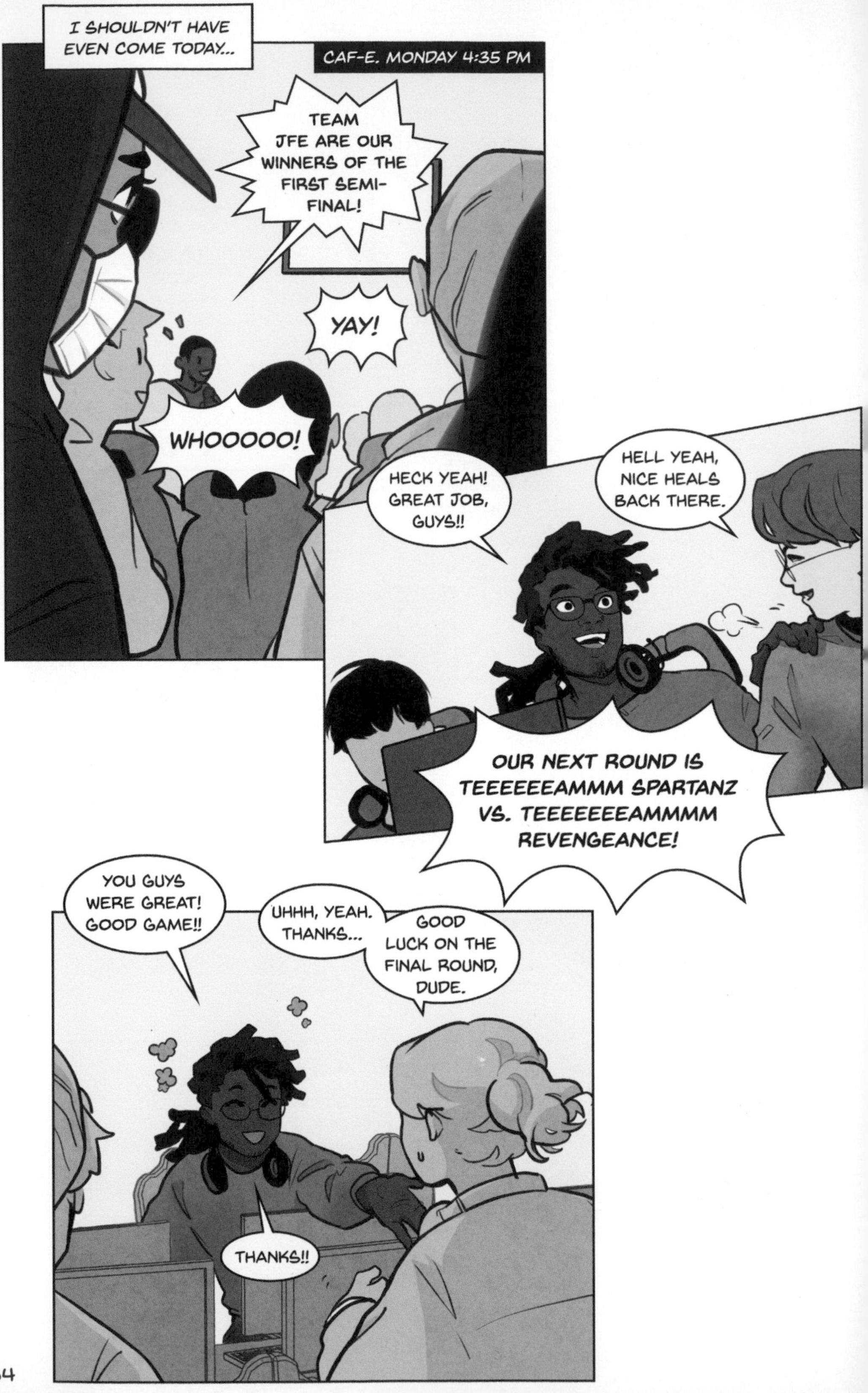

I SHOULDN'T HAVE EVEN COME TODAY...
CAF-E. MONDAY 4:35 PM
TEAM JFE ARE OUR WINNERS OF THE FIRST SEMI-FINAL!
YAY!
WHOOOOO!
HECK YEAH! GREAT JOB, GUYS!!
HELL YEAH, NICE HEALS BACK THERE.
OUR NEXT ROUND IS TEEEEEEAMMM SPARTANZ VS. TEEEEEEEAMMMM REVENGEANCE!
YOU GUYS WERE GREAT! GOOD GAME!!
UHHH, YEAH. THANKS...
GOOD LUCK ON THE FINAL ROUND, DUDE.
THANKS!!

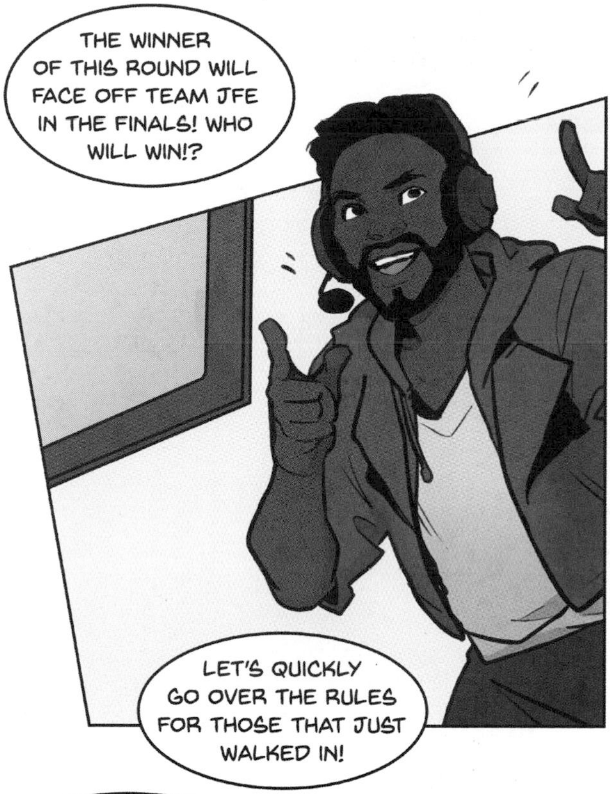
THE WINNER OF THIS ROUND WILL FACE OFF TEAM JFE IN THE FINALS! WHO WILL WIN!?
LET'S QUICKLY GO OVER THE RULES FOR THOSE THAT JUST WALKED IN!

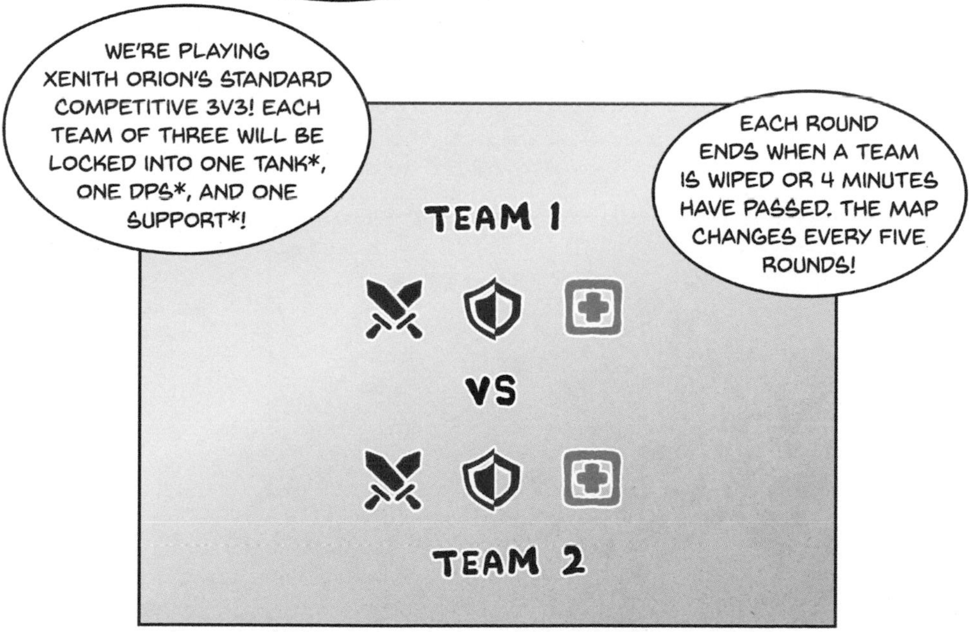
WE'RE PLAYING XENITH ORION'S STANDARD COMPETITIVE 3V3! EACH TEAM OF THREE WILL BE LOCKED INTO ONE TANK*, ONE DPS*, AND ONE SUPPORT*!
EACH ROUND ENDS WHEN A TEAM IS WIPED OR 4 MINUTES HAVE PASSED. THE MAP CHANGES EVERY FIVE ROUNDS!
TEAM 1
VS
TEAM 2

*TANK- CHARACTER THAT SHIELDS THEIR TEAMMATES WITH THEIR DEFENSIVE ABILITIES AND HIGH HEALTH POINTS (HP).

*DPS- CHARACTER THAT DEALS THE MOST DAMAGE. IN CHARGE OF KILLING.

*SUPPORT- CHARACTER THAT HEALS AND SUPPORTS THEIR TEAMMATES. SHOULD BE PROTECTED.

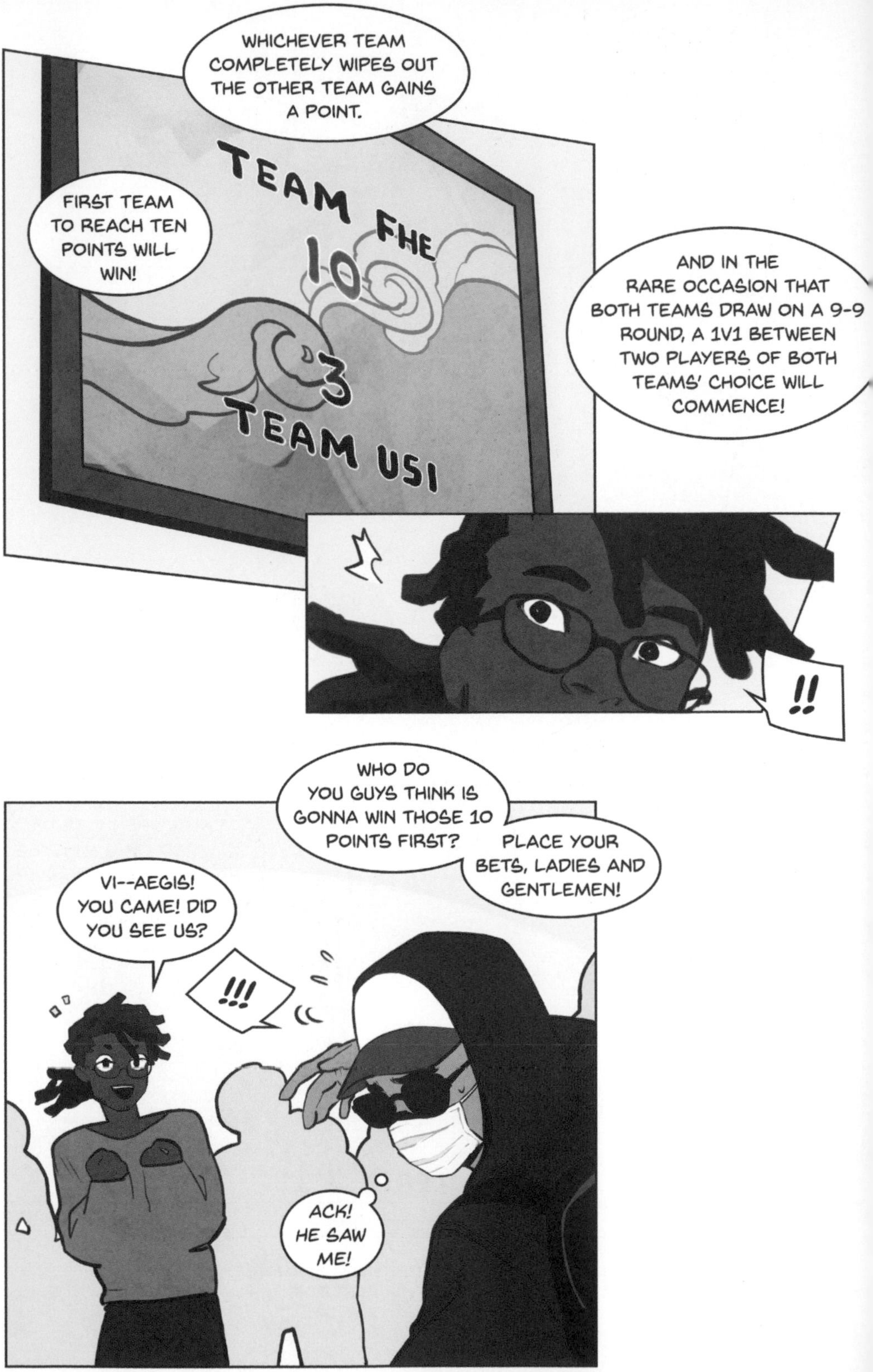
WHICHEVER TEAM COMPLETELY WIPES OUT THE OTHER TEAM GAINS A POINT.
TEAM FHE
10
3
TEAM USI
FIRST TEAM TO REACH TEN POINTS WILL WIN!
AND IN THE RARE OCCASION THAT BOTH TEAMS DRAW ON A 9-9 ROUND, A 1V1 BETWEEN TWO PLAYERS OF BOTH TEAMS' CHOICE WILL COMMENCE!
!!
WHO DO YOU GUYS THINK IS GONNA WIN THOSE 10 POINTS FIRST?
PLACE YOUR BETS, LADIES AND GENTLEMEN!
VI--AEGIS! YOU CAME! DID YOU SEE US?
!!!
ACK! HE SAW ME!

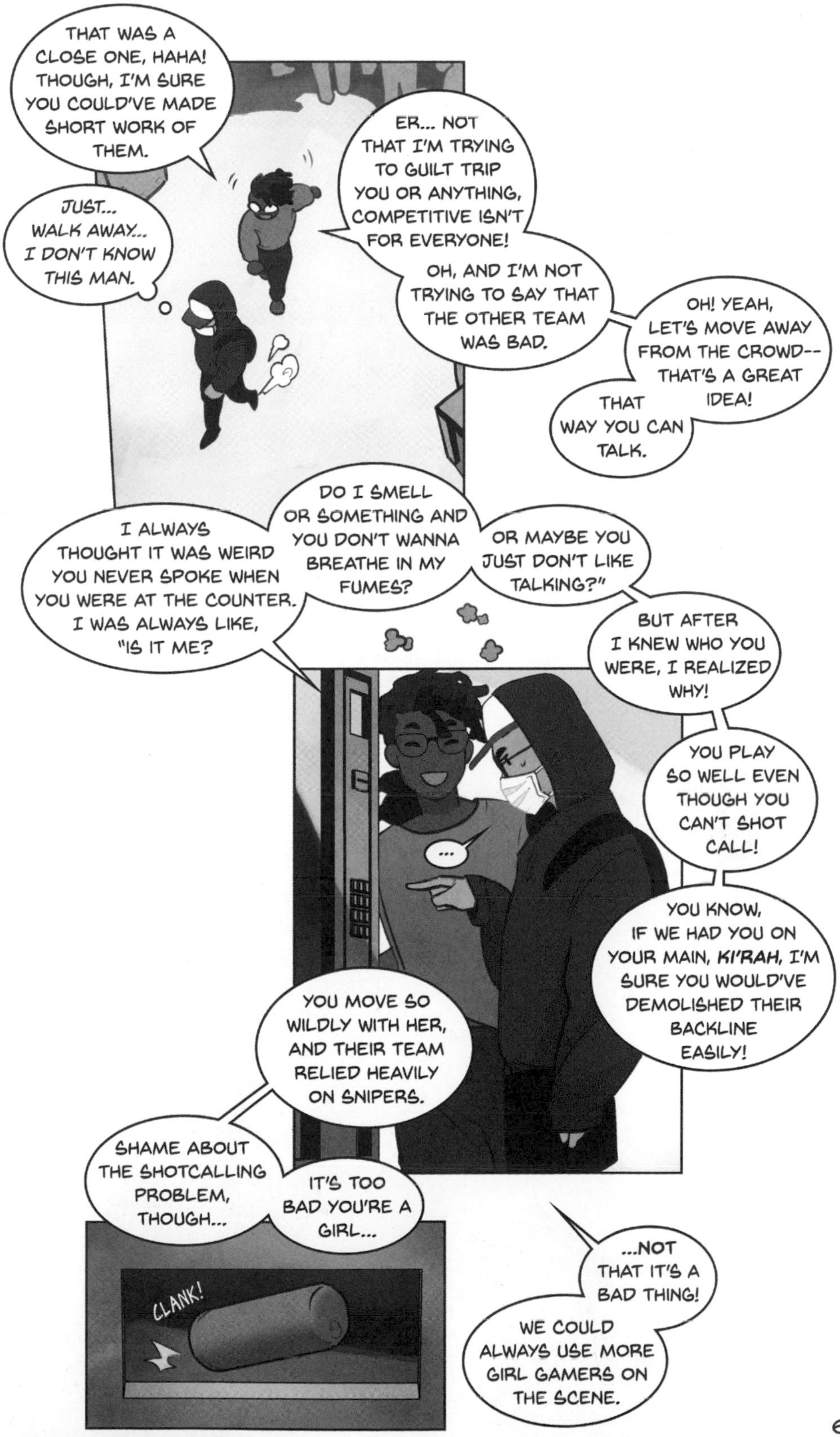
THAT WAS A CLOSE ONE, HAHA! THOUGH, I'M SURE YOU COULD'VE MADE SHORT WORK OF THEM.
ER... NOT THAT I'M TRYING TO GUILT TRIP YOU OR ANYTHING, COMPETITIVE ISN'T FOR EVERYONE!
JUST... WALK AWAY... I DON'T KNOW THIS MAN.
OH, AND I'M NOT TRYING TO SAY THAT THE OTHER TEAM WAS BAD.
OH! YEAH, LET'S MOVE AWAY FROM THE CROWD-- THAT'S A GREAT IDEA!
THAT WAY YOU CAN TALK.
I ALWAYS THOUGHT IT WAS WEIRD YOU NEVER SPOKE WHEN YOU WERE AT THE COUNTER. I WAS ALWAYS LIKE, "IS IT ME?
DO I SMELL OR SOMETHING AND YOU DON'T WANNA BREATHE IN MY FUMES?
OR MAYBE YOU JUST DON'T LIKE TALKING?"
BUT AFTER I KNEW WHO YOU WERE, I REALIZED WHY!
YOU PLAY SO WELL EVEN THOUGH YOU CAN'T SHOT CALL!
...
YOU KNOW, IF WE HAD YOU ON YOUR MAIN, ***KI'RAH***, I'M SURE YOU WOULD'VE DEMOLISHED THEIR BACKLINE EASILY!
YOU MOVE SO WILDLY WITH HER, AND THEIR TEAM RELIED HEAVILY ON SNIPERS.
SHAME ABOUT THE SHOTCALLING PROBLEM, THOUGH...
IT'S TOO BAD YOU'RE A GIRL...
CLANK!
...NOT THAT IT'S A BAD THING!
WE COULD ALWAYS USE MORE GIRL GAMERS ON THE SCENE.

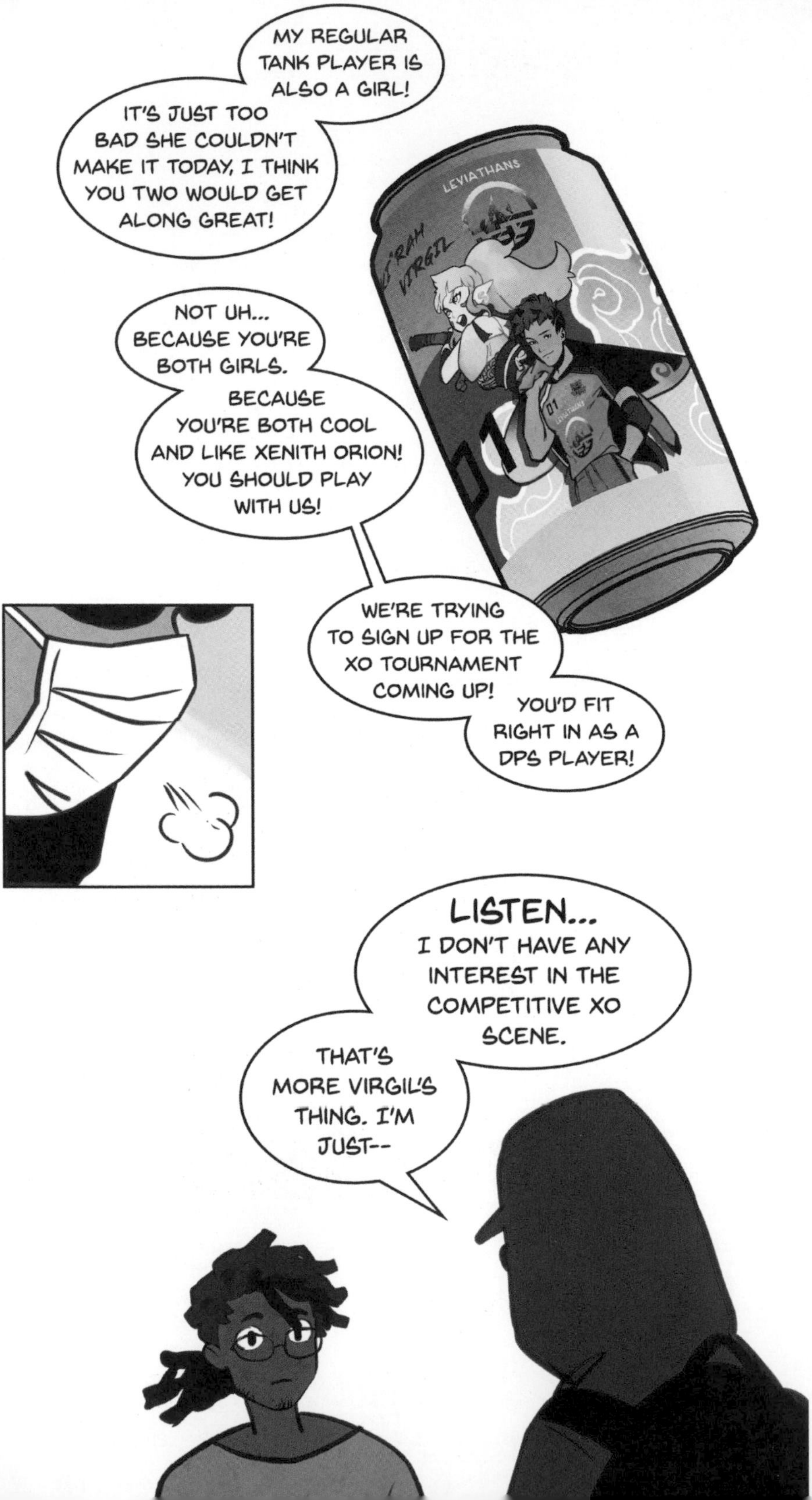
MY REGULAR TANK PLAYER IS ALSO A GIRL!
IT'S JUST TOO BAD SHE COULDN'T MAKE IT TODAY, I THINK YOU TWO WOULD GET ALONG GREAT!
LEVIATHANS
NOT UH... BECAUSE YOU'RE BOTH GIRLS.
BECAUSE YOU'RE BOTH COOL AND LIKE XENITH ORION! YOU SHOULD PLAY WITH US!
WE'RE TRYING TO SIGN UP FOR THE XO TOURNAMENT COMING UP!
YOU'D FIT RIGHT IN AS A DPS PLAYER!
LISTEN... I DON'T HAVE ANY INTEREST IN THE COMPETITIVE XO SCENE.
THAT'S MORE VIRGIL'S THING. I'M JUST--

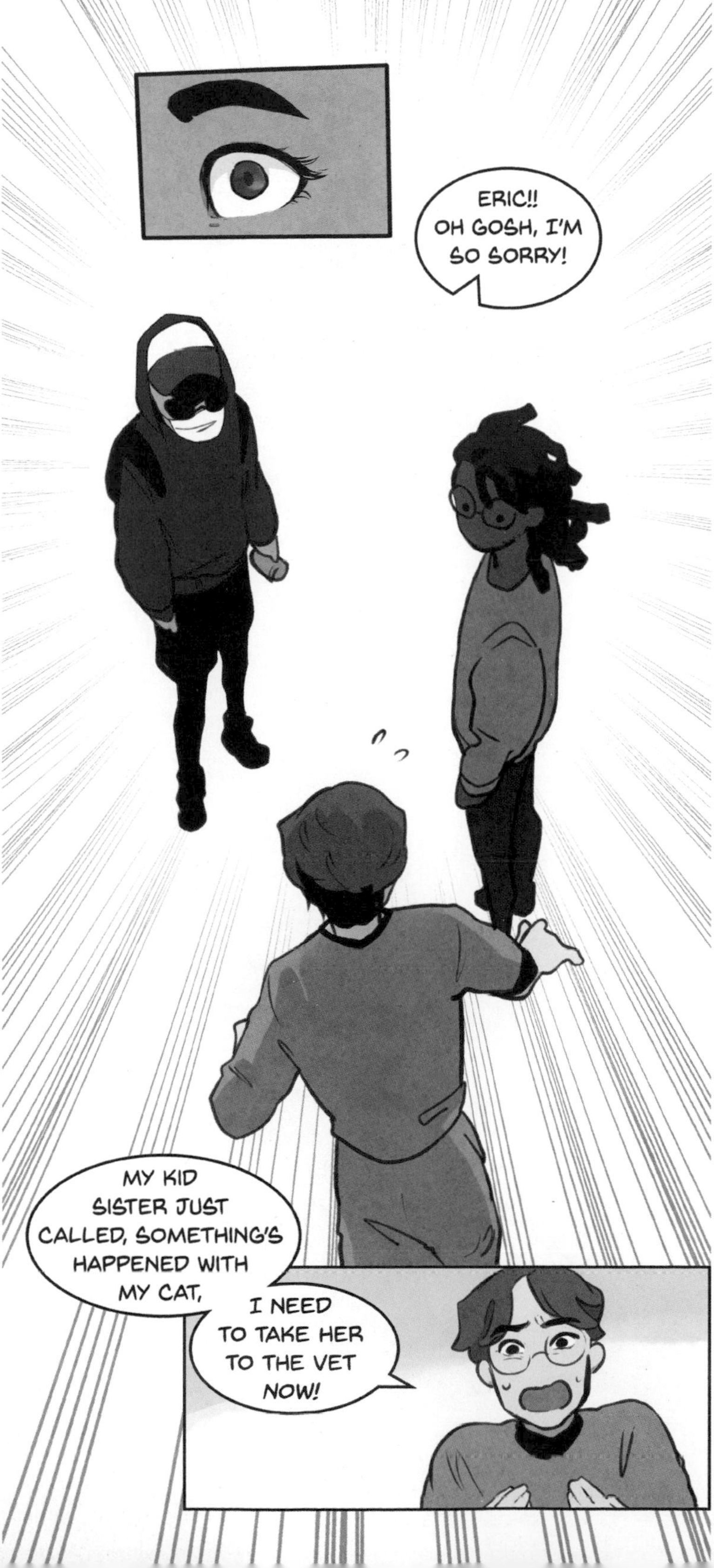
ERIC!!
OH GOSH, I'M SO SORRY!
MY KID SISTER JUST CALLED, SOMETHING'S HAPPENED WITH MY CAT,
I NEED TO TAKE HER TO THE VET NOW!

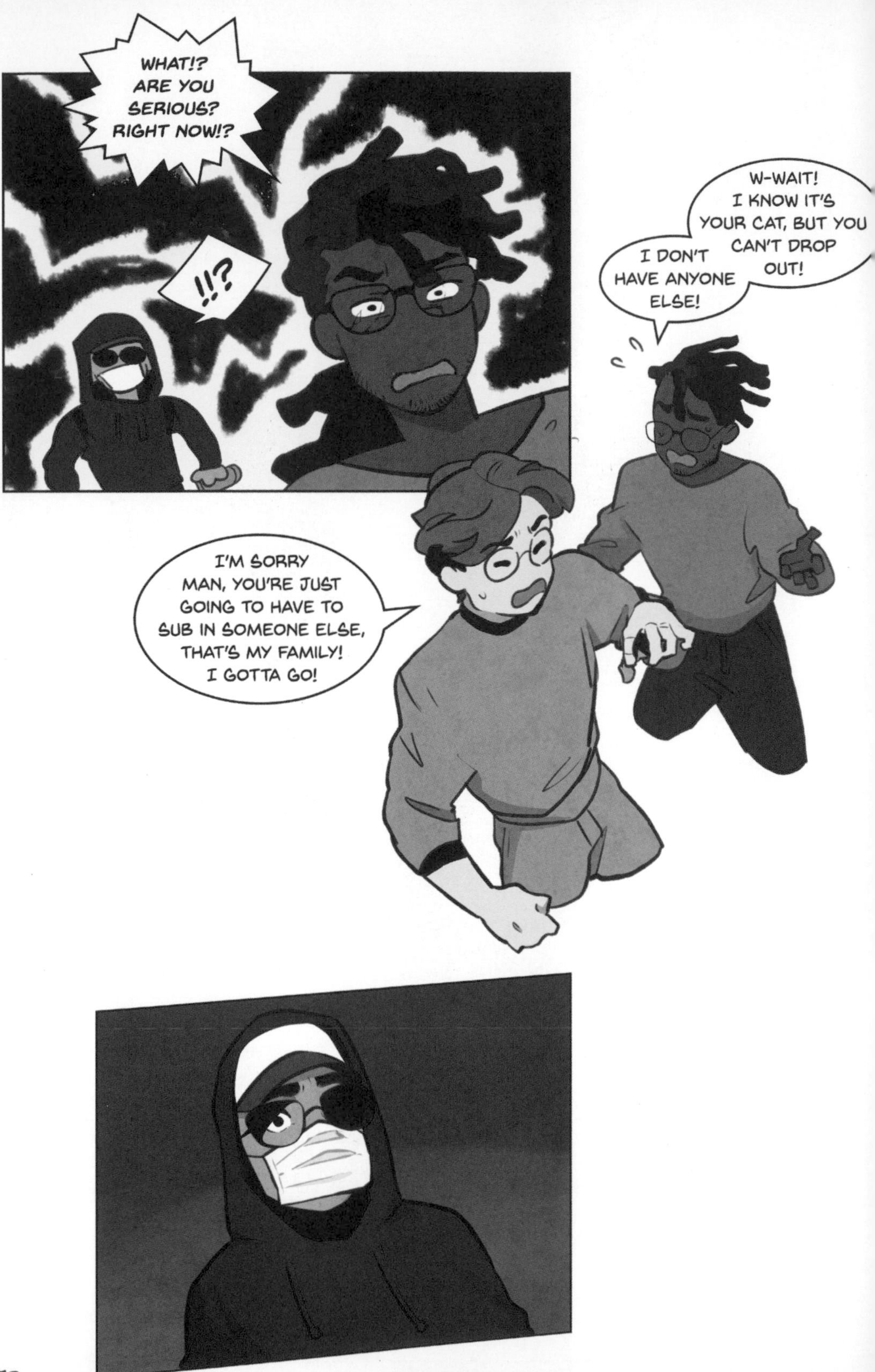
WHAT!? ARE YOU SERIOUS? RIGHT NOW!?
!!?
W-WAIT! I KNOW IT'S YOUR CAT, BUT YOU CAN'T DROP OUT!
I DON'T HAVE ANYONE ELSE!
I'M SORRY MAN, YOU'RE JUST GOING TO HAVE TO SUB IN SOMEONE ELSE, THAT'S MY FAMILY! I GOTTA GO!

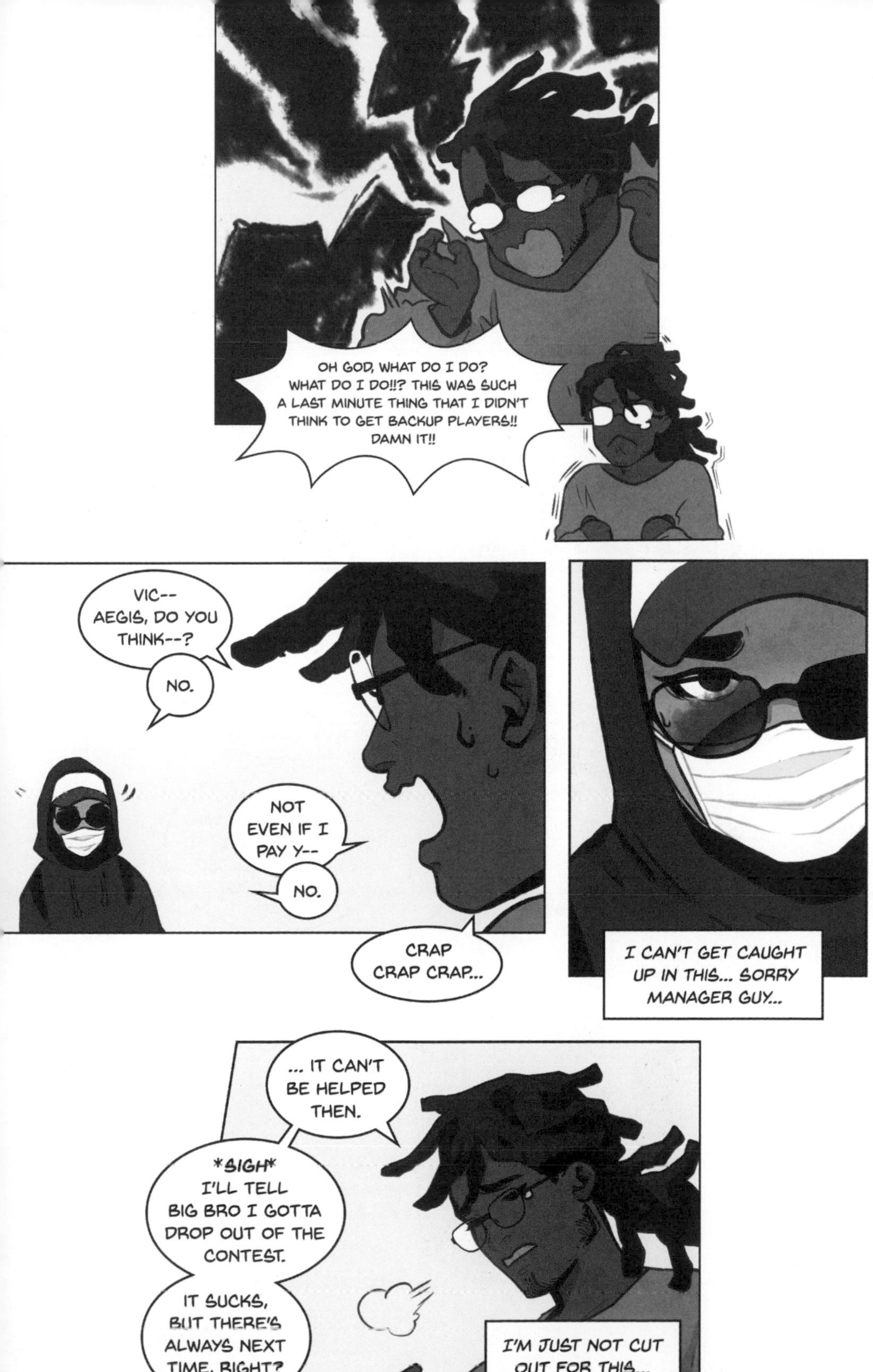
OH GOD, WHAT DO I DO? WHAT DO I DO!!? THIS WAS SUCH A LAST MINUTE THING THAT I DIDN'T THINK TO GET BACKUP PLAYERS!! DAMN IT!!
VIC-- AEGIS, DO YOU THINK--?
NO.
NOT EVEN IF I PAY Y--
NO.
CRAP CRAP CRAP...
I CAN'T GET CAUGHT UP IN THIS... SORRY MANAGER GUY...
... IT CAN'T BE HELPED THEN.
SIGH I'LL TELL BIG BRO I GOTTA DROP OUT OF THE CONTEST.
IT SUCKS, BUT THERE'S ALWAYS NEXT TIME, RIGHT?
I'M JUST NOT CUT OUT FOR THIS...

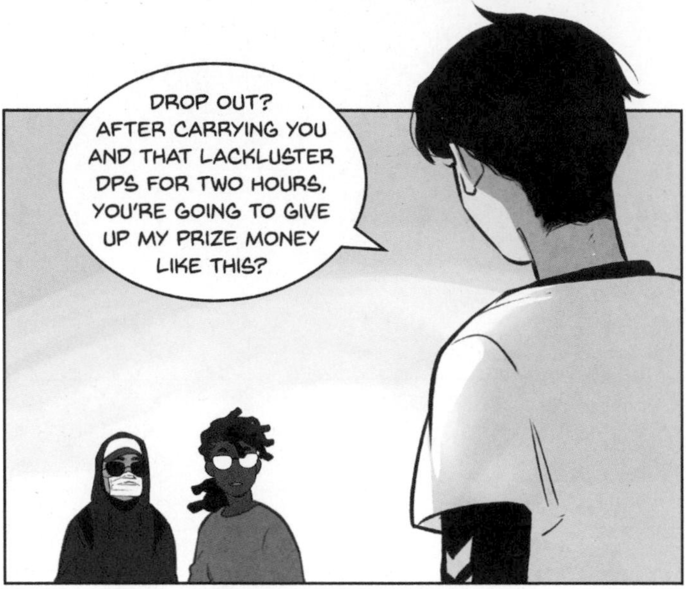
DROP OUT? AFTER CARRYING YOU AND THAT LACKLUSTER DPS FOR TWO HOURS, YOU'RE GOING TO GIVE UP MY PRIZE MONEY LIKE THIS?

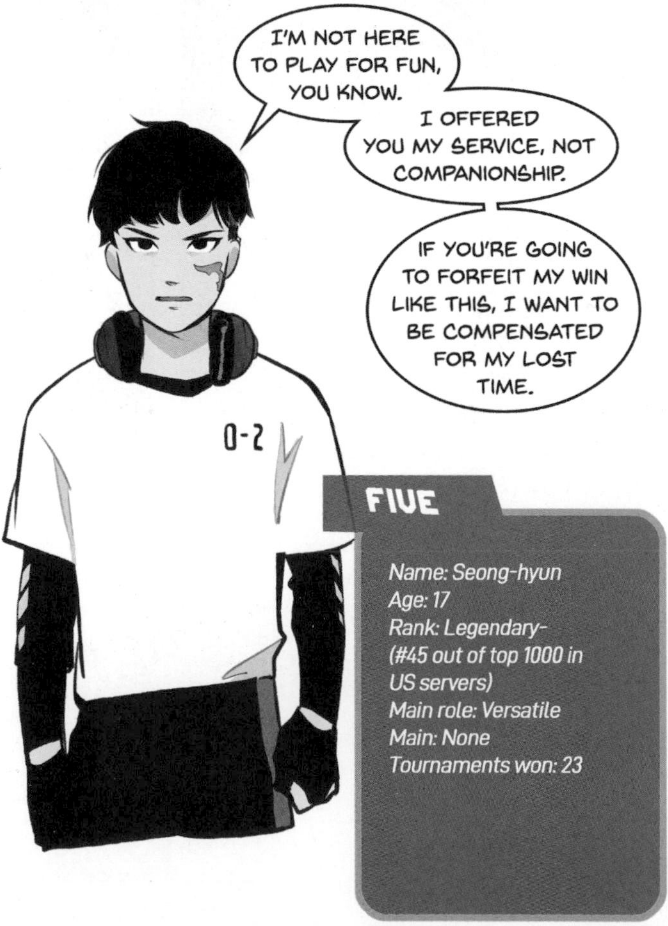
I'M NOT HERE TO PLAY FOR FUN, YOU KNOW.
I OFFERED YOU MY SERVICE, NOT COMPANIONSHIP.
IF YOU'RE GOING TO FORFEIT MY WIN LIKE THIS, I WANT TO BE COMPENSATED FOR MY LOST TIME.
0-2
FIVE
Name: Seong-hyun
Age: 17
Rank: Legendary-
(#45 out of top 1000 in
US servers)
Main role: Versatile
Main: None
Tournaments won: 23

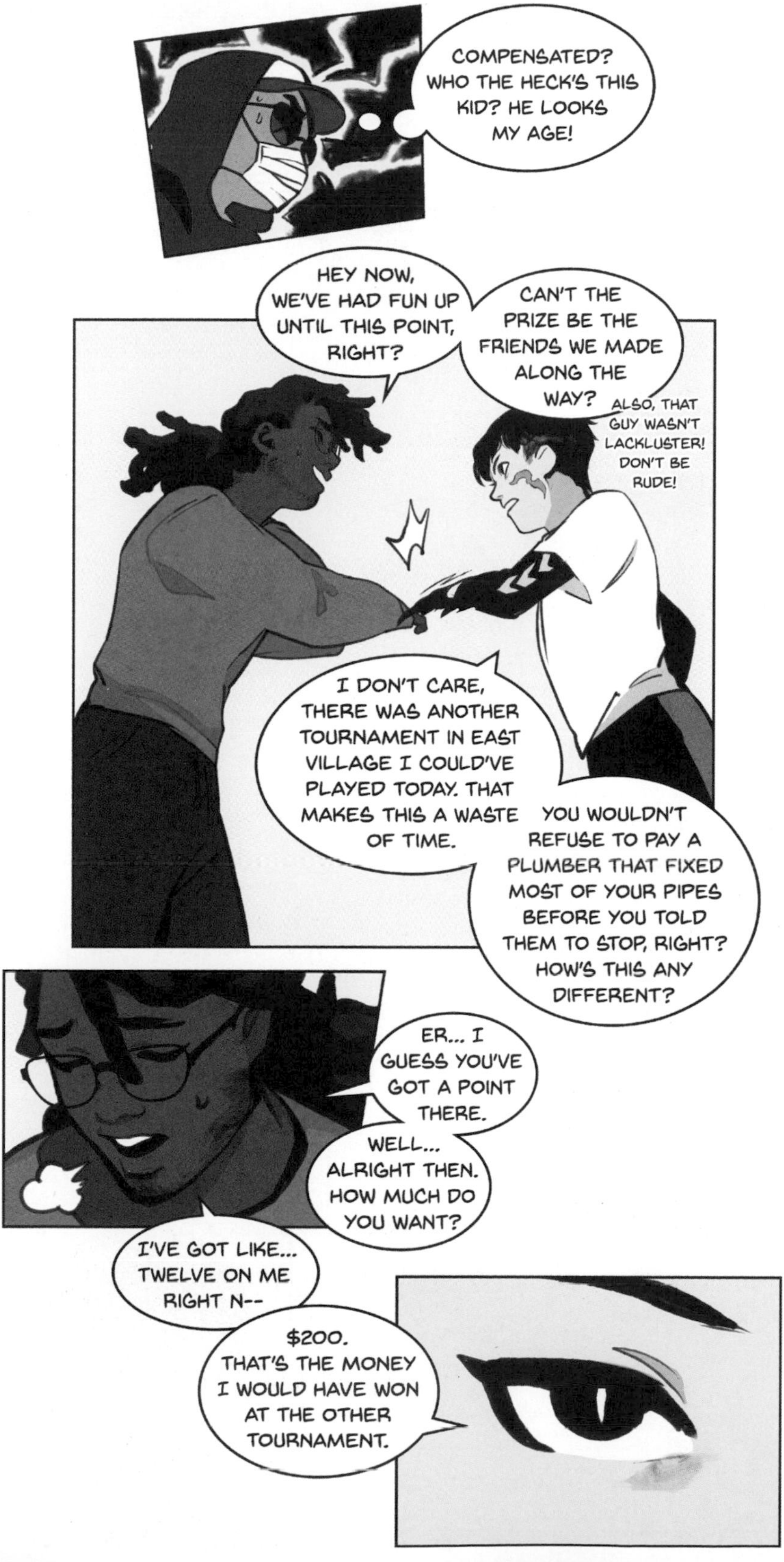

COMPENSATED? WHO THE HECK'S THIS KID? HE LOOKS MY AGE!
HEY NOW, WE'VE HAD FUN UP UNTIL THIS POINT, RIGHT?
CAN'T THE PRIZE BE THE FRIENDS WE MADE ALONG THE WAY?
ALSO, THAT GUY WASN'T LACKLUSTER! DON'T BE RUDE!
I DON'T CARE, THERE WAS ANOTHER TOURNAMENT IN EAST VILLAGE I COULD'VE PLAYED TODAY. THAT MAKES THIS A WASTE OF TIME.
YOU WOULDN'T REFUSE TO PAY A PLUMBER THAT FIXED MOST OF YOUR PIPES BEFORE YOU TOLD THEM TO STOP, RIGHT? HOW'S THIS ANY DIFFERENT?
ER... I GUESS YOU'VE GOT A POINT THERE.
WELL... ALRIGHT THEN. HOW MUCH DO YOU WANT?
I'VE GOT LIKE... TWELVE ON ME RIGHT N--
$200. THAT'S THE MONEY I WOULD HAVE WON AT THE OTHER TOURNAMENT.

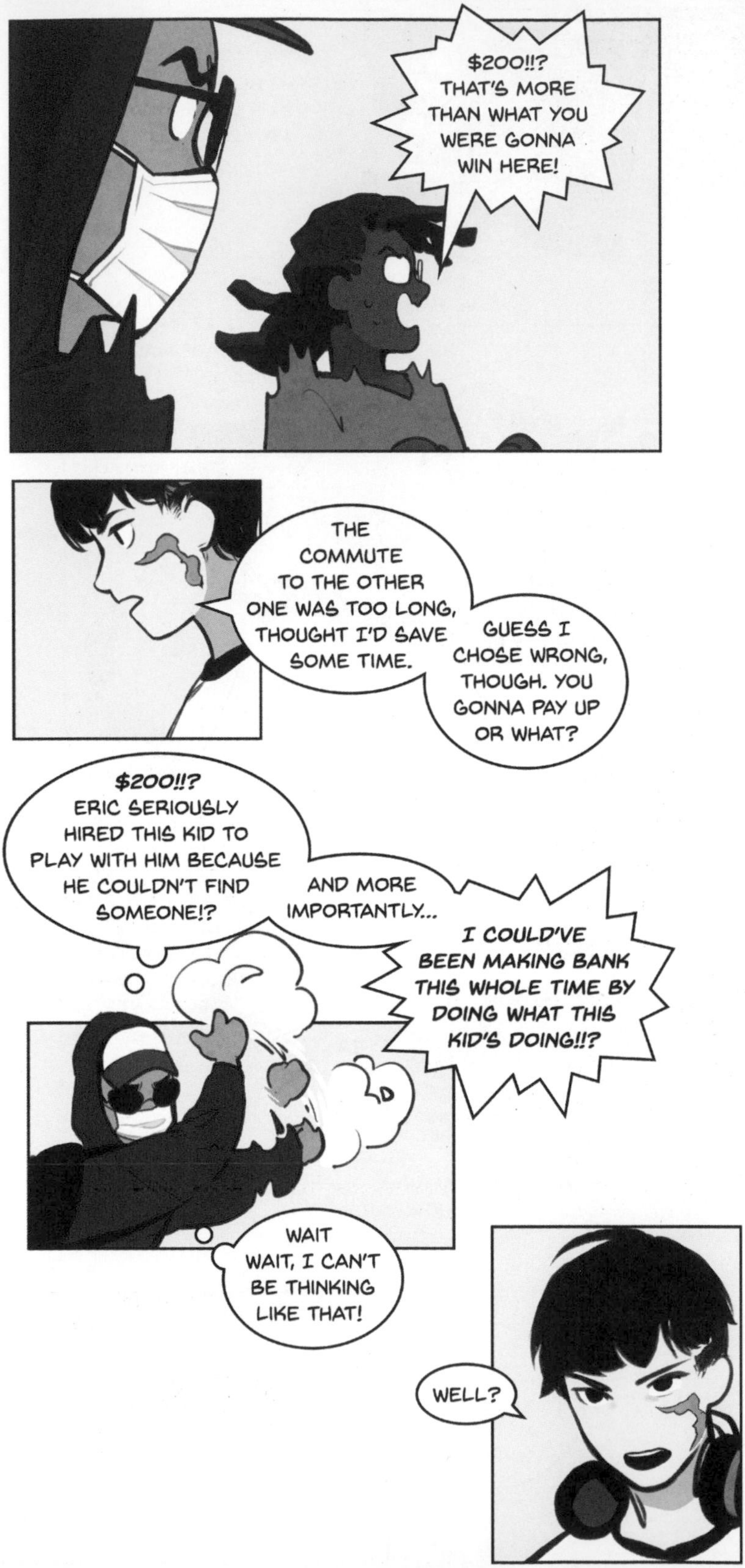
$200!!? THAT'S MORE THAN WHAT YOU WERE GONNA WIN HERE!
THE COMMUTE TO THE OTHER ONE WAS TOO LONG, THOUGHT I'D SAVE SOME TIME.
GUESS I CHOSE WRONG, THOUGH. YOU GONNA PAY UP OR WHAT?
$200!!? ERIC SERIOUSLY HIRED THIS KID TO PLAY WITH HIM BECAUSE HE COULDN'T FIND SOMEONE!?
AND MORE IMPORTANTLY...
I COULD'VE BEEN MAKING BANK THIS WHOLE TIME BY DOING WHAT THIS KID'S DOING!!?
WAIT WAIT, I CAN'T BE THINKING LIKE THAT!
WELL?

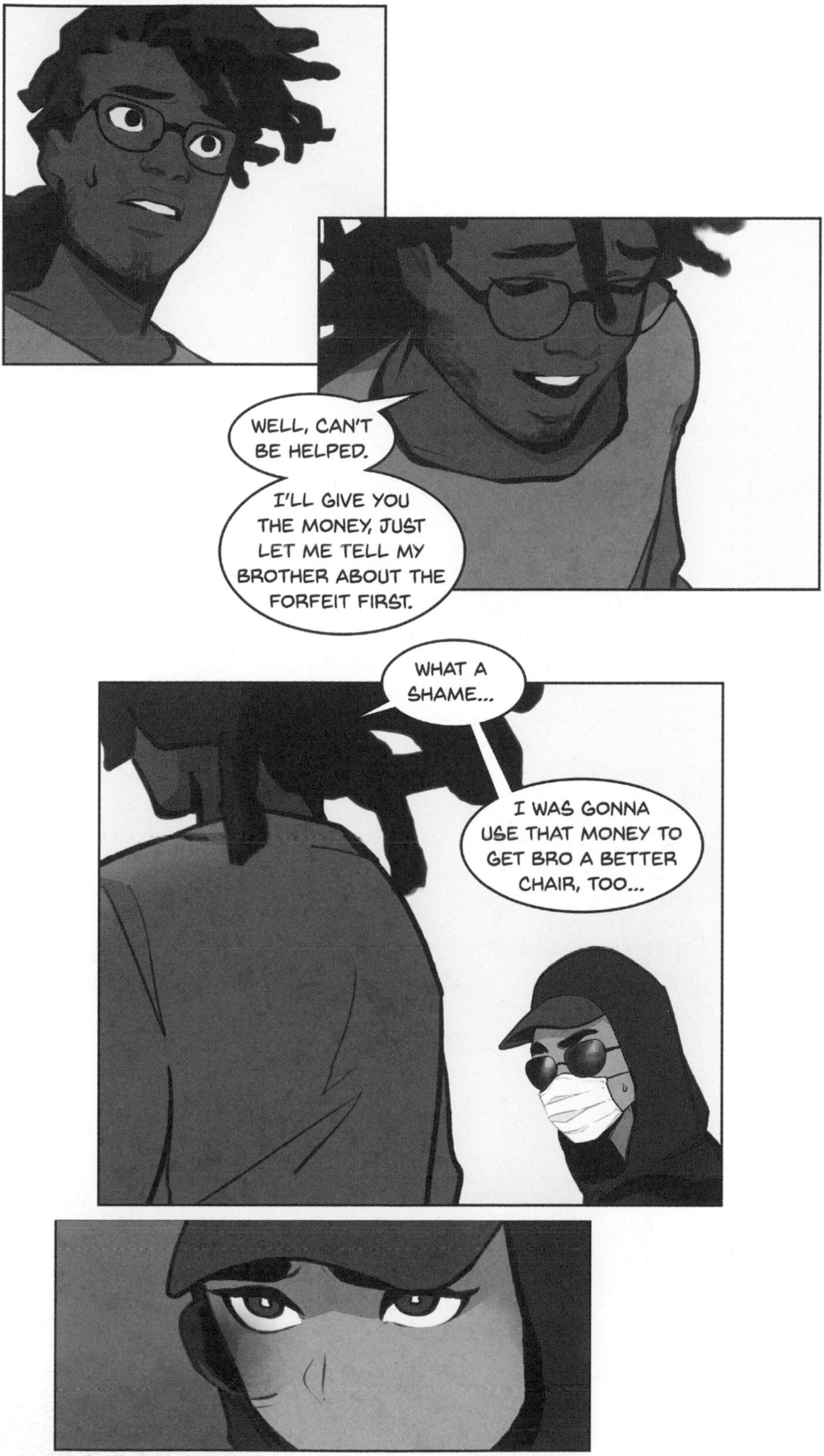
WELL, CAN'T BE HELPED.
I'LL GIVE YOU THE MONEY, JUST LET ME TELL MY BROTHER ABOUT THE FORFEIT FIRST.
WHAT A SHAME...
I WAS GONNA USE THAT MONEY TO GET BRO A BETTER CHAIR, TOO...

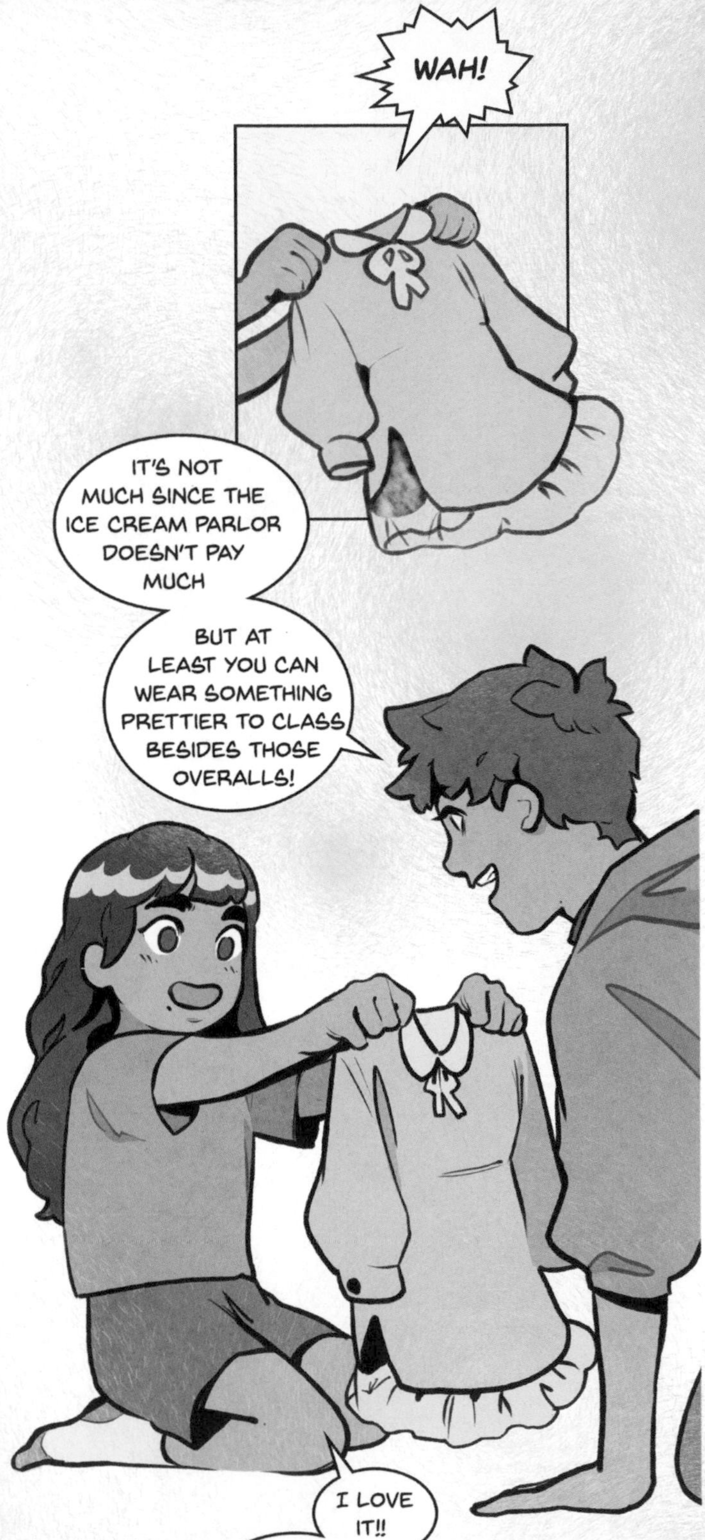
WAH!
IT'S NOT MUCH SINCE THE ICE CREAM PARLOR DOESN'T PAY MUCH
BUT AT LEAST YOU CAN WEAR SOMETHING PRETTIER TO CLASS BESIDES THOSE OVERALLS!
I LOVE IT!!
THANK YOU, VEEVEE!

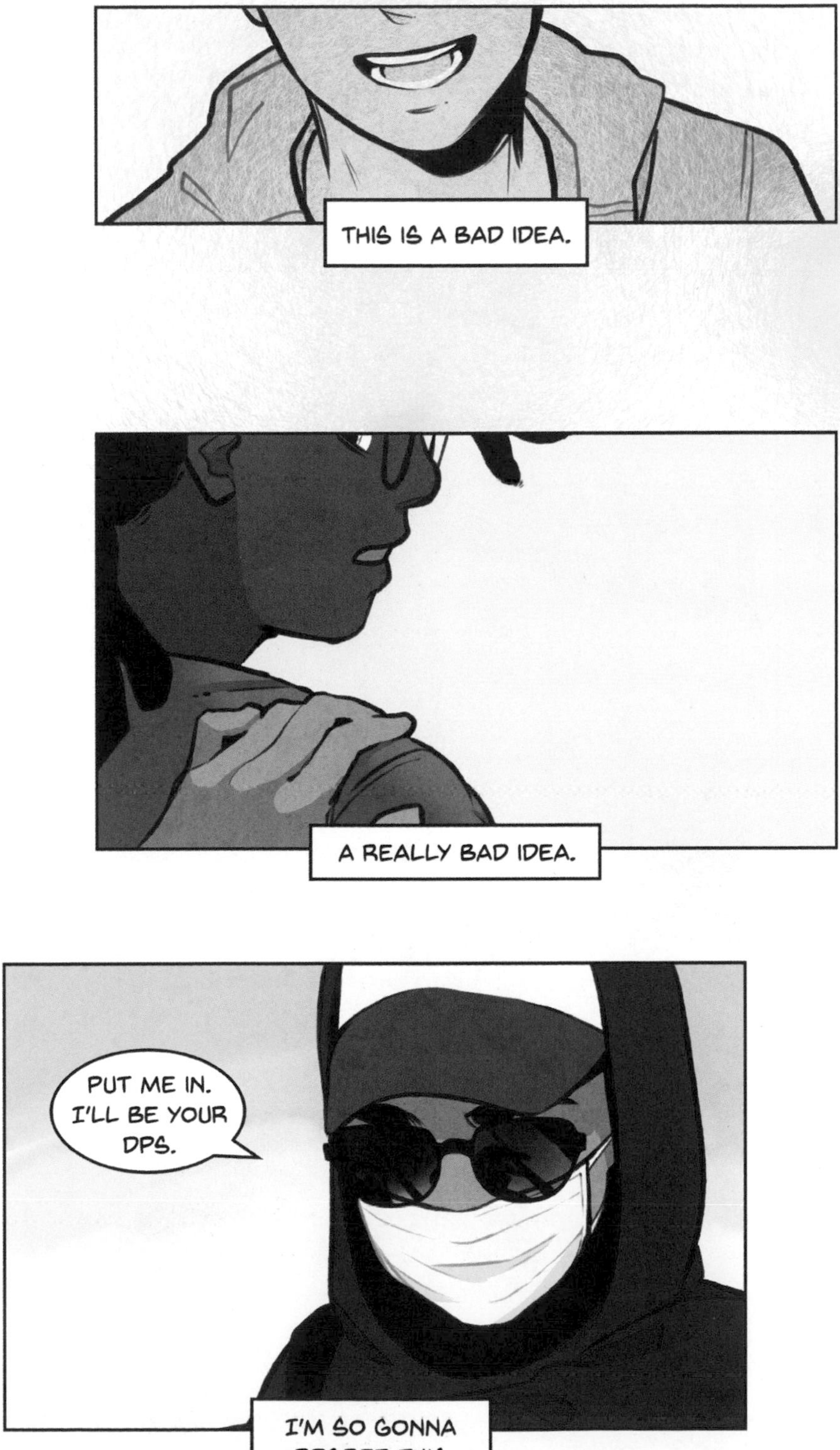
THIS IS A BAD IDEA.
A REALLY BAD IDEA.
PUT ME IN. I'LL BE YOUR DPS.
I'M SO GONNA REGRET THIS.

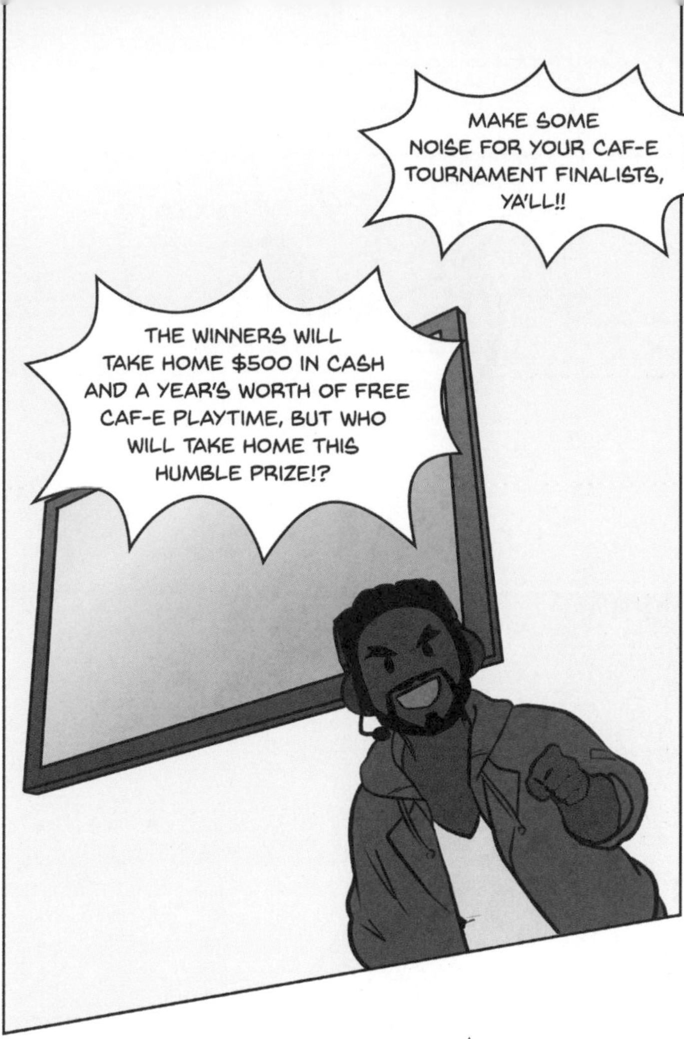
MAKE SOME NOISE FOR YOUR CAF-E TOURNAMENT FINALISTS, YA'LL!!
THE WINNERS WILL TAKE HOME $500 IN CASH AND A YEAR'S WORTH OF FREE CAF-E PLAYTIME, BUT WHO WILL TAKE HOME THIS HUMBLE PRIZE!?

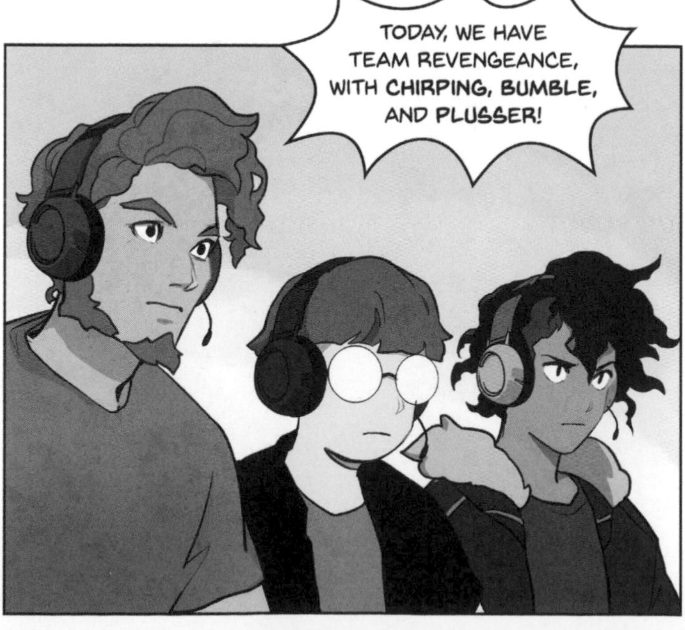
TODAY, WE HAVE TEAM REVENGEANCE, WITH CHIRPING, BUMBLE, AND PLUSSER!

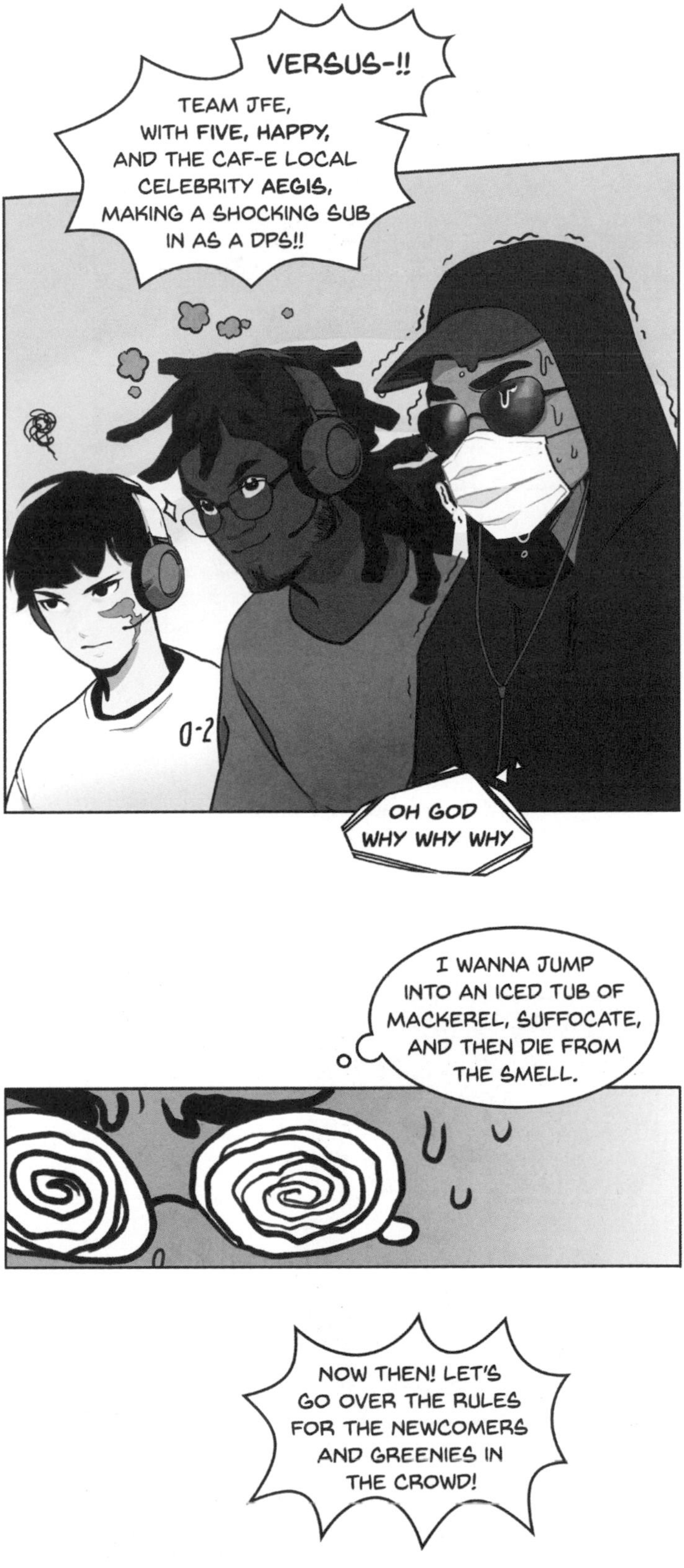
VERSUS-!!
TEAM JFE, WITH FIVE, HAPPY, AND THE CAF-E LOCAL CELEBRITY AEGIS, MAKING A SHOCKING SUB IN AS A DPS!!
0-2
OH GOD WHY WHY WHY
I WANNA JUMP INTO AN ICED TUB OF MACKEREL, SUFFOCATE, AND THEN DIE FROM THE SMELL.
NOW THEN! LET'S GO OVER THE RULES FOR THE NEWCOMERS AND GREENIES IN THE CROWD!

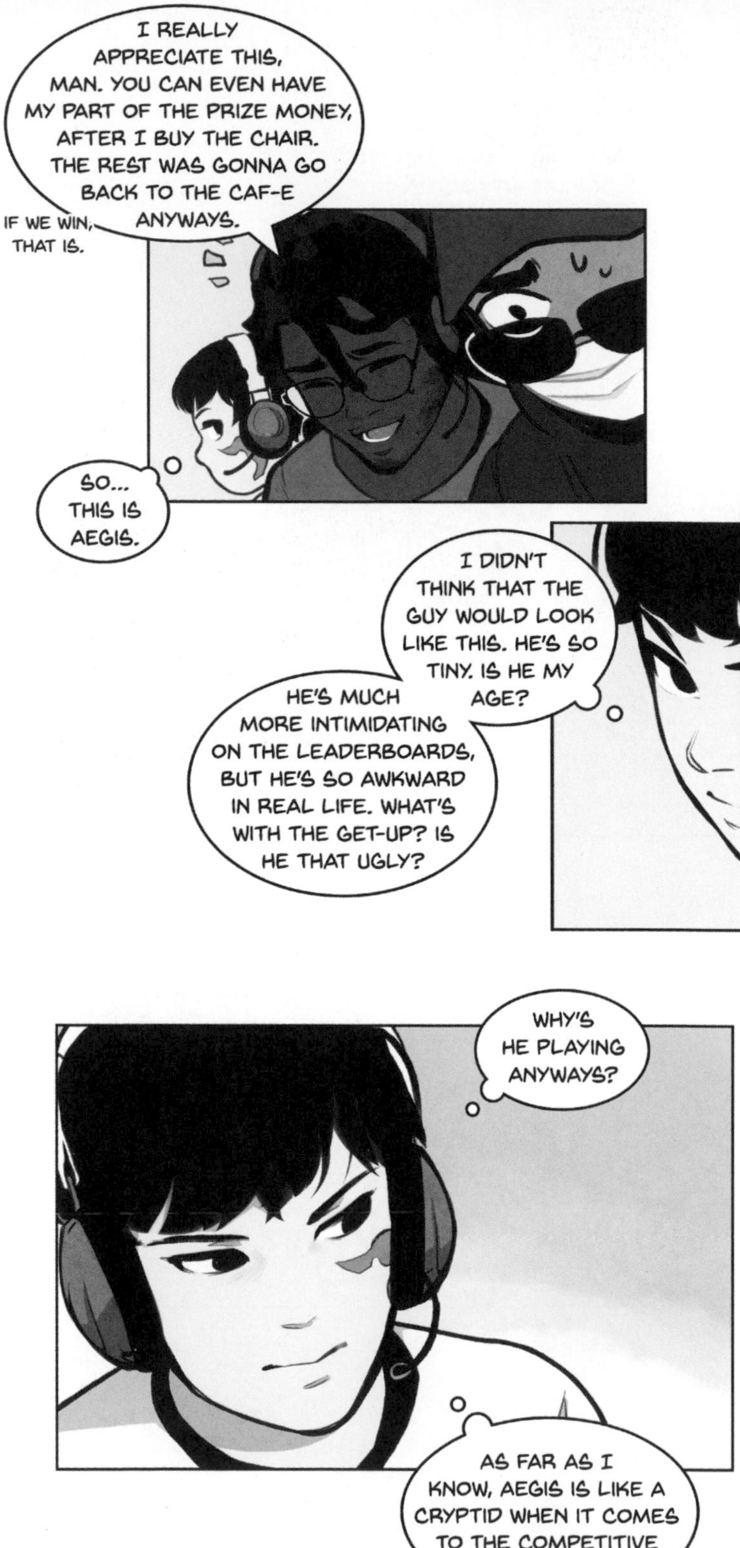
I REALLY APPRECIATE THIS, MAN. YOU CAN EVEN HAVE MY PART OF THE PRIZE MONEY, AFTER I BUY THE CHAIR. THE REST WAS GONNA GO BACK TO THE CAF-E ANYWAYS.
IF WE WIN, THAT IS.
SO... THIS IS AEGIS.
I DIDN'T THINK THAT THE GUY WOULD LOOK LIKE THIS. HE'S SO TINY. IS HE MY AGE?
HE'S MUCH MORE INTIMIDATING ON THE LEADERBOARDS, BUT HE'S SO AWKWARD IN REAL LIFE. WHAT'S WITH THE GET-UP? IS HE THAT UGLY?
WHY'S HE PLAYING ANYWAYS?
AS FAR AS I KNOW, AEGIS IS LIKE A CRYPTID WHEN IT COMES TO THE COMPETITIVE SCENE...

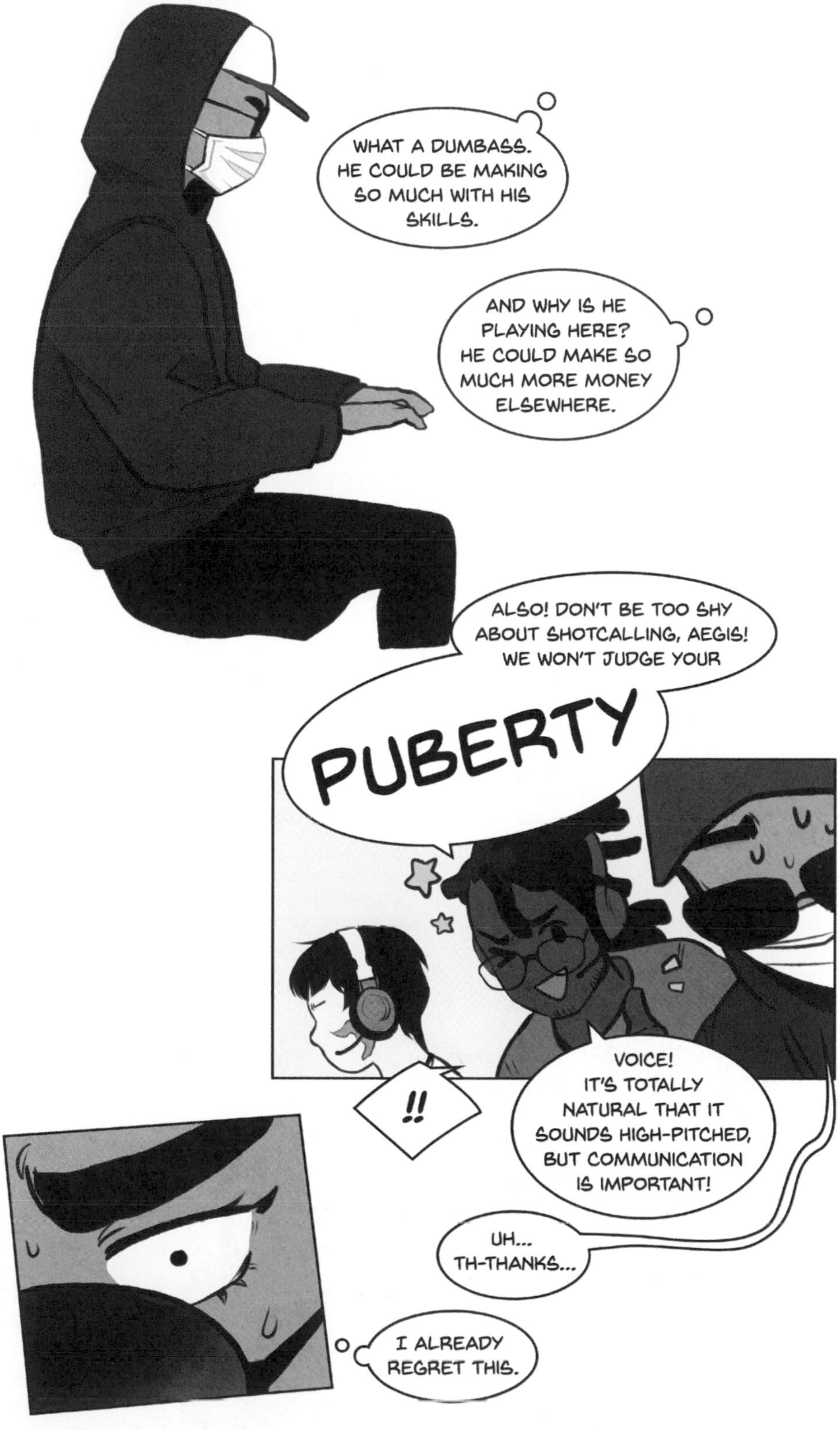
WHAT A DUMBASS. HE COULD BE MAKING SO MUCH WITH HIS SKILLS.
AND WHY IS HE PLAYING HERE? HE COULD MAKE SO MUCH MORE MONEY ELSEWHERE.
ALSO! DON'T BE TOO SHY ABOUT SHOTCALLING, AEGIS! WE WON'T JUDGE YOUR
PUBERTY
VOICE! IT'S TOTALLY NATURAL THAT IT SOUNDS HIGH-PITCHED, BUT COMMUNICATION IS IMPORTANT!
!!
UH... TH-THANKS...
I ALREADY REGRET THIS.

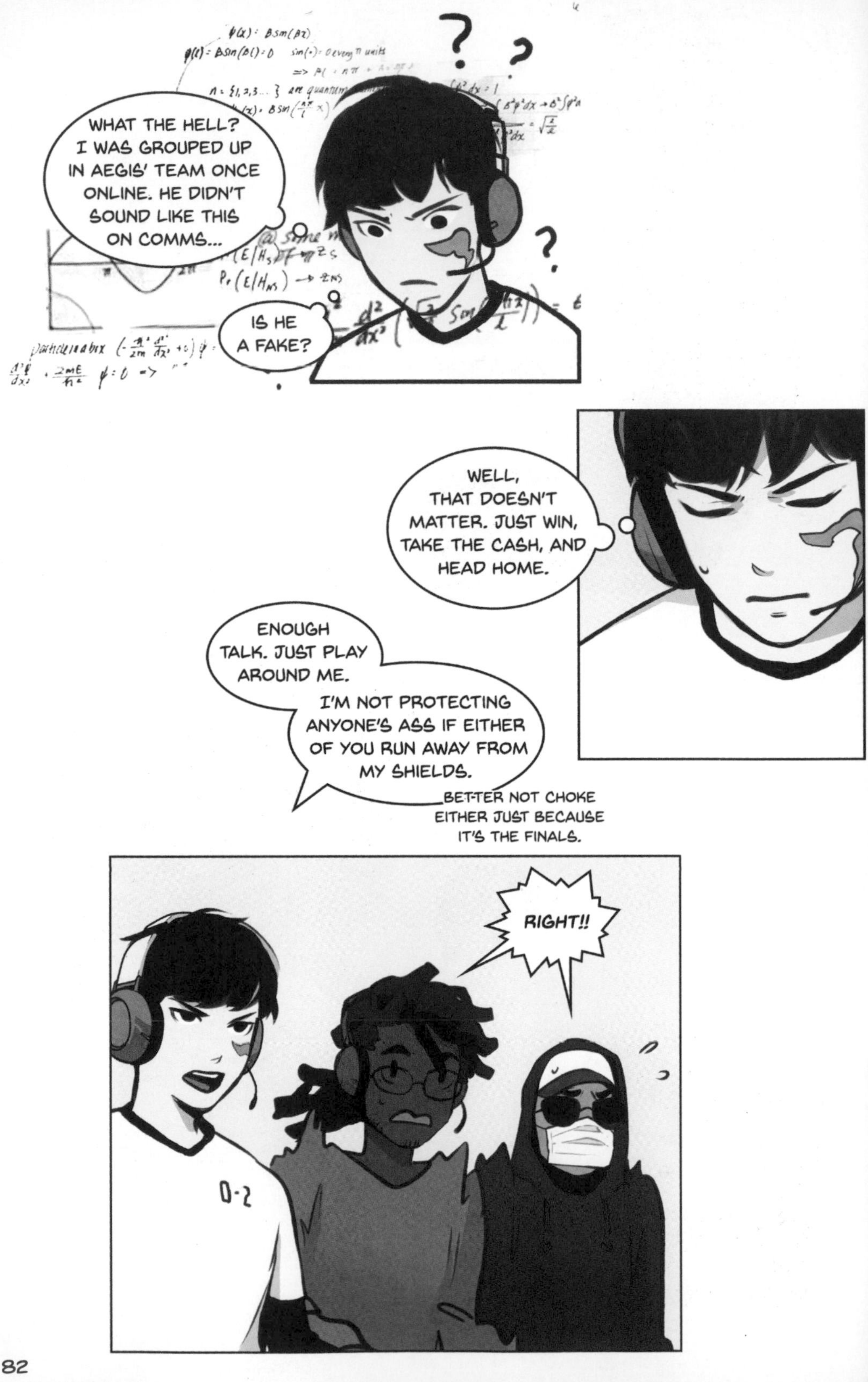
WHAT THE HELL? I WAS GROUPED UP IN AEGIS' TEAM ONCE ONLINE. HE DIDN'T SOUND LIKE THIS ON COMMS...
IS HE A FAKE?
WELL, THAT DOESN'T MATTER. JUST WIN, TAKE THE CASH, AND HEAD HOME.
ENOUGH TALK. JUST PLAY AROUND ME.
I'M NOT PROTECTING ANYONE'S ASS IF EITHER OF YOU RUN AWAY FROM MY SHIELDS.
BETTER NOT CHOKE EITHER JUST BECAUSE IT'S THE FINALS.
RIGHT!!
O-2

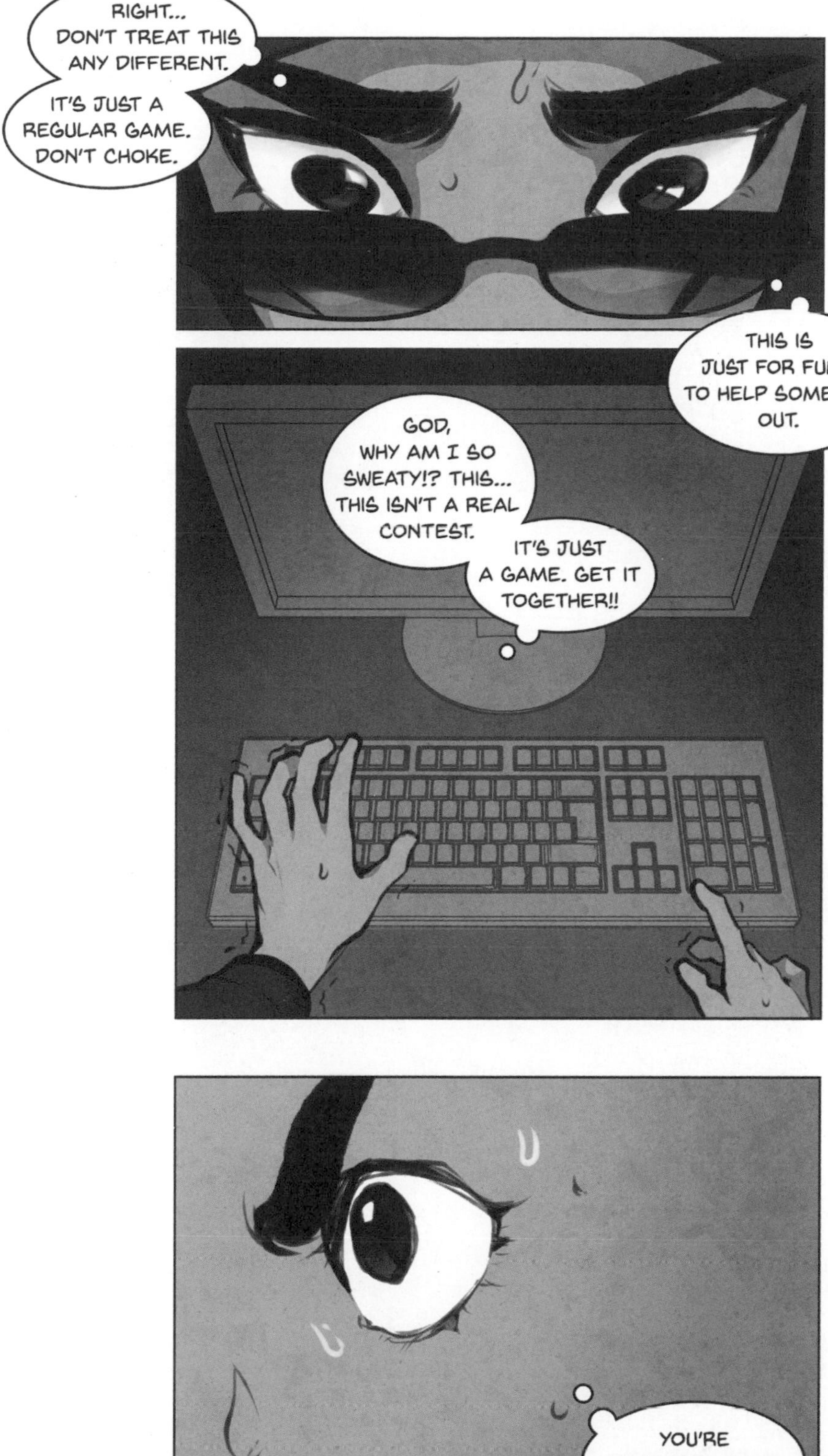
RIGHT... DON'T TREAT THIS ANY DIFFERENT.
IT'S JUST A REGULAR GAME. DON'T CHOKE.
THIS IS JUST FOR FUN... TO HELP SOMEONE OUT.
GOD, WHY AM I SO SWEATY!? THIS... THIS ISN'T A REAL CONTEST.
IT'S JUST A GAME. GET IT TOGETHER!!
YOU'RE *NOT* VICKY RIGHT NOW!

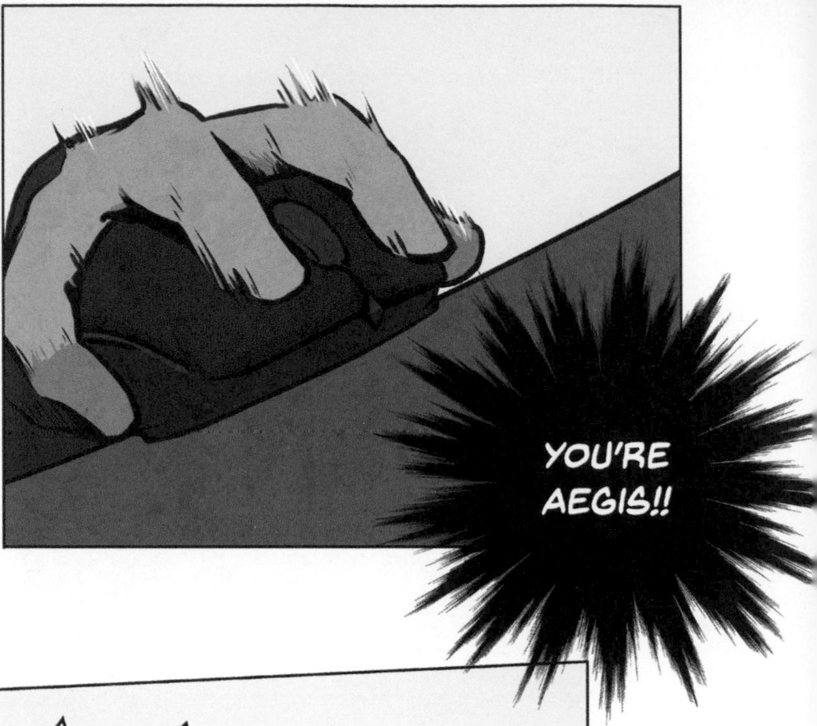
YOU'RE AEGIS!!

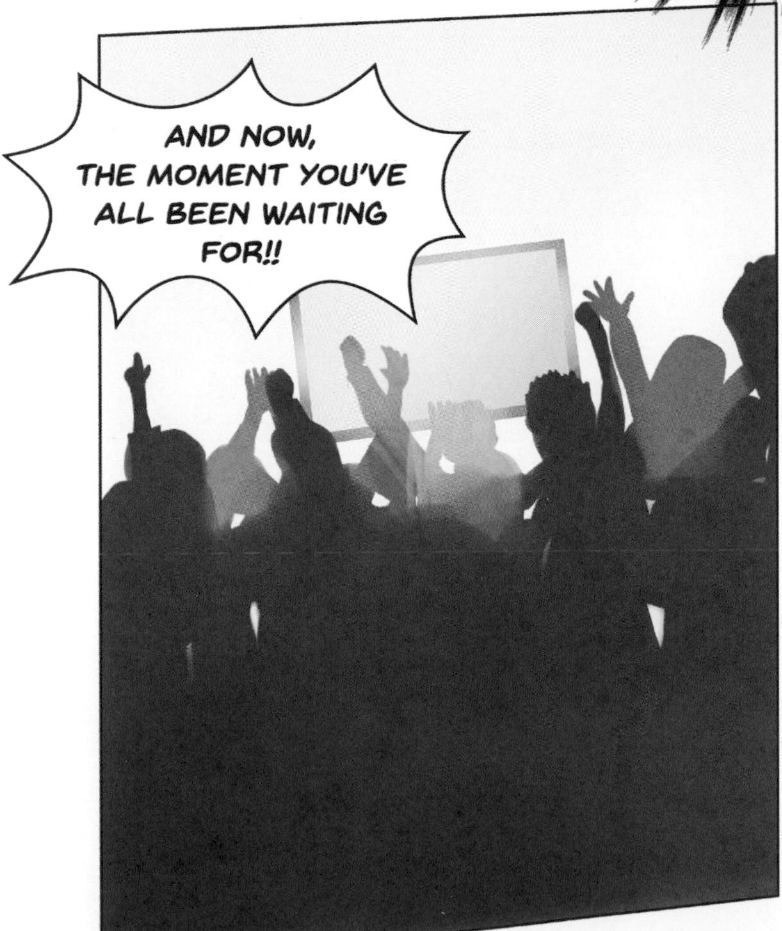
AND NOW, THE MOMENT YOU'VE ALL BEEN WAITING FOR!!

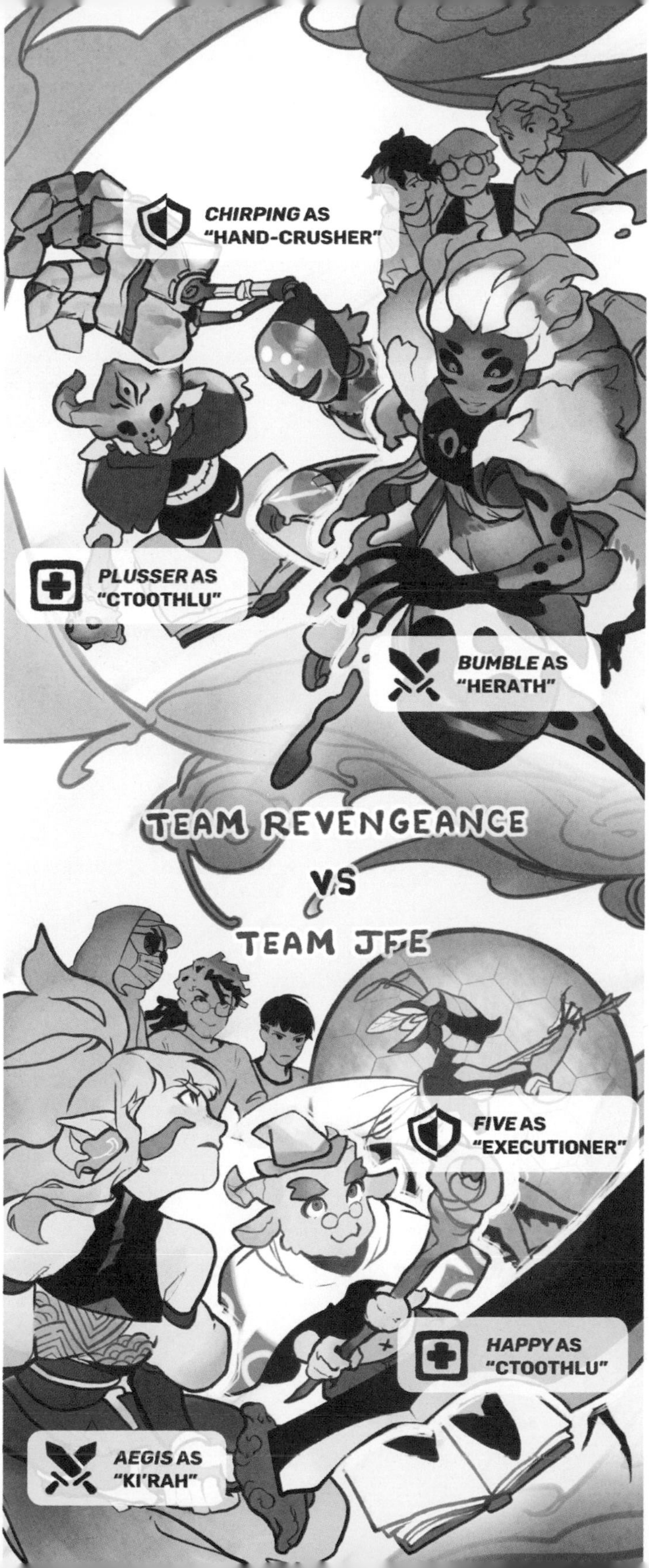
CHIRPING AS
"HAND-CRUSHER"
PLUSSER AS
"CTOOTHLU"
BUMBLE AS
"HERATH"
TEAM REVENGEANCE
VS
TEAM JFE
FIVE AS
"EXECUTIONER"
HAPPY AS
"CTOOTHLU"
AEGIS AS
"KI'RAH"

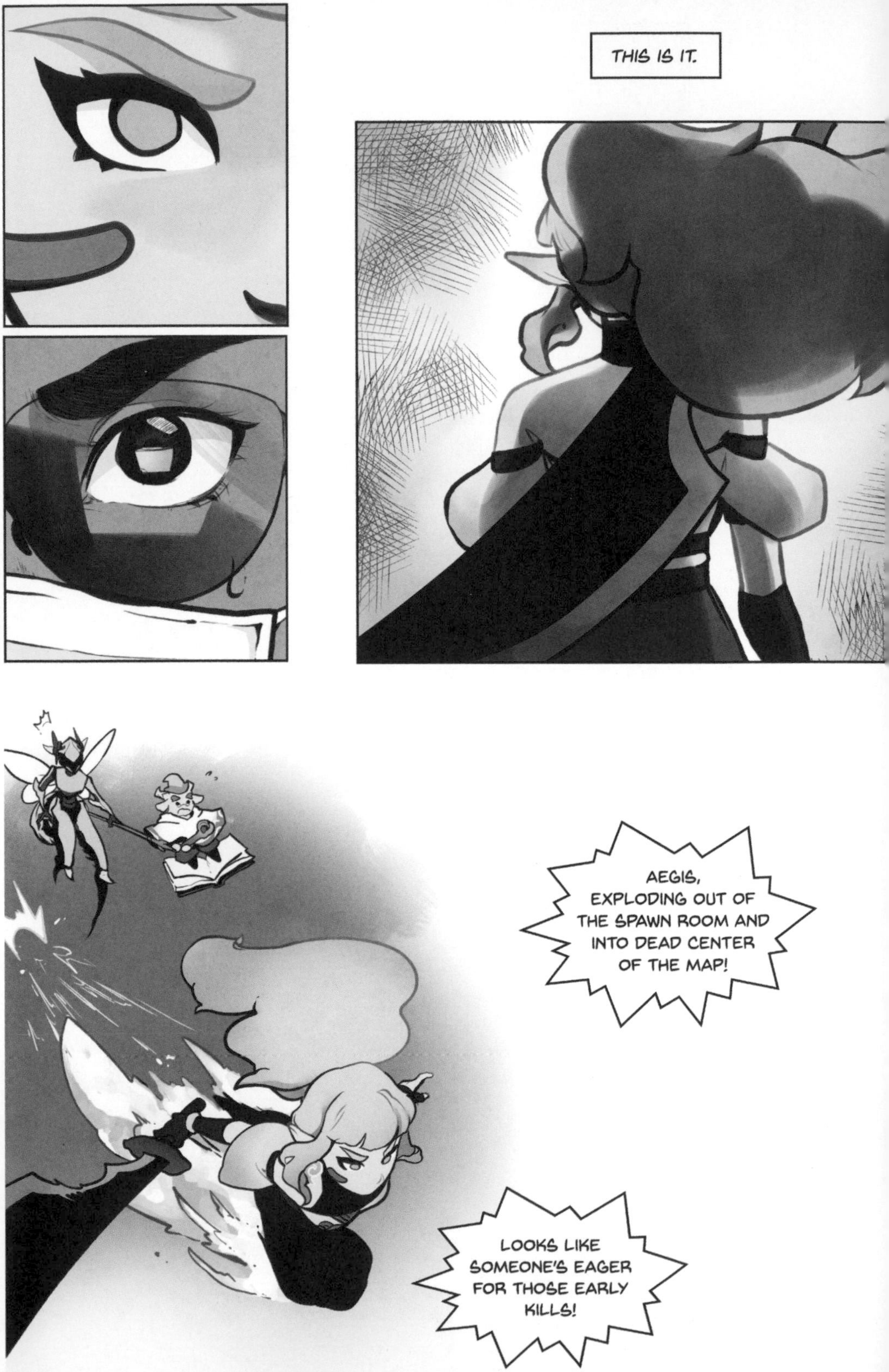
THIS IS IT.
AEGIS, EXPLODING OUT OF THE SPAWN ROOM AND INTO DEAD CENTER OF THE MAP!
LOOKS LIKE SOMEONE'S EAGER FOR THOSE EARLY KILLS!

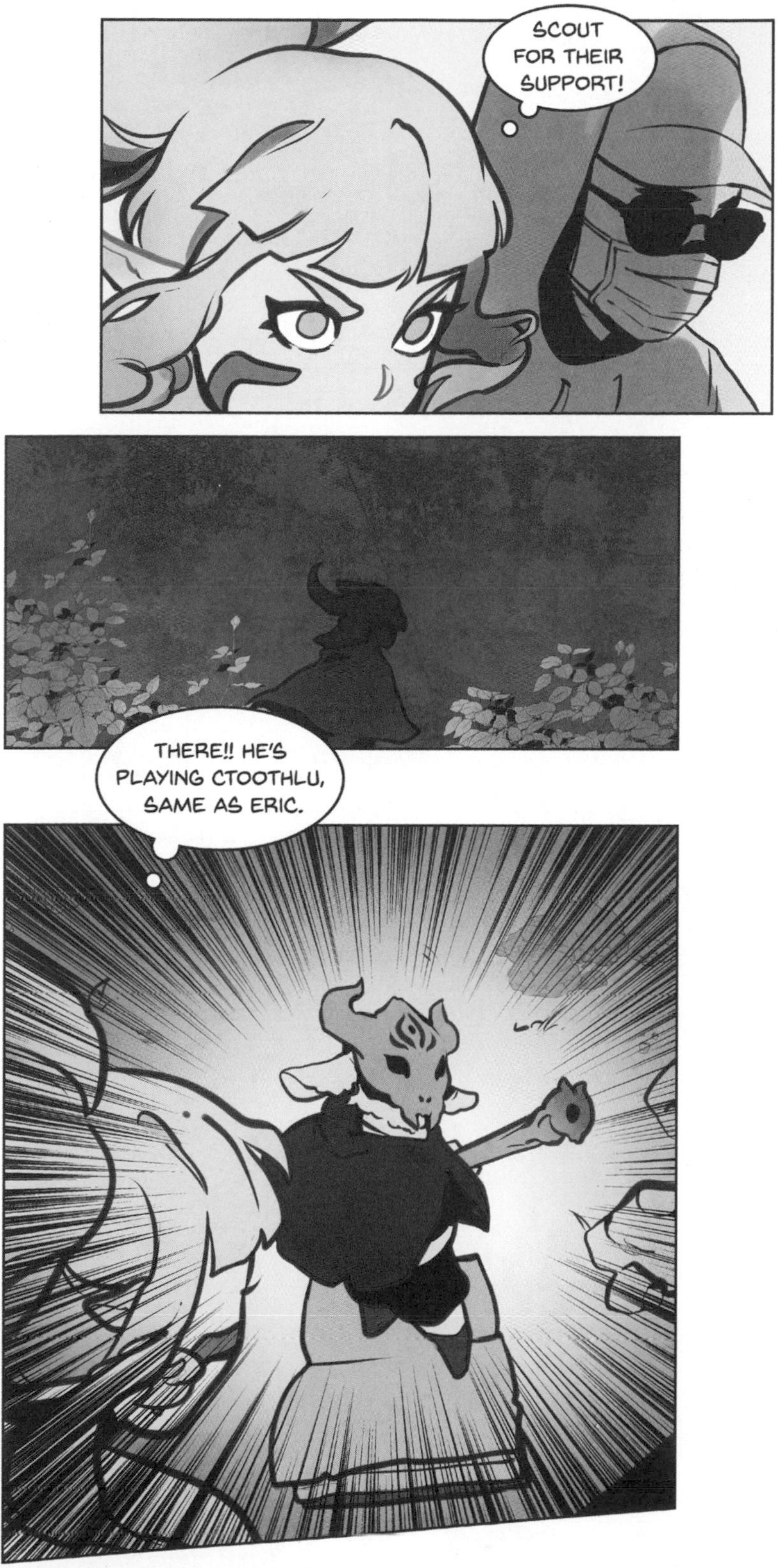
SCOUT FOR THEIR SUPPORT!
THERE!! HE'S PLAYING CTOOTHLU, SAME AS ERIC.

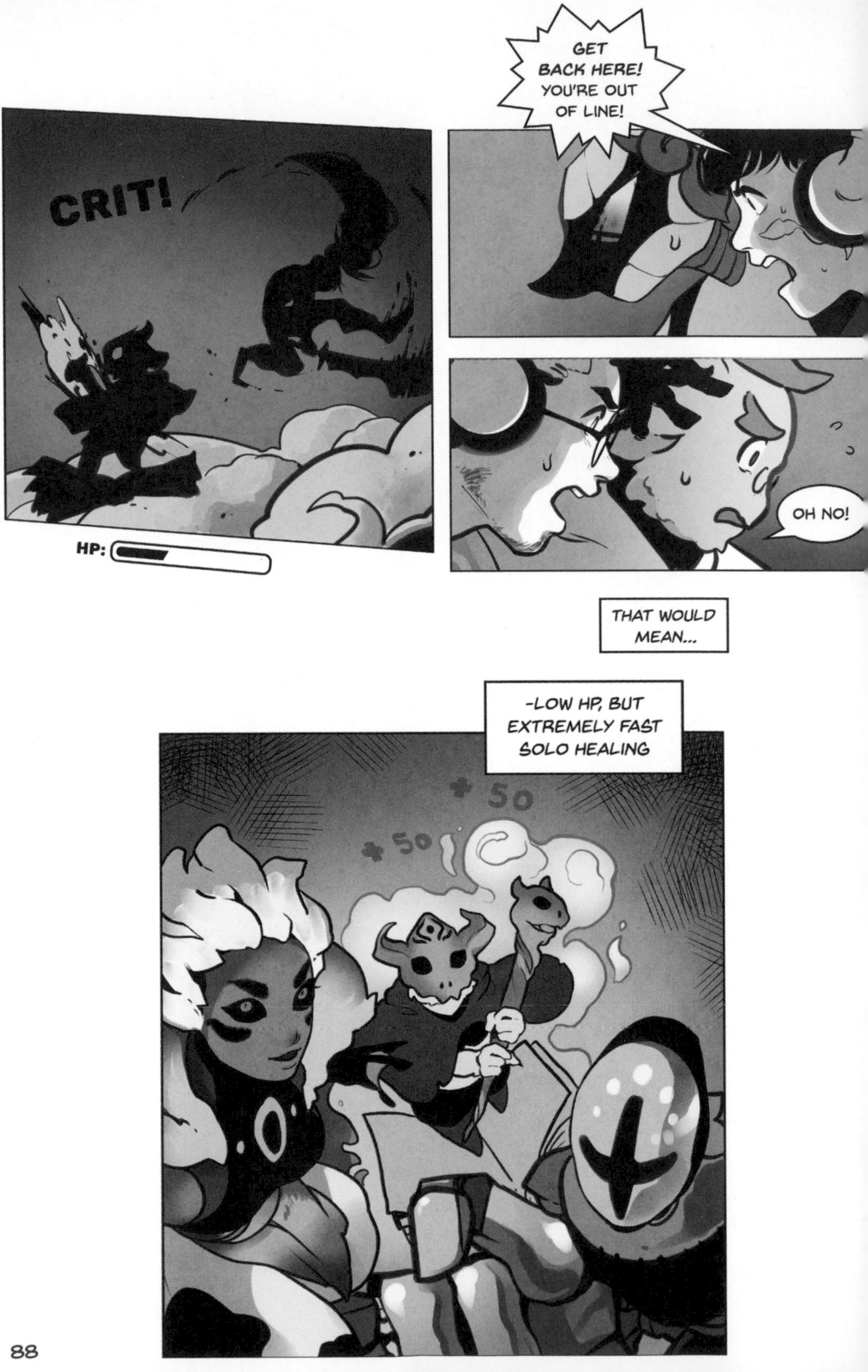
CRIT!
HP:
GET BACK HERE! YOU'RE OUT OF LINE!
OH NO!
THAT WOULD MEAN...
-LOW HP, BUT EXTREMELY FAST SOLO HEALING
+50
+50

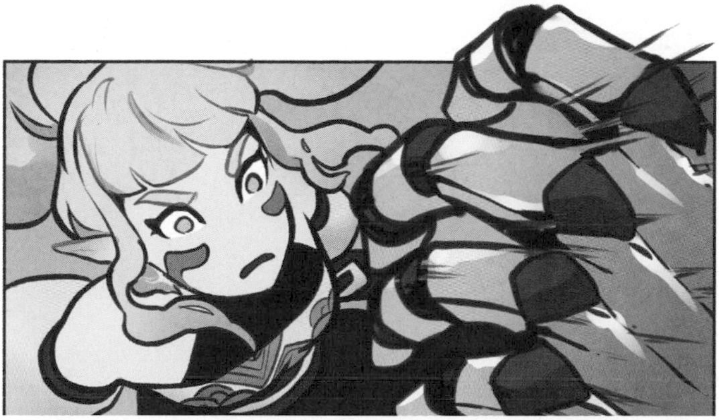

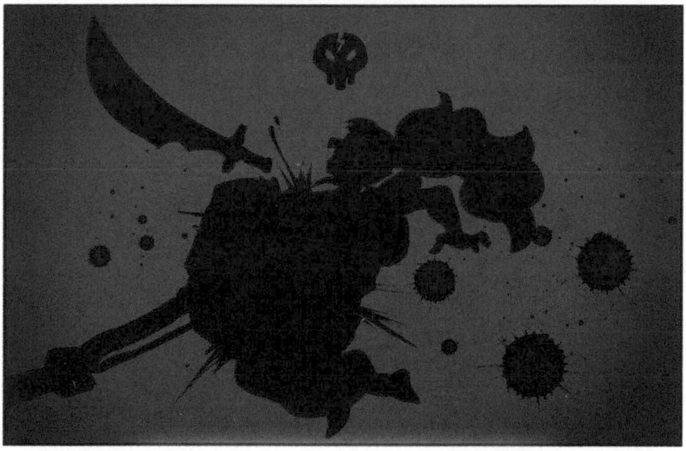

AEGIS KILLED BY CHIRPING

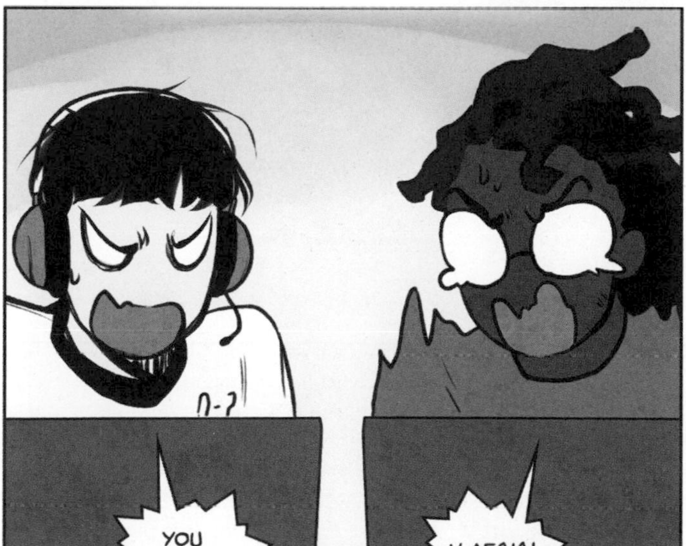
YOU IDIOT!
V-AEGIS!

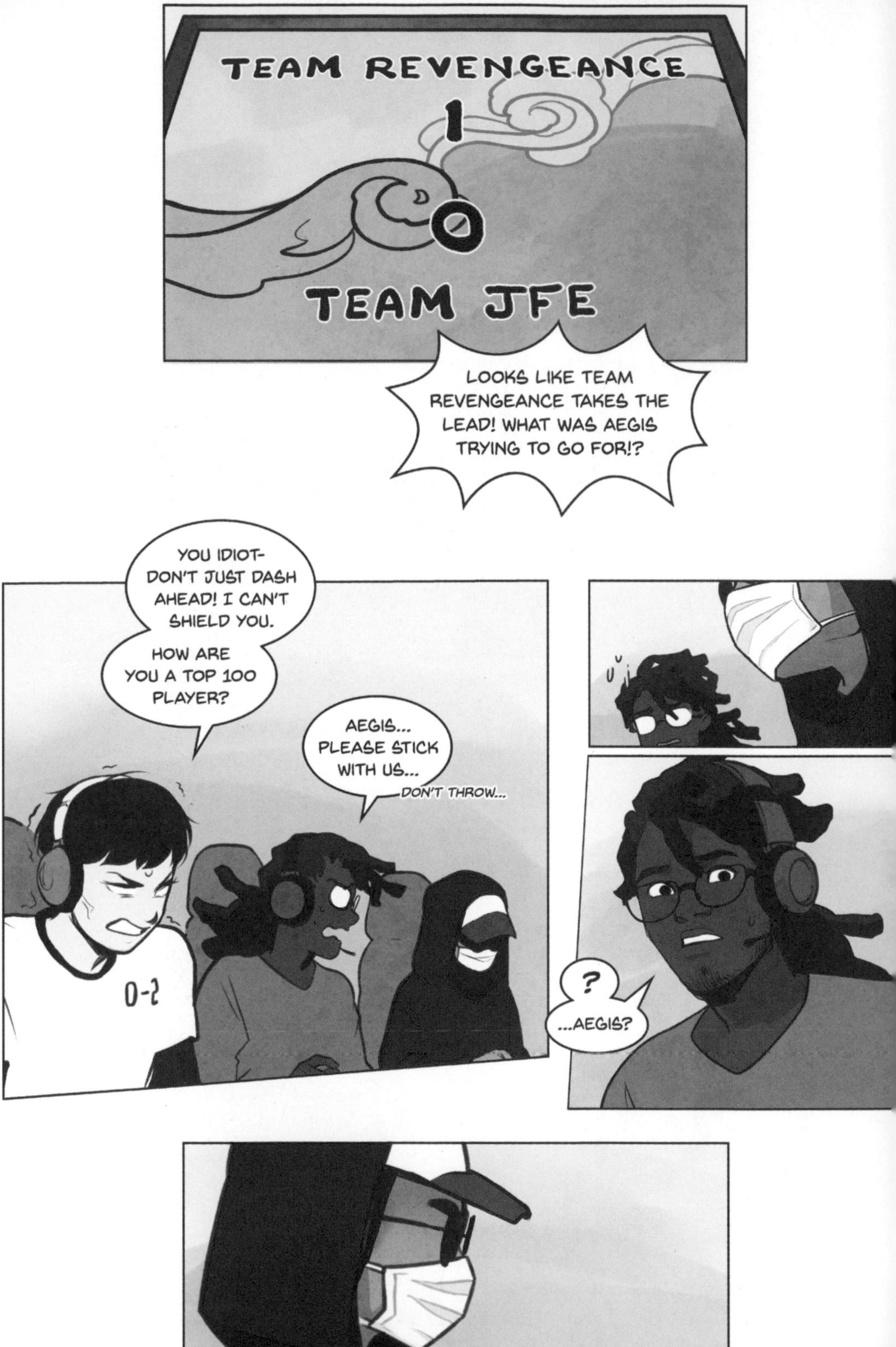
TEAM REVENGEANCE
1
0
TEAM JFE
LOOKS LIKE TEAM REVENGEANCE TAKES THE LEAD! WHAT WAS AEGIS TRYING TO GO FOR!?
YOU IDIOT- DON'T JUST DASH AHEAD! I CAN'T SHIELD YOU.
HOW ARE YOU A TOP 100 PLAYER?
AEGIS... PLEASE STICK WITH US...
DON'T THROW...
0-2
?
...AEGIS?

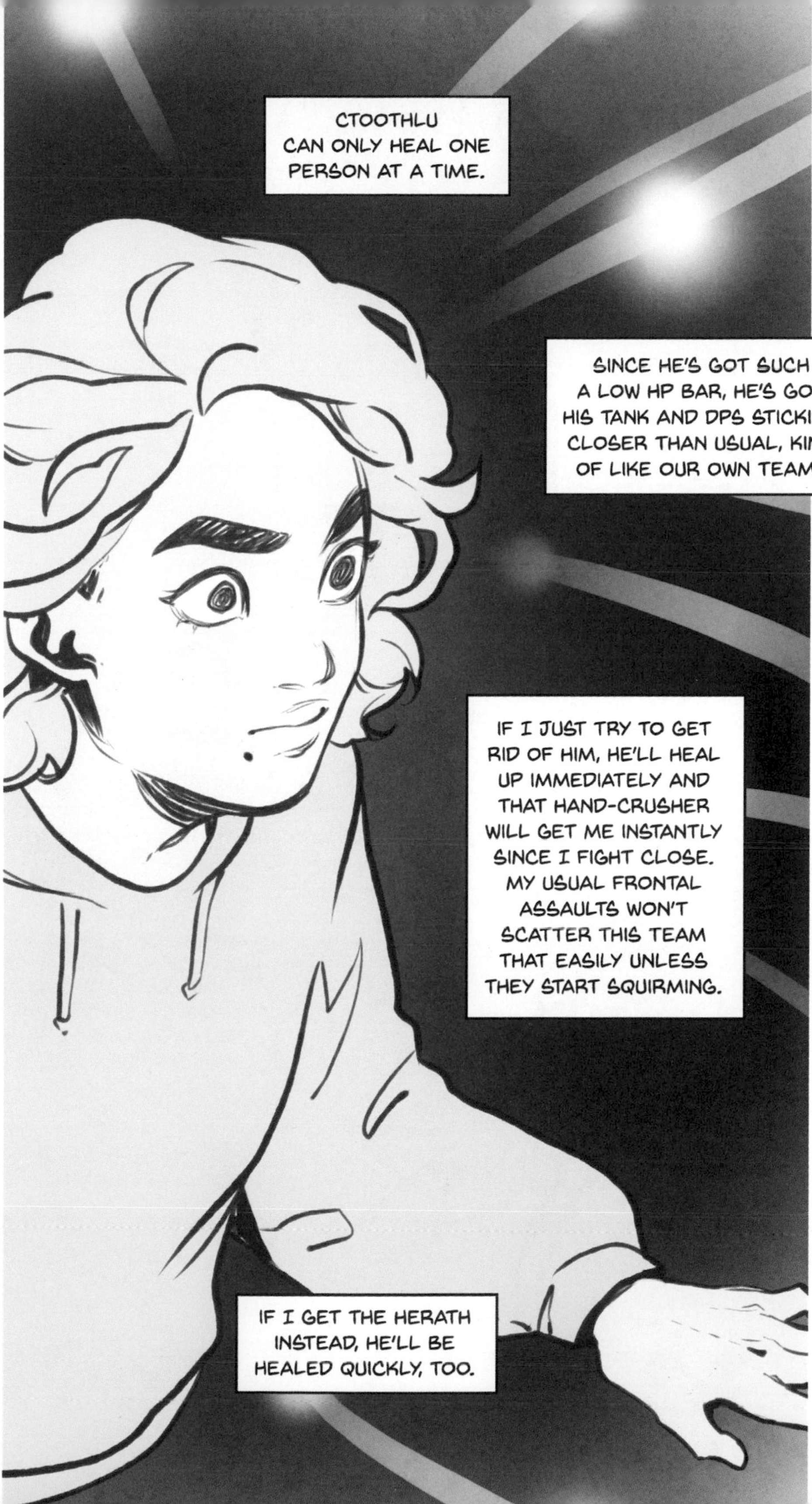
CTOOTHLU CAN ONLY HEAL ONE PERSON AT A TIME.
SINCE HE'S GOT SUCH A LOW HP BAR, HE'S GOT HIS TANK AND DPS STICKING CLOSER THAN USUAL, KIND OF LIKE OUR OWN TEAM...
IF I JUST TRY TO GET RID OF HIM, HE'LL HEAL UP IMMEDIATELY AND THAT HAND-CRUSHER WILL GET ME INSTANTLY SINCE I FIGHT CLOSE. MY USUAL FRONTAL ASSAULTS WON'T SCATTER THIS TEAM THAT EASILY UNLESS THEY START SQUIRMING.
IF I GET THE HERATH INSTEAD, HE'LL BE HEALED QUICKLY, TOO.

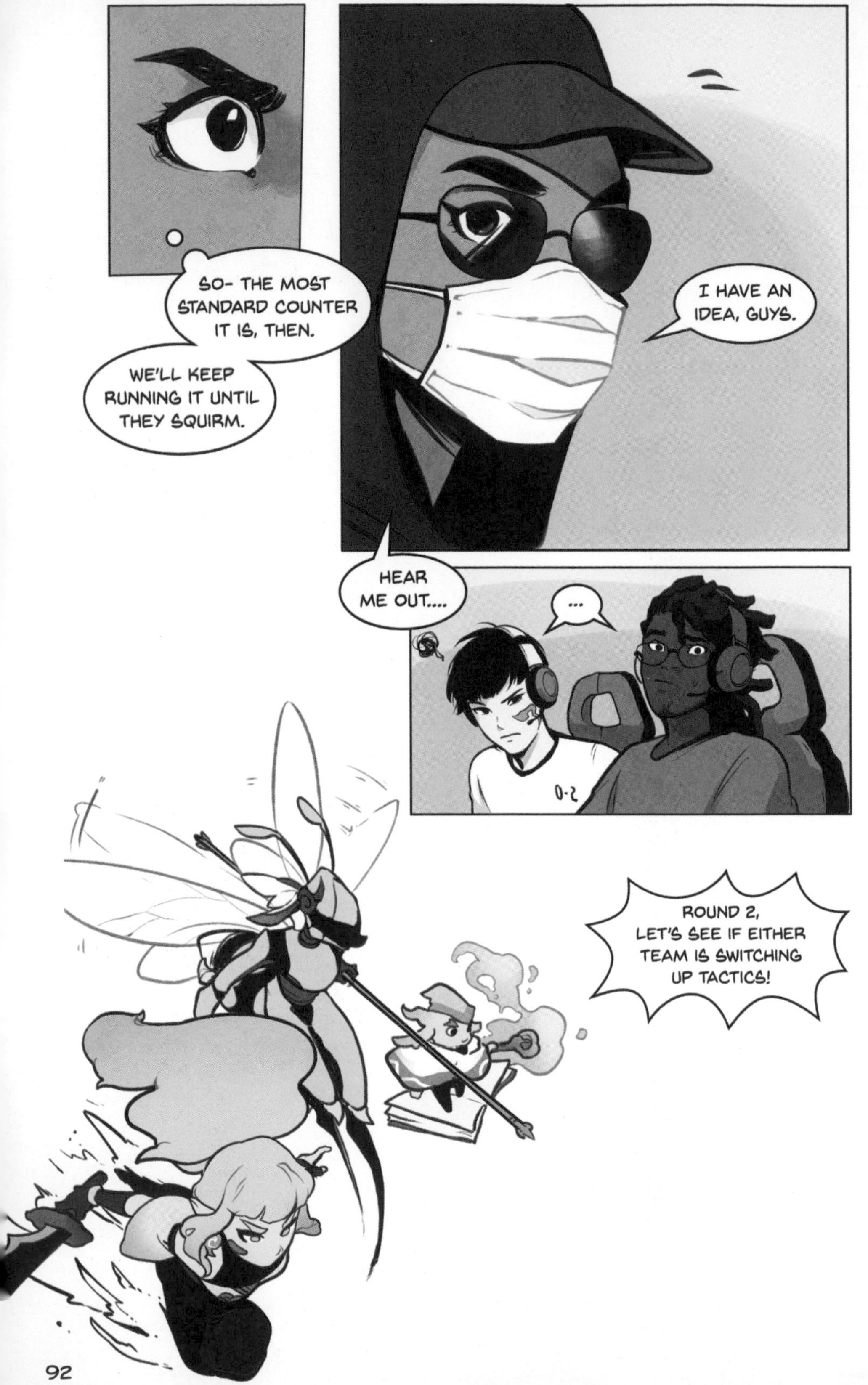
SO- THE MOST STANDARD COUNTER IT IS, THEN.
WE'LL KEEP RUNNING IT UNTIL THEY SQUIRM.
I HAVE AN IDEA, GUYS.
HEAR ME OUT....
...
ROUND 2, LET'S SEE IF EITHER TEAM IS SWITCHING UP TACTICS!

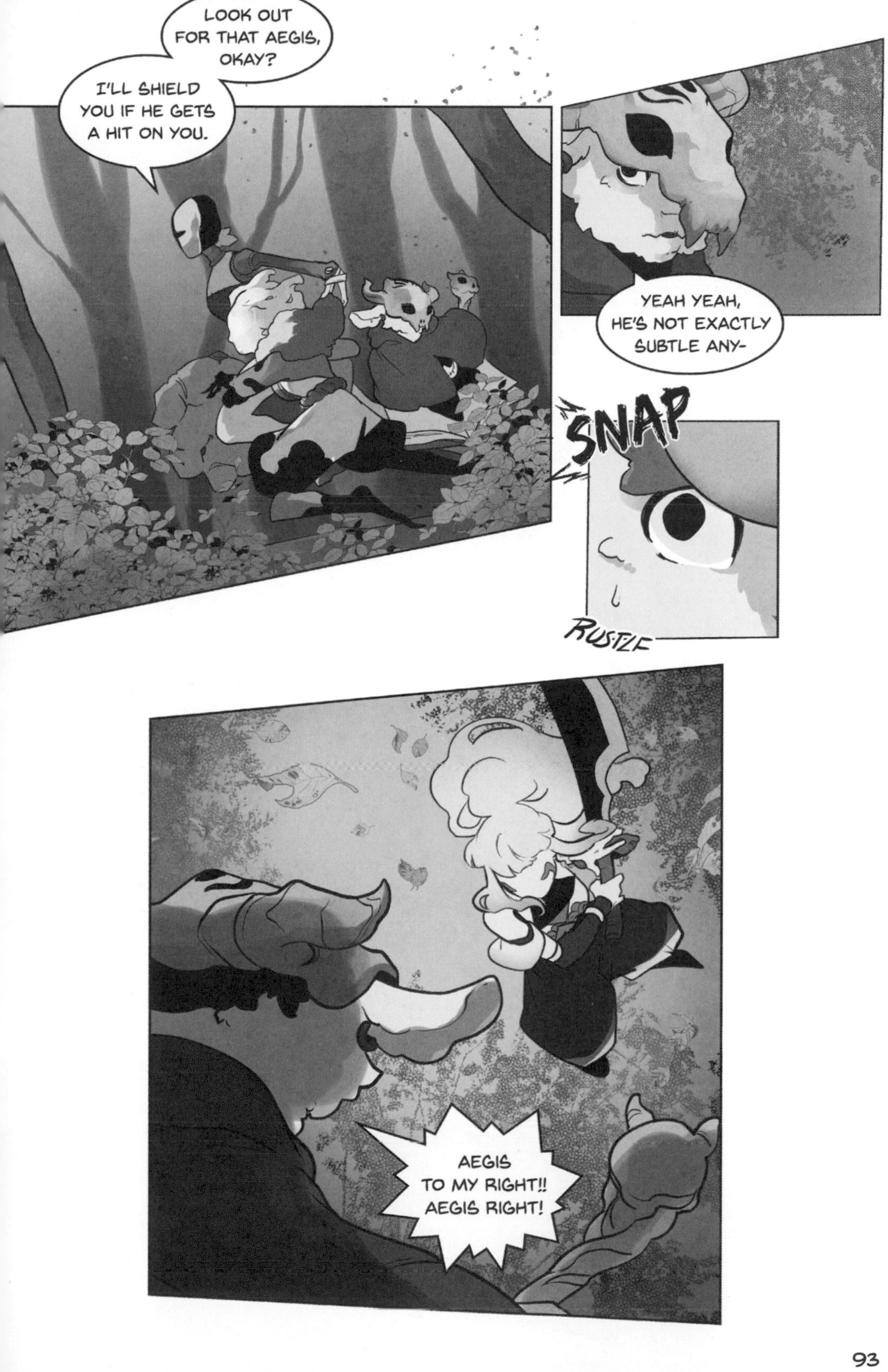
LOOK OUT FOR THAT AEGIS, OKAY?
I'LL SHIELD YOU IF HE GETS A HIT ON YOU.
YEAH YEAH, HE'S NOT EXACTLY SUBTLE ANY-
SNAP
RUSTLE
AEGIS TO MY RIGHT!! AEGIS RIGHT!

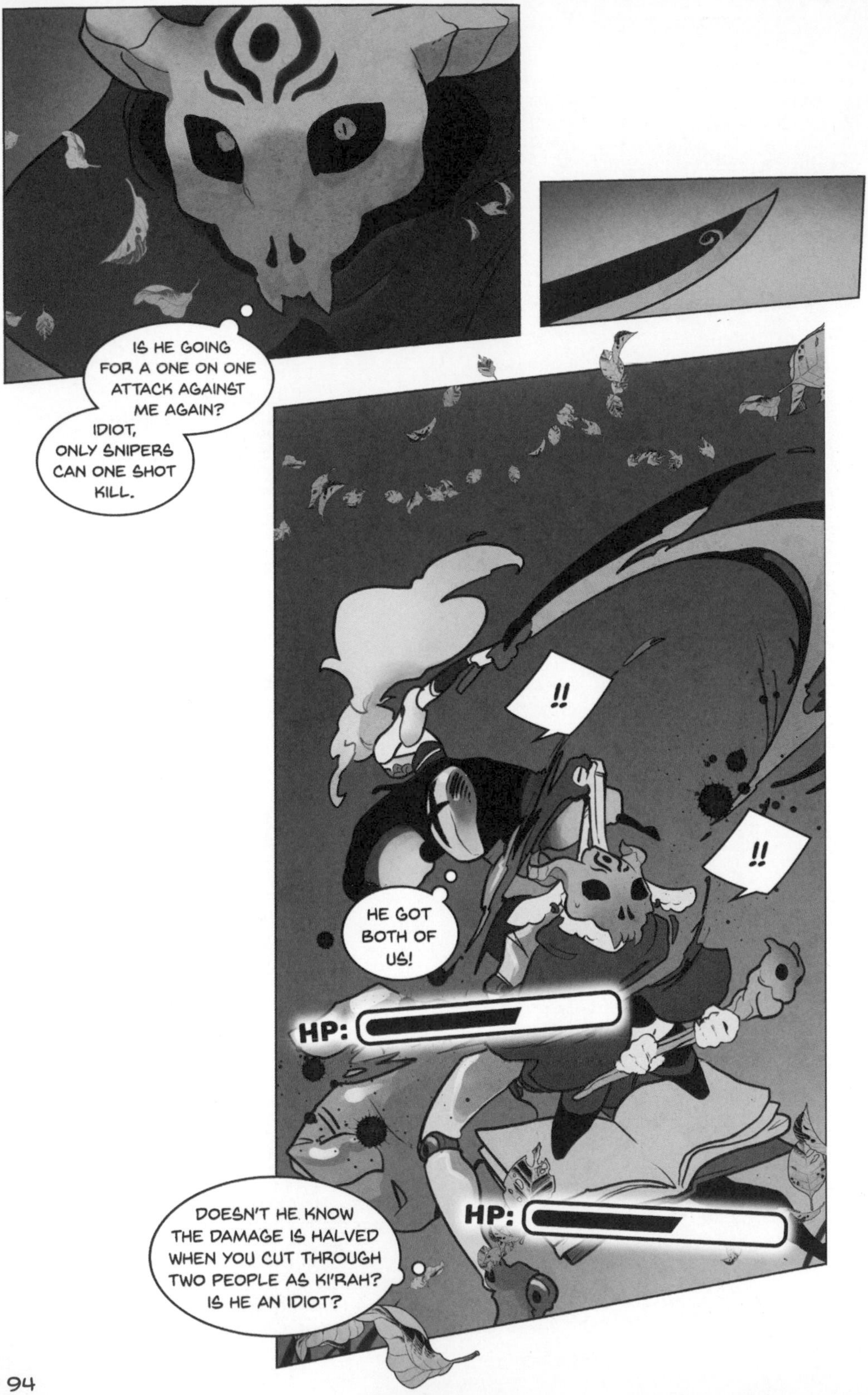

IS HE GOING FOR A ONE ON ONE ATTACK AGAINST ME AGAIN?
IDIOT, ONLY SNIPERS CAN ONE SHOT KILL.
!!
!!
HE GOT BOTH OF US!
HP:
HP:
DOESN'T HE KNOW THE DAMAGE IS HALVED WHEN YOU CUT THROUGH TWO PEOPLE AS KI'RAH? IS HE AN IDIOT?

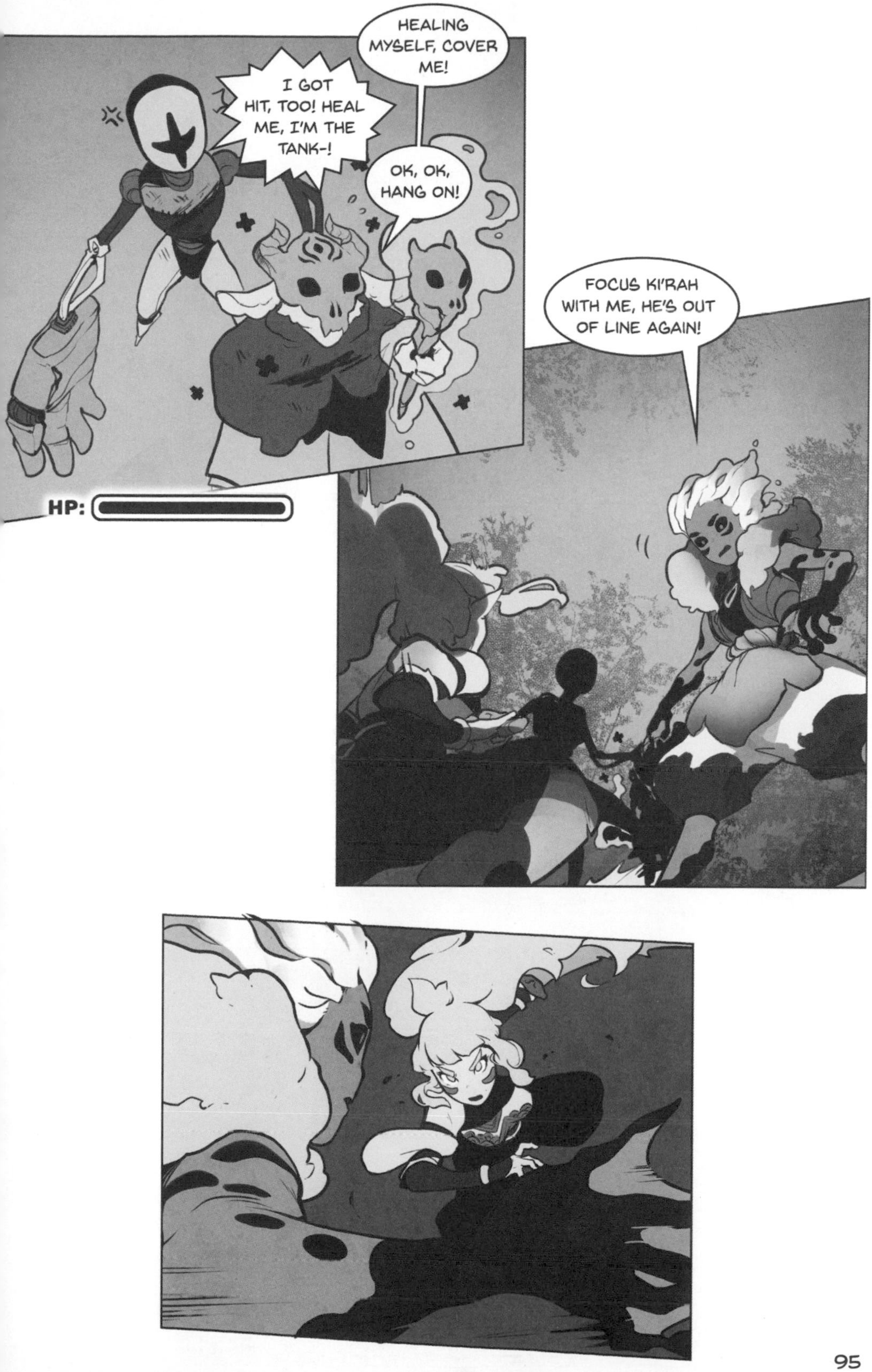
HEALING MYSELF, COVER ME!
I GOT HIT, TOO! HEAL ME, I'M THE TANK-!
OK, OK, HANG ON!
HP:
FOCUS KI'RAH WITH ME, HE'S OUT OF LINE AGAIN!

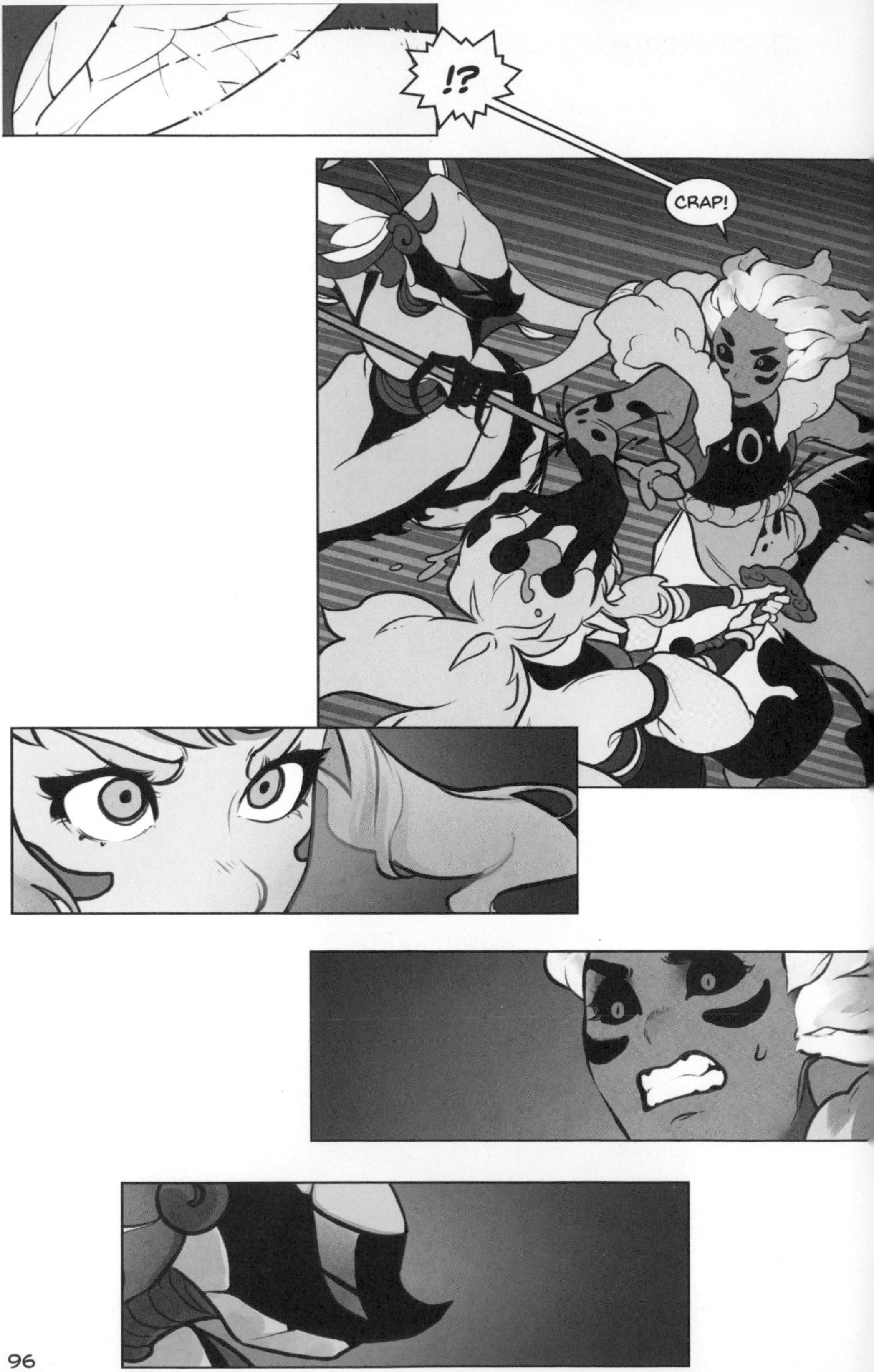
!?
CRAP!

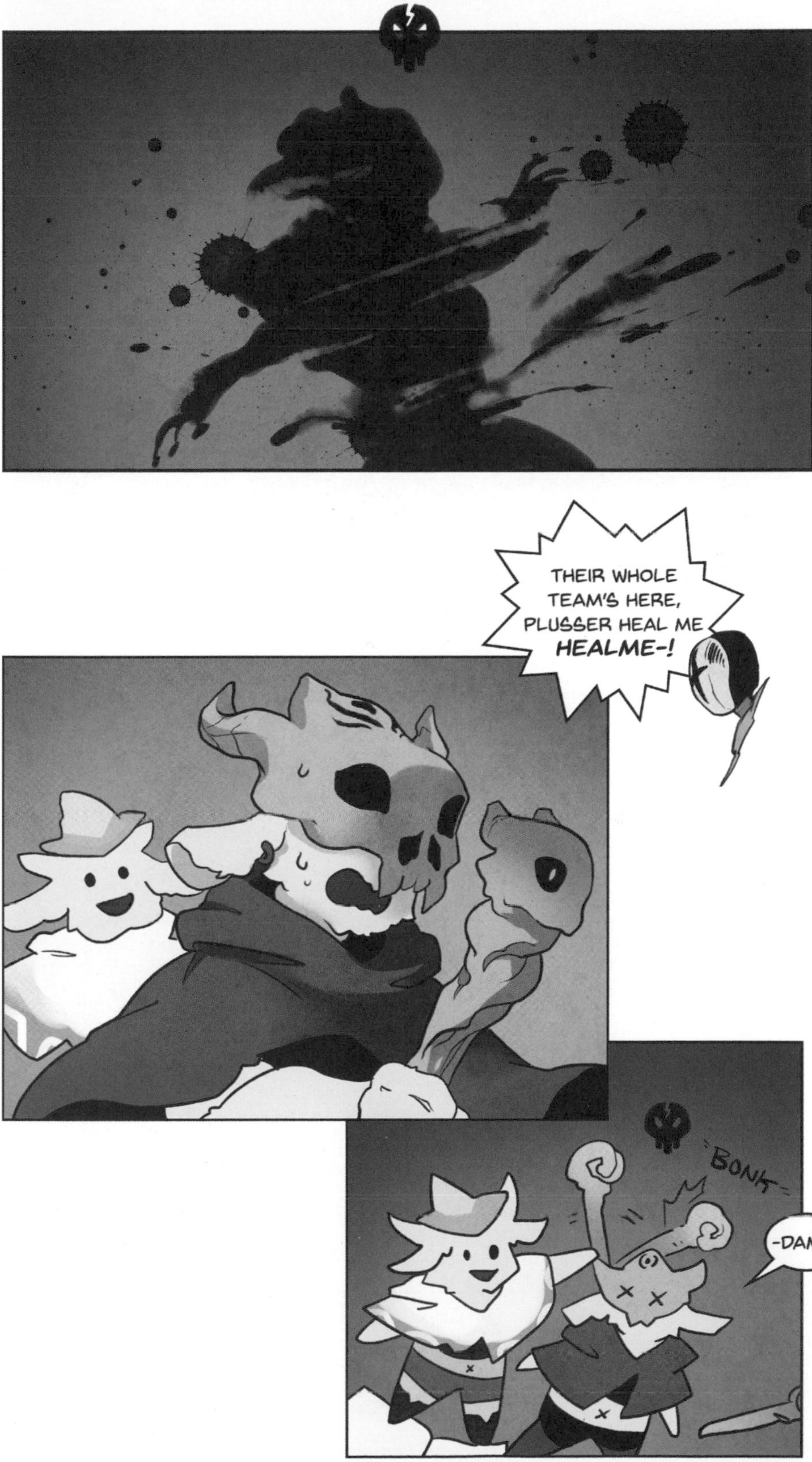
THEIR WHOLE TEAM'S HERE, PLUSSER HEAL ME **HEALME-!**
BONK
-DAMN.

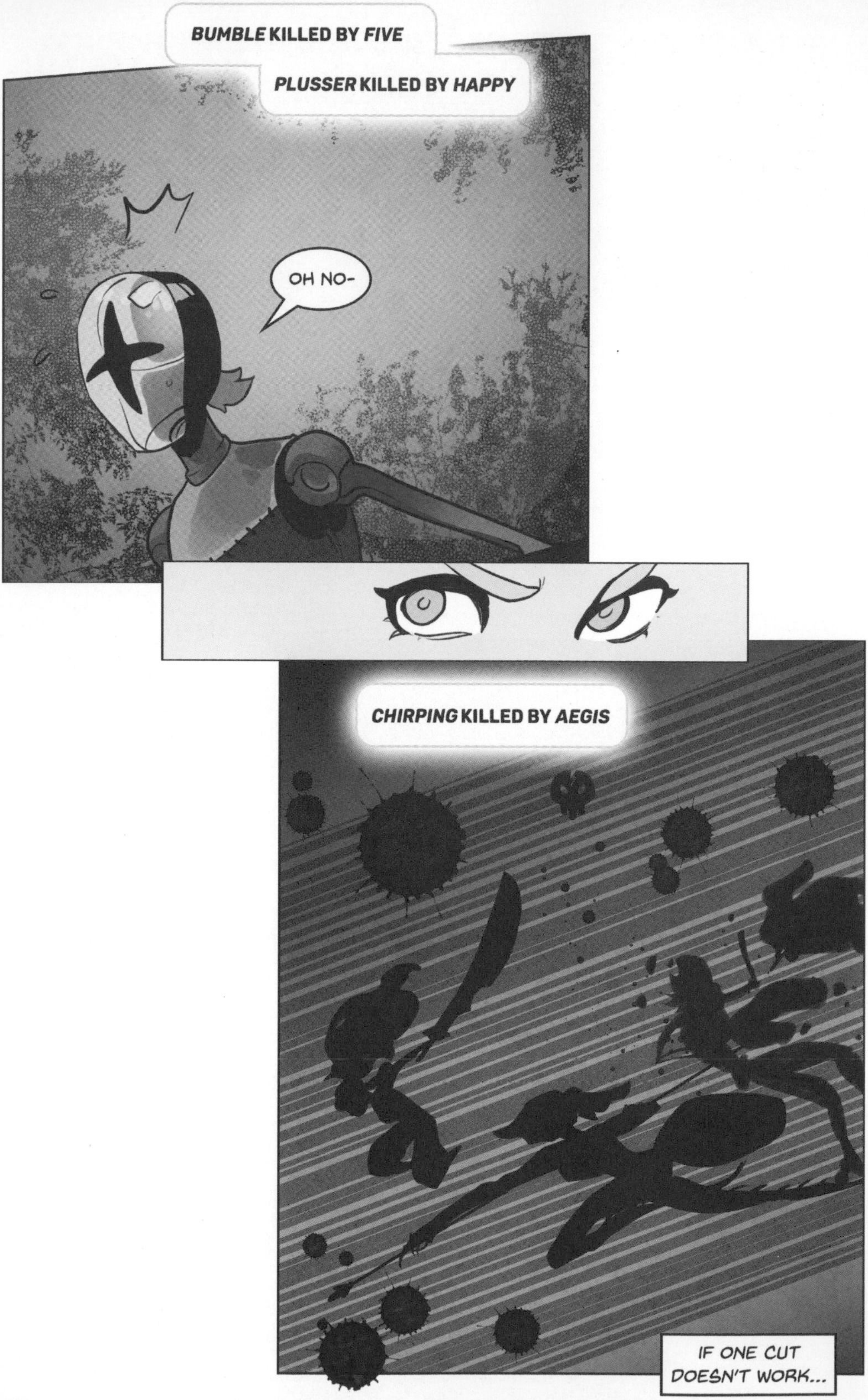
BUMBLE KILLED BY *FIVE*
PLUSSER KILLED BY *HAPPY*
OH NO-
CHIRPING KILLED BY *AEGIS*
IF ONE CUT DOESN'T WORK...

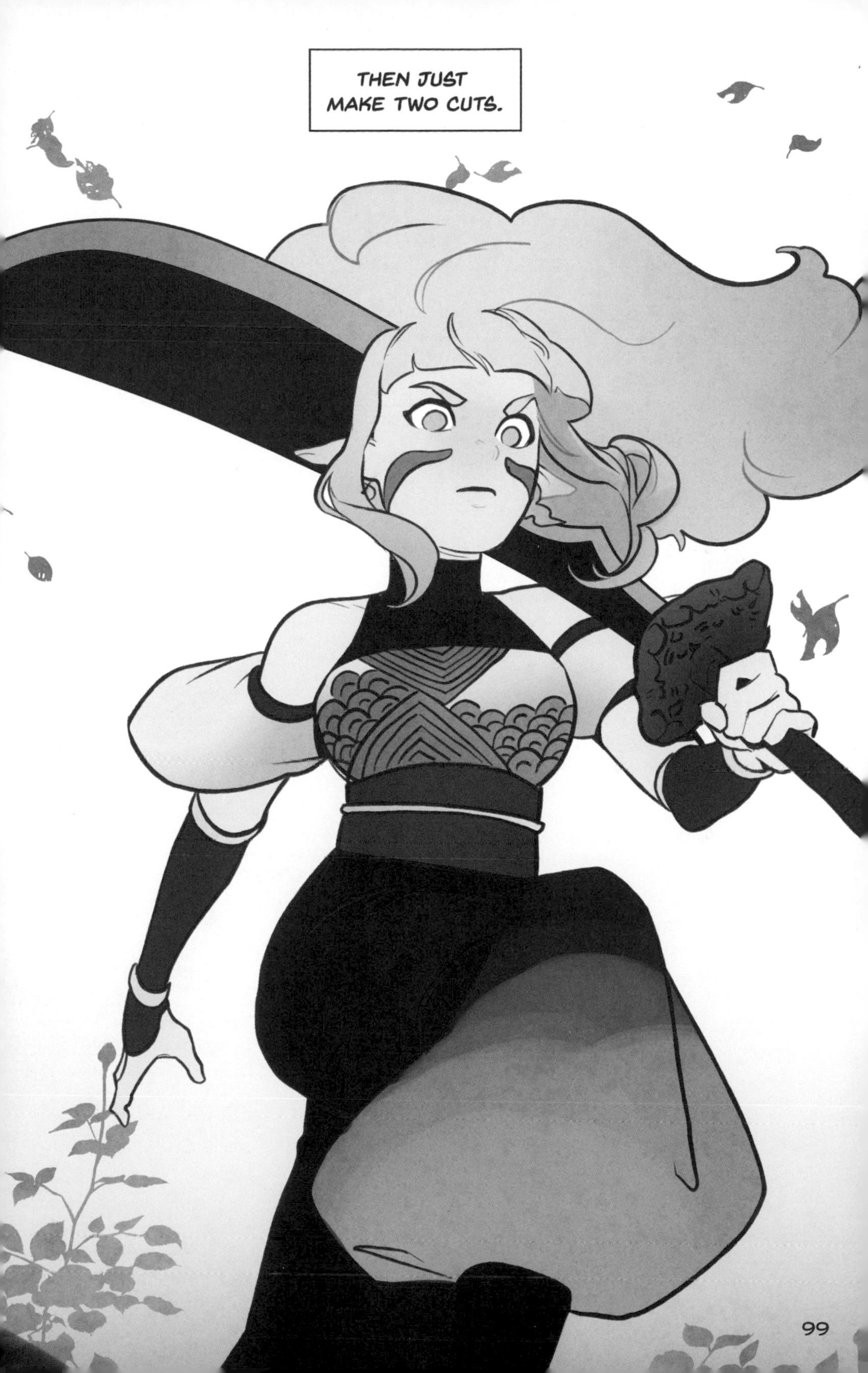
THEN JUST
MAKE TWO CUTS.

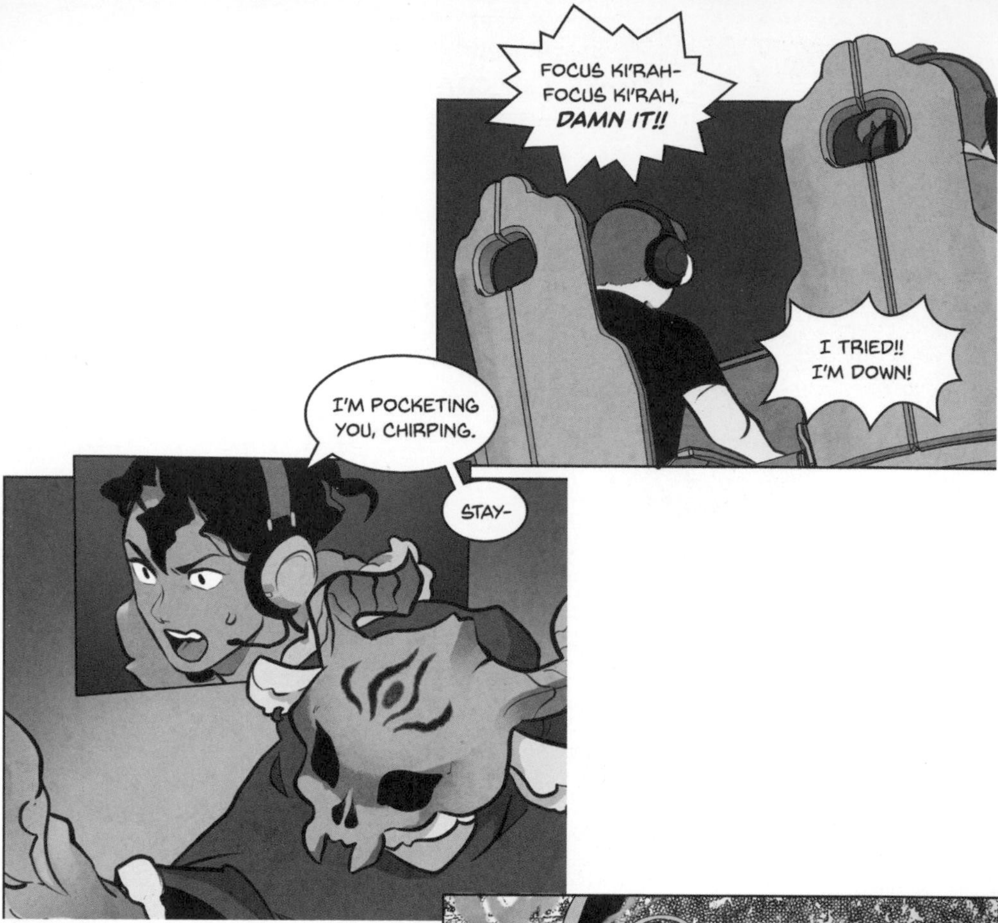
FOCUS KI'RAH-
FOCUS KI'RAH,
DAMN IT!!
I TRIED!!
I'M DOWN!
I'M POCKETING
YOU, CHIRPING.
STAY-
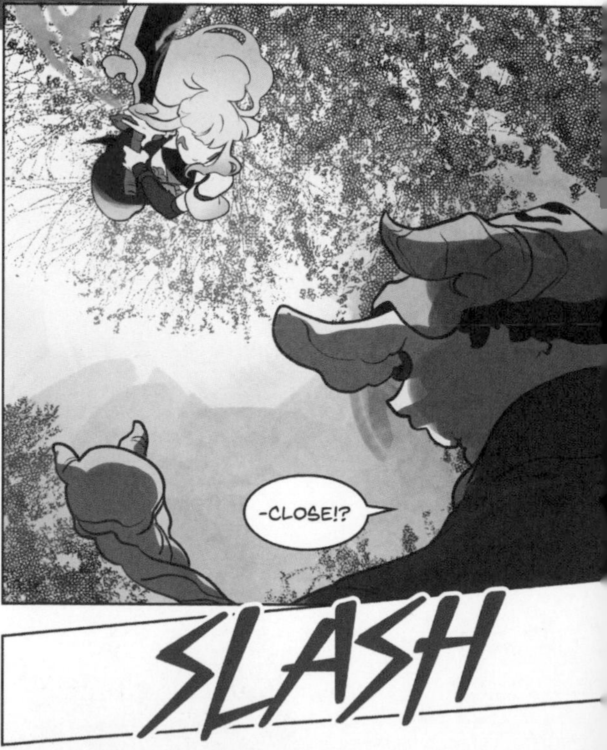
-CLOSE!?
SLASH

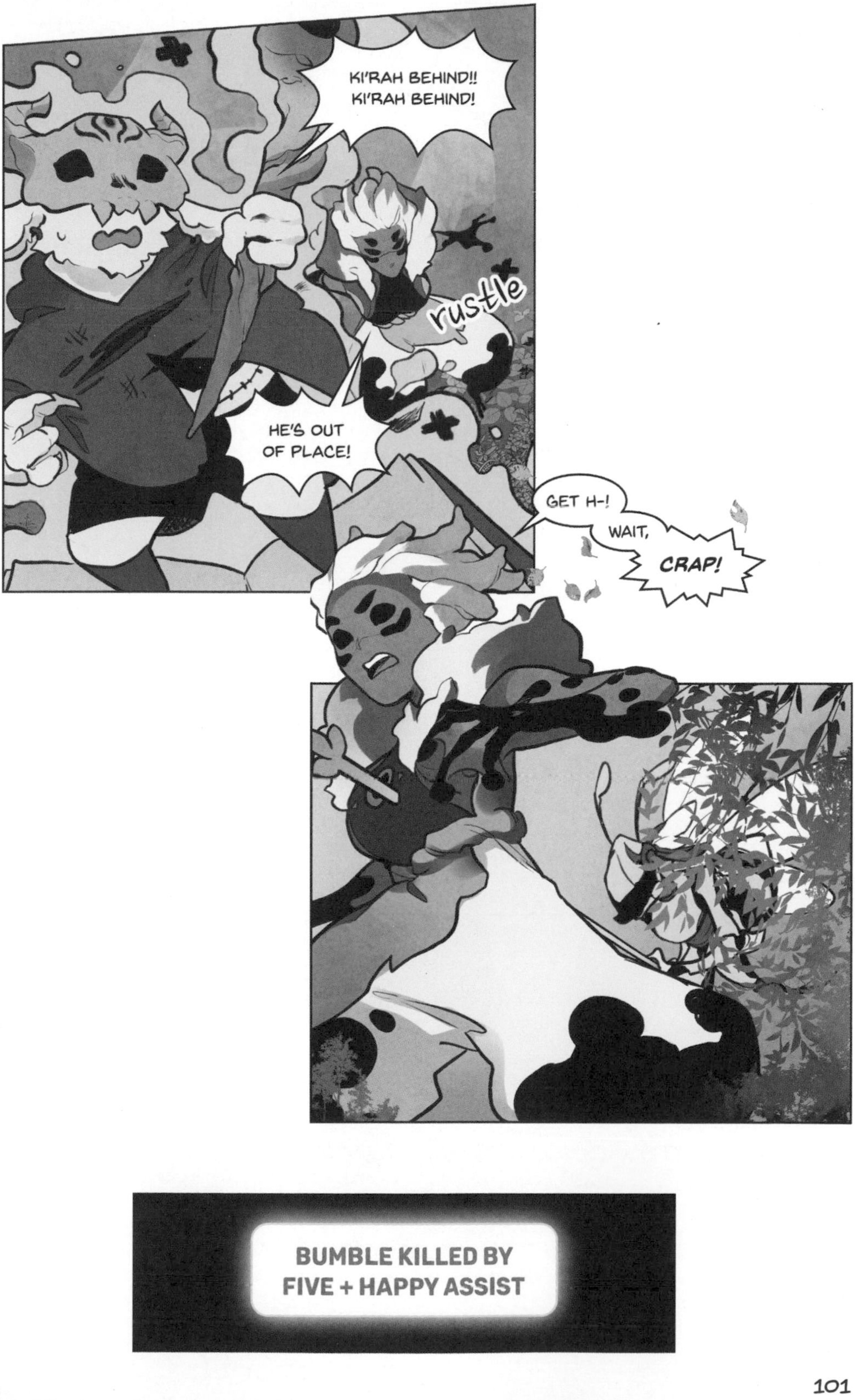
KI'RAH BEHIND!!
KI'RAH BEHIND!
rustle
HE'S OUT OF PLACE!
GET H-!
WAIT,
CRAP!

BUMBLE KILLED BY FIVE + HAPPY ASSIST

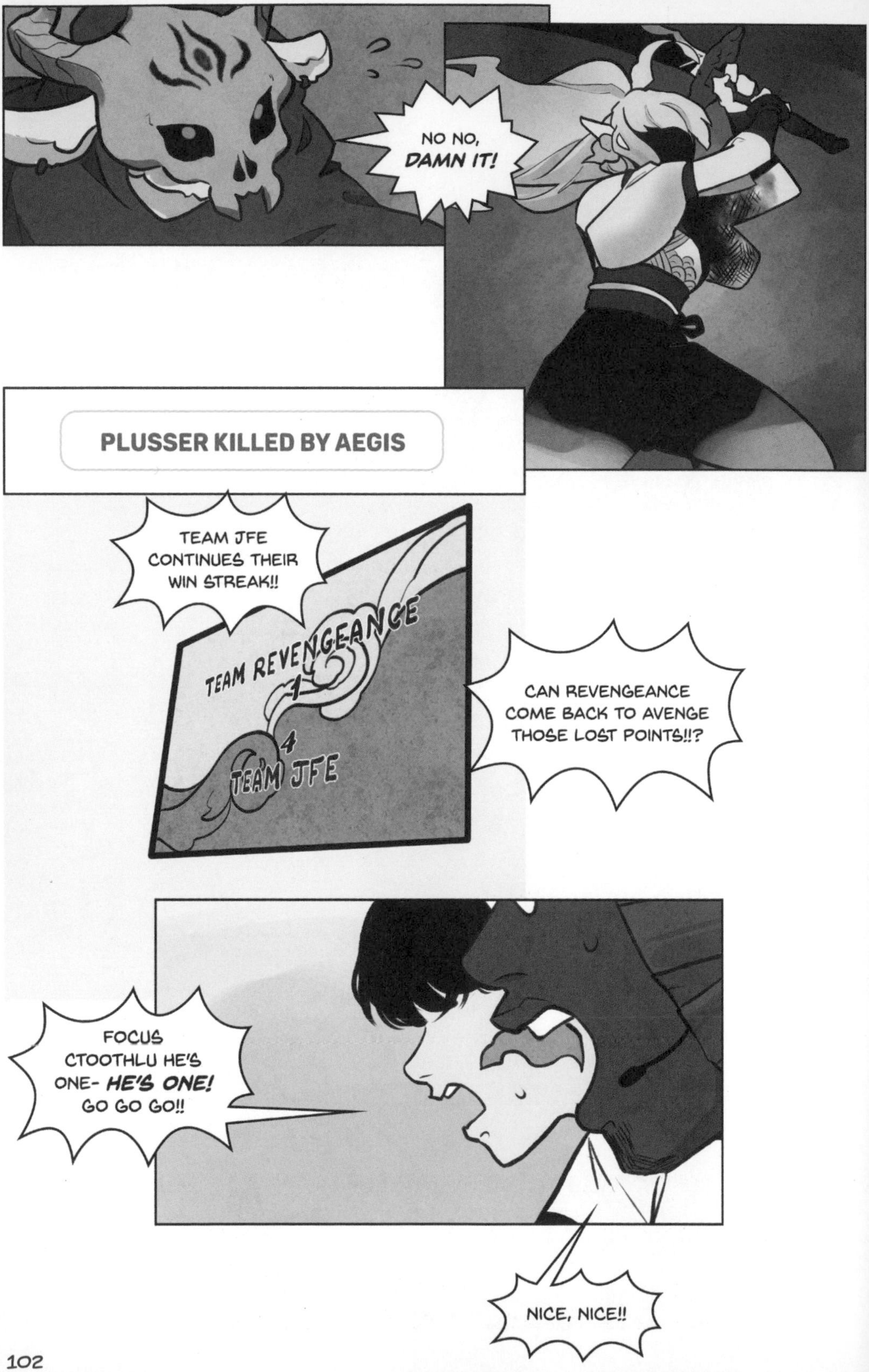
NO NO, DAMN IT!
PLUSSER KILLED BY AEGIS
TEAM JFE CONTINUES THEIR WIN STREAK!!
TEAM REVENGEANCE
1
4
TEAM JFE
CAN REVENGEANCE COME BACK TO AVENGE THOSE LOST POINTS!!?
FOCUS CTOOTHLU HE'S ONE- HE'S ONE! GO GO GO!!
NICE, NICE!!

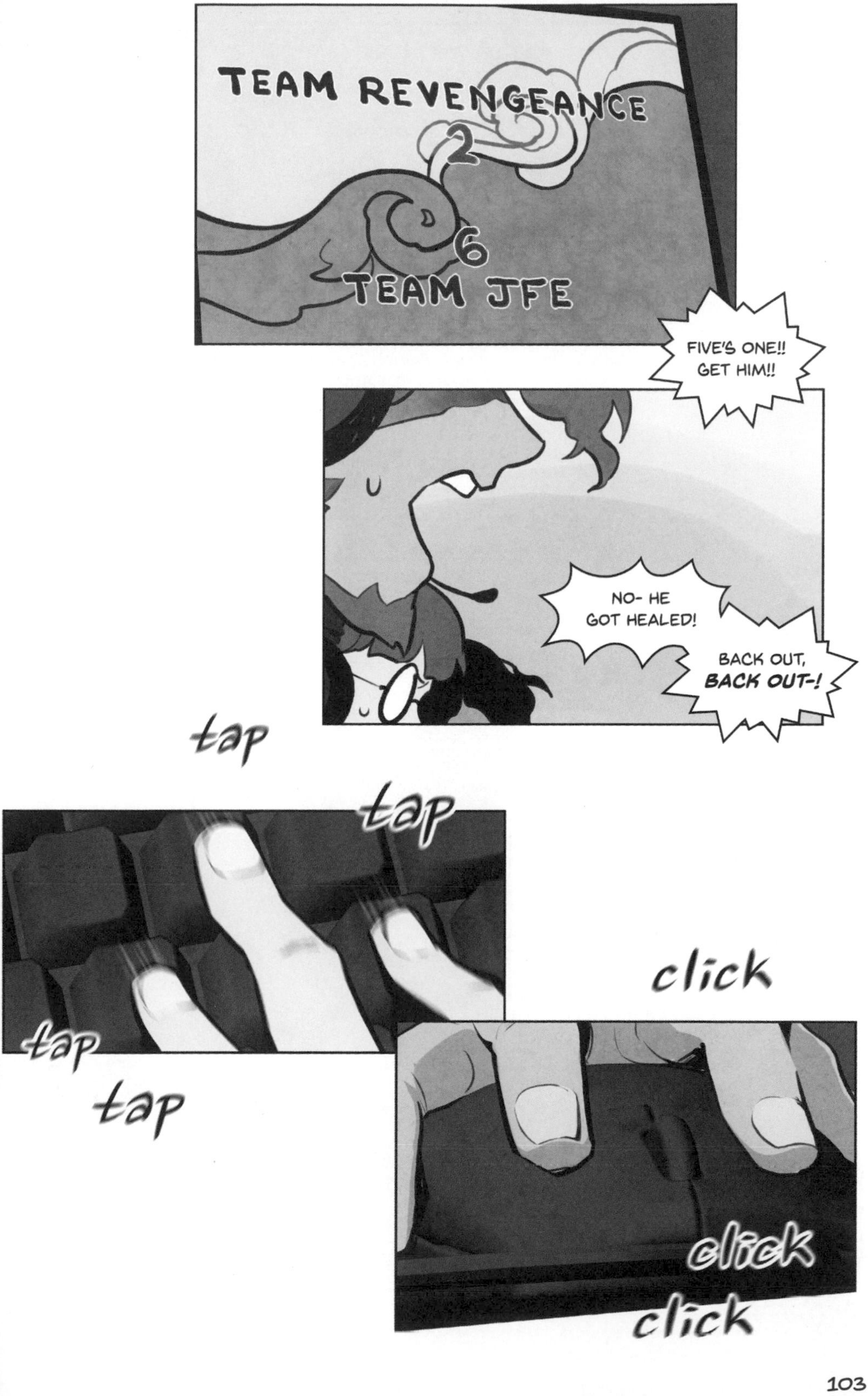
TEAM REVENGEANCE
2
6
TEAM JFE
FIVE'S ONE!! GET HIM!!
NO- HE GOT HEALED!
BACK OUT, **BACK OUT-!**
tap
tap
tap
tap
click
click
click

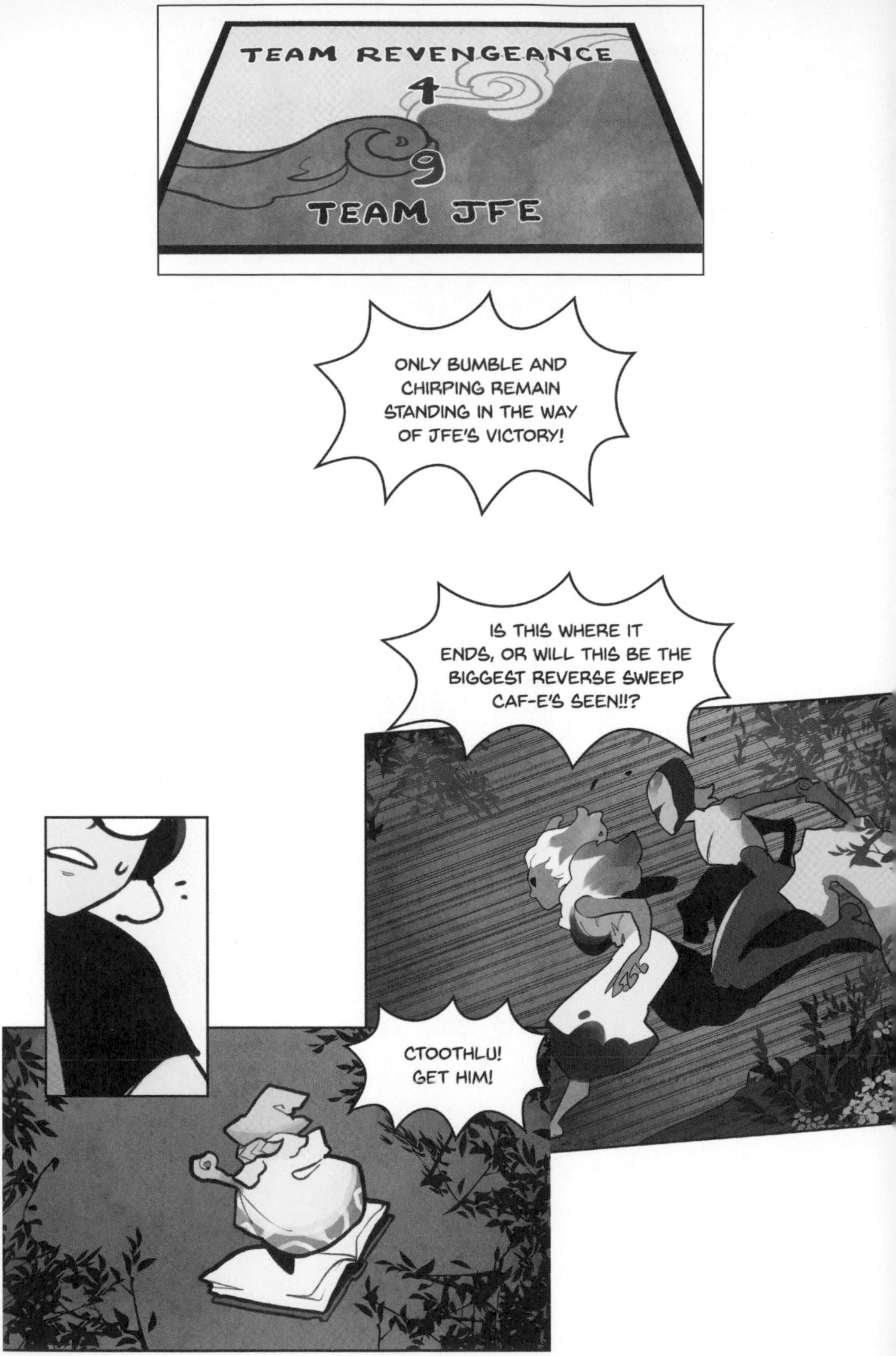
TEAM REVENGEANCE
4
9
TEAM JFE
ONLY BUMBLE AND CHIRPING REMAIN STANDING IN THE WAY OF JFE'S VICTORY!
IS THIS WHERE IT ENDS, OR WILL THIS BE THE BIGGEST REVERSE SWEEP CAF-E'S SEEN!!?
CTOOTHLU! GET HIM!

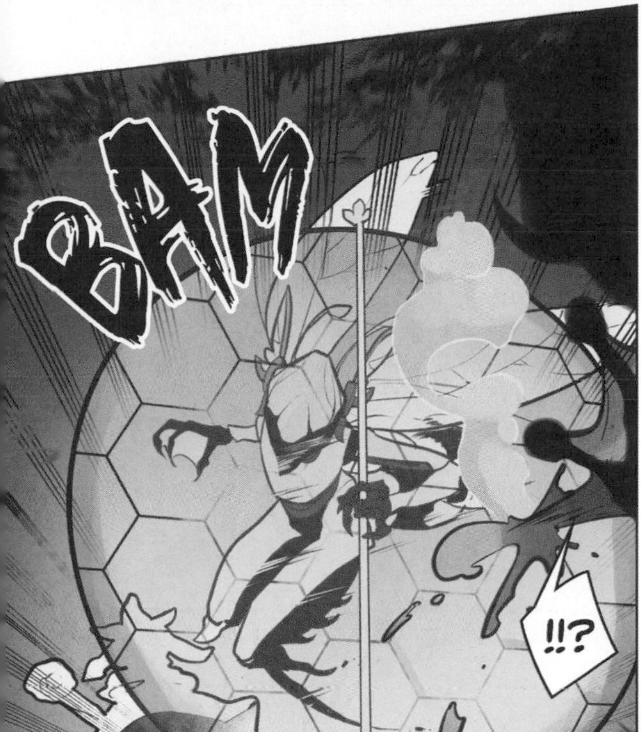
BAM
!!?
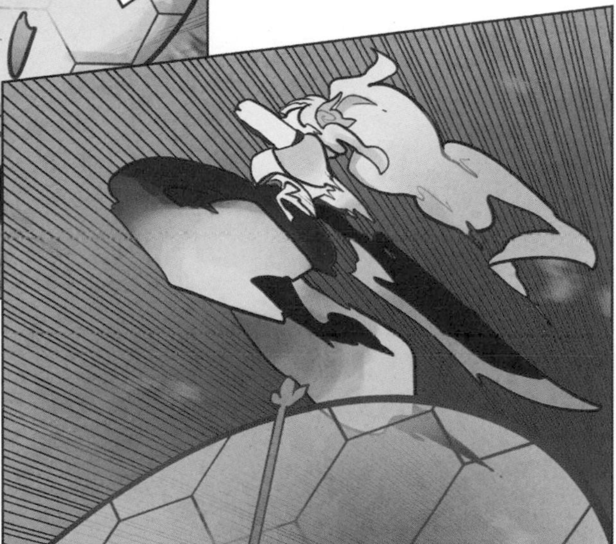
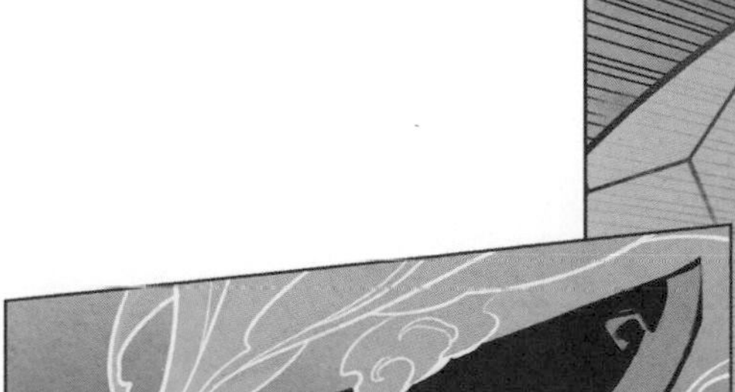

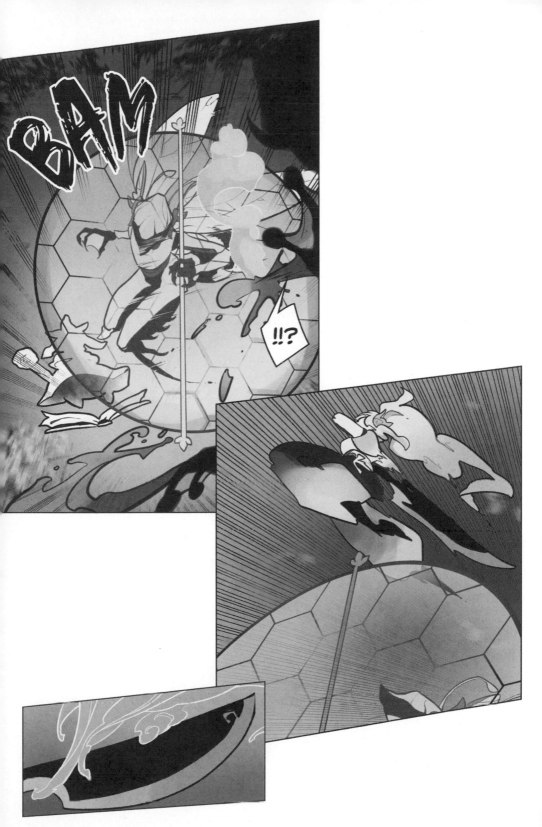

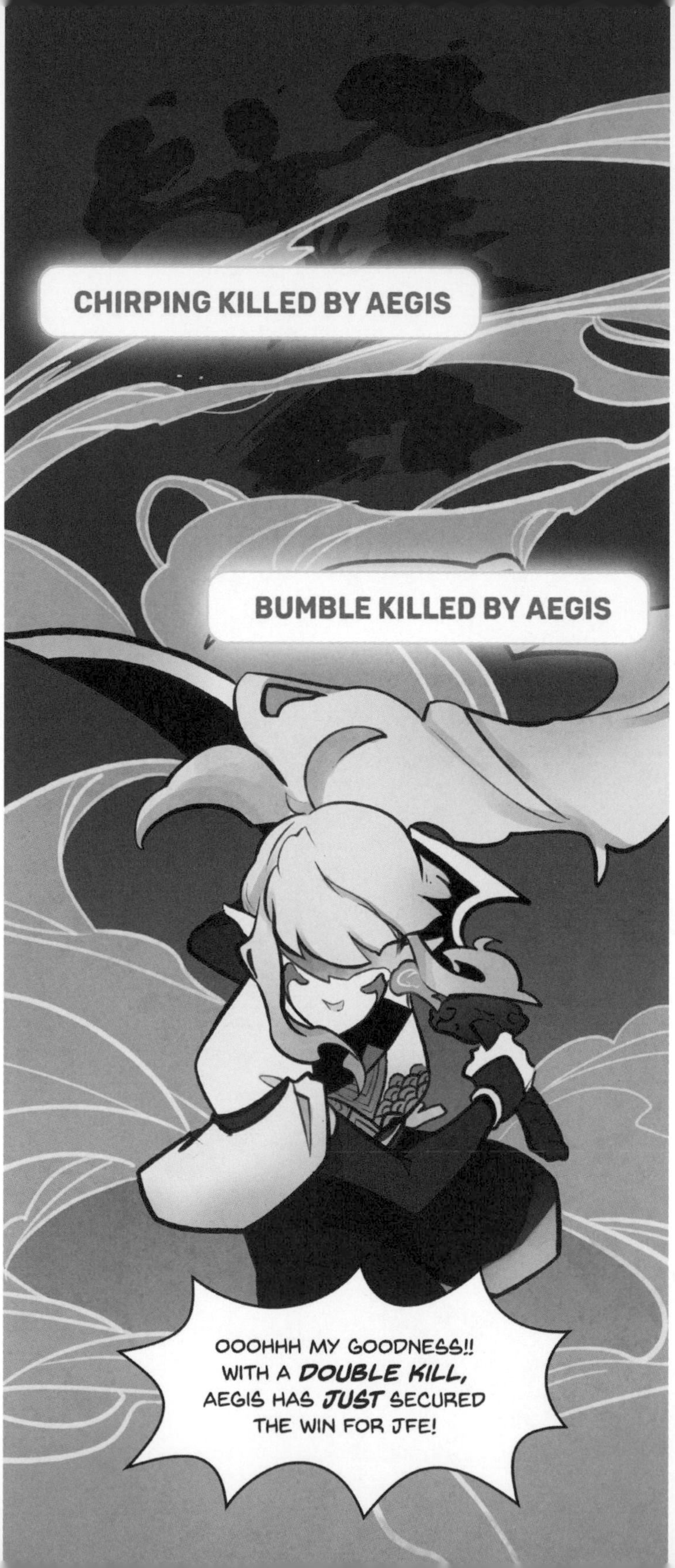
CHIRPING KILLED BY AEGIS
BUMBLE KILLED BY AEGIS
OOOHHH MY GOODNESS!! WITH A DOUBLE KILL, AEGIS HAS JUST SECURED THE WIN FOR JFE!

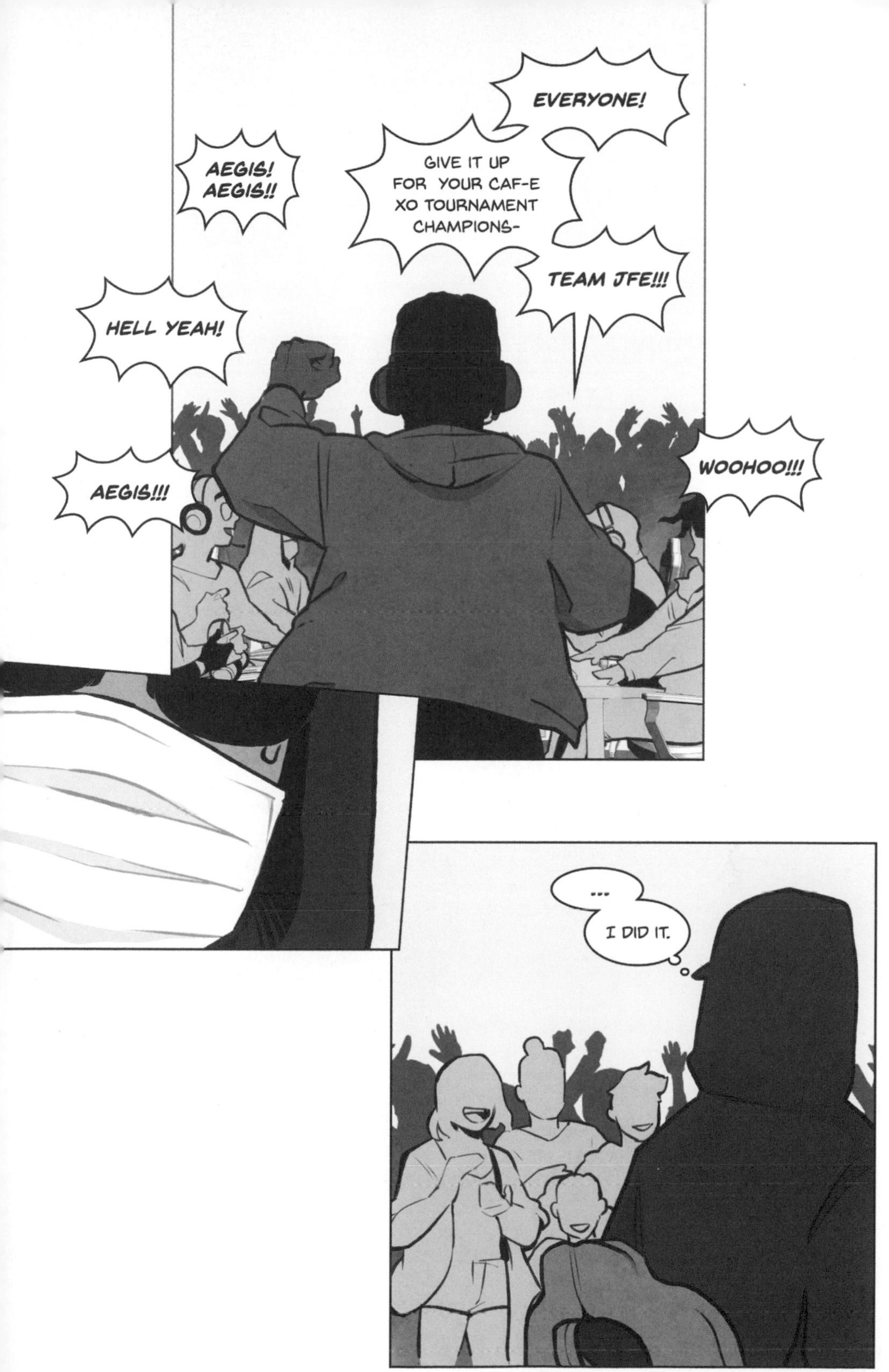

AEGIS! AEGIS!!
GIVE IT UP FOR YOUR CAF-E XO TOURNAMENT CHAMPIONS-
EVERYONE!
TEAM JFE!!!
HELL YEAH!
AEGIS!!!
WOOHOO!!!
...
I DID IT.

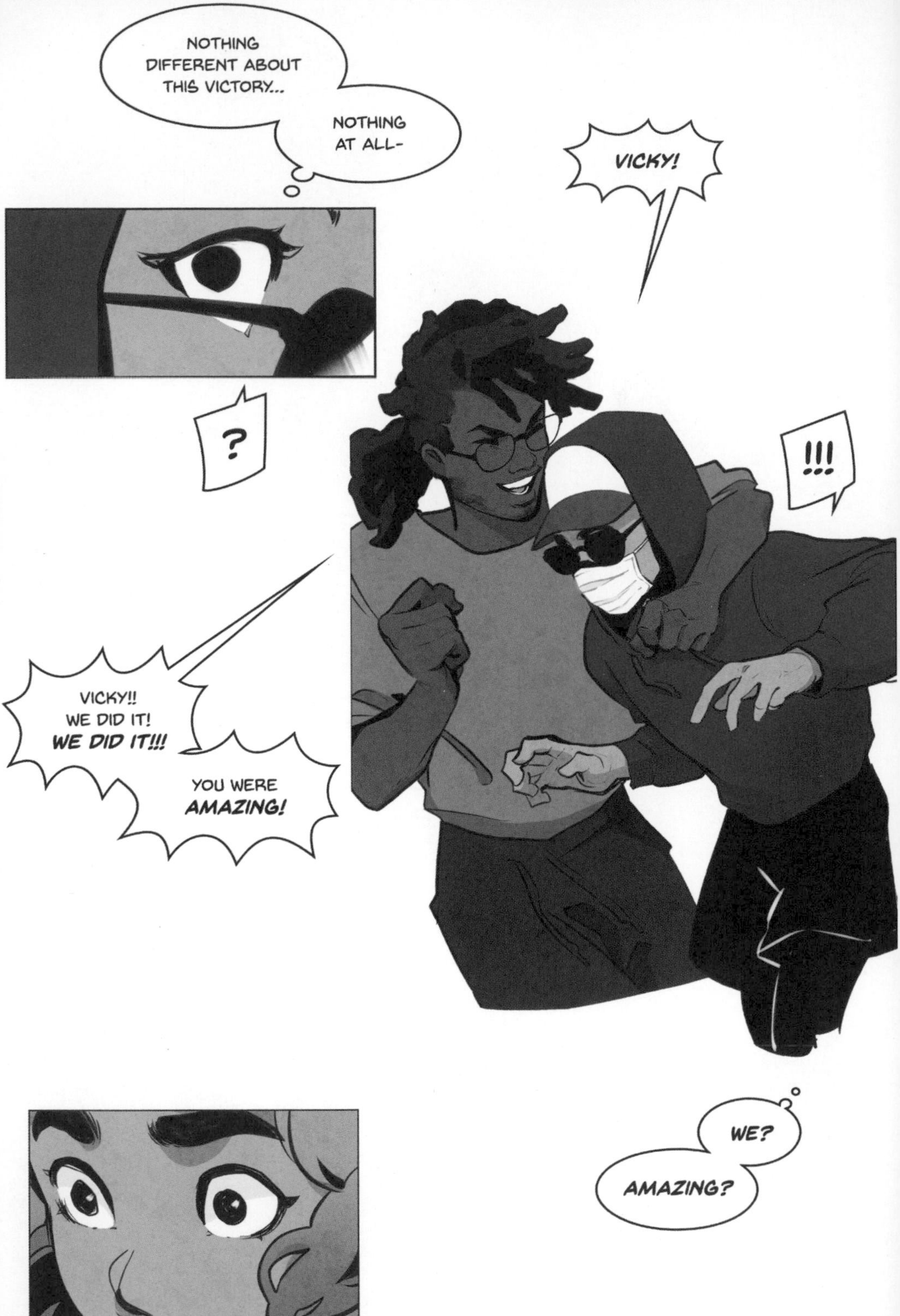
NOTHING DIFFERENT ABOUT THIS VICTORY...
NOTHING AT ALL-
VICKY!
?
!!!
VICKY!! WE DID IT! WE DID IT!!!
YOU WERE AMAZING!
WE?
AMAZING?

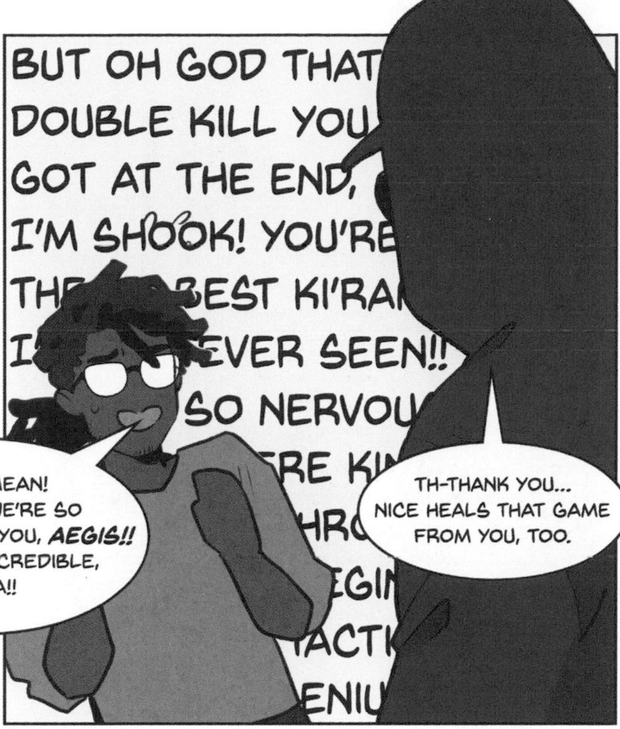
AH- I MEAN! LUCKY!! WE'RE SO LUCKY TO HAVE YOU, AEGIS!! YOU WERE INCREDIBLE, HAHA!!
TH-THANK YOU... NICE HEALS THAT GAME FROM YOU, TOO.

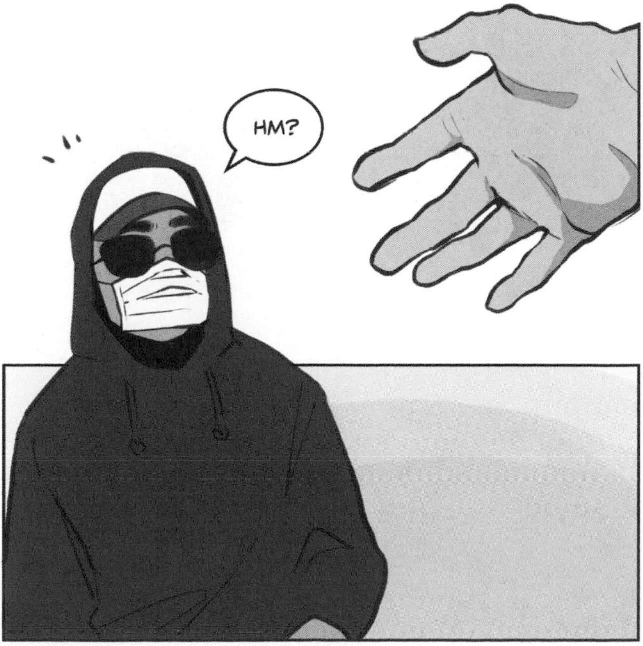
HM?

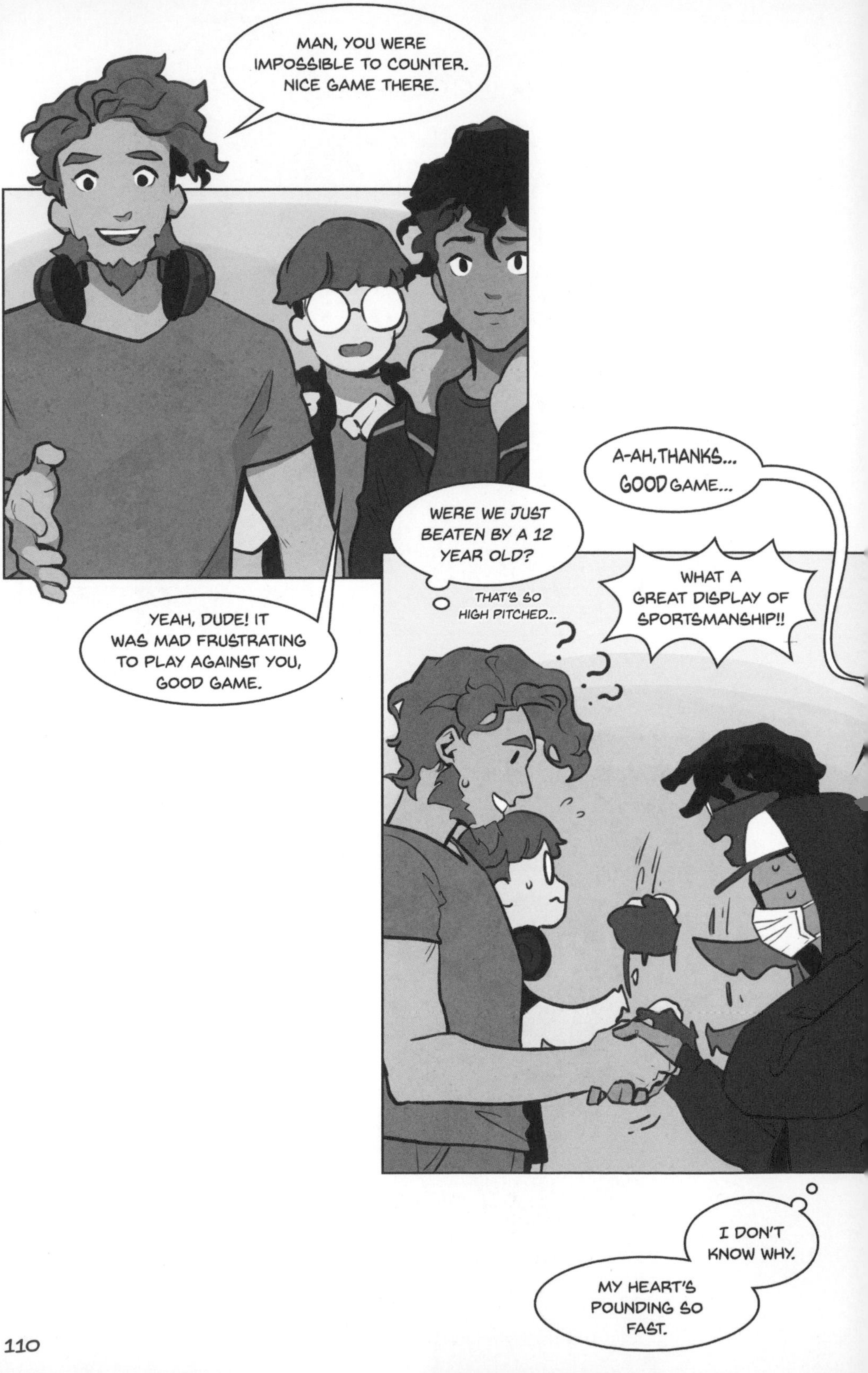
MAN, YOU WERE IMPOSSIBLE TO COUNTER. NICE GAME THERE.
YEAH, DUDE! IT WAS MAD FRUSTRATING TO PLAY AGAINST YOU, GOOD GAME.
A-AH, THANKS... GOOD GAME...
WERE WE JUST BEATEN BY A 12 YEAR OLD?
THAT'S SO HIGH PITCHED...
WHAT A GREAT DISPLAY OF SPORTSMANSHIP!!
I DON'T KNOW WHY.
MY HEART'S POUNDING SO FAST.

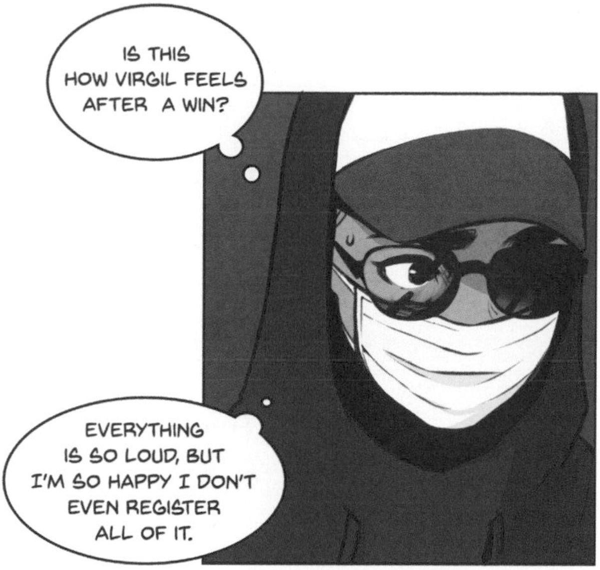
IS THIS HOW VIRGIL FEELS AFTER A WIN?
EVERYTHING IS SO LOUD, BUT I'M SO HAPPY I DON'T EVEN REGISTER ALL OF IT.

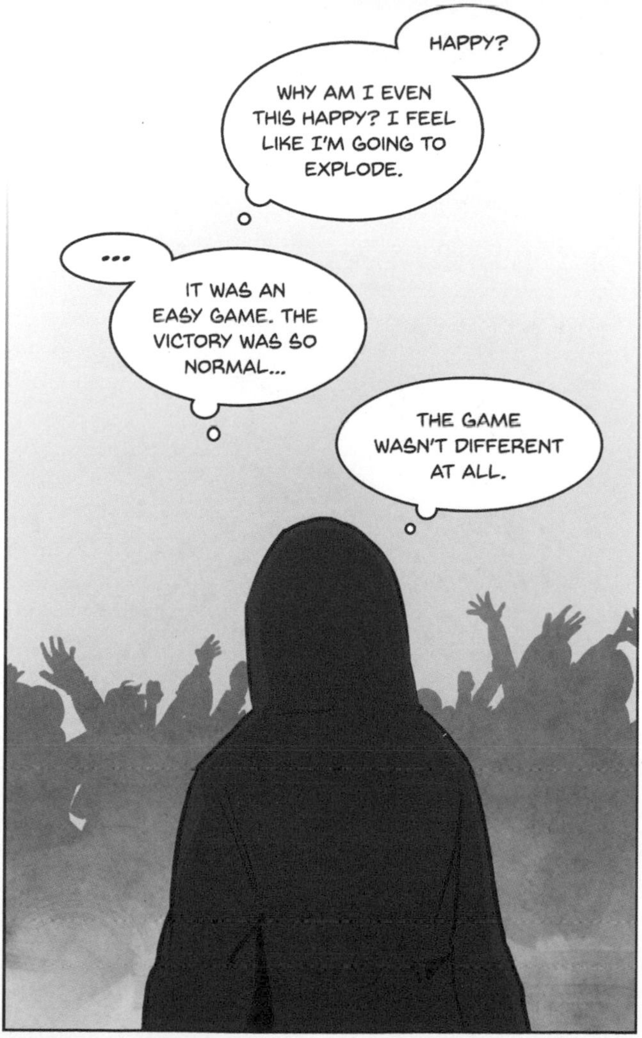
HAPPY?
WHY AM I EVEN THIS HAPPY? I FEEL LIKE I'M GOING TO EXPLODE.
...
IT WAS AN EASY GAME. THE VICTORY WAS SO NORMAL...
THE GAME WASN'T DIFFERENT AT ALL.

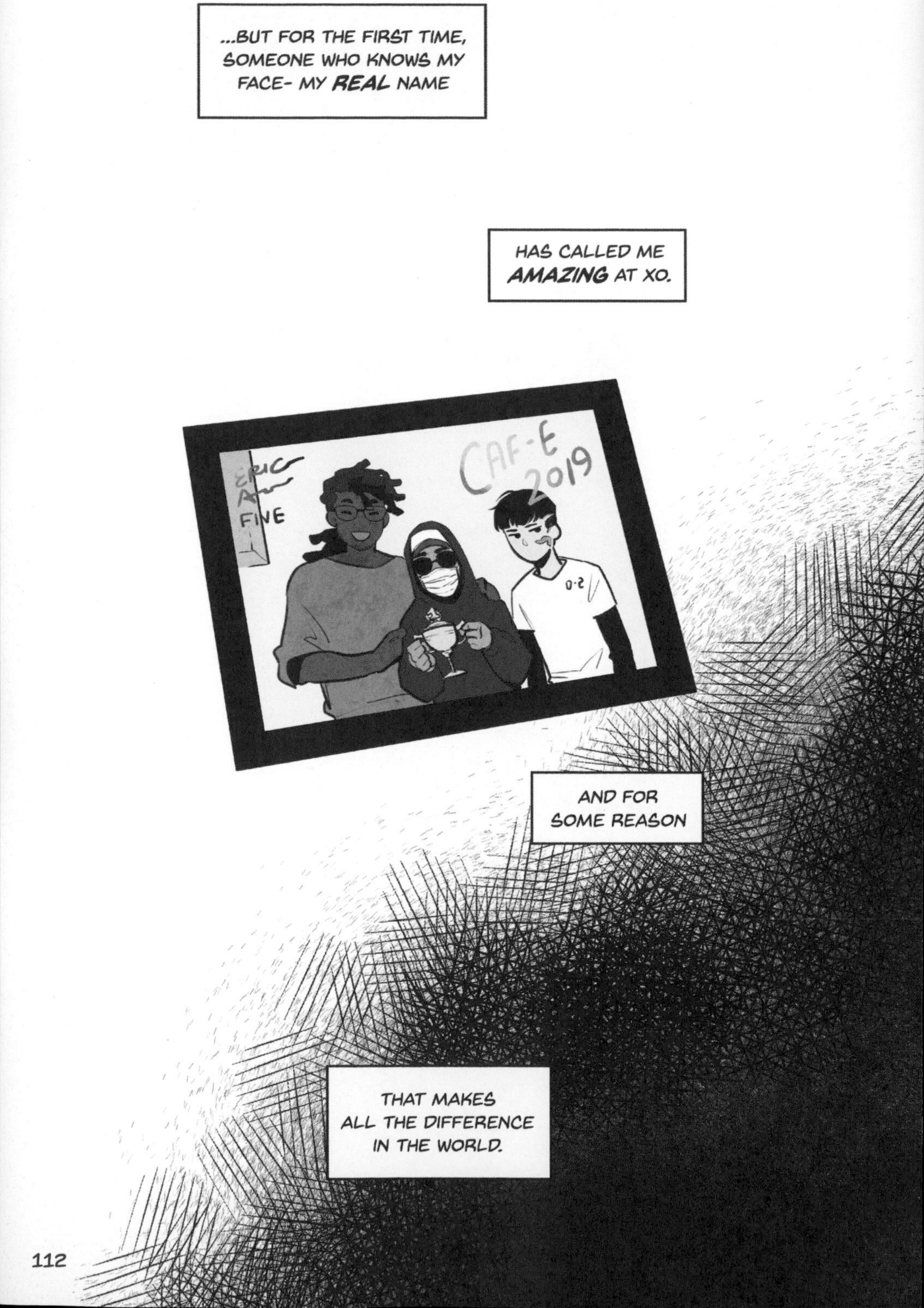
...BUT FOR THE FIRST TIME, SOMEONE WHO KNOWS MY FACE- MY **REAL** NAME
HAS CALLED ME **AMAZING** AT XO.
CAF-E 2019
AND FOR SOME REASON
THAT MAKES ALL THE DIFFERENCE IN THE WORLD.

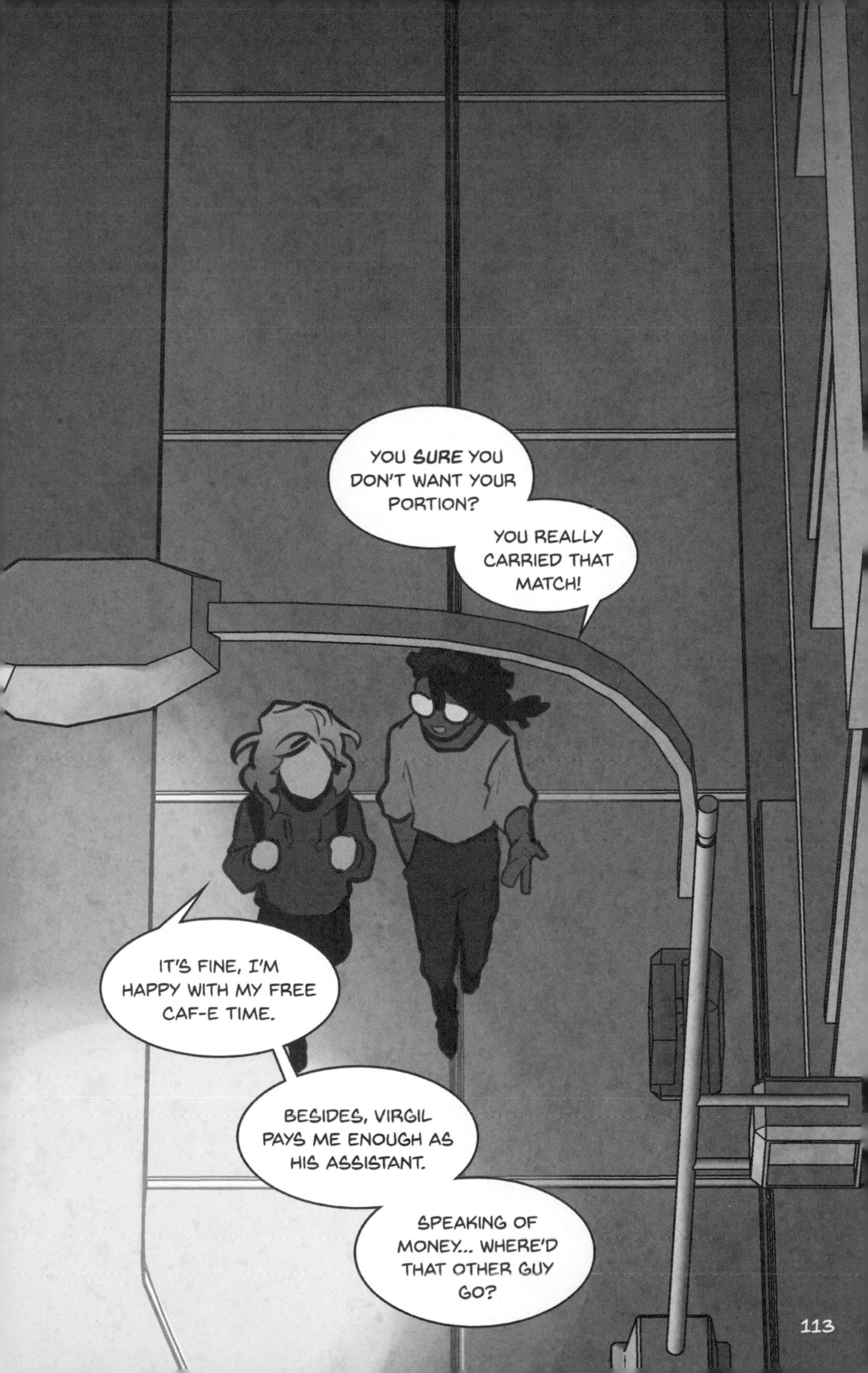
YOU SURE YOU DON'T WANT YOUR PORTION?
YOU REALLY CARRIED THAT MATCH!
IT'S FINE, I'M HAPPY WITH MY FREE CAF-E TIME.
BESIDES, VIRGIL PAYS ME ENOUGH AS HIS ASSISTANT.
SPEAKING OF MONEY... WHERE'D THAT OTHER GUY GO?

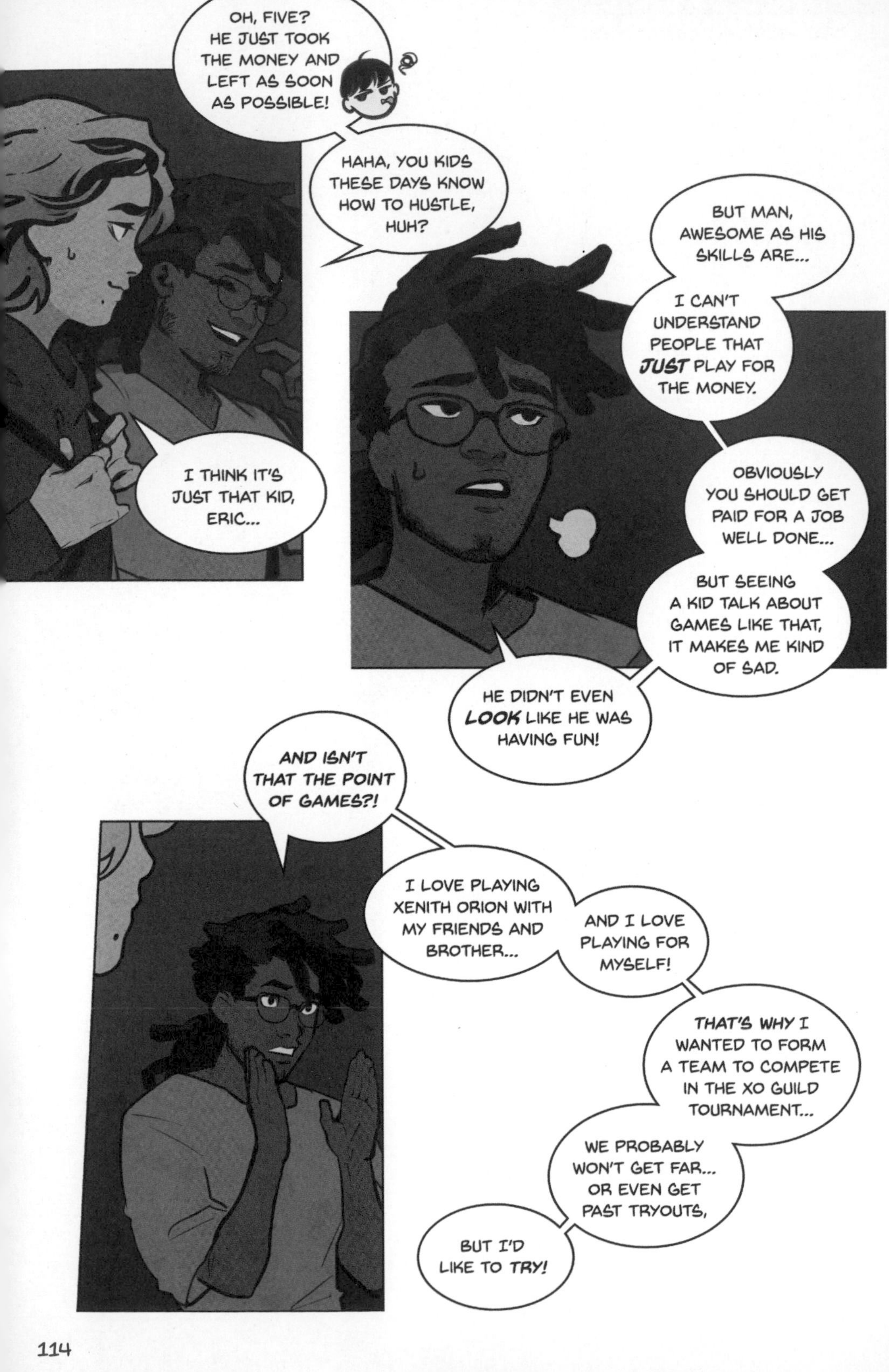
OH, FIVE? HE JUST TOOK THE MONEY AND LEFT AS SOON AS POSSIBLE!
HAHA, YOU KIDS THESE DAYS KNOW HOW TO HUSTLE, HUH?
I THINK IT'S JUST THAT KID, ERIC...
BUT MAN, AWESOME AS HIS SKILLS ARE...
I CAN'T UNDERSTAND PEOPLE THAT JUST PLAY FOR THE MONEY.
OBVIOUSLY YOU SHOULD GET PAID FOR A JOB WELL DONE...
BUT SEEING A KID TALK ABOUT GAMES LIKE THAT, IT MAKES ME KIND OF SAD.
HE DIDN'T EVEN LOOK LIKE HE WAS HAVING FUN!
AND ISN'T THAT THE POINT OF GAMES?!
I LOVE PLAYING XENITH ORION WITH MY FRIENDS AND BROTHER...
AND I LOVE PLAYING FOR MYSELF!
THAT'S WHY I WANTED TO FORM A TEAM TO COMPETE IN THE XO GUILD TOURNAMENT...
WE PROBABLY WON'T GET FAR... OR EVEN GET PAST TRYOUTS,
BUT I'D LIKE TO TRY!

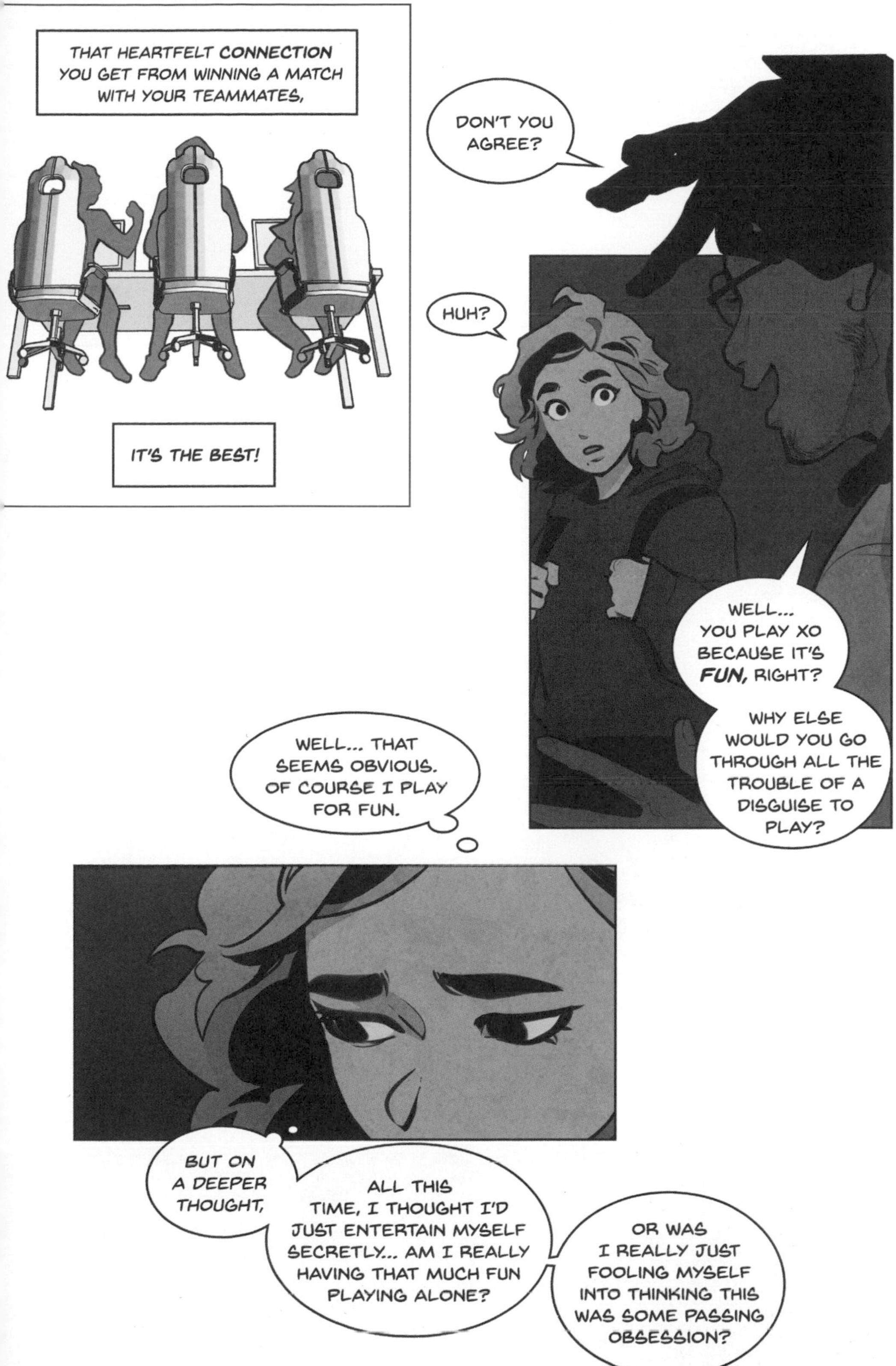
THAT HEARTFELT CONNECTION YOU GET FROM WINNING A MATCH WITH YOUR TEAMMATES,
IT'S THE BEST!
DON'T YOU AGREE?
HUH?
WELL... YOU PLAY XO BECAUSE IT'S FUN, RIGHT?
WHY ELSE WOULD YOU GO THROUGH ALL THE TROUBLE OF A DISGUISE TO PLAY?
WELL... THAT SEEMS OBVIOUS. OF COURSE I PLAY FOR FUN.
BUT ON A DEEPER THOUGHT,
ALL THIS TIME, I THOUGHT I'D JUST ENTERTAIN MYSELF SECRETLY... AM I REALLY HAVING THAT MUCH FUN PLAYING ALONE?
OR WAS I REALLY JUST FOOLING MYSELF INTO THINKING THIS WAS SOME PASSING OBSESSION?

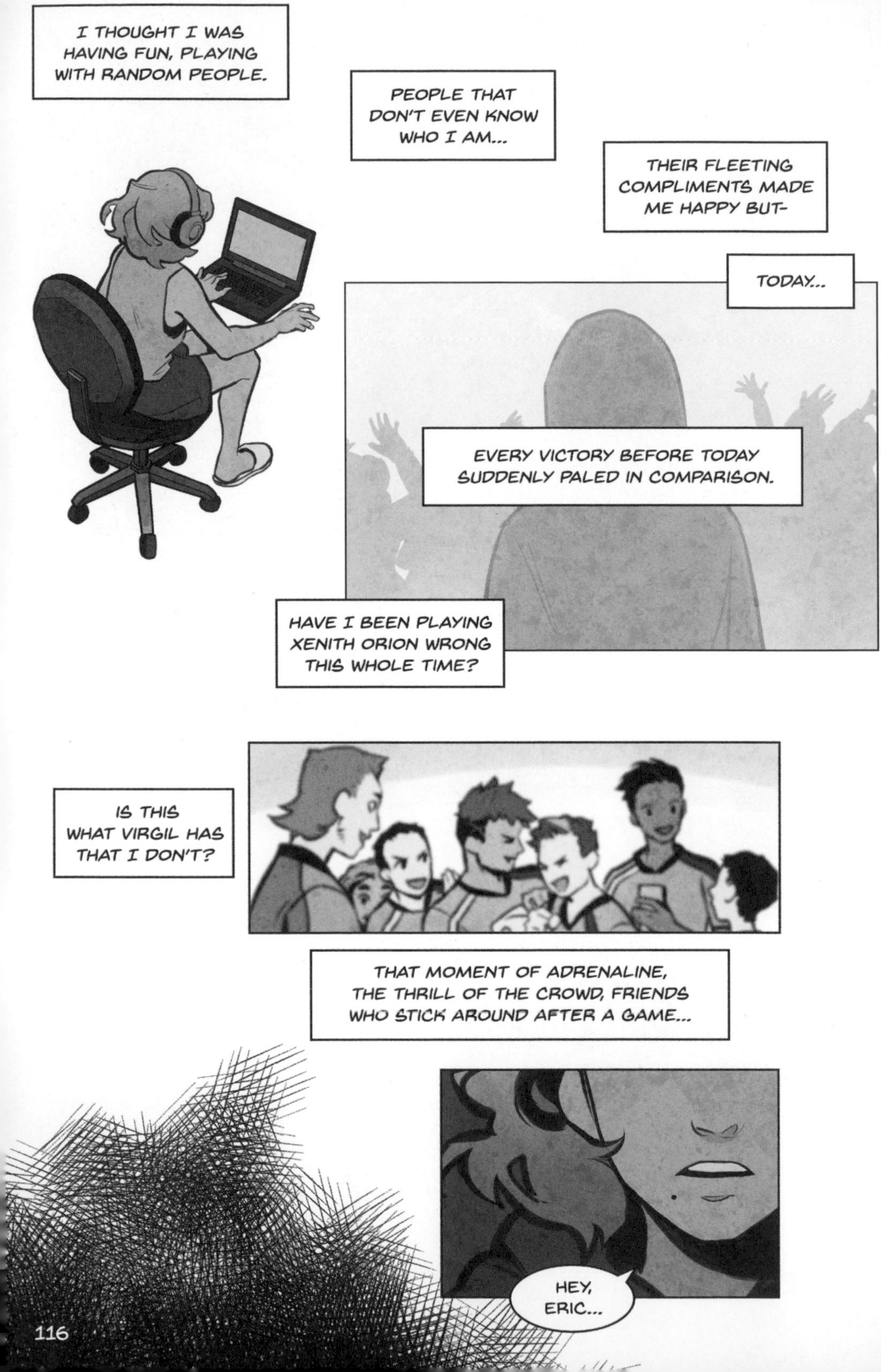
I THOUGHT I WAS HAVING FUN, PLAYING WITH RANDOM PEOPLE.
PEOPLE THAT DON'T EVEN KNOW WHO I AM...
THEIR FLEETING COMPLIMENTS MADE ME HAPPY BUT-
TODAY...
EVERY VICTORY BEFORE TODAY SUDDENLY PALED IN COMPARISON.
HAVE I BEEN PLAYING XENITH ORION WRONG THIS WHOLE TIME?
IS THIS WHAT VIRGIL HAS THAT I DON'T?
THAT MOMENT OF ADRENALINE, THE THRILL OF THE CROWD, FRIENDS WHO STICK AROUND AFTER A GAME...
HEY, ERIC...

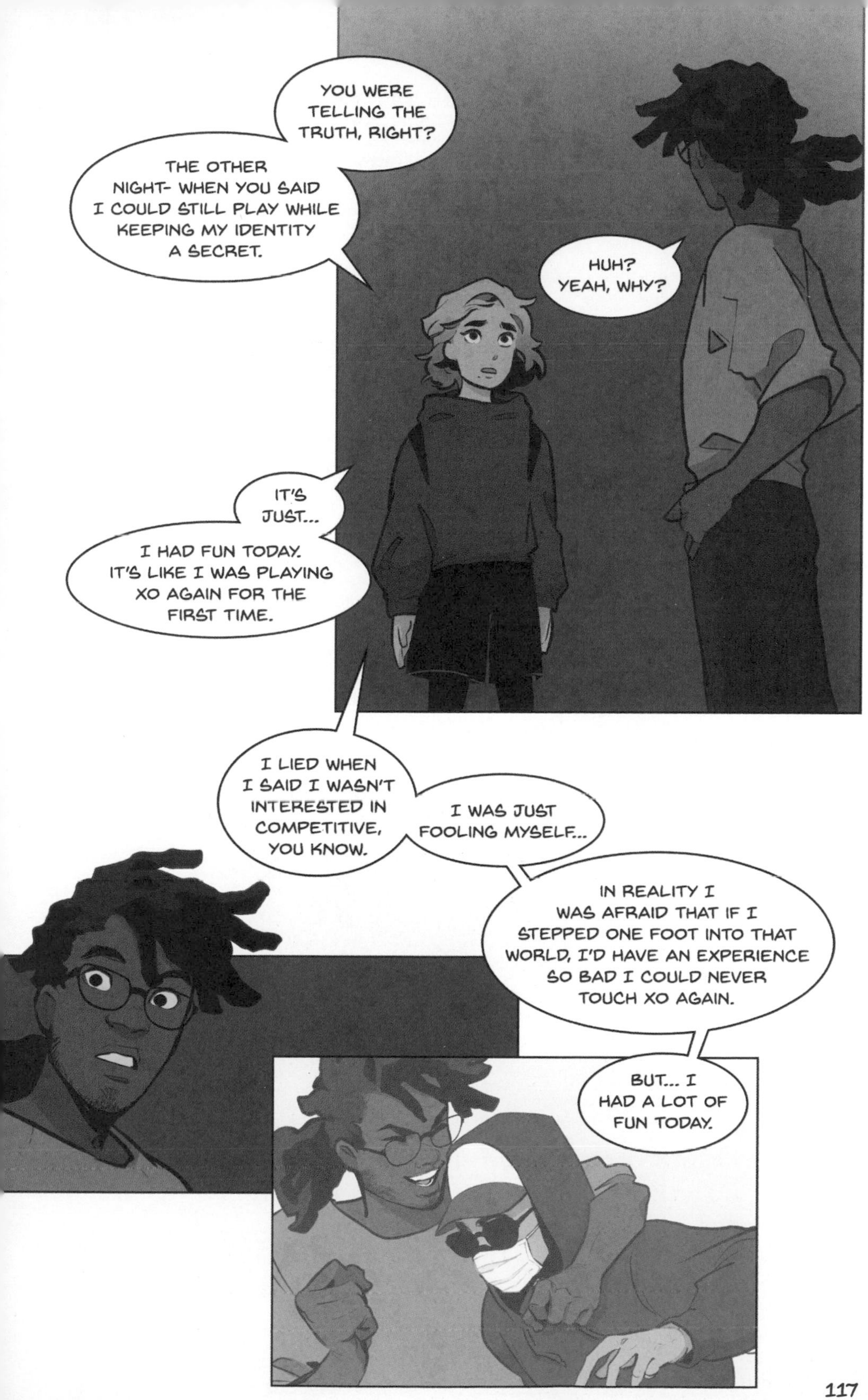
YOU WERE TELLING THE TRUTH, RIGHT?
THE OTHER NIGHT- WHEN YOU SAID I COULD STILL PLAY WHILE KEEPING MY IDENTITY A SECRET.
HUH? YEAH, WHY?
IT'S JUST...
I HAD FUN TODAY. IT'S LIKE I WAS PLAYING XO AGAIN FOR THE FIRST TIME.
I LIED WHEN I SAID I WASN'T INTERESTED IN COMPETITIVE, YOU KNOW.
I WAS JUST FOOLING MYSELF...
IN REALITY I WAS AFRAID THAT IF I STEPPED ONE FOOT INTO THAT WORLD, I'D HAVE AN EXPERIENCE SO BAD I COULD NEVER TOUCH XO AGAIN.
BUT... I HAD A LOT OF FUN TODAY.

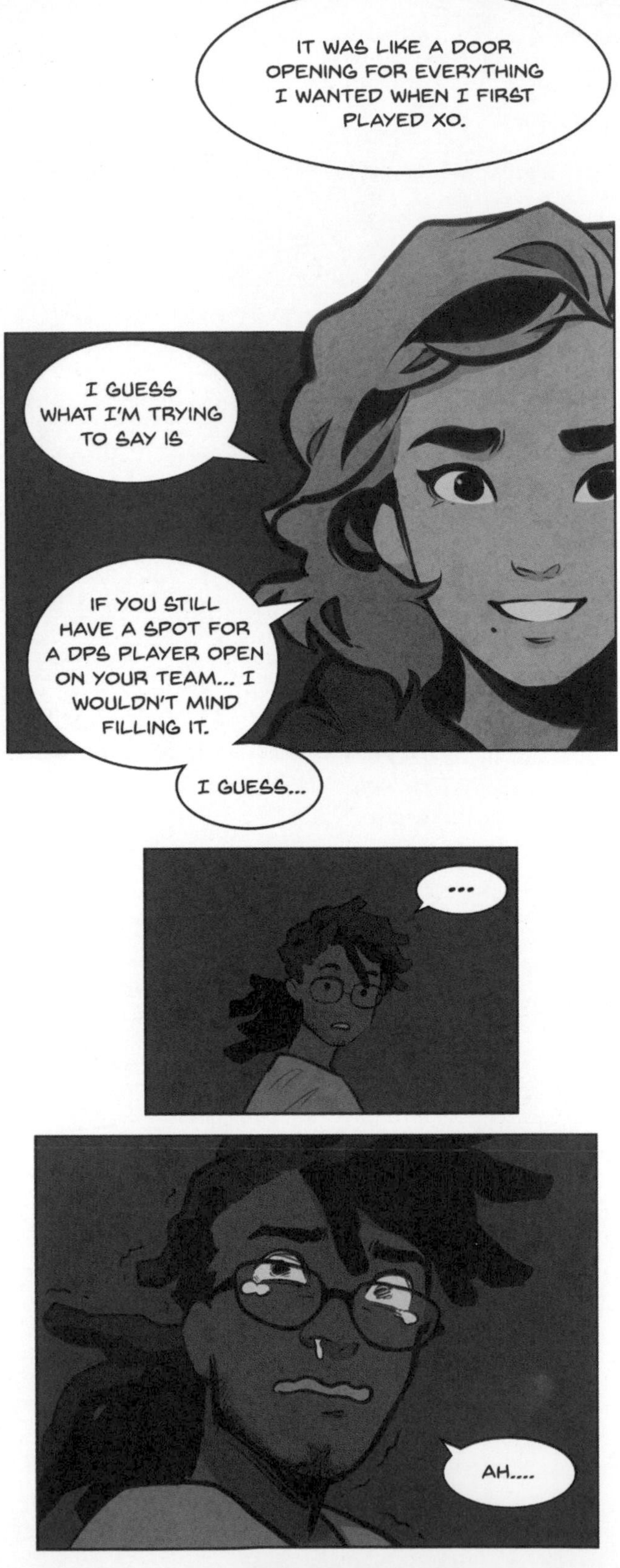
IT WAS LIKE A DOOR OPENING FOR EVERYTHING I WANTED WHEN I FIRST PLAYED XO.
I GUESS WHAT I'M TRYING TO SAY IS
IF YOU STILL HAVE A SPOT FOR A DPS PLAYER OPEN ON YOUR TEAM... I WOULDN'T MIND FILLING IT.
I GUESS...
...
AH....

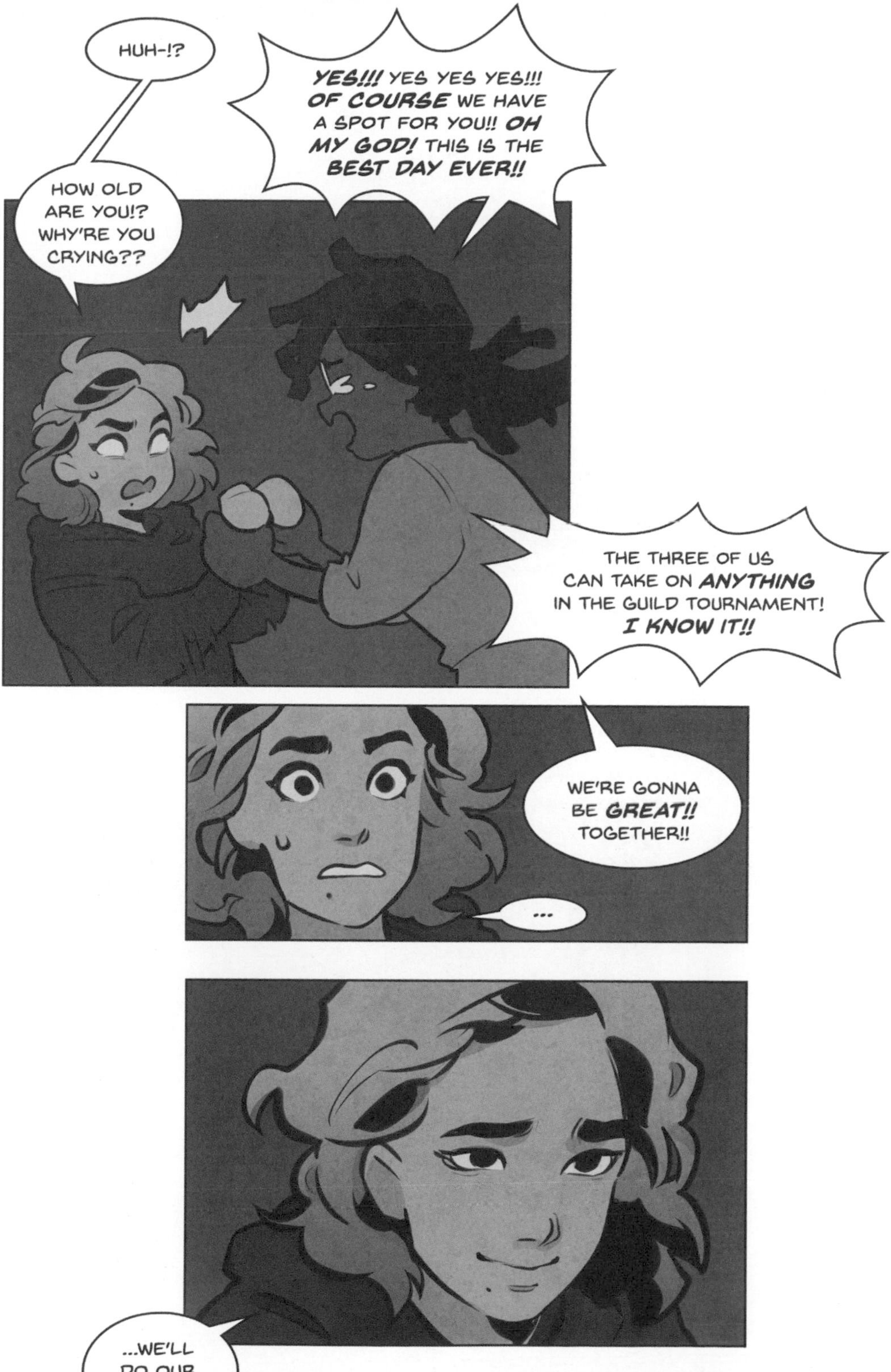
HUH-!?
YES!!! YES YES YES!!! OF COURSE WE HAVE A SPOT FOR YOU!! OH MY GOD! THIS IS THE BEST DAY EVER!!
HOW OLD ARE YOU!? WHY'RE YOU CRYING??
THE THREE OF US CAN TAKE ON ANYTHING IN THE GUILD TOURNAMENT! I KNOW IT!!
WE'RE GONNA BE GREAT!! TOGETHER!!
...
...WE'LL DO OUR BEST...!

CHAPTER 3: COMING CLEAN

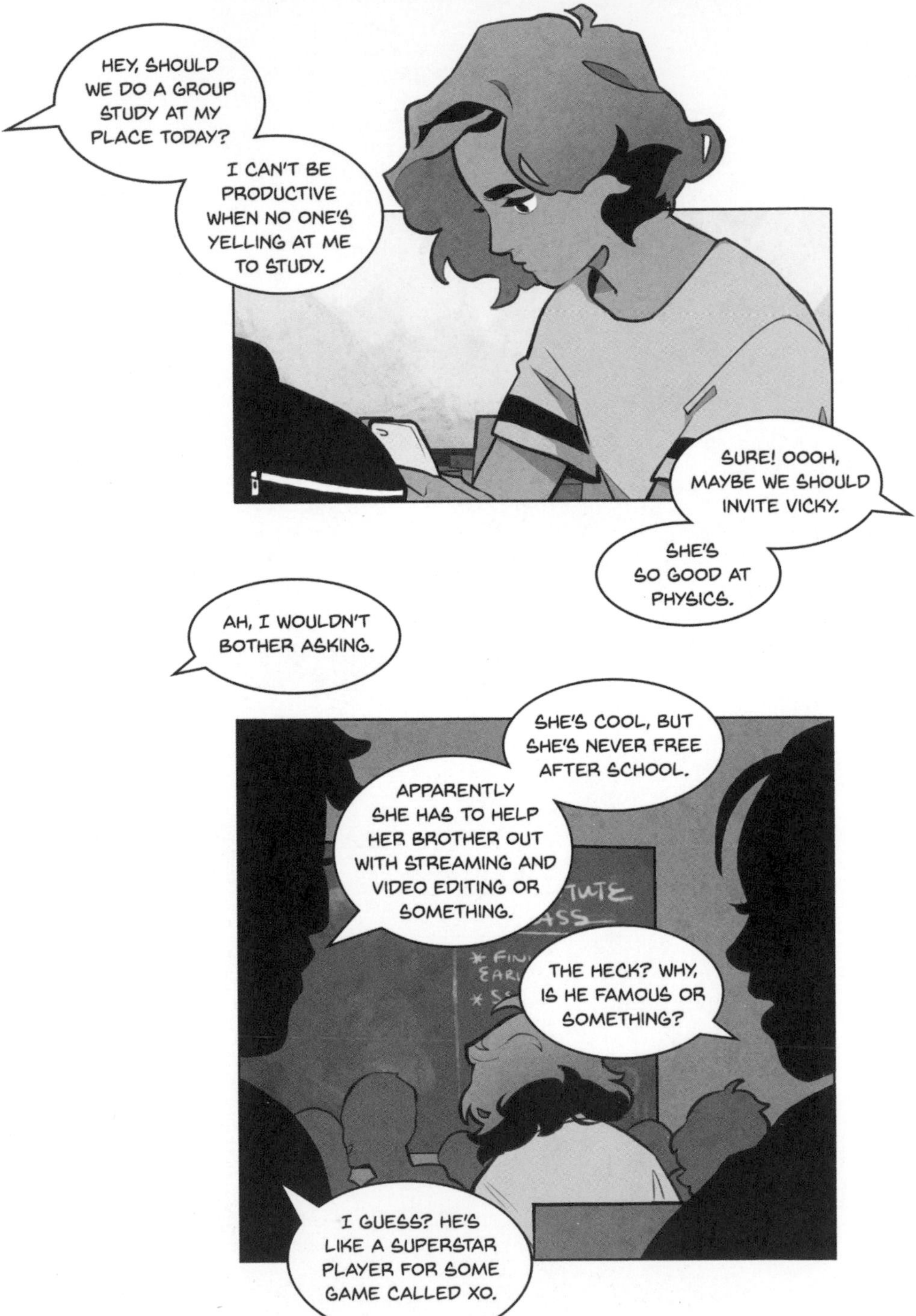

HEY, SHOULD WE DO A GROUP STUDY AT MY PLACE TODAY?
I CAN'T BE PRODUCTIVE WHEN NO ONE'S YELLING AT ME TO STUDY.
SURE! OOOH, MAYBE WE SHOULD INVITE VICKY.
SHE'S SO GOOD AT PHYSICS.
AH, I WOULDN'T BOTHER ASKING.
SHE'S COOL, BUT SHE'S NEVER FREE AFTER SCHOOL.
APPARENTLY SHE HAS TO HELP HER BROTHER OUT WITH STREAMING AND VIDEO EDITING OR SOMETHING.
THE HECK? WHY, IS HE FAMOUS OR SOMETHING?
I GUESS? HE'S LIKE A SUPERSTAR PLAYER FOR SOME GAME CALLED XO.

WHAT?! NO WAY! I LOVE XENITH ORION! IS HE A TOP PLAYER?

VELZOR   08:56 PM   43%

Eric

Today 9:51

Don't forget!! We're scrimming tomorrow (´ ω `)
Swing by after school!
Our tank is so excited to meet you!

I'll be there, promise.
I'm kind of nervous, I've never scrimmed before

Omg!! Baby's first scrim...
∑(д゚ ;)

I'll bring donuts to celebrate then!!

in HS, that's not a baby you old ma

at? I can't hear you over my creaking old bones...

AHEM.

?!

VICK--!!

SO LOUD!

MM MHHNNN... EEEGEEZ... MHHRHHY.

(I MEAN... AEGIS... SORRY.)

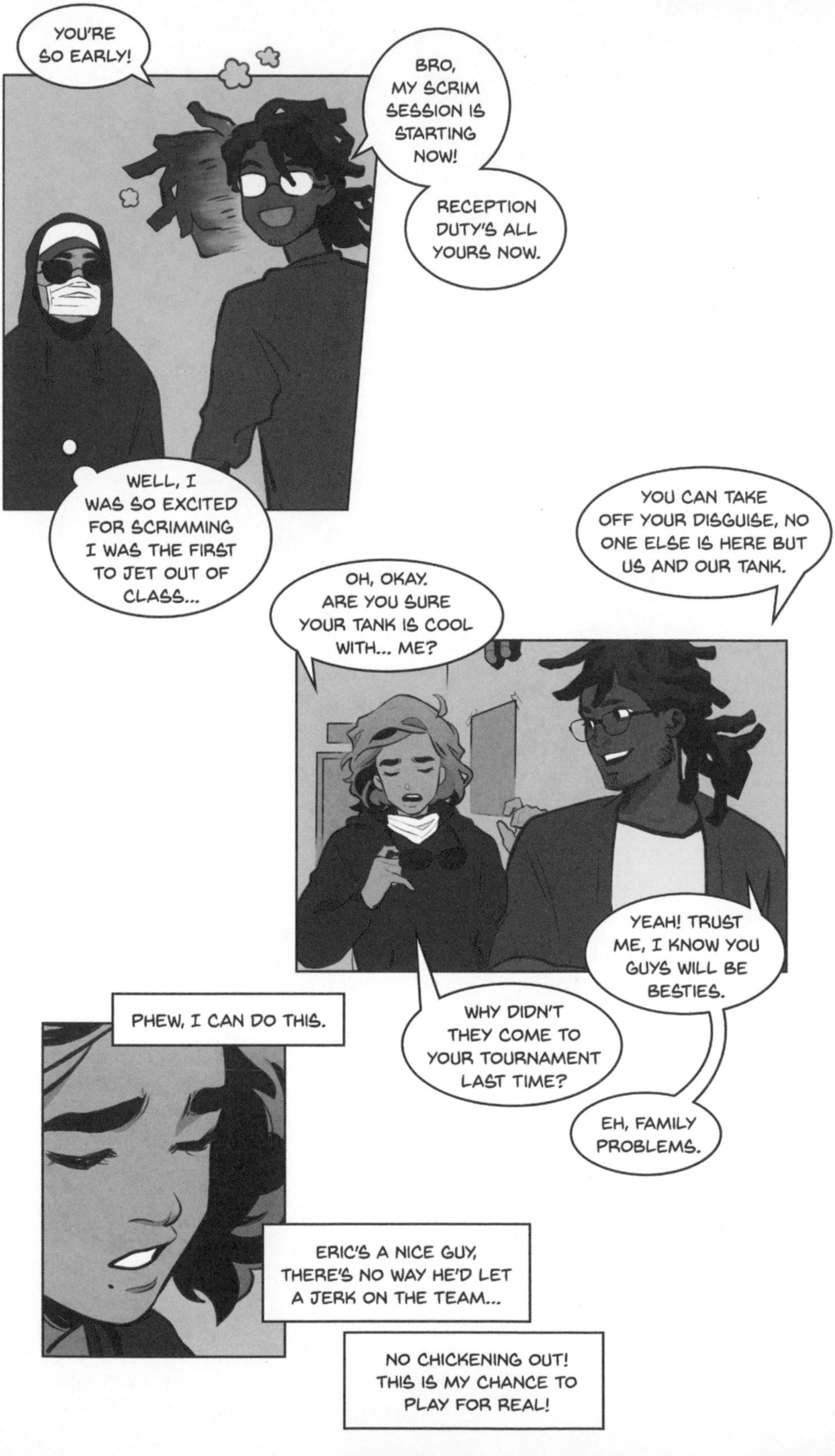
YOU'RE SO EARLY!
BRO, MY SCRIM SESSION IS STARTING NOW!
RECEPTION DUTY'S ALL YOURS NOW.
WELL, I WAS SO EXCITED FOR SCRIMMING I WAS THE FIRST TO JET OUT OF CLASS...
YOU CAN TAKE OFF YOUR DISGUISE, NO ONE ELSE IS HERE BUT US AND OUR TANK.
OH, OKAY. ARE YOU SURE YOUR TANK IS COOL WITH... ME?
YEAH! TRUST ME, I KNOW YOU GUYS WILL BE BESTIES.
WHY DIDN'T THEY COME TO YOUR TOURNAMENT LAST TIME?
EH, FAMILY PROBLEMS.
PHEW, I CAN DO THIS.
ERIC'S A NICE GUY, THERE'S NO WAY HE'D LET A JERK ON THE TEAM...
NO CHICKENING OUT! THIS IS MY CHANCE TO PLAY FOR REAL!

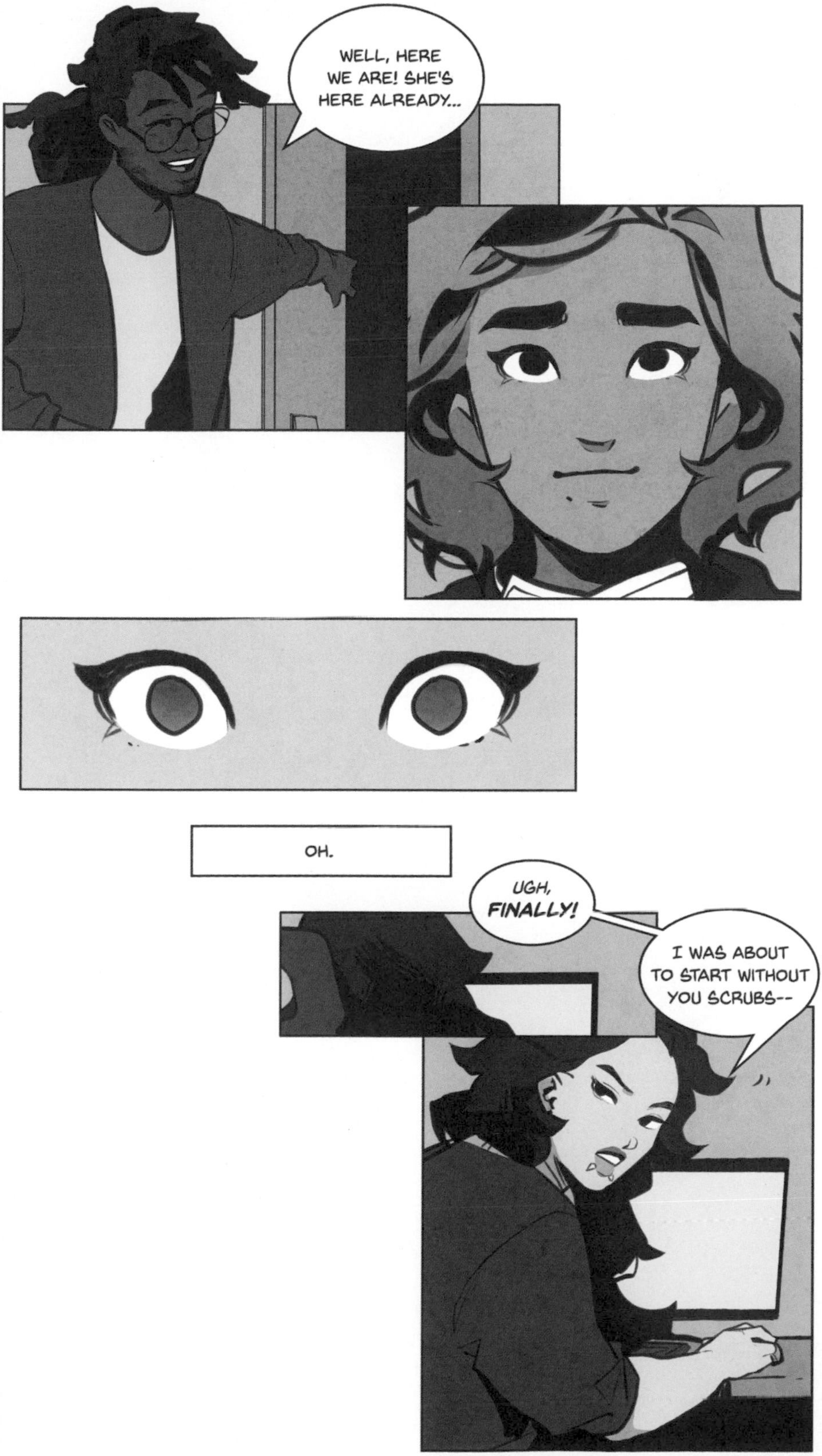
WELL, HERE WE ARE! SHE'S HERE ALREADY...
OH.
UGH, FINALLY!
I WAS ABOUT TO START WITHOUT YOU SCRUBS--

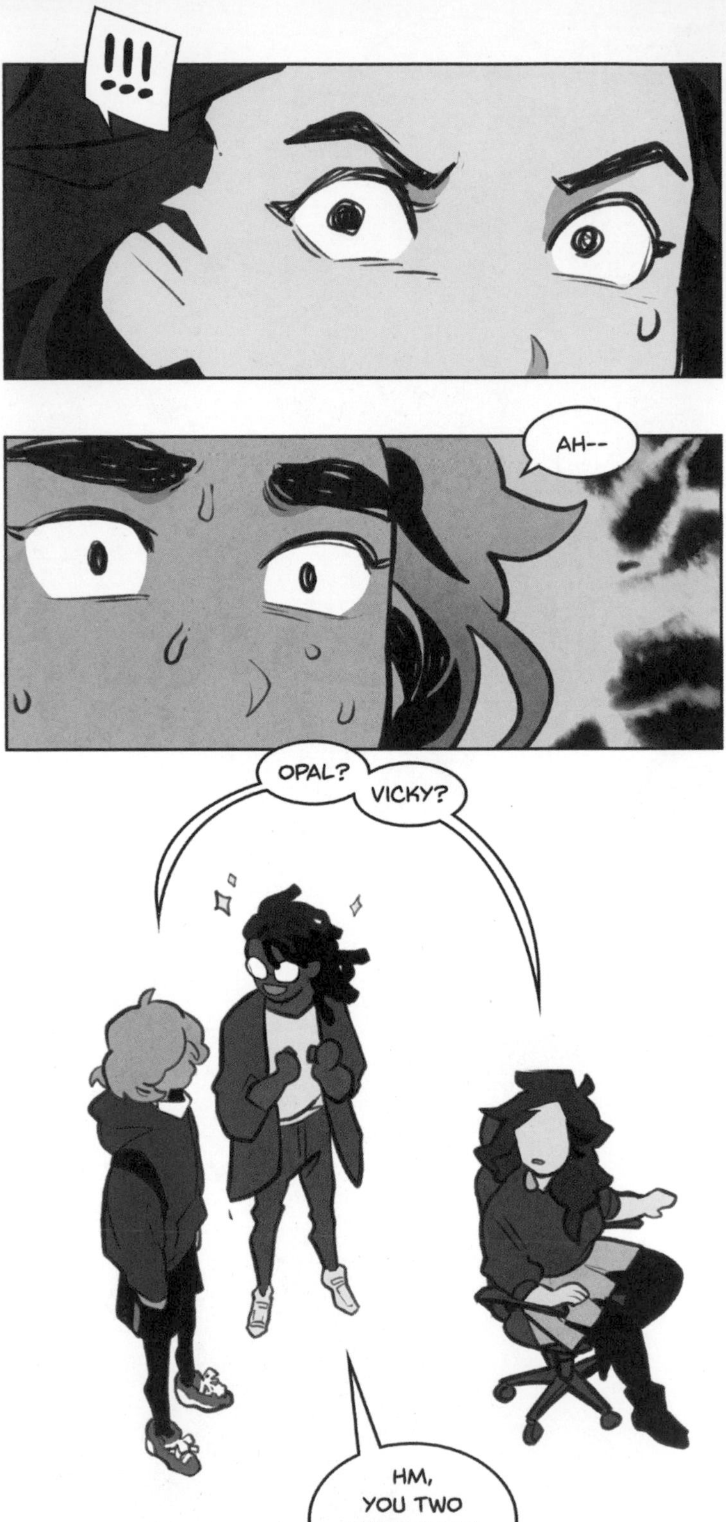
!!!
AH--
OPAL?
VICKY?
HM, YOU TWO KNOW EACH OTHER?

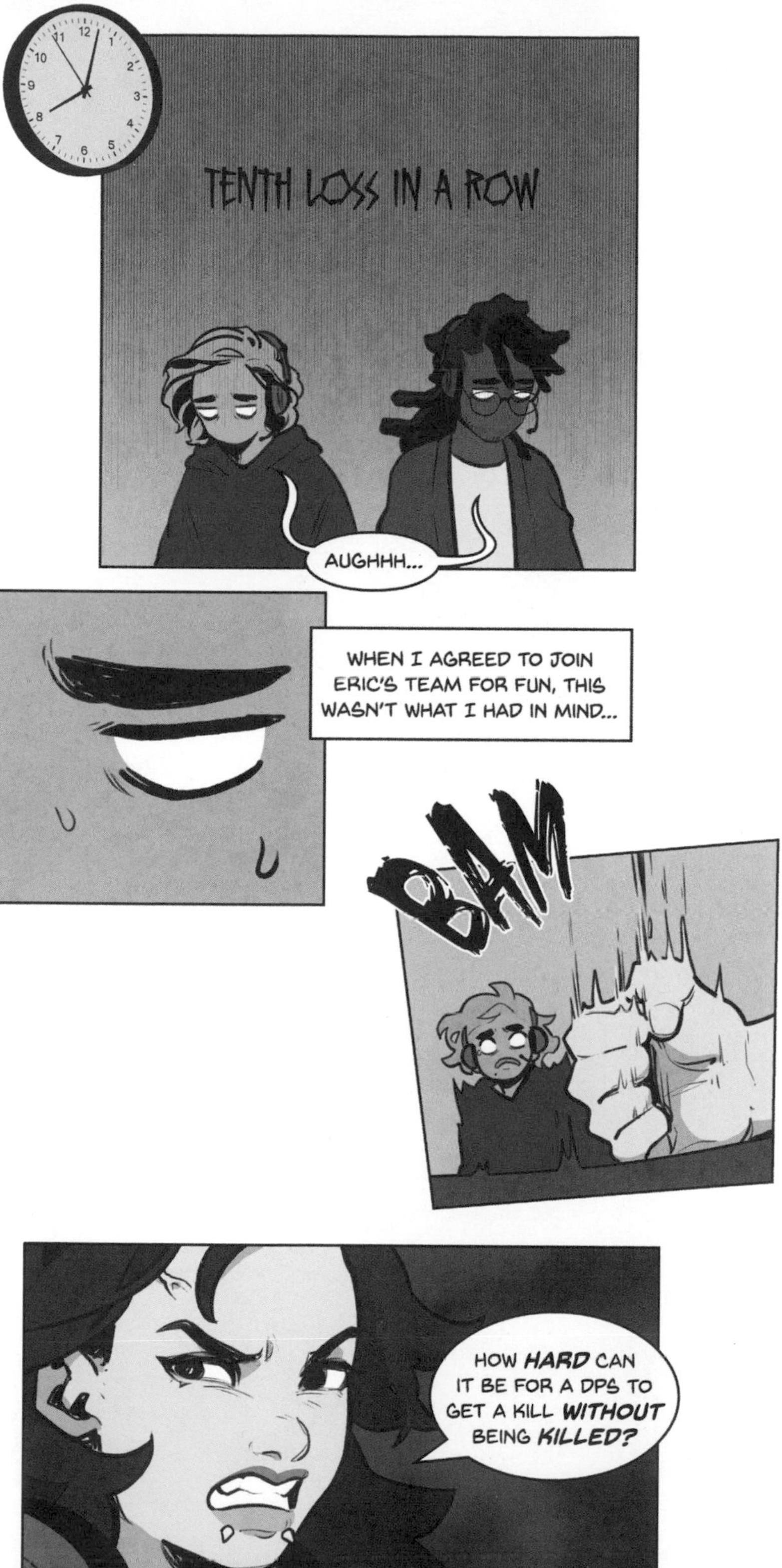
TENTH LOSS IN A ROW
AUGHHH...
WHEN I AGREED TO JOIN ERIC'S TEAM FOR FUN, THIS WASN'T WHAT I HAD IN MIND...
BAM
HOW **HARD** CAN IT BE FOR A DPS TO GET A KILL **WITHOUT** BEING **KILLED?**

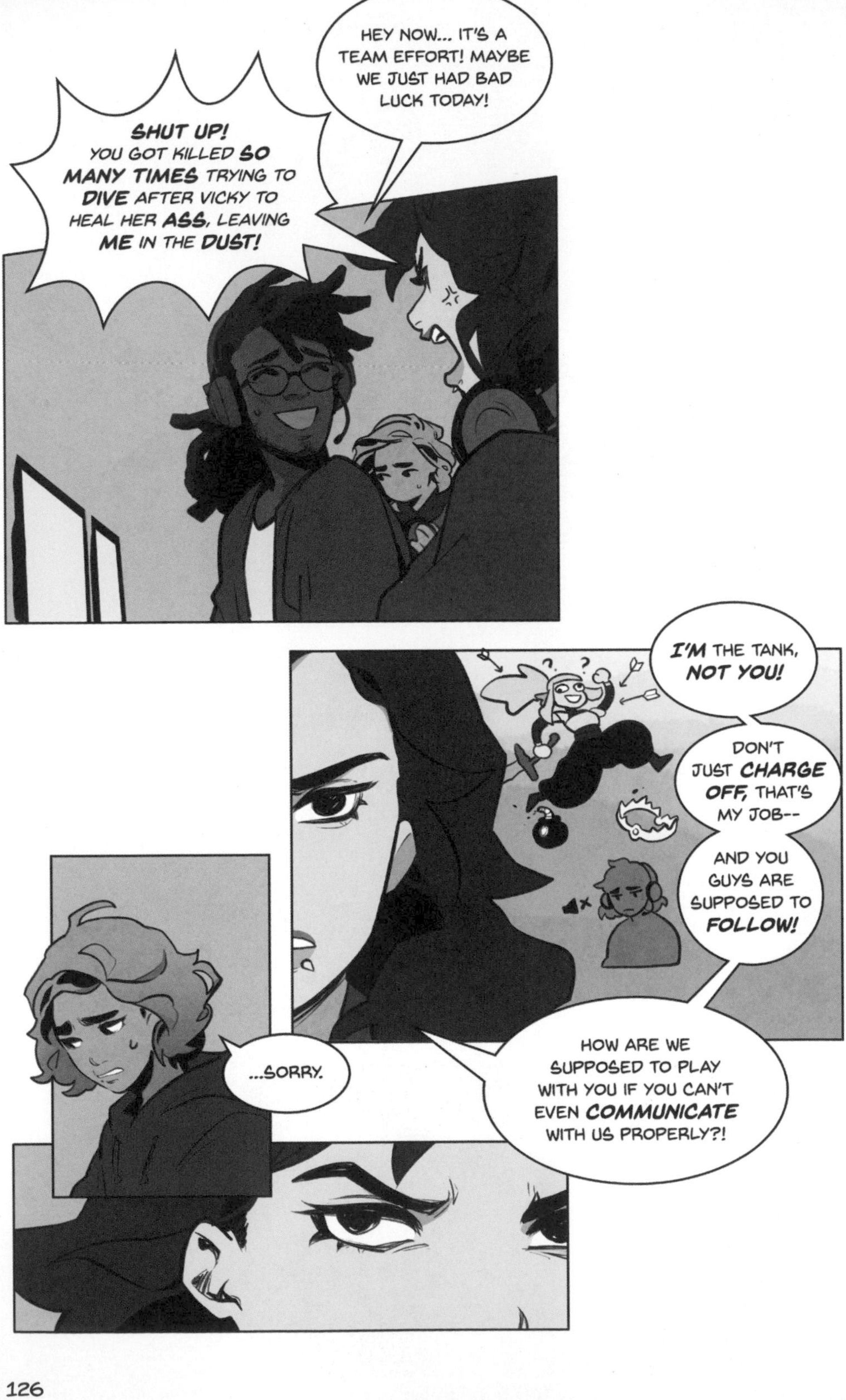
HEY NOW... IT'S A TEAM EFFORT! MAYBE WE JUST HAD BAD LUCK TODAY!
SHUT UP! YOU GOT KILLED SO MANY TIMES TRYING TO DIVE AFTER VICKY TO HEAL HER ASS, LEAVING ME IN THE DUST!
I'M THE TANK, NOT YOU!
DON'T JUST CHARGE OFF, THAT'S MY JOB--
AND YOU GUYS ARE SUPPOSED TO FOLLOW!
HOW ARE WE SUPPOSED TO PLAY WITH YOU IF YOU CAN'T EVEN COMMUNICATE WITH US PROPERLY?!
...SORRY.

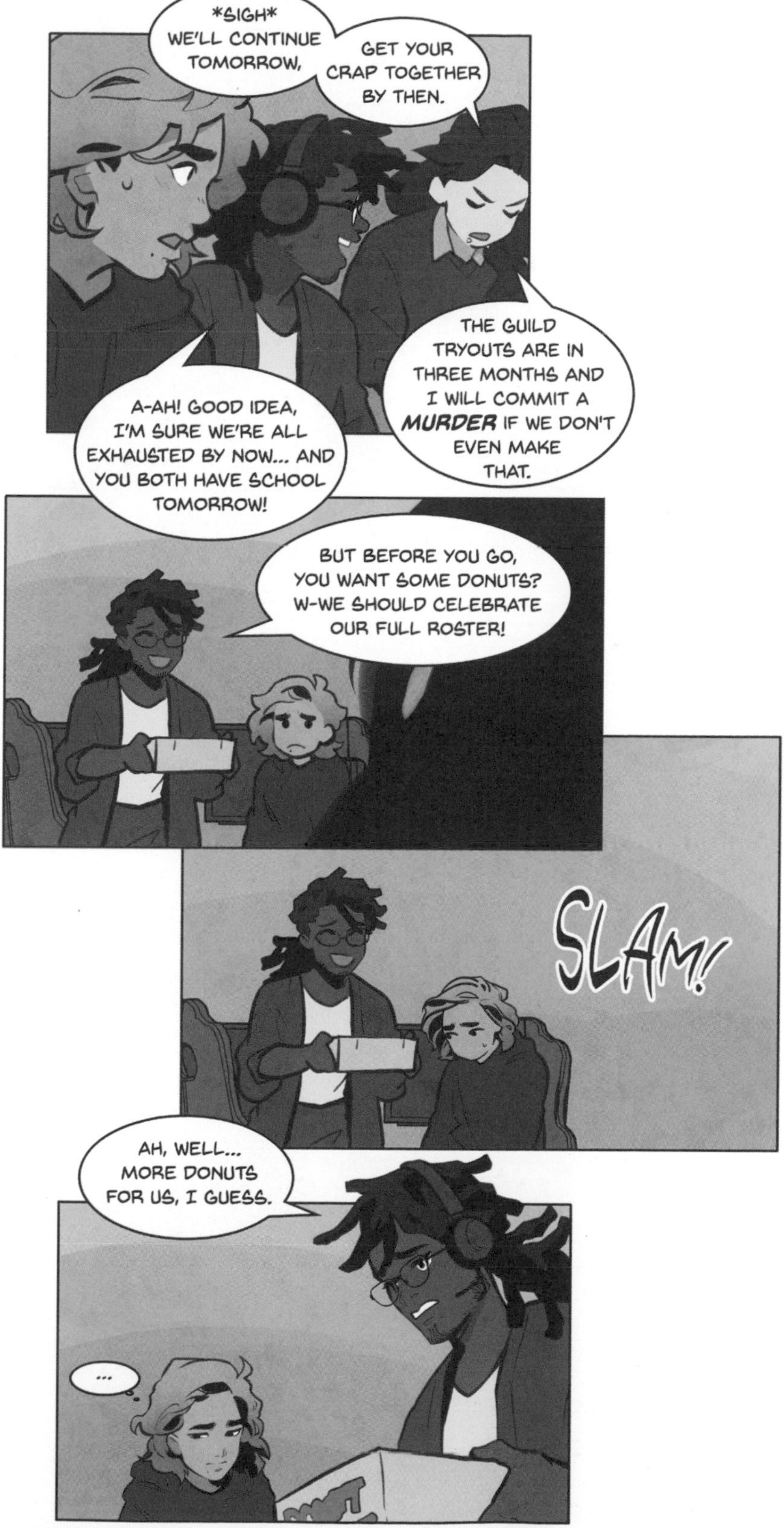
SIGH WE'LL CONTINUE TOMORROW,
GET YOUR CRAP TOGETHER BY THEN.
A-AH! GOOD IDEA, I'M SURE WE'RE ALL EXHAUSTED BY NOW... AND YOU BOTH HAVE SCHOOL TOMORROW!
THE GUILD TRYOUTS ARE IN THREE MONTHS AND I WILL COMMIT A MURDER IF WE DON'T EVEN MAKE THAT.
BUT BEFORE YOU GO, YOU WANT SOME DONUTS? W-WE SHOULD CELEBRATE OUR FULL ROSTER!
SLAM!
AH, WELL... MORE DONUTS FOR US, I GUESS.
...

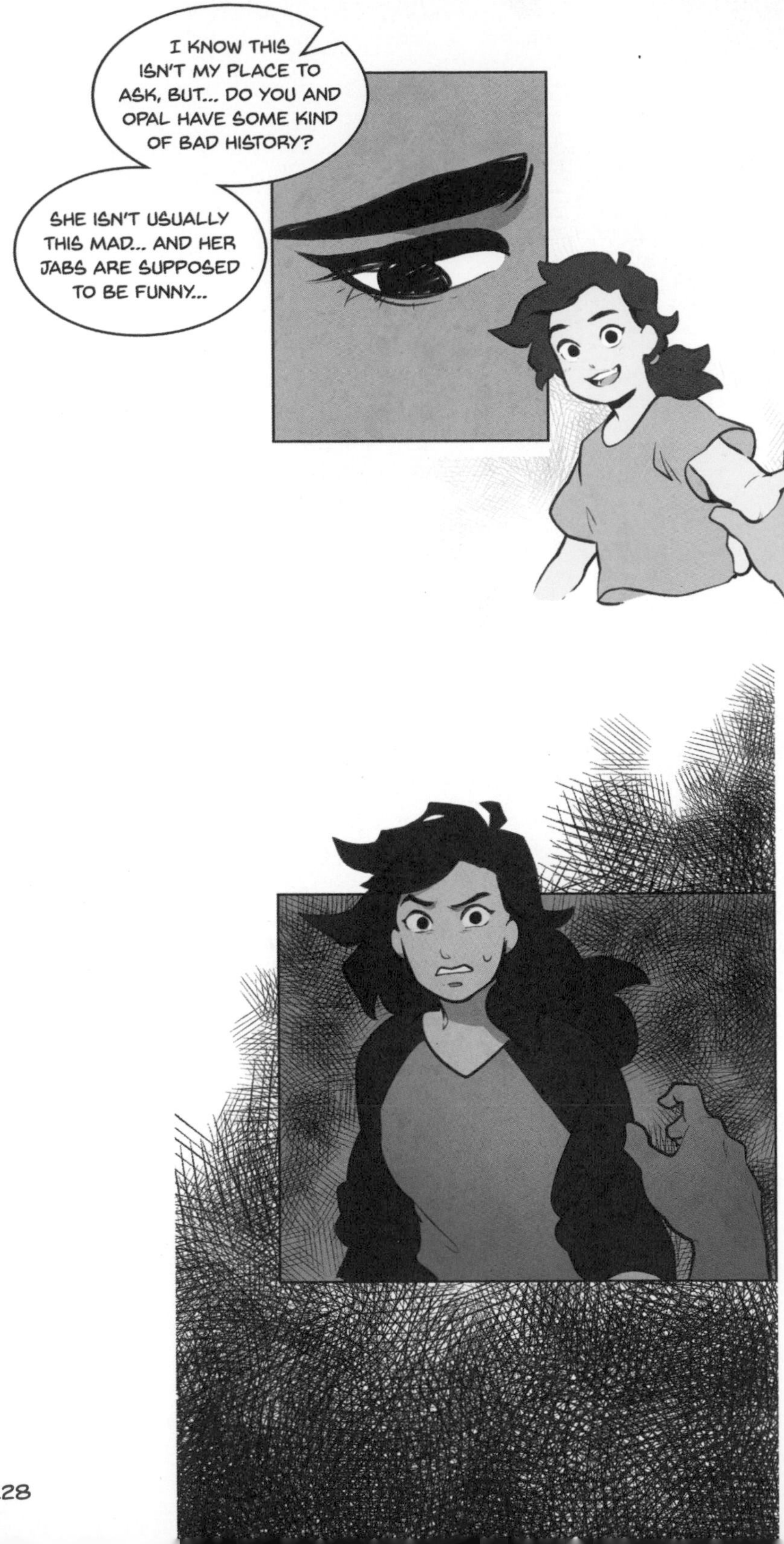
I KNOW THIS ISN'T MY PLACE TO ASK, BUT... DO YOU AND OPAL HAVE SOME KIND OF BAD HISTORY?
SHE ISN'T USUALLY THIS MAD... AND HER JABS ARE SUPPOSED TO BE FUNNY...

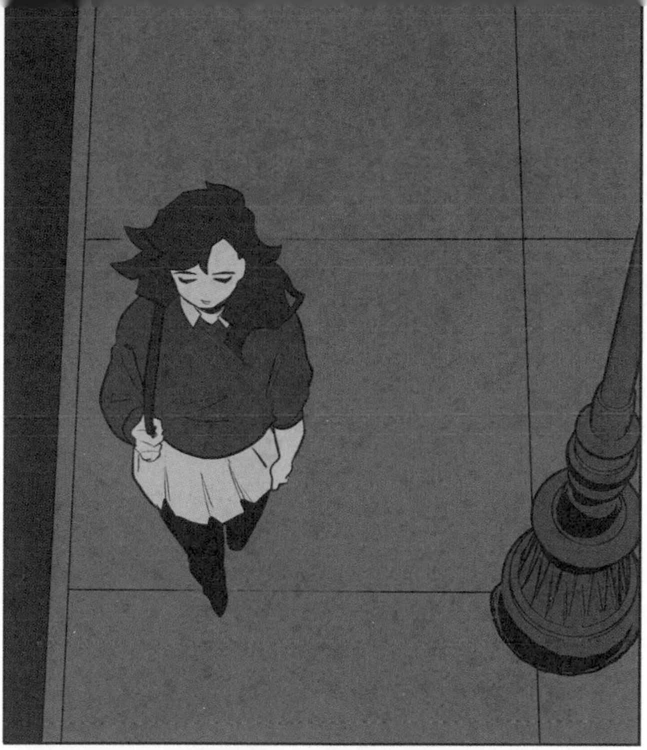

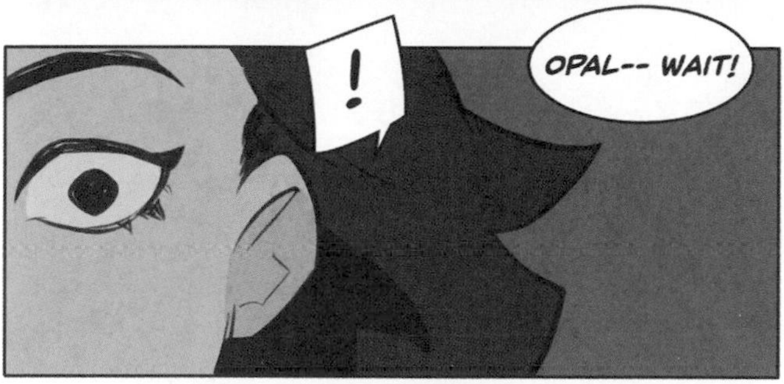
!
OPAL-- WAIT!

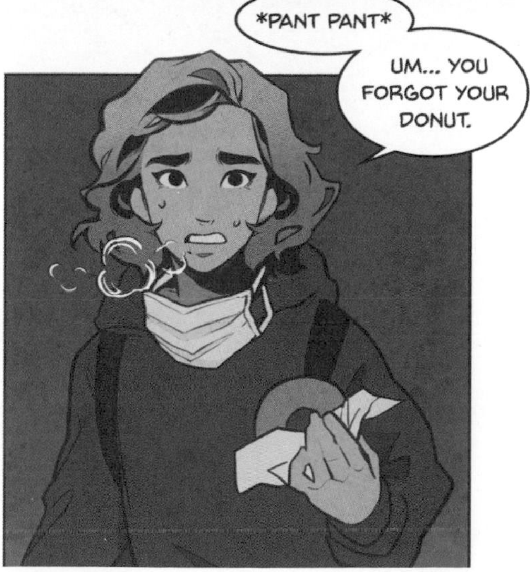
PANT PANT
UM... YOU FORGOT YOUR DONUT.

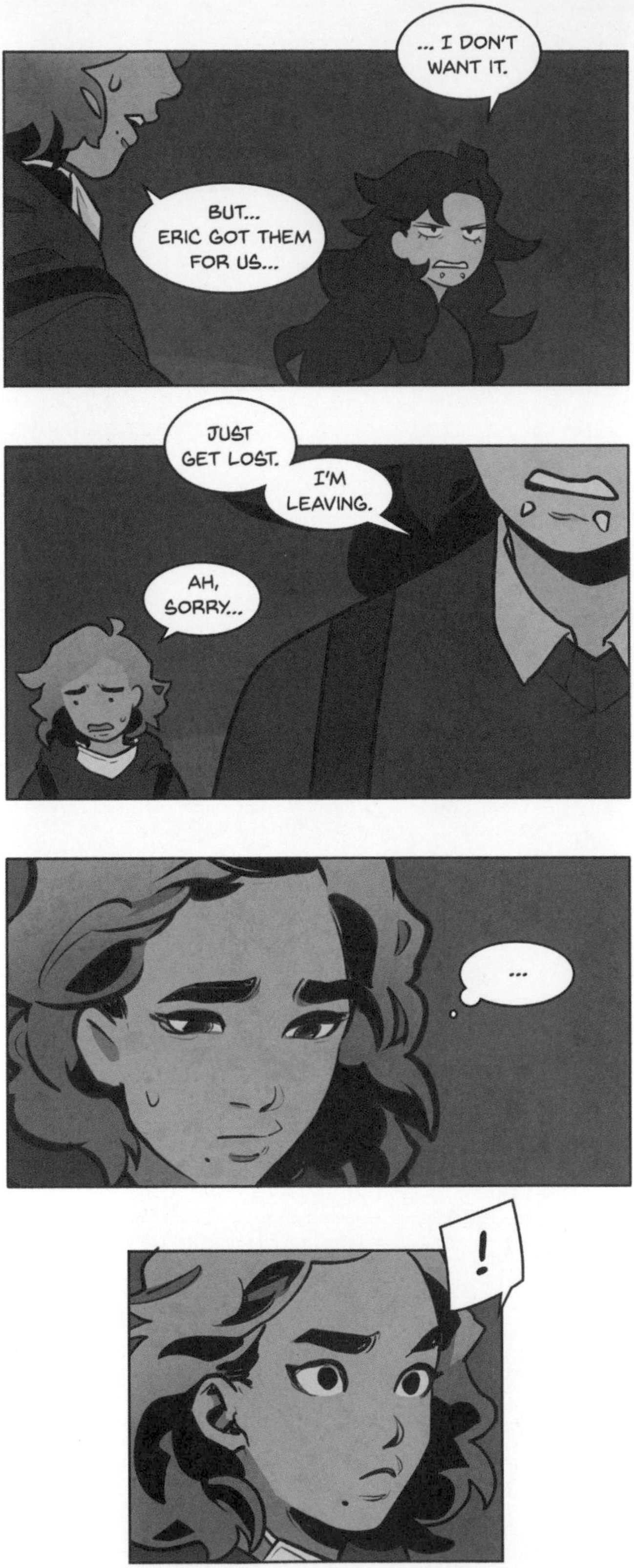
... I DON'T WANT IT.
BUT... ERIC GOT THEM FOR US...
JUST GET LOST.
I'M LEAVING.
AH, SORRY...
...
!

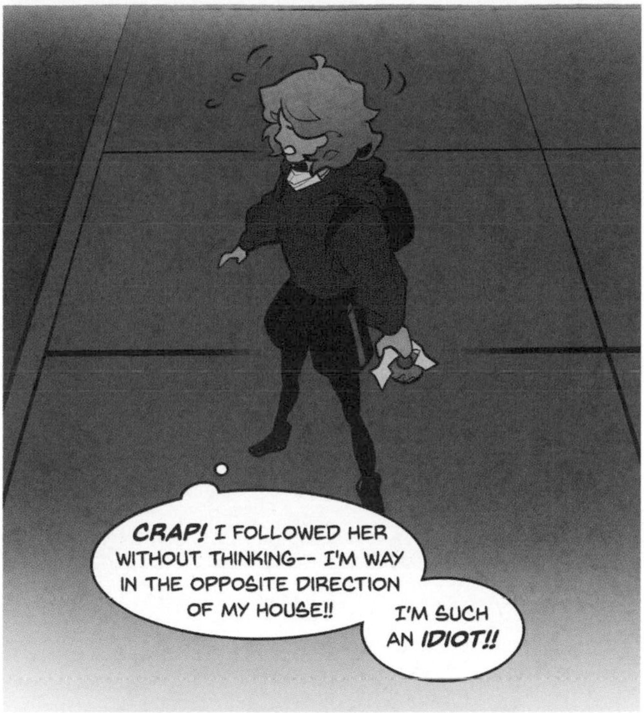
CRAP! I FOLLOWED HER WITHOUT THINKING-- I'M WAY IN THE OPPOSITE DIRECTION OF MY HOUSE!!
I'M SUCH AN IDIOT!!

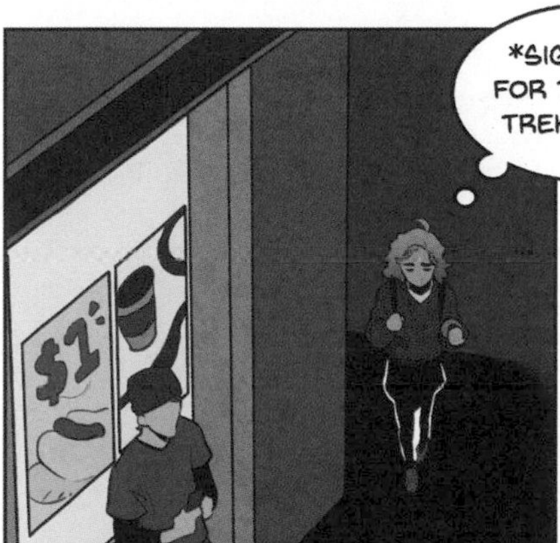
SIGH TIME FOR THE LONG TREK HOME...
$2

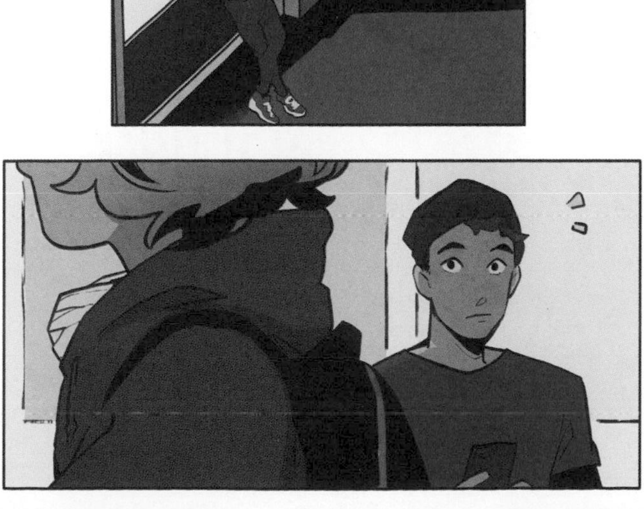

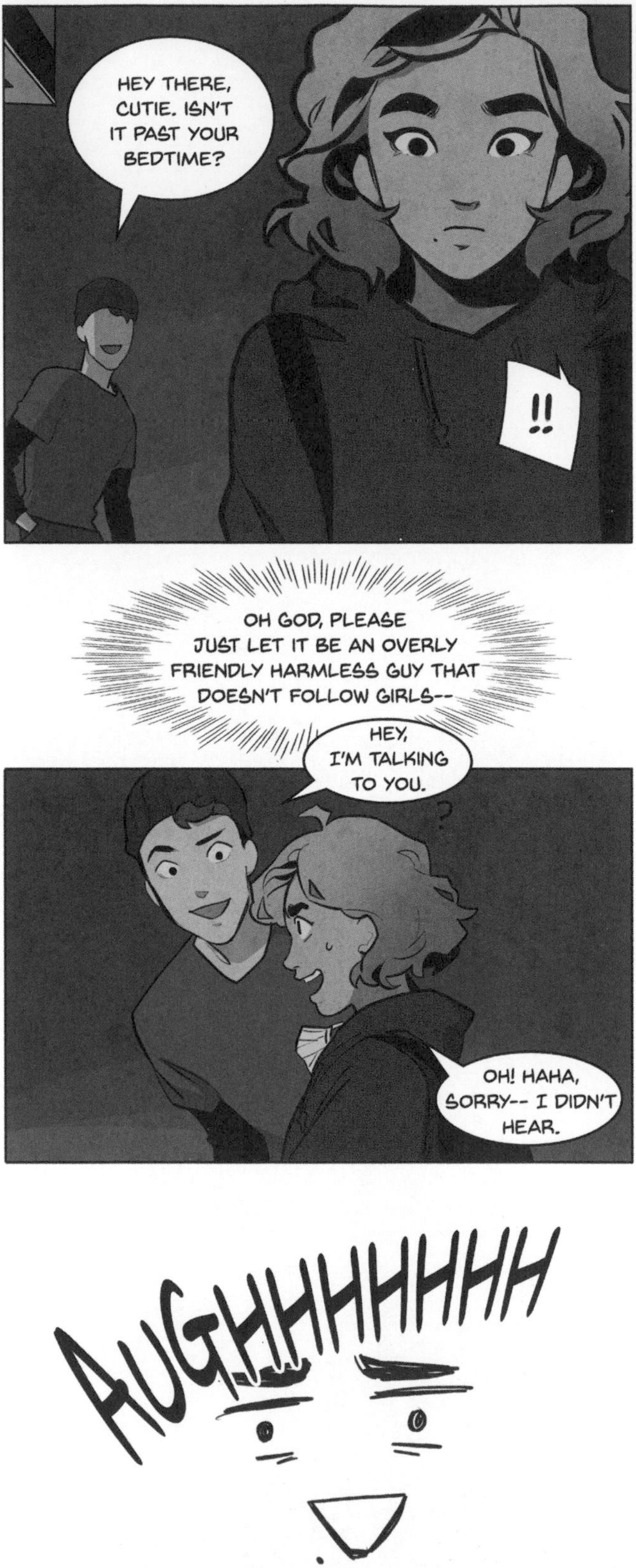
HEY THERE, CUTIE. ISN'T IT PAST YOUR BEDTIME?
!!
OH GOD, PLEASE JUST LET IT BE AN OVERLY FRIENDLY HARMLESS GUY THAT DOESN'T FOLLOW GIRLS--
HEY, I'M TALKING TO YOU.
?
OH! HAHA, SORRY-- I DIDN'T HEAR.
AUGHHHHHHH

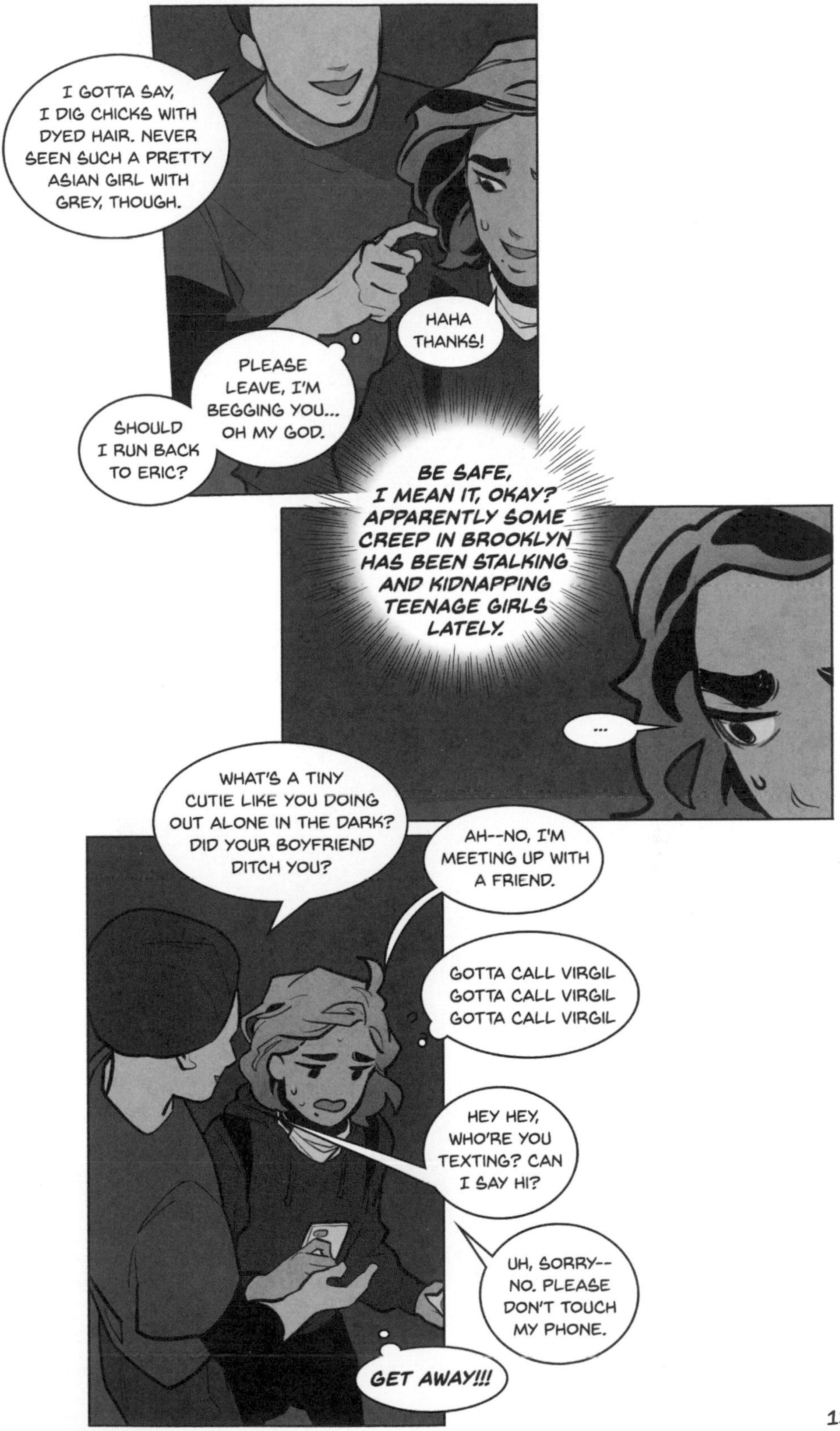
I GOTTA SAY, I DIG CHICKS WITH DYED HAIR. NEVER SEEN SUCH A PRETTY ASIAN GIRL WITH GREY, THOUGH.
HAHA THANKS!
PLEASE LEAVE, I'M BEGGING YOU... OH MY GOD.
SHOULD I RUN BACK TO ERIC?
BE SAFE, I MEAN IT, OKAY? APPARENTLY SOME CREEP IN BROOKLYN HAS BEEN STALKING AND KIDNAPPING TEENAGE GIRLS LATELY.
...
WHAT'S A TINY CUTIE LIKE YOU DOING OUT ALONE IN THE DARK? DID YOUR BOYFRIEND DITCH YOU?
AH--NO, I'M MEETING UP WITH A FRIEND.
GOTTA CALL VIRGIL GOTTA CALL VIRGIL GOTTA CALL VIRGIL
HEY HEY, WHO'RE YOU TEXTING? CAN I SAY HI?
UH, SORRY-- NO. PLEASE DON'T TOUCH MY PHONE.
GET AWAY!!!

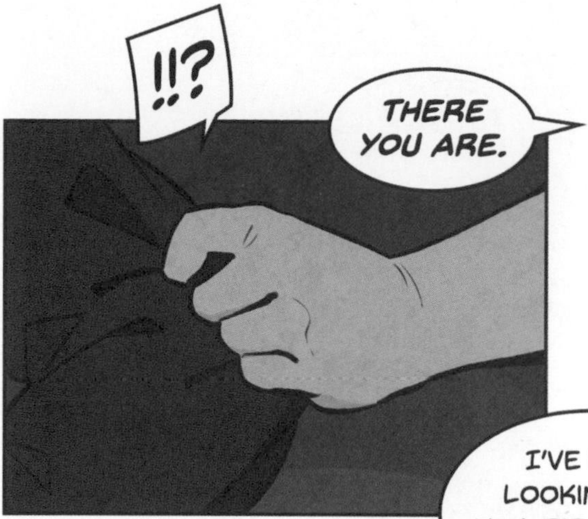
!!?
THERE YOU ARE.

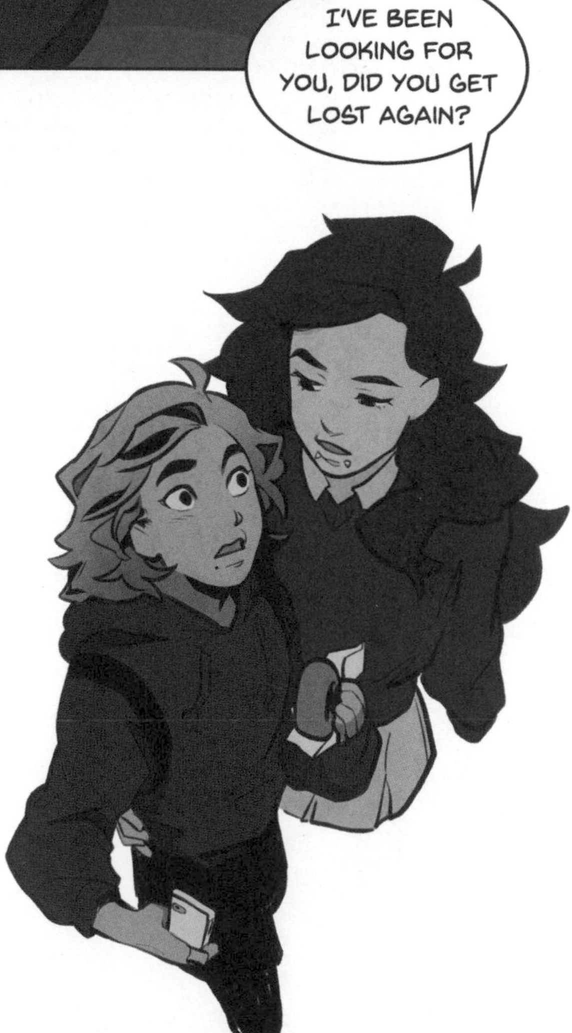
I'VE BEEN LOOKING FOR YOU, DID YOU GET LOST AGAIN?

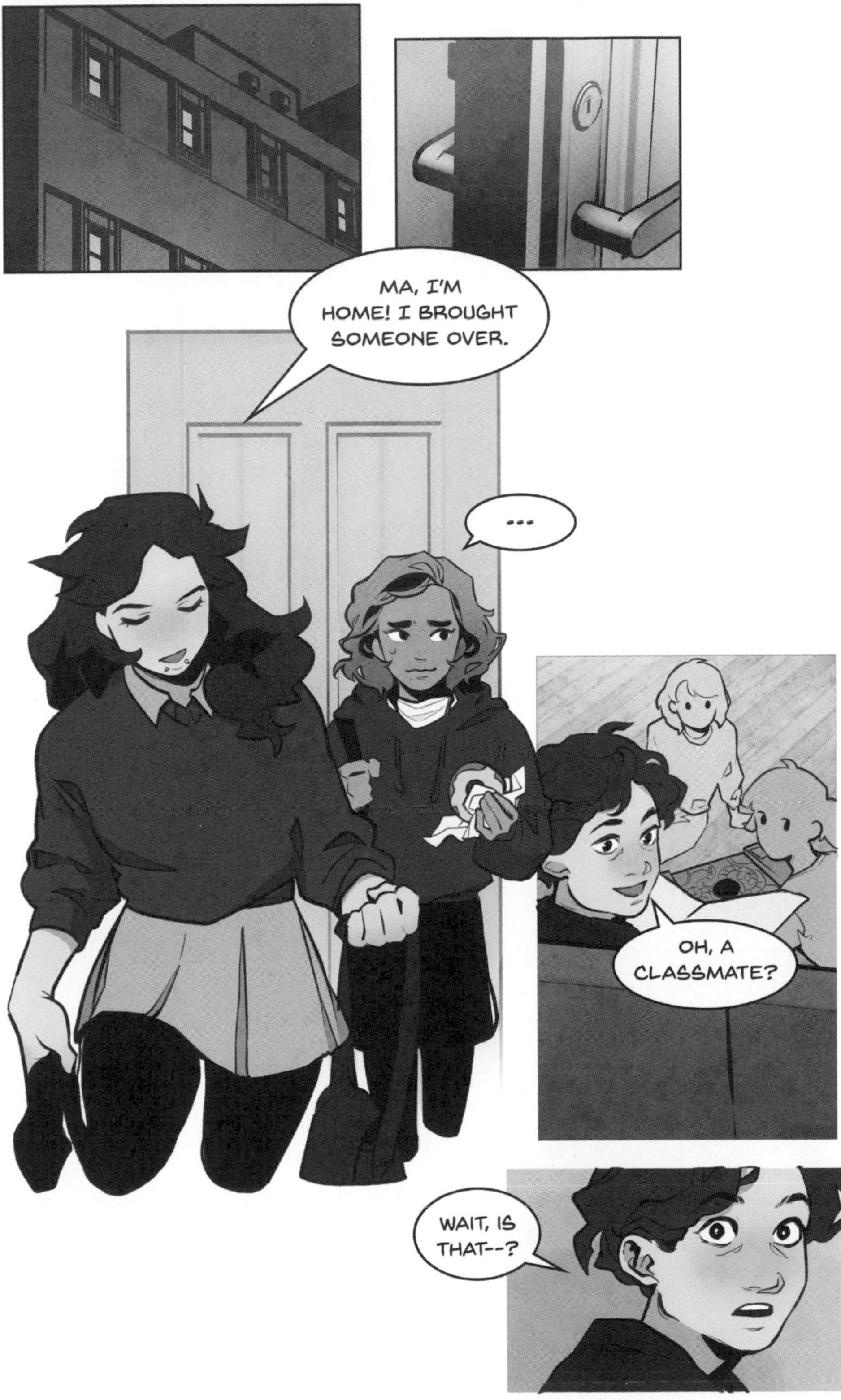
MA, I'M HOME! I BROUGHT SOMEONE OVER.
...
OH, A CLASSMATE?
WAIT, IS THAT--?

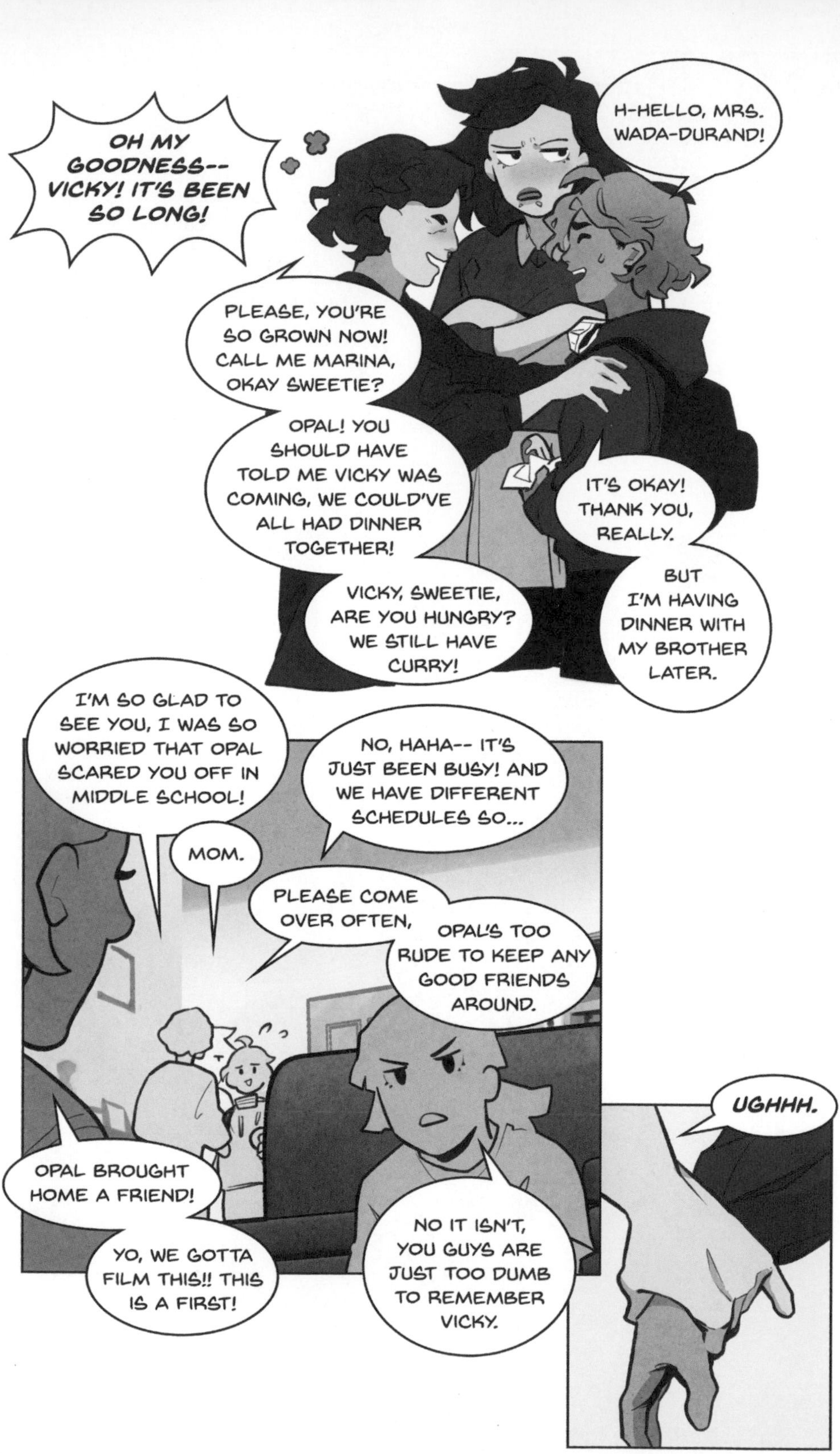
OH MY GOODNESS-- VICKY! IT'S BEEN SO LONG!
H-HELLO, MRS. WADA-DURAND!
PLEASE, YOU'RE SO GROWN NOW! CALL ME MARINA, OKAY SWEETIE?
OPAL! YOU SHOULD HAVE TOLD ME VICKY WAS COMING, WE COULD'VE ALL HAD DINNER TOGETHER!
IT'S OKAY! THANK YOU, REALLY.
VICKY, SWEETIE, ARE YOU HUNGRY? WE STILL HAVE CURRY!
BUT I'M HAVING DINNER WITH MY BROTHER LATER.
I'M SO GLAD TO SEE YOU, I WAS SO WORRIED THAT OPAL SCARED YOU OFF IN MIDDLE SCHOOL!
NO, HAHA-- IT'S JUST BEEN BUSY! AND WE HAVE DIFFERENT SCHEDULES SO...
MOM.
PLEASE COME OVER OFTEN,
OPAL'S TOO RUDE TO KEEP ANY GOOD FRIENDS AROUND.
OPAL BROUGHT HOME A FRIEND!
YO, WE GOTTA FILM THIS!! THIS IS A FIRST!
NO IT ISN'T, YOU GUYS ARE JUST TOO DUMB TO REMEMBER VICKY.
UGHHH.

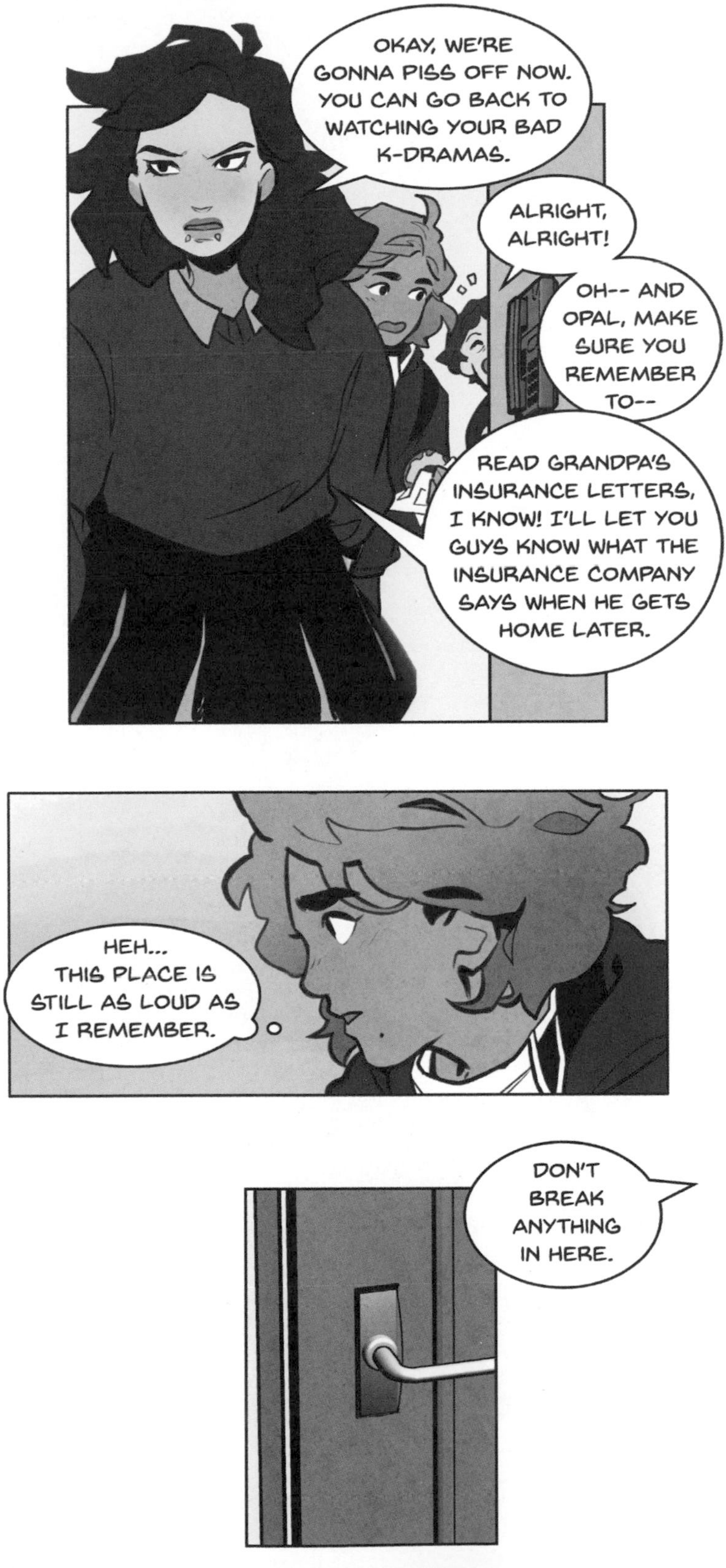
OKAY, WE'RE GONNA PISS OFF NOW. YOU CAN GO BACK TO WATCHING YOUR BAD K-DRAMAS.
ALRIGHT, ALRIGHT!
OH-- AND OPAL, MAKE SURE YOU REMEMBER TO--
READ GRANDPA'S INSURANCE LETTERS, I KNOW! I'LL LET YOU GUYS KNOW WHAT THE INSURANCE COMPANY SAYS WHEN HE GETS HOME LATER.
HEH... THIS PLACE IS STILL AS LOUD AS I REMEMBER.
DON'T BREAK ANYTHING IN HERE.

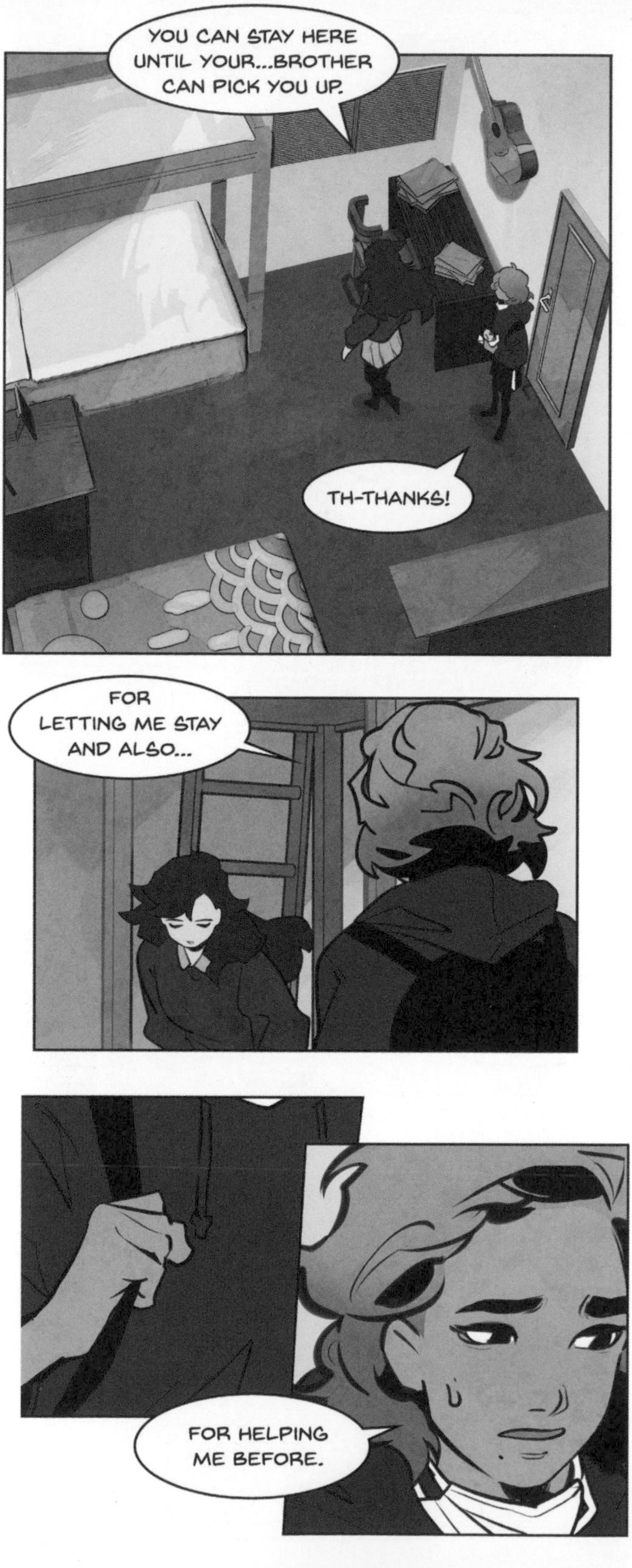
YOU CAN STAY HERE UNTIL YOUR...BROTHER CAN PICK YOU UP.
TH-THANKS!
FOR LETTING ME STAY AND ALSO...
FOR HELPING ME BEFORE.

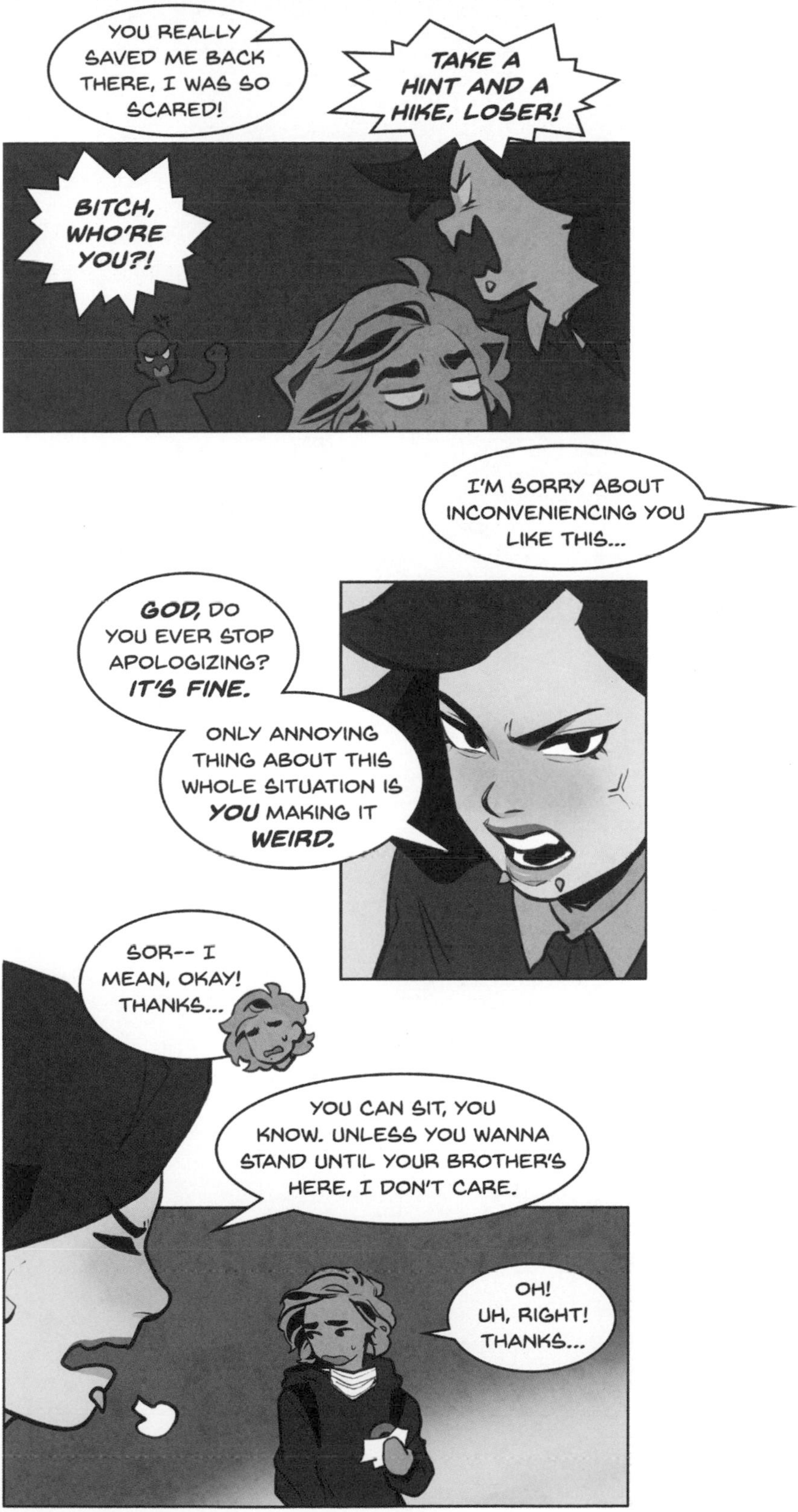
YOU REALLY SAVED ME BACK THERE, I WAS SO SCARED!
TAKE A HINT AND A HIKE, LOSER!
BITCH, WHO'RE YOU?!
I'M SORRY ABOUT INCONVENIENCING YOU LIKE THIS...
GOD, DO YOU EVER STOP APOLOGIZING? IT'S FINE.
ONLY ANNOYING THING ABOUT THIS WHOLE SITUATION IS YOU MAKING IT WEIRD.
SOR-- I MEAN, OKAY! THANKS...
YOU CAN SIT, YOU KNOW. UNLESS YOU WANNA STAND UNTIL YOUR BROTHER'S HERE, I DON'T CARE.
OH! UH, RIGHT! THANKS...

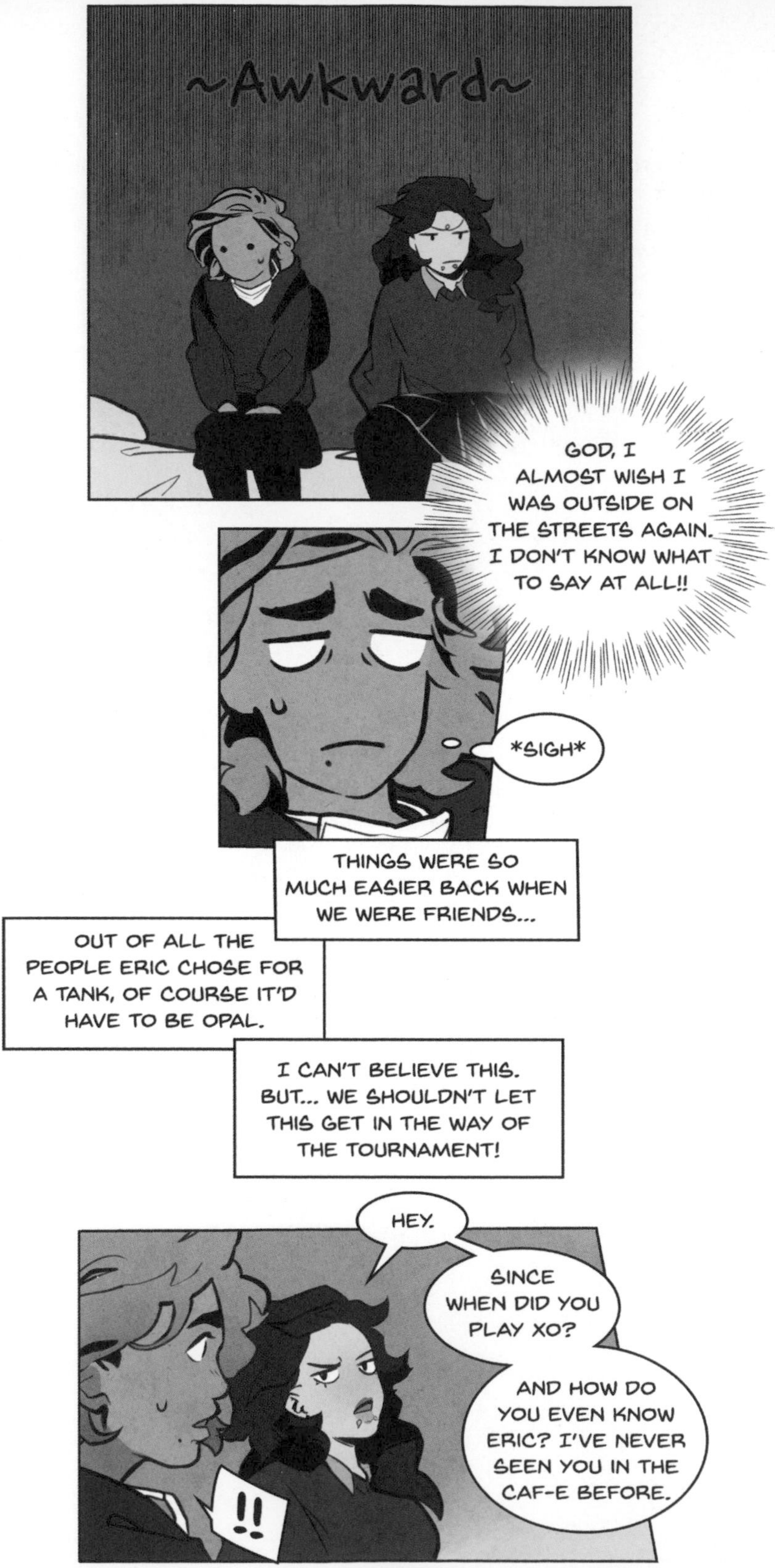
~Awkward~
GOD, I ALMOST WISH I WAS OUTSIDE ON THE STREETS AGAIN. I DON'T KNOW WHAT TO SAY AT ALL!!
SIGH
THINGS WERE SO MUCH EASIER BACK WHEN WE WERE FRIENDS...
OUT OF ALL THE PEOPLE ERIC CHOSE FOR A TANK, OF COURSE IT'D HAVE TO BE OPAL.
I CAN'T BELIEVE THIS. BUT... WE SHOULDN'T LET THIS GET IN THE WAY OF THE TOURNAMENT!
HEY.
SINCE WHEN DID YOU PLAY XO?
AND HOW DO YOU EVEN KNOW ERIC? I'VE NEVER SEEN YOU IN THE CAF-E BEFORE.
!!

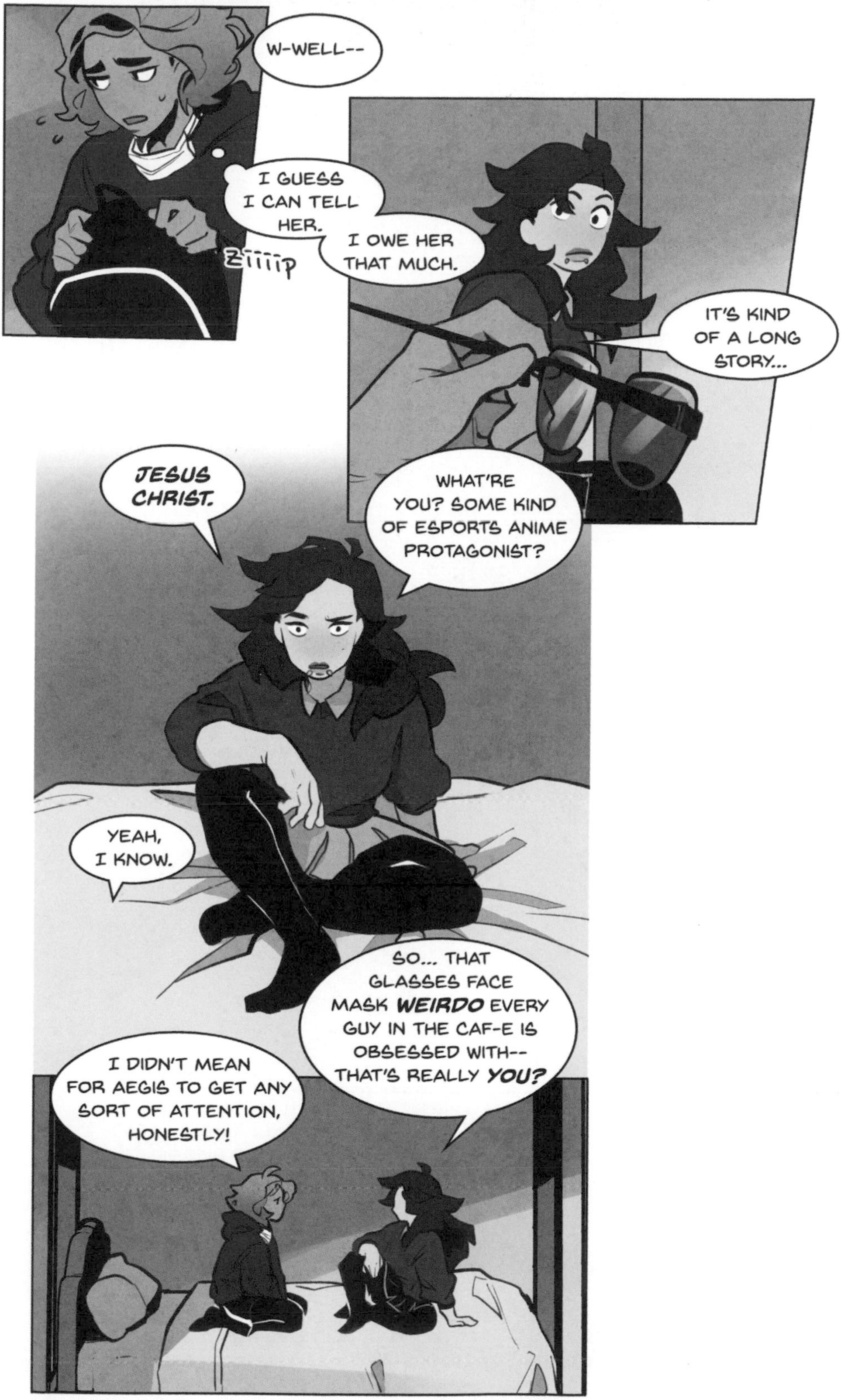
W-WELL--
I GUESS I CAN TELL HER.
I OWE HER THAT MUCH.
ZIIIIP
IT'S KIND OF A LONG STORY...
JESUS CHRIST.
WHAT'RE YOU? SOME KIND OF ESPORTS ANIME PROTAGONIST?
YEAH, I KNOW.
SO... THAT GLASSES FACE MASK WEIRDO EVERY GUY IN THE CAF-E IS OBSESSED WITH-- THAT'S REALLY YOU?
I DIDN'T MEAN FOR AEGIS TO GET ANY SORT OF ATTENTION, HONESTLY!

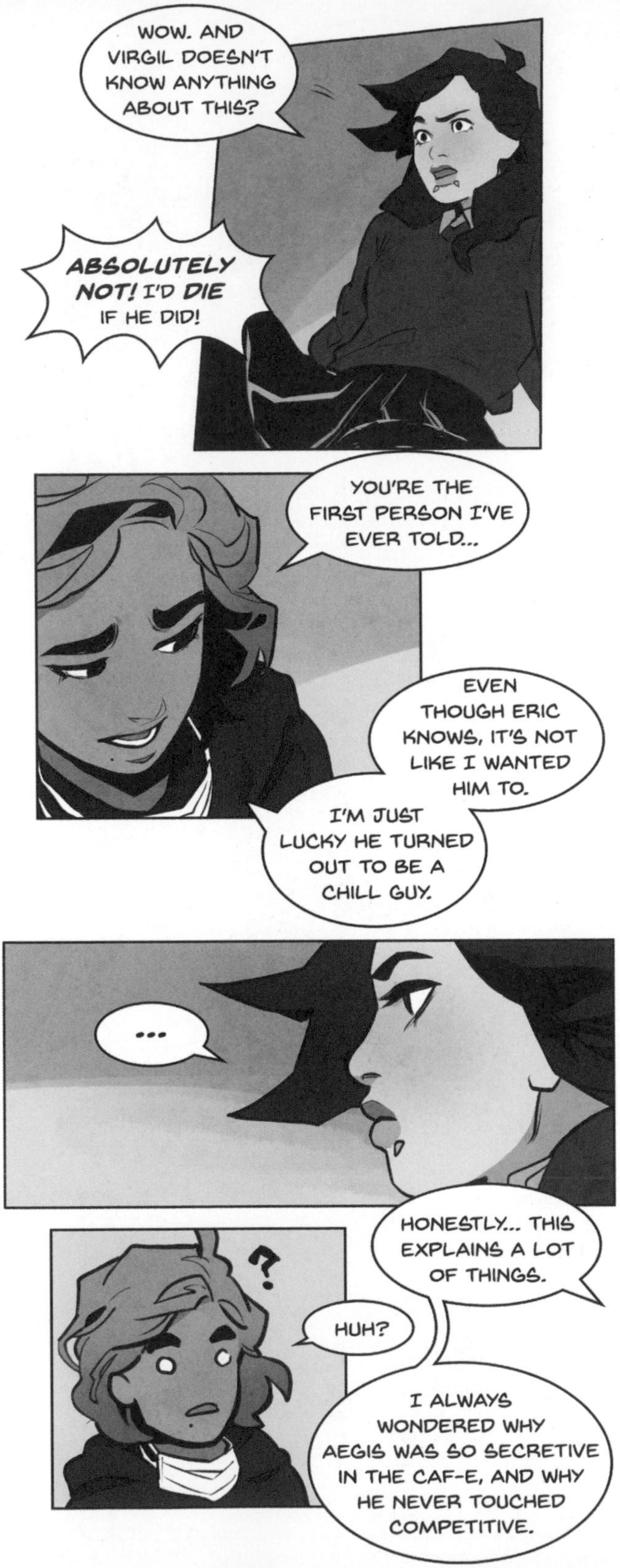
WOW. AND VIRGIL DOESN'T KNOW ANYTHING ABOUT THIS?
ABSOLUTELY NOT! I'D DIE IF HE DID!
YOU'RE THE FIRST PERSON I'VE EVER TOLD...
EVEN THOUGH ERIC KNOWS, IT'S NOT LIKE I WANTED HIM TO.
I'M JUST LUCKY HE TURNED OUT TO BE A CHILL GUY.
...
HONESTLY... THIS EXPLAINS A LOT OF THINGS.
?
HUH?
I ALWAYS WONDERED WHY AEGIS WAS SO SECRETIVE IN THE CAF-E, AND WHY HE NEVER TOUCHED COMPETITIVE.

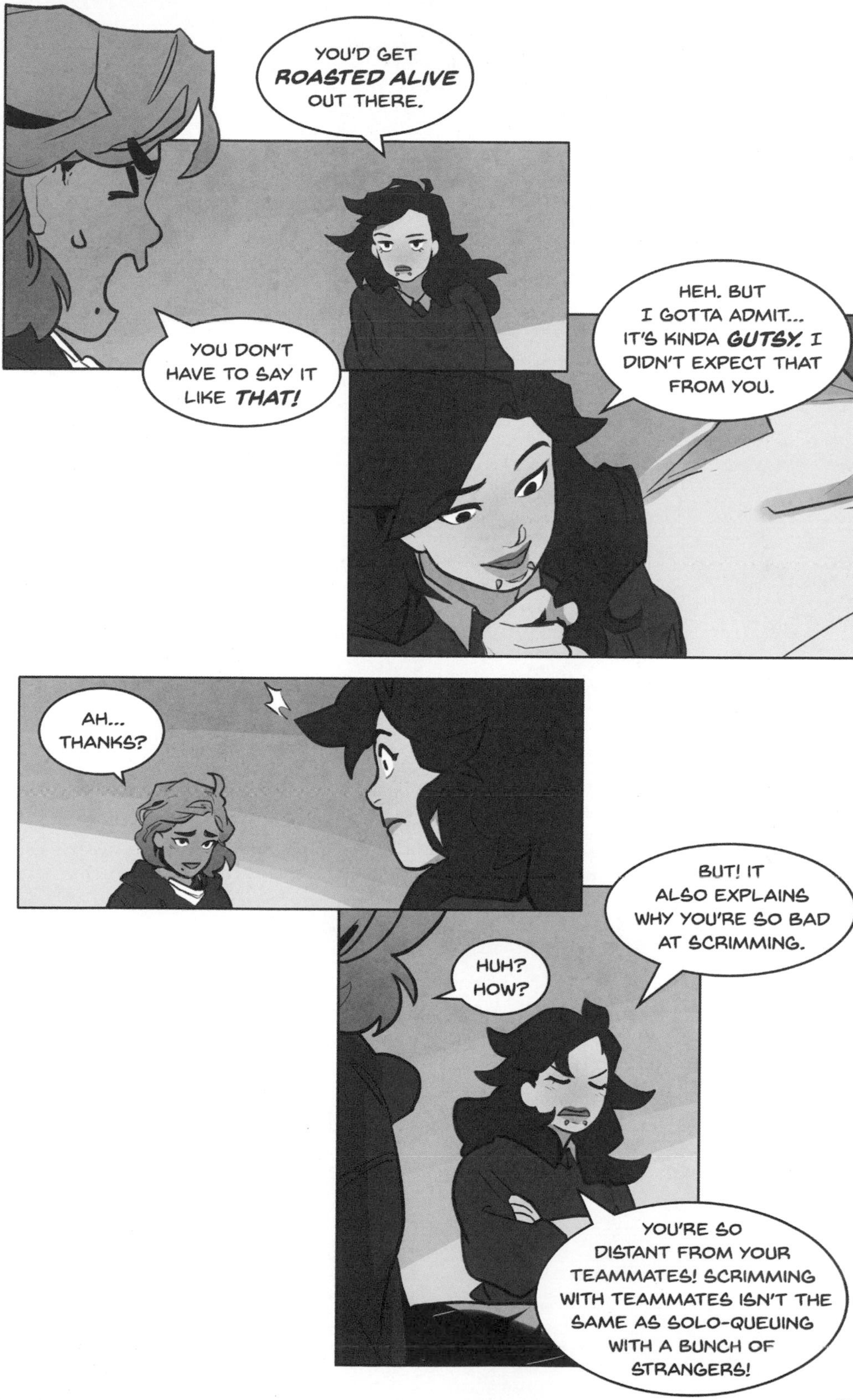
YOU'D GET ROASTED ALIVE OUT THERE.
YOU DON'T HAVE TO SAY IT LIKE THAT!
HEH. BUT I GOTTA ADMIT... IT'S KINDA GUTSY. I DIDN'T EXPECT THAT FROM YOU.
AH... THANKS?
BUT! IT ALSO EXPLAINS WHY YOU'RE SO BAD AT SCRIMMING.
HUH? HOW?
YOU'RE SO DISTANT FROM YOUR TEAMMATES! SCRIMMING WITH TEAMMATES ISN'T THE SAME AS SOLO-QUEUING WITH A BUNCH OF STRANGERS!

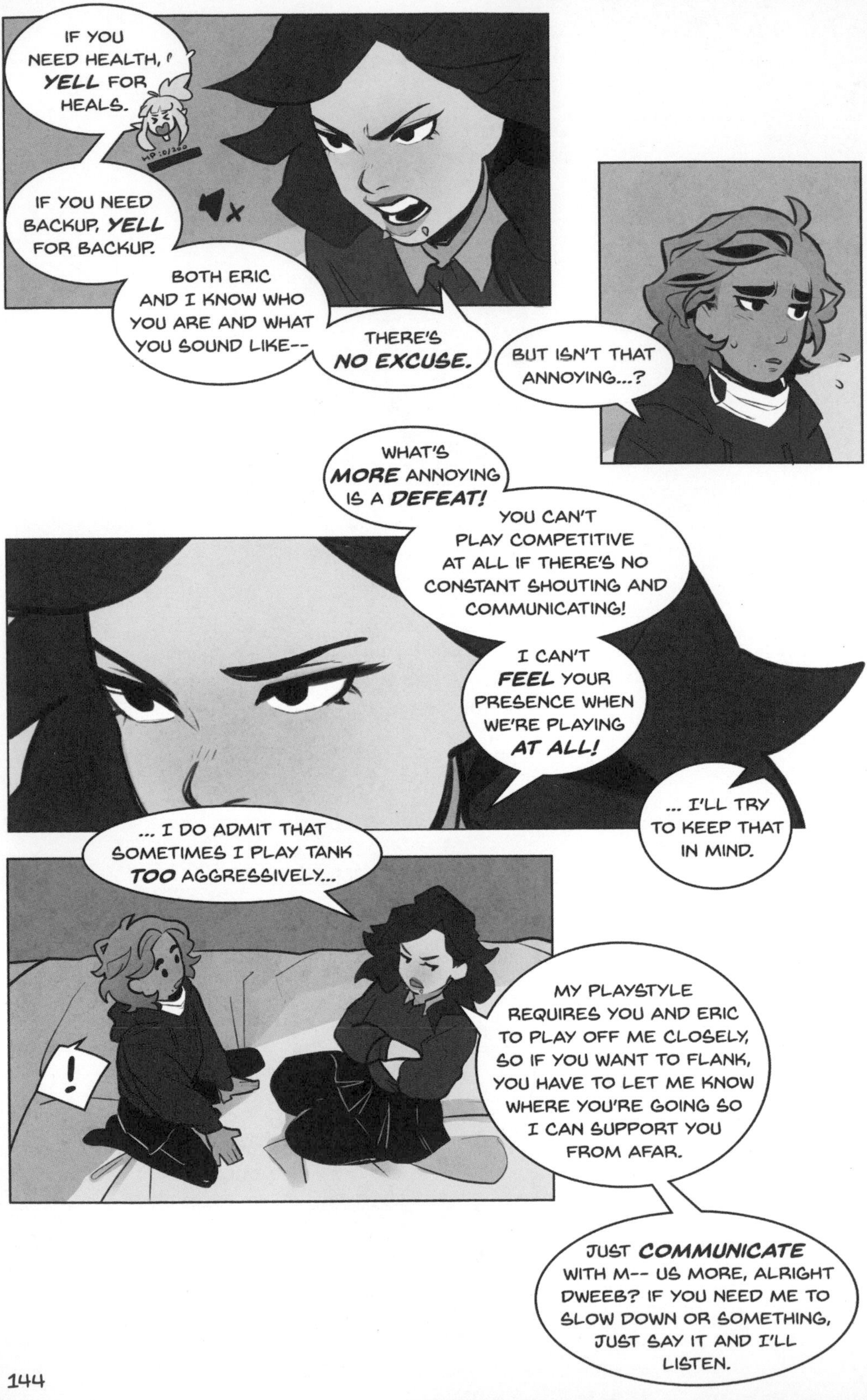
IF YOU NEED HEALTH, **YELL** FOR HEALS.
IF YOU NEED BACKUP, **YELL** FOR BACKUP.
BOTH ERIC AND I KNOW WHO YOU ARE AND WHAT YOU SOUND LIKE--
THERE'S **NO EXCUSE.**
BUT ISN'T THAT ANNOYING...?
WHAT'S **MORE** ANNOYING IS A **DEFEAT!**
YOU CAN'T PLAY COMPETITIVE AT ALL IF THERE'S NO CONSTANT SHOUTING AND COMMUNICATING!
I CAN'T **FEEL** YOUR PRESENCE WHEN WE'RE PLAYING **AT ALL!**
... I'LL TRY TO KEEP THAT IN MIND.
... I DO ADMIT THAT SOMETIMES I PLAY TANK **TOO** AGGRESSIVELY...
!
MY PLAYSTYLE REQUIRES YOU AND ERIC TO PLAY OFF ME CLOSELY, SO IF YOU WANT TO FLANK, YOU HAVE TO LET ME KNOW WHERE YOU'RE GOING SO I CAN SUPPORT YOU FROM AFAR.
JUST **COMMUNICATE** WITH M-- US MORE, ALRIGHT DWEEB? IF YOU NEED ME TO SLOW DOWN OR SOMETHING, JUST SAY IT AND I'LL LISTEN.

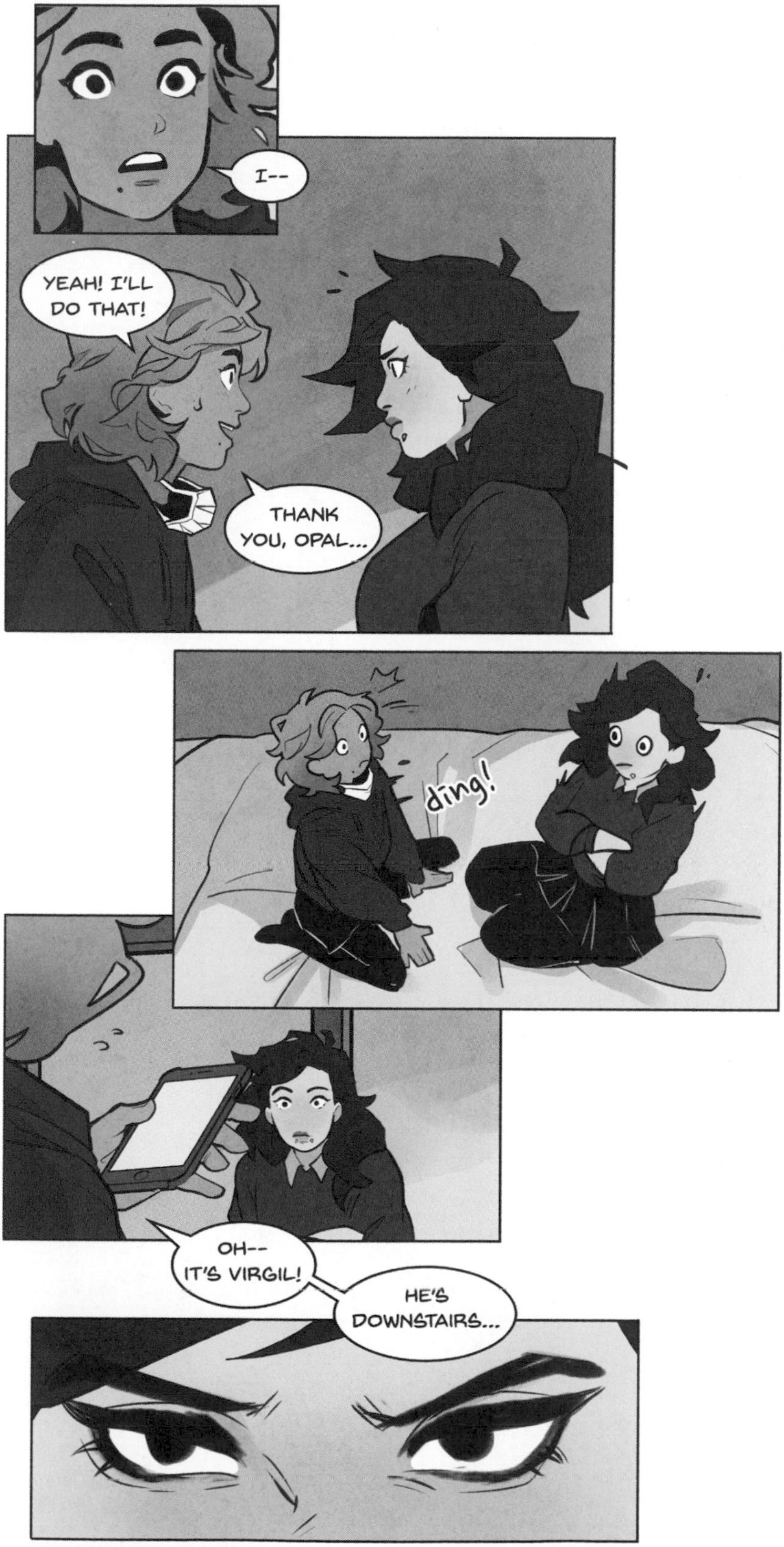
I--
YEAH! I'LL DO THAT!
THANK YOU, OPAL...
ding!
OH-- IT'S VIRGIL!
HE'S DOWNSTAIRS...

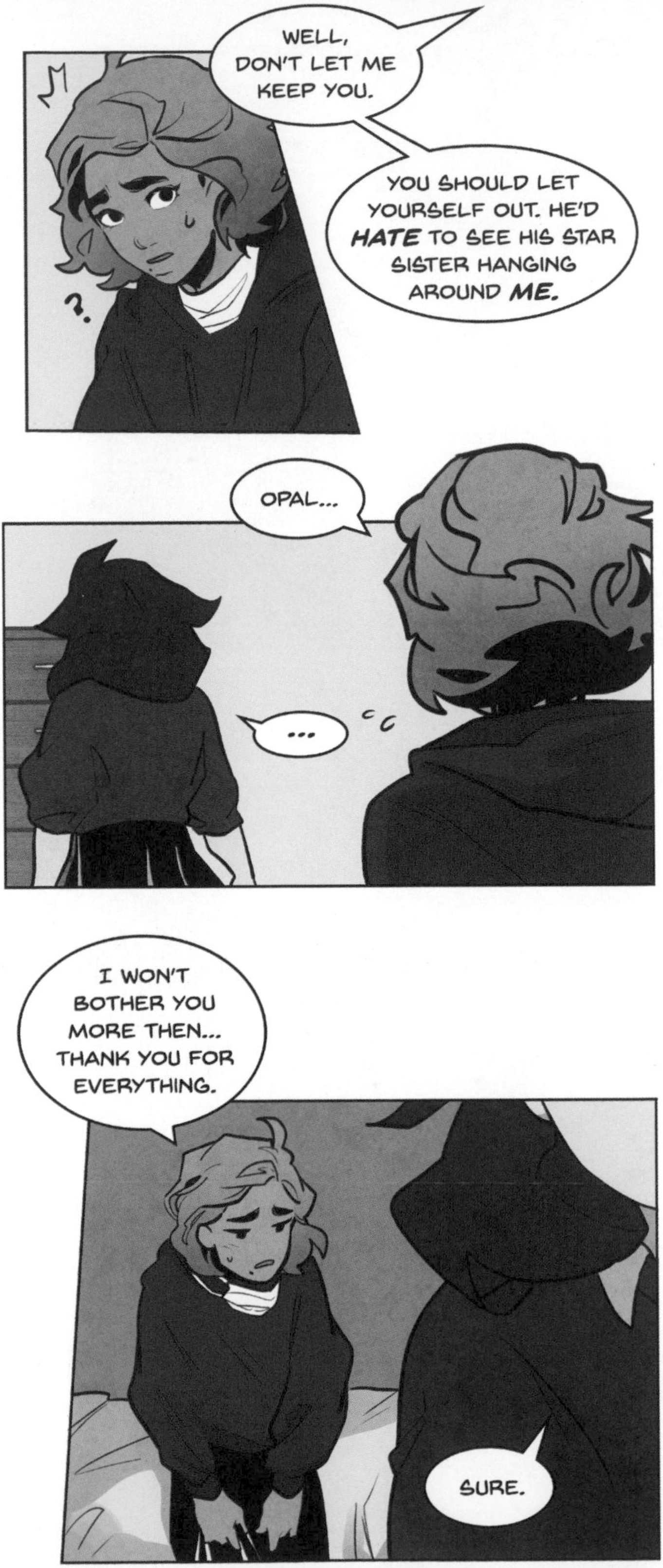
WELL, DON'T LET ME KEEP YOU.
YOU SHOULD LET YOURSELF OUT. HE'D **HATE** TO SEE HIS STAR SISTER HANGING AROUND **ME.**
?
OPAL...
...
I WON'T BOTHER YOU MORE THEN... THANK YOU FOR EVERYTHING.
SURE.

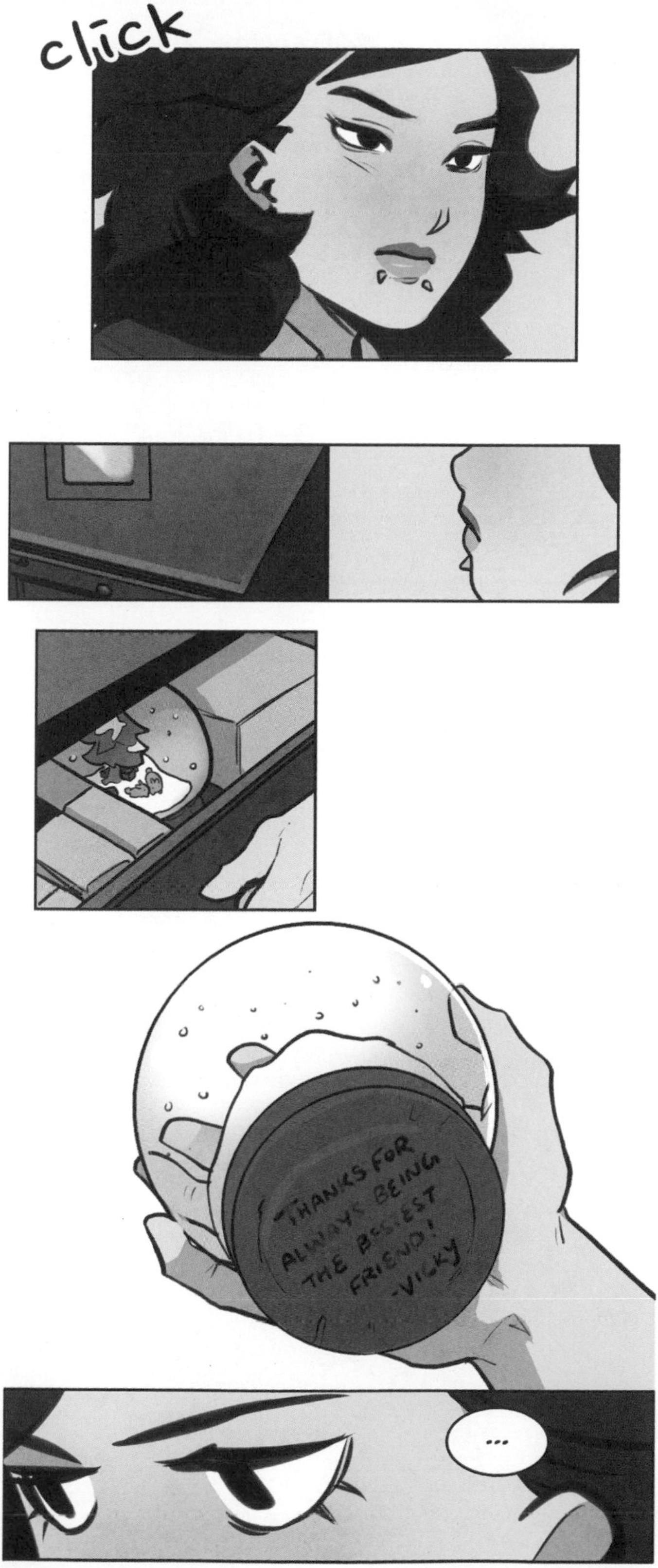
click
THANKS FOR ALWAYS BEING THE BESTEST FRIEND! -VICKY
...

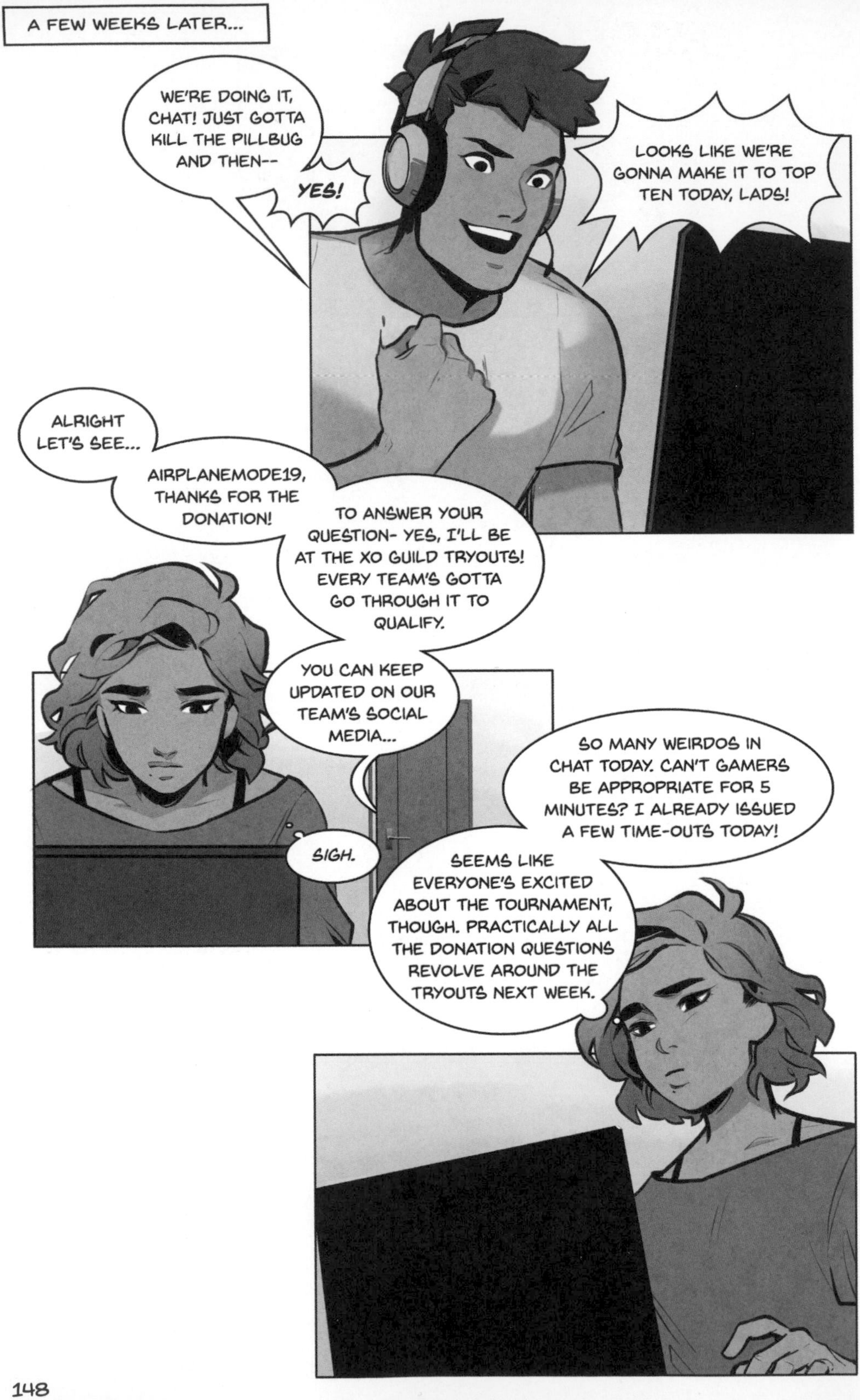
A FEW WEEKS LATER...
WE'RE DOING IT, CHAT! JUST GOTTA KILL THE PILLBUG AND THEN--
YES!
LOOKS LIKE WE'RE GONNA MAKE IT TO TOP TEN TODAY, LADS!
ALRIGHT LET'S SEE...
AIRPLANEMODE19, THANKS FOR THE DONATION!
TO ANSWER YOUR QUESTION- YES, I'LL BE AT THE XO GUILD TRYOUTS! EVERY TEAM'S GOTTA GO THROUGH IT TO QUALIFY.
YOU CAN KEEP UPDATED ON OUR TEAM'S SOCIAL MEDIA...
SIGH.
SO MANY WEIRDOS IN CHAT TODAY. CAN'T GAMERS BE APPROPRIATE FOR 5 MINUTES? I ALREADY ISSUED A FEW TIME-OUTS TODAY!
SEEMS LIKE EVERYONE'S EXCITED ABOUT THE TOURNAMENT, THOUGH. PRACTICALLY ALL THE DONATION QUESTIONS REVOLVE AROUND THE TRYOUTS NEXT WEEK.

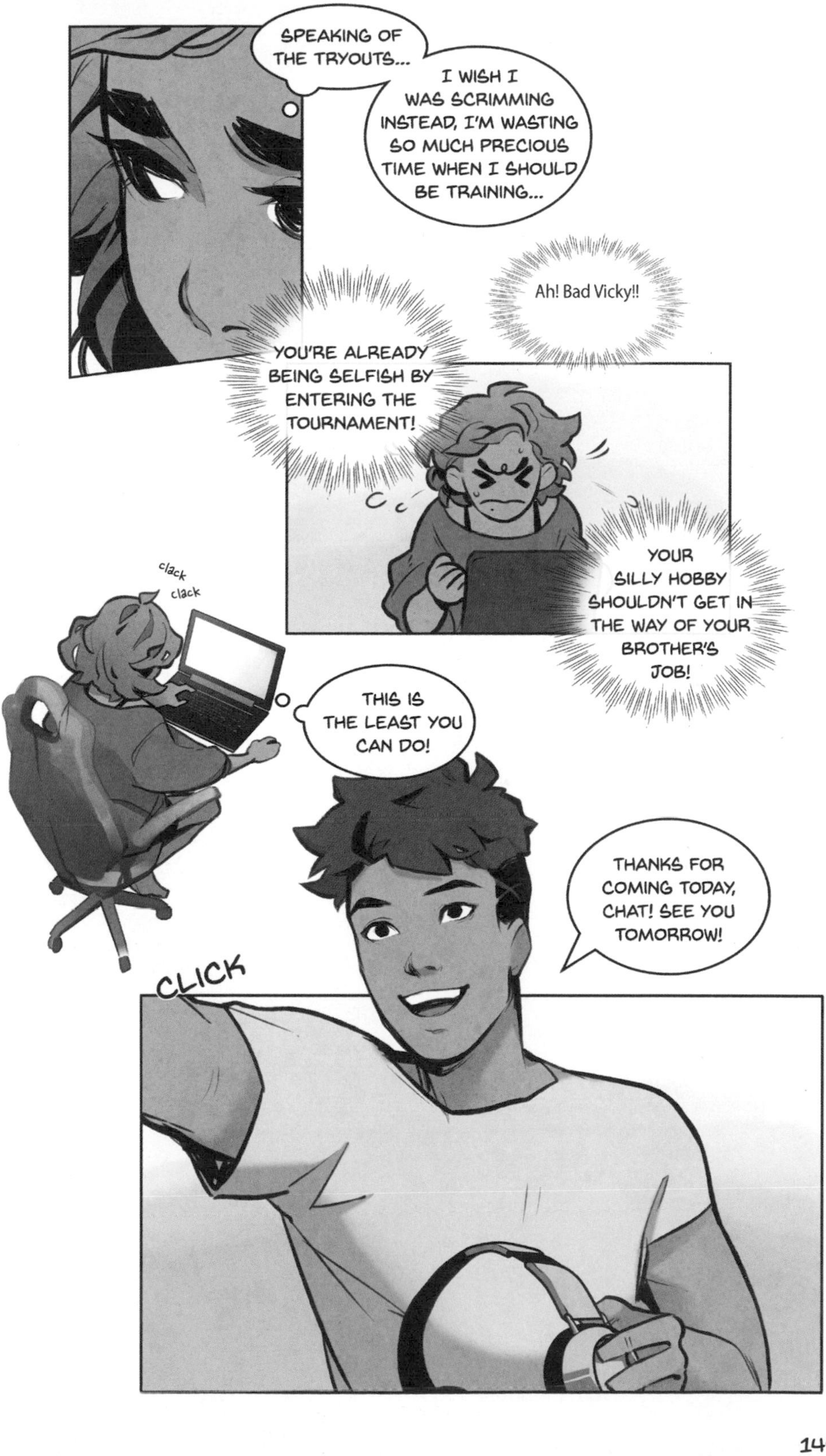
SPEAKING OF THE TRYOUTS...
I WISH I WAS SCRIMMING INSTEAD, I'M WASTING SO MUCH PRECIOUS TIME WHEN I SHOULD BE TRAINING...
Ah! Bad Vicky!!
YOU'RE ALREADY BEING SELFISH BY ENTERING THE TOURNAMENT!
YOUR SILLY HOBBY SHOULDN'T GET IN THE WAY OF YOUR BROTHER'S JOB!
clack
clack
THIS IS THE LEAST YOU CAN DO!
THANKS FOR COMING TODAY, CHAT! SEE YOU TOMORROW!
CLICK

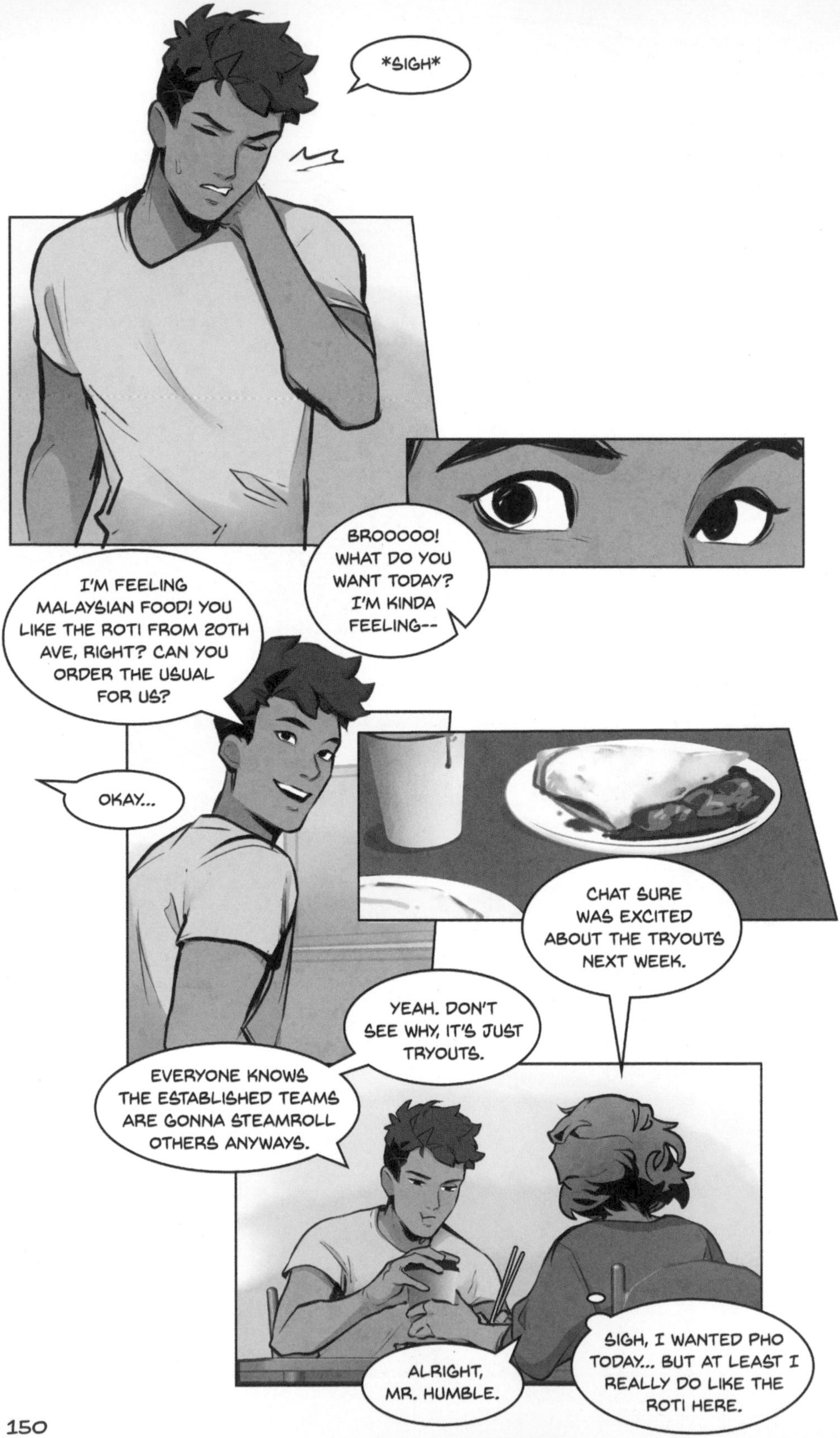
SIGH
BROOOOO! WHAT DO YOU WANT TODAY? I'M KINDA FEELING--
I'M FEELING MALAYSIAN FOOD! YOU LIKE THE ROTI FROM 20TH AVE, RIGHT? CAN YOU ORDER THE USUAL FOR US?
OKAY...
CHAT SURE WAS EXCITED ABOUT THE TRYOUTS NEXT WEEK.
YEAH. DON'T SEE WHY, IT'S JUST TRYOUTS.
EVERYONE KNOWS THE ESTABLISHED TEAMS ARE GONNA STEAMROLL OTHERS ANYWAYS.
ALRIGHT, MR. HUMBLE.
SIGH, I WANTED PHO TODAY... BUT AT LEAST I REALLY DO LIKE THE ROTI HERE.

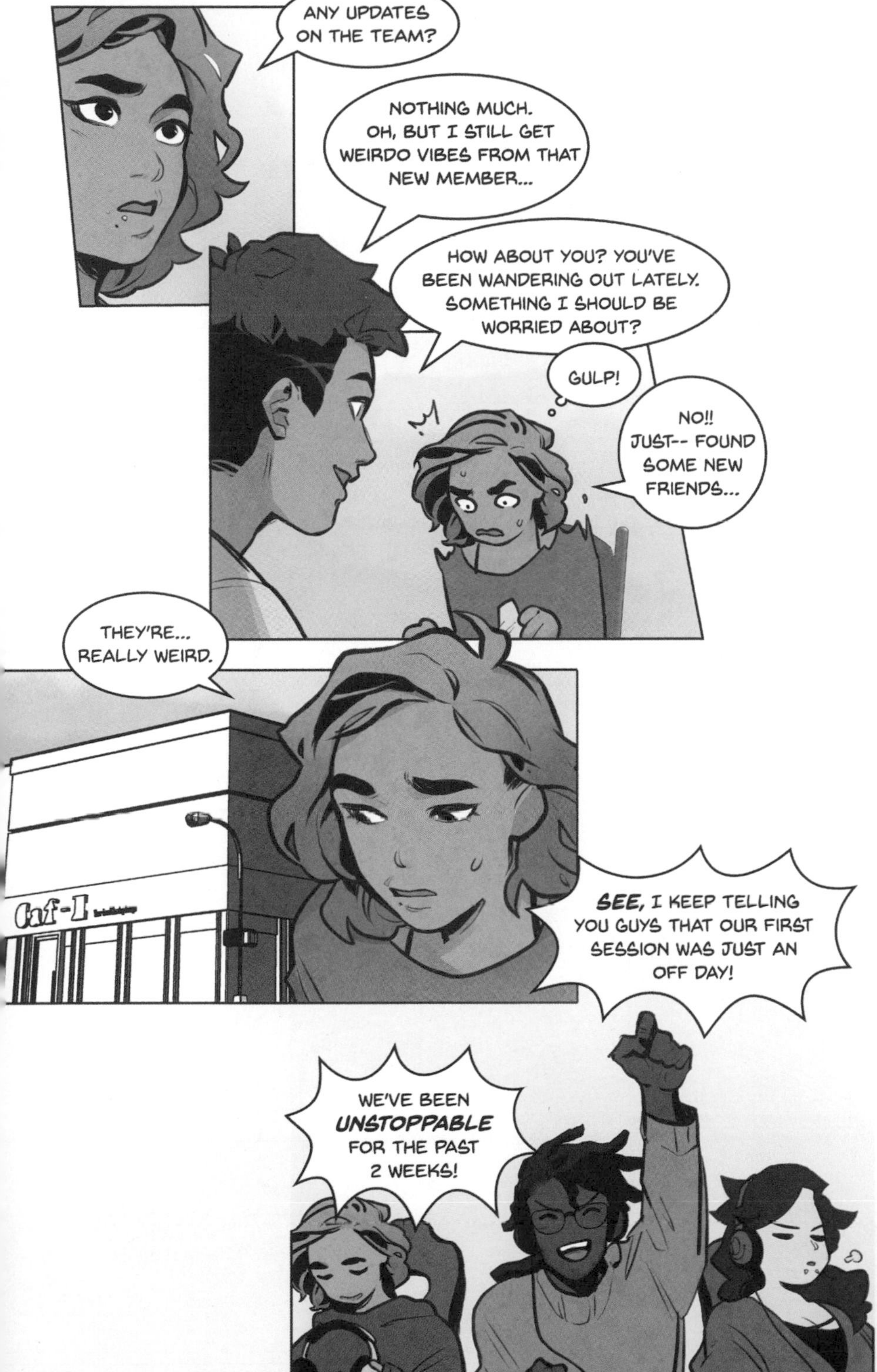
ANY UPDATES ON THE TEAM?
NOTHING MUCH. OH, BUT I STILL GET WEIRDO VIBES FROM THAT NEW MEMBER...
HOW ABOUT YOU? YOU'VE BEEN WANDERING OUT LATELY. SOMETHING I SHOULD BE WORRIED ABOUT?
GULP!
NO!! JUST-- FOUND SOME NEW FRIENDS...
THEY'RE... REALLY WEIRD.
Caf-I
SEE, I KEEP TELLING YOU GUYS THAT OUR FIRST SESSION WAS JUST AN OFF DAY!
WE'VE BEEN UNSTOPPABLE FOR THE PAST 2 WEEKS!

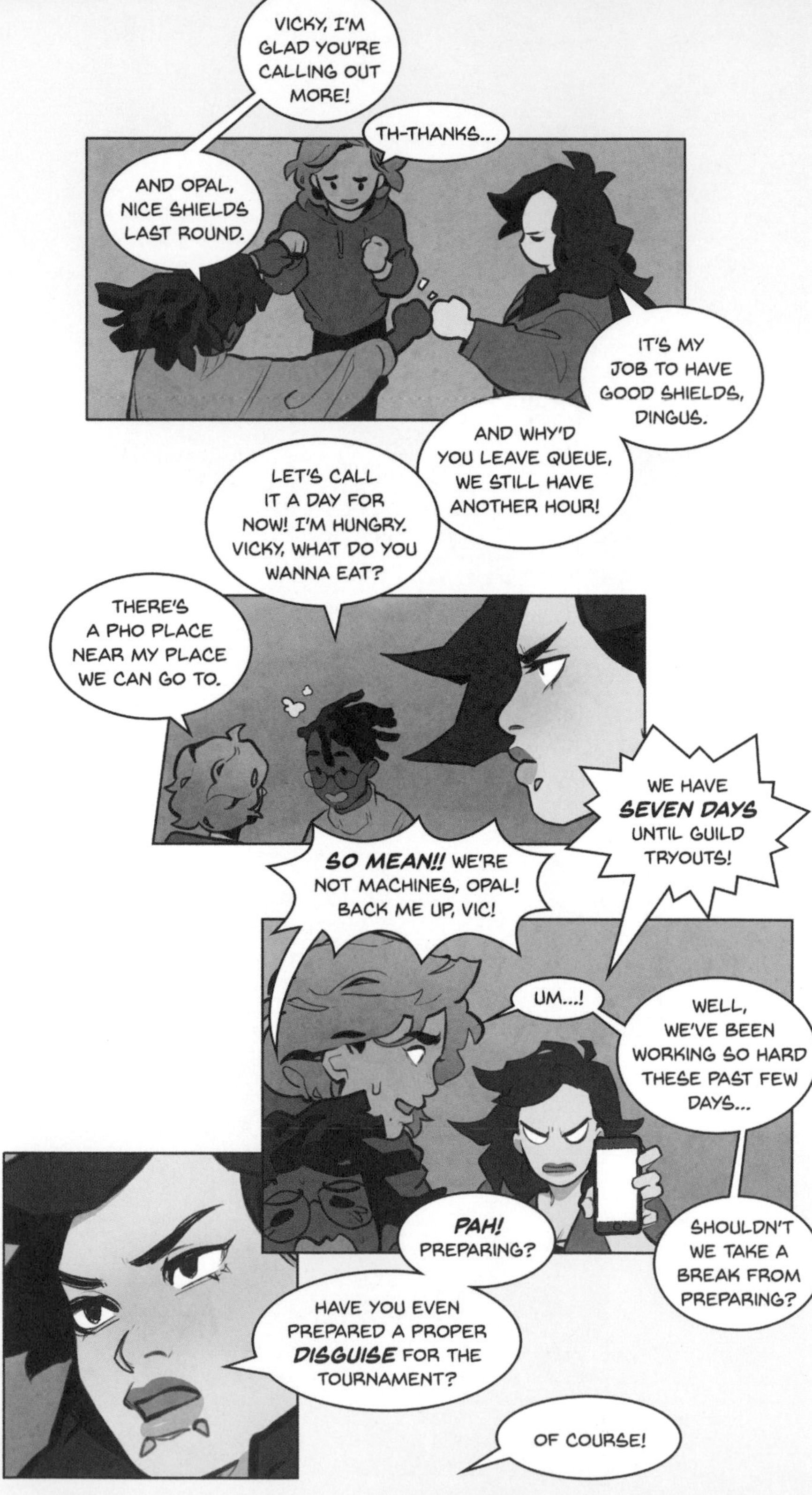

VICKY, I'M GLAD YOU'RE CALLING OUT MORE!
TH-THANKS...
AND OPAL, NICE SHIELDS LAST ROUND.
IT'S MY JOB TO HAVE GOOD SHIELDS, DINGUS.
AND WHY'D YOU LEAVE QUEUE, WE STILL HAVE ANOTHER HOUR!
LET'S CALL IT A DAY FOR NOW! I'M HUNGRY. VICKY, WHAT DO YOU WANNA EAT?
THERE'S A PHO PLACE NEAR MY PLACE WE CAN GO TO.
WE HAVE **SEVEN DAYS** UNTIL GUILD TRYOUTS!
SO MEAN!! WE'RE NOT MACHINES, OPAL! BACK ME UP, VIC!
UM...!
WELL, WE'VE BEEN WORKING SO HARD THESE PAST FEW DAYS...
SHOULDN'T WE TAKE A BREAK FROM PREPARING?
PAH! PREPARING?
HAVE YOU EVEN PREPARED A PROPER **DISGUISE** FOR THE TOURNAMENT?
OF COURSE!

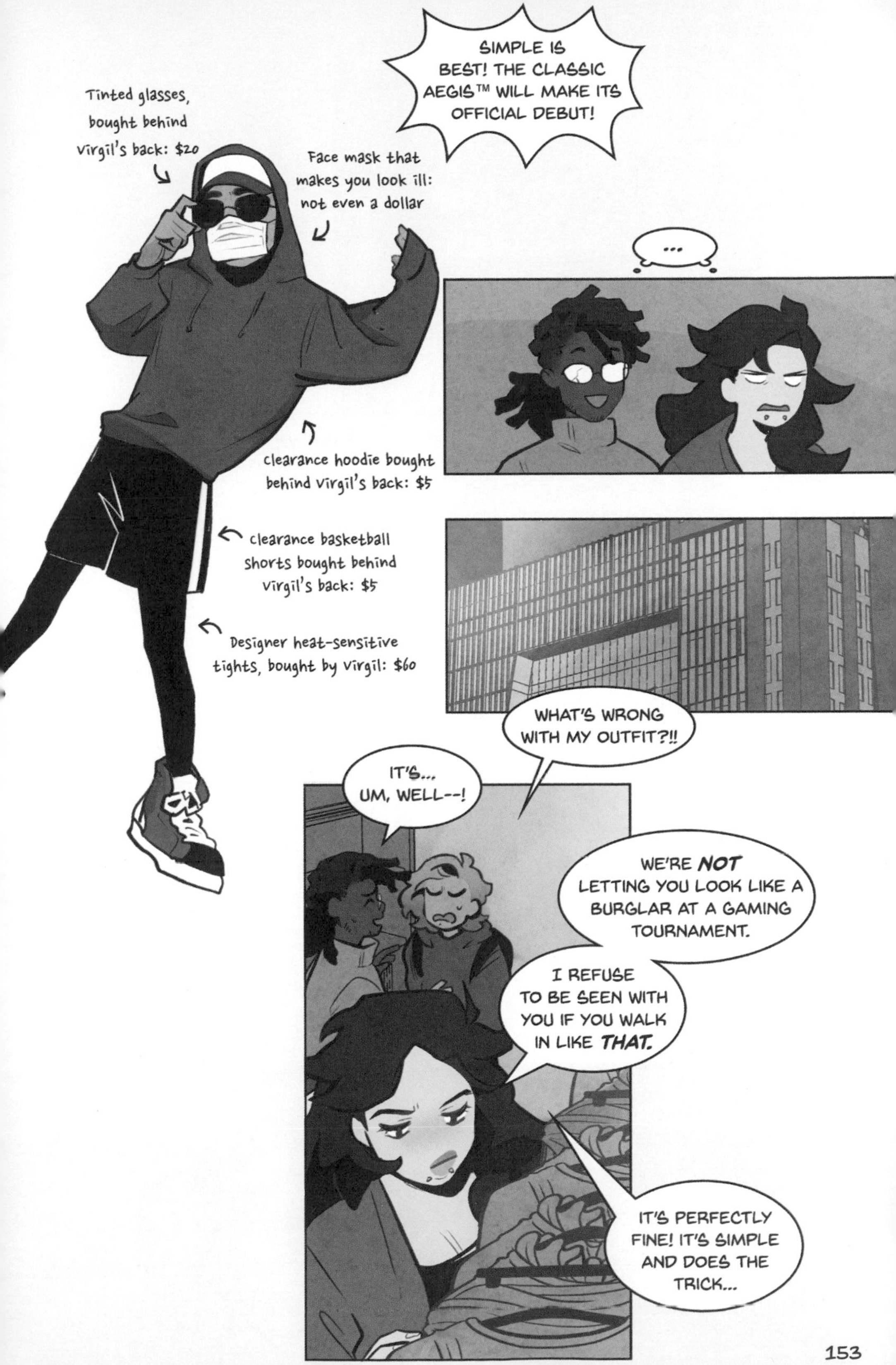
SIMPLE IS BEST! THE CLASSIC AEGIS™ WILL MAKE ITS OFFICIAL DEBUT!
Tinted glasses, bought behind Virgil's back: $20
Face mask that makes you look ill: not even a dollar
clearance hoodie bought behind Virgil's back: $5
clearance basketball shorts bought behind Virgil's back: $5
Designer heat-sensitive tights, bought by Virgil: $60
...
WHAT'S WRONG WITH MY OUTFIT?!!
IT'S... UM, WELL--!
WE'RE NOT LETTING YOU LOOK LIKE A BURGLAR AT A GAMING TOURNAMENT.
I REFUSE TO BE SEEN WITH YOU IF YOU WALK IN LIKE THAT.
IT'S PERFECTLY FINE! IT'S SIMPLE AND DOES THE TRICK...

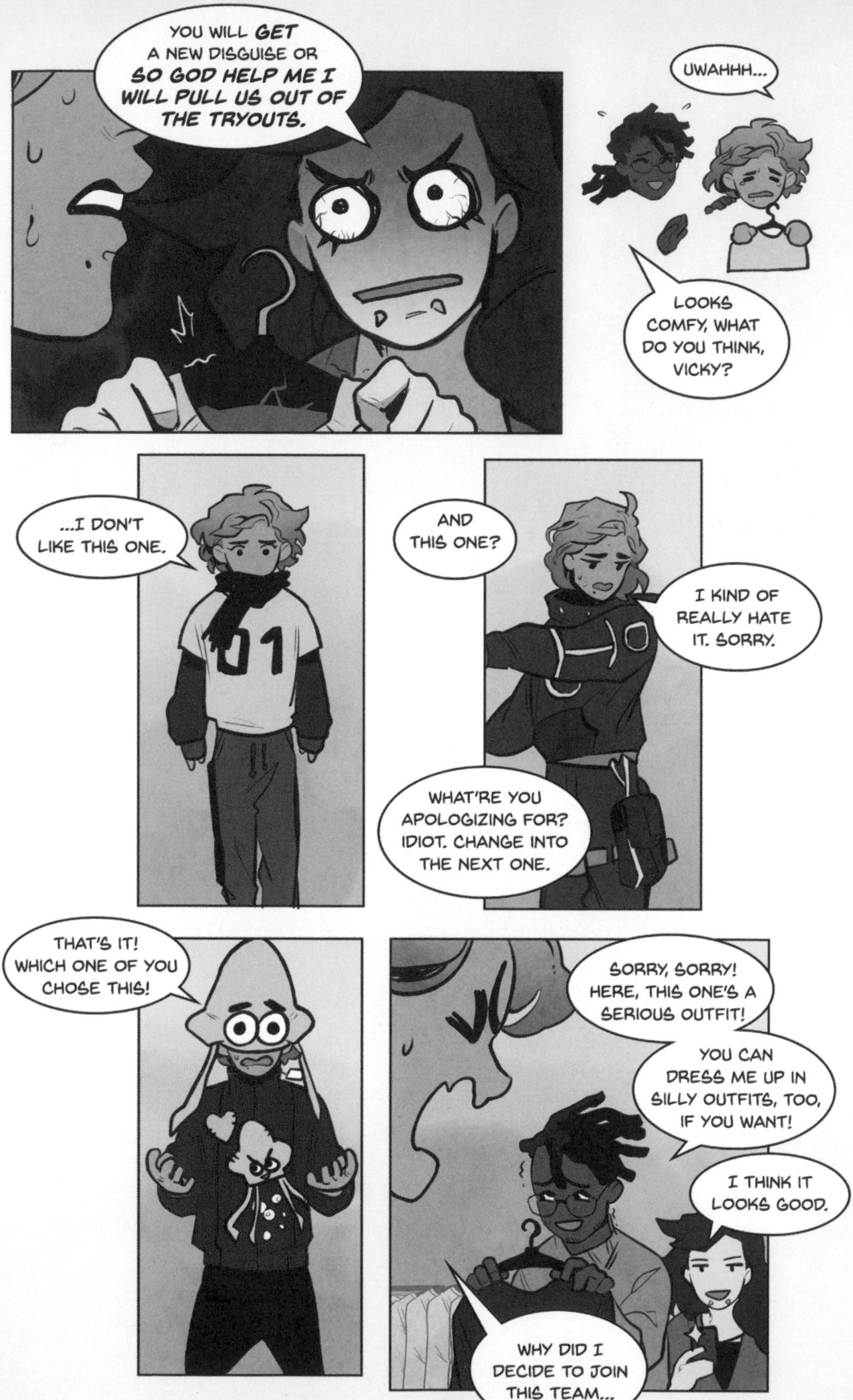
YOU WILL **GET** A NEW DISGUISE OR **SO GOD HELP ME I WILL PULL US OUT OF THE TRYOUTS.**
UWAHHH...
LOOKS COMFY, WHAT DO YOU THINK, VICKY?
...I DON'T LIKE THIS ONE.
AND THIS ONE?
I KIND OF REALLY HATE IT. SORRY.
WHAT'RE YOU APOLOGIZING FOR? IDIOT. CHANGE INTO THE NEXT ONE.
THAT'S IT! WHICH ONE OF YOU CHOSE THIS!
SORRY, SORRY! HERE, THIS ONE'S A SERIOUS OUTFIT!
YOU CAN DRESS ME UP IN SILLY OUTFITS, TOO, IF YOU WANT!
I THINK IT LOOKS GOOD.
WHY DID I DECIDE TO JOIN THIS TEAM...

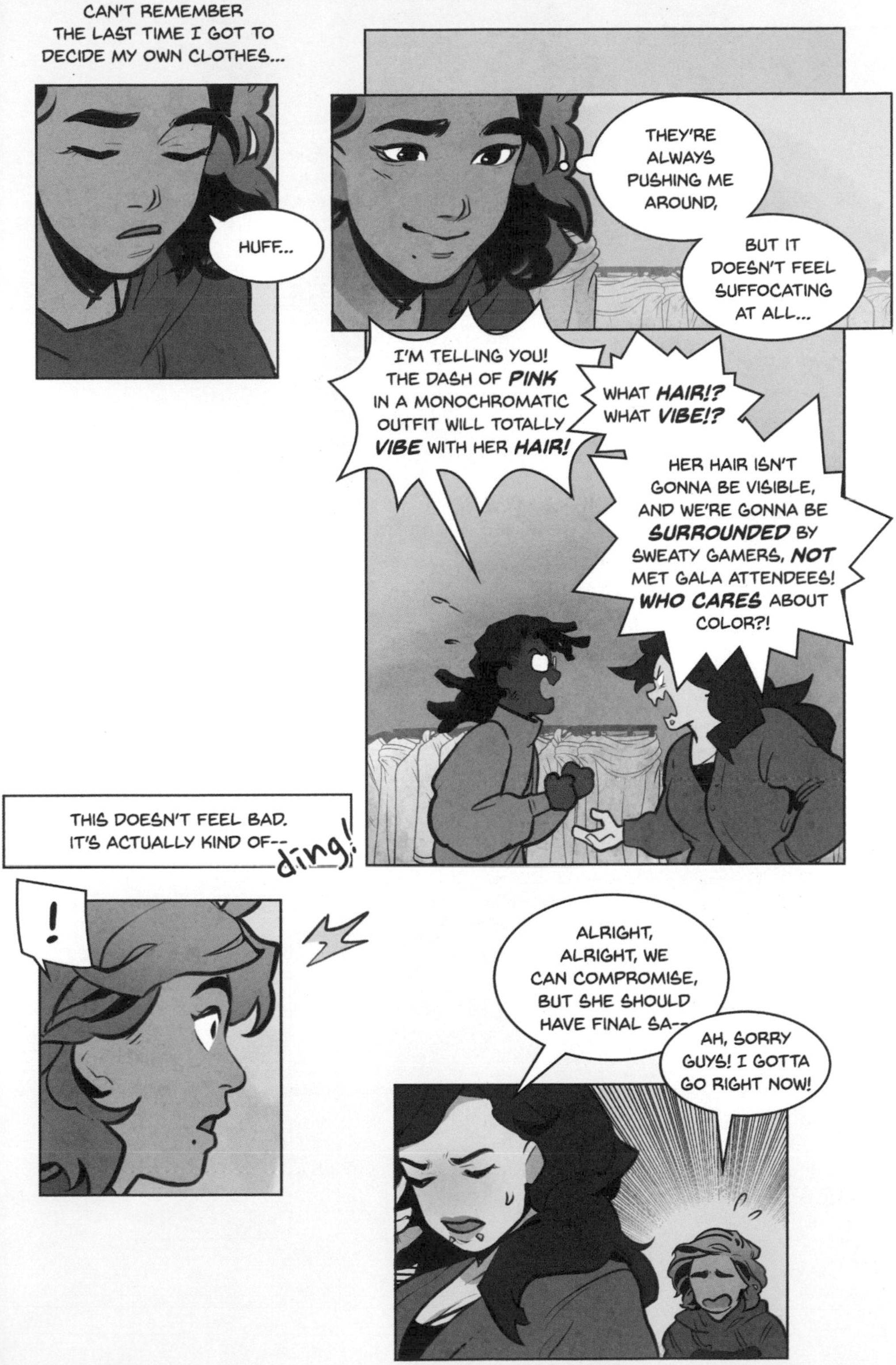
CAN'T REMEMBER THE LAST TIME I GOT TO DECIDE MY OWN CLOTHES...
HUFF...
THEY'RE ALWAYS PUSHING ME AROUND,
BUT IT DOESN'T FEEL SUFFOCATING AT ALL...
I'M TELLING YOU! THE DASH OF PINK IN A MONOCHROMATIC OUTFIT WILL TOTALLY VIBE WITH HER HAIR!
WHAT HAIR!? WHAT VIBE!?
HER HAIR ISN'T GONNA BE VISIBLE, AND WE'RE GONNA BE SURROUNDED BY SWEATY GAMERS, NOT MET GALA ATTENDEES! WHO CARES ABOUT COLOR?!
THIS DOESN'T FEEL BAD. IT'S ACTUALLY KIND OF--
ding!
!
ALRIGHT, ALRIGHT, WE CAN COMPROMISE, BUT SHE SHOULD HAVE FINAL SA--
AH, SORRY GUYS! I GOTTA GO RIGHT NOW!

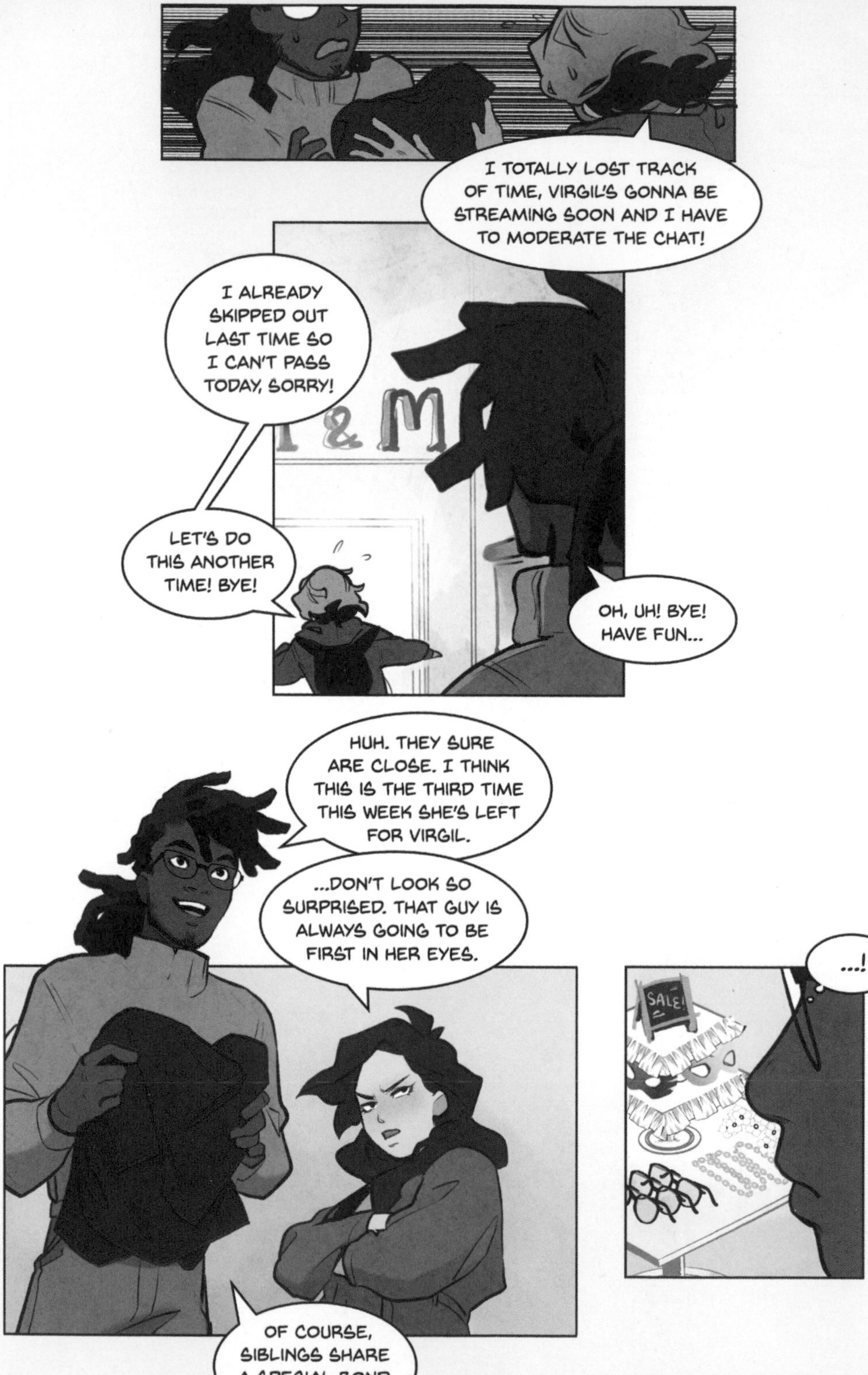
I TOTALLY LOST TRACK OF TIME, VIRGIL'S GONNA BE STREAMING SOON AND I HAVE TO MODERATE THE CHAT!
I ALREADY SKIPPED OUT LAST TIME SO I CAN'T PASS TODAY, SORRY!
LET'S DO THIS ANOTHER TIME! BYE!
OH, UH! BYE! HAVE FUN...
HUH. THEY SURE ARE CLOSE. I THINK THIS IS THE THIRD TIME THIS WEEK SHE'S LEFT FOR VIRGIL.
...DON'T LOOK SO SURPRISED. THAT GUY IS ALWAYS GOING TO BE FIRST IN HER EYES.
OF COURSE, SIBLINGS SHARE A SPECIAL BOND, YOU KNOW!
SALE!
...!

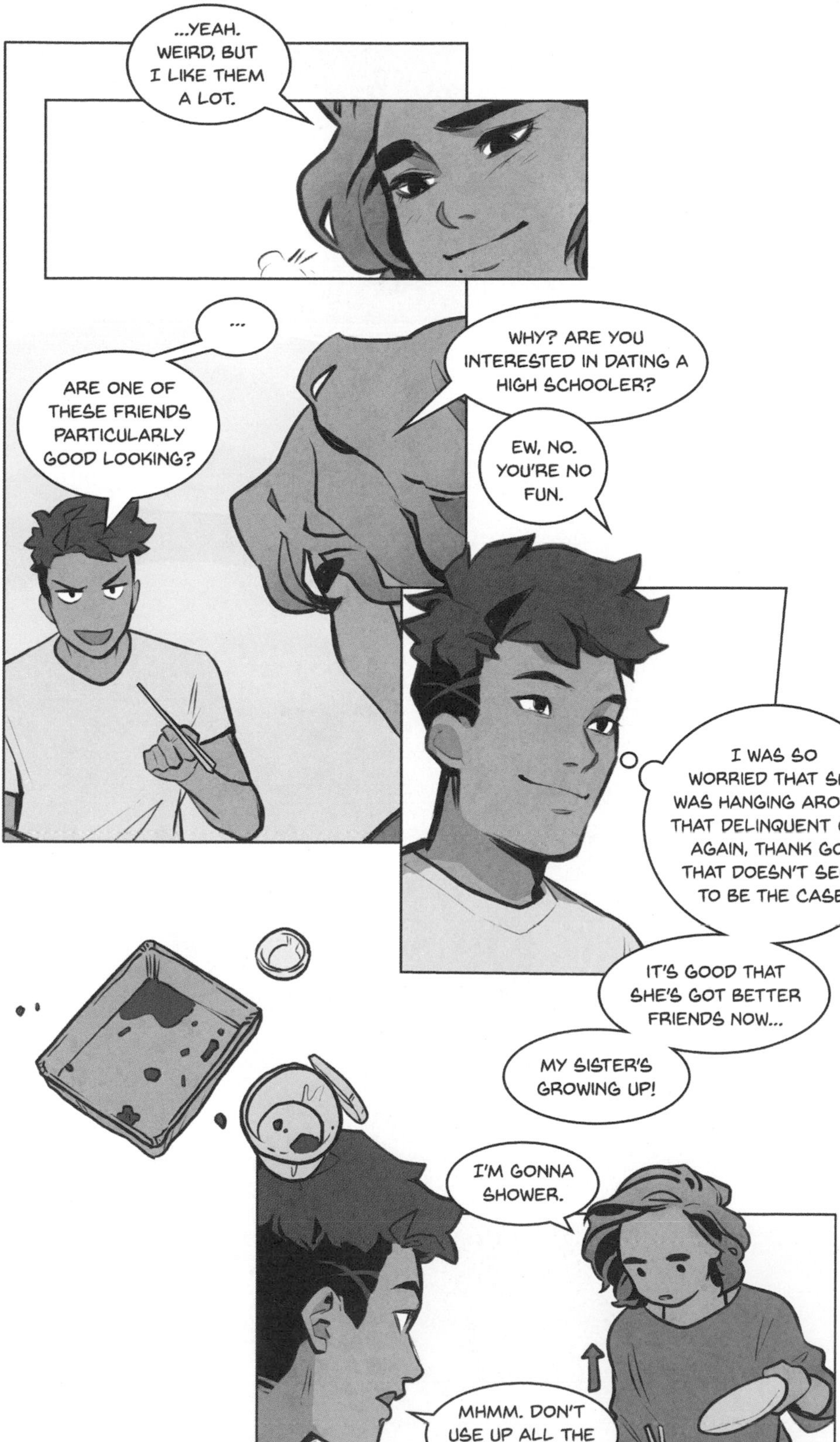
...YEAH. WEIRD, BUT I LIKE THEM A LOT.
...
ARE ONE OF THESE FRIENDS PARTICULARLY GOOD LOOKING?
WHY? ARE YOU INTERESTED IN DATING A HIGH SCHOOLER?
EW, NO. YOU'RE NO FUN.
I WAS SO WORRIED THAT SHE WAS HANGING AROUND THAT DELINQUENT GIRL AGAIN, THANK GOD THAT DOESN'T SEEM TO BE THE CASE.
IT'S GOOD THAT SHE'S GOT BETTER FRIENDS NOW...
MY SISTER'S GROWING UP!
I'M GONNA SHOWER.
MHMM. DON'T USE UP ALL THE HOT WATER.

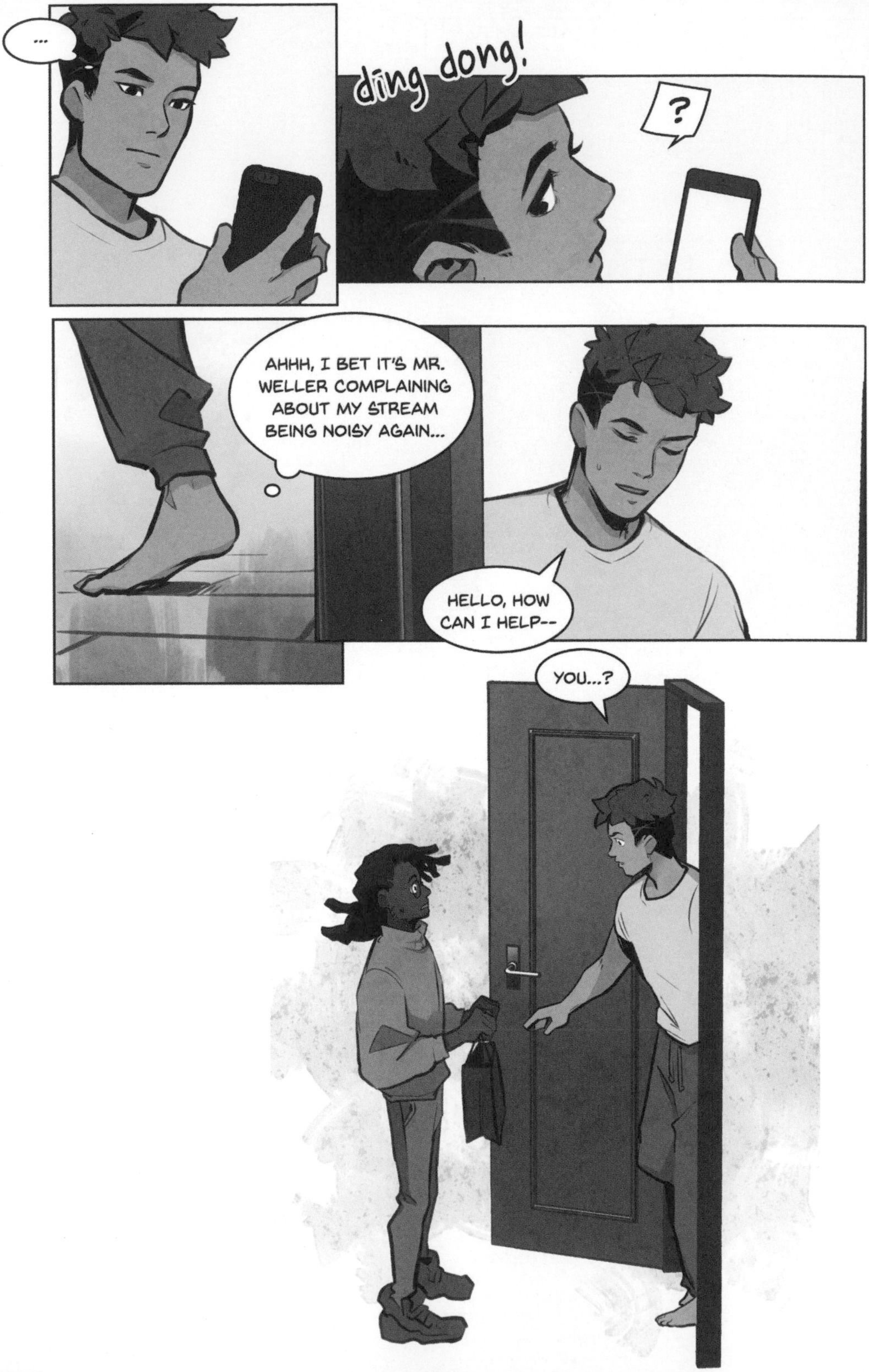
...
ding dong!
?
AHHH, I BET IT'S MR. WELLER COMPLAINING ABOUT MY STREAM BEING NOISY AGAIN...
HELLO, HOW CAN I HELP--
YOU...?

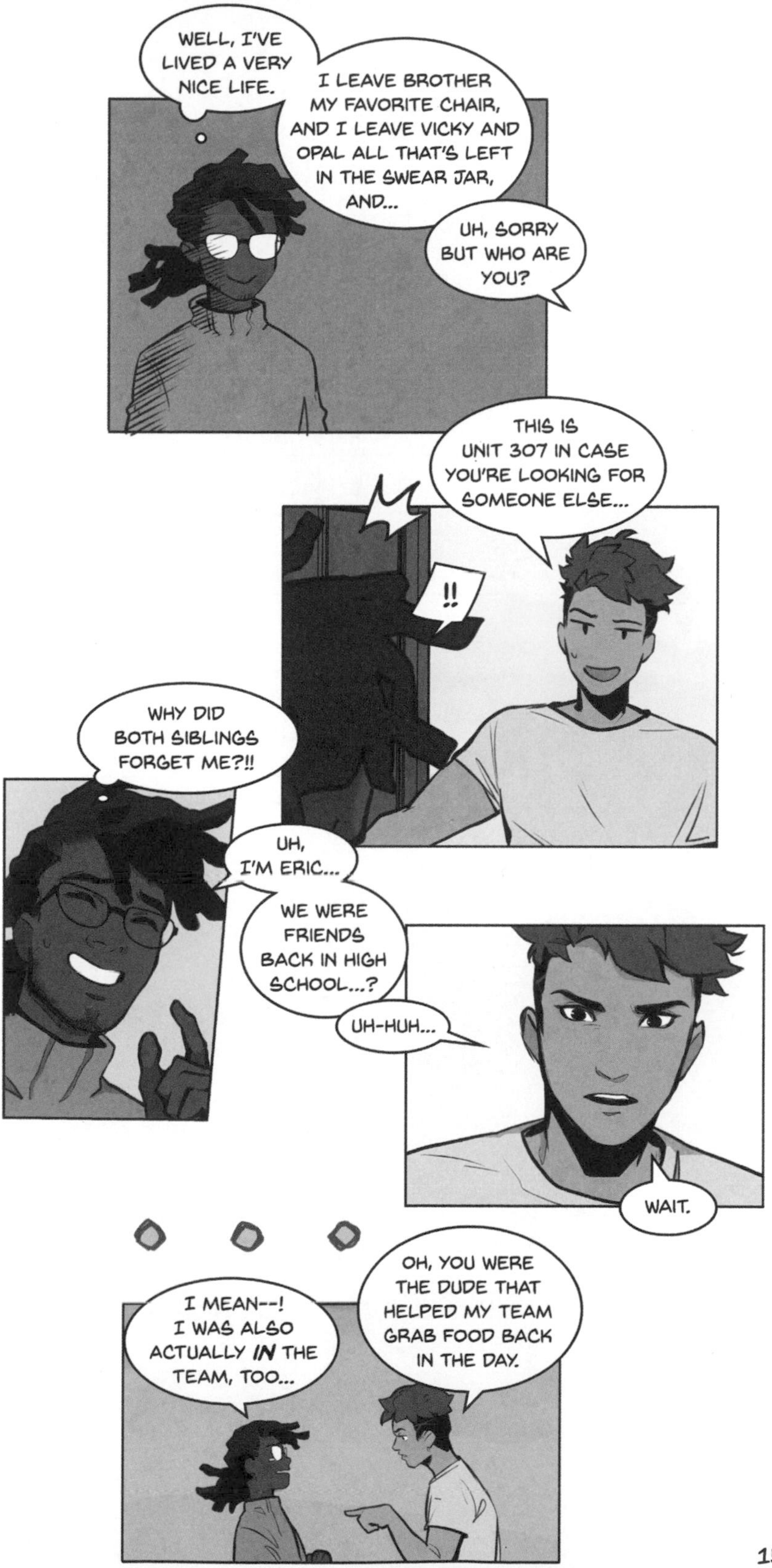

WELL, I'VE LIVED A VERY NICE LIFE.
I LEAVE BROTHER MY FAVORITE CHAIR, AND I LEAVE VICKY AND OPAL ALL THAT'S LEFT IN THE SWEAR JAR, AND...
UH, SORRY BUT WHO ARE YOU?
THIS IS UNIT 307 IN CASE YOU'RE LOOKING FOR SOMEONE ELSE...
!!
WHY DID BOTH SIBLINGS FORGET ME?!!
UH, I'M ERIC...
WE WERE FRIENDS BACK IN HIGH SCHOOL...?
UH-HUH...
WAIT.
I MEAN--! I WAS ALSO ACTUALLY *IN* THE TEAM, TOO...
OH, YOU WERE THE DUDE THAT HELPED MY TEAM GRAB FOOD BACK IN THE DAY.

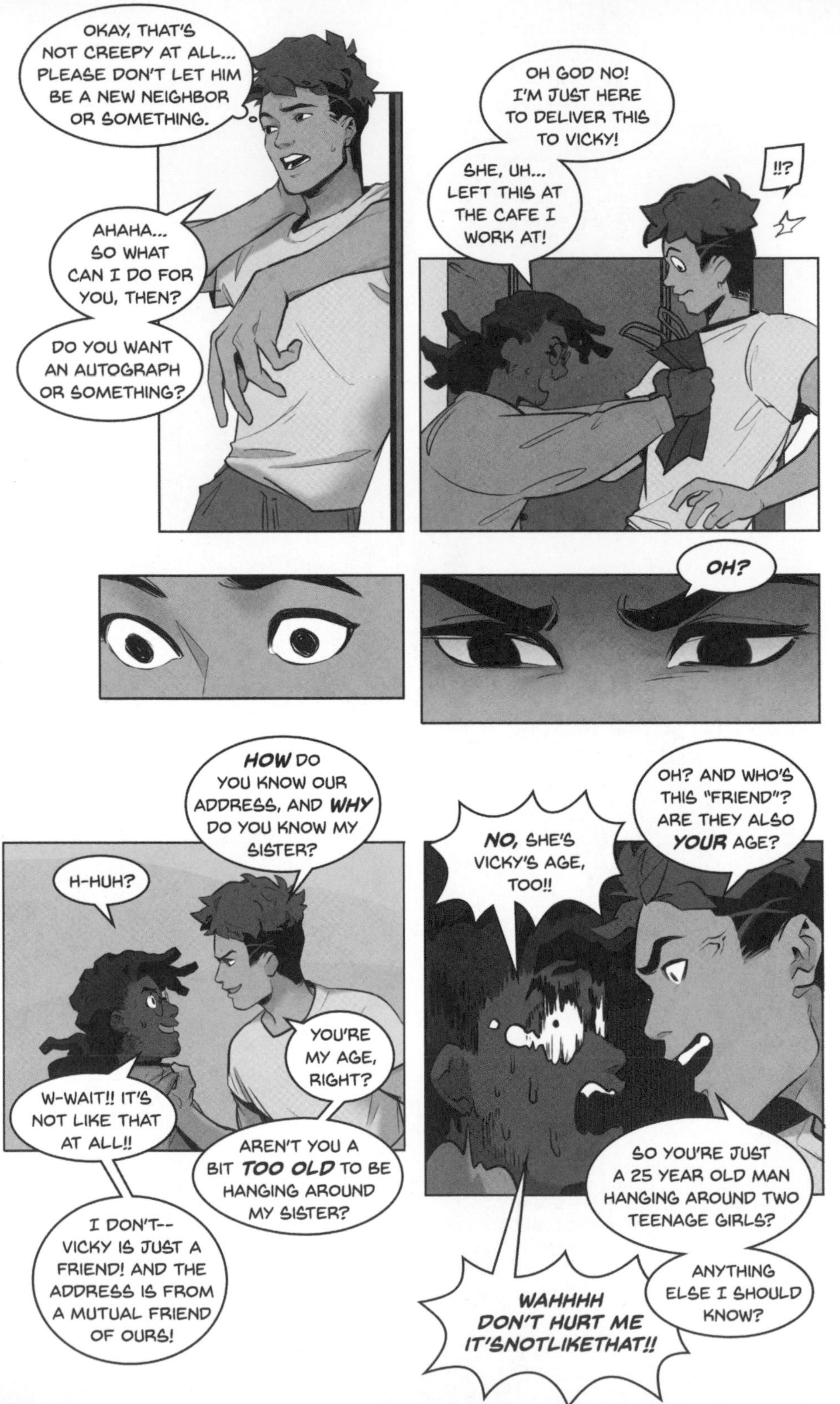
OKAY, THAT'S NOT CREEPY AT ALL... PLEASE DON'T LET HIM BE A NEW NEIGHBOR OR SOMETHING.
AHAHA... SO WHAT CAN I DO FOR YOU, THEN?
DO YOU WANT AN AUTOGRAPH OR SOMETHING?
OH GOD NO! I'M JUST HERE TO DELIVER THIS TO VICKY!
SHE, UH... LEFT THIS AT THE CAFE I WORK AT!
!!?
OH?
H-HUH?
HOW DO YOU KNOW OUR ADDRESS, AND WHY DO YOU KNOW MY SISTER?
YOU'RE MY AGE, RIGHT?
W-WAIT!! IT'S NOT LIKE THAT AT ALL!!
AREN'T YOU A BIT TOO OLD TO BE HANGING AROUND MY SISTER?
I DON'T-- VICKY IS JUST A FRIEND! AND THE ADDRESS IS FROM A MUTUAL FRIEND OF OURS!
OH? AND WHO'S THIS "FRIEND"? ARE THEY ALSO YOUR AGE?
NO, SHE'S VICKY'S AGE, TOO!!
SO YOU'RE JUST A 25 YEAR OLD MAN HANGING AROUND TWO TEENAGE GIRLS?
ANYTHING ELSE I SHOULD KNOW?
WAHHHH DON'T HURT ME IT'SNOTLIKETHAT!!

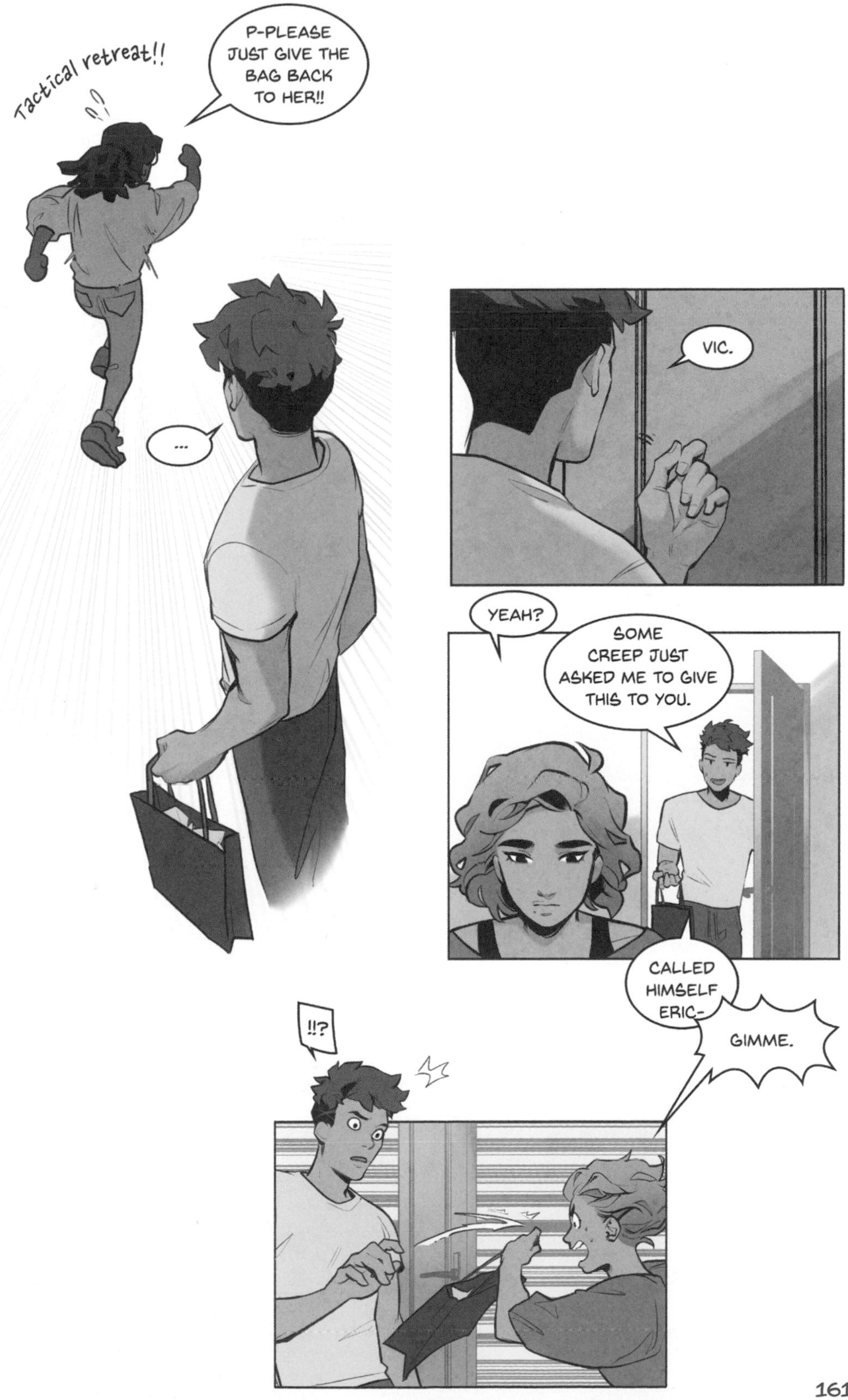
Tactical retreat!!
P-PLEASE JUST GIVE THE BAG BACK TO HER!!
...
VIC.
YEAH?
SOME CREEP JUST ASKED ME TO GIVE THIS TO YOU.
CALLED HIMSELF ERIC-
GIMME.
!!?

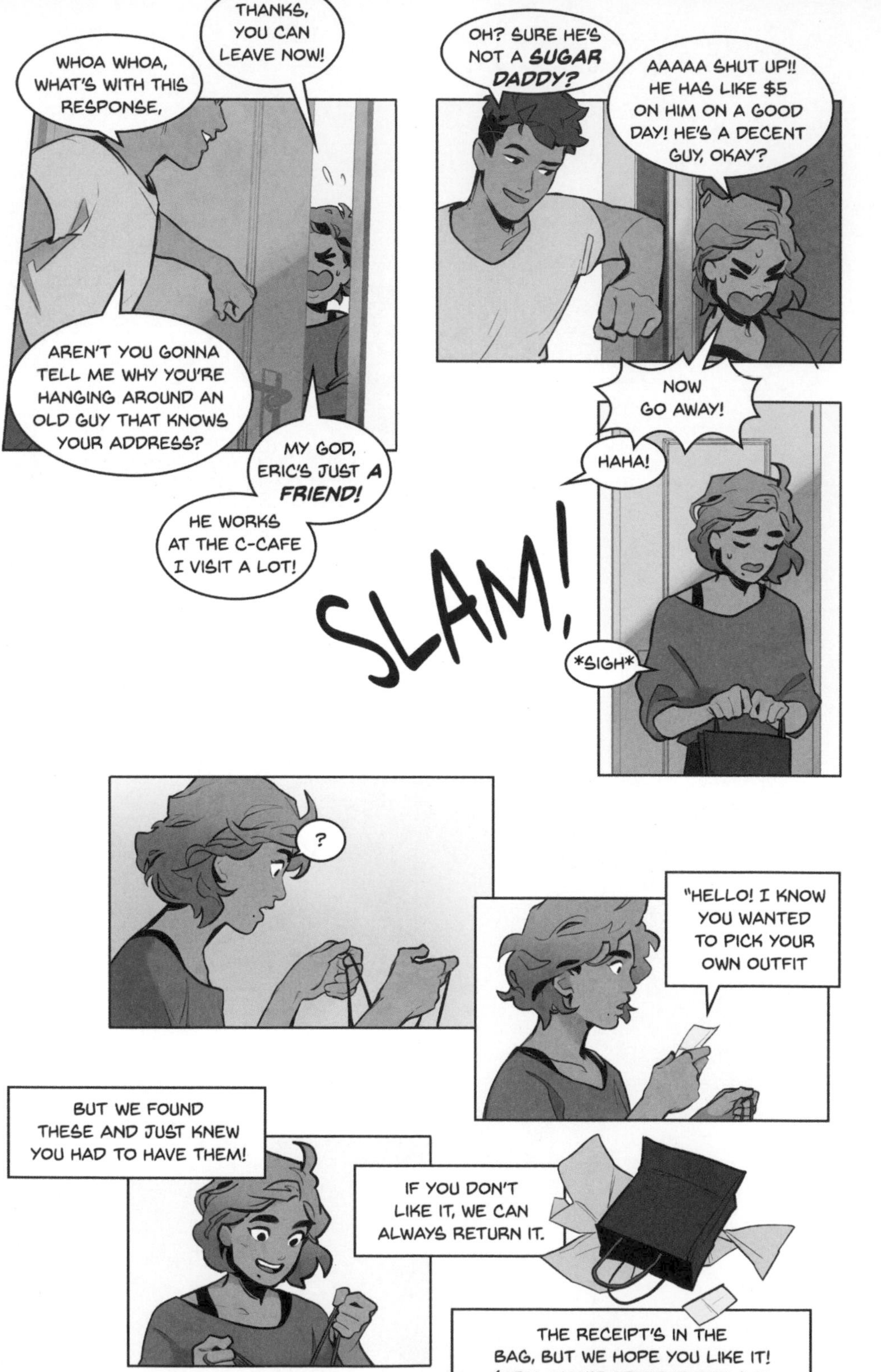
THANKS, YOU CAN LEAVE NOW!
WHOA WHOA, WHAT'S WITH THIS RESPONSE,
AREN'T YOU GONNA TELL ME WHY YOU'RE HANGING AROUND AN OLD GUY THAT KNOWS YOUR ADDRESS?
MY GOD, ERIC'S JUST **A FRIEND!**
HE WORKS AT THE C-CAFE I VISIT A LOT!
OH? SURE HE'S NOT A ***SUGAR DADDY?***
AAAAA SHUT UP!! HE HAS LIKE $5 ON HIM ON A GOOD DAY! HE'S A DECENT GUY, OKAY?
NOW GO AWAY!
HAHA!
SLAM!
SIGH
?
"HELLO! I KNOW YOU WANTED TO PICK YOUR OWN OUTFIT
BUT WE FOUND THESE AND JUST KNEW YOU HAD TO HAVE THEM!
IF YOU DON'T LIKE IT, WE CAN ALWAYS RETURN IT.
THE RECEIPT'S IN THE BAG, BUT WE HOPE YOU LIKE IT! (OPAL WON'T ADMIT IT, BUT SHE THINKS YOU'D LOOK COOL IN THESE.)"

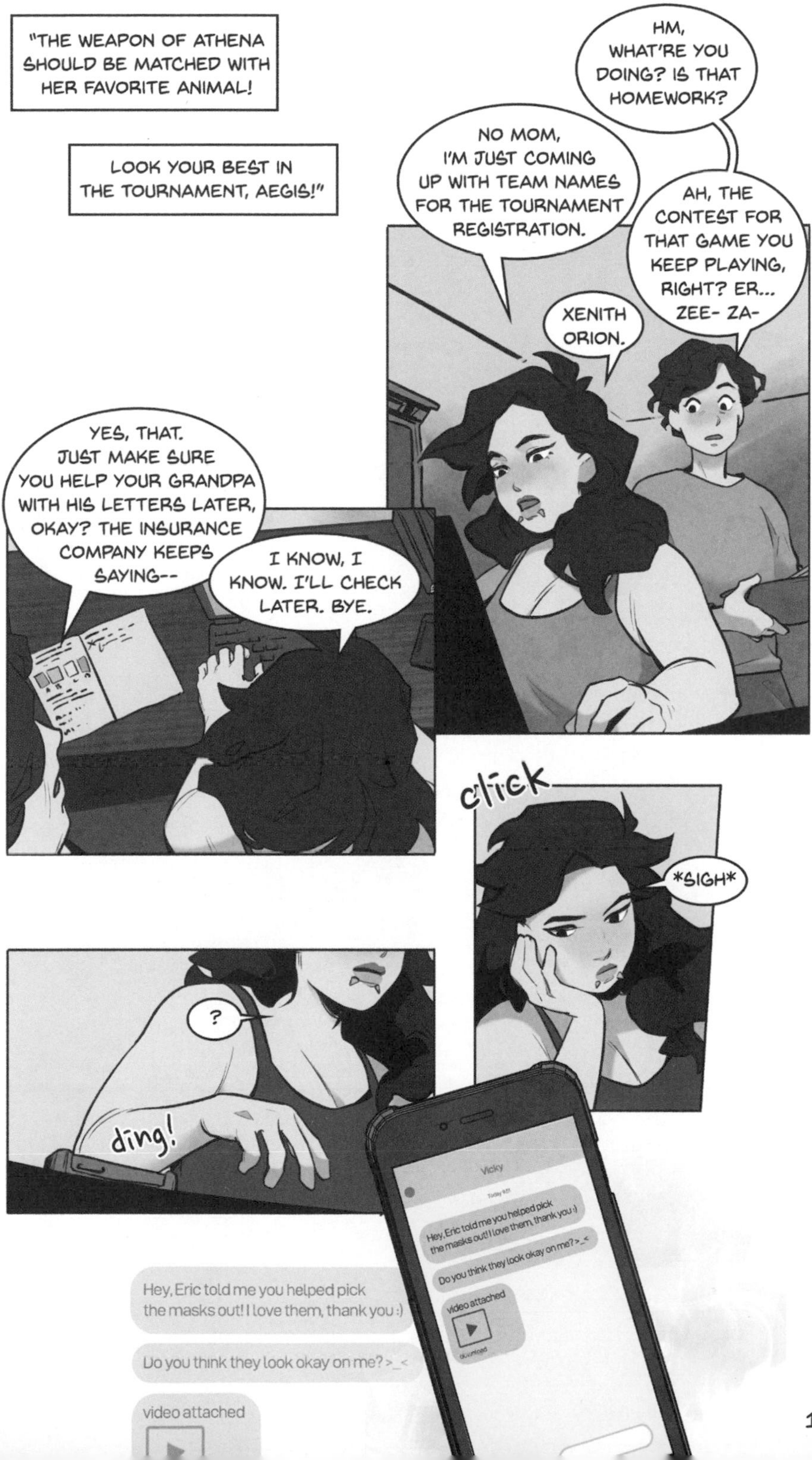
"THE WEAPON OF ATHENA SHOULD BE MATCHED WITH HER FAVORITE ANIMAL!
LOOK YOUR BEST IN THE TOURNAMENT, AEGIS!"
HM, WHAT'RE YOU DOING? IS THAT HOMEWORK?
NO MOM, I'M JUST COMING UP WITH TEAM NAMES FOR THE TOURNAMENT REGISTRATION.
AH, THE CONTEST FOR THAT GAME YOU KEEP PLAYING, RIGHT? ER... ZEE- ZA-
XENITH ORION.
YES, THAT. JUST MAKE SURE YOU HELP YOUR GRANDPA WITH HIS LETTERS LATER, OKAY? THE INSURANCE COMPANY KEEPS SAYING--
I KNOW, I KNOW. I'LL CHECK LATER. BYE.
click
SIGH
?
ding!
Vicky
Hey, Eric told me you helped pick the masks out! I love them, thank you :)
Do you think they look okay on me? >_<
video attached

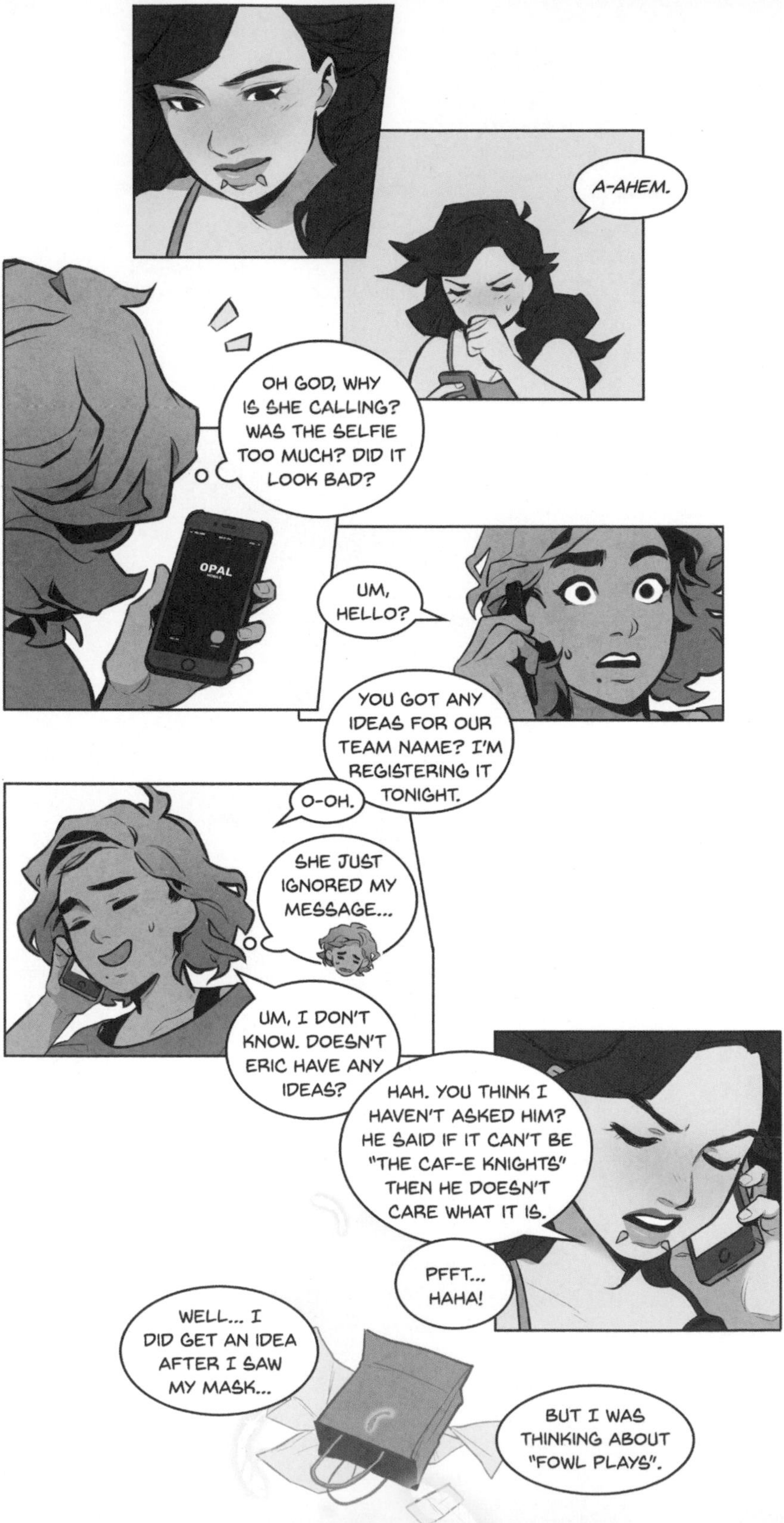

A-AHEM.
OH GOD, WHY IS SHE CALLING? WAS THE SELFIE TOO MUCH? DID IT LOOK BAD?
OPAL
UM, HELLO?
YOU GOT ANY IDEAS FOR OUR TEAM NAME? I'M REGISTERING IT TONIGHT.
O-OH.
SHE JUST IGNORED MY MESSAGE...
UM, I DON'T KNOW. DOESN'T ERIC HAVE ANY IDEAS?
HAH. YOU THINK I HAVEN'T ASKED HIM? HE SAID IF IT CAN'T BE "THE CAF-E KNIGHTS" THEN HE DOESN'T CARE WHAT IT IS.
PFFT... HAHA!
WELL... I DID GET AN IDEA AFTER I SAW MY MASK...
BUT I WAS THINKING ABOUT "FOWL PLAYS".

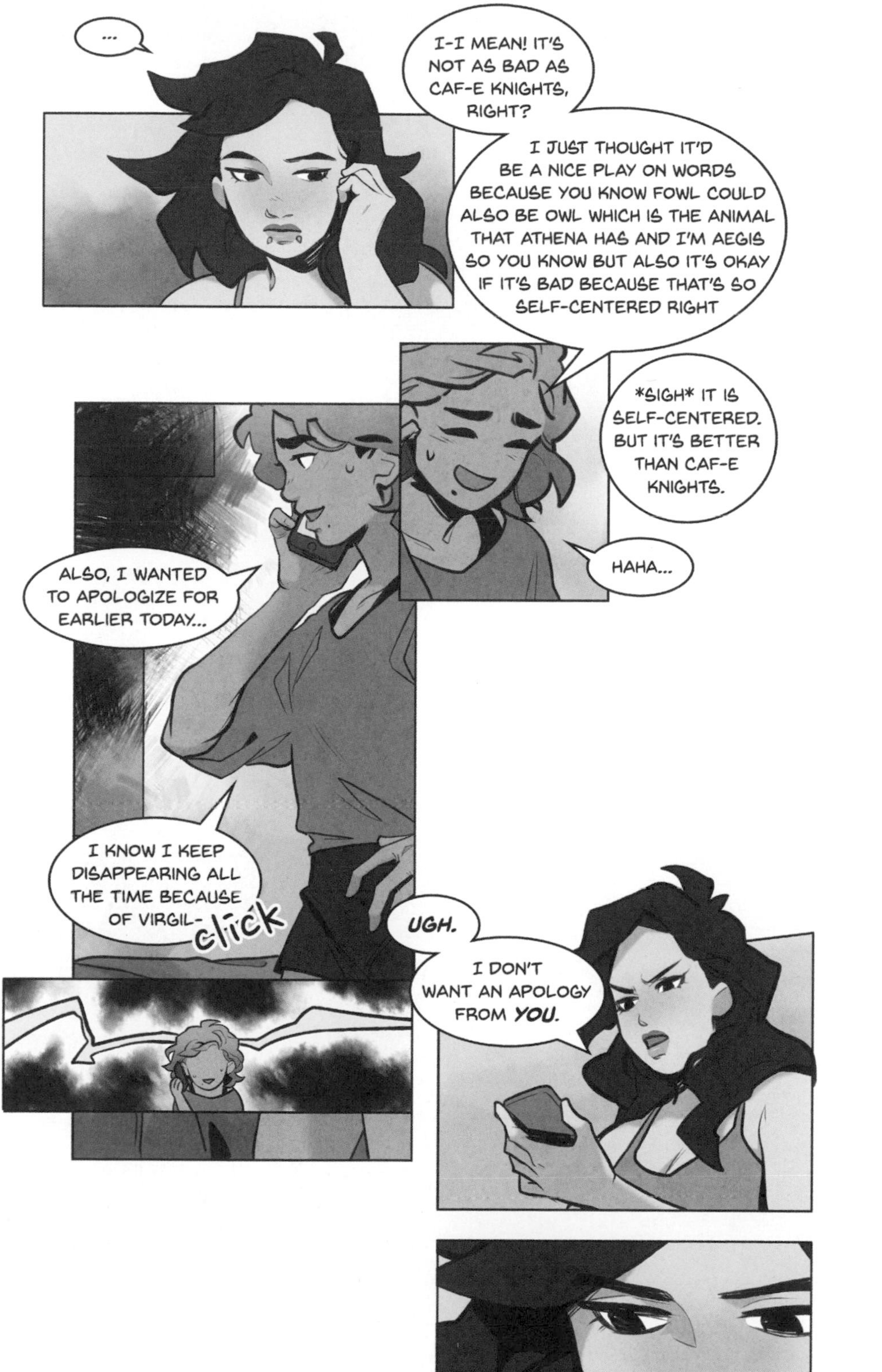
...
I-I MEAN! IT'S NOT AS BAD AS CAF-E KNIGHTS, RIGHT?
I JUST THOUGHT IT'D BE A NICE PLAY ON WORDS BECAUSE YOU KNOW FOWL COULD ALSO BE OWL WHICH IS THE ANIMAL THAT ATHENA HAS AND I'M AEGIS SO YOU KNOW BUT ALSO IT'S OKAY IF IT'S BAD BECAUSE THAT'S SO SELF-CENTERED RIGHT
SIGH IT IS SELF-CENTERED. BUT IT'S BETTER THAN CAF-E KNIGHTS.
HAHA...
ALSO, I WANTED TO APOLOGIZE FOR EARLIER TODAY...
I KNOW I KEEP DISAPPEARING ALL THE TIME BECAUSE OF VIRGIL-
click
UGH.
I DON'T WANT AN APOLOGY FROM YOU.

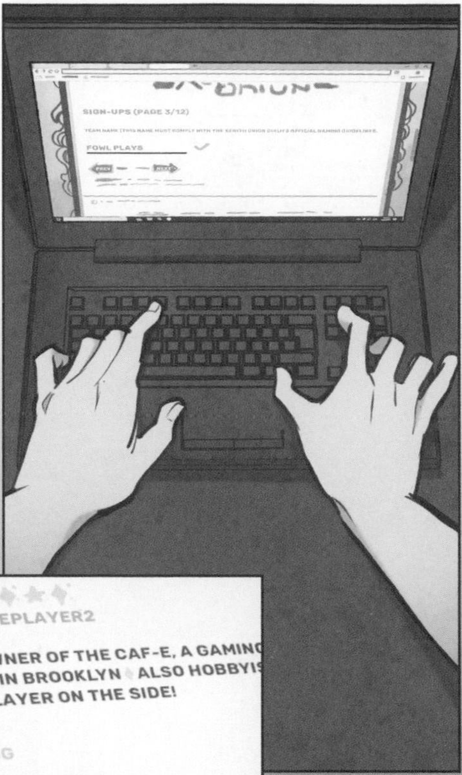
SIGN-UPS (PAGE 3/12)
FOWL PLAYS

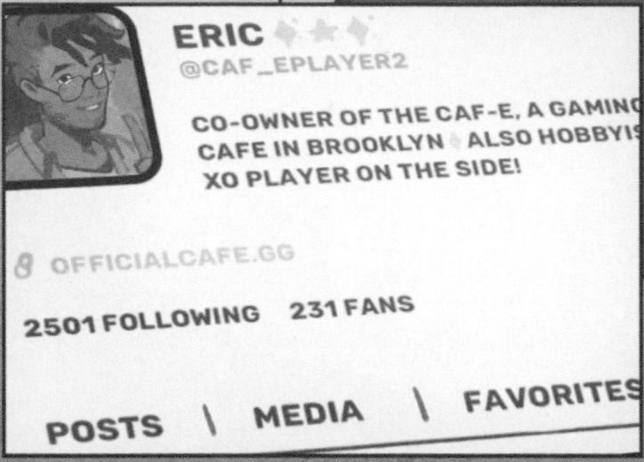
ERIC
@CAF_EPLAYER2
CO-OWNER OF THE CAF-E, A GAMIN
CAFE IN BROOKLYN ALSO HOBBYIS
XO PLAYER ON THE SIDE!
OFFICIALCAFE.GG
2501 FOLLOWING 231 FANS
POSTS | MEDIA | FAVORITES

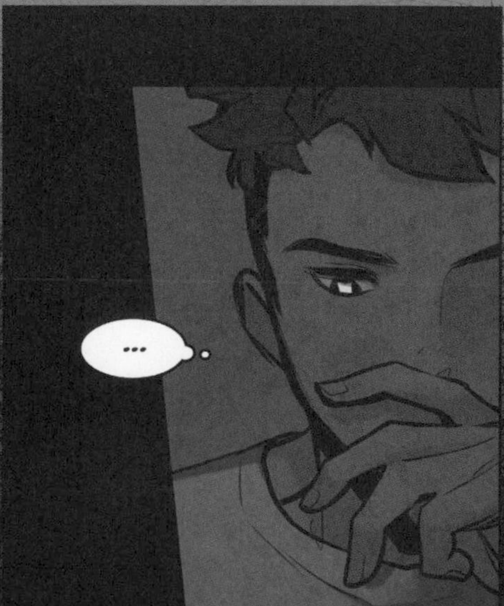
...

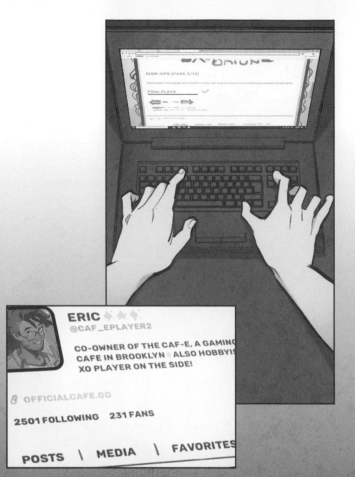

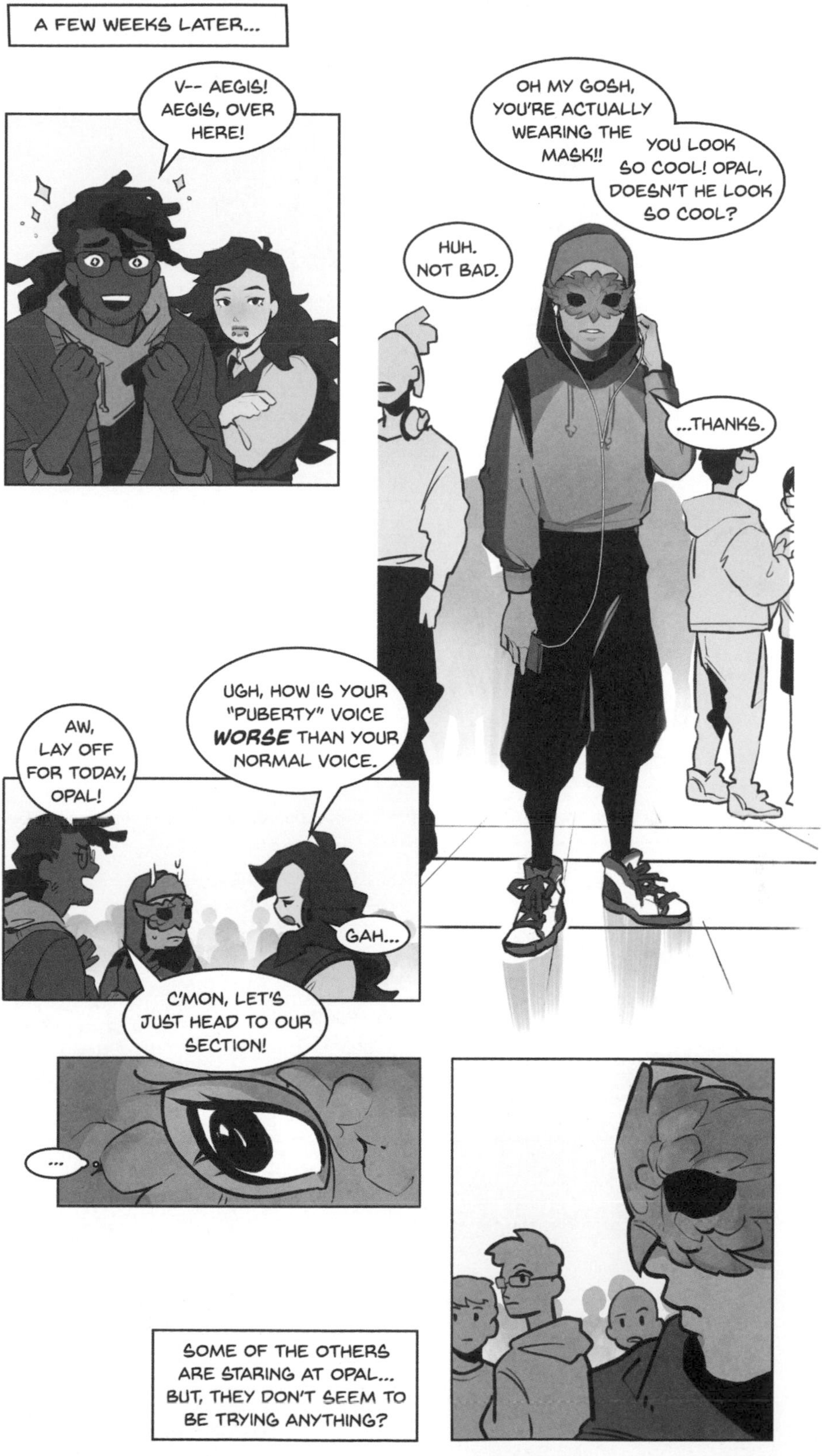
A FEW WEEKS LATER...
V-- AEGIS! AEGIS, OVER HERE!
OH MY GOSH, YOU'RE ACTUALLY WEARING THE MASK!!
YOU LOOK SO COOL! OPAL, DOESN'T HE LOOK SO COOL?
HUH. NOT BAD.
...THANKS.
AW, LAY OFF FOR TODAY, OPAL!
UGH, HOW IS YOUR "PUBERTY" VOICE WORSE THAN YOUR NORMAL VOICE.
GAH...
C'MON, LET'S JUST HEAD TO OUR SECTION!
...
SOME OF THE OTHERS ARE STARING AT OPAL... BUT, THEY DON'T SEEM TO BE TRYING ANYTHING?

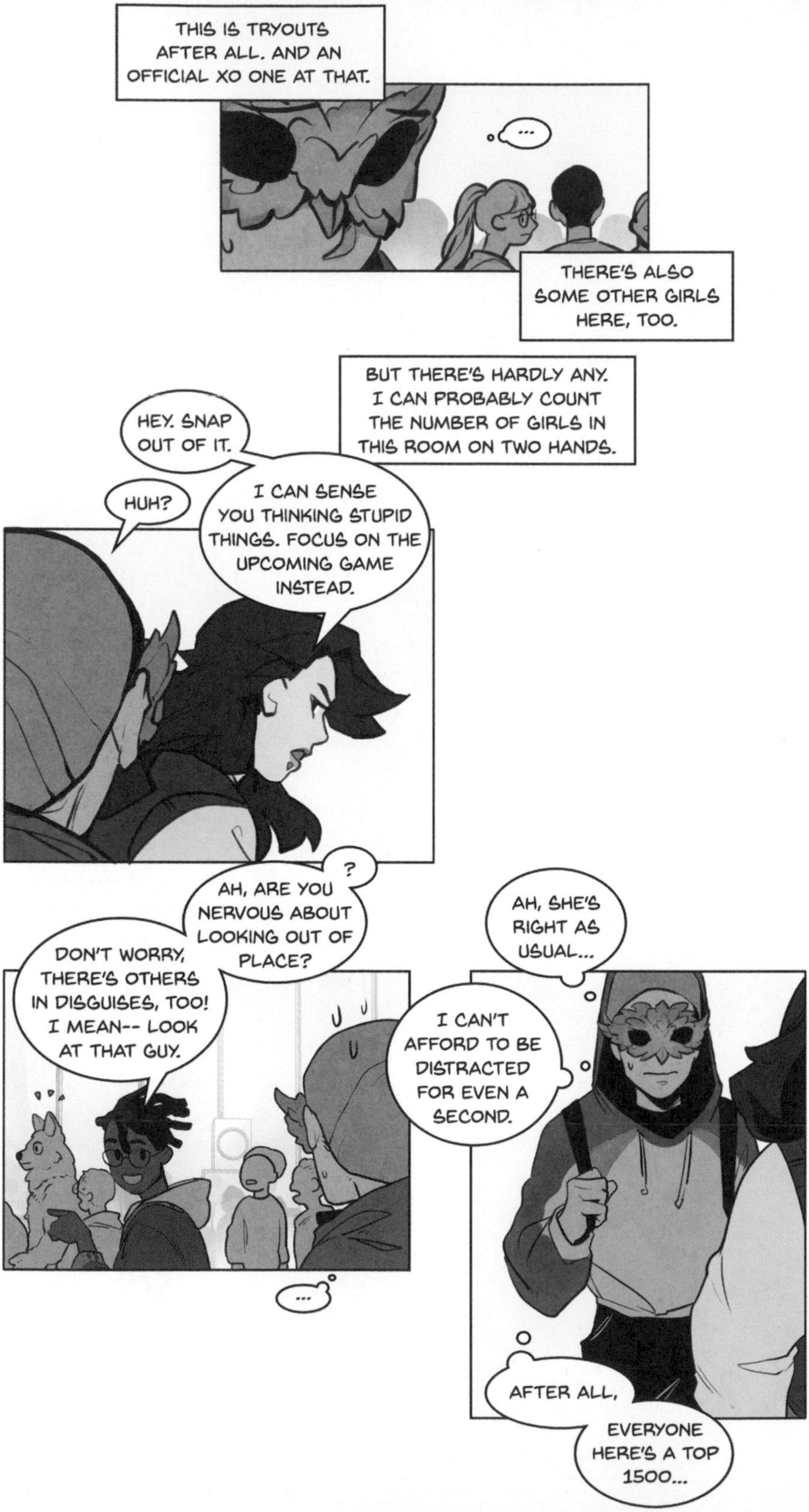
THIS IS TRYOUTS AFTER ALL. AND AN OFFICIAL XO ONE AT THAT.
...
THERE'S ALSO SOME OTHER GIRLS HERE, TOO.
BUT THERE'S HARDLY ANY. I CAN PROBABLY COUNT THE NUMBER OF GIRLS IN THIS ROOM ON TWO HANDS.
HEY. SNAP OUT OF IT.
HUH?
I CAN SENSE YOU THINKING STUPID THINGS. FOCUS ON THE UPCOMING GAME INSTEAD.
?
AH, ARE YOU NERVOUS ABOUT LOOKING OUT OF PLACE?
DON'T WORRY, THERE'S OTHERS IN DISGUISES, TOO! I MEAN-- LOOK AT THAT GUY.
...
AH, SHE'S RIGHT AS USUAL...
I CAN'T AFFORD TO BE DISTRACTED FOR EVEN A SECOND.
AFTER ALL,
EVERYONE HERE'S A TOP 1500...

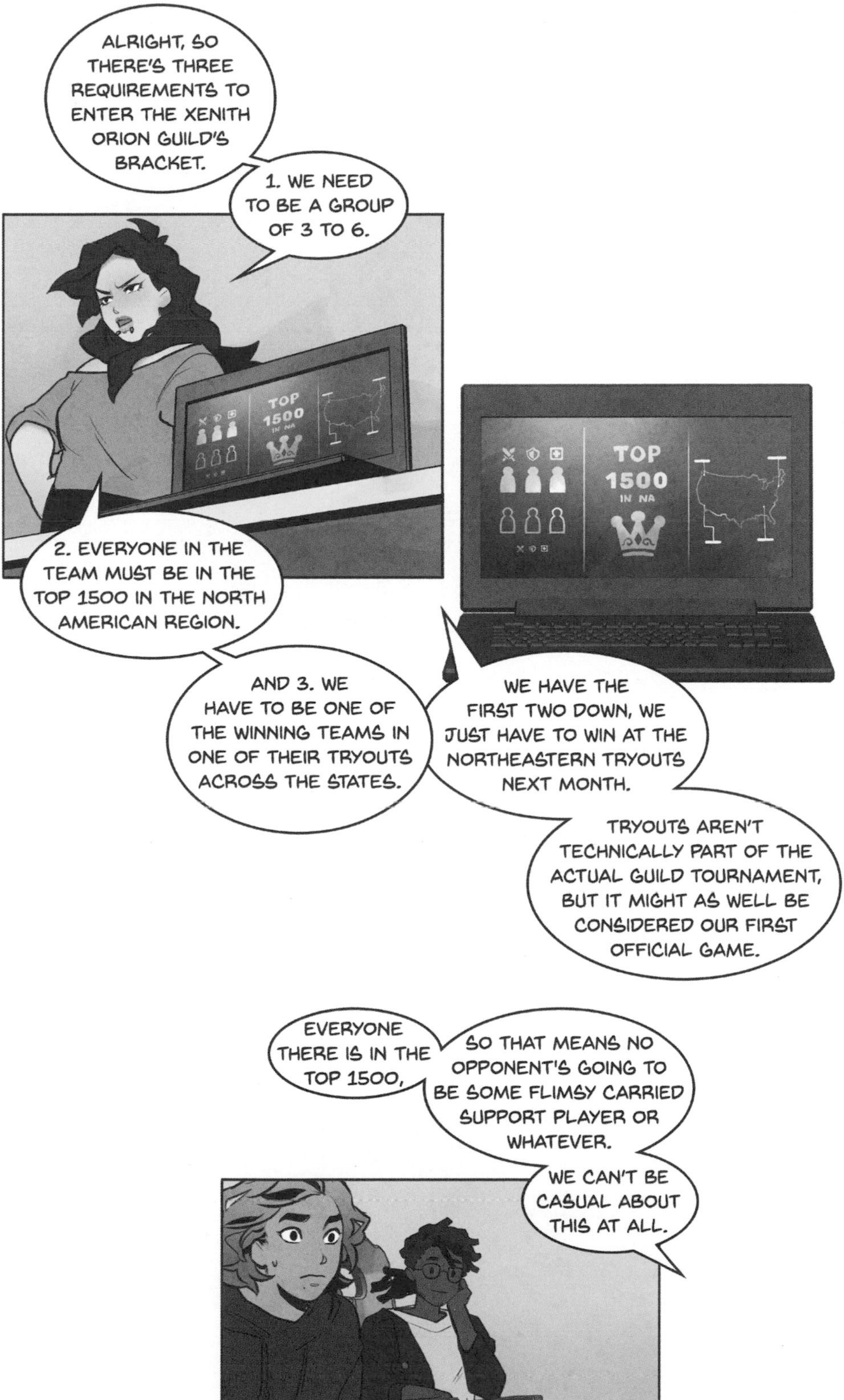
ALRIGHT, SO THERE'S THREE REQUIREMENTS TO ENTER THE XENITH ORION GUILD'S BRACKET.
1. WE NEED TO BE A GROUP OF 3 TO 6.
TOP 1500 IN NA
2. EVERYONE IN THE TEAM MUST BE IN THE TOP 1500 IN THE NORTH AMERICAN REGION.
TOP 1500 IN NA
AND 3. WE HAVE TO BE ONE OF THE WINNING TEAMS IN ONE OF THEIR TRYOUTS ACROSS THE STATES.
WE HAVE THE FIRST TWO DOWN, WE JUST HAVE TO WIN AT THE NORTHEASTERN TRYOUTS NEXT MONTH.
TRYOUTS AREN'T TECHNICALLY PART OF THE ACTUAL GUILD TOURNAMENT, BUT IT MIGHT AS WELL BE CONSIDERED OUR FIRST OFFICIAL GAME.
EVERYONE THERE IS IN THE TOP 1500,
SO THAT MEANS NO OPPONENT'S GOING TO BE SOME FLIMSY CARRIED SUPPORT PLAYER OR WHATEVER.
WE CAN'T BE CASUAL ABOUT THIS AT ALL.

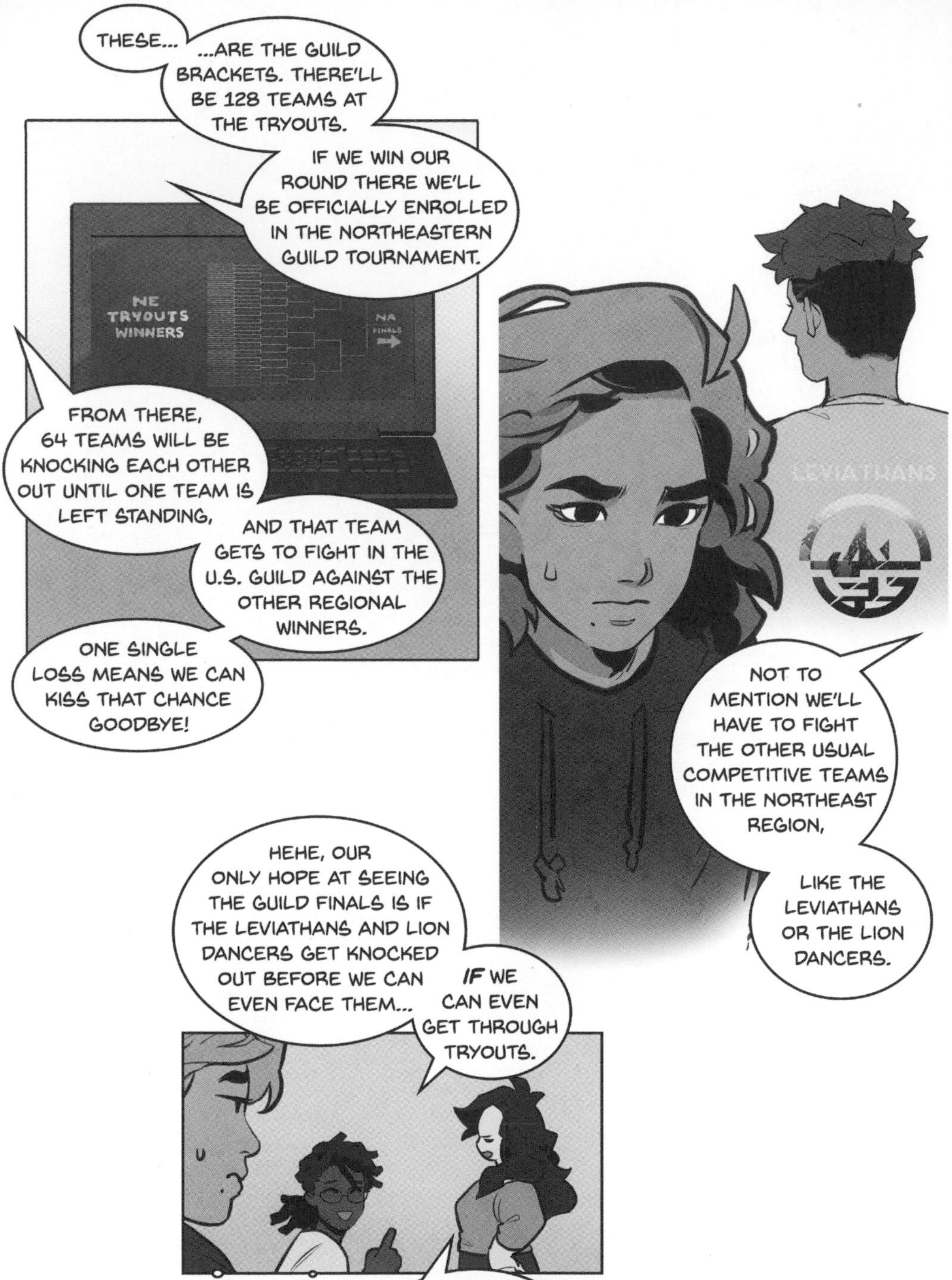
THESE...
...ARE THE GUILD BRACKETS. THERE'LL BE 128 TEAMS AT THE TRYOUTS.
IF WE WIN OUR ROUND THERE WE'LL BE OFFICIALLY ENROLLED IN THE NORTHEASTERN GUILD TOURNAMENT.
NE TRYOUTS WINNERS
NA FINALS
FROM THERE, 64 TEAMS WILL BE KNOCKING EACH OTHER OUT UNTIL ONE TEAM IS LEFT STANDING,
AND THAT TEAM GETS TO FIGHT IN THE U.S. GUILD AGAINST THE OTHER REGIONAL WINNERS.
ONE SINGLE LOSS MEANS WE CAN KISS THAT CHANCE GOODBYE!
LEVIATHANS
NOT TO MENTION WE'LL HAVE TO FIGHT THE OTHER USUAL COMPETITIVE TEAMS IN THE NORTHEAST REGION,
LIKE THE LEVIATHANS OR THE LION DANCERS.
HEHE, OUR ONLY HOPE AT SEEING THE GUILD FINALS IS IF THE LEVIATHANS AND LION DANCERS GET KNOCKED OUT BEFORE WE CAN EVEN FACE THEM...
IF WE CAN EVEN GET THROUGH TRYOUTS.
TYRANT...
IF WE DON'T MAKE IT THROUGH THE TRYOUTS, I'LL SKIN YOU TWO ALIVE AND MOUNT YOUR FLESH IN MY ROOM.

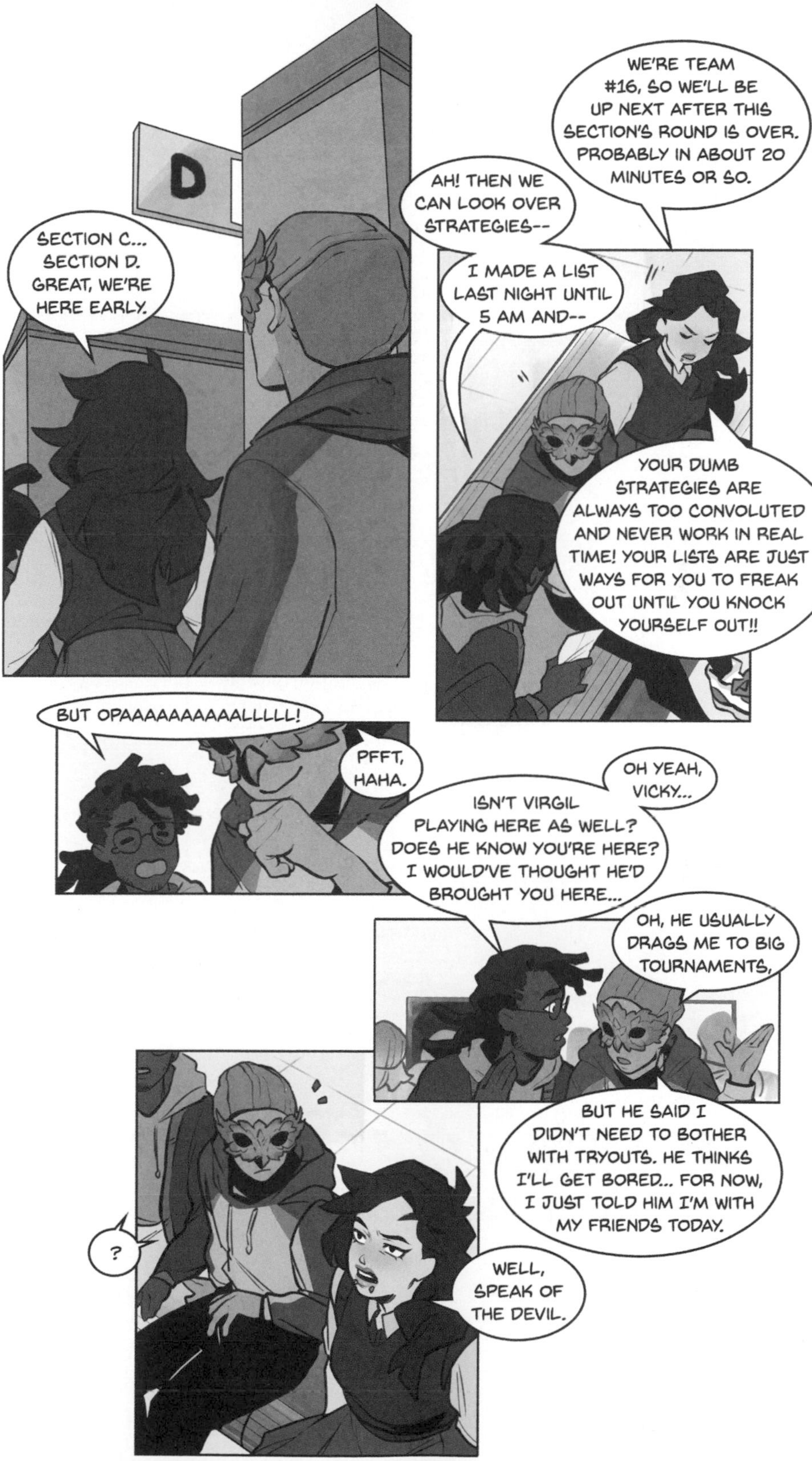
SECTION C... SECTION D. GREAT, WE'RE HERE EARLY.
AH! THEN WE CAN LOOK OVER STRATEGIES--
WE'RE TEAM #16, SO WE'LL BE UP NEXT AFTER THIS SECTION'S ROUND IS OVER. PROBABLY IN ABOUT 20 MINUTES OR SO.
I MADE A LIST LAST NIGHT UNTIL 5 AM AND--
YOUR DUMB STRATEGIES ARE ALWAYS TOO CONVOLUTED AND NEVER WORK IN REAL TIME! YOUR LISTS ARE JUST WAYS FOR YOU TO FREAK OUT UNTIL YOU KNOCK YOURSELF OUT!!
BUT OPAAAAAAAAAALLLLL!
PFFT, HAHA.
OH YEAH, VICKY...
ISN'T VIRGIL PLAYING HERE AS WELL? DOES HE KNOW YOU'RE HERE? I WOULD'VE THOUGHT HE'D BROUGHT YOU HERE...
OH, HE USUALLY DRAGS ME TO BIG TOURNAMENTS,
BUT HE SAID I DIDN'T NEED TO BOTHER WITH TRYOUTS. HE THINKS I'LL GET BORED... FOR NOW, I JUST TOLD HIM I'M WITH MY FRIENDS TODAY.
?
WELL, SPEAK OF THE DEVIL.

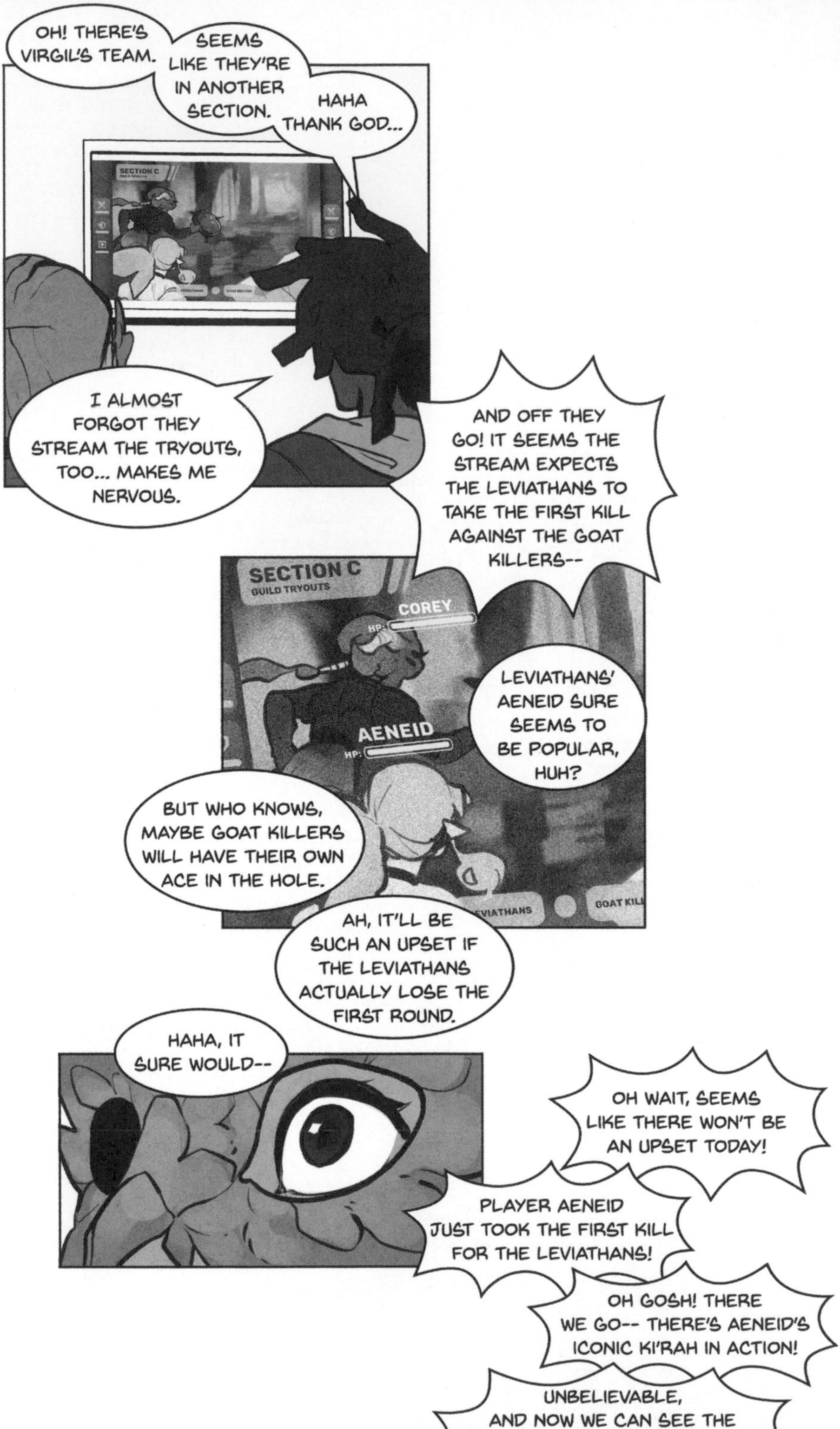
OH! THERE'S VIRGIL'S TEAM.
SEEMS LIKE THEY'RE IN ANOTHER SECTION.
HAHA THANK GOD...
I ALMOST FORGOT THEY STREAM THE TRYOUTS, TOO... MAKES ME NERVOUS.
AND OFF THEY GO! IT SEEMS THE STREAM EXPECTS THE LEVIATHANS TO TAKE THE FIRST KILL AGAINST THE GOAT KILLERS--
SECTION C
GUILD TRYOUTS
COREY
HP:
LEVIATHANS' AENEID SURE SEEMS TO BE POPULAR, HUH?
AENEID
HP:
BUT WHO KNOWS, MAYBE GOAT KILLERS WILL HAVE THEIR OWN ACE IN THE HOLE.
AH, IT'LL BE SUCH AN UPSET IF THE LEVIATHANS ACTUALLY LOSE THE FIRST ROUND.
HAHA, IT SURE WOULD--
OH WAIT, SEEMS LIKE THERE WON'T BE AN UPSET TODAY!
PLAYER AENEID JUST TOOK THE FIRST KILL FOR THE LEVIATHANS!
OH GOSH! THERE WE GO-- THERE'S AENEID'S ICONIC KI'RAH IN ACTION!
UNBELIEVABLE, AND NOW WE CAN SEE THE GOAT KILLERS RETREATING JUST AFTER LOSING THEIR TANK...

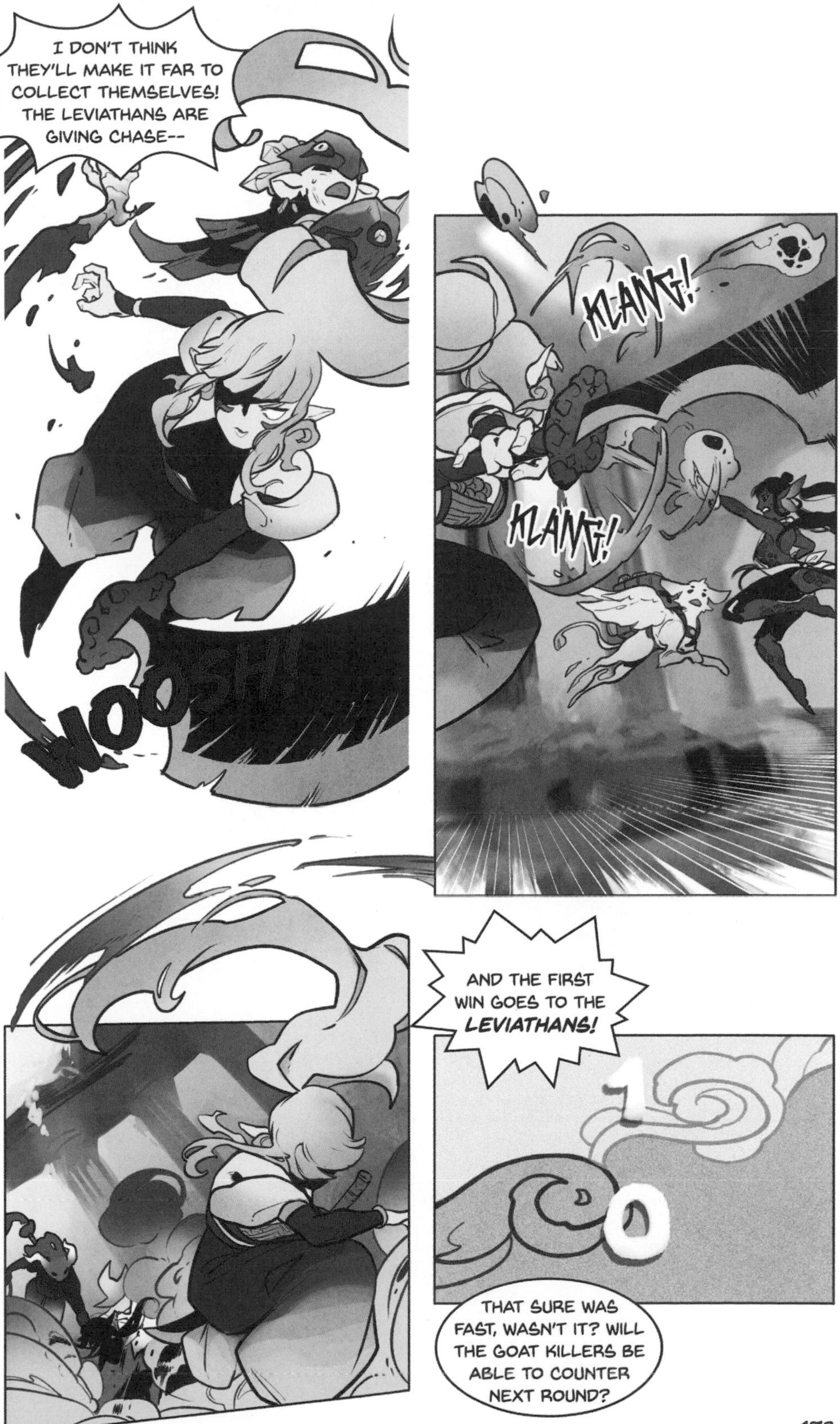
I DON'T THINK THEY'LL MAKE IT FAR TO COLLECT THEMSELVES! THE LEVIATHANS ARE GIVING CHASE--
WOOSH!!
KLANG!
KLANG!
AND THE FIRST WIN GOES TO THE *LEVIATHANS!*
1
0
THAT SURE WAS FAST, WASN'T IT? WILL THE GOAT KILLERS BE ABLE TO COUNTER NEXT ROUND?

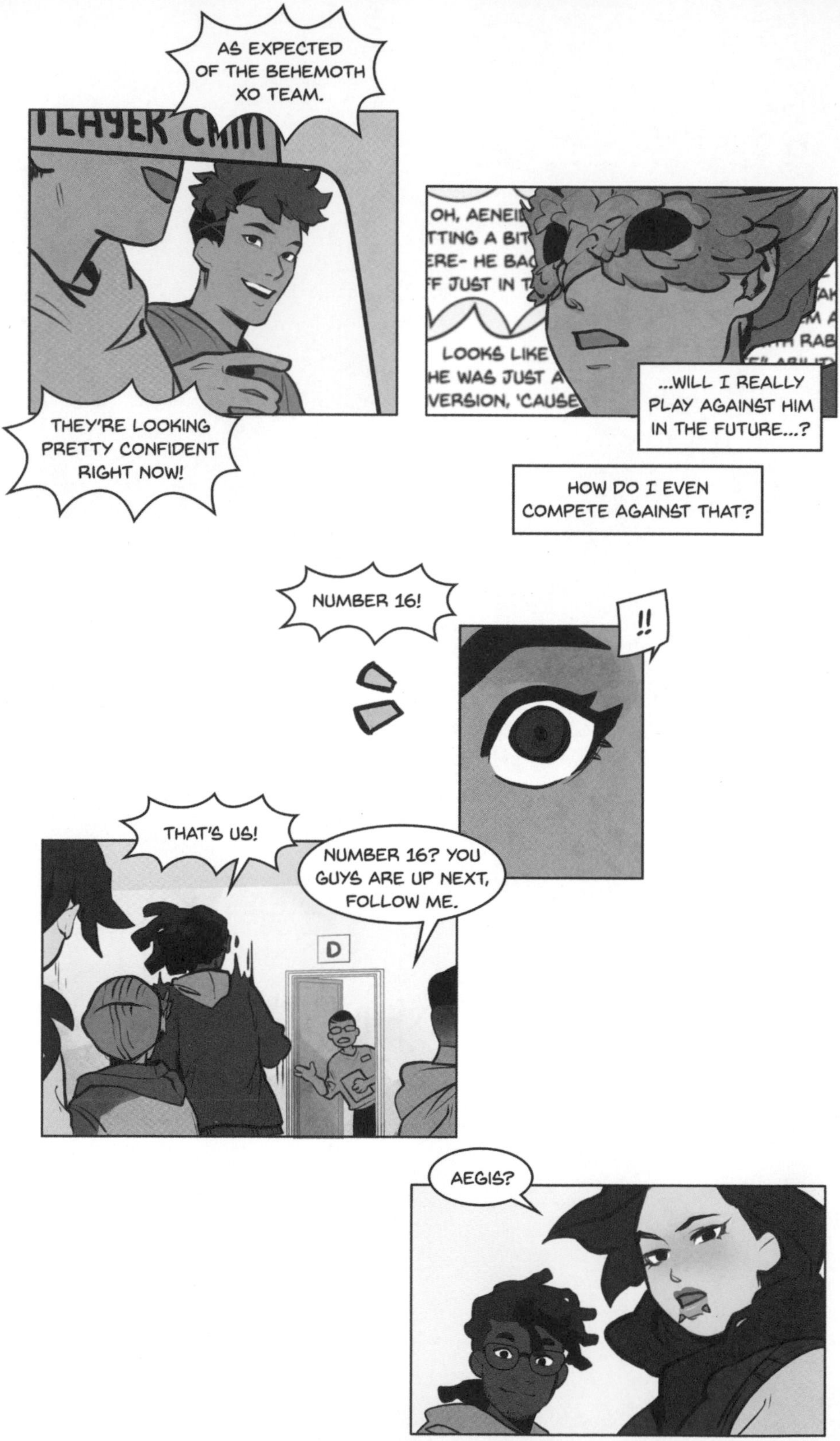
AS EXPECTED OF THE BEHEMOTH XO TEAM.
THEY'RE LOOKING PRETTY CONFIDENT RIGHT NOW!
...WILL I REALLY PLAY AGAINST HIM IN THE FUTURE...?
HOW DO I EVEN COMPETE AGAINST THAT?
NUMBER 16!
!!
THAT'S US!
NUMBER 16? YOU GUYS ARE UP NEXT, FOLLOW ME.
D
AEGIS?

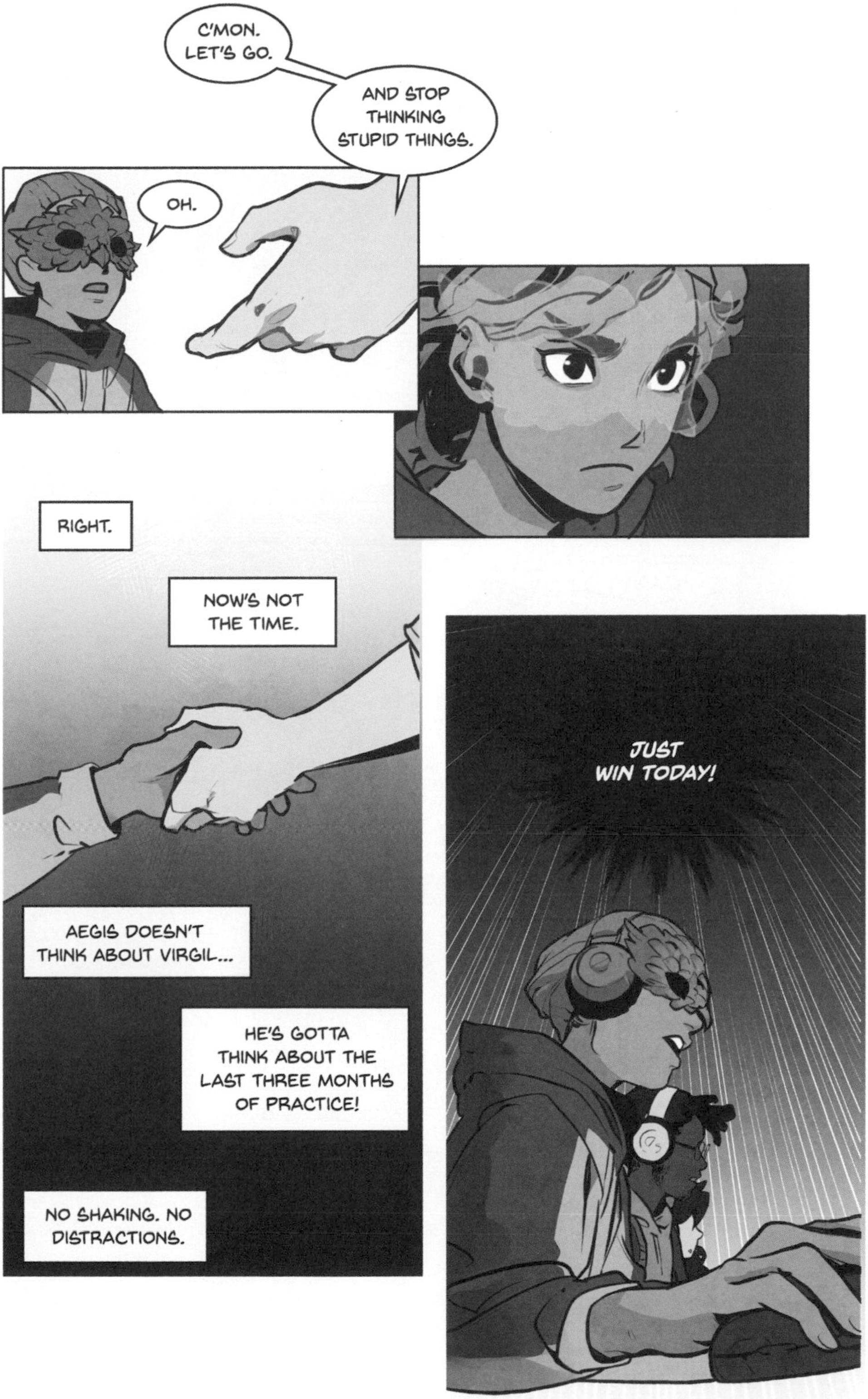
C'MON. LET'S GO.
AND STOP THINKING STUPID THINGS.
OH.
RIGHT.
NOW'S NOT THE TIME.
AEGIS DOESN'T THINK ABOUT VIRGIL...
HE'S GOTTA THINK ABOUT THE LAST THREE MONTHS OF PRACTICE!
NO SHAKING. NO DISTRACTIONS.
JUST WIN TODAY!

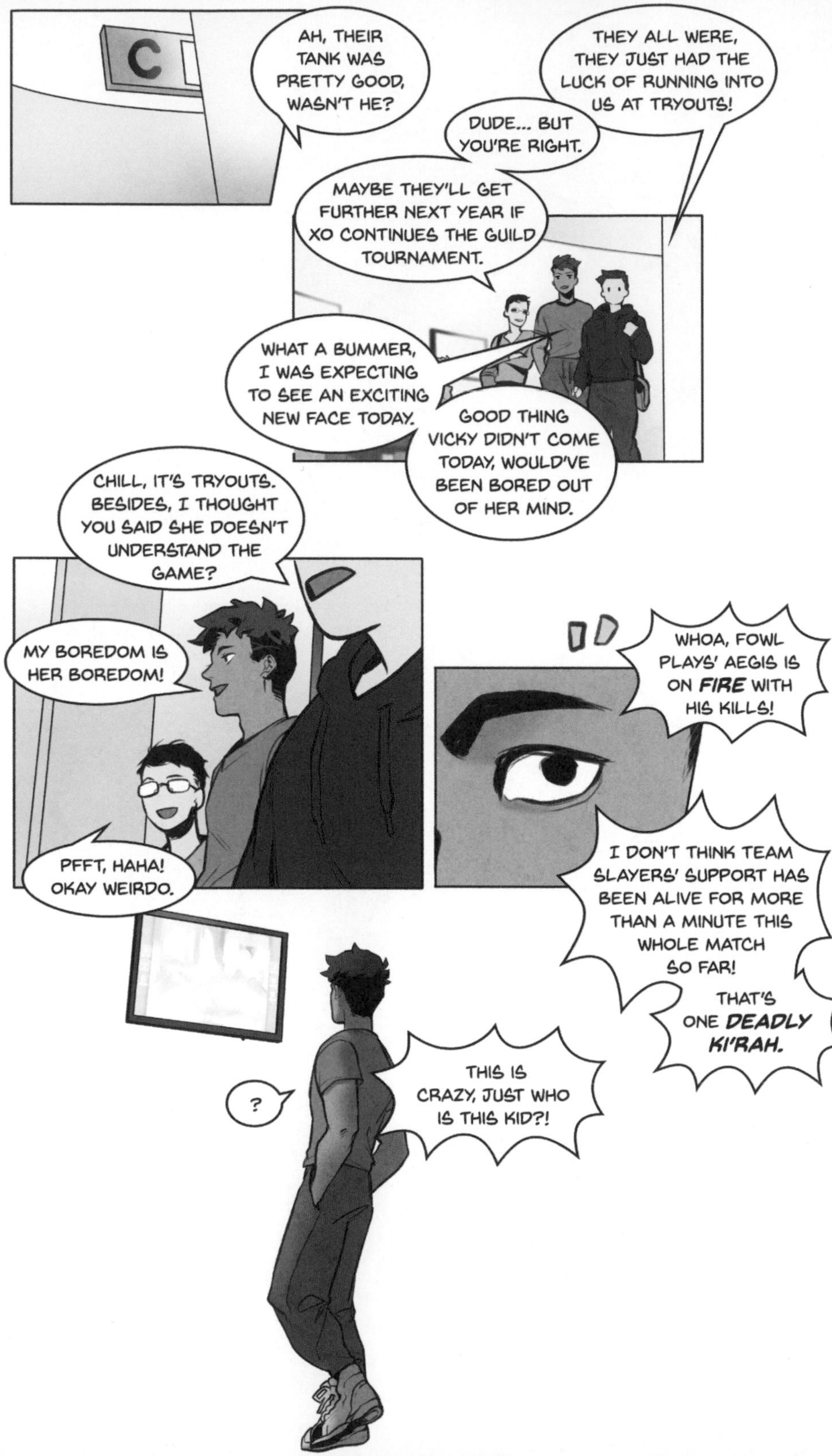
AH, THEIR TANK WAS PRETTY GOOD, WASN'T HE?
THEY ALL WERE, THEY JUST HAD THE LUCK OF RUNNING INTO US AT TRYOUTS!
DUDE... BUT YOU'RE RIGHT.
MAYBE THEY'LL GET FURTHER NEXT YEAR IF XO CONTINUES THE GUILD TOURNAMENT.
WHAT A BUMMER, I WAS EXPECTING TO SEE AN EXCITING NEW FACE TODAY.
GOOD THING VICKY DIDN'T COME TODAY, WOULD'VE BEEN BORED OUT OF HER MIND.
CHILL, IT'S TRYOUTS. BESIDES, I THOUGHT YOU SAID SHE DOESN'T UNDERSTAND THE GAME?
MY BOREDOM IS HER BOREDOM!
PFFT, HAHA! OKAY WEIRDO.
WHOA, FOWL PLAYS' AEGIS IS ON **FIRE** WITH HIS KILLS!
I DON'T THINK TEAM SLAYERS' SUPPORT HAS BEEN ALIVE FOR MORE THAN A MINUTE THIS WHOLE MATCH SO FAR!
THAT'S ONE **DEADLY KI'RAH.**
?
THIS IS CRAZY, JUST WHO IS THIS KID?!

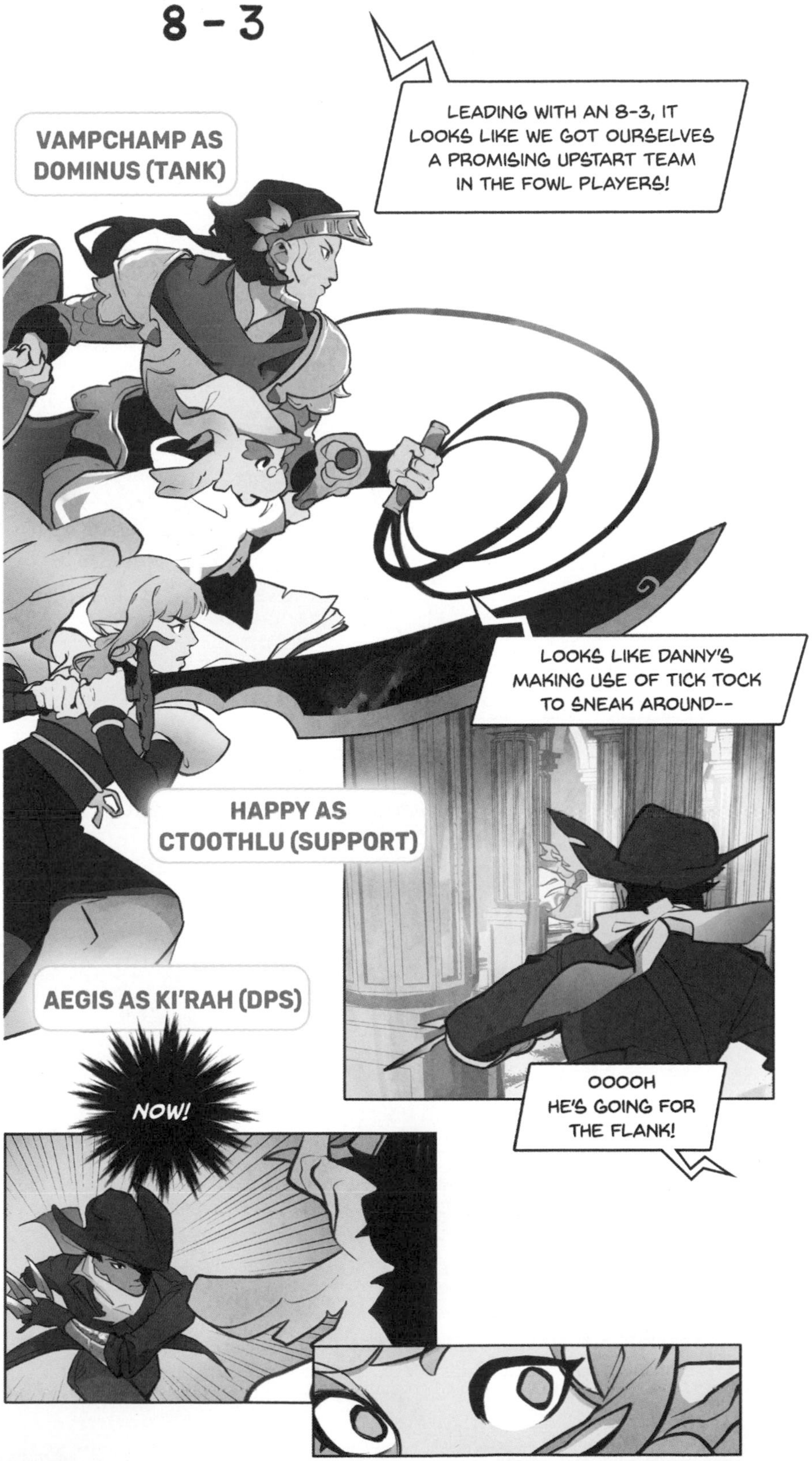
8 - 3
VAMPCHAMP AS DOMINUS (TANK)
LEADING WITH AN 8-3, IT LOOKS LIKE WE GOT OURSELVES A PROMISING UPSTART TEAM IN THE FOWL PLAYERS!
HAPPY AS CTOOTHLU (SUPPORT)
AEGIS AS KI'RAH (DPS)
LOOKS LIKE DANNY'S MAKING USE OF TICK TOCK TO SNEAK AROUND--
OOOOH HE'S GOING FOR THE FLANK!
NOW!

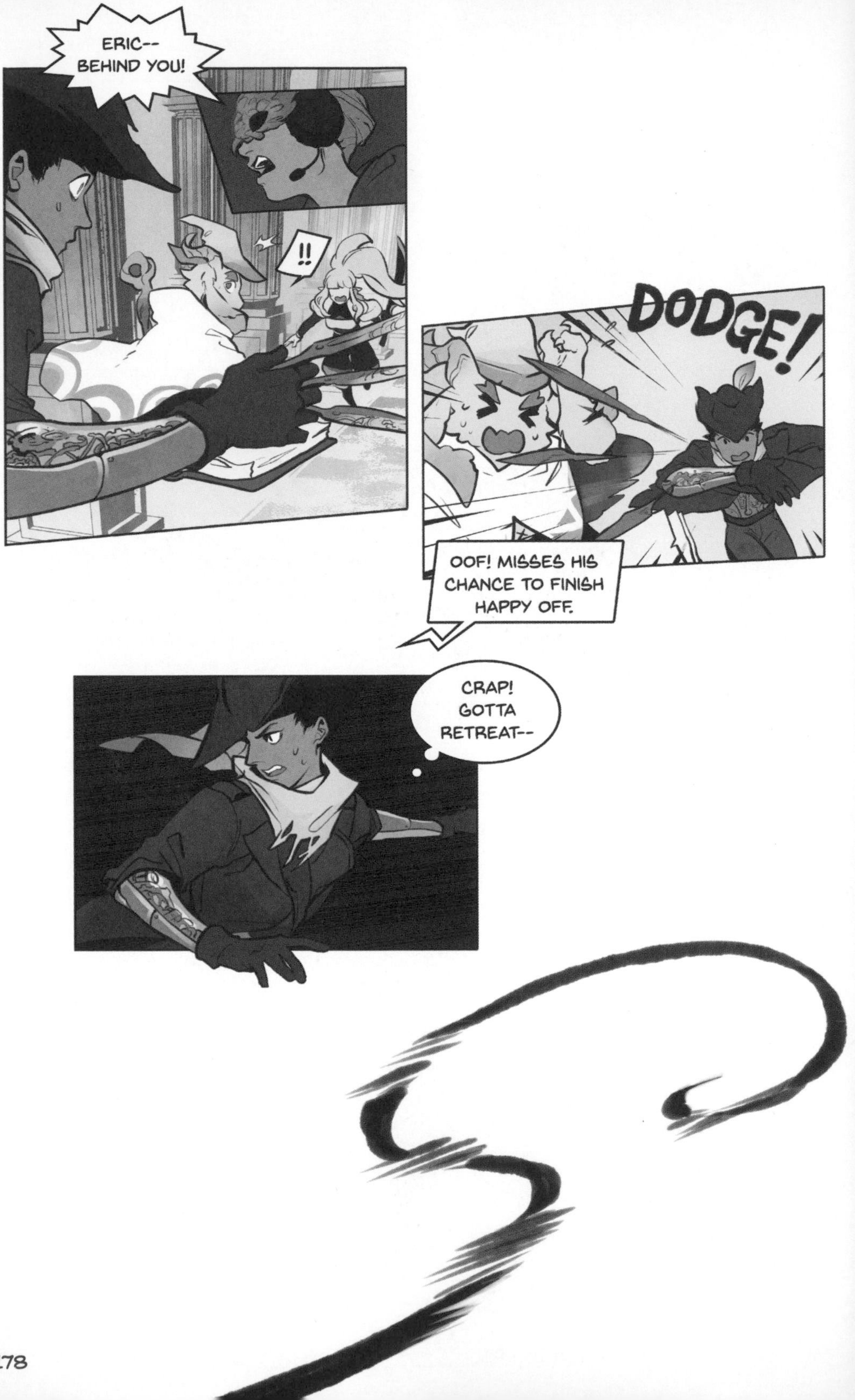
ERIC--
BEHIND YOU!
!!
DODGE!
OOF! MISSES HIS CHANCE TO FINISH HAPPY OFF.
CRAP! GOTTA RETREAT--

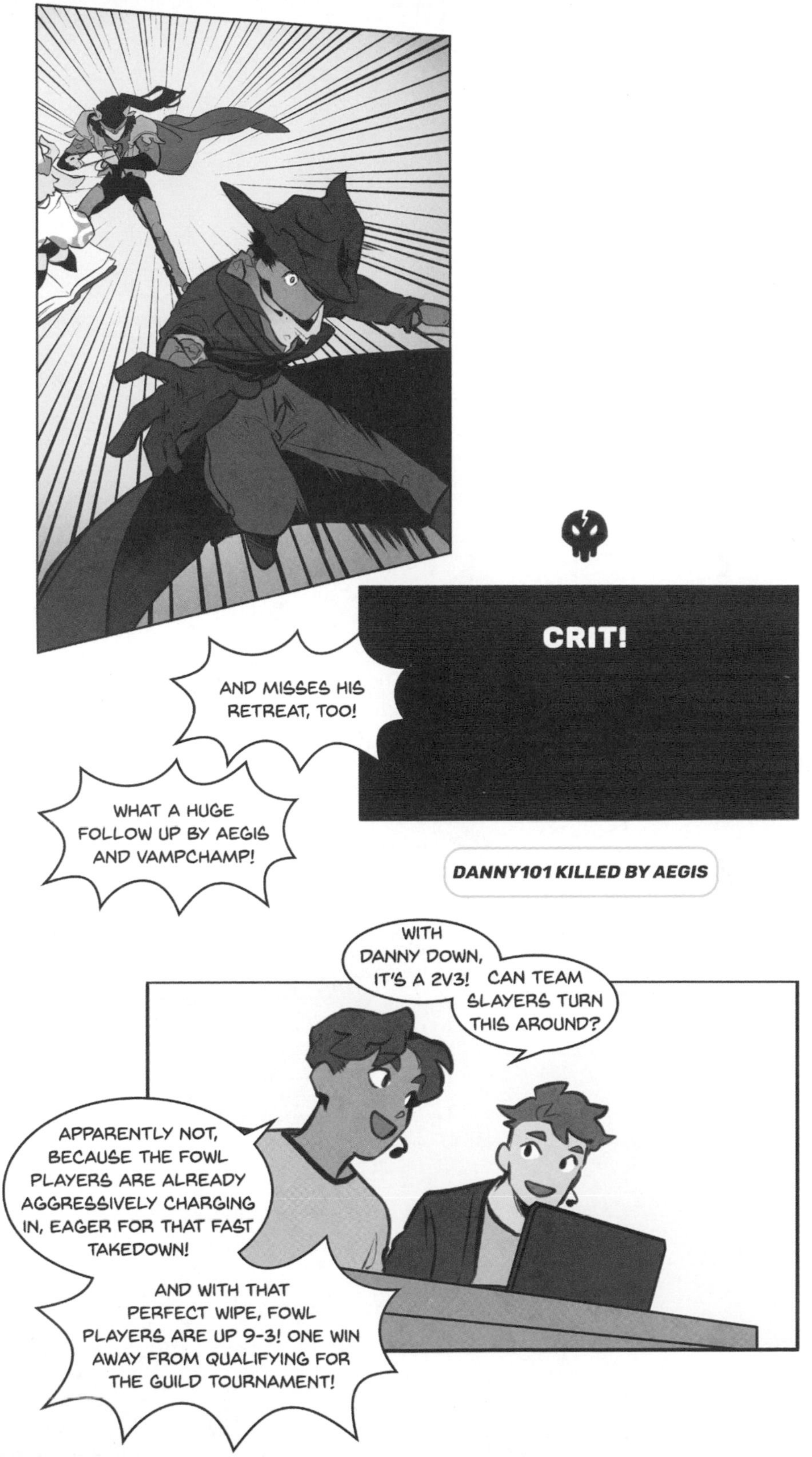
CRIT!
AND MISSES HIS RETREAT, TOO!
WHAT A HUGE FOLLOW UP BY AEGIS AND VAMPCHAMP!
DANNY101 KILLED BY AEGIS
WITH DANNY DOWN, IT'S A 2V3! CAN TEAM SLAYERS TURN THIS AROUND?
APPARENTLY NOT, BECAUSE THE FOWL PLAYERS ARE ALREADY AGGRESSIVELY CHARGING IN, EAGER FOR THAT FAST TAKEDOWN!
AND WITH THAT PERFECT WIPE, FOWL PLAYERS ARE UP 9-3! ONE WIN AWAY FROM QUALIFYING FOR THE GUILD TOURNAMENT!

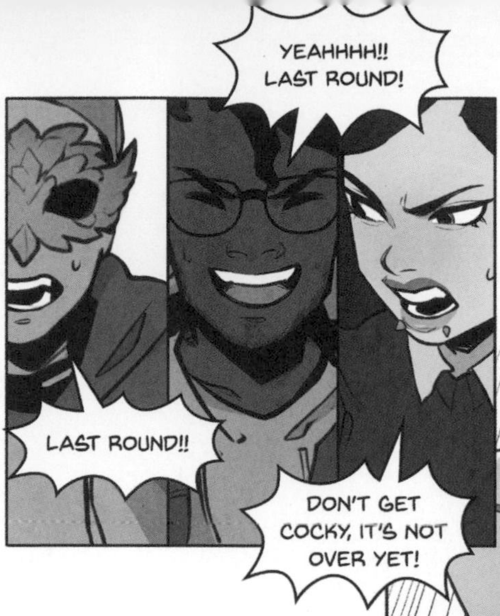
YEAHHHH!! LAST ROUND!
LAST ROUND!!
DON'T GET COCKY, IT'S NOT OVER YET!

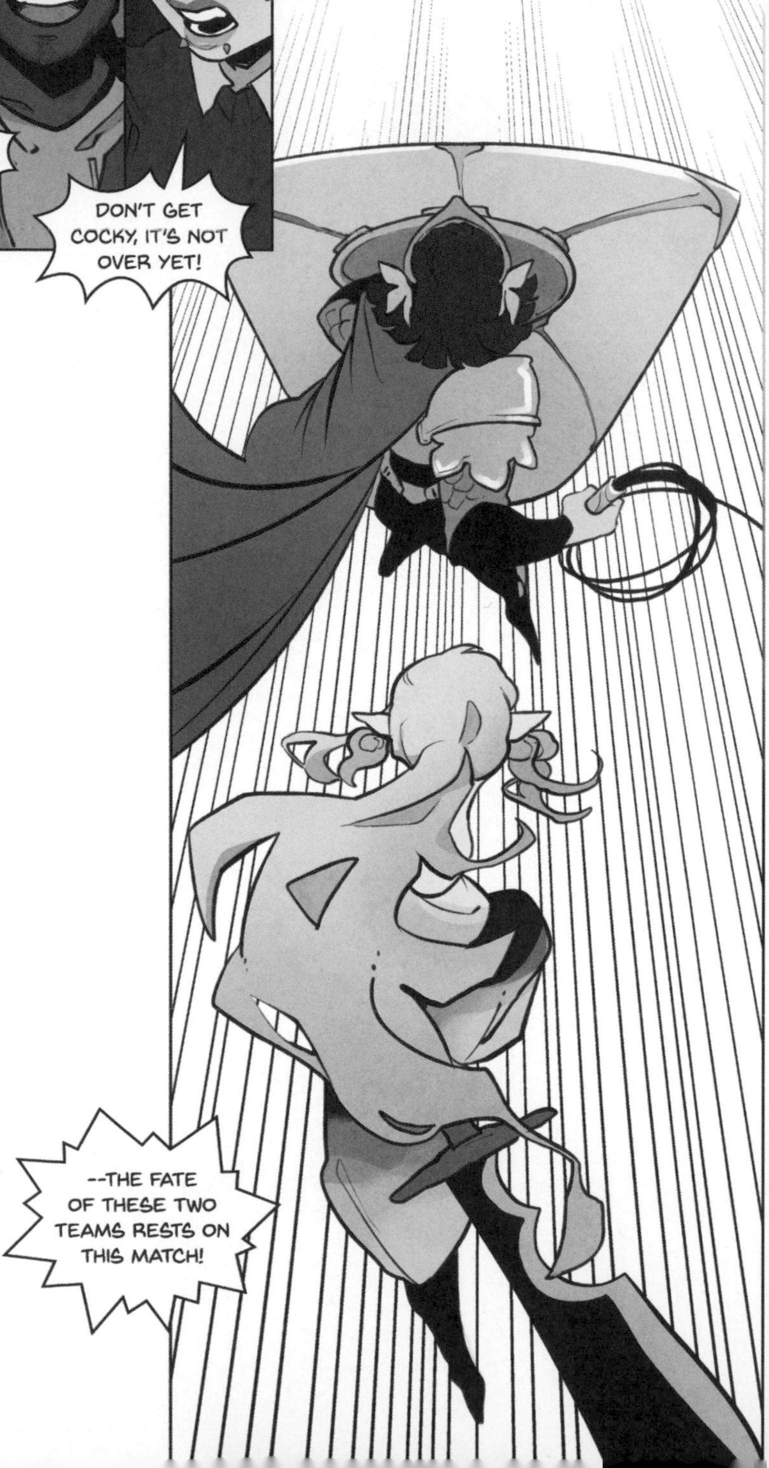
--THE FATE OF THESE TWO TEAMS RESTS ON THIS MATCH!

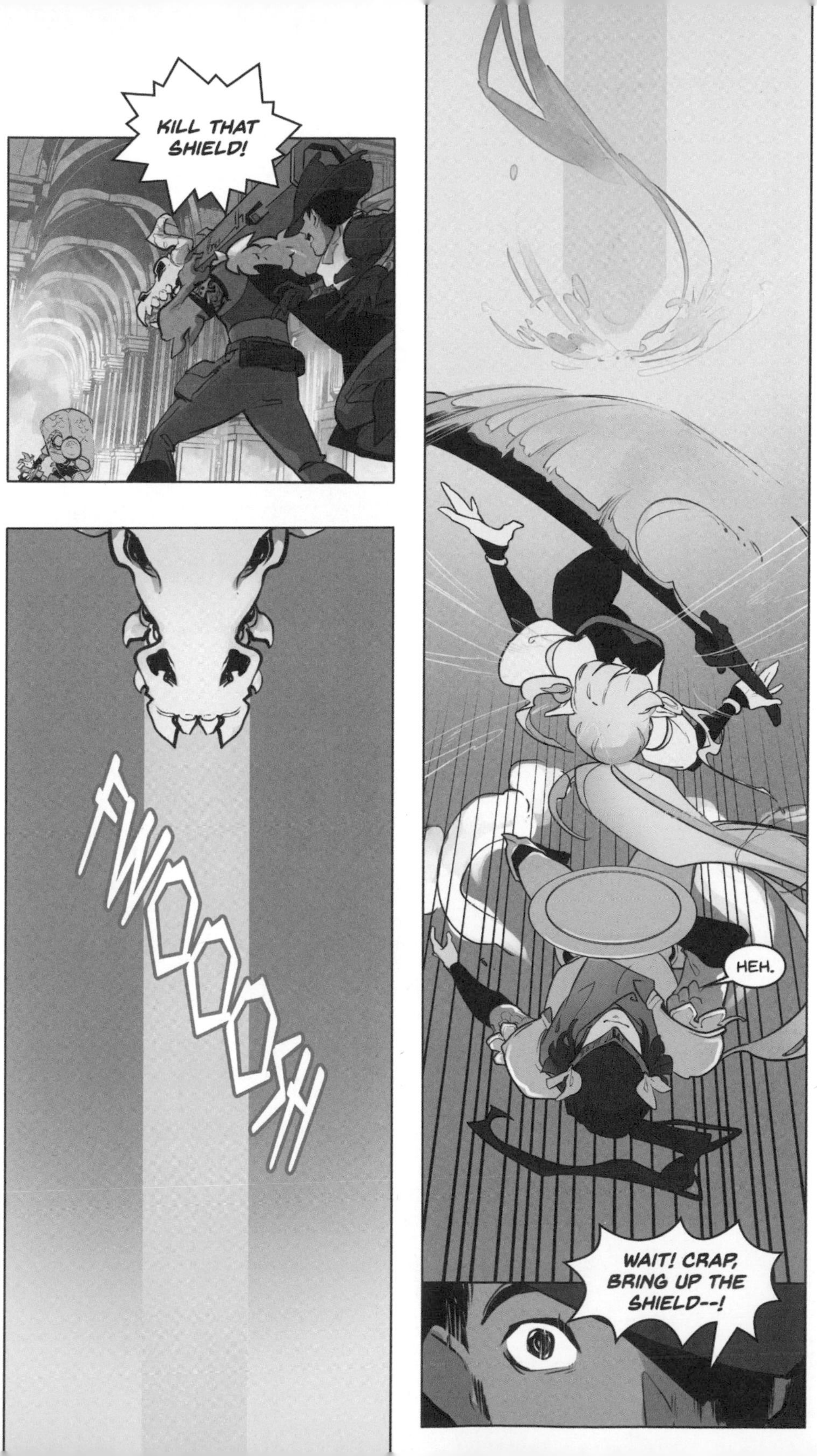
KILL THAT SHIELD!
FWOOOSH
HEH.
WAIT! CRAP, BRING UP THE SHIELD--!

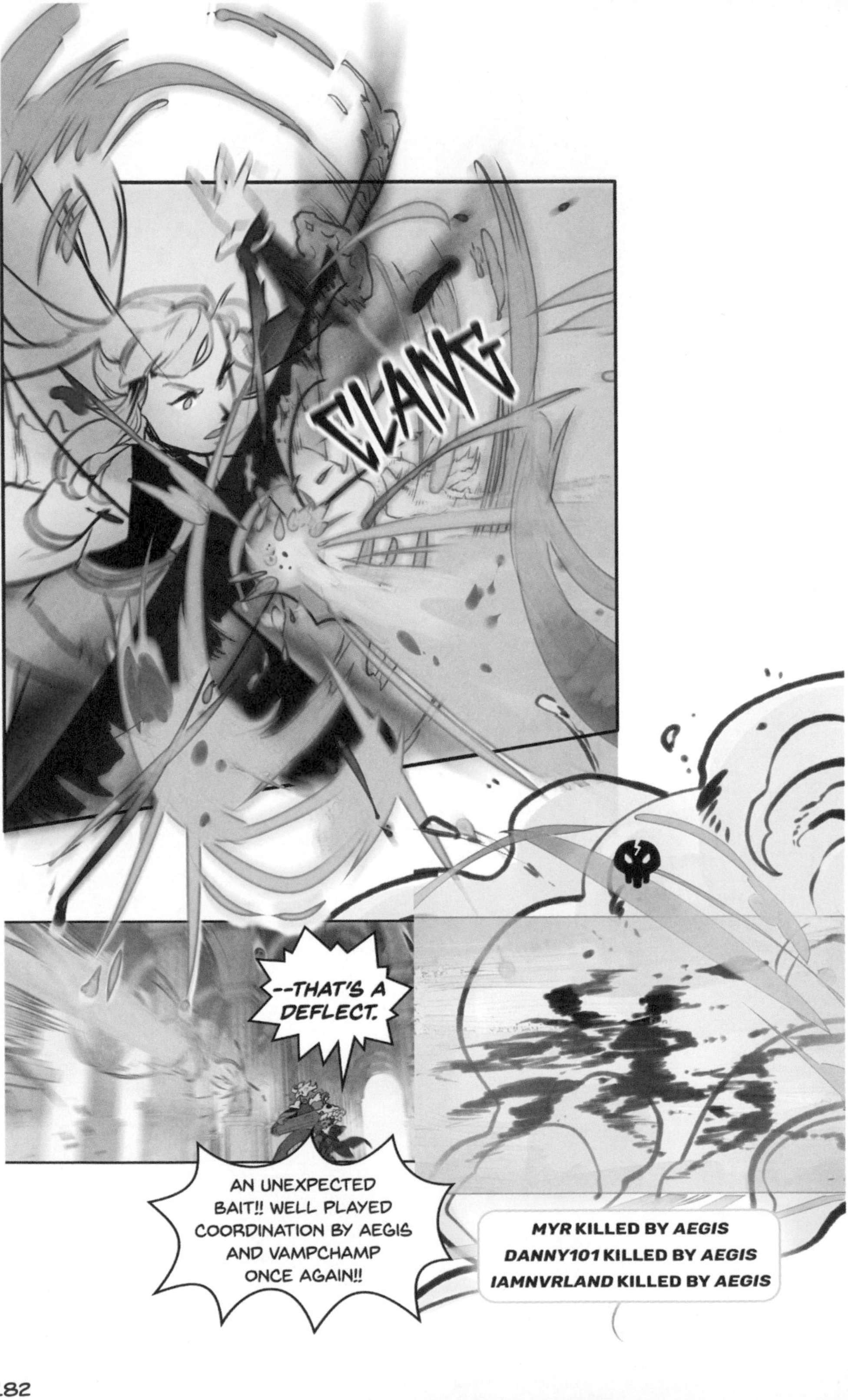
CLANG
--THAT'S A DEFLECT.
AN UNEXPECTED BAIT!! WELL PLAYED COORDINATION BY AEGIS AND VAMPCHAMP ONCE AGAIN!!
MYR KILLED BY AEGIS
DANNY101 KILLED BY AEGIS
IAMNVRLAND KILLED BY AEGIS

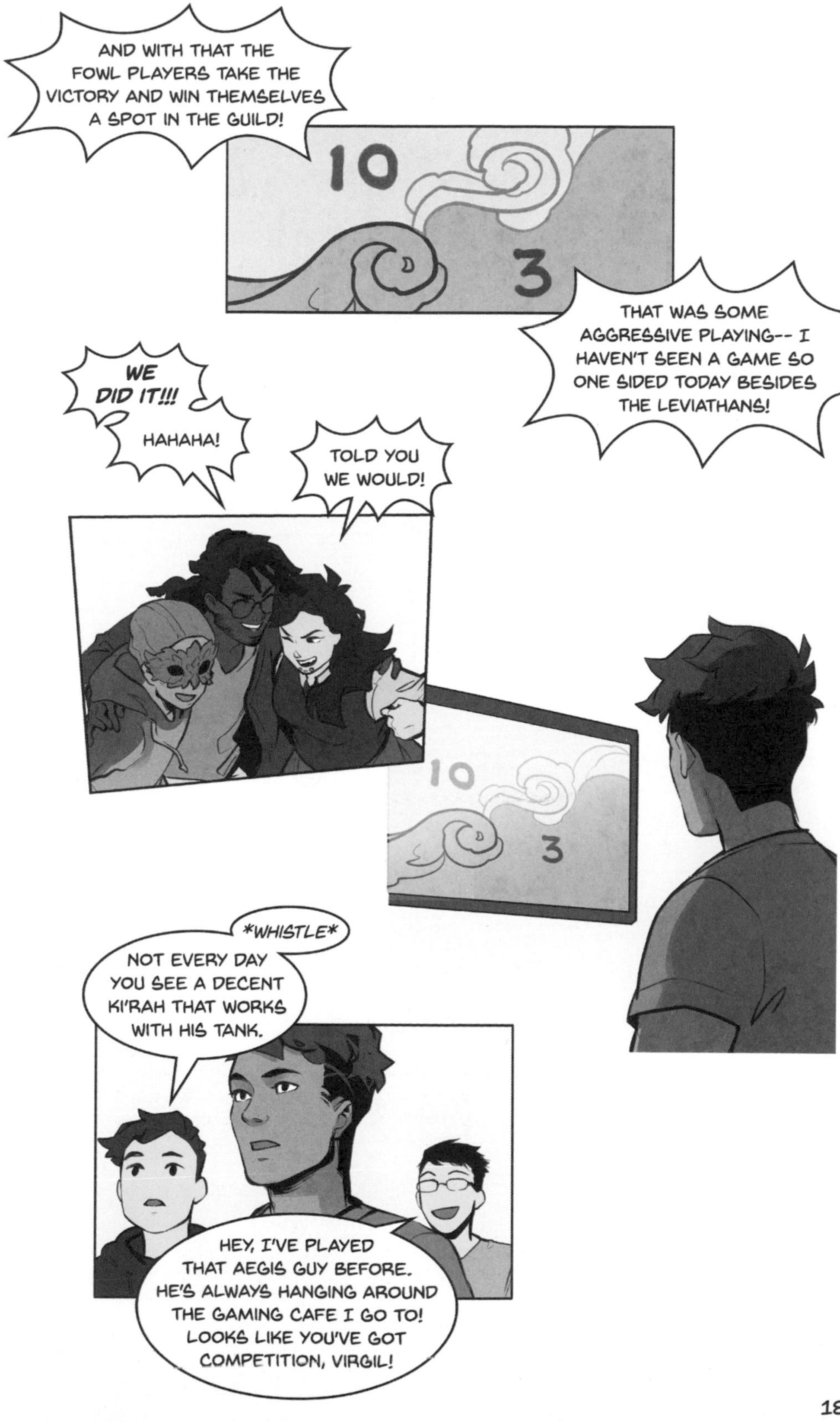
AND WITH THAT THE FOWL PLAYERS TAKE THE VICTORY AND WIN THEMSELVES A SPOT IN THE GUILD!
10
3
THAT WAS SOME AGGRESSIVE PLAYING-- I HAVEN'T SEEN A GAME SO ONE SIDED TODAY BESIDES THE LEVIATHANS!
WE DID IT!!!
HAHAHA!
TOLD YOU WE WOULD!
10
3
WHISTLE
NOT EVERY DAY YOU SEE A DECENT KI'RAH THAT WORKS WITH HIS TANK.
HEY, I'VE PLAYED THAT AEGIS GUY BEFORE. HE'S ALWAYS HANGING AROUND THE GAMING CAFE I GO TO! LOOKS LIKE YOU'VE GOT COMPETITION, VIRGIL!

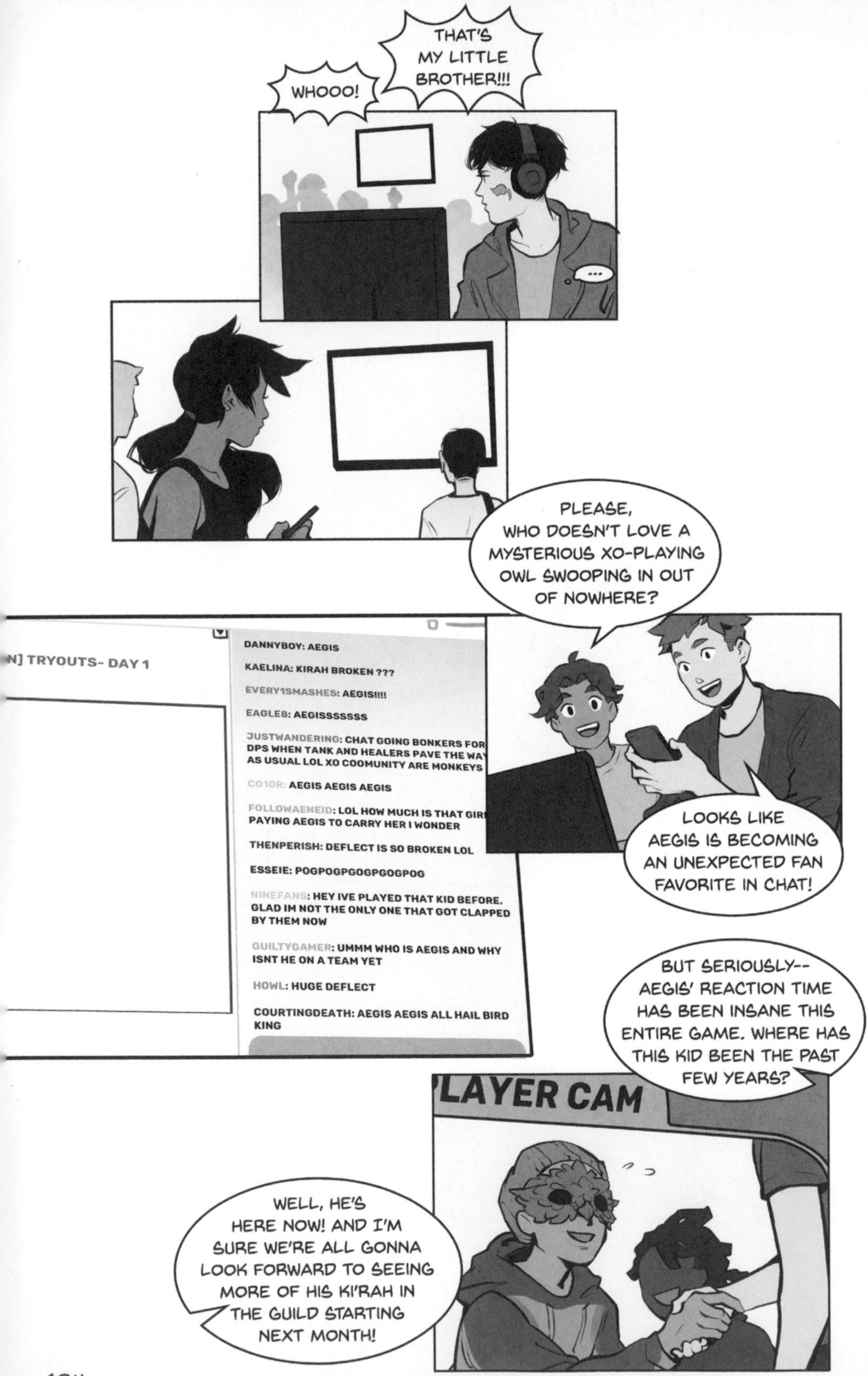
WHOOO!
THAT'S MY LITTLE BROTHER!!!
...
N] TRYOUTS- DAY 1
DANNYBOY: AEGIS
KAELINA: KIRAH BROKEN ???
EVERY1SMASHES: AEGIS!!!!
EAGLE8: AEGISSSSSSS
JUSTWANDERING: CHAT GOING BONKERS FOR DPS WHEN TANK AND HEALERS PAVE THE WAY AS USUAL LOL XO COOMUNITY ARE MONKEYS
CO1OR: AEGIS AEGIS AEGIS
FOLLOWAENEID: LOL HOW MUCH IS THAT GIRL PAYING AEGIS TO CARRY HER I WONDER
THENPERISH: DEFLECT IS SO BROKEN LOL
ESSEIE: POGPOGPGOGPGOGPOG
NINEFANS: HEY IVE PLAYED THAT KID BEFORE. GLAD IM NOT THE ONLY ONE THAT GOT CLAPPED BY THEM NOW
GUILTYGAMER: UMMM WHO IS AEGIS AND WHY ISNT HE ON A TEAM YET
HOWL: HUGE DEFLECT
COURTINGDEATH: AEGIS AEGIS ALL HAIL BIRD KING
PLEASE, WHO DOESN'T LOVE A MYSTERIOUS XO-PLAYING OWL SWOOPING IN OUT OF NOWHERE?
LOOKS LIKE AEGIS IS BECOMING AN UNEXPECTED FAN FAVORITE IN CHAT!
BUT SERIOUSLY-- AEGIS' REACTION TIME HAS BEEN INSANE THIS ENTIRE GAME. WHERE HAS THIS KID BEEN THE PAST FEW YEARS?
PLAYER CAM
WELL, HE'S HERE NOW! AND I'M SURE WE'RE ALL GONNA LOOK FORWARD TO SEEING MORE OF HIS KI'RAH IN THE GUILD STARTING NEXT MONTH!

CHAPTER 4: NOT A DREAM

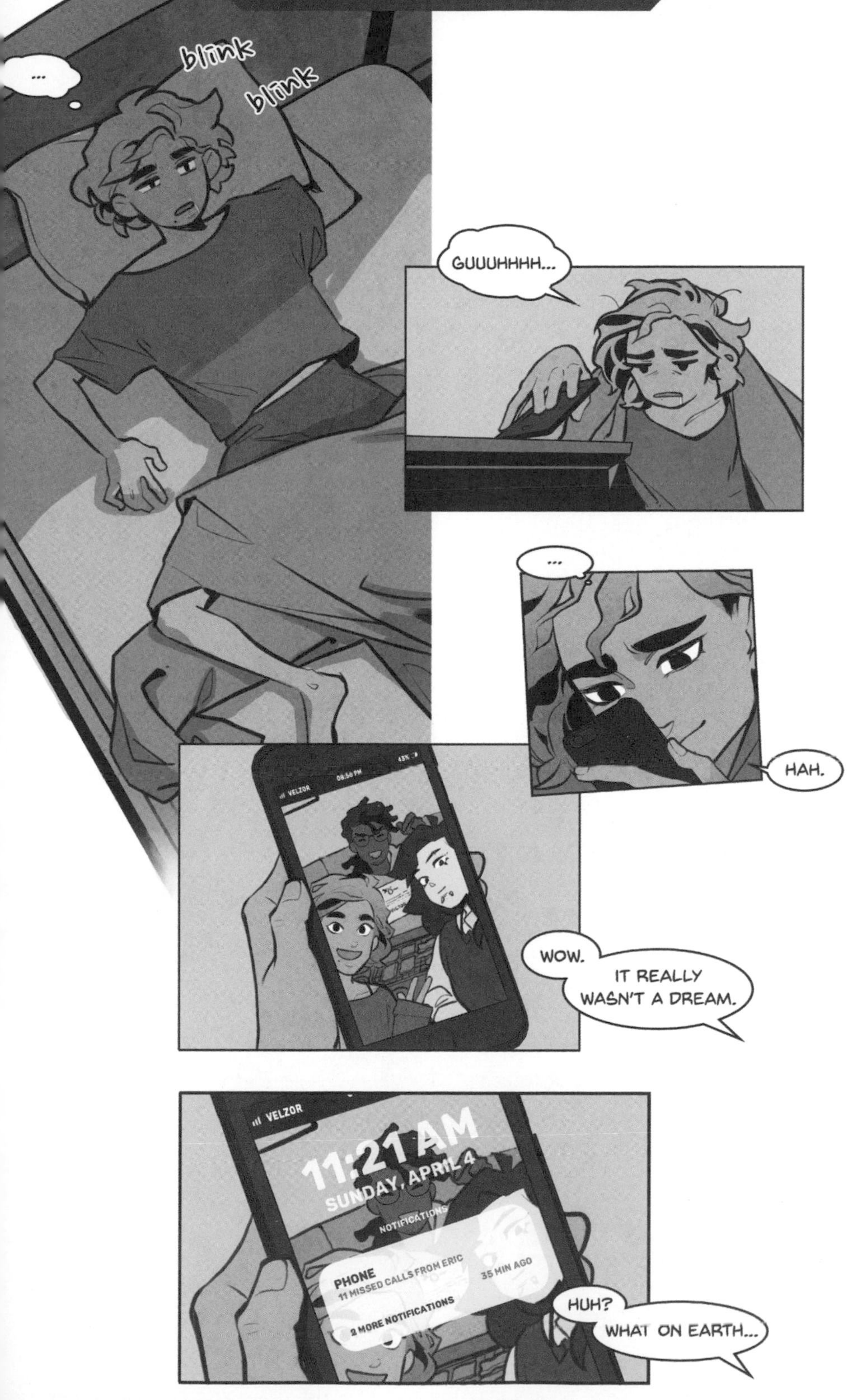
...
blink
blink
GUUUHHHH...
...
HAH.
VELZOR
WOW.
IT REALLY WASN'T A DREAM.
VELZOR
11:21 AM
SUNDAY, APRIL 4
NOTIFICATIONS
PHONE
11 MISSED CALLS FROM ERIC
35 MIN AGO
2 MORE NOTIFICATIONS
HUH?
WHAT ON EARTH...

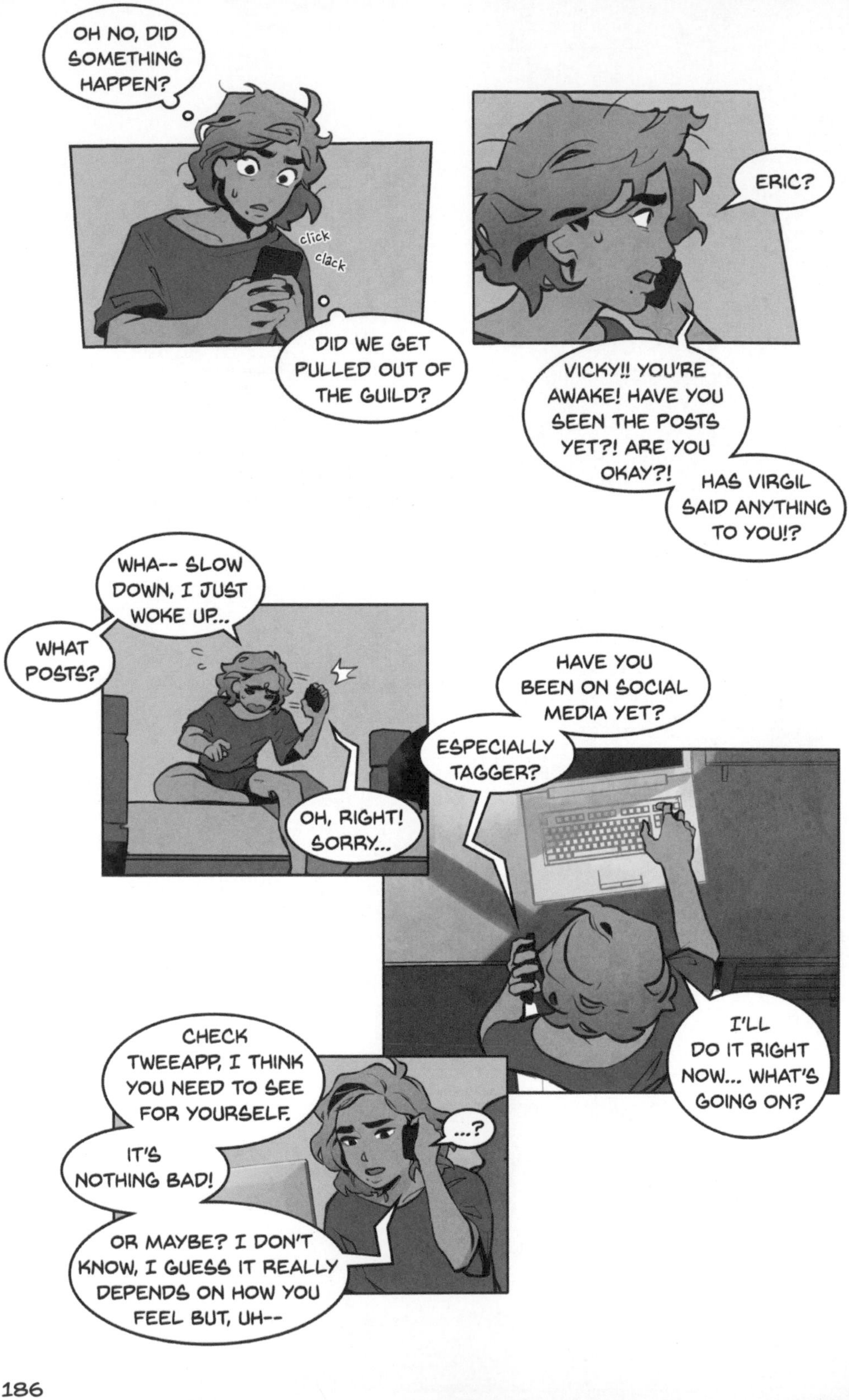
OH NO, DID SOMETHING HAPPEN?
click
clack
DID WE GET PULLED OUT OF THE GUILD?
ERIC?
VICKY!! YOU'RE AWAKE! HAVE YOU SEEN THE POSTS YET?! ARE YOU OKAY?!
HAS VIRGIL SAID ANYTHING TO YOU!?
WHA-- SLOW DOWN, I JUST WOKE UP...
WHAT POSTS?
OH, RIGHT! SORRY...
HAVE YOU BEEN ON SOCIAL MEDIA YET?
ESPECIALLY TAGGER?
I'LL DO IT RIGHT NOW... WHAT'S GOING ON?
CHECK TWEEAPP, I THINK YOU NEED TO SEE FOR YOURSELF.
IT'S NOTHING BAD!
...?
OR MAYBE? I DON'T KNOW, I GUESS IT REALLY DEPENDS ON HOW YOU FEEL BUT, UH--

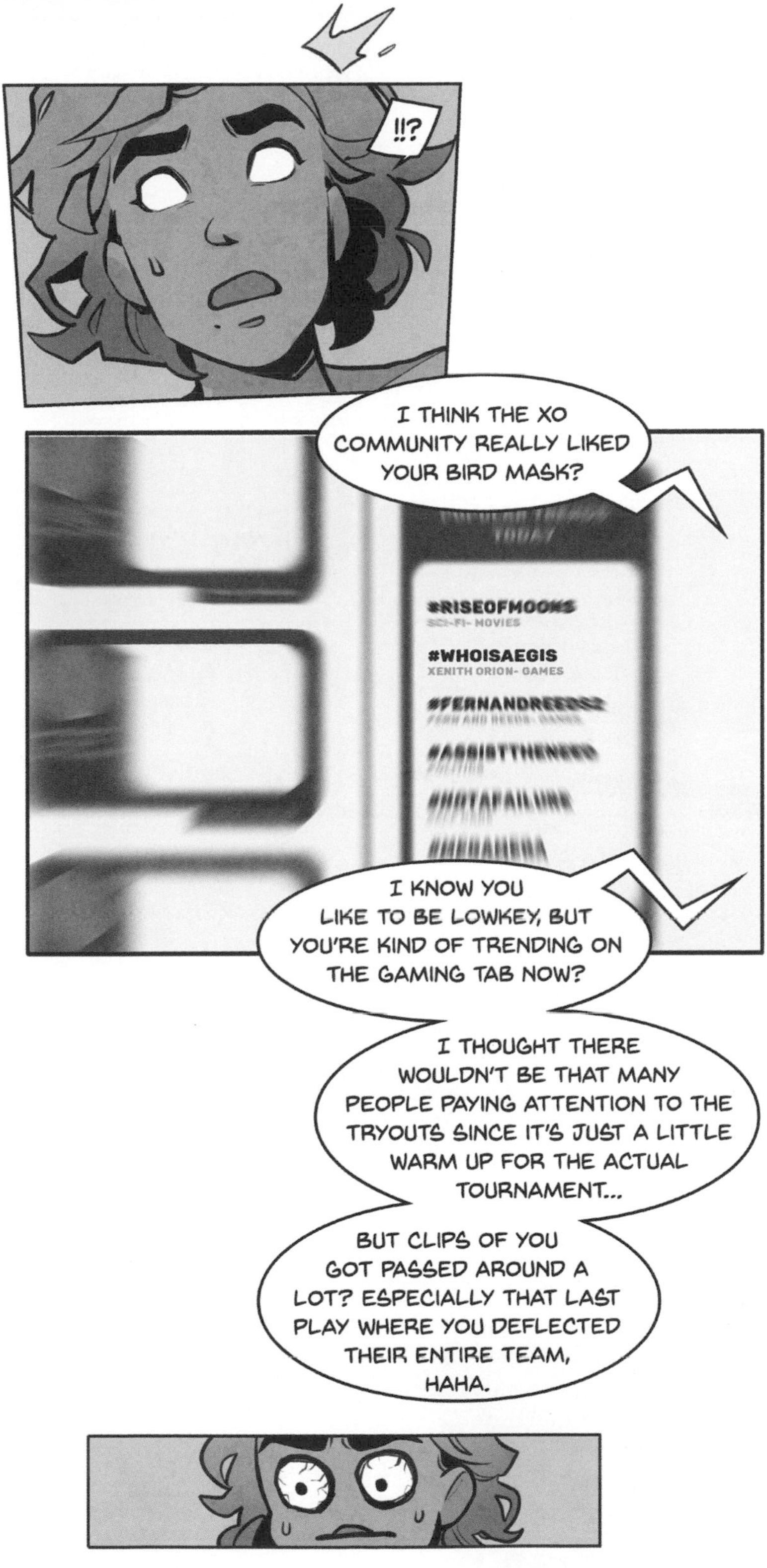
!!?
I THINK THE XO COMMUNITY REALLY LIKED YOUR BIRD MASK?
#RISEOFMOONS
SCI-FI- MOVIES
#WHOISAEGIS
XENITH ORION- GAMES
I KNOW YOU LIKE TO BE LOWKEY, BUT YOU'RE KIND OF TRENDING ON THE GAMING TAB NOW?
I THOUGHT THERE WOULDN'T BE THAT MANY PEOPLE PAYING ATTENTION TO THE TRYOUTS SINCE IT'S JUST A LITTLE WARM UP FOR THE ACTUAL TOURNAMENT...
BUT CLIPS OF YOU GOT PASSED AROUND A LOT? ESPECIALLY THAT LAST PLAY WHERE YOU DEFLECTED THEIR ENTIRE TEAM, HAHA.

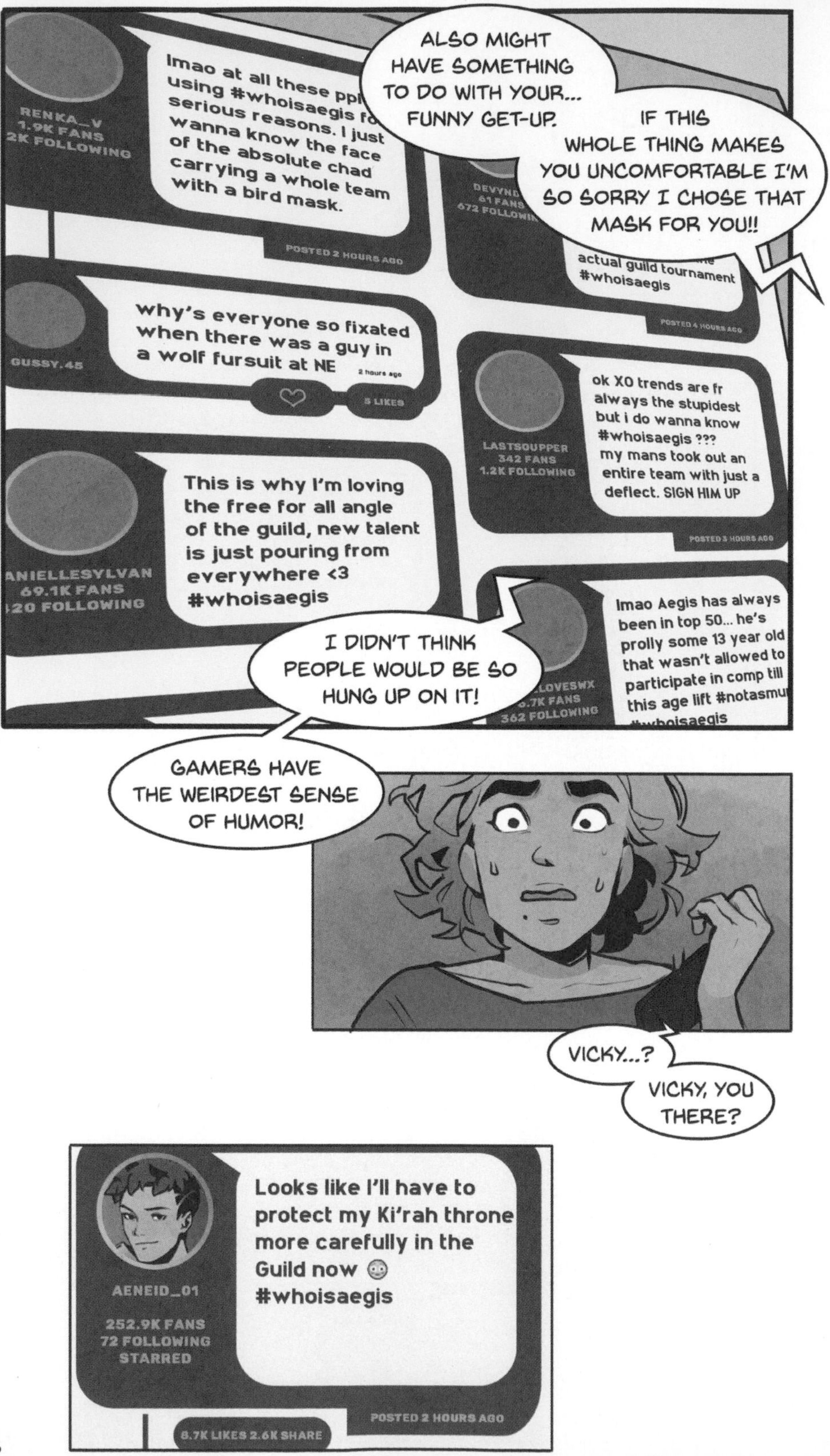
RENKA_V
1.9K FANS
2K FOLLOWING
lmao at all these ppl using #whoisaegis for serious reasons. I just wanna know the face of the absolute chad carrying a whole team with a bird mask.
POSTED 2 HOURS AGO
ALSO MIGHT HAVE SOMETHING TO DO WITH YOUR... FUNNY GET-UP.
IF THIS WHOLE THING MAKES YOU UNCOMFORTABLE I'M SO SORRY I CHOSE THAT MASK FOR YOU!!
61 FANS
672 FOLLOWING
actual guild tournament
#whoisaegis
POSTED 4 HOURS AGO
GUSSY.45
why's everyone so fixated when there was a guy in a wolf fursuit at NE
2 hours ago
5 LIKES
LASTSOUPPER
342 FANS
1.2K FOLLOWING
ok XO trends are fr always the stupidest but i do wanna know #whoisaegis ???
my mans took out an entire team with just a deflect. SIGN HIM UP
POSTED 3 HOURS AGO
ANIELLESYLVAN
69.1K FANS
20 FOLLOWING
This is why I'm loving the free for all angle of the guild, new talent is just pouring from everywhere <3
#whoisaegis
lmao Aegis has always been in top 50... he's prolly some 13 year old that wasn't allowed to participate in comp till this age lift
362 FOLLOWING
I DIDN'T THINK PEOPLE WOULD BE SO HUNG UP ON IT!
GAMERS HAVE THE WEIRDEST SENSE OF HUMOR!
VICKY...?
VICKY, YOU THERE?
Looks like I'll have to protect my Ki'rah throne more carefully in the Guild now
#whoisaegis
AENEID_01
252.9K FANS
72 FOLLOWING
STARRED
POSTED 2 HOURS AGO
8.7K LIKES 2.6K SHARE

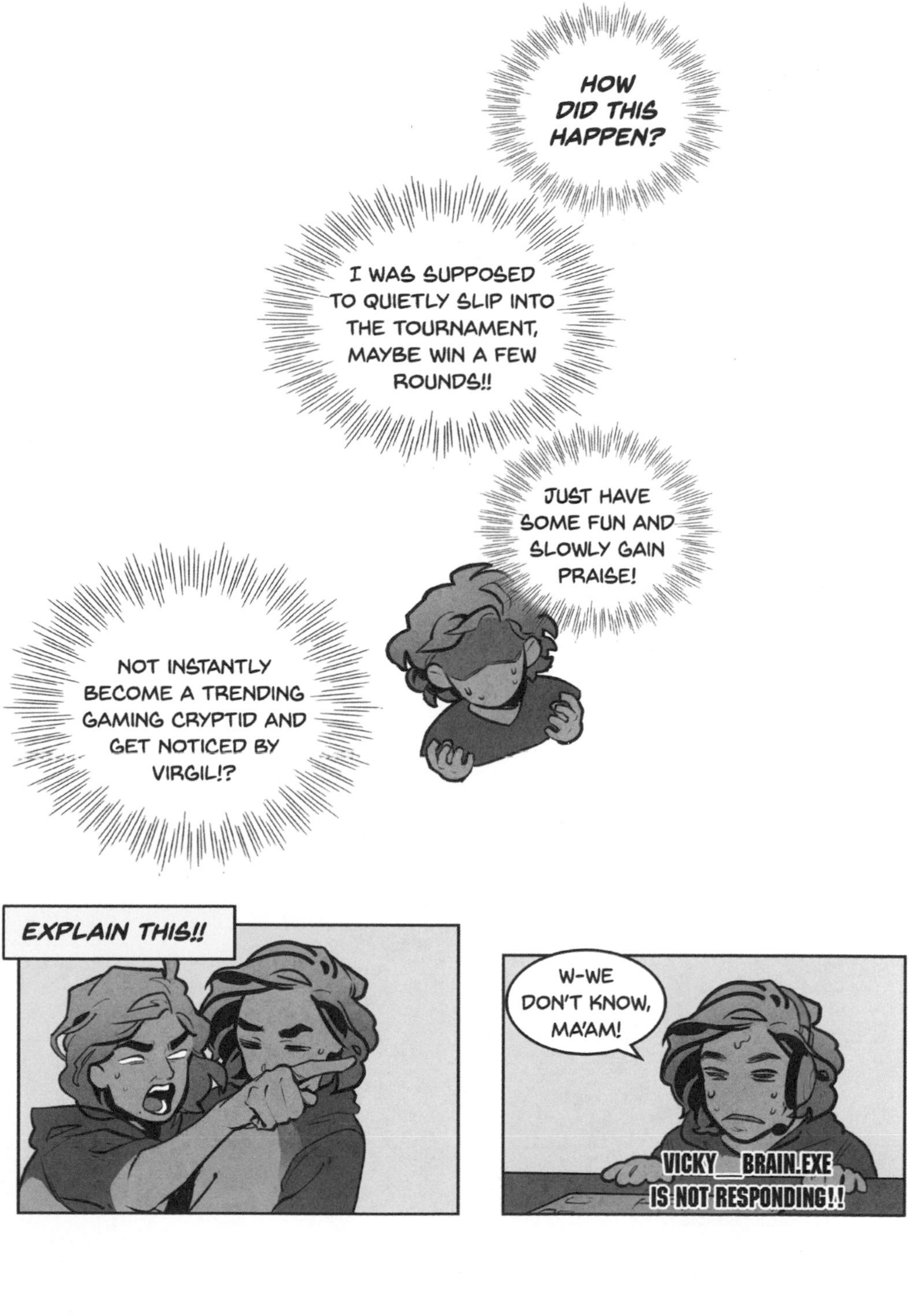
HOW DID THIS HAPPEN?
I WAS SUPPOSED TO QUIETLY SLIP INTO THE TOURNAMENT, MAYBE WIN A FEW ROUNDS!!
JUST HAVE SOME FUN AND SLOWLY GAIN PRAISE!
NOT INSTANTLY BECOME A TRENDING GAMING CRYPTID AND GET NOTICED BY VIRGIL!?
EXPLAIN THIS!!
W-WE DON'T KNOW, MA'AM!
VICKY__BRAIN.EXE IS NOT RESPONDING!!

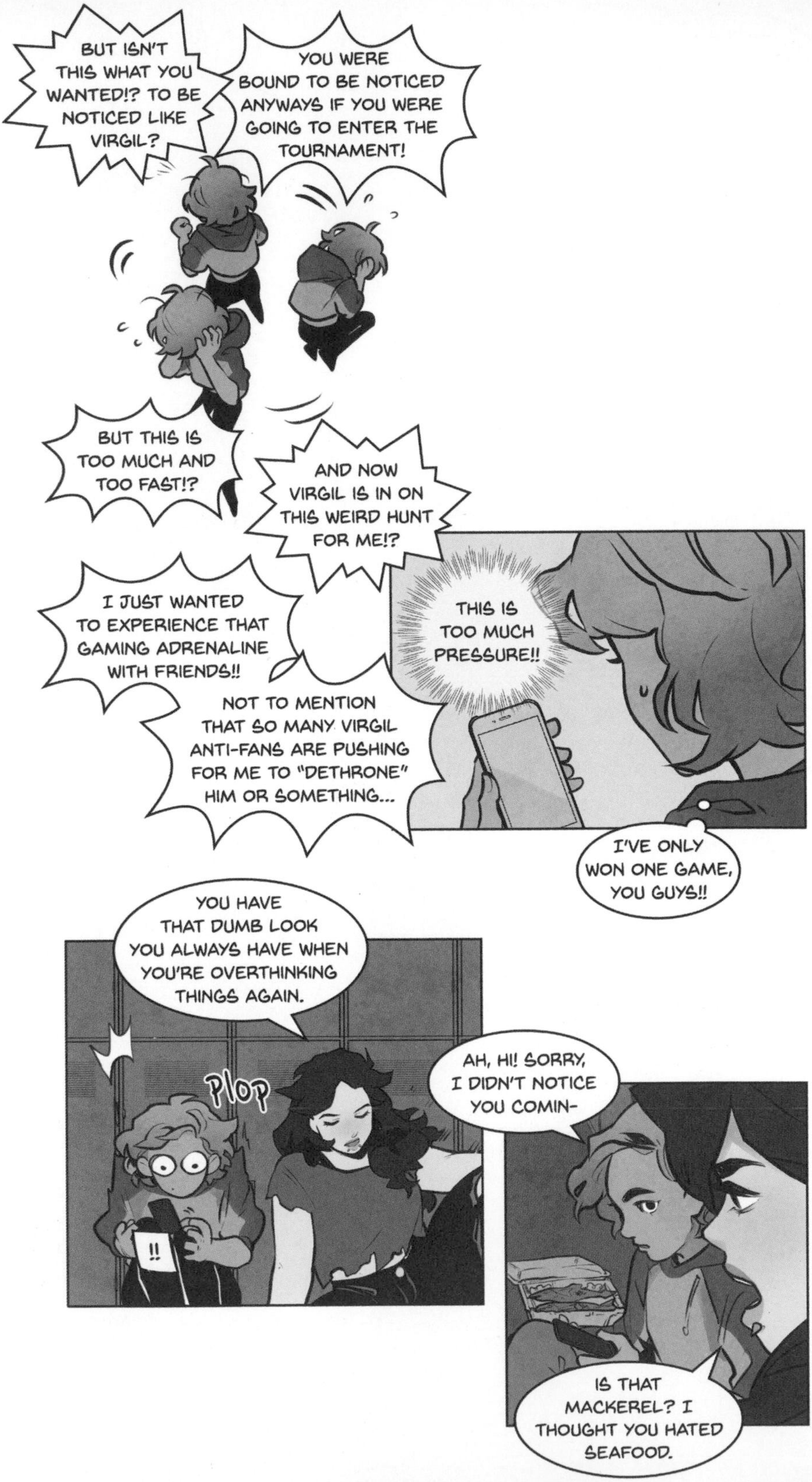
BUT ISN'T THIS WHAT YOU WANTED!? TO BE NOTICED LIKE VIRGIL?
YOU WERE BOUND TO BE NOTICED ANYWAYS IF YOU WERE GOING TO ENTER THE TOURNAMENT!
BUT THIS IS TOO MUCH AND TOO FAST!?
AND NOW VIRGIL IS IN ON THIS WEIRD HUNT FOR ME!?
I JUST WANTED TO EXPERIENCE THAT GAMING ADRENALINE WITH FRIENDS!!
NOT TO MENTION THAT SO MANY VIRGIL ANTI-FANS ARE PUSHING FOR ME TO "DETHRONE" HIM OR SOMETHING...
THIS IS TOO MUCH PRESSURE!!
I'VE ONLY WON ONE GAME, YOU GUYS!!
YOU HAVE THAT DUMB LOOK YOU ALWAYS HAVE WHEN YOU'RE OVERTHINKING THINGS AGAIN.
Plop
!!
AH, HI! SORRY, I DIDN'T NOTICE YOU COMIN-
IS THAT MACKEREL? I THOUGHT YOU HATED SEAFOOD.

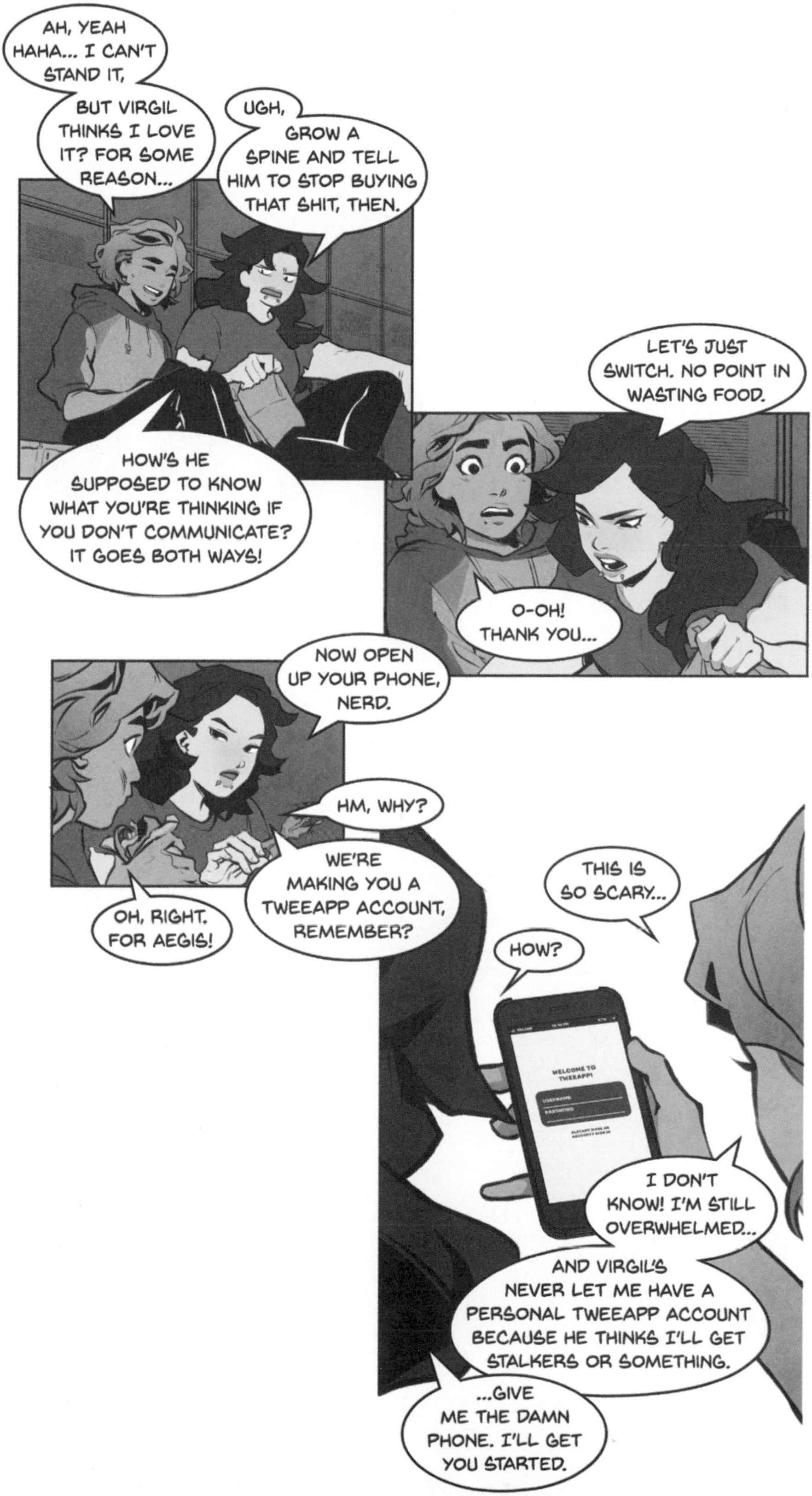
AH, YEAH HAHA... I CAN'T STAND IT,
BUT VIRGIL THINKS I LOVE IT? FOR SOME REASON...
UGH, GROW A SPINE AND TELL HIM TO STOP BUYING THAT SHIT, THEN.
HOW'S HE SUPPOSED TO KNOW WHAT YOU'RE THINKING IF YOU DON'T COMMUNICATE? IT GOES BOTH WAYS!
LET'S JUST SWITCH. NO POINT IN WASTING FOOD.
O-OH! THANK YOU...
NOW OPEN UP YOUR PHONE, NERD.
HM, WHY?
WE'RE MAKING YOU A TWEEAPP ACCOUNT, REMEMBER?
OH, RIGHT. FOR AEGIS!
THIS IS SO SCARY...
HOW?
I DON'T KNOW! I'M STILL OVERWHELMED...
AND VIRGIL'S NEVER LET ME HAVE A PERSONAL TWEEAPP ACCOUNT BECAUSE HE THINKS I'LL GET STALKERS OR SOMETHING.
...GIVE ME THE DAMN PHONE. I'LL GET YOU STARTED.

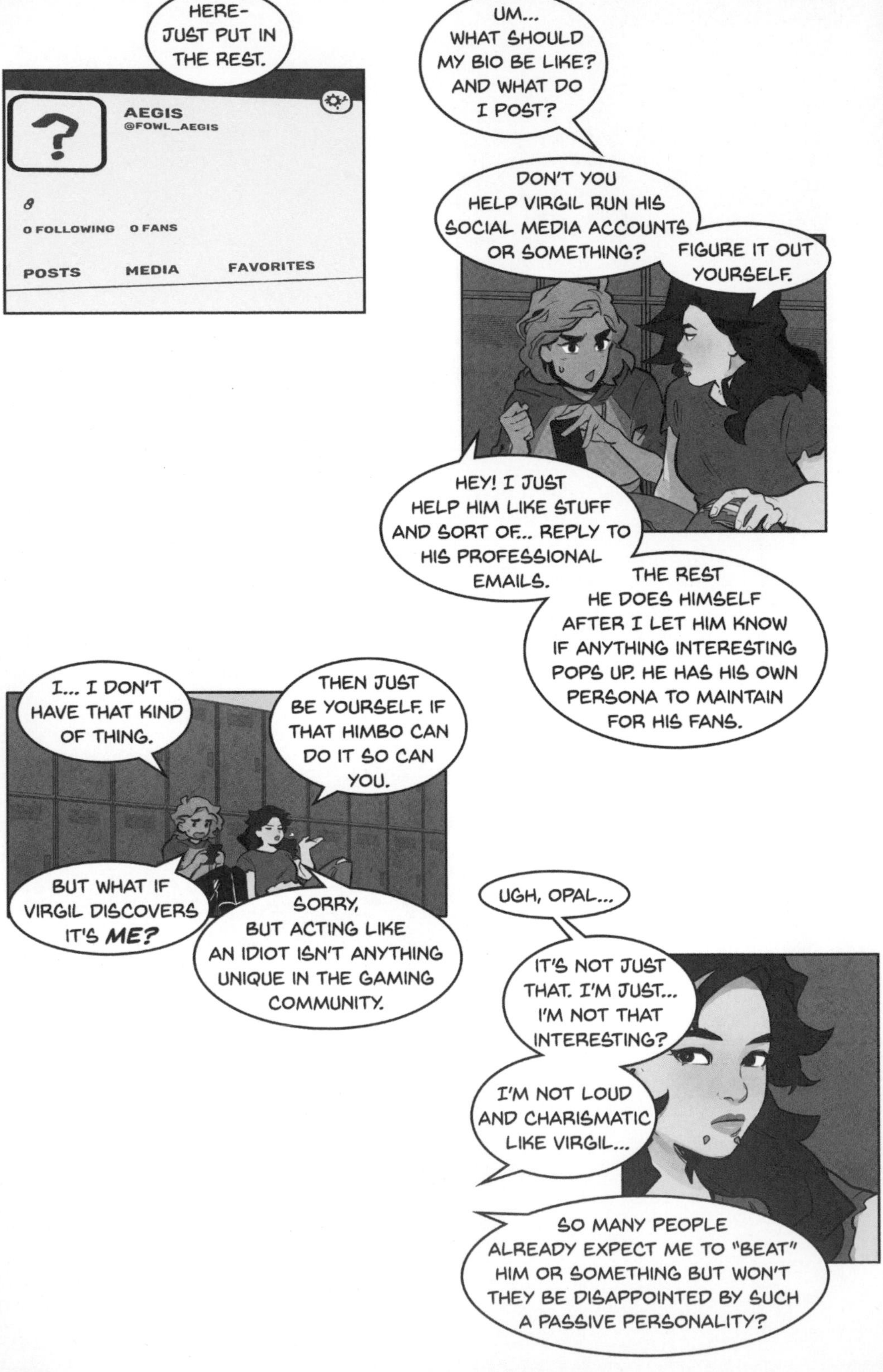
HERE- JUST PUT IN THE REST.
AEGIS
@FOWL_AEGIS
0 FOLLOWING 0 FANS
POSTS MEDIA FAVORITES
UM... WHAT SHOULD MY BIO BE LIKE? AND WHAT DO I POST?
DON'T YOU HELP VIRGIL RUN HIS SOCIAL MEDIA ACCOUNTS OR SOMETHING?
FIGURE IT OUT YOURSELF.
HEY! I JUST HELP HIM LIKE STUFF AND SORT OF... REPLY TO HIS PROFESSIONAL EMAILS.
THE REST HE DOES HIMSELF AFTER I LET HIM KNOW IF ANYTHING INTERESTING POPS UP. HE HAS HIS OWN PERSONA TO MAINTAIN FOR HIS FANS.
I... I DON'T HAVE THAT KIND OF THING.
THEN JUST BE YOURSELF. IF THAT HIMBO CAN DO IT SO CAN YOU.
BUT WHAT IF VIRGIL DISCOVERS IT'S *ME?*
SORRY, BUT ACTING LIKE AN IDIOT ISN'T ANYTHING UNIQUE IN THE GAMING COMMUNITY.
UGH, OPAL...
IT'S NOT JUST THAT. I'M JUST... I'M NOT THAT INTERESTING?
I'M NOT LOUD AND CHARISMATIC LIKE VIRGIL...
SO MANY PEOPLE ALREADY EXPECT ME TO "BEAT" HIM OR SOMETHING BUT WON'T THEY BE DISAPPOINTED BY SUCH A PASSIVE PERSONALITY?

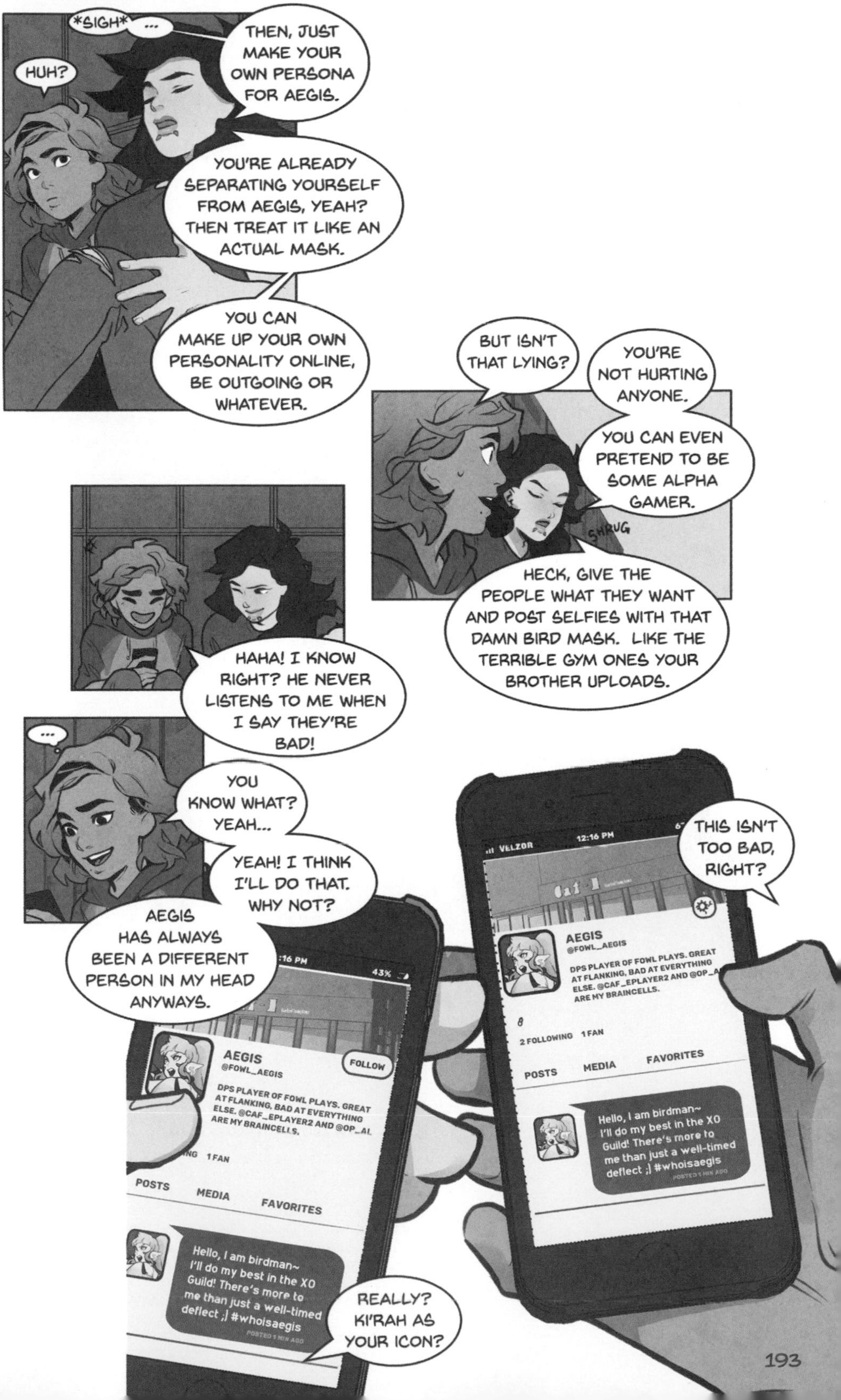
SIGH
...
THEN, JUST MAKE YOUR OWN PERSONA FOR AEGIS.
HUH?
YOU'RE ALREADY SEPARATING YOURSELF FROM AEGIS, YEAH? THEN TREAT IT LIKE AN ACTUAL MASK.
YOU CAN MAKE UP YOUR OWN PERSONALITY ONLINE, BE OUTGOING OR WHATEVER.
BUT ISN'T THAT LYING?
YOU'RE NOT HURTING ANYONE.
YOU CAN EVEN PRETEND TO BE SOME ALPHA GAMER.
SHRUG
HECK, GIVE THE PEOPLE WHAT THEY WANT AND POST SELFIES WITH THAT DAMN BIRD MASK. LIKE THE TERRIBLE GYM ONES YOUR BROTHER UPLOADS.
HAHA! I KNOW RIGHT? HE NEVER LISTENS TO ME WHEN I SAY THEY'RE BAD!
...
YOU KNOW WHAT? YEAH...
YEAH! I THINK I'LL DO THAT. WHY NOT?
AEGIS HAS ALWAYS BEEN A DIFFERENT PERSON IN MY HEAD ANYWAYS.
VELZOR
12:16 PM
AEGIS
@FOWL_AEGIS
DPS PLAYER OF FOWL PLAYS. GREAT AT FLANKING, BAD AT EVERYTHING ELSE. @CAF_EPLAYER2 AND @OP_A ARE MY BRAINCELLS.
2 FOLLOWING 1 FAN
POSTS MEDIA FAVORITES
Hello, I am birdman~ I'll do my best in the XO Guild! There's more to me than just a well-timed deflect ;] #whoisaegis
POSTED 1 MIN AGO
THIS ISN'T TOO BAD, RIGHT?
AEGIS
@FOWL_AEGIS
FOLLOW
DPS PLAYER OF FOWL PLAYS. GREAT AT FLANKING, BAD AT EVERYTHING ELSE. @CAF_EPLAYER2 AND @OP_AL ARE MY BRAINCELLS.
1 FAN
POSTS MEDIA FAVORITES
Hello, I am birdman~ I'll do my best in the XO Guild! There's more to me than just a well-timed deflect ;] #whoisaegis
REALLY? KI'RAH AS YOUR ICON?

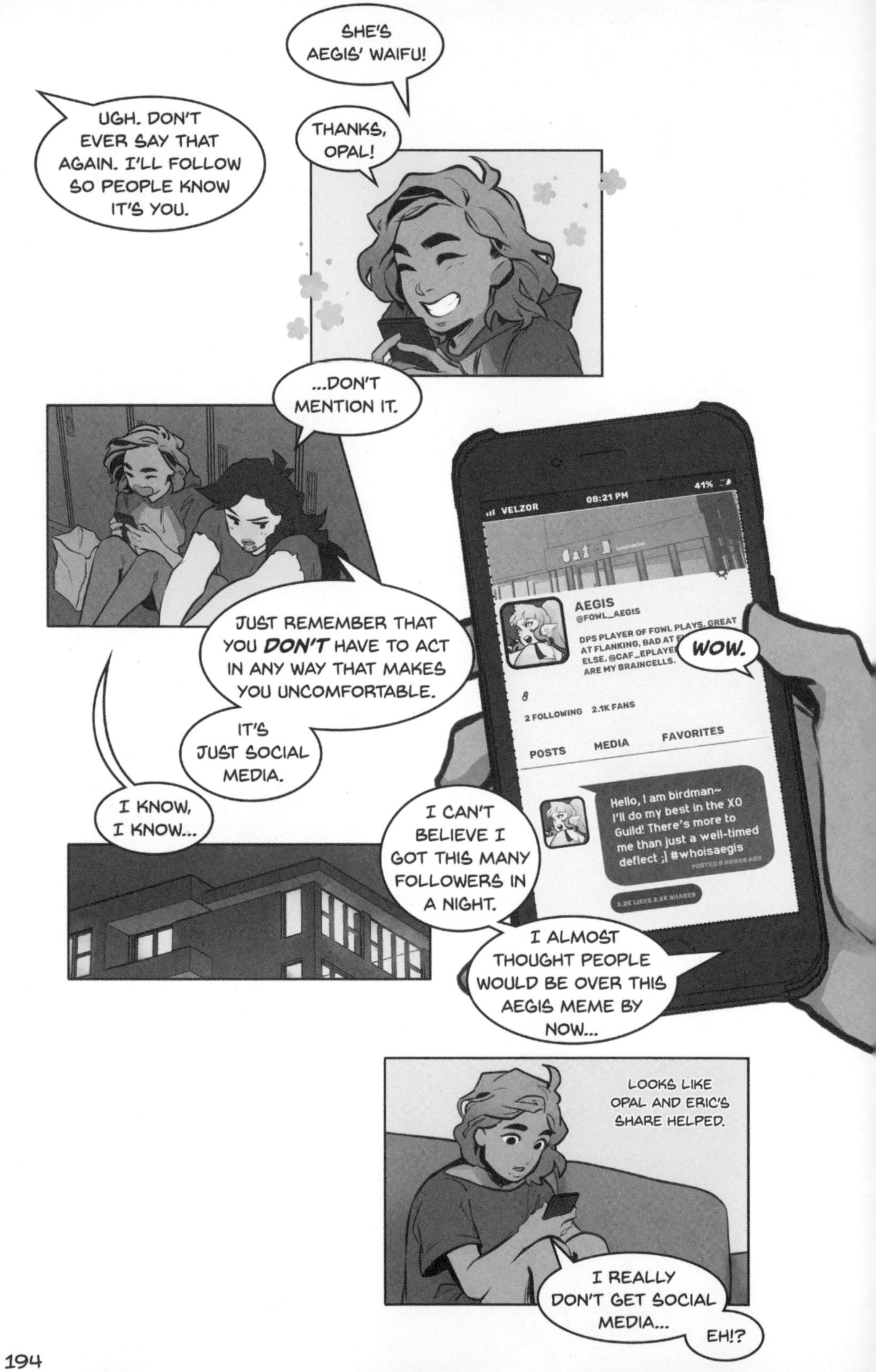
SHE'S AEGIS' WAIFU!
UGH. DON'T EVER SAY THAT AGAIN. I'LL FOLLOW SO PEOPLE KNOW IT'S YOU.
THANKS, OPAL!
...DON'T MENTION IT.
JUST REMEMBER THAT YOU ***DON'T*** HAVE TO ACT IN ANY WAY THAT MAKES YOU UNCOMFORTABLE.
IT'S JUST SOCIAL MEDIA.
I KNOW, I KNOW...
VELZOR
08:21 PM
41%
AEGIS
@FOWL_AEGIS
DPS PLAYER OF FOWL PLAYS, GREAT AT FLANKING, BAD AT E
ELSE. @CAF_EPLAYE
ARE MY BRAINCELLS.
WOW.
2 FOLLOWING 2.1K FANS
POSTS
MEDIA
FAVORITES
Hello, I am birdman~ I'll do my best in the XO Guild! There's more to me than just a well-timed deflect ;] #whoisaegis
POSTED 8 HOURS AGO
I CAN'T BELIEVE I GOT THIS MANY FOLLOWERS IN A NIGHT.
I ALMOST THOUGHT PEOPLE WOULD BE OVER THIS AEGIS MEME BY NOW...
LOOKS LIKE OPAL AND ERIC'S SHARE HELPED.
I REALLY DON'T GET SOCIAL MEDIA...
EH!?

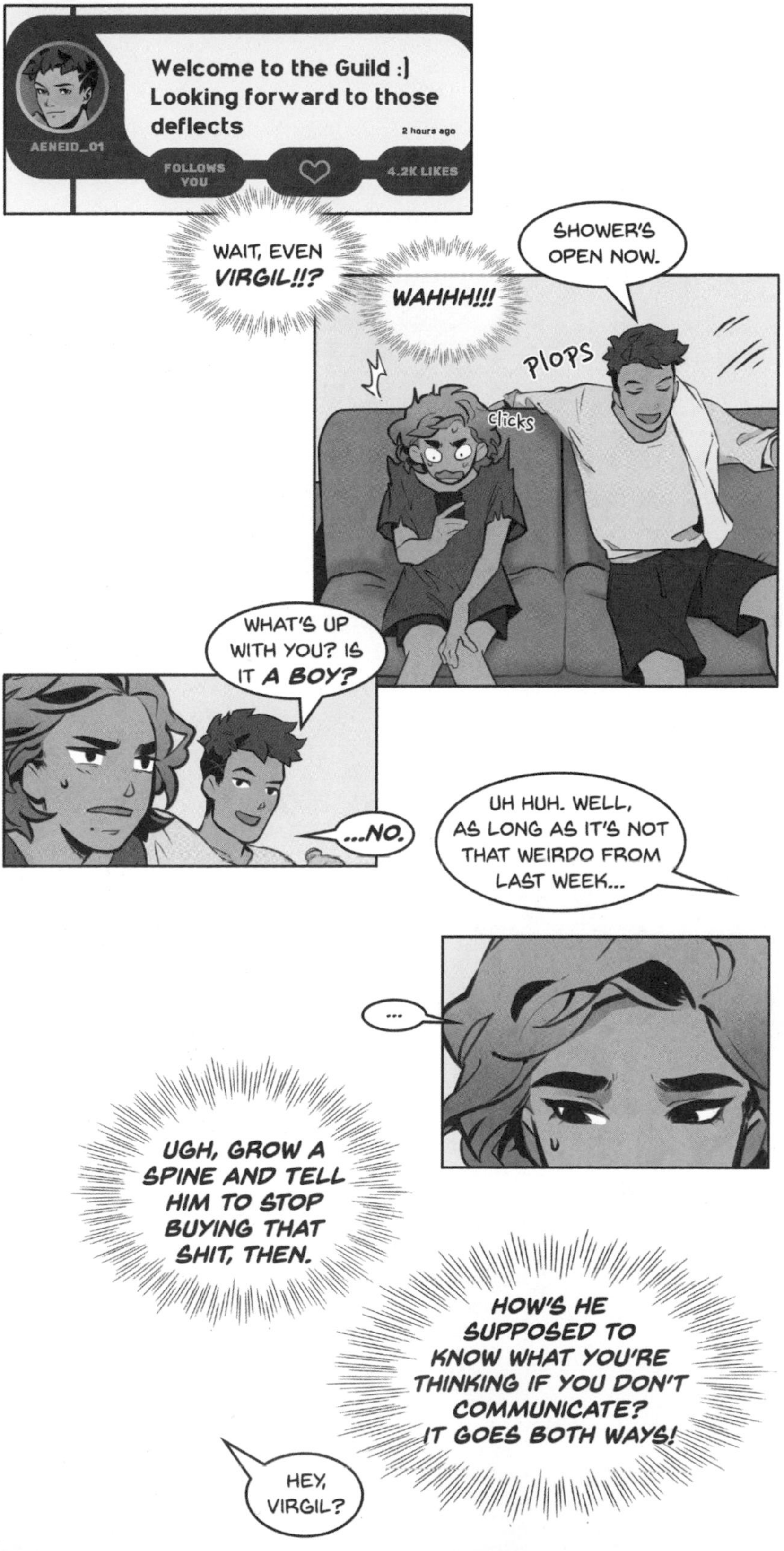
Welcome to the Guild :)
Looking forward to those deflects
2 hours ago
AENEID_01
FOLLOWS YOU
4.2K LIKES
WAIT, EVEN VIRGIL!!?
SHOWER'S OPEN NOW.
WAHHH!!!
PLOPS
clicks
WHAT'S UP WITH YOU? IS IT A BOY?
...NO.
UH HUH. WELL, AS LONG AS IT'S NOT THAT WEIRDO FROM LAST WEEK...
...
UGH, GROW A SPINE AND TELL HIM TO STOP BUYING THAT SHIT, THEN.
HOW'S HE SUPPOSED TO KNOW WHAT YOU'RE THINKING IF YOU DON'T COMMUNICATE? IT GOES BOTH WAYS!
HEY, VIRGIL?

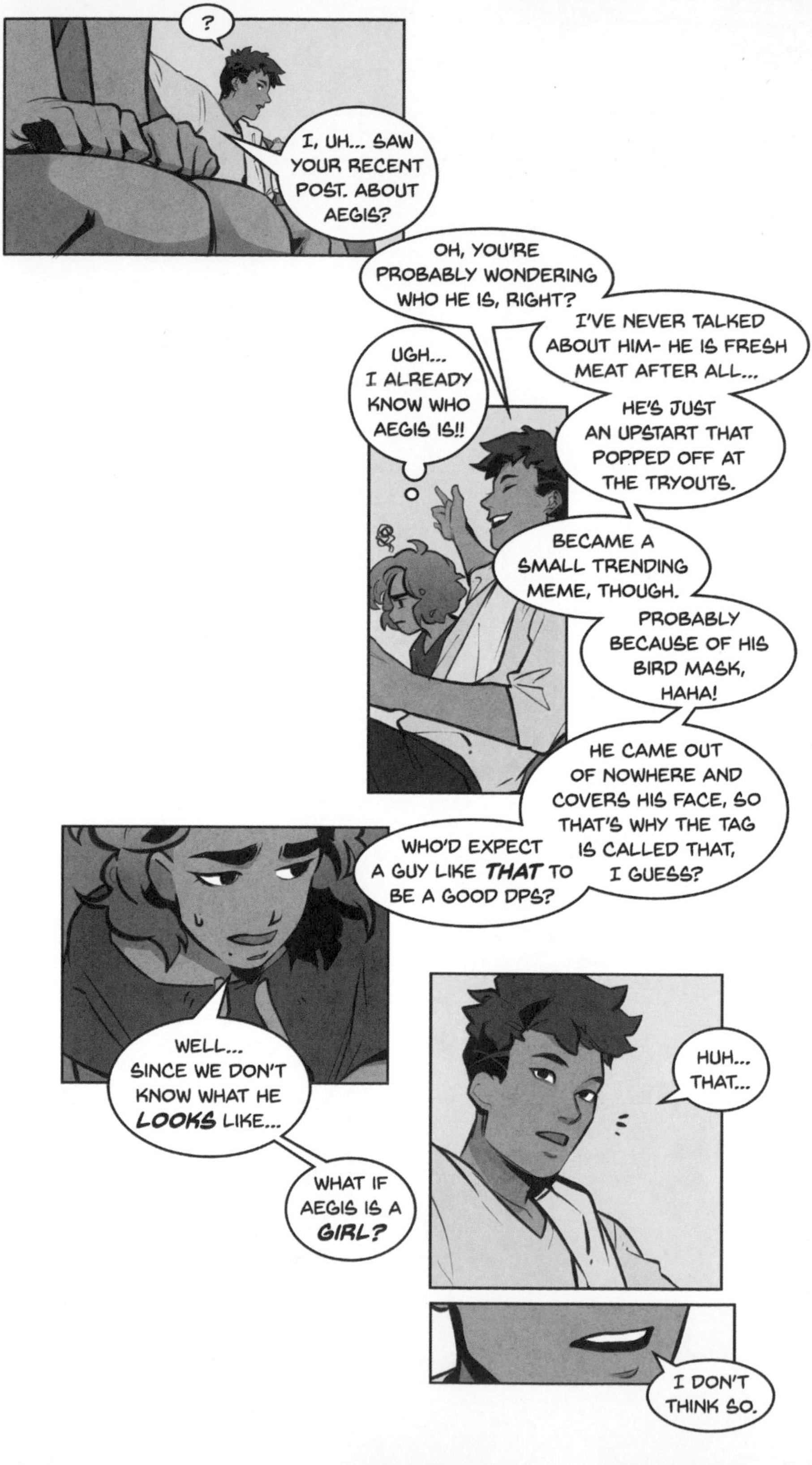
?
I, UH... SAW YOUR RECENT POST. ABOUT AEGIS?
OH, YOU'RE PROBABLY WONDERING WHO HE IS, RIGHT?
I'VE NEVER TALKED ABOUT HIM- HE IS FRESH MEAT AFTER ALL...
UGH... I ALREADY KNOW WHO AEGIS IS!!
HE'S JUST AN UPSTART THAT POPPED OFF AT THE TRYOUTS.
BECAME A SMALL TRENDING MEME, THOUGH.
PROBABLY BECAUSE OF HIS BIRD MASK, HAHA!
HE CAME OUT OF NOWHERE AND COVERS HIS FACE, SO THAT'S WHY THE TAG IS CALLED THAT, I GUESS?
WHO'D EXPECT A GUY LIKE ***THAT*** TO BE A GOOD DPS?
WELL... SINCE WE DON'T KNOW WHAT HE ***LOOKS*** LIKE...
WHAT IF AEGIS IS A ***GIRL?***
HUH... THAT...
I DON'T THINK SO.

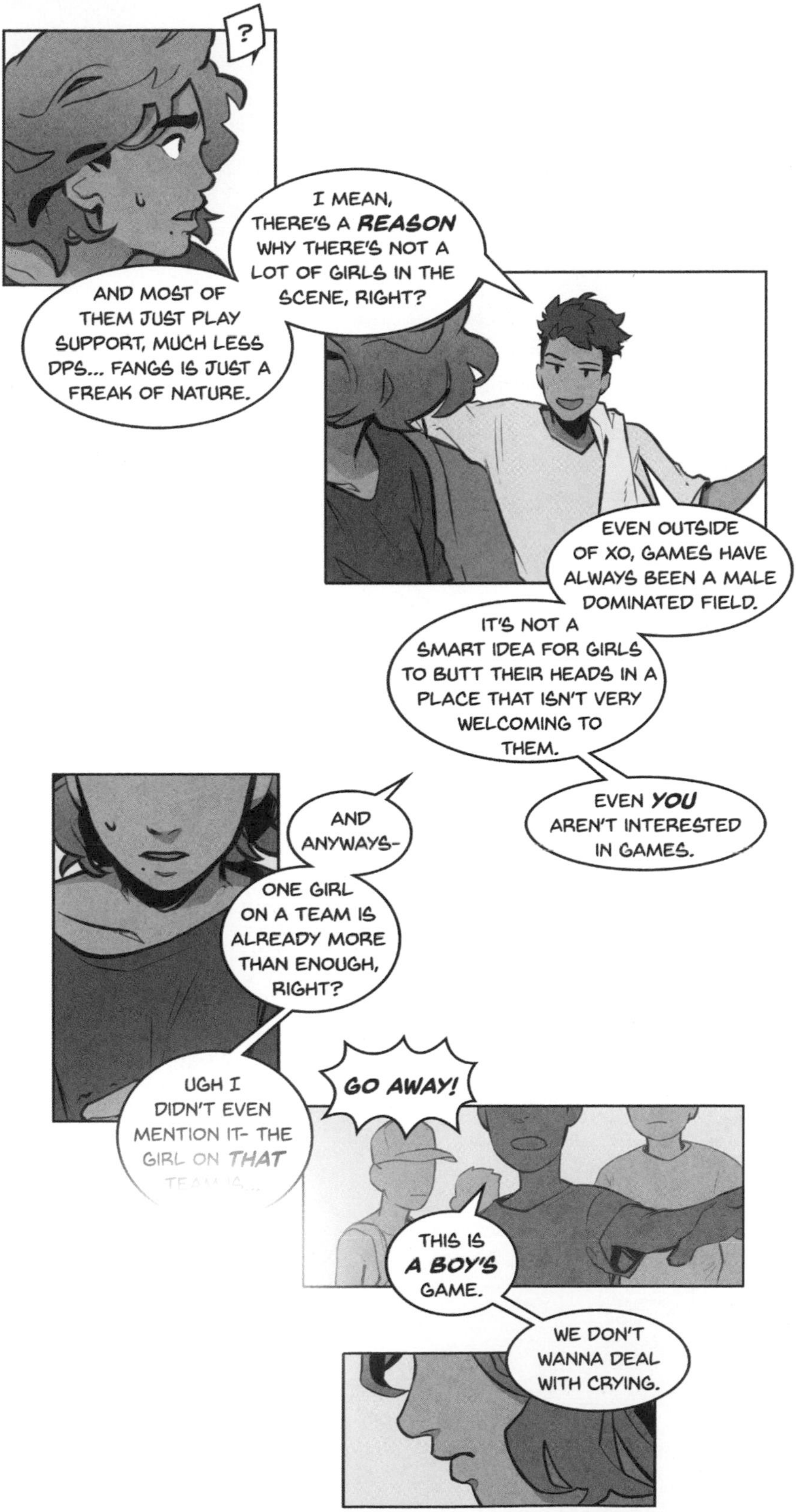
?
I MEAN, THERE'S A ***REASON*** WHY THERE'S NOT A LOT OF GIRLS IN THE SCENE, RIGHT?
AND MOST OF THEM JUST PLAY SUPPORT, MUCH LESS DPS... FANGS IS JUST A FREAK OF NATURE.
EVEN OUTSIDE OF XO, GAMES HAVE ALWAYS BEEN A MALE DOMINATED FIELD.
IT'S NOT A SMART IDEA FOR GIRLS TO BUTT THEIR HEADS IN A PLACE THAT ISN'T VERY WELCOMING TO THEM.
EVEN ***YOU*** AREN'T INTERESTED IN GAMES.
AND ANYWAYS-
ONE GIRL ON A TEAM IS ALREADY MORE THAN ENOUGH, RIGHT?
UGH I DIDN'T EVEN MENTION IT- THE GIRL ON *THAT*
GO AWAY!
THIS IS ***A BOY'S*** GAME.
WE DON'T WANNA DEAL WITH CRYING.

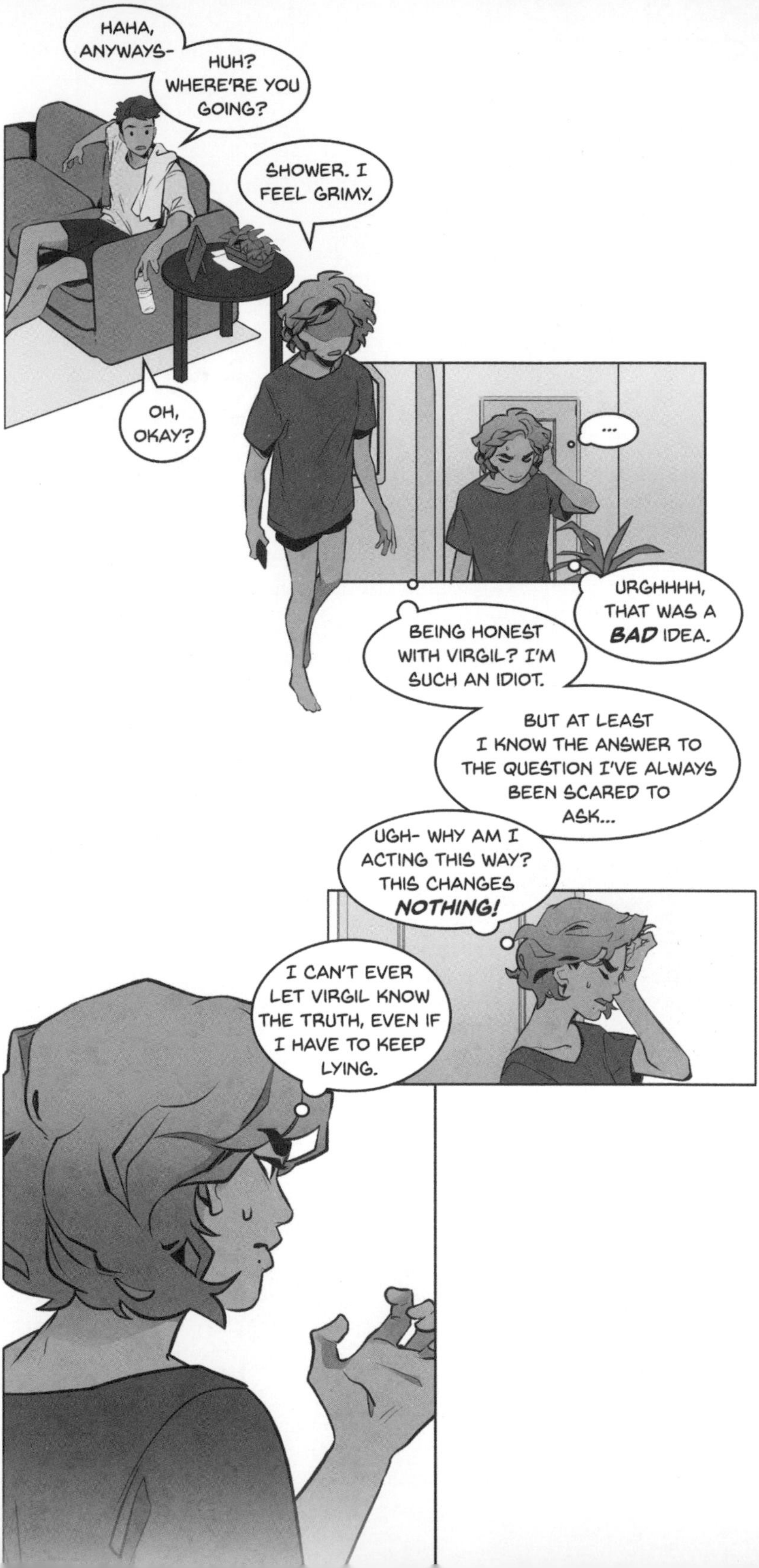
HAHA, ANYWAYS-
HUH? WHERE'RE YOU GOING?
SHOWER. I FEEL GRIMY.
OH, OKAY?
...
URGHHHH, THAT WAS A **BAD** IDEA.
BEING HONEST WITH VIRGIL? I'M SUCH AN IDIOT.
BUT AT LEAST I KNOW THE ANSWER TO THE QUESTION I'VE ALWAYS BEEN SCARED TO ASK...
UGH- WHY AM I ACTING THIS WAY? THIS CHANGES ***NOTHING!***
I CAN'T EVER LET VIRGIL KNOW THE TRUTH, EVEN IF I HAVE TO KEEP LYING.

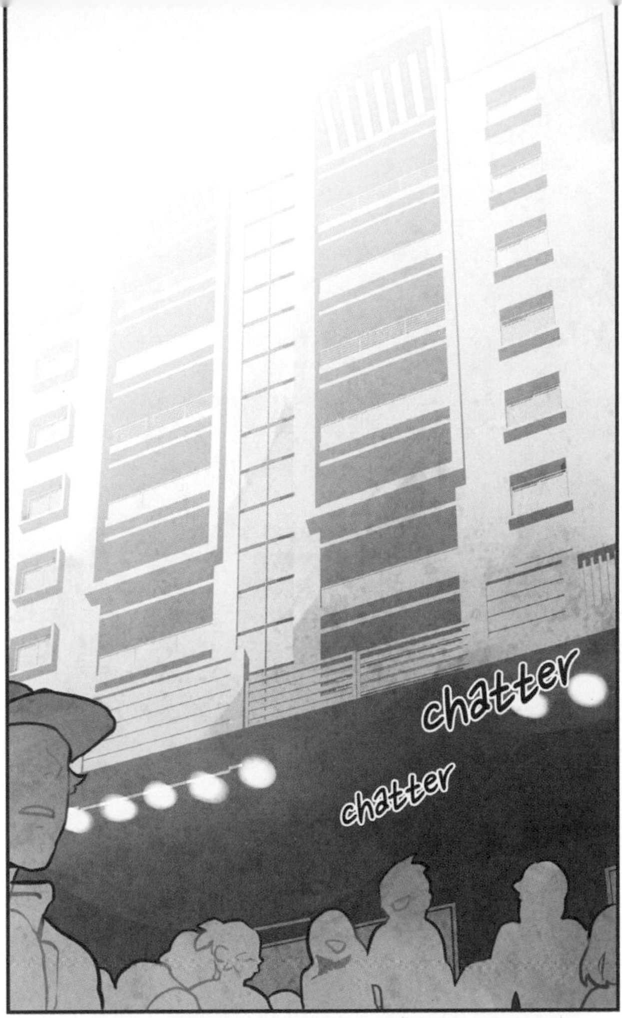
chatter
chatter

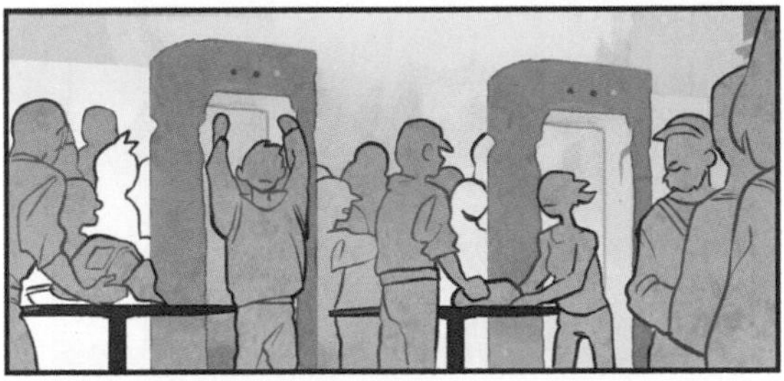

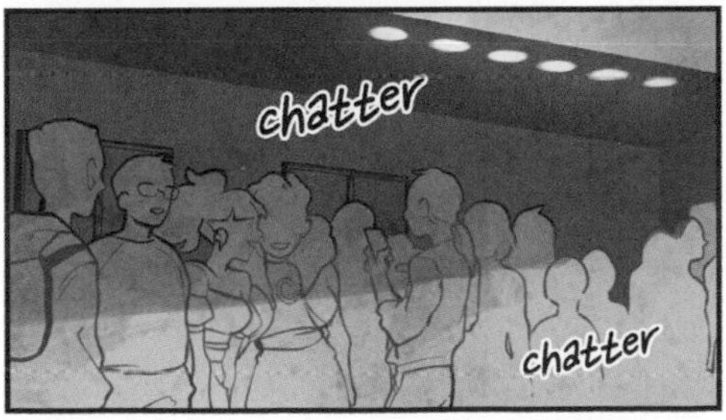
chatter
chatter

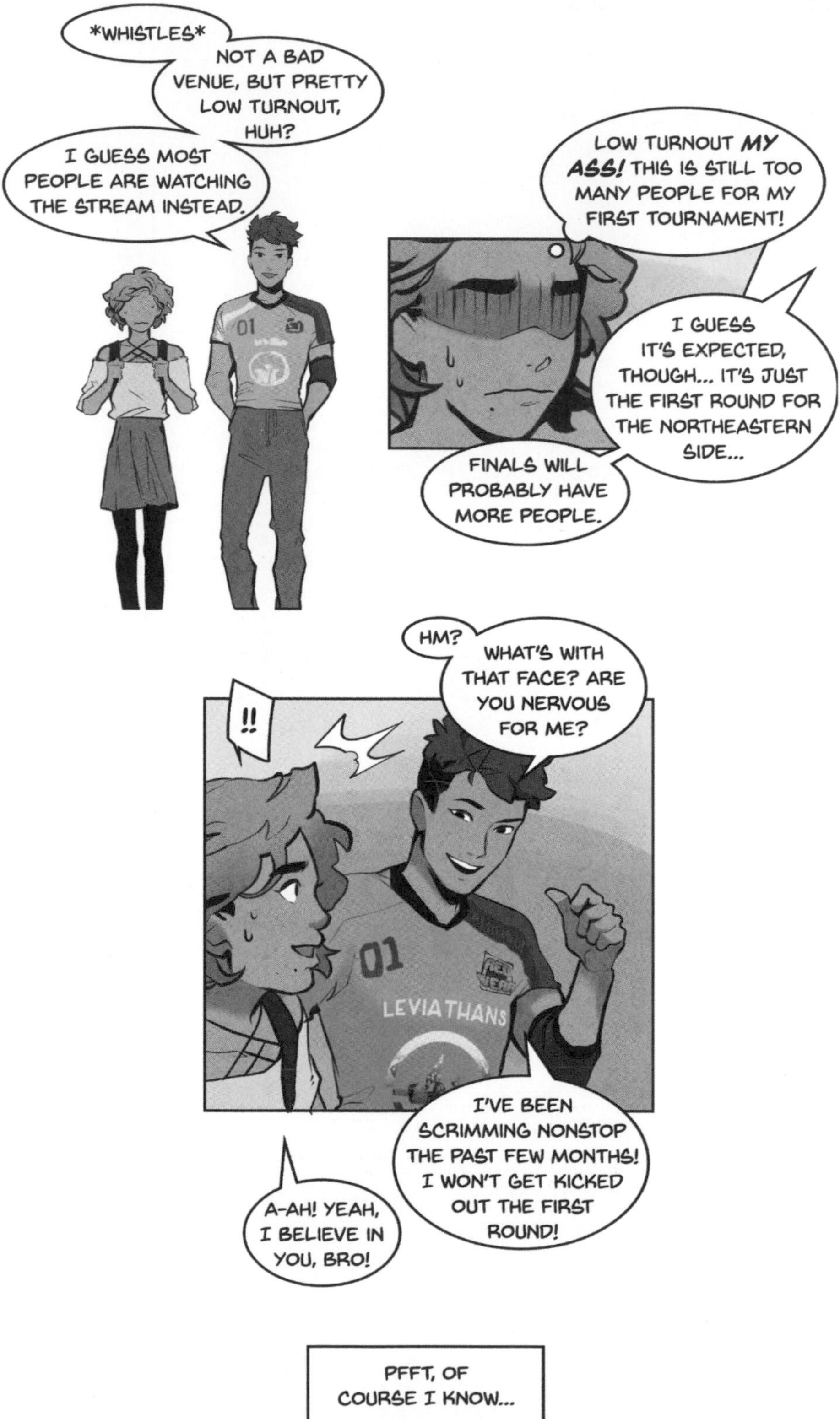
WHISTLES
NOT A BAD VENUE, BUT PRETTY LOW TURNOUT, HUH?
I GUESS MOST PEOPLE ARE WATCHING THE STREAM INSTEAD.
LOW TURNOUT **MY ASS!** THIS IS STILL TOO MANY PEOPLE FOR MY FIRST TOURNAMENT!
I GUESS IT'S EXPECTED, THOUGH... IT'S JUST THE FIRST ROUND FOR THE NORTHEASTERN SIDE...
FINALS WILL PROBABLY HAVE MORE PEOPLE.
HM?
WHAT'S WITH THAT FACE? ARE YOU NERVOUS FOR ME?
!!
01
LEVIATHANS
I'VE BEEN SCRIMMING NONSTOP THE PAST FEW MONTHS! I WON'T GET KICKED OUT THE FIRST ROUND!
A-AH! YEAH, I BELIEVE IN YOU, BRO!
PFFT, OF COURSE I KNOW...

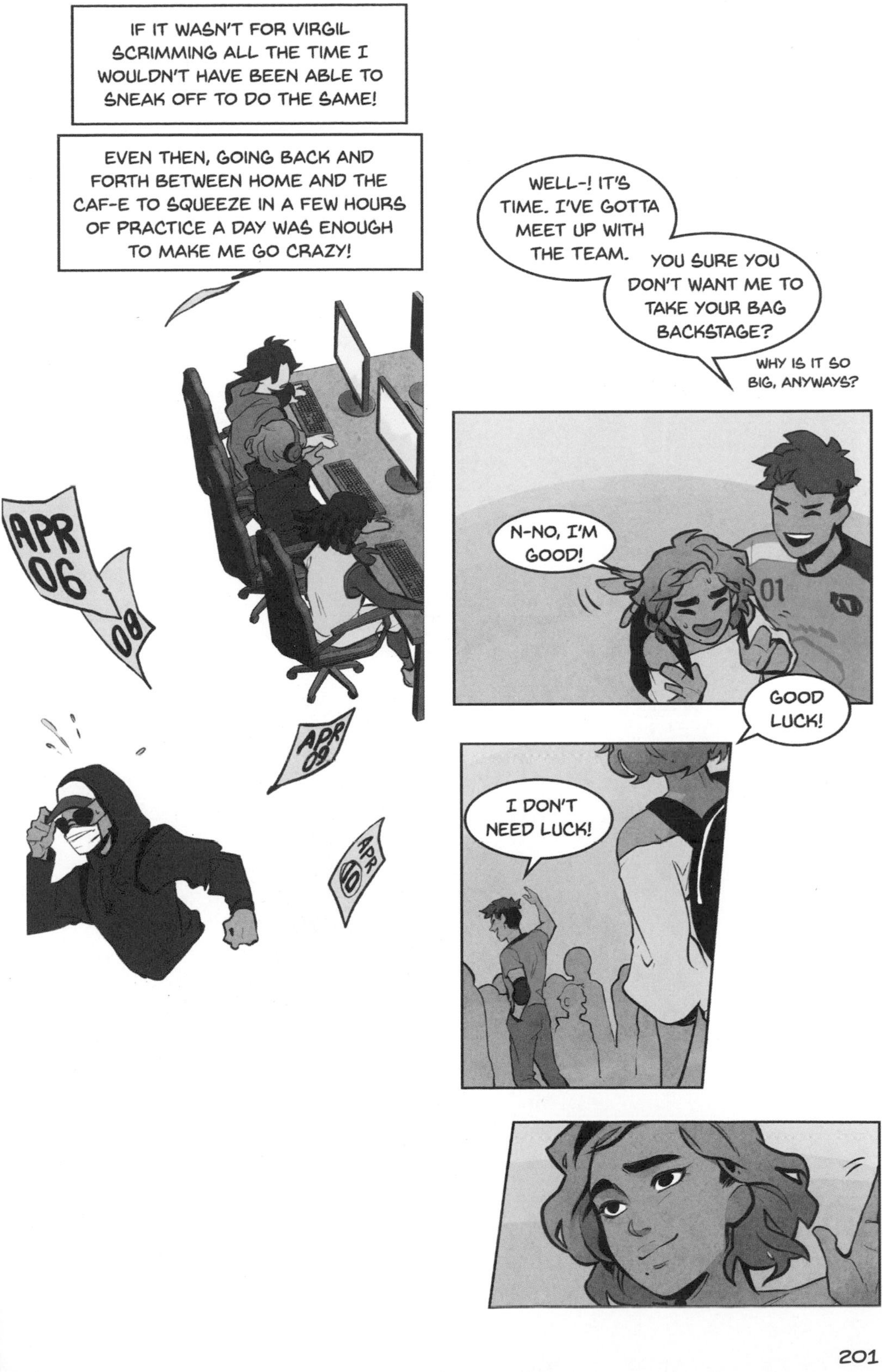
IF IT WASN'T FOR VIRGIL SCRIMMING ALL THE TIME I WOULDN'T HAVE BEEN ABLE TO SNEAK OFF TO DO THE SAME!
EVEN THEN, GOING BACK AND FORTH BETWEEN HOME AND THE CAF-E TO SQUEEZE IN A FEW HOURS OF PRACTICE A DAY WAS ENOUGH TO MAKE ME GO CRAZY!
APR 06
08
APR 09
APR 10
WELL-! IT'S TIME. I'VE GOTTA MEET UP WITH THE TEAM.
YOU SURE YOU DON'T WANT ME TO TAKE YOUR BAG BACKSTAGE?
WHY IS IT SO BIG, ANYWAYS?
N-NO, I'M GOOD!
01
GOOD LUCK!
I DON'T NEED LUCK!

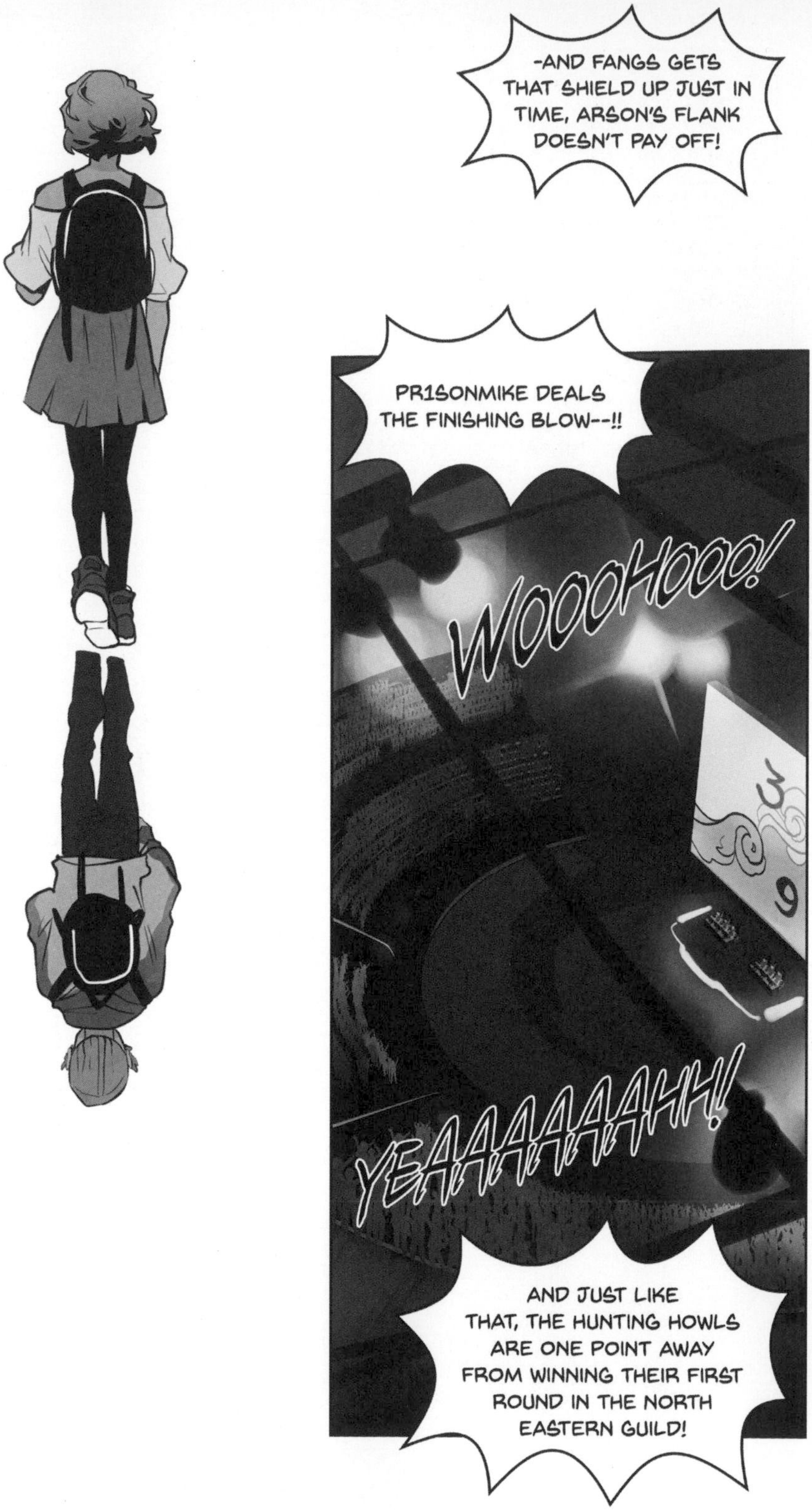
-AND FANGS GETS THAT SHIELD UP JUST IN TIME, ARSON'S FLANK DOESN'T PAY OFF!
PR1SONMIKE DEALS THE FINISHING BLOW--!!
WOOOHOOO!
YEAAAAAAHH!
AND JUST LIKE THAT, THE HUNTING HOWLS ARE ONE POINT AWAY FROM WINNING THEIR FIRST ROUND IN THE NORTH EASTERN GUILD!

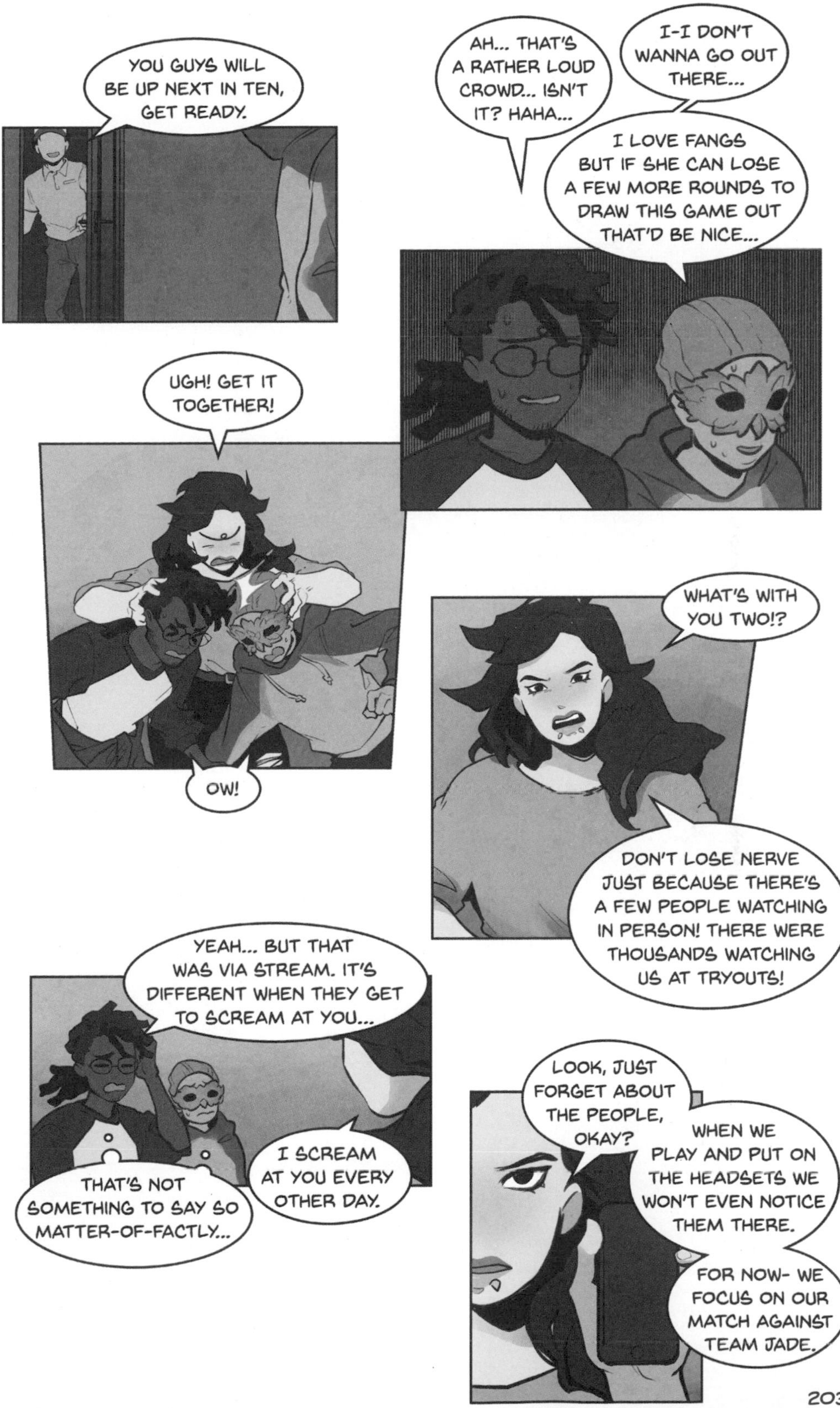
YOU GUYS WILL BE UP NEXT IN TEN, GET READY.
AH... THAT'S A RATHER LOUD CROWD... ISN'T IT? HAHA...
I-I DON'T WANNA GO OUT THERE...
I LOVE FANGS BUT IF SHE CAN LOSE A FEW MORE ROUNDS TO DRAW THIS GAME OUT THAT'D BE NICE...
UGH! GET IT TOGETHER!
OW!
WHAT'S WITH YOU TWO!?
DON'T LOSE NERVE JUST BECAUSE THERE'S A FEW PEOPLE WATCHING IN PERSON! THERE WERE THOUSANDS WATCHING US AT TRYOUTS!
YEAH... BUT THAT WAS VIA STREAM. IT'S DIFFERENT WHEN THEY GET TO SCREAM AT YOU...
I SCREAM AT YOU EVERY OTHER DAY.
THAT'S NOT SOMETHING TO SAY SO MATTER-OF-FACTLY...
LOOK, JUST FORGET ABOUT THE PEOPLE, OKAY?
WHEN WE PLAY AND PUT ON THE HEADSETS WE WON'T EVEN NOTICE THEM THERE.
FOR NOW- WE FOCUS ON OUR MATCH AGAINST TEAM JADE.

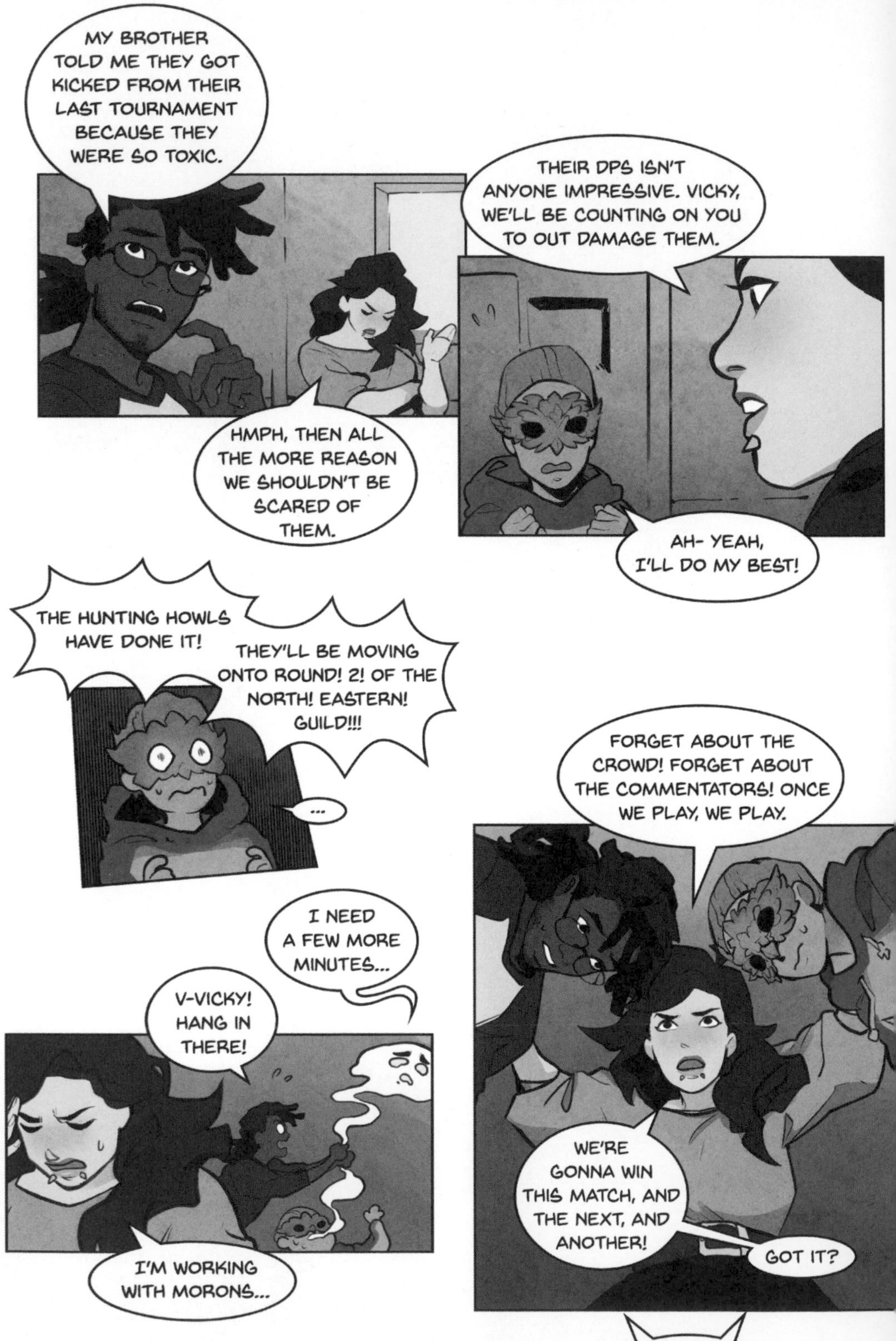
MY BROTHER TOLD ME THEY GOT KICKED FROM THEIR LAST TOURNAMENT BECAUSE THEY WERE SO TOXIC.
HMPH, THEN ALL THE MORE REASON WE SHOULDN'T BE SCARED OF THEM.
THEIR DPS ISN'T ANYONE IMPRESSIVE. VICKY, WE'LL BE COUNTING ON YOU TO OUT DAMAGE THEM.
AH- YEAH, I'LL DO MY BEST!
THE HUNTING HOWLS HAVE DONE IT!
THEY'LL BE MOVING ONTO ROUND! 2! OF THE NORTH! EASTERN! GUILD!!!
...
I NEED A FEW MORE MINUTES...
V-VICKY! HANG IN THERE!
I'M WORKING WITH MORONS...
FORGET ABOUT THE CROWD! FORGET ABOUT THE COMMENTATORS! ONCE WE PLAY, WE PLAY.
WE'RE GONNA WIN THIS MATCH, AND THE NEXT, AND ANOTHER!
GOT IT?
G-GOT IT!

AT THAT TIME, I THOUGHT ERIC AND I WOULD HAVE THE MOST PROBLEMS...

THE CROWD WAS SO LOUD, WE'VE NEVER EXPERIENCED ANYTHING LIKE IT...

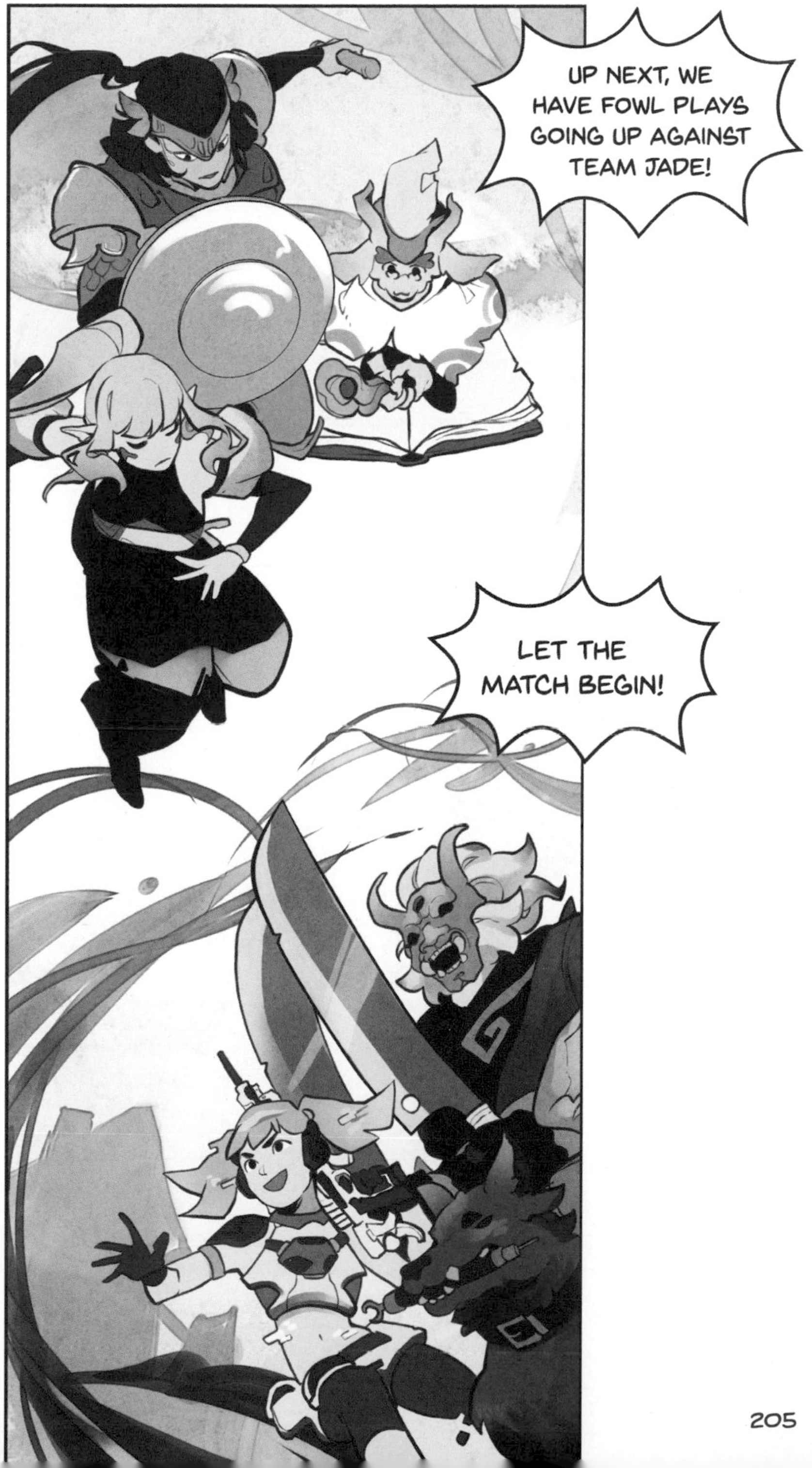
UP NEXT, WE HAVE FOWL PLAYS GOING UP AGAINST TEAM JADE!
LET THE MATCH BEGIN!

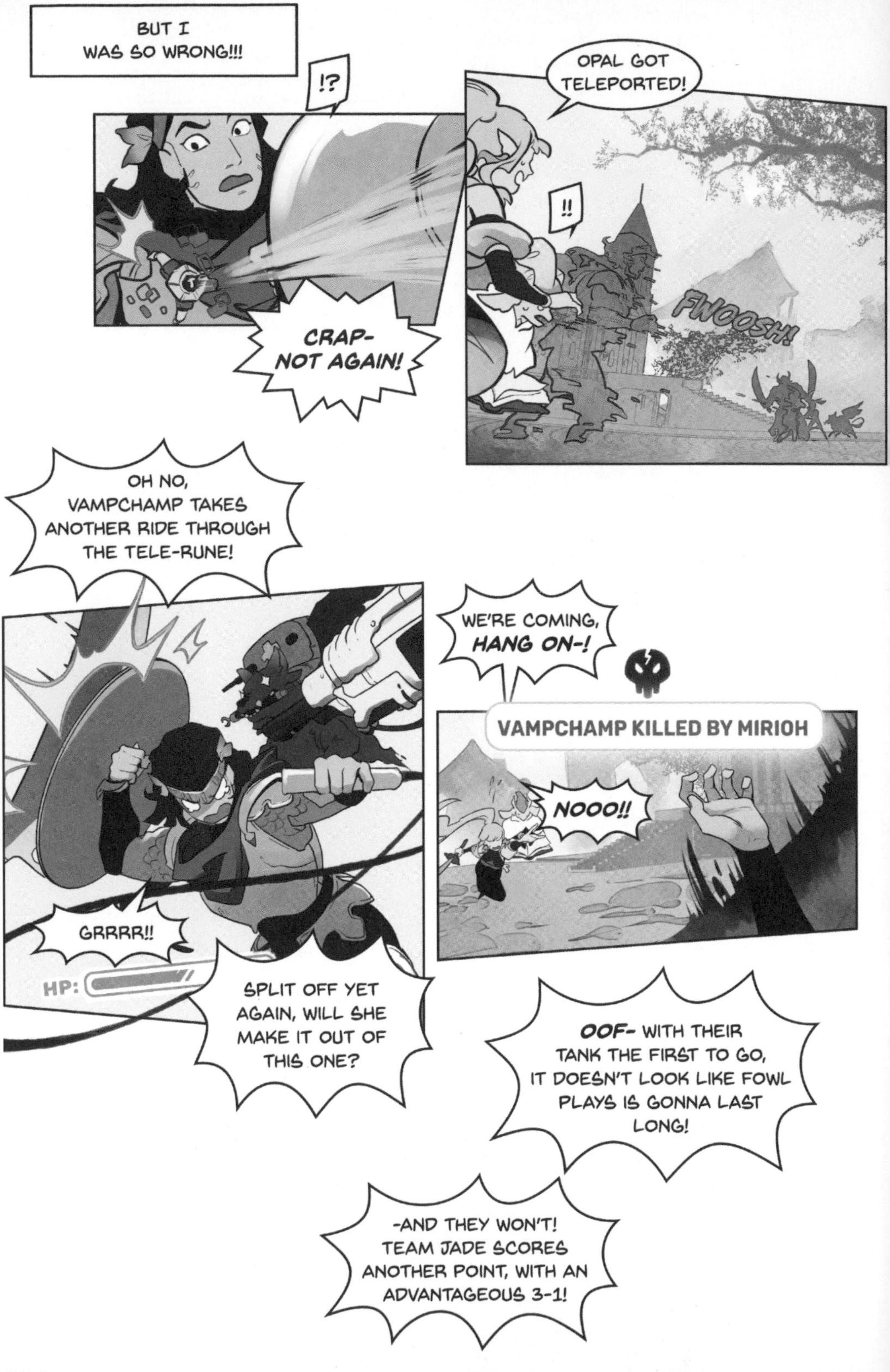
BUT I WAS SO WRONG!!!
!?
CRAP- NOT AGAIN!
OPAL GOT TELEPORTED!
!!
FWOOSH!
OH NO, VAMPCHAMP TAKES ANOTHER RIDE THROUGH THE TELE-RUNE!
GRRRR!!
HP:
SPLIT OFF YET AGAIN, WILL SHE MAKE IT OUT OF THIS ONE?
WE'RE COMING, HANG ON-!
VAMPCHAMP KILLED BY MIRIOH
NOOO!!
OOF- WITH THEIR TANK THE FIRST TO GO, IT DOESN'T LOOK LIKE FOWL PLAYS IS GONNA LAST LONG!
-AND THEY WON'T! TEAM JADE SCORES ANOTHER POINT, WITH AN ADVANTAGEOUS 3-1!

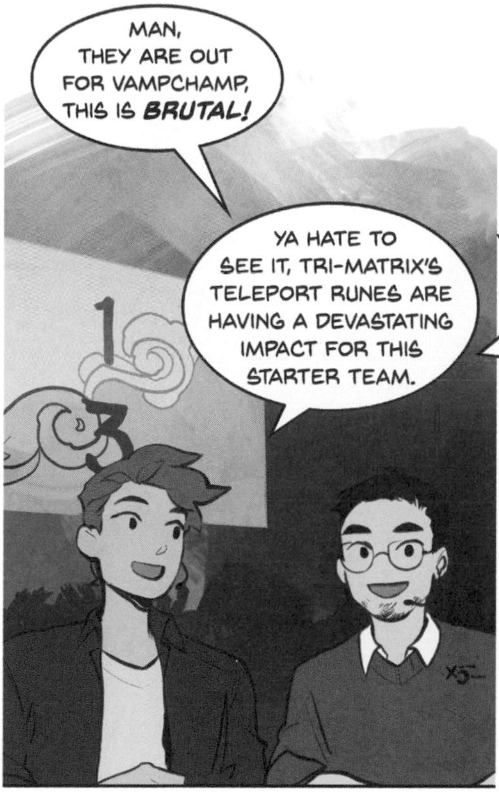
MAN, THEY ARE OUT FOR VAMPCHAMP, THIS IS ***BRUTAL!***
YA HATE TO SEE IT, TRI-MATRIX'S TELEPORT RUNES ARE HAVING A DEVASTATING IMPACT FOR THIS STARTER TEAM.

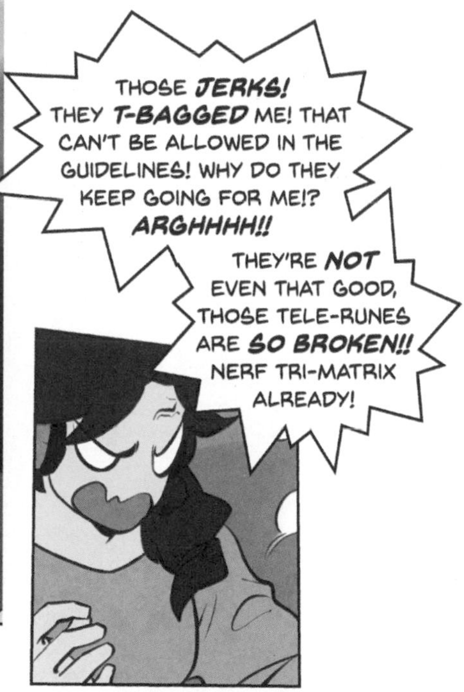
THOSE ***JERKS!*** THEY ***T-BAGGED*** ME! THAT CAN'T BE ALLOWED IN THE GUIDELINES! WHY DO THEY KEEP GOING FOR ME!? ***ARGHHHH!!***
THEY'RE ***NOT*** EVEN THAT GOOD, THOSE TELE-RUNES ARE ***SO BROKEN!!*** NERF TRI-MATRIX ALREADY!

*T-BAG: TO MAKE A CHARACTER CROUCH AND UNCROUCH QUICKLY ON TOP OF ANOTHER CHARACTER OR A CHARACTER'S CORPSE. IT'S USUALLY DEROGATORY AND BAD MANNERED.

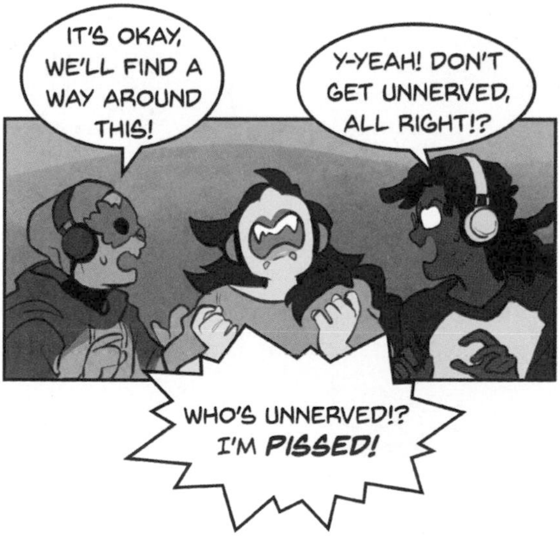
IT'S OKAY, WE'LL FIND A WAY AROUND THIS!
Y-YEAH! DON'T GET UNNERVED, ALL RIGHT!?
WHO'S UNNERVED!? I'M ***PISSED!***

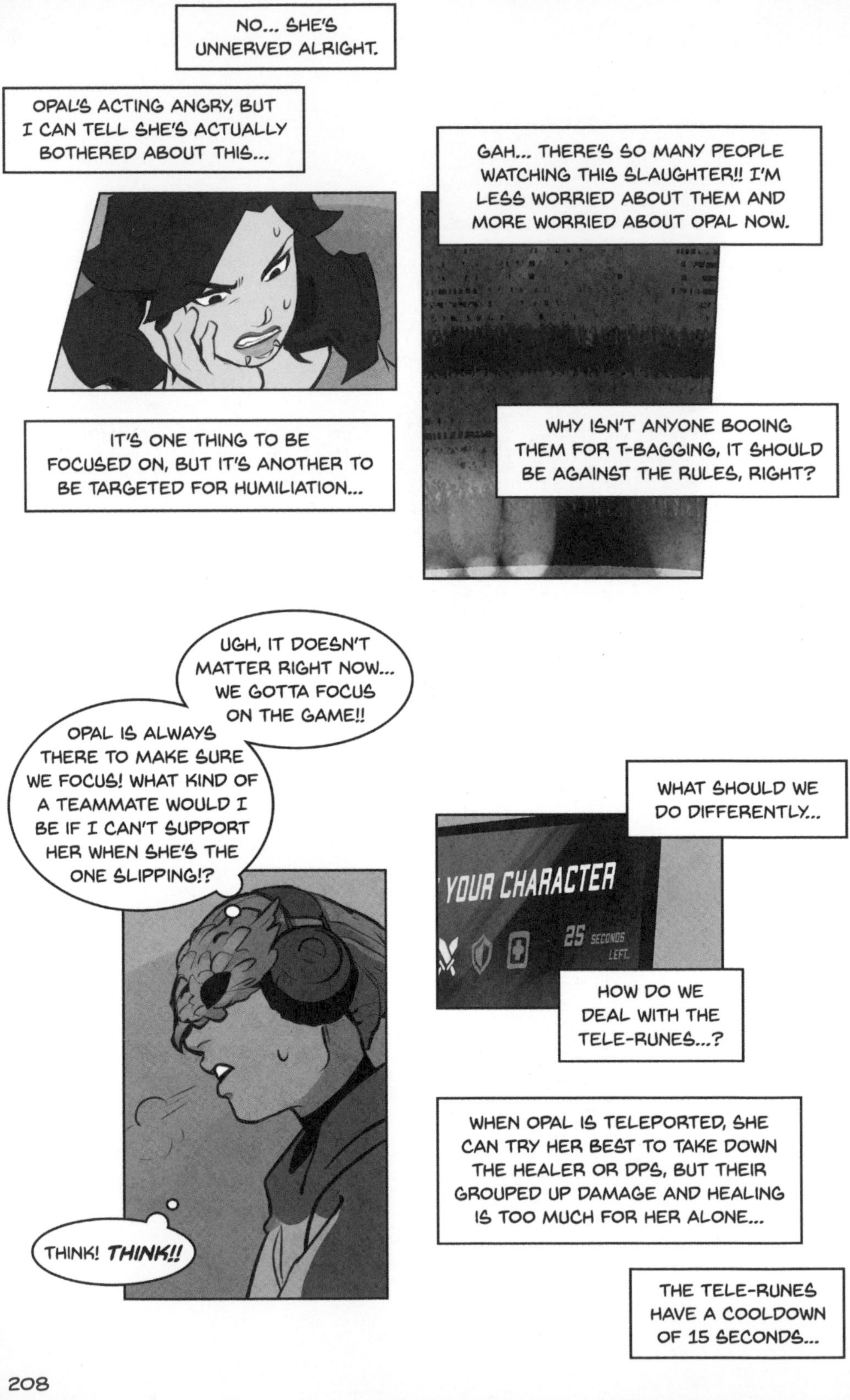
NO... SHE'S UNNERVED ALRIGHT.
OPAL'S ACTING ANGRY, BUT I CAN TELL SHE'S ACTUALLY BOTHERED ABOUT THIS...
IT'S ONE THING TO BE FOCUSED ON, BUT IT'S ANOTHER TO BE TARGETED FOR HUMILIATION...
GAH... THERE'S SO MANY PEOPLE WATCHING THIS SLAUGHTER!! I'M LESS WORRIED ABOUT THEM AND MORE WORRIED ABOUT OPAL NOW.
WHY ISN'T ANYONE BOOING THEM FOR T-BAGGING, IT SHOULD BE AGAINST THE RULES, RIGHT?
UGH, IT DOESN'T MATTER RIGHT NOW... WE GOTTA FOCUS ON THE GAME!!
OPAL IS ALWAYS THERE TO MAKE SURE WE FOCUS! WHAT KIND OF A TEAMMATE WOULD I BE IF I CAN'T SUPPORT HER WHEN SHE'S THE ONE SLIPPING!?
THINK! ***THINK!!***
WHAT SHOULD WE DO DIFFERENTLY...
YOUR CHARACTER
25 SECONDS LEFT.
HOW DO WE DEAL WITH THE TELE-RUNES...?
WHEN OPAL IS TELEPORTED, SHE CAN TRY HER BEST TO TAKE DOWN THE HEALER OR DPS, BUT THEIR GROUPED UP DAMAGE AND HEALING IS TOO MUCH FOR HER ALONE...
THE TELE-RUNES HAVE A COOLDOWN OF 15 SECONDS...

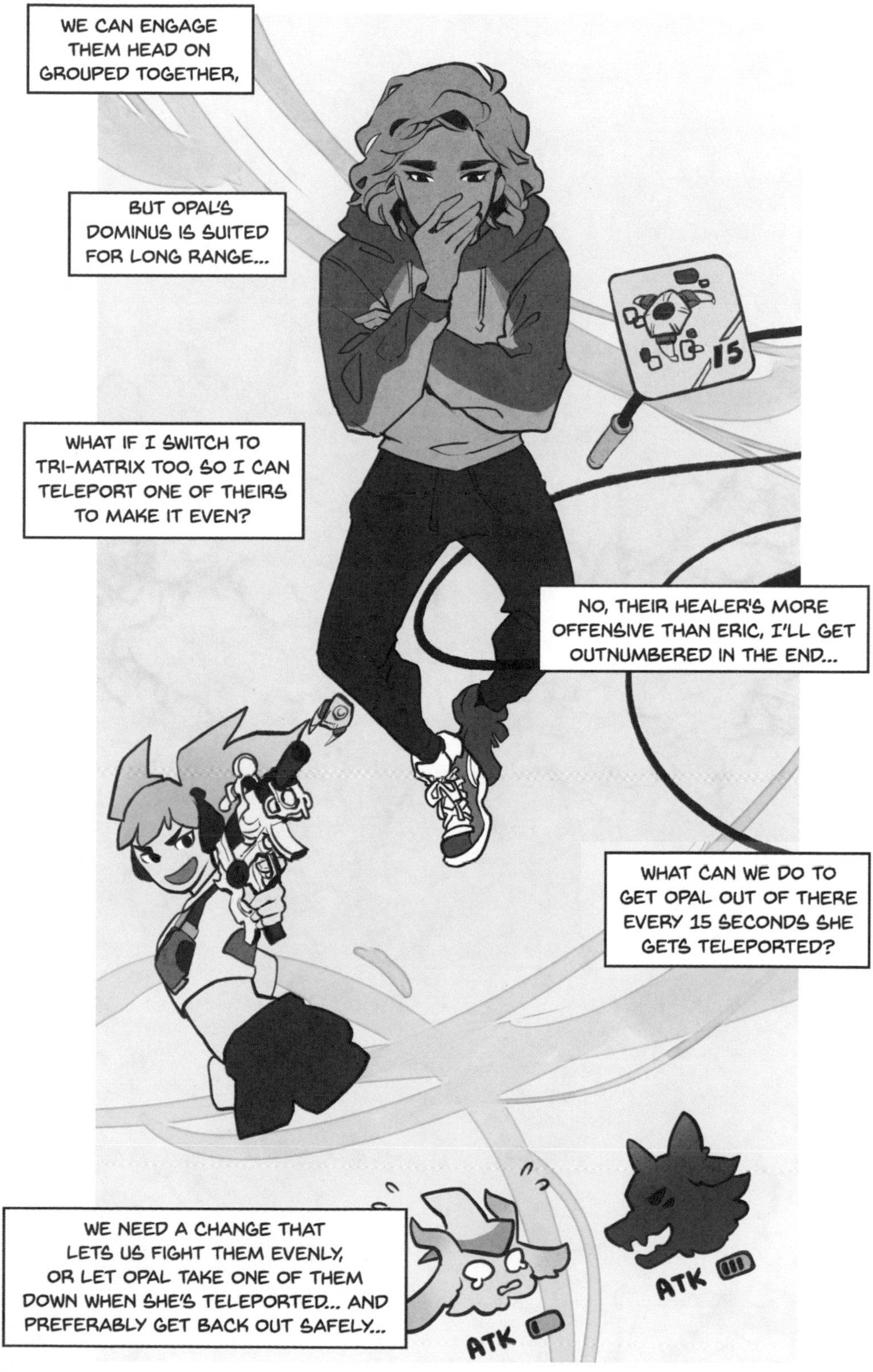
WE CAN ENGAGE THEM HEAD ON GROUPED TOGETHER,
BUT OPAL'S DOMINUS IS SUITED FOR LONG RANGE...
15
WHAT IF I SWITCH TO TRI-MATRIX TOO, SO I CAN TELEPORT ONE OF THEIRS TO MAKE IT EVEN?
NO, THEIR HEALER'S MORE OFFENSIVE THAN ERIC, I'LL GET OUTNUMBERED IN THE END...
WHAT CAN WE DO TO GET OPAL OUT OF THERE EVERY 15 SECONDS SHE GETS TELEPORTED?
WE NEED A CHANGE THAT LETS US FIGHT THEM EVENLY, OR LET OPAL TAKE ONE OF THEM DOWN WHEN SHE'S TELEPORTED... AND PREFERABLY GET BACK OUT SAFELY...
ATK
ATK

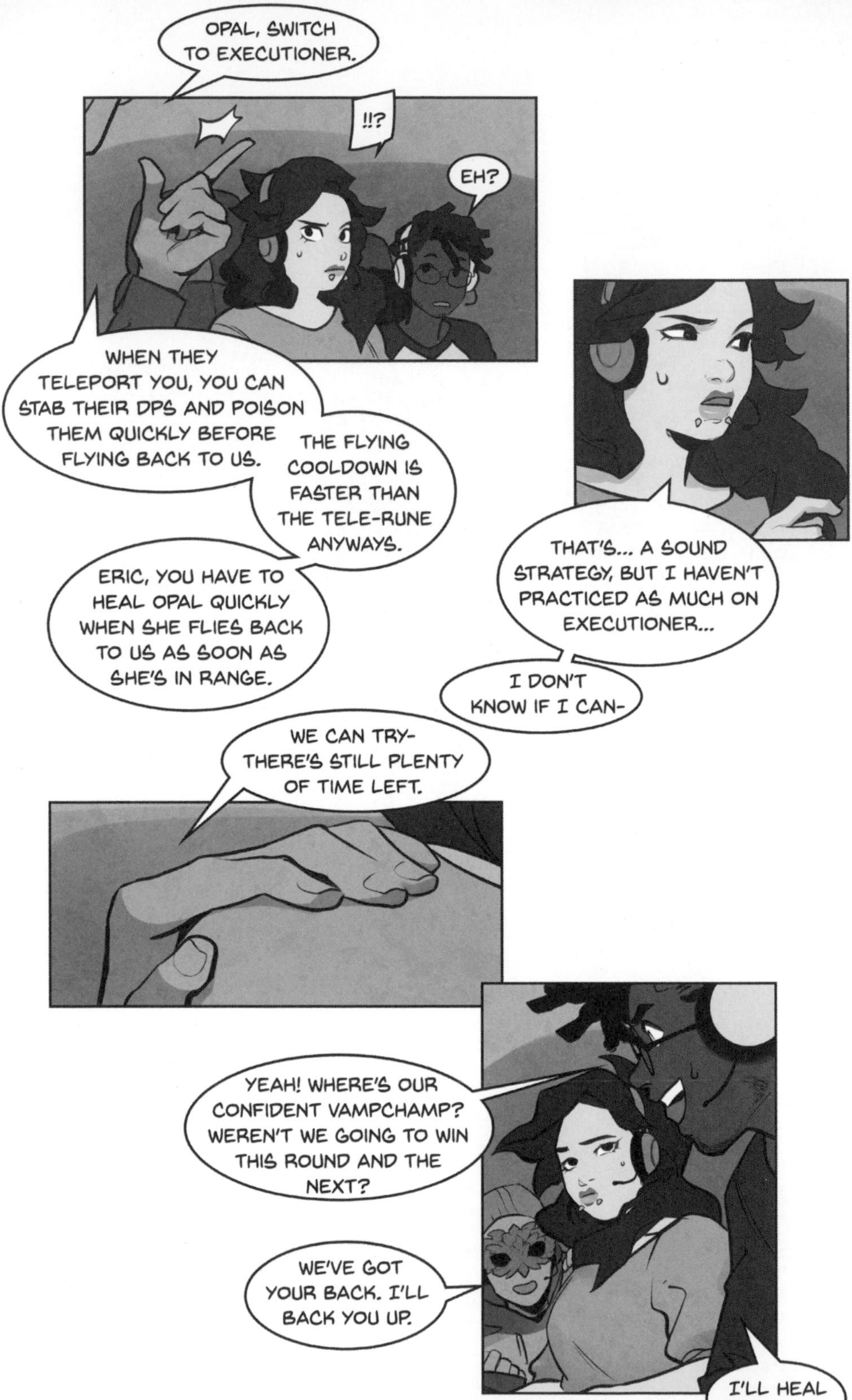
OPAL, SWITCH TO EXECUTIONER.
!!?
EH?
WHEN THEY TELEPORT YOU, YOU CAN STAB THEIR DPS AND POISON THEM QUICKLY BEFORE FLYING BACK TO US.
THE FLYING COOLDOWN IS FASTER THAN THE TELE-RUNE ANYWAYS.
ERIC, YOU HAVE TO HEAL OPAL QUICKLY WHEN SHE FLIES BACK TO US AS SOON AS SHE'S IN RANGE.
THAT'S... A SOUND STRATEGY, BUT I HAVEN'T PRACTICED AS MUCH ON EXECUTIONER...
I DON'T KNOW IF I CAN-
WE CAN TRY- THERE'S STILL PLENTY OF TIME LEFT.
YEAH! WHERE'S OUR CONFIDENT VAMPCHAMP? WEREN'T WE GOING TO WIN THIS ROUND AND THE NEXT?
WE'VE GOT YOUR BACK. I'LL BACK YOU UP.
I'LL HEAL YOU UP!

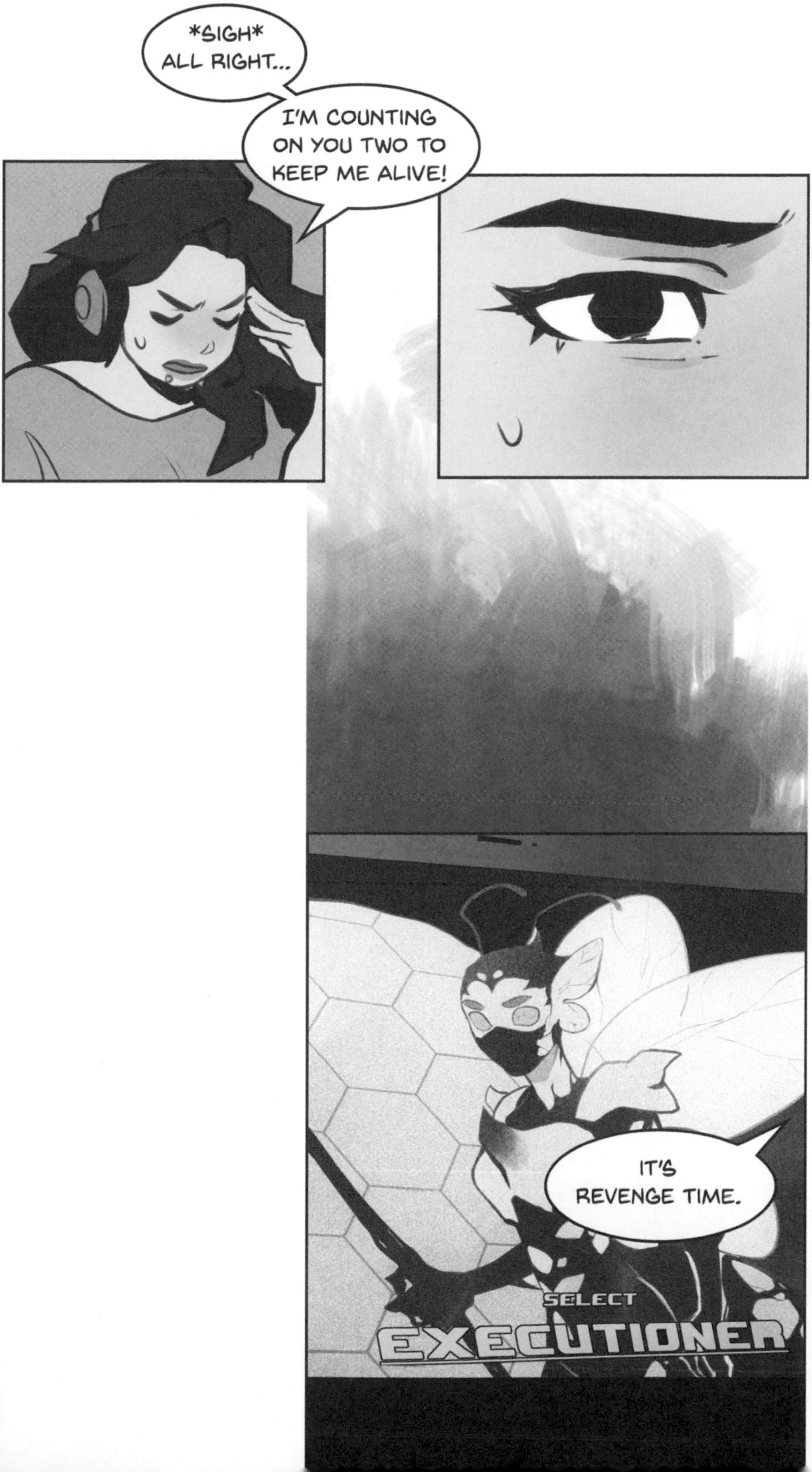
SIGH ALL RIGHT...
I'M COUNTING ON YOU TWO TO KEEP ME ALIVE!
IT'S REVENGE TIME.
SELECT
EXECUTIONER

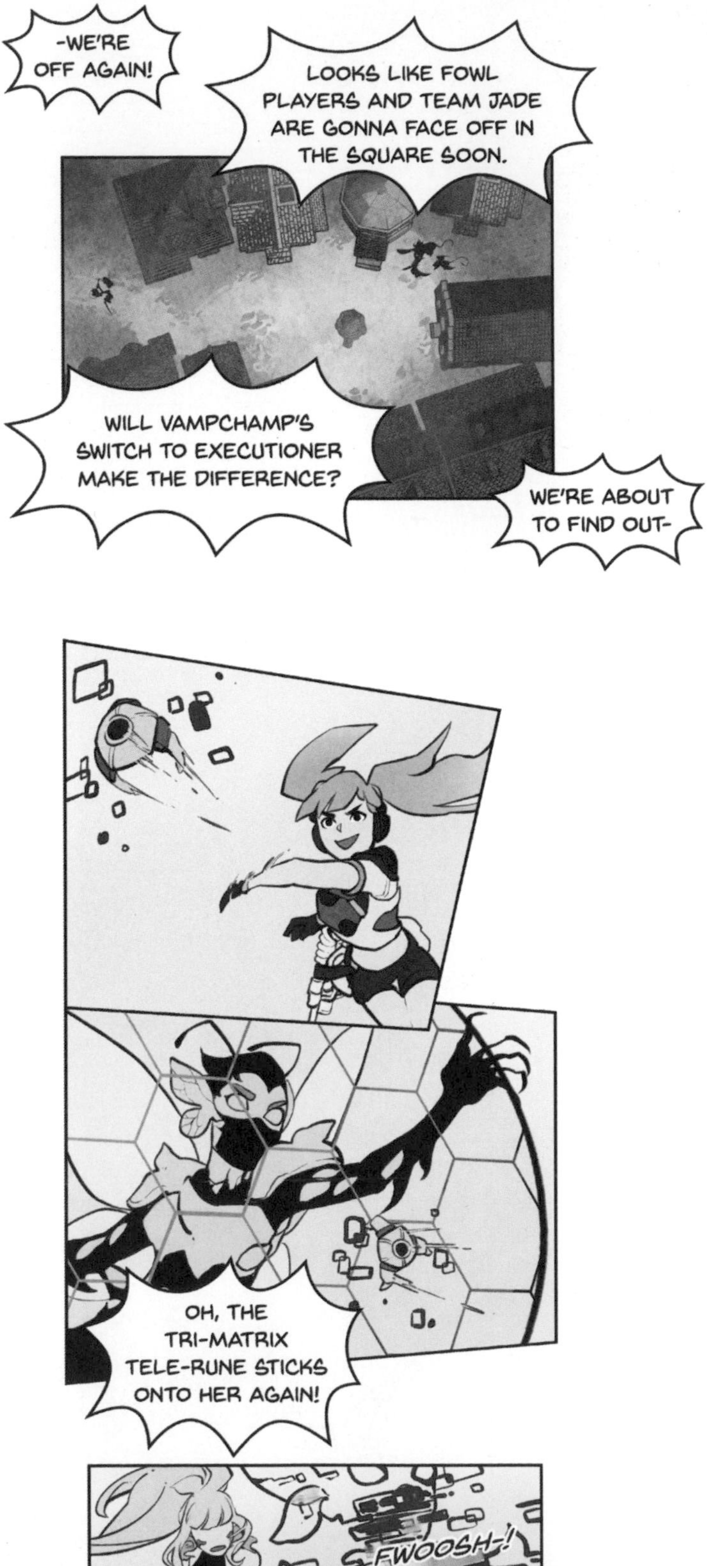
-WE'RE OFF AGAIN!
LOOKS LIKE FOWL PLAYERS AND TEAM JADE ARE GONNA FACE OFF IN THE SQUARE SOON.
WILL VAMPCHAMP'S SWITCH TO EXECUTIONER MAKE THE DIFFERENCE?
WE'RE ABOUT TO FIND OUT-
OH, THE TRI-MATRIX TELE-RUNE STICKS ONTO HER AGAIN!
FWOOSH-!

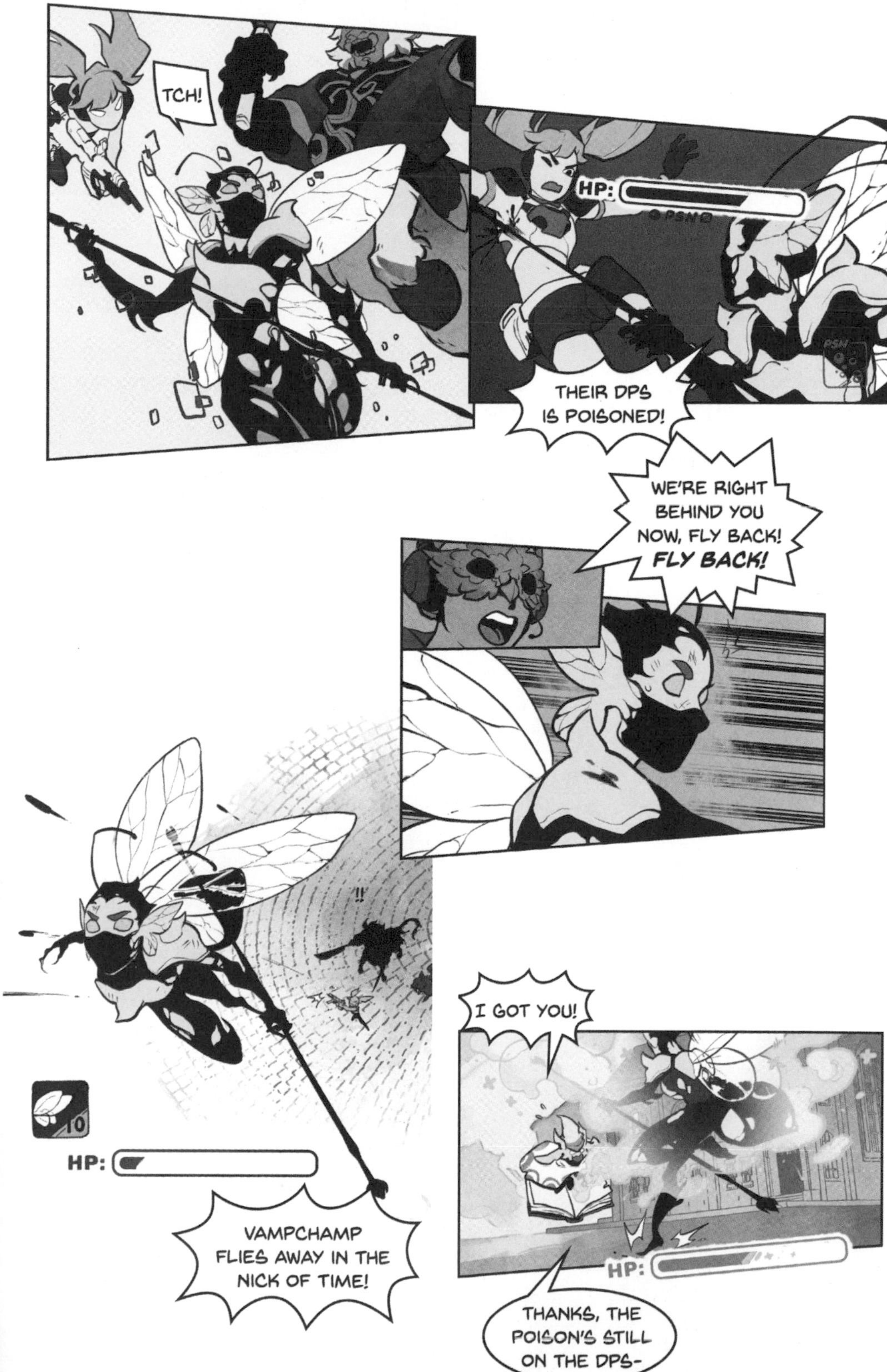
TCH!
HP:
THEIR DPS IS POISONED!
WE'RE RIGHT BEHIND YOU NOW, FLY BACK! FLY BACK!
10
HP:
VAMPCHAMP FLIES AWAY IN THE NICK OF TIME!
I GOT YOU!
HP:
THANKS, THE POISON'S STILL ON THE DPS-

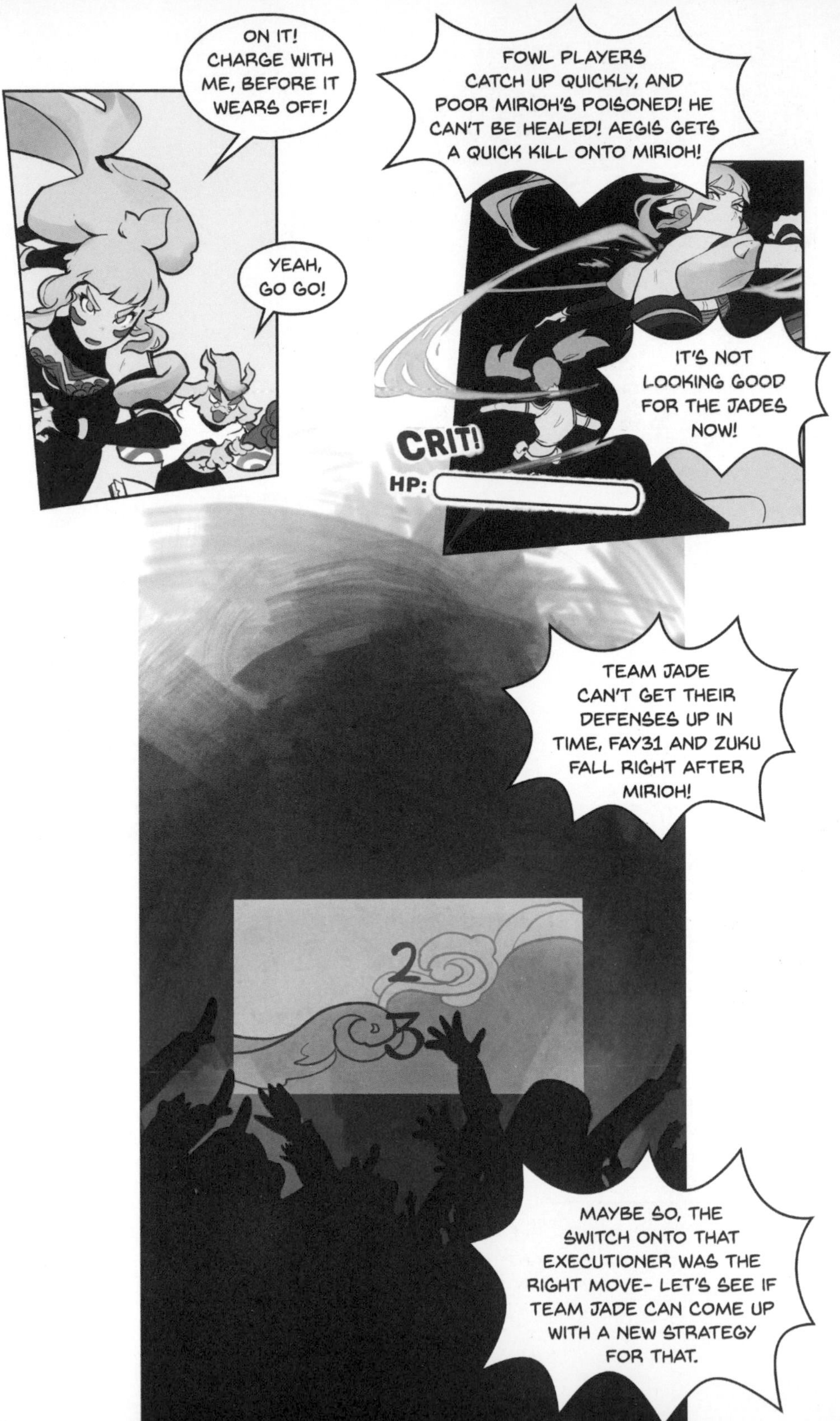
ON IT! CHARGE WITH ME, BEFORE IT WEARS OFF!
YEAH, GO GO!
FOWL PLAYERS CATCH UP QUICKLY, AND POOR MIRIOH'S POISONED! HE CAN'T BE HEALED! AEGIS GETS A QUICK KILL ONTO MIRIOH!
CRIT!
HP:
IT'S NOT LOOKING GOOD FOR THE JADES NOW!
TEAM JADE CAN'T GET THEIR DEFENSES UP IN TIME, FAY31 AND ZUKU FALL RIGHT AFTER MIRIOH!
2
3
MAYBE SO, THE SWITCH ONTO THAT EXECUTIONER WAS THE RIGHT MOVE- LET'S SEE IF TEAM JADE CAN COME UP WITH A NEW STRATEGY FOR THAT.

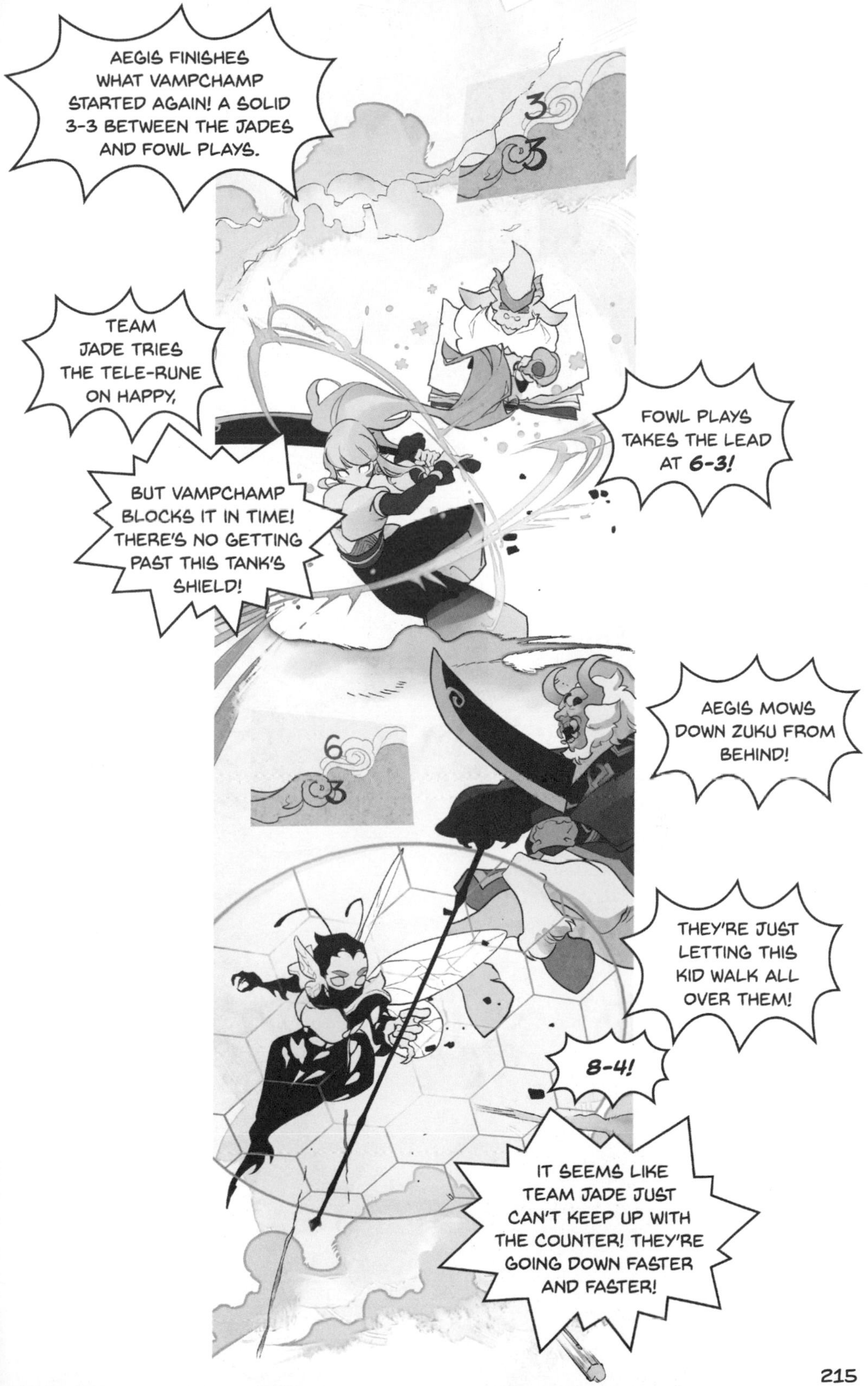
AEGIS FINISHES WHAT VAMPCHAMP STARTED AGAIN! A SOLID 3-3 BETWEEN THE JADES AND FOWL PLAYS.
3
3
TEAM JADE TRIES THE TELE-RUNE ON HAPPY,
BUT VAMPCHAMP BLOCKS IT IN TIME! THERE'S NO GETTING PAST THIS TANK'S SHIELD!
FOWL PLAYS TAKES THE LEAD AT 6-3!
6
3
AEGIS MOWS DOWN ZUKU FROM BEHIND!
THEY'RE JUST LETTING THIS KID WALK ALL OVER THEM!
8-4!
IT SEEMS LIKE TEAM JADE JUST CAN'T KEEP UP WITH THE COUNTER! THEY'RE GOING DOWN FASTER AND FASTER!

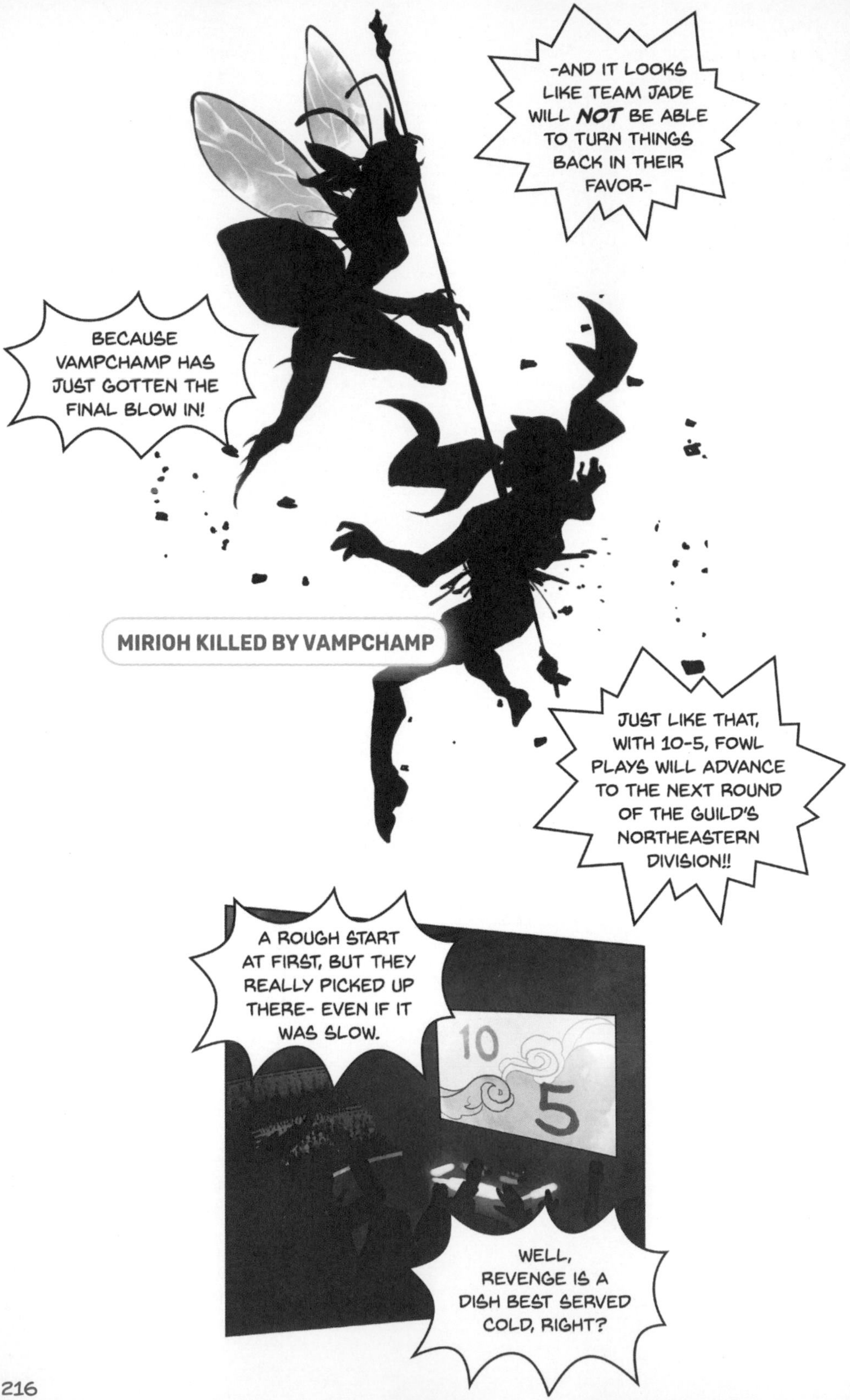
-AND IT LOOKS LIKE TEAM JADE WILL NOT BE ABLE TO TURN THINGS BACK IN THEIR FAVOR-
BECAUSE VAMPCHAMP HAS JUST GOTTEN THE FINAL BLOW IN!
MIRIOH KILLED BY VAMPCHAMP
JUST LIKE THAT, WITH 10-5, FOWL PLAYS WILL ADVANCE TO THE NEXT ROUND OF THE GUILD'S NORTHEASTERN DIVISION!!
A ROUGH START AT FIRST, BUT THEY REALLY PICKED UP THERE- EVEN IF IT WAS SLOW.
10
5
WELL, REVENGE IS A DISH BEST SERVED COLD, RIGHT?

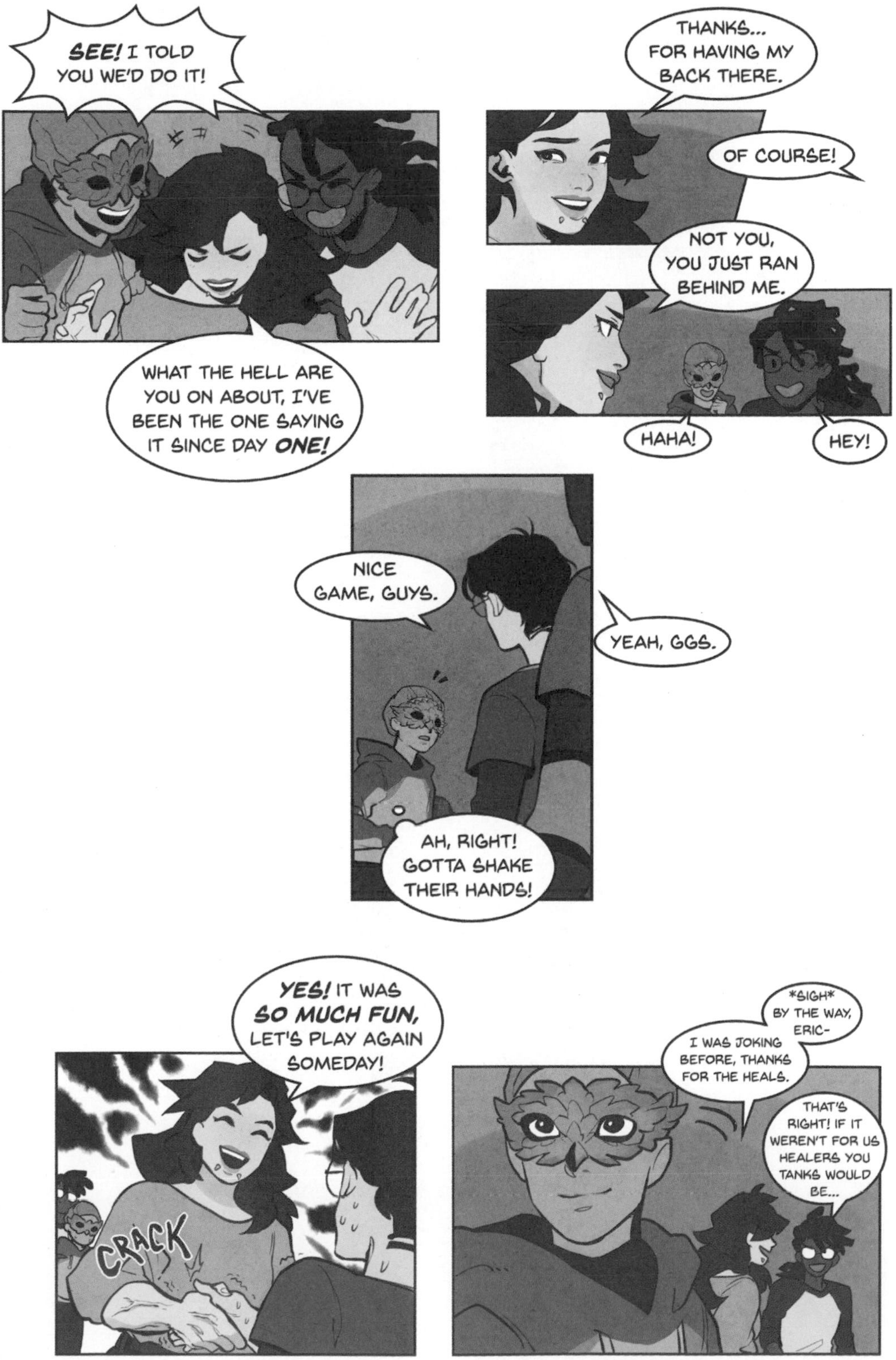
SEE! I TOLD YOU WE'D DO IT!
WHAT THE HELL ARE YOU ON ABOUT, I'VE BEEN THE ONE SAYING IT SINCE DAY ONE!
THANKS... FOR HAVING MY BACK THERE.
OF COURSE!
NOT YOU, YOU JUST RAN BEHIND ME.
HAHA!
HEY!
NICE GAME, GUYS.
YEAH, GGS.
AH, RIGHT! GOTTA SHAKE THEIR HANDS!
YES! IT WAS SO MUCH FUN, LET'S PLAY AGAIN SOMEDAY!
CRACK
SIGH BY THE WAY, ERIC-
I WAS JOKING BEFORE, THANKS FOR THE HEALS.
THAT'S RIGHT! IF IT WEREN'T FOR US HEALERS YOU TANKS WOULD BE...

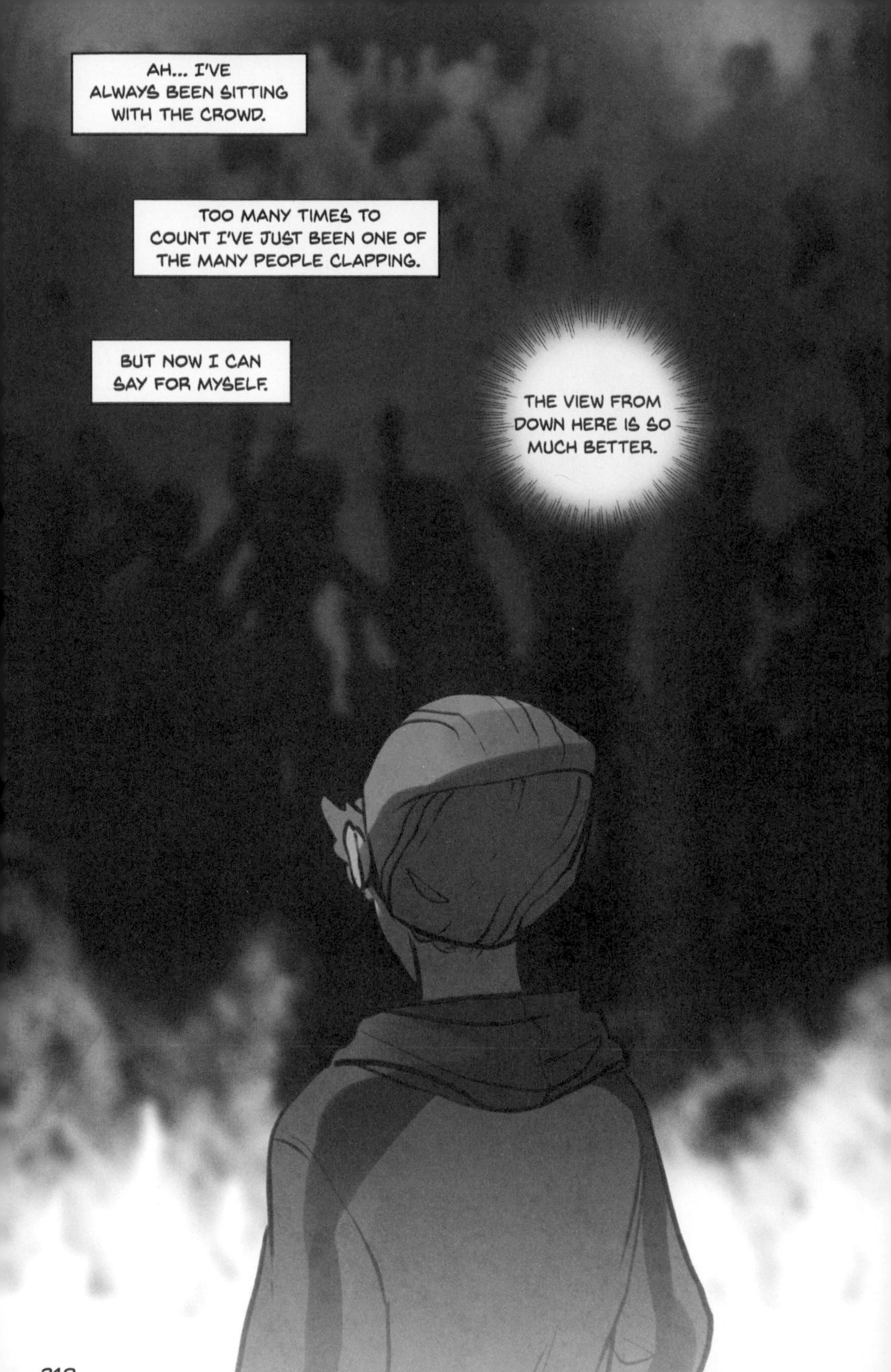
AH... I'VE ALWAYS BEEN SITTING WITH THE CROWD.
TOO MANY TIMES TO COUNT I'VE JUST BEEN ONE OF THE MANY PEOPLE CLAPPING.
BUT NOW I CAN SAY FOR MYSELF.
THE VIEW FROM DOWN HERE IS SO MUCH BETTER.

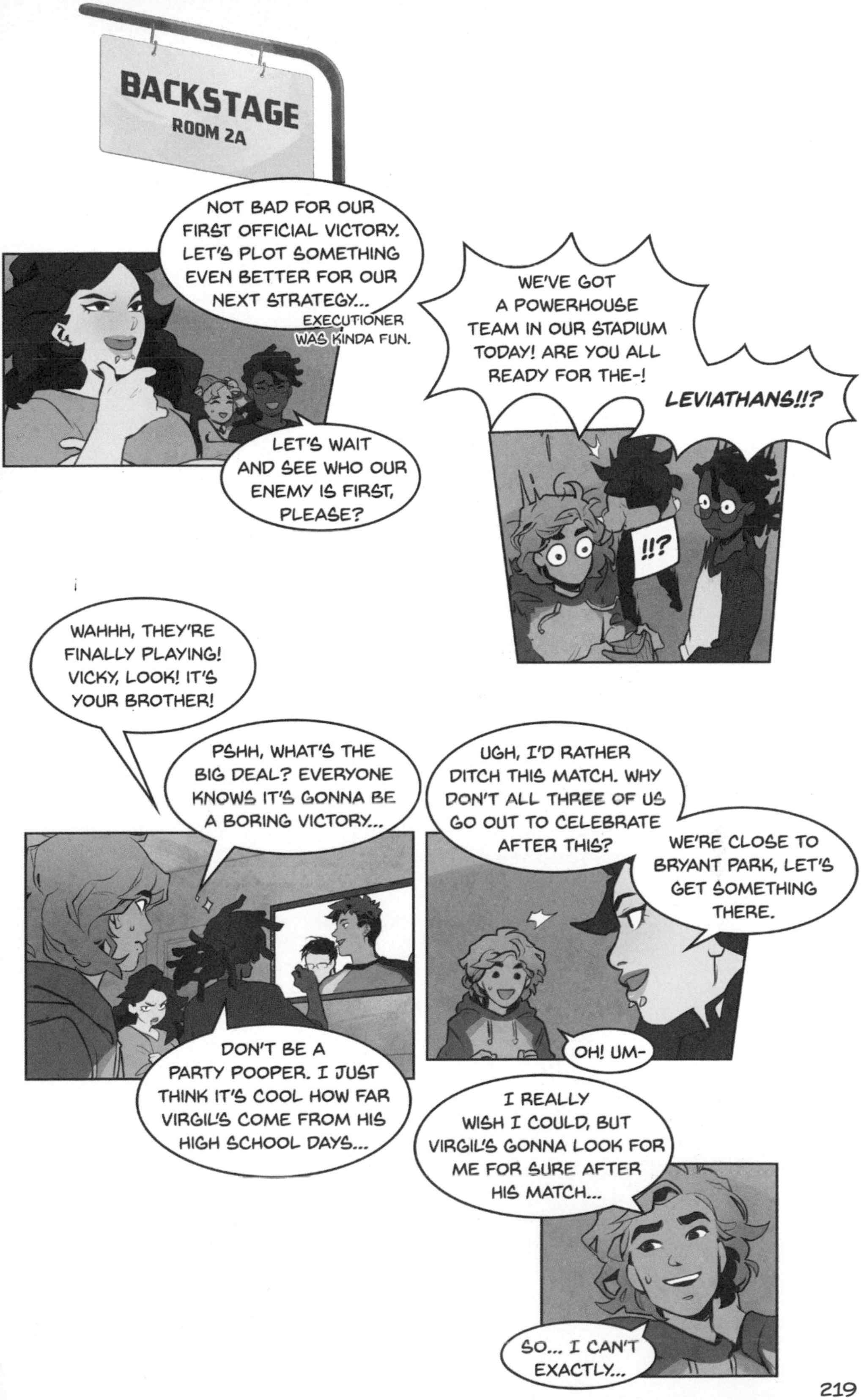
BACKSTAGE
ROOM 2A
NOT BAD FOR OUR FIRST OFFICIAL VICTORY. LET'S PLOT SOMETHING EVEN BETTER FOR OUR NEXT STRATEGY...
EXECUTIONER WAS KINDA FUN.
LET'S WAIT AND SEE WHO OUR ENEMY IS FIRST, PLEASE?
WE'VE GOT A POWERHOUSE TEAM IN OUR STADIUM TODAY! ARE YOU ALL READY FOR THE-!
LEVIATHANS!!?
!!?
WAHHH, THEY'RE FINALLY PLAYING! VICKY, LOOK! IT'S YOUR BROTHER!
PSHH, WHAT'S THE BIG DEAL? EVERYONE KNOWS IT'S GONNA BE A BORING VICTORY...
DON'T BE A PARTY POOPER. I JUST THINK IT'S COOL HOW FAR VIRGIL'S COME FROM HIS HIGH SCHOOL DAYS...
UGH, I'D RATHER DITCH THIS MATCH. WHY DON'T ALL THREE OF US GO OUT TO CELEBRATE AFTER THIS?
WE'RE CLOSE TO BRYANT PARK, LET'S GET SOMETHING THERE.
OH! UM-
I REALLY WISH I COULD, BUT VIRGIL'S GONNA LOOK FOR ME FOR SURE AFTER HIS MATCH...
SO... I CAN'T EXACTLY...

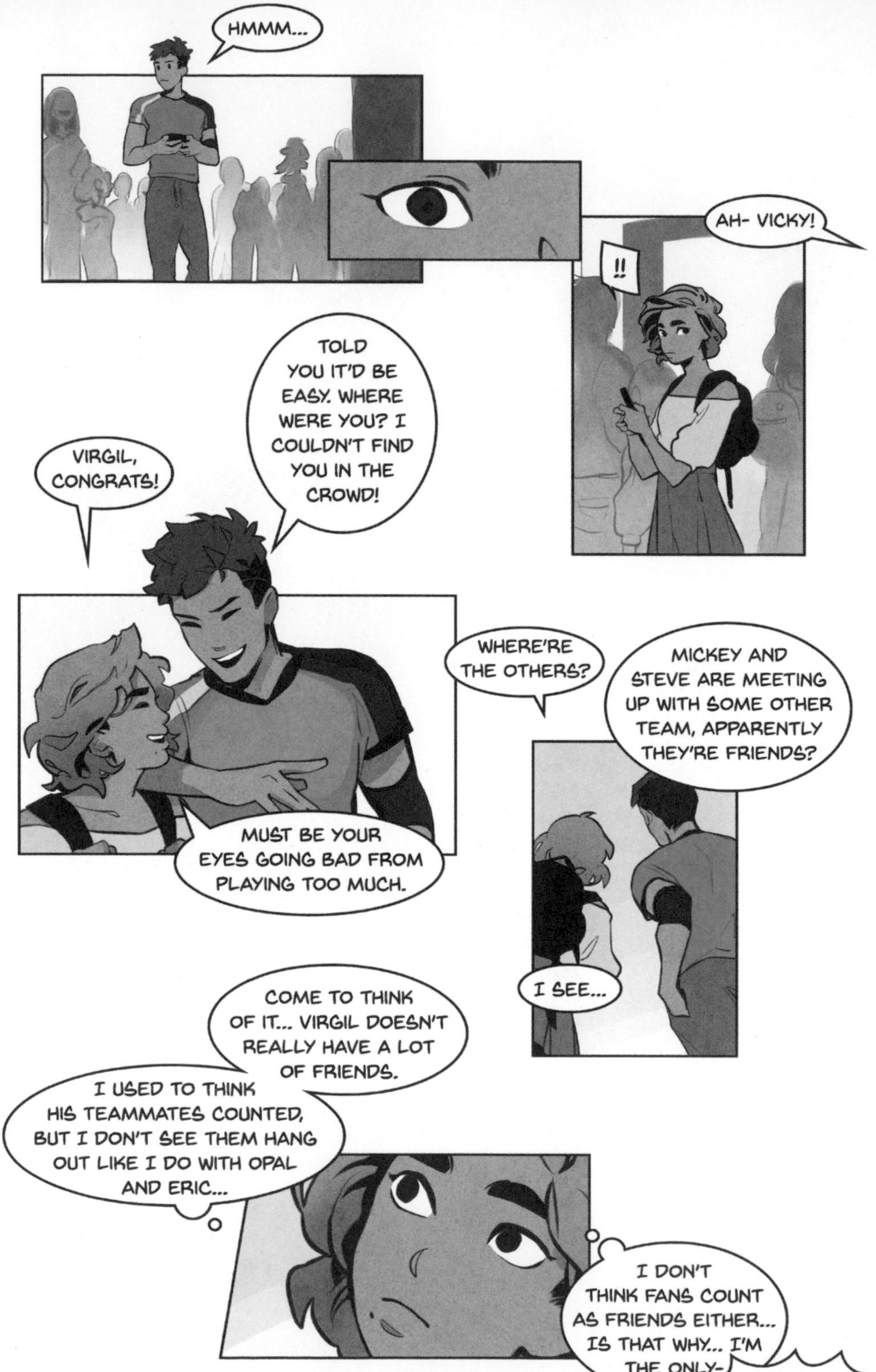
HMMM...
AH- VICKY!
!!
VIRGIL, CONGRATS!
TOLD YOU IT'D BE EASY. WHERE WERE YOU? I COULDN'T FIND YOU IN THE CROWD!
MUST BE YOUR EYES GOING BAD FROM PLAYING TOO MUCH.
WHERE'RE THE OTHERS?
MICKEY AND STEVE ARE MEETING UP WITH SOME OTHER TEAM, APPARENTLY THEY'RE FRIENDS?
I SEE...
COME TO THINK OF IT... VIRGIL DOESN'T REALLY HAVE A LOT OF FRIENDS.
I USED TO THINK HIS TEAMMATES COUNTED, BUT I DON'T SEE THEM HANG OUT LIKE I DO WITH OPAL AND ERIC...
I DON'T THINK FANS COUNT AS FRIENDS EITHER... IS THAT WHY... I'M THE ONLY-
GASP! OH WOW!

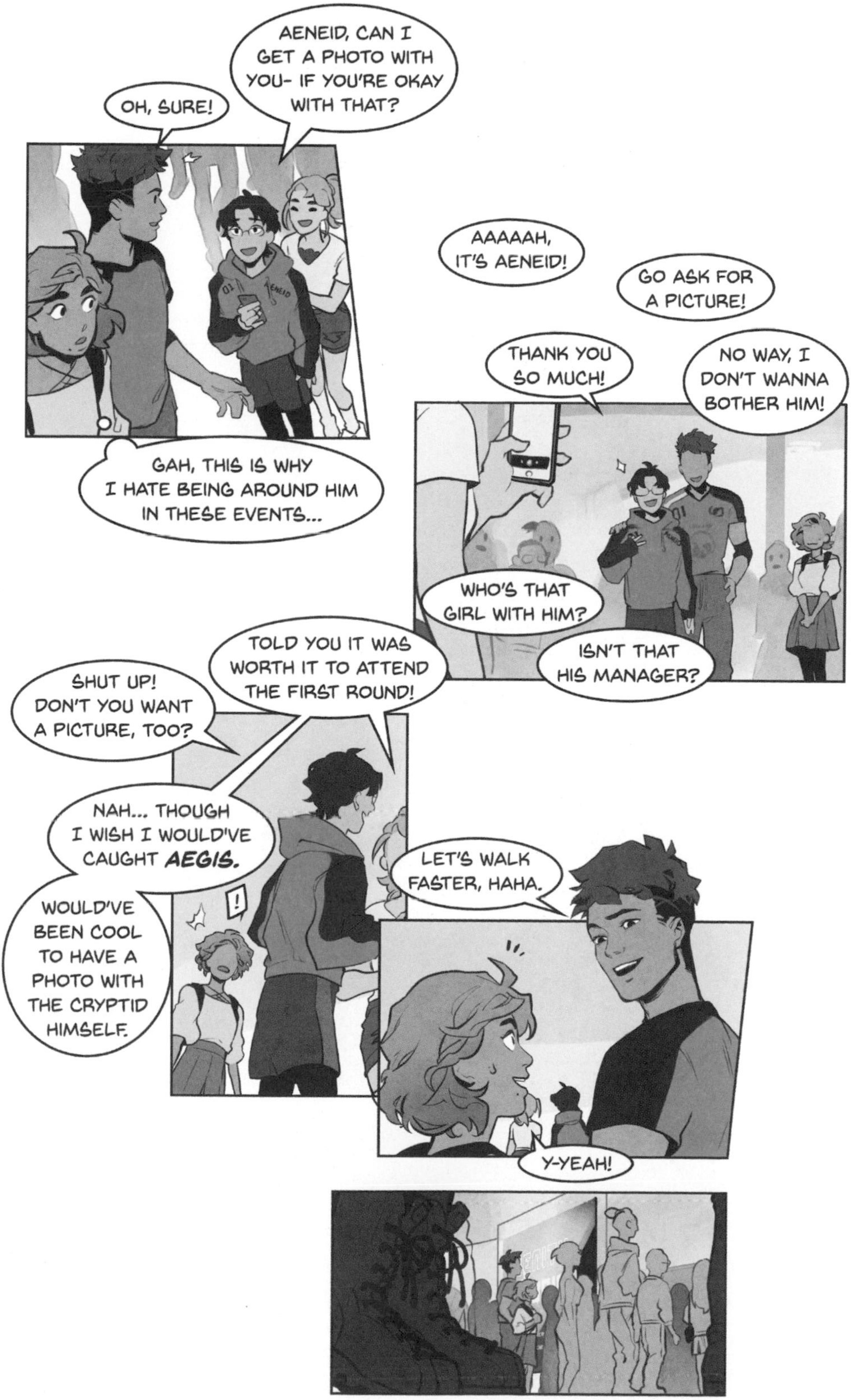
AENEID, CAN I GET A PHOTO WITH YOU- IF YOU'RE OKAY WITH THAT?
OH, SURE!
GAH, THIS IS WHY I HATE BEING AROUND HIM IN THESE EVENTS...
AAAAAH, IT'S AENEID!
GO ASK FOR A PICTURE!
THANK YOU SO MUCH!
NO WAY, I DON'T WANNA BOTHER HIM!
WHO'S THAT GIRL WITH HIM?
ISN'T THAT HIS MANAGER?
SHUT UP! DON'T YOU WANT A PICTURE, TOO?
TOLD YOU IT WAS WORTH IT TO ATTEND THE FIRST ROUND!
NAH... THOUGH I WISH I WOULD'VE CAUGHT **AEGIS.**
WOULD'VE BEEN COOL TO HAVE A PHOTO WITH THE CRYPTID HIMSELF.
!
LET'S WALK FASTER, HAHA.
Y-YEAH!

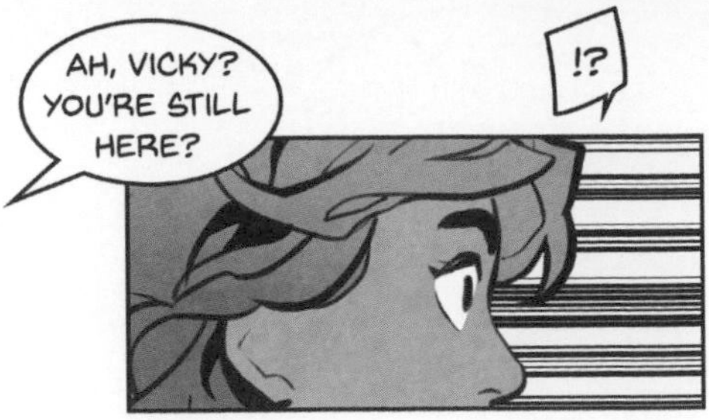
AH, VICKY? YOU'RE STILL HERE?
!?

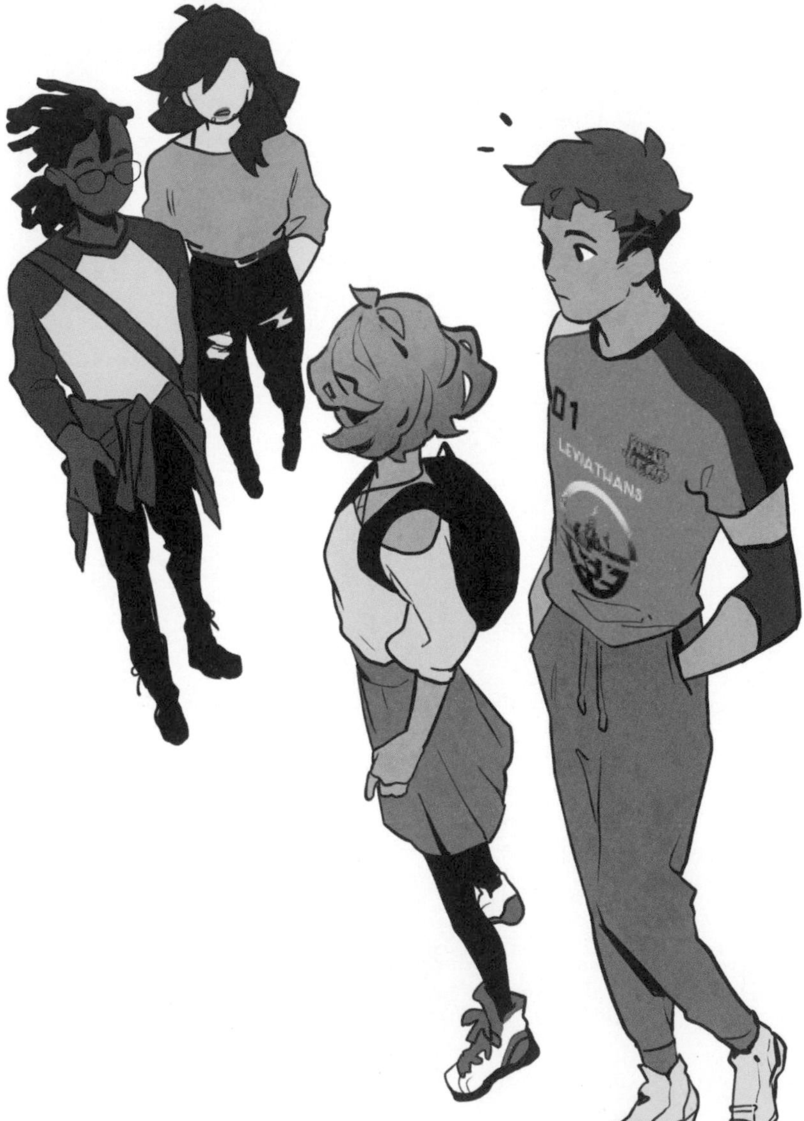
01
LEVIATHANS

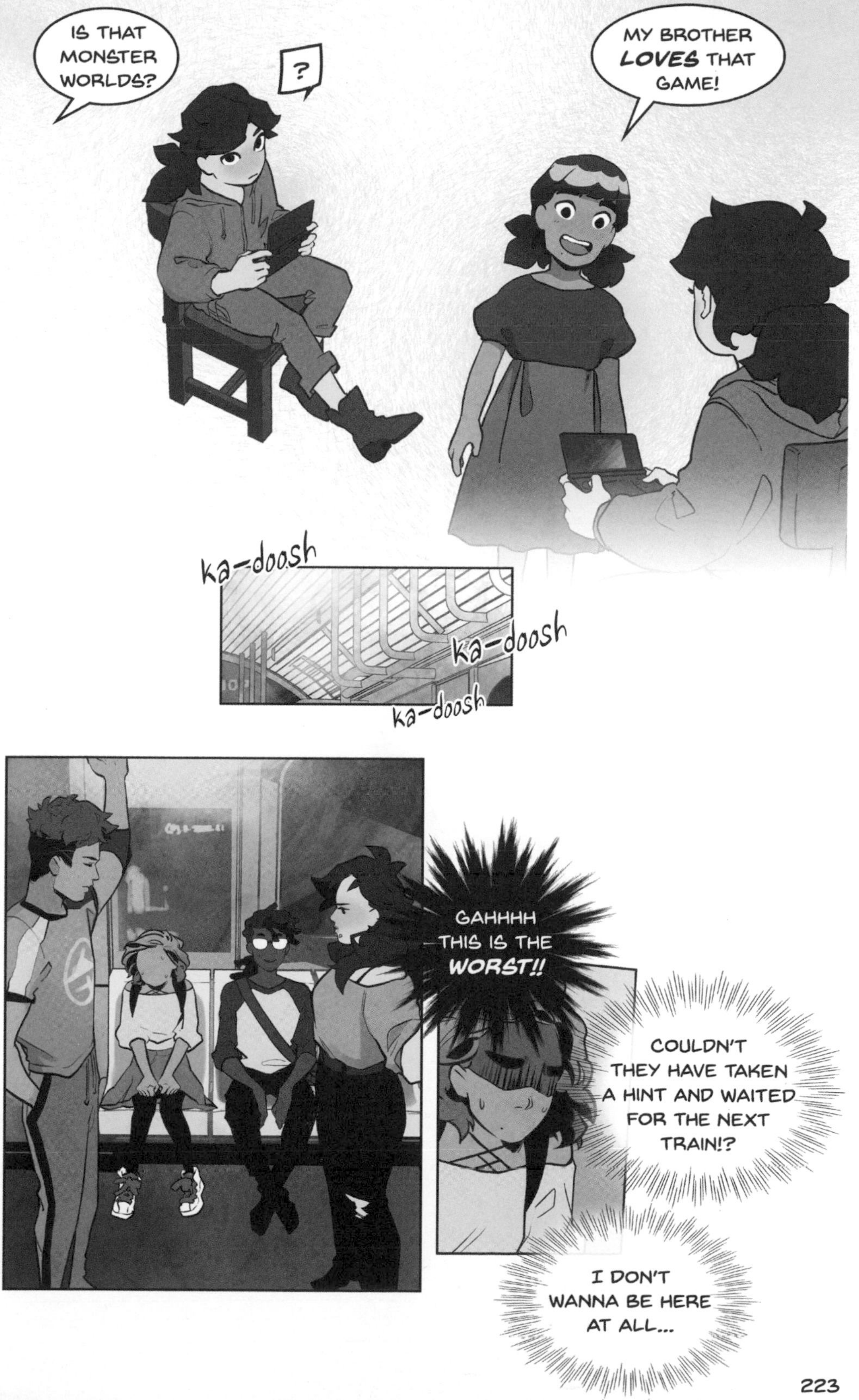
IS THAT MONSTER WORLDS?
?
MY BROTHER LOVES THAT GAME!
ka-doosh
ka-doosh
ka-doosh
GAHHHH THIS IS THE WORST!!
COULDN'T THEY HAVE TAKEN A HINT AND WAITED FOR THE NEXT TRAIN!?
I DON'T WANNA BE HERE AT ALL...

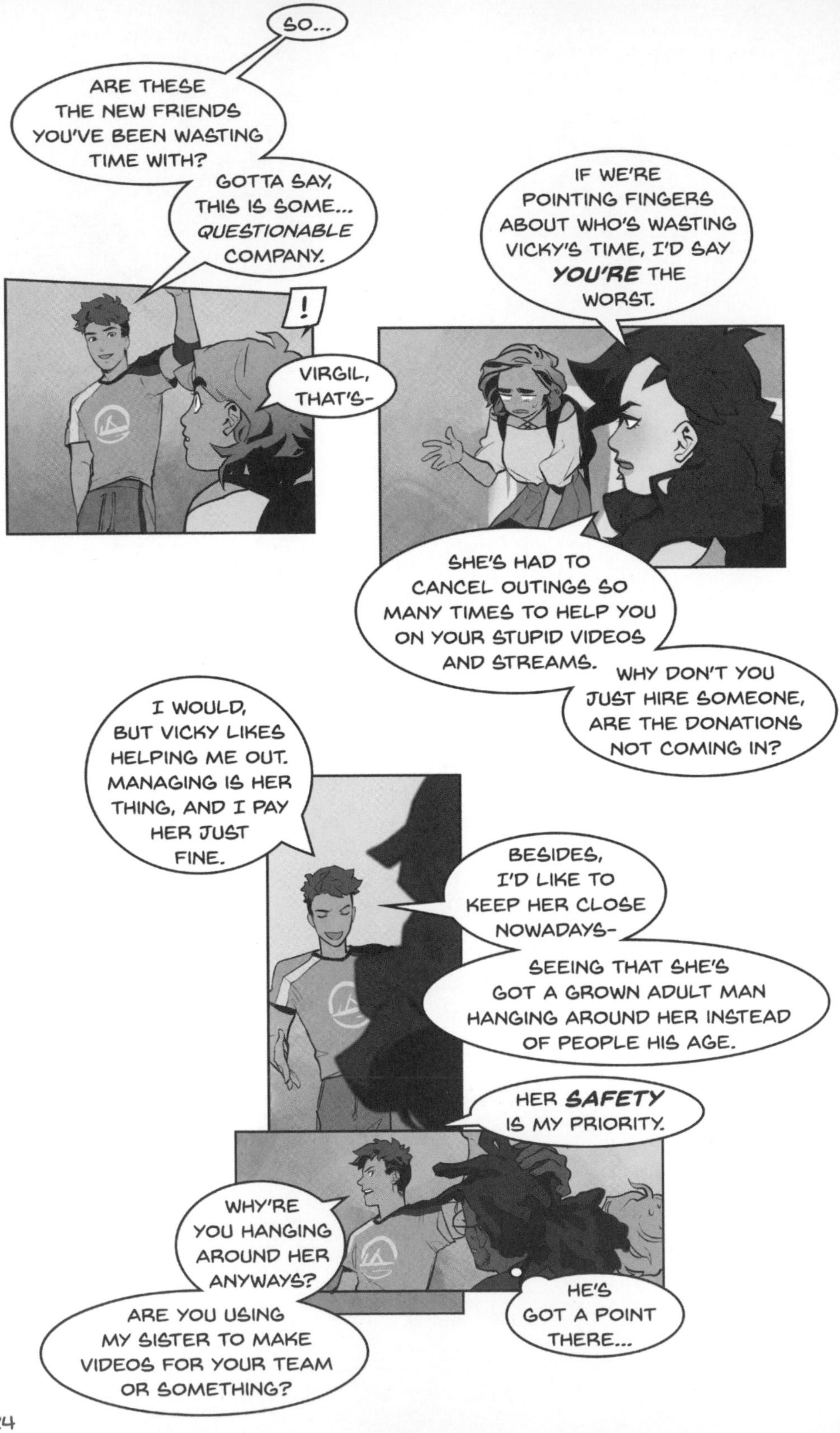
SO...
ARE THESE THE NEW FRIENDS YOU'VE BEEN WASTING TIME WITH?
GOTTA SAY, THIS IS SOME... QUESTIONABLE COMPANY.
!
VIRGIL, THAT'S-
IF WE'RE POINTING FINGERS ABOUT WHO'S WASTING VICKY'S TIME, I'D SAY YOU'RE THE WORST.
SHE'S HAD TO CANCEL OUTINGS SO MANY TIMES TO HELP YOU ON YOUR STUPID VIDEOS AND STREAMS.
WHY DON'T YOU JUST HIRE SOMEONE, ARE THE DONATIONS NOT COMING IN?
I WOULD, BUT VICKY LIKES HELPING ME OUT. MANAGING IS HER THING, AND I PAY HER JUST FINE.
BESIDES, I'D LIKE TO KEEP HER CLOSE NOWADAYS-
SEEING THAT SHE'S GOT A GROWN ADULT MAN HANGING AROUND HER INSTEAD OF PEOPLE HIS AGE.
HER SAFETY IS MY PRIORITY.
WHY'RE YOU HANGING AROUND HER ANYWAYS?
ARE YOU USING MY SISTER TO MAKE VIDEOS FOR YOUR TEAM OR SOMETHING?
HE'S GOT A POINT THERE...

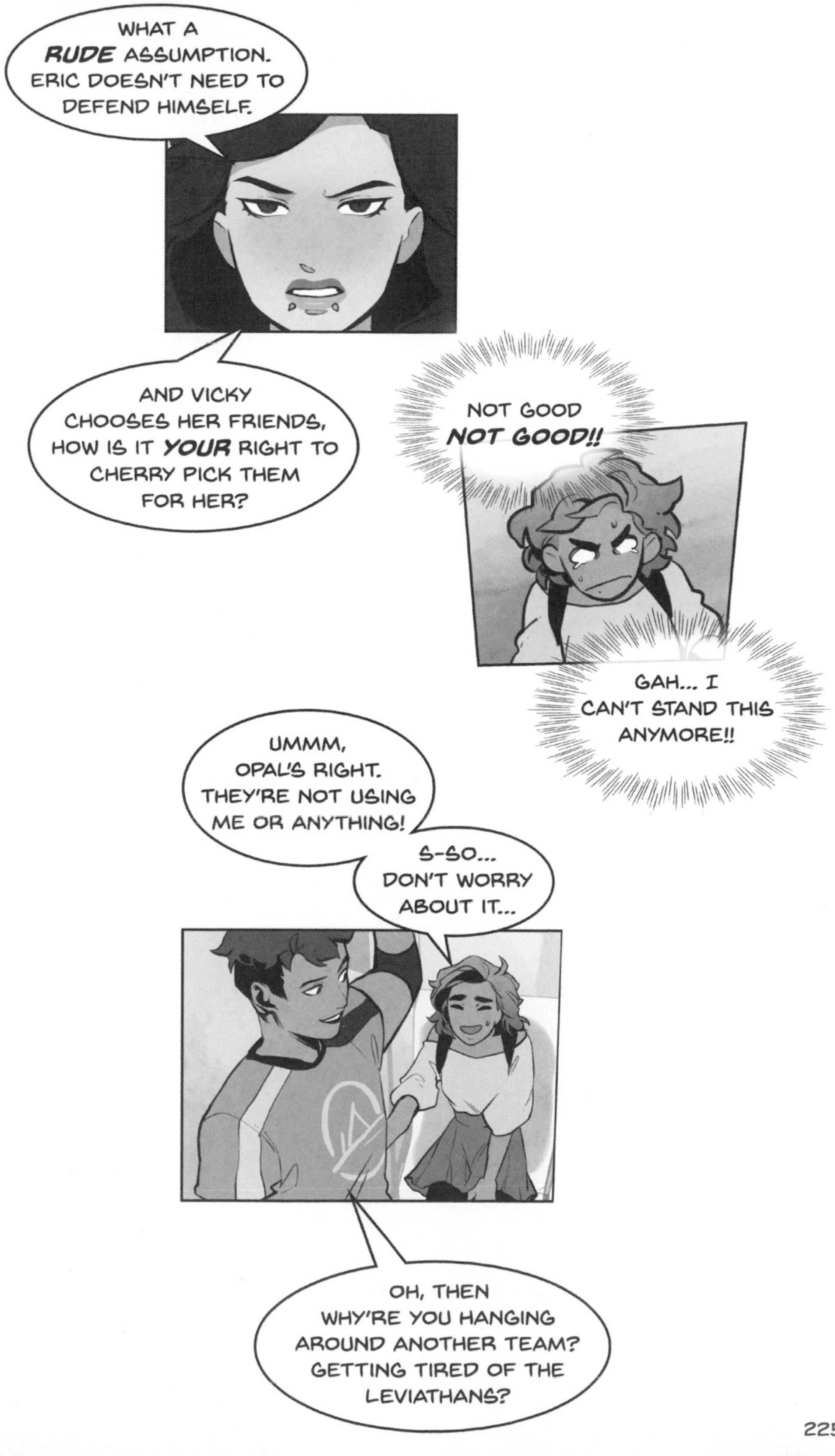
WHAT A *RUDE* ASSUMPTION. ERIC DOESN'T NEED TO DEFEND HIMSELF.
AND VICKY CHOOSES HER FRIENDS, HOW IS IT *YOUR* RIGHT TO CHERRY PICK THEM FOR HER?
NOT GOOD *NOT GOOD!!*
GAH... I CAN'T STAND THIS ANYMORE!!
UMMM, OPAL'S RIGHT. THEY'RE NOT USING ME OR ANYTHING!
S-SO... DON'T WORRY ABOUT IT...
OH, THEN WHY'RE YOU HANGING AROUND ANOTHER TEAM? GETTING TIRED OF THE LEVIATHANS?

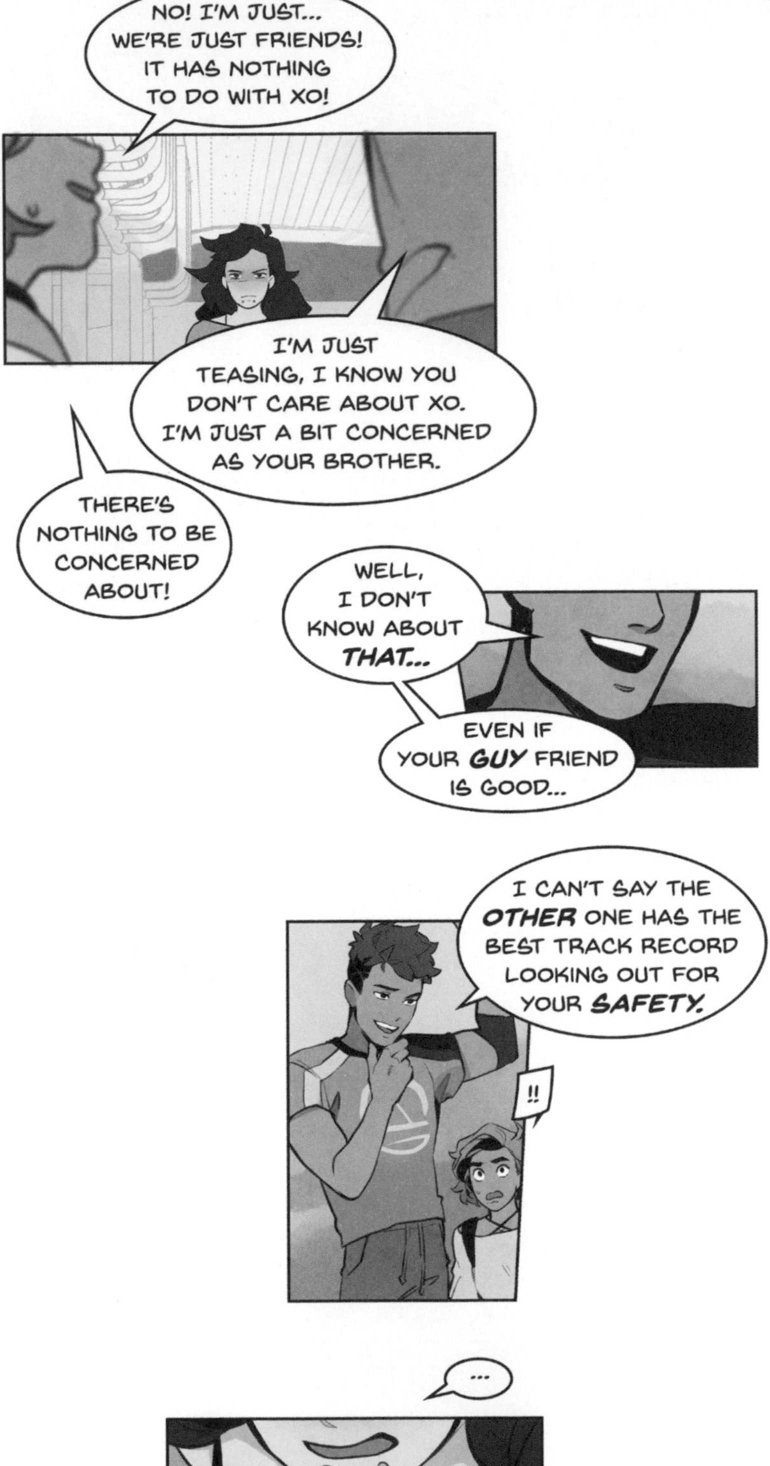
NO! I'M JUST... WE'RE JUST FRIENDS! IT HAS NOTHING TO DO WITH XO!
I'M JUST TEASING, I KNOW YOU DON'T CARE ABOUT XO. I'M JUST A BIT CONCERNED AS YOUR BROTHER.
THERE'S NOTHING TO BE CONCERNED ABOUT!
WELL, I DON'T KNOW ABOUT THAT...
EVEN IF YOUR GUY FRIEND IS GOOD...
I CAN'T SAY THE OTHER ONE HAS THE BEST TRACK RECORD LOOKING OUT FOR YOUR SAFETY.
!!
...

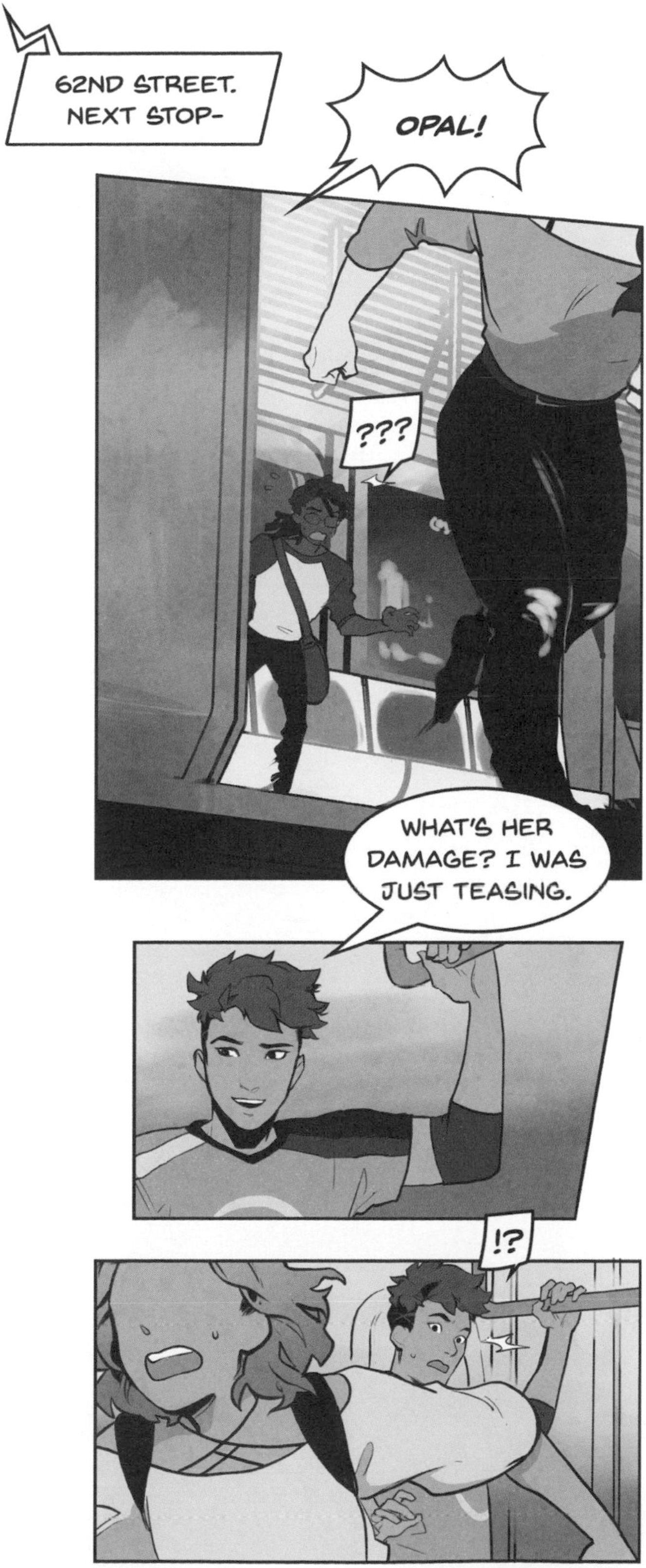
62ND STREET. NEXT STOP-
OPAL!
???
WHAT'S HER DAMAGE? I WAS JUST TEASING.
!?

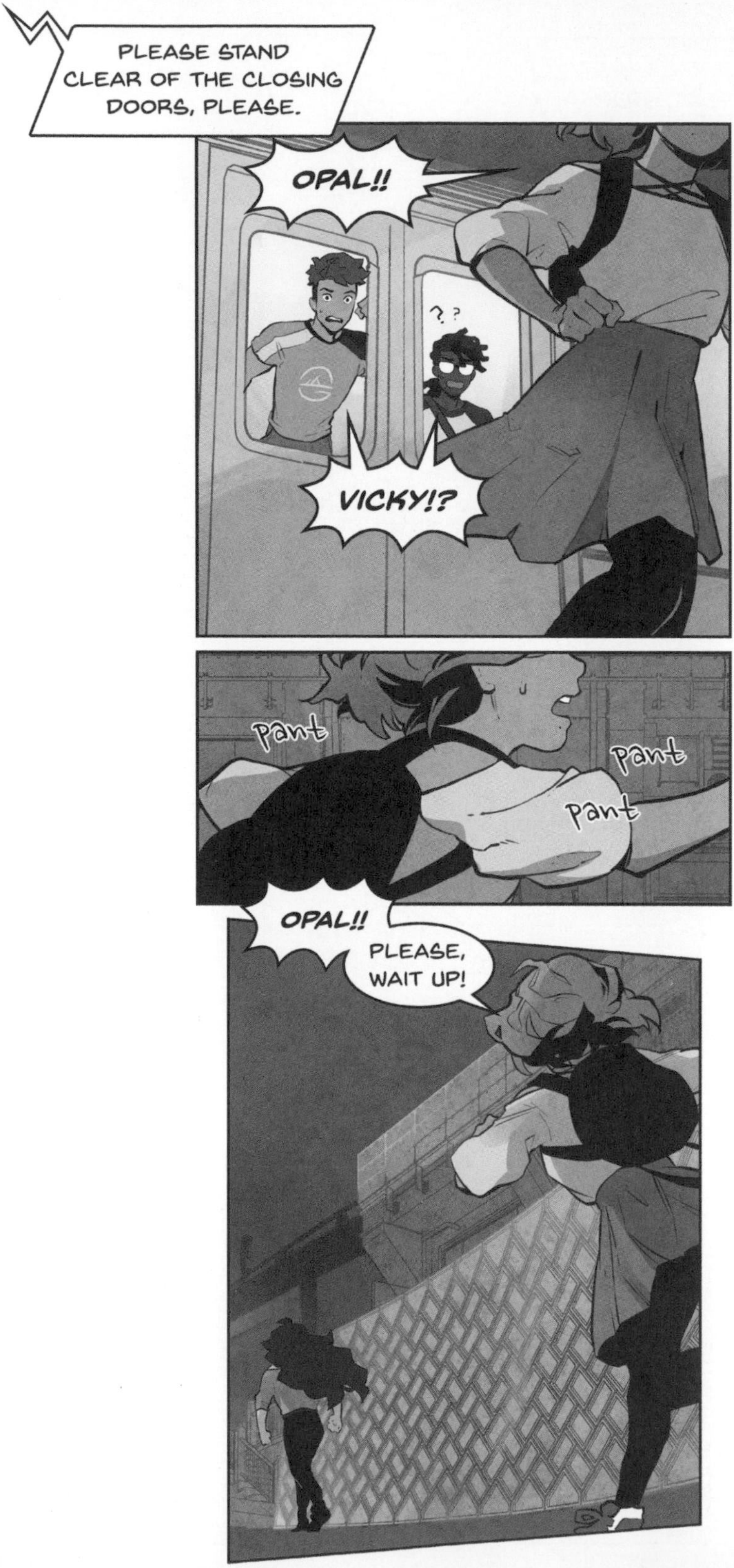
PLEASE STAND CLEAR OF THE CLOSING DOORS, PLEASE.
OPAL!!
? ?
VICKY!?
pant
pant
pant
OPAL!!
PLEASE, WAIT UP!

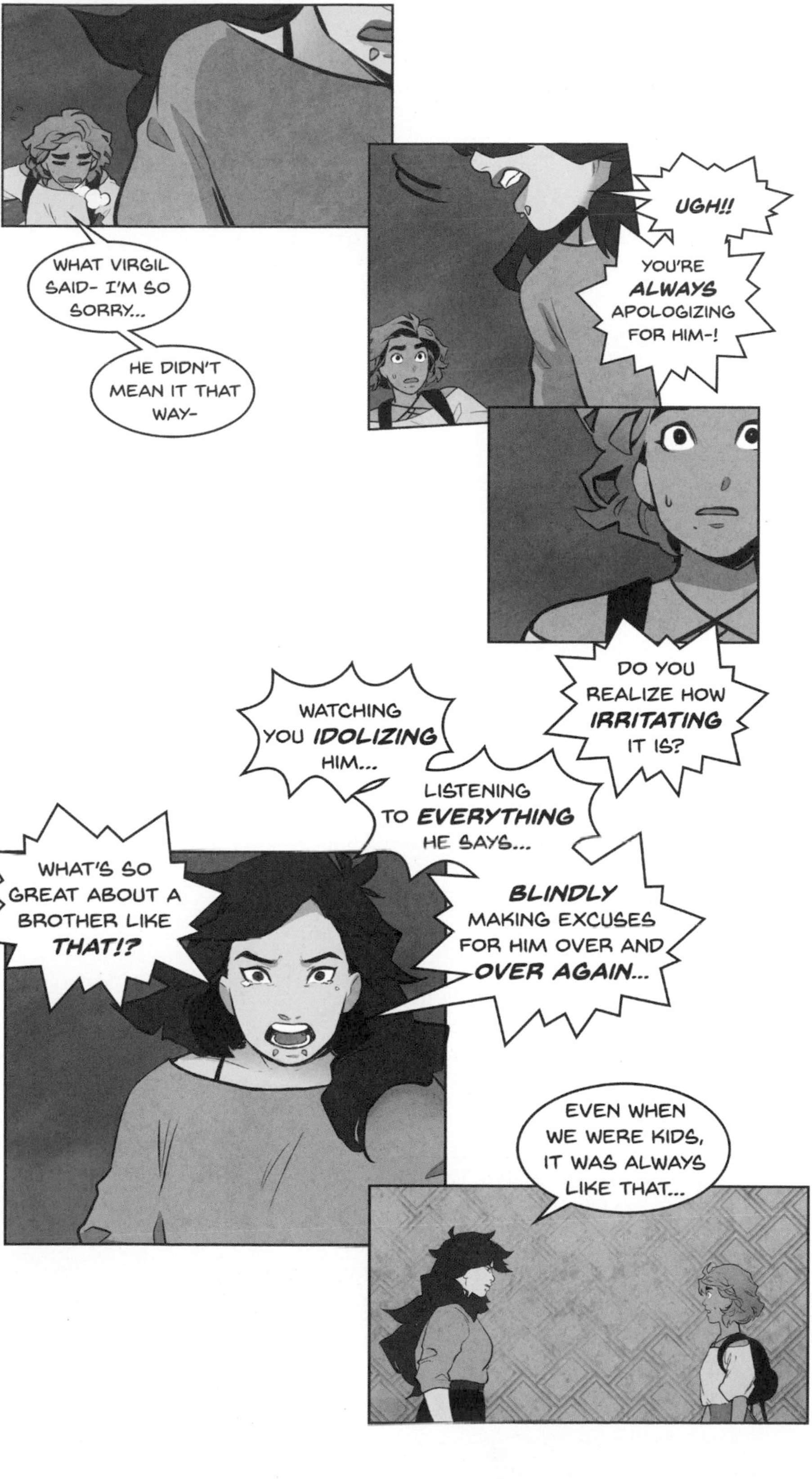
WHAT VIRGIL SAID- I'M SO SORRY...
HE DIDN'T MEAN IT THAT WAY-
UGH!!
YOU'RE ALWAYS APOLOGIZING FOR HIM-!
DO YOU REALIZE HOW IRRITATING IT IS?
WATCHING YOU IDOLIZING HIM...
LISTENING TO EVERYTHING HE SAYS...
BLINDLY MAKING EXCUSES FOR HIM OVER AND OVER AGAIN...
WHAT'S SO GREAT ABOUT A BROTHER LIKE THAT!?
EVEN WHEN WE WERE KIDS, IT WAS ALWAYS LIKE THAT...

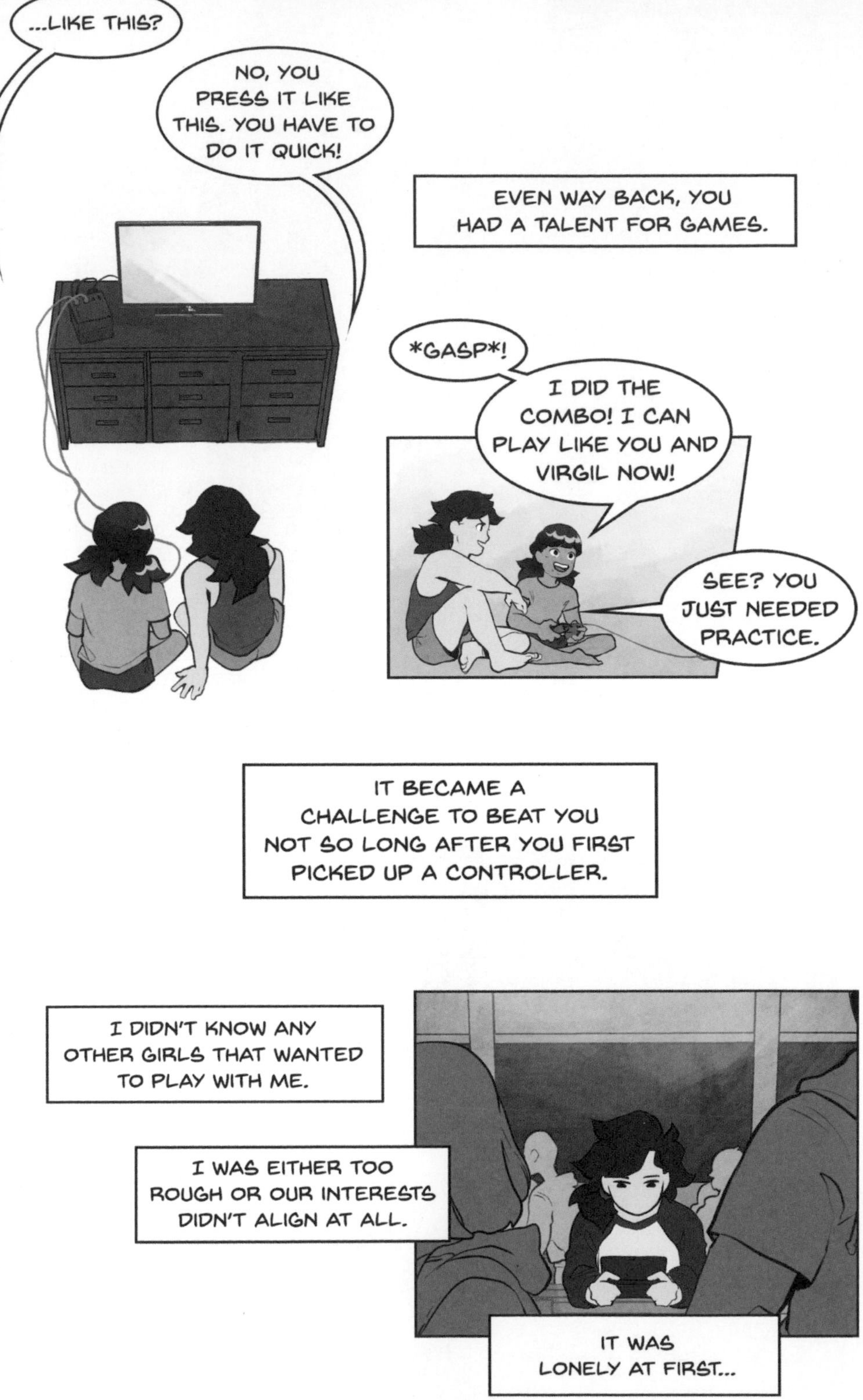
...LIKE THIS?
NO, YOU PRESS IT LIKE THIS. YOU HAVE TO DO IT QUICK!
EVEN WAY BACK, YOU HAD A TALENT FOR GAMES.
GASP!
I DID THE COMBO! I CAN PLAY LIKE YOU AND VIRGIL NOW!
SEE? YOU JUST NEEDED PRACTICE.
IT BECAME A CHALLENGE TO BEAT YOU NOT SO LONG AFTER YOU FIRST PICKED UP A CONTROLLER.
I DIDN'T KNOW ANY OTHER GIRLS THAT WANTED TO PLAY WITH ME.
I WAS EITHER TOO ROUGH OR OUR INTERESTS DIDN'T ALIGN AT ALL.
IT WAS LONELY AT FIRST...

BUT IT WAS FINE–

–WHEN YOU CAME ALONG.

HAPPY BIRTHDAY, OPAL!

I DIDN'T NEED ANYONE ELSE WHEN WE FILLED EACH OTHER'S DAYS WITH GOOD MEMORIES.

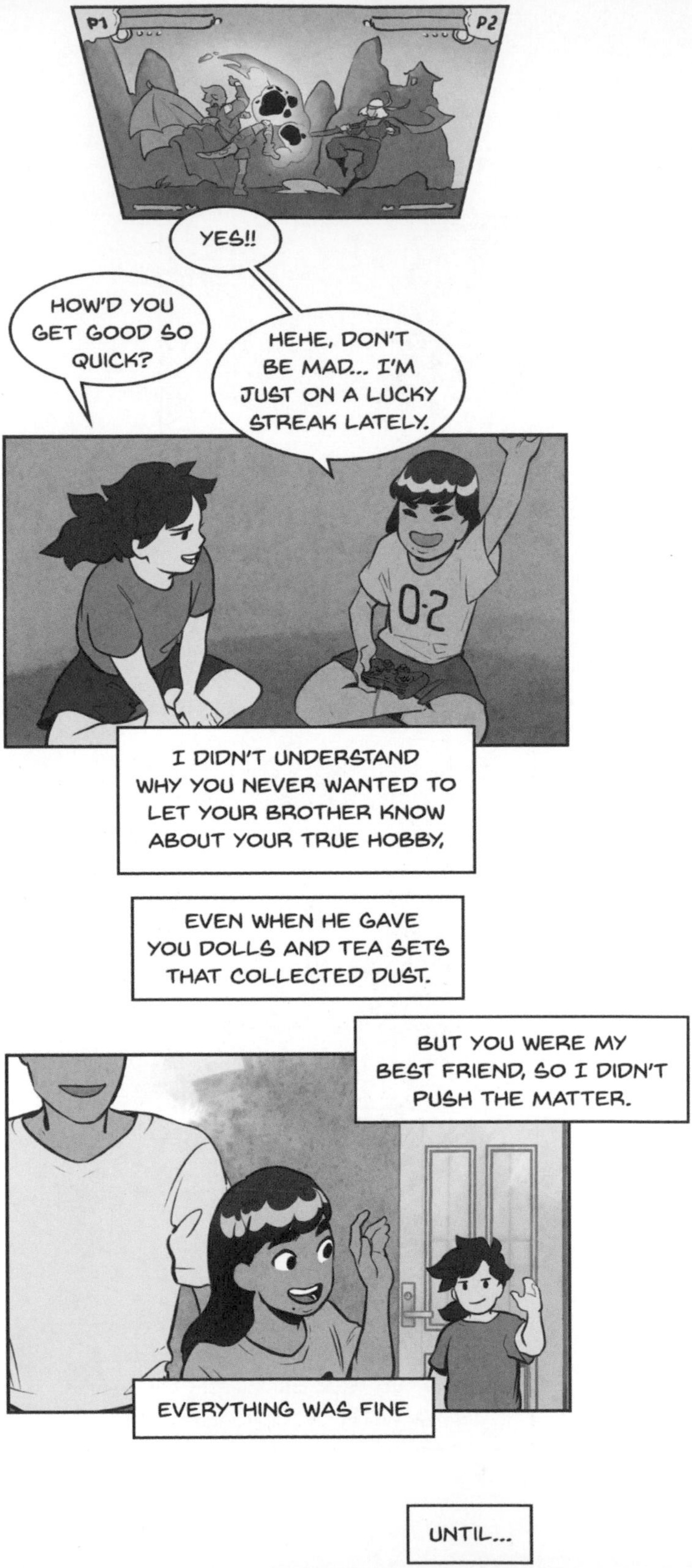
P1
P2
YES!!
HOW'D YOU GET GOOD SO QUICK?
HEHE, DON'T BE MAD... I'M JUST ON A LUCKY STREAK LATELY.
0-2
I DIDN'T UNDERSTAND WHY YOU NEVER WANTED TO LET YOUR BROTHER KNOW ABOUT YOUR TRUE HOBBY,
EVEN WHEN HE GAVE YOU DOLLS AND TEA SETS THAT COLLECTED DUST.
BUT YOU WERE MY BEST FRIEND, SO I DIDN'T PUSH THE MATTER.
EVERYTHING WAS FINE
UNTIL...

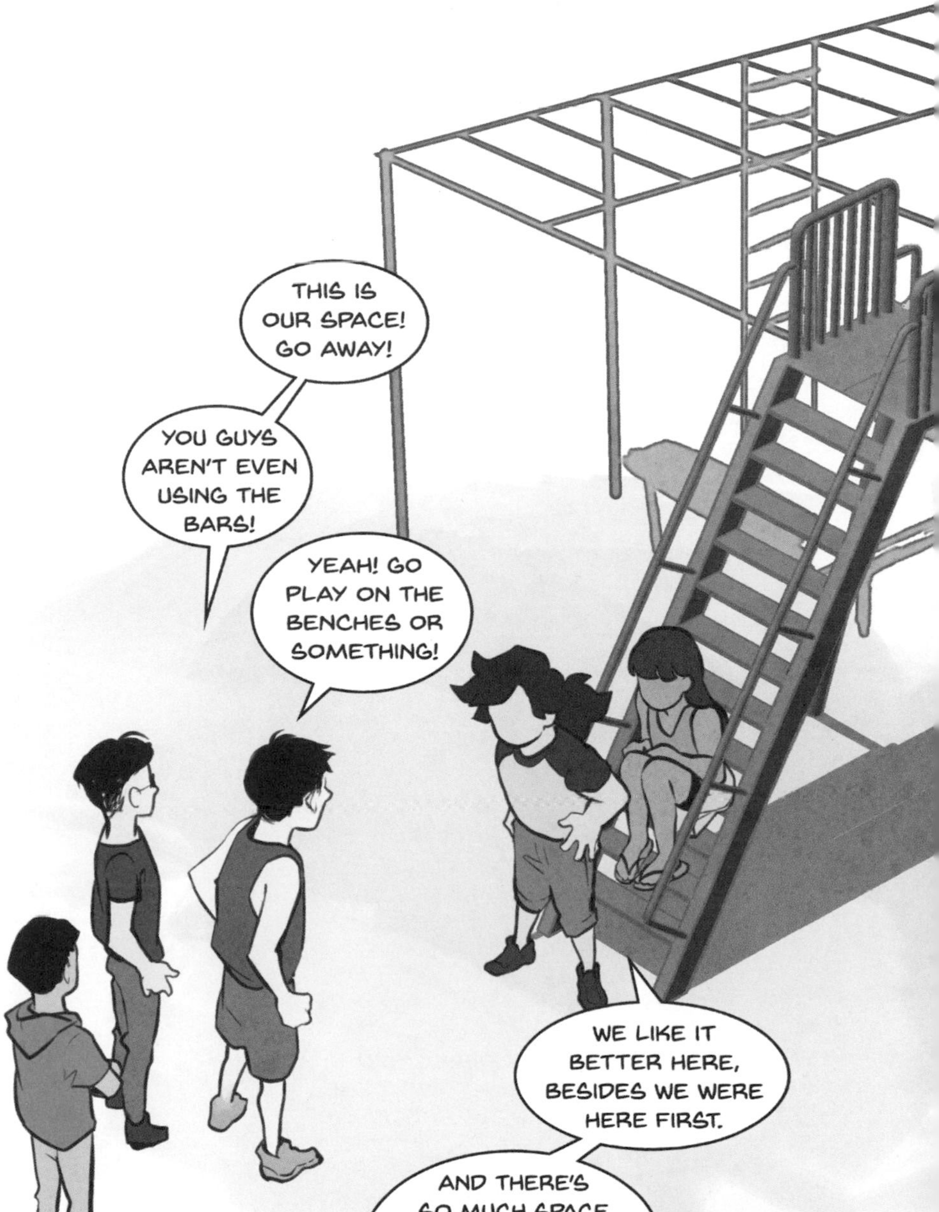
THIS IS OUR SPACE! GO AWAY!
YOU GUYS AREN'T EVEN USING THE BARS!
YEAH! GO PLAY ON THE BENCHES OR SOMETHING!
WE LIKE IT BETTER HERE, BESIDES WE WERE HERE FIRST.
AND THERE'S SO MUCH SPACE HERE, YOU GUYS CAN STILL PLAY ON THE BARS ANYWAYS.

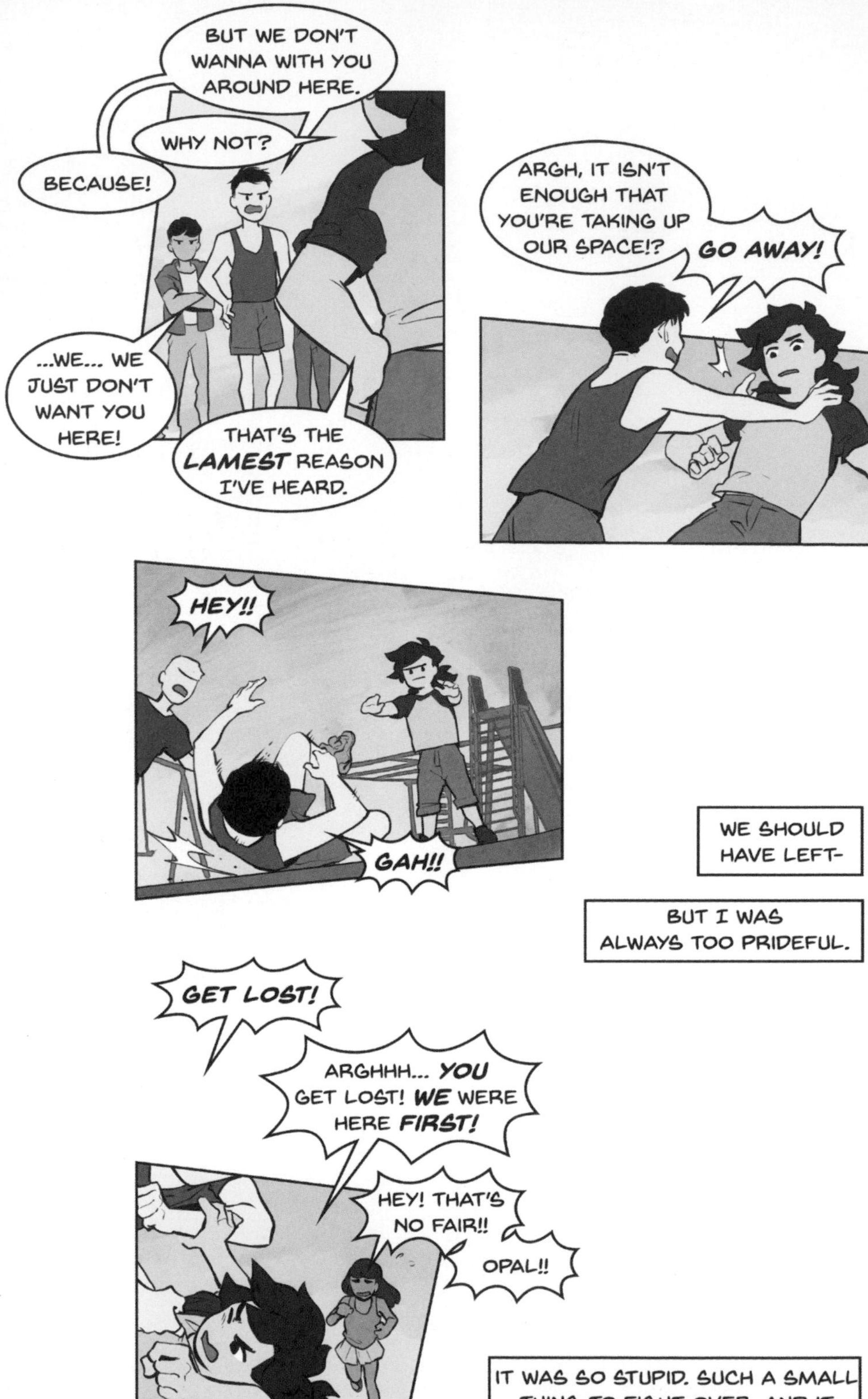
BUT WE DON'T WANNA WITH YOU AROUND HERE.
WHY NOT?
BECAUSE!
...WE... WE JUST DON'T WANT YOU HERE!
THAT'S THE **LAMEST** REASON I'VE HEARD.
ARGH, IT ISN'T ENOUGH THAT YOU'RE TAKING UP OUR SPACE!?
GO AWAY!
HEY!!
GAH!!
WE SHOULD HAVE LEFT-
BUT I WAS ALWAYS TOO PRIDEFUL.
GET LOST!
ARGHHH... ***YOU*** GET LOST! ***WE*** WERE HERE ***FIRST!***
HEY! THAT'S NO FAIR!!
OPAL!!
IT WAS SO STUPID. SUCH A SMALL THING TO FIGHT OVER, AND IT CHANGED EVERYTHING.

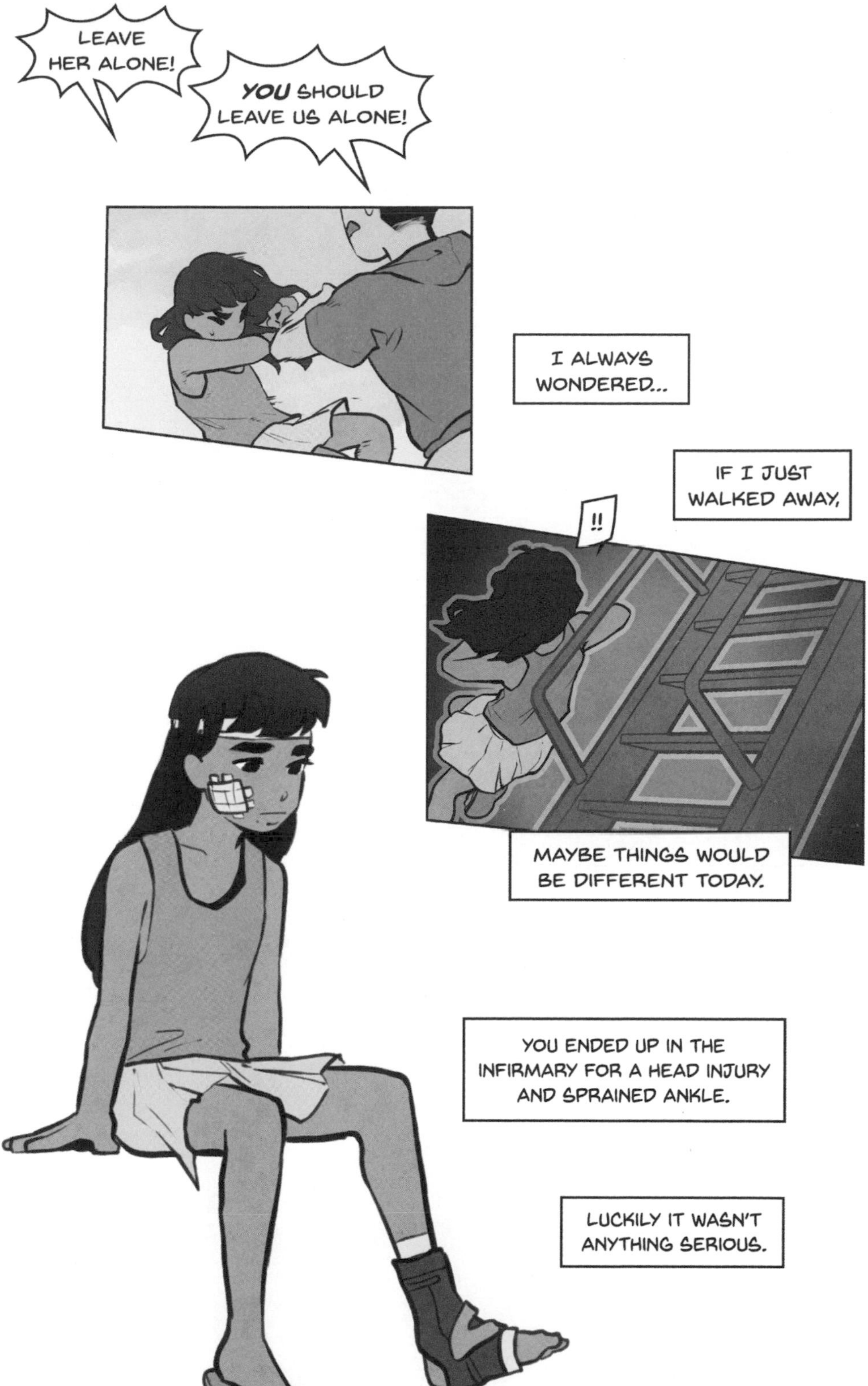
LEAVE HER ALONE!
YOU SHOULD LEAVE US ALONE!
I ALWAYS WONDERED...
IF I JUST WALKED AWAY,
!!
MAYBE THINGS WOULD BE DIFFERENT TODAY.
YOU ENDED UP IN THE INFIRMARY FOR A HEAD INJURY AND SPRAINED ANKLE.
LUCKILY IT WASN'T ANYTHING SERIOUS.

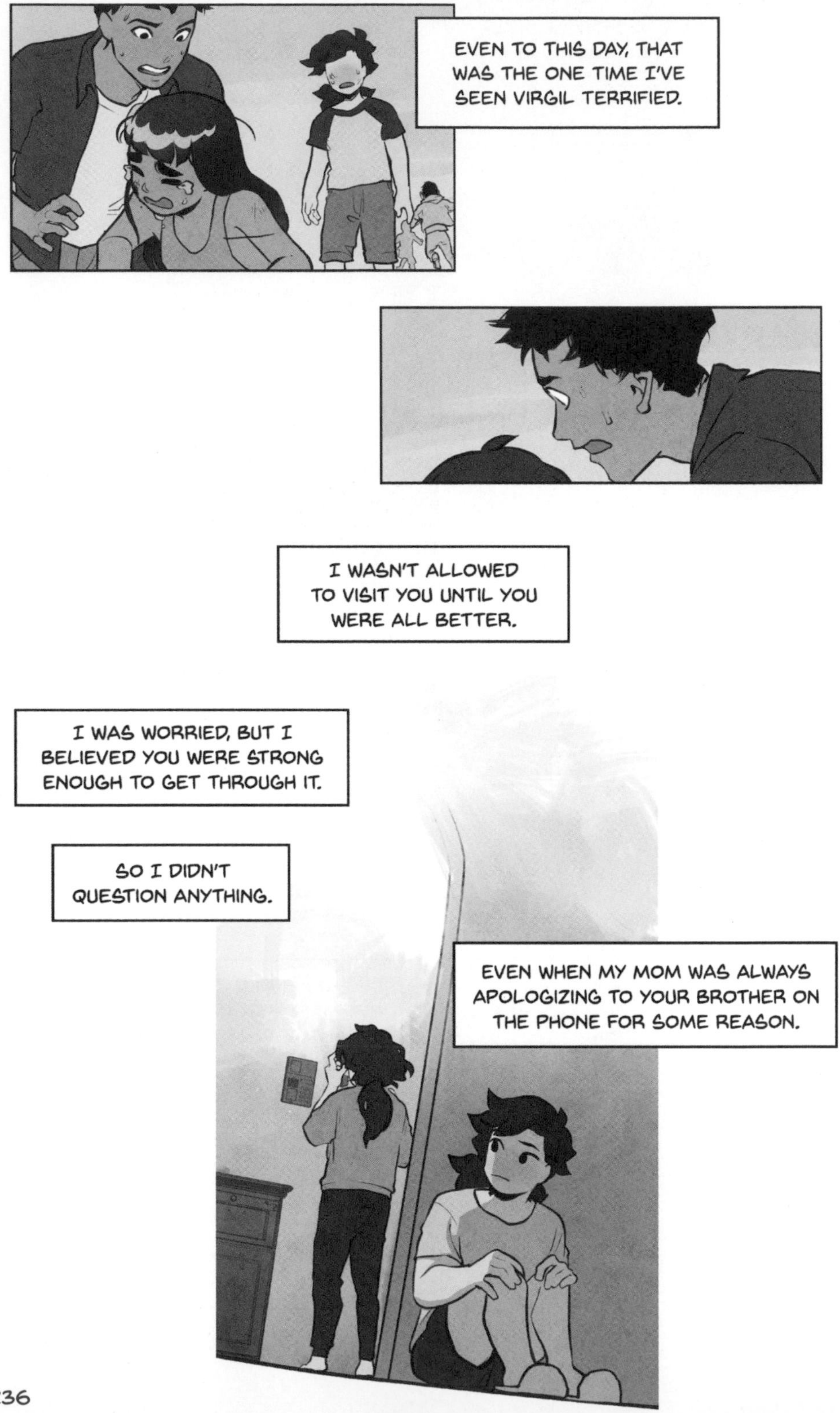
EVEN TO THIS DAY, THAT WAS THE ONE TIME I'VE SEEN VIRGIL TERRIFIED.
I WASN'T ALLOWED TO VISIT YOU UNTIL YOU WERE ALL BETTER.
I WAS WORRIED, BUT I BELIEVED YOU WERE STRONG ENOUGH TO GET THROUGH IT.
SO I DIDN'T QUESTION ANYTHING.
EVEN WHEN MY MOM WAS ALWAYS APOLOGIZING TO YOUR BROTHER ON THE PHONE FOR SOME REASON.

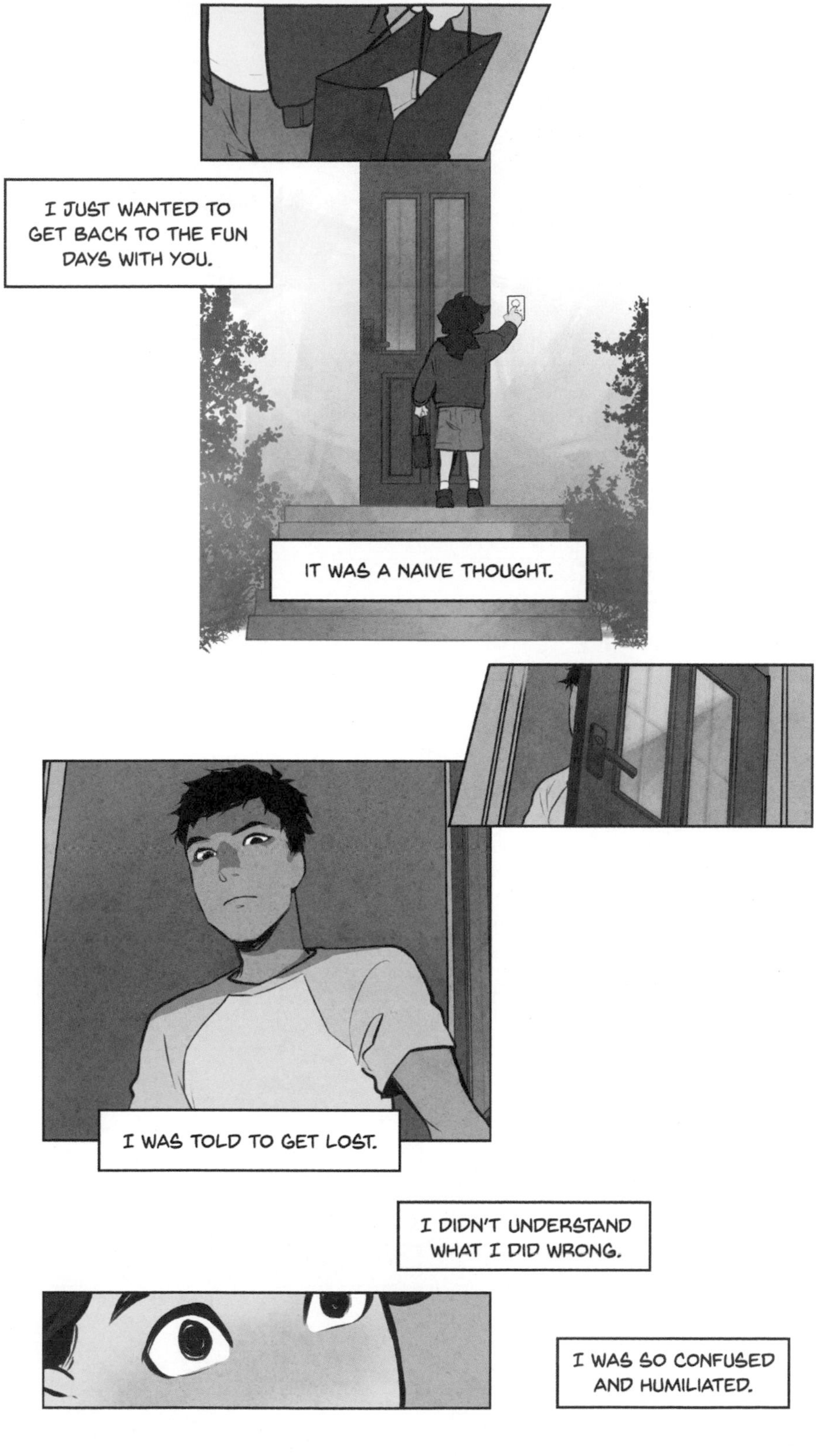
I JUST WANTED TO GET BACK TO THE FUN DAYS WITH YOU.
IT WAS A NAIVE THOUGHT.
I WAS TOLD TO GET LOST.
I DIDN'T UNDERSTAND WHAT I DID WRONG.
I WAS SO CONFUSED AND HUMILIATED.

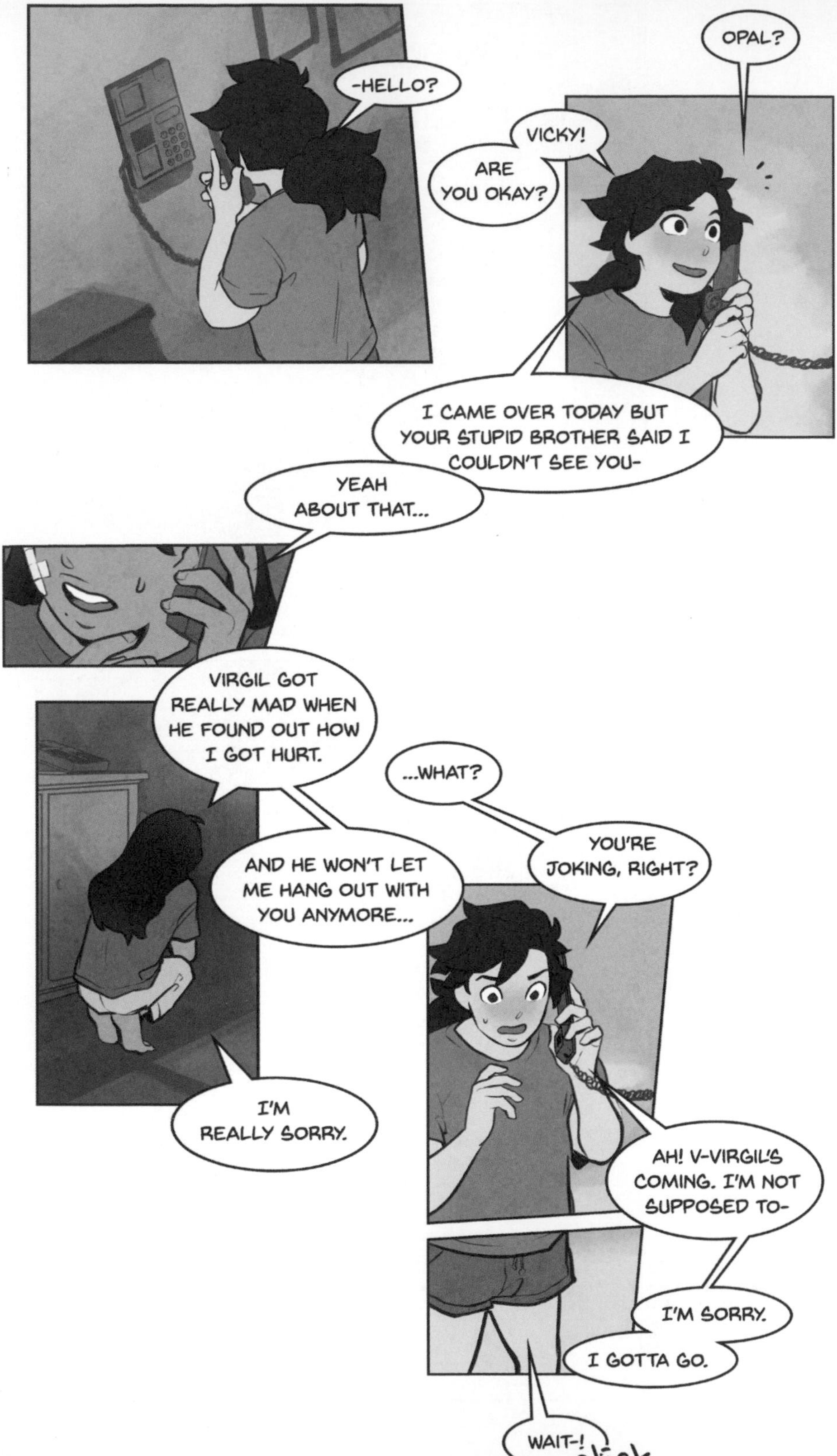
-HELLO?
OPAL?
VICKY!
ARE YOU OKAY?
I CAME OVER TODAY BUT YOUR STUPID BROTHER SAID I COULDN'T SEE YOU-
YEAH ABOUT THAT...
VIRGIL GOT REALLY MAD WHEN HE FOUND OUT HOW I GOT HURT.
AND HE WON'T LET ME HANG OUT WITH YOU ANYMORE...
I'M REALLY SORRY.
...WHAT?
YOU'RE JOKING, RIGHT?
AH! V-VIRGIL'S COMING. I'M NOT SUPPOSED TO-
I'M SORRY.
I GOTTA GO.
WAIT-!
click

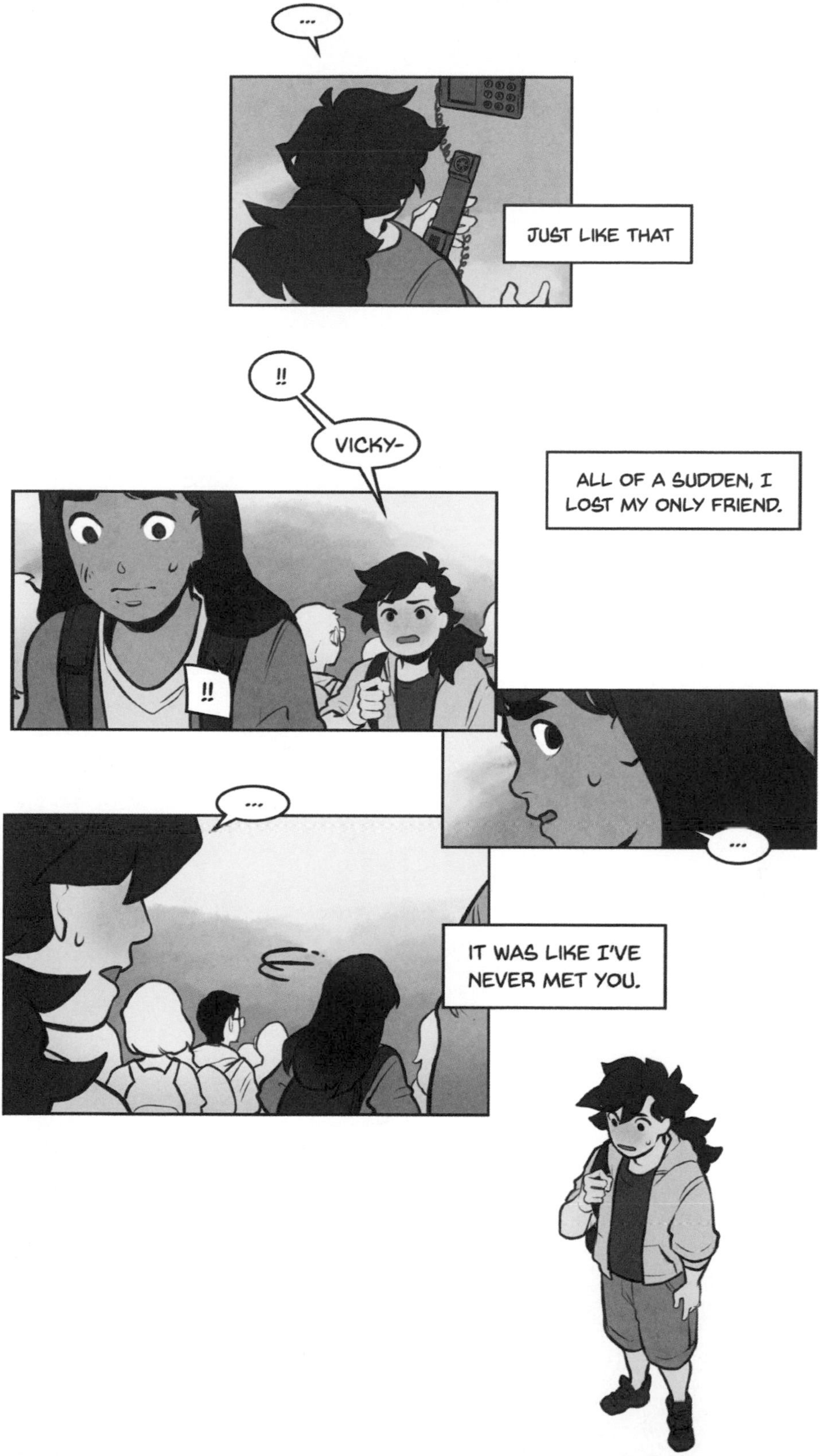
...
JUST LIKE THAT
!!
VICKY-
!!
ALL OF A SUDDEN, I LOST MY ONLY FRIEND.
...
...
IT WAS LIKE I'VE NEVER MET YOU.

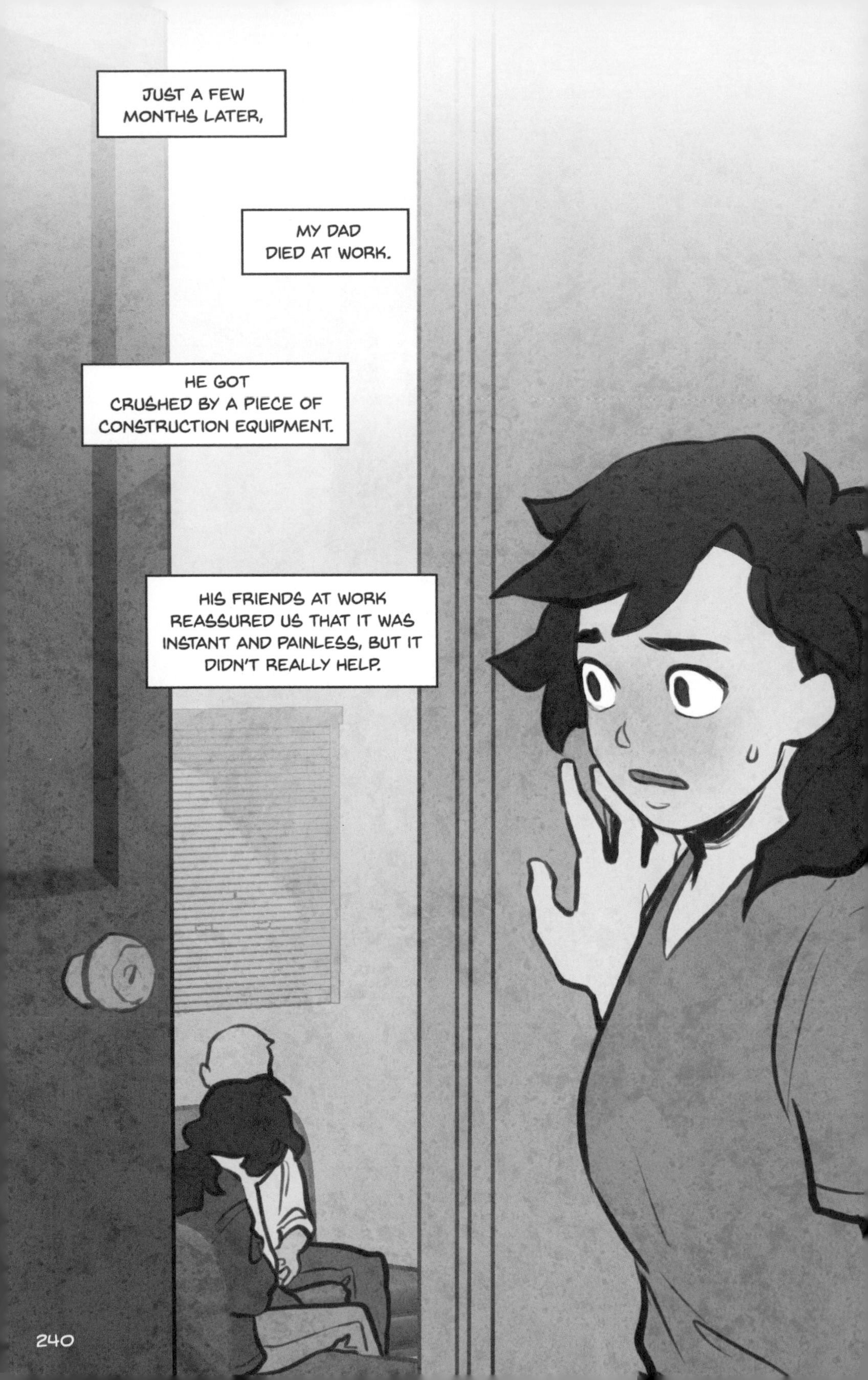
JUST A FEW MONTHS LATER,
MY DAD DIED AT WORK.
HE GOT CRUSHED BY A PIECE OF CONSTRUCTION EQUIPMENT.
HIS FRIENDS AT WORK REASSURED US THAT IT WAS INSTANT AND PAINLESS, BUT IT DIDN'T REALLY HELP.

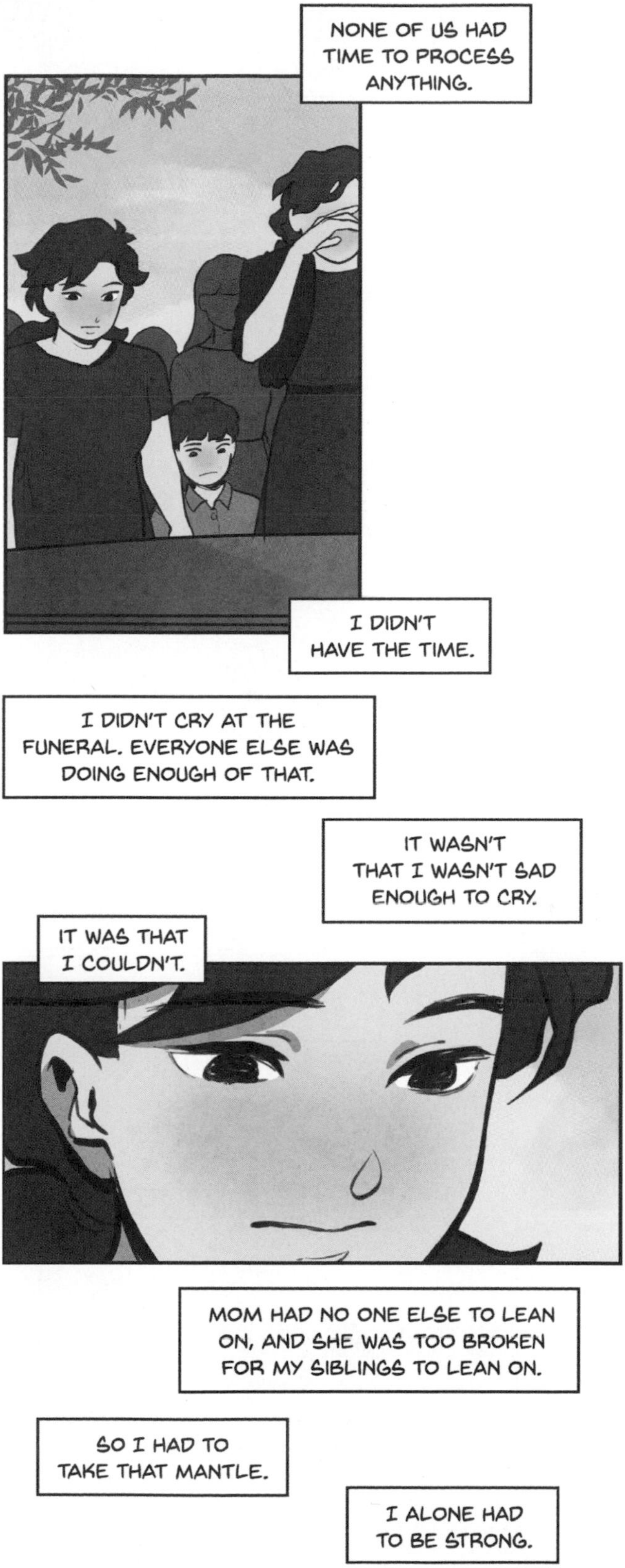
NONE OF US HAD TIME TO PROCESS ANYTHING.
I DIDN'T HAVE THE TIME.
I DIDN'T CRY AT THE FUNERAL. EVERYONE ELSE WAS DOING ENOUGH OF THAT.
IT WASN'T THAT I WASN'T SAD ENOUGH TO CRY.
IT WAS THAT I COULDN'T.
MOM HAD NO ONE ELSE TO LEAN ON, AND SHE WAS TOO BROKEN FOR MY SIBLINGS TO LEAN ON.
SO I HAD TO TAKE THAT MANTLE.
I ALONE HAD TO BE STRONG.

BUT THAT DIDN'T
MEAN I WASN'T LONELY.

I COULDN'T OPEN
UP TO ANYONE ABOUT MY
FEELINGS, EVEN AT HOME.

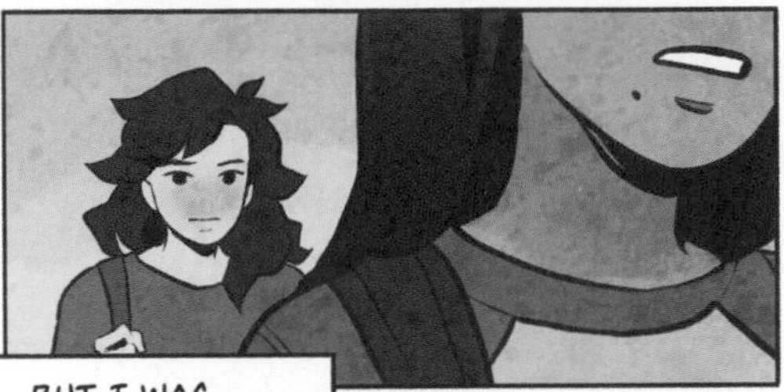

BUT I WAS
HOPING YOU WOULD
HAVE REACHED OUT.

GIVEN ME A
SHOULDER TO CRY ON.

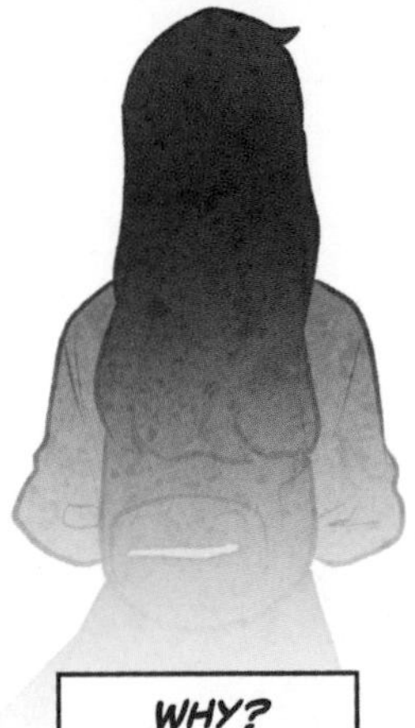

EVEN JUST IN
SECRET, FOR JUST
A MOMENT.

BUT YOU DIDN'T
LOOK MY WAY.

WHY?

WHY WERE YOU
ALWAYS LOOKING AT
VIRGIL INSTEAD?

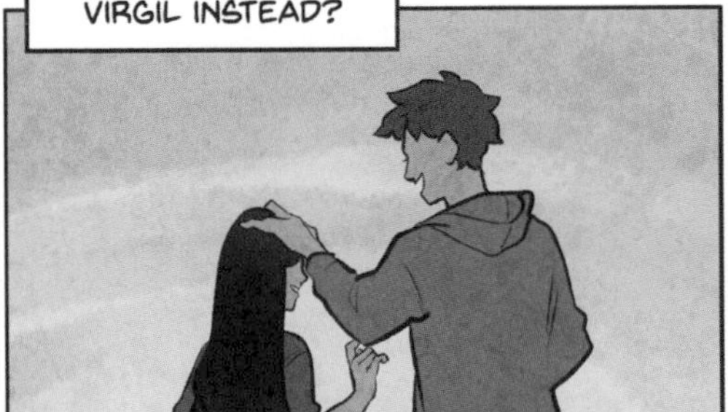

WAS I ***NEVER***
WORTH IT TO YOU?

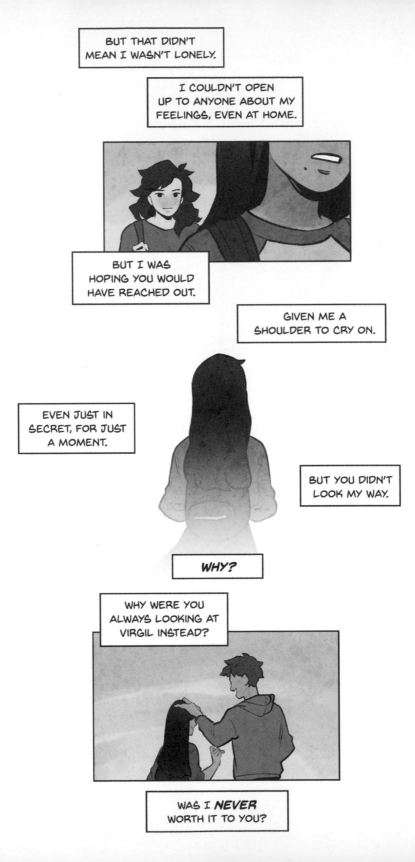

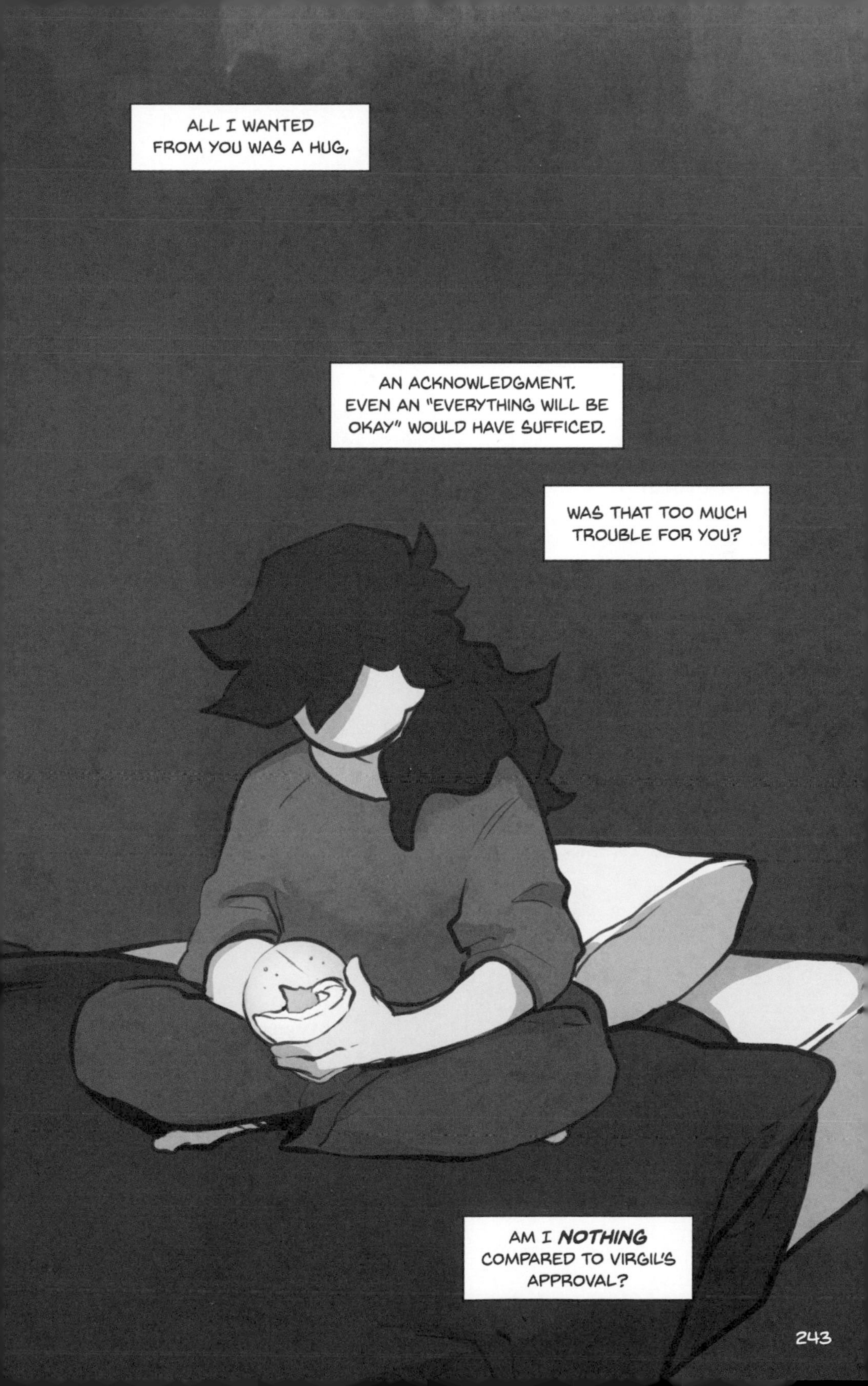
ALL I WANTED FROM YOU WAS A HUG,
AN ACKNOWLEDGMENT. EVEN AN "EVERYTHING WILL BE OKAY" WOULD HAVE SUFFICED.
WAS THAT TOO MUCH TROUBLE FOR YOU?
AM I ***NOTHING*** COMPARED TO VIRGIL'S APPROVAL?

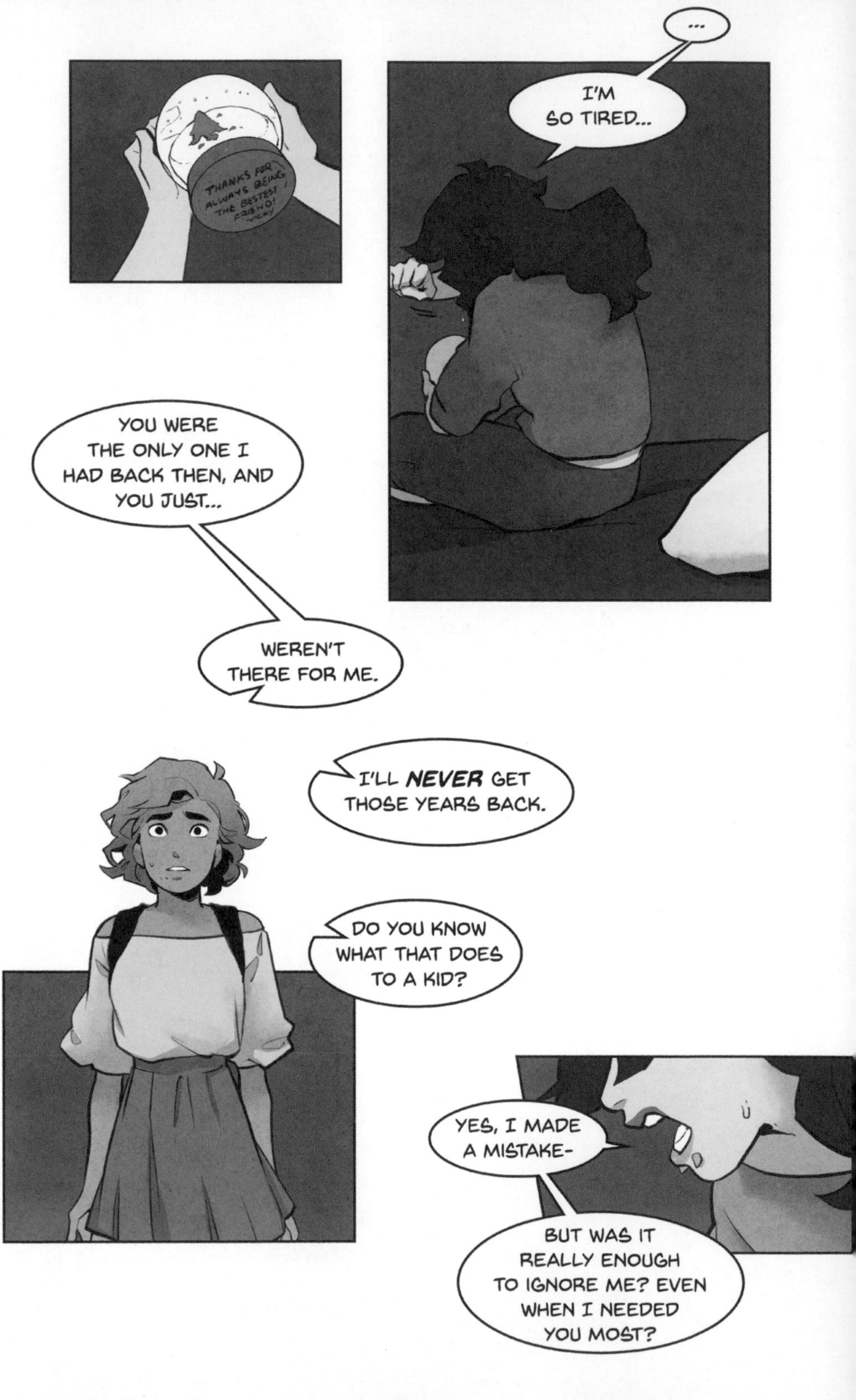
THANKS FOR ALWAYS BEING THE BESTEST FRIEND!
...
I'M SO TIRED...
YOU WERE THE ONLY ONE I HAD BACK THEN, AND YOU JUST...
WEREN'T THERE FOR ME.
I'LL **NEVER** GET THOSE YEARS BACK.
DO YOU KNOW WHAT THAT DOES TO A KID?
YES, I MADE A MISTAKE-
BUT WAS IT REALLY ENOUGH TO IGNORE ME? EVEN WHEN I NEEDED YOU MOST?

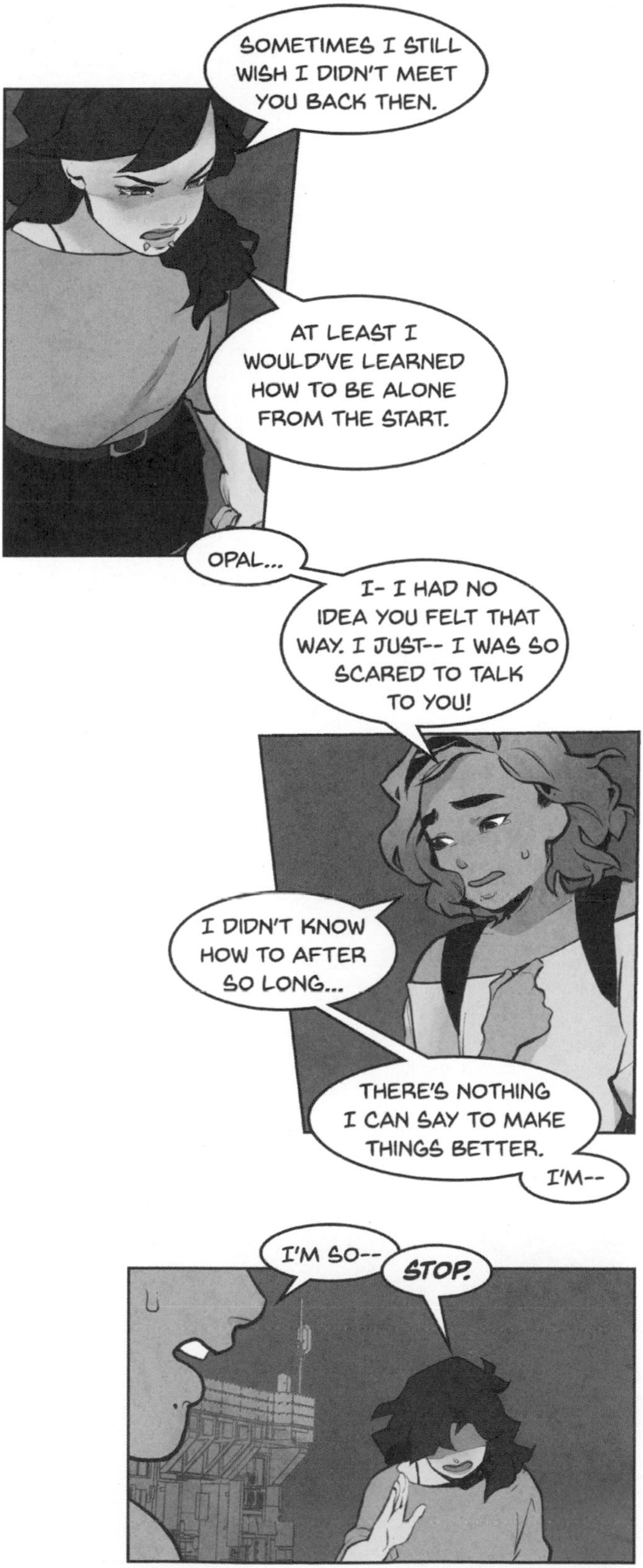
SOMETIMES I STILL WISH I DIDN'T MEET YOU BACK THEN.
AT LEAST I WOULD'VE LEARNED HOW TO BE ALONE FROM THE START.
OPAL...
I- I HAD NO IDEA YOU FELT THAT WAY. I JUST-- I WAS SO SCARED TO TALK TO YOU!
I DIDN'T KNOW HOW TO AFTER SO LONG...
THERE'S NOTHING I CAN SAY TO MAKE THINGS BETTER.
I'M--
I'M SO--
STOP.

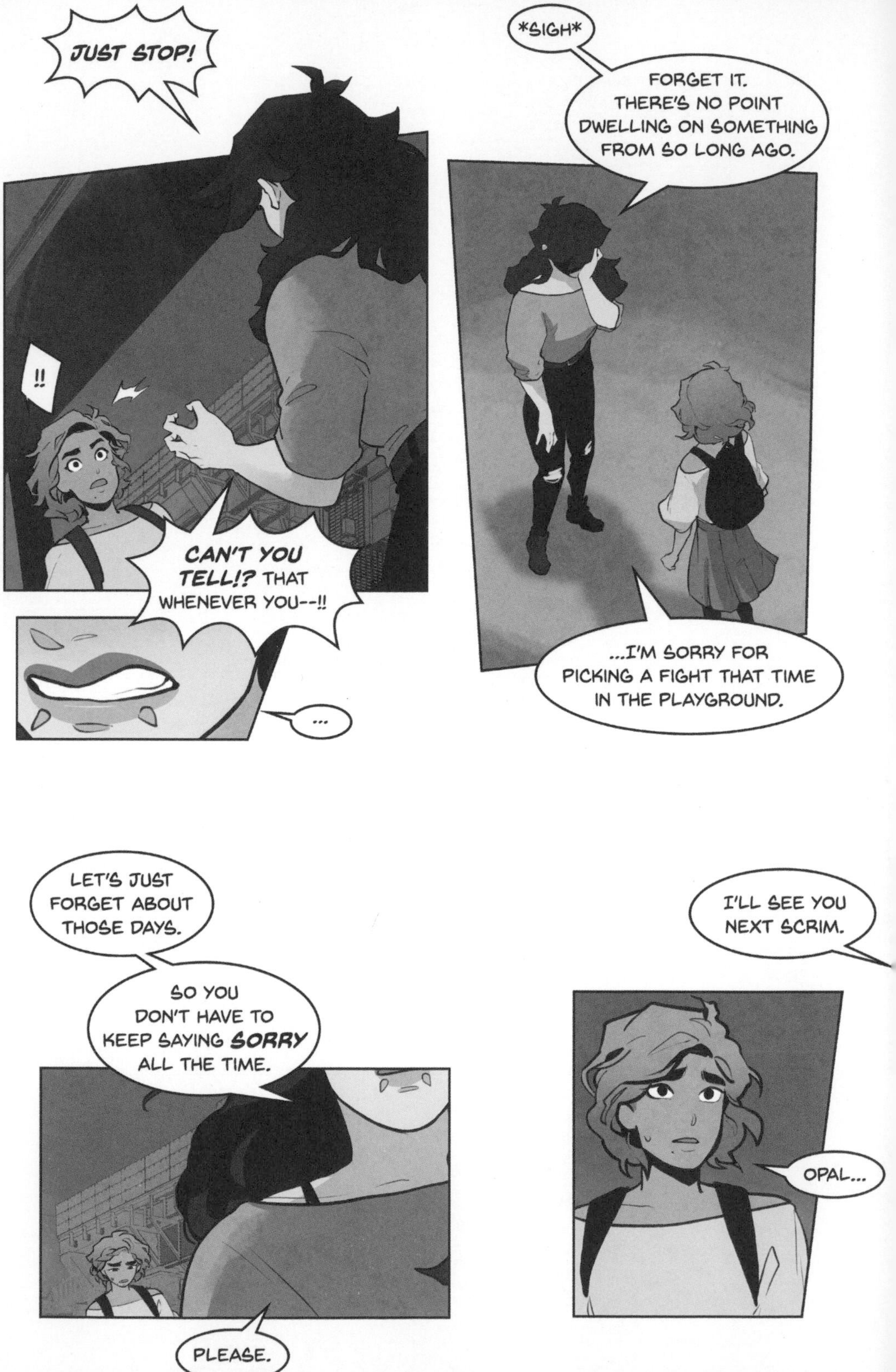
JUST STOP!
!!
CAN'T YOU TELL!? THAT WHENEVER YOU--!!
...
SIGH
FORGET IT. THERE'S NO POINT DWELLING ON SOMETHING FROM SO LONG AGO.
...I'M SORRY FOR PICKING A FIGHT THAT TIME IN THE PLAYGROUND.
LET'S JUST FORGET ABOUT THOSE DAYS.
SO YOU DON'T HAVE TO KEEP SAYING SORRY ALL THE TIME.
PLEASE.
I'LL SEE YOU NEXT SCRIM.
OPAL...

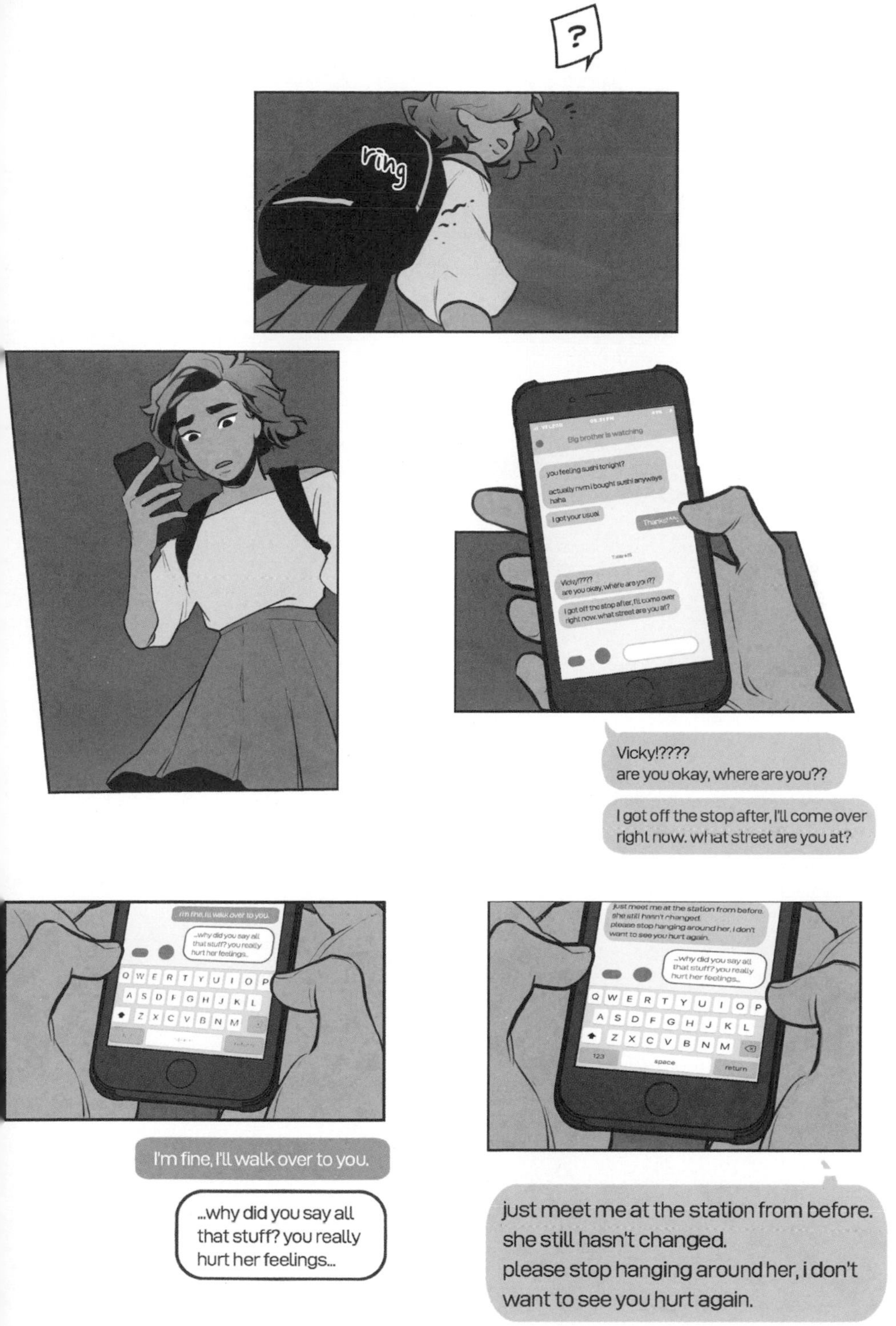
?
ring
Vicky!????
are you okay, where are you??
I got off the stop after, I'll come over right now. what street are you at?
I'm fine, I'll walk over to you.
...why did you say all that stuff? you really hurt her feelings...
just meet me at the station from before.
she still hasn't changed.
please stop hanging around her, i don't want to see you hurt again.

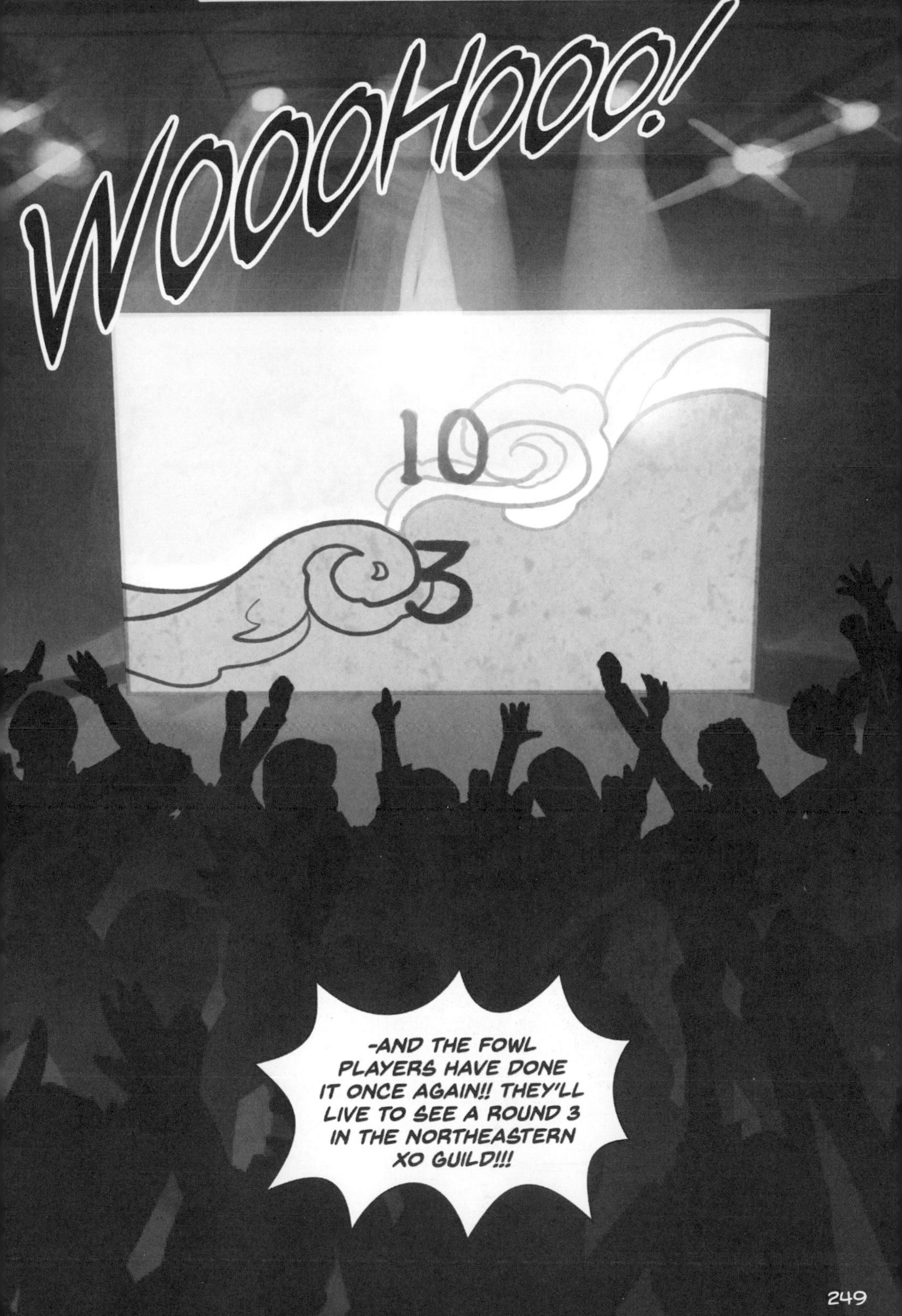
WOOOHOOO!
10
3
-AND THE FOWL PLAYERS HAVE DONE IT ONCE AGAIN!! THEY'LL LIVE TO SEE A ROUND 3 IN THE NORTHEASTERN XO GUILD!!!

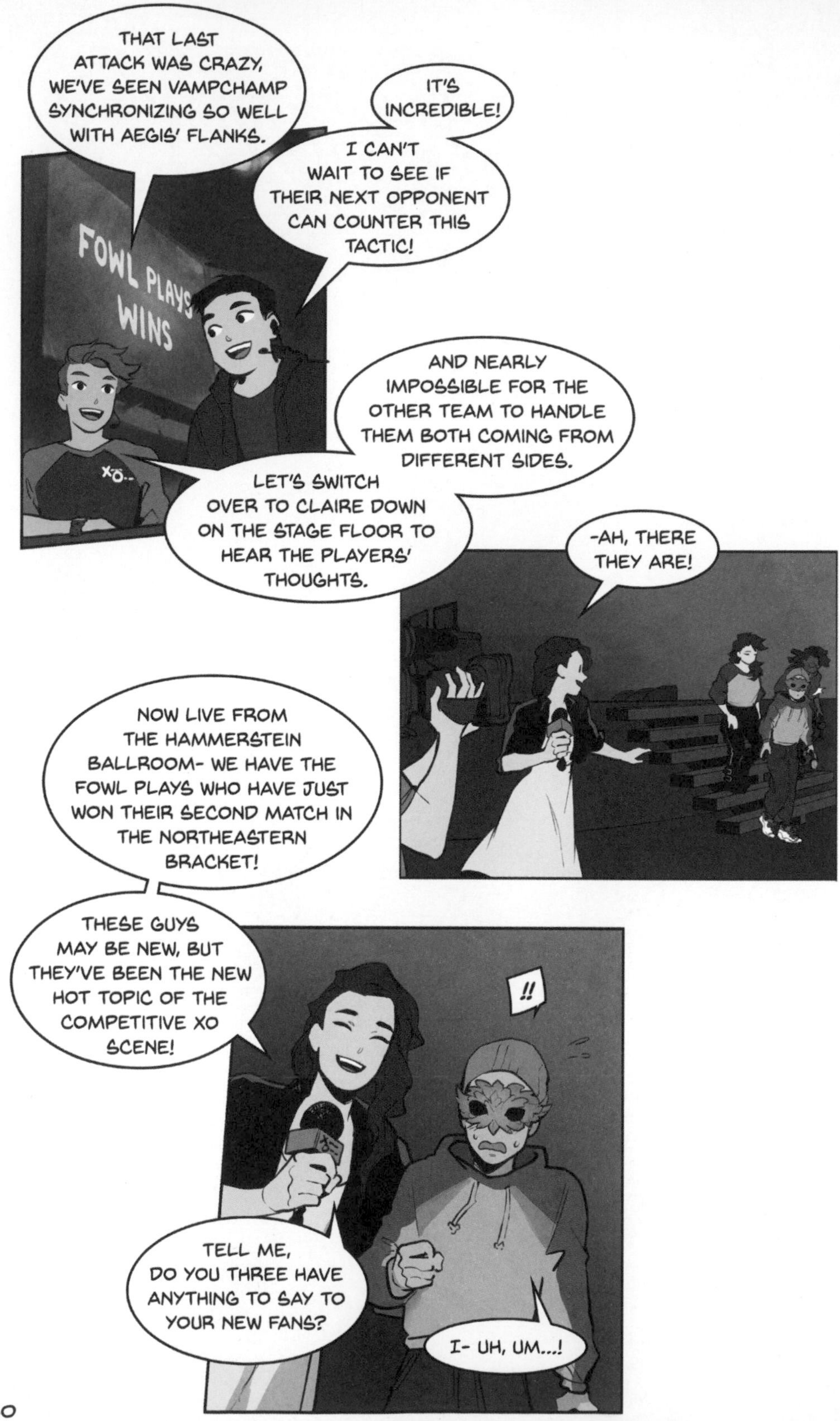
THAT LAST ATTACK WAS CRAZY, WE'VE SEEN VAMPCHAMP SYNCHRONIZING SO WELL WITH AEGIS' FLANKS.
IT'S INCREDIBLE!
I CAN'T WAIT TO SEE IF THEIR NEXT OPPONENT CAN COUNTER THIS TACTIC!
FOWL PLAYS WINS
AND NEARLY IMPOSSIBLE FOR THE OTHER TEAM TO HANDLE THEM BOTH COMING FROM DIFFERENT SIDES.
LET'S SWITCH OVER TO CLAIRE DOWN ON THE STAGE FLOOR TO HEAR THE PLAYERS' THOUGHTS.
-AH, THERE THEY ARE!
NOW LIVE FROM THE HAMMERSTEIN BALLROOM- WE HAVE THE FOWL PLAYS WHO HAVE JUST WON THEIR SECOND MATCH IN THE NORTHEASTERN BRACKET!
THESE GUYS MAY BE NEW, BUT THEY'VE BEEN THE NEW HOT TOPIC OF THE COMPETITIVE XO SCENE!
!!
TELL ME, DO YOU THREE HAVE ANYTHING TO SAY TO YOUR NEW FANS?
I- UH, UM...!

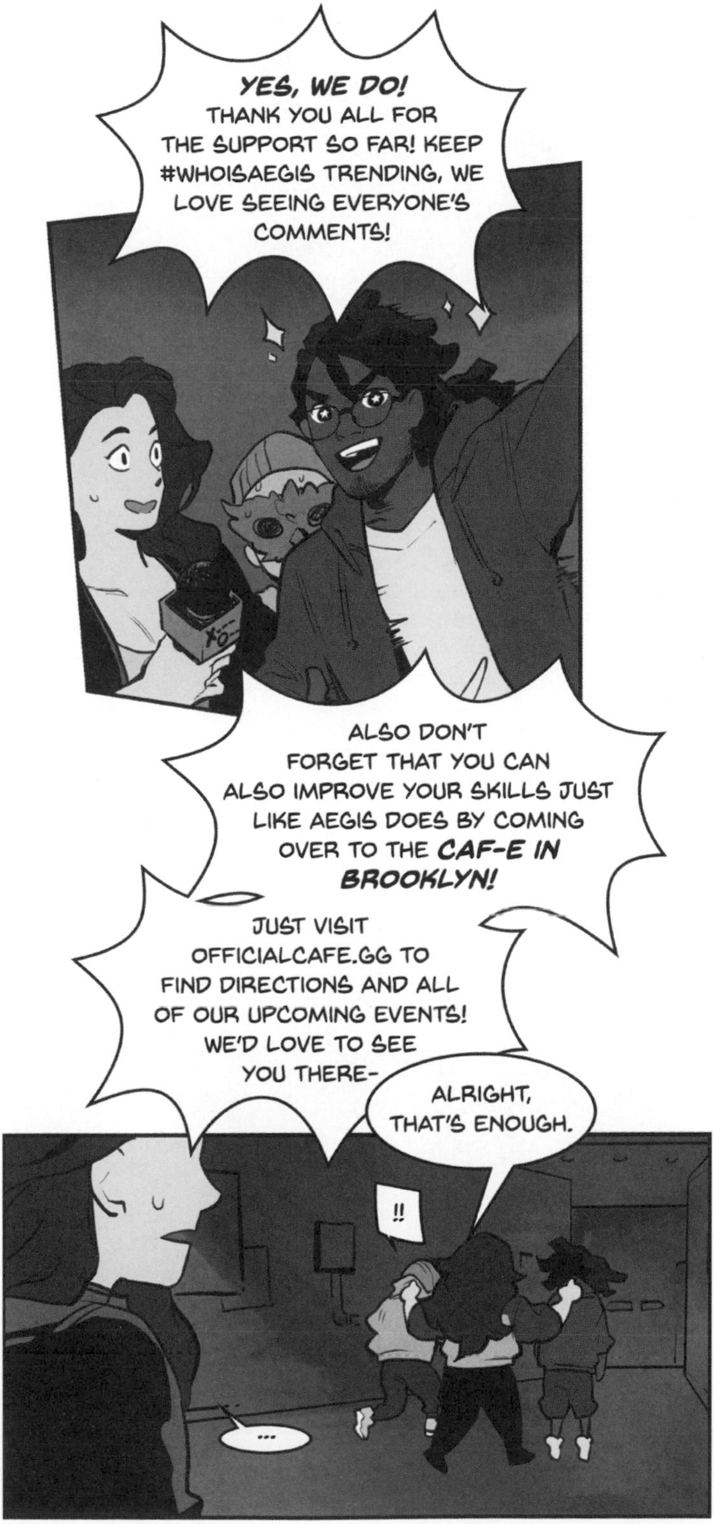
YES, WE DO! THANK YOU ALL FOR THE SUPPORT SO FAR! KEEP #WHOISAEGIS TRENDING, WE LOVE SEEING EVERYONE'S COMMENTS!
ALSO DON'T FORGET THAT YOU CAN ALSO IMPROVE YOUR SKILLS JUST LIKE AEGIS DOES BY COMING OVER TO THE CAF-E IN BROOKLYN!
JUST VISIT OFFICIALCAFE.GG TO FIND DIRECTIONS AND ALL OF OUR UPCOMING EVENTS! WE'D LOVE TO SEE YOU THERE-
ALRIGHT, THAT'S ENOUGH.
!!
...

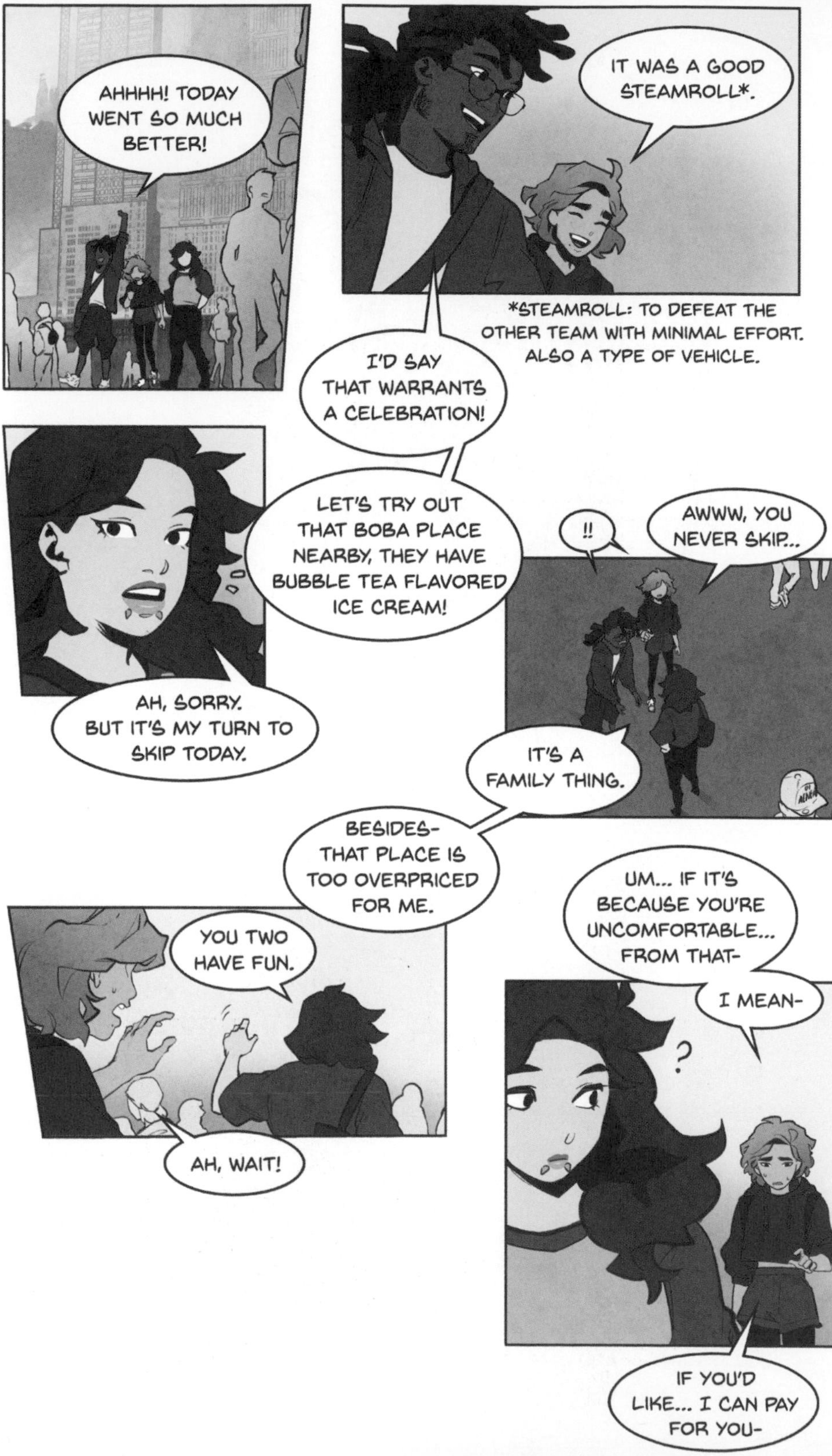
AHHHH! TODAY WENT SO MUCH BETTER!
IT WAS A GOOD STEAMROLL*.
*STEAMROLL: TO DEFEAT THE OTHER TEAM WITH MINIMAL EFFORT. ALSO A TYPE OF VEHICLE.
I'D SAY THAT WARRANTS A CELEBRATION!
LET'S TRY OUT THAT BOBA PLACE NEARBY, THEY HAVE BUBBLE TEA FLAVORED ICE CREAM!
AH, SORRY. BUT IT'S MY TURN TO SKIP TODAY.
!!
AWWW, YOU NEVER SKIP...
IT'S A FAMILY THING.
BESIDES- THAT PLACE IS TOO OVERPRICED FOR ME.
YOU TWO HAVE FUN.
AH, WAIT!
UM... IF IT'S BECAUSE YOU'RE UNCOMFORTABLE... FROM THAT-
I MEAN-
?
IF YOU'D LIKE... I CAN PAY FOR YOU-

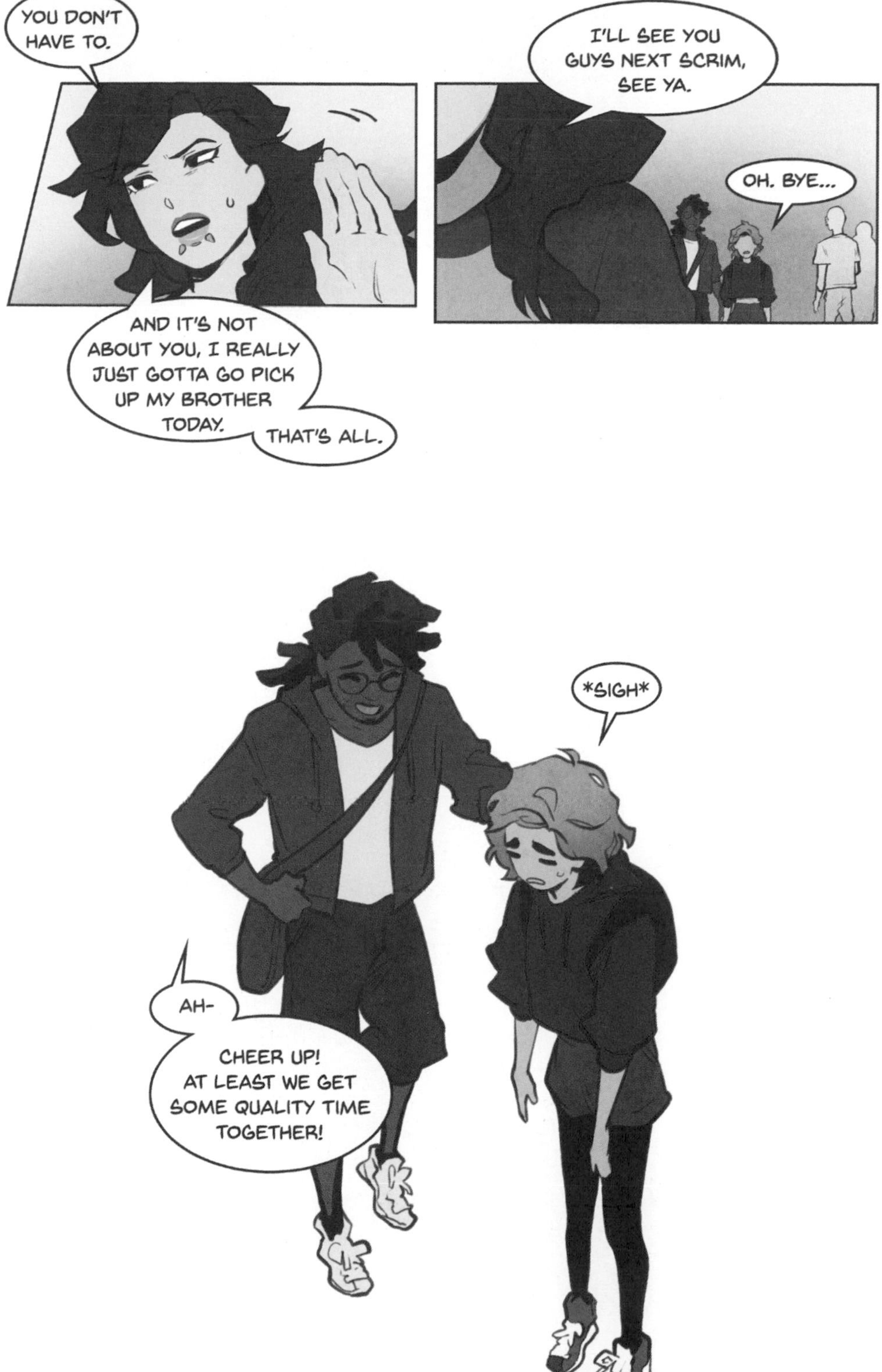
YOU DON'T HAVE TO.
AND IT'S NOT ABOUT YOU, I REALLY JUST GOTTA GO PICK UP MY BROTHER TODAY.
THAT'S ALL.
I'LL SEE YOU GUYS NEXT SCRIM, SEE YA.
OH, BYE...
SIGH
AH-
CHEER UP! AT LEAST WE GET SOME QUALITY TIME TOGETHER!

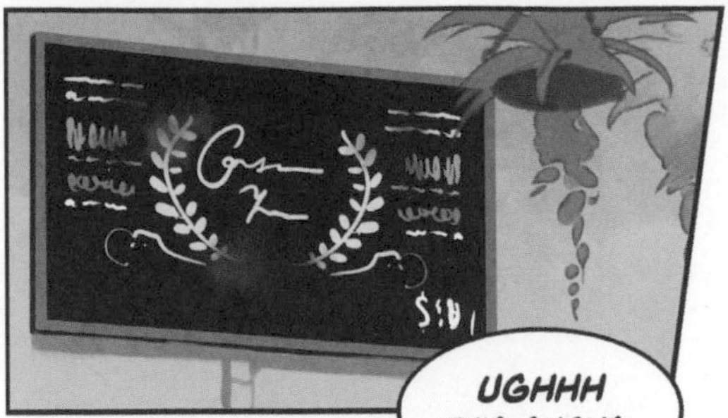

UGHHH
THIS SUCKS.

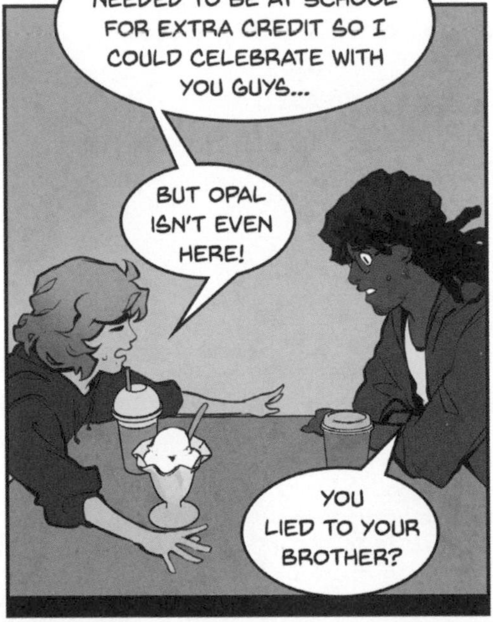

I EVEN TOLD VIRGIL I NEEDED TO BE AT SCHOOL FOR EXTRA CREDIT SO I COULD CELEBRATE WITH YOU GUYS...
BUT OPAL ISN'T EVEN HERE!
YOU LIED TO YOUR BROTHER?

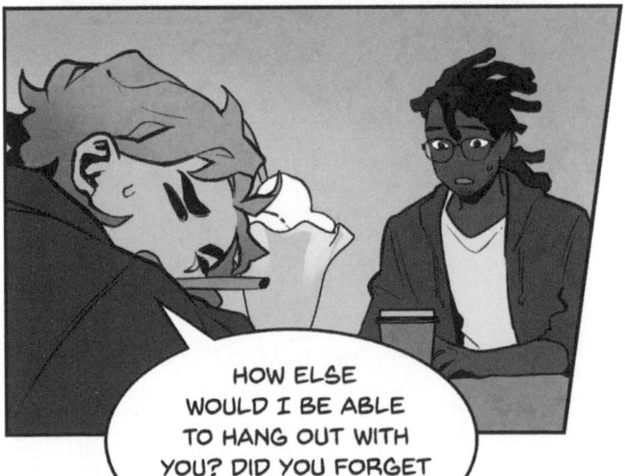

HOW ELSE WOULD I BE ABLE TO HANG OUT WITH YOU? DID YOU FORGET ***LAST WEEK?***

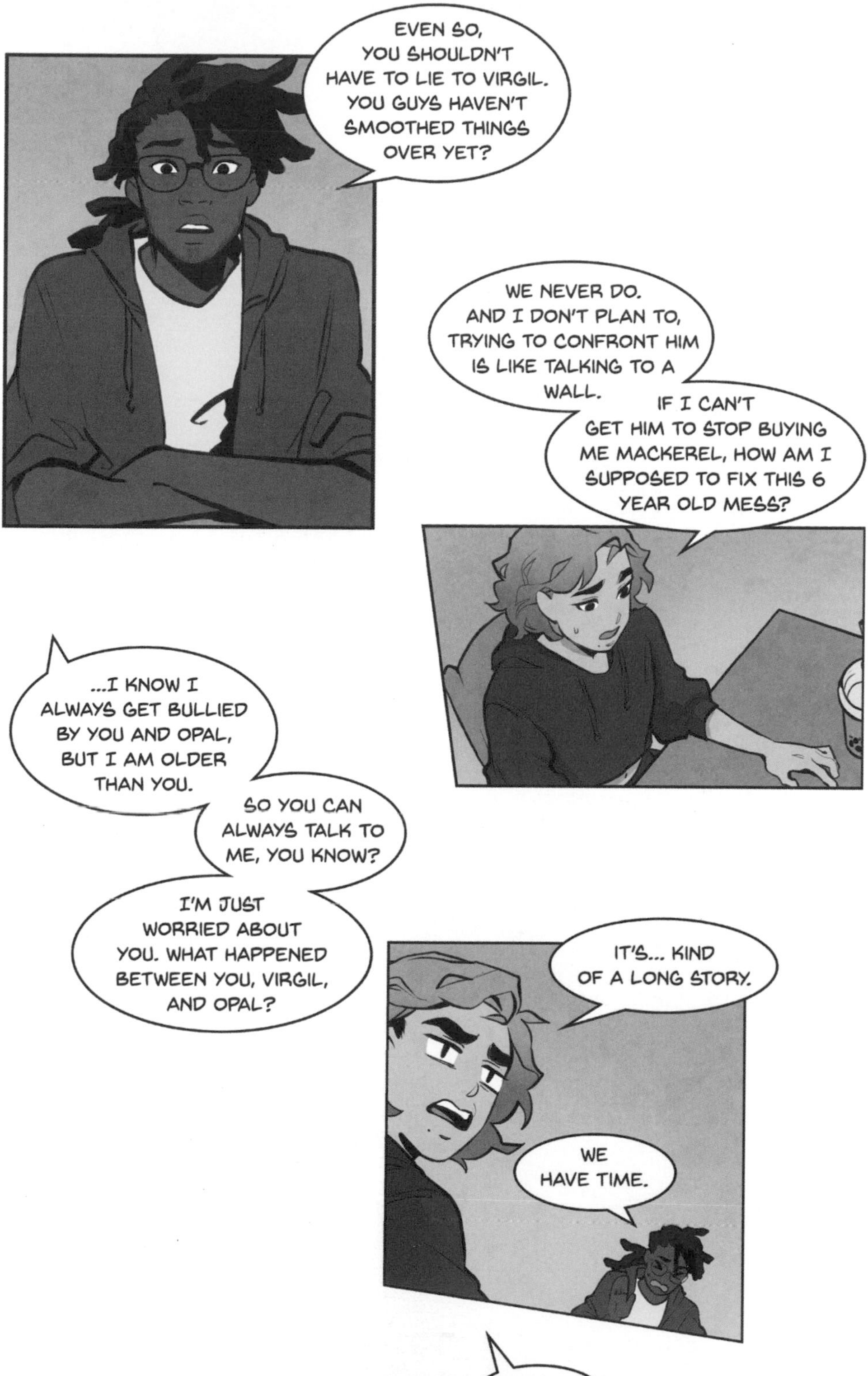
EVEN SO, YOU SHOULDN'T HAVE TO LIE TO VIRGIL. YOU GUYS HAVEN'T SMOOTHED THINGS OVER YET?
WE NEVER DO. AND I DON'T PLAN TO, TRYING TO CONFRONT HIM IS LIKE TALKING TO A WALL.
IF I CAN'T GET HIM TO STOP BUYING ME MACKEREL, HOW AM I SUPPOSED TO FIX THIS 6 YEAR OLD MESS?
...I KNOW I ALWAYS GET BULLIED BY YOU AND OPAL, BUT I AM OLDER THAN YOU.
SO YOU CAN ALWAYS TALK TO ME, YOU KNOW?
I'M JUST WORRIED ABOUT YOU. WHAT HAPPENED BETWEEN YOU, VIRGIL, AND OPAL?
IT'S... KIND OF A LONG STORY.
WE HAVE TIME.
WELL...

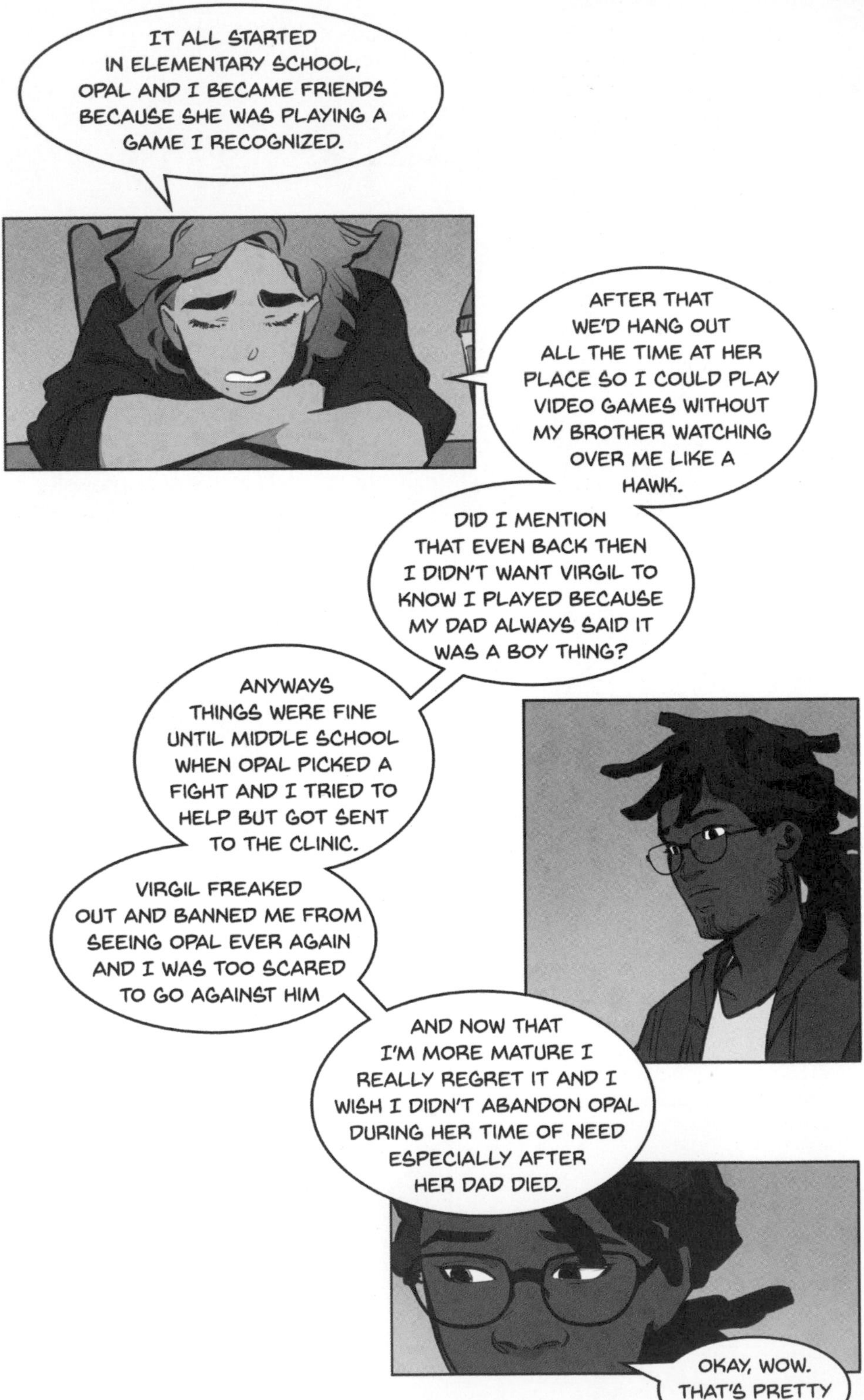
IT ALL STARTED IN ELEMENTARY SCHOOL, OPAL AND I BECAME FRIENDS BECAUSE SHE WAS PLAYING A GAME I RECOGNIZED.
AFTER THAT WE'D HANG OUT ALL THE TIME AT HER PLACE SO I COULD PLAY VIDEO GAMES WITHOUT MY BROTHER WATCHING OVER ME LIKE A HAWK.
DID I MENTION THAT EVEN BACK THEN I DIDN'T WANT VIRGIL TO KNOW I PLAYED BECAUSE MY DAD ALWAYS SAID IT WAS A BOY THING?
ANYWAYS THINGS WERE FINE UNTIL MIDDLE SCHOOL WHEN OPAL PICKED A FIGHT AND I TRIED TO HELP BUT GOT SENT TO THE CLINIC.
VIRGIL FREAKED OUT AND BANNED ME FROM SEEING OPAL EVER AGAIN AND I WAS TOO SCARED TO GO AGAINST HIM
AND NOW THAT I'M MORE MATURE I REALLY REGRET IT AND I WISH I DIDN'T ABANDON OPAL DURING HER TIME OF NEED ESPECIALLY AFTER HER DAD DIED.
OKAY, WOW. THAT'S PRETTY LONG.

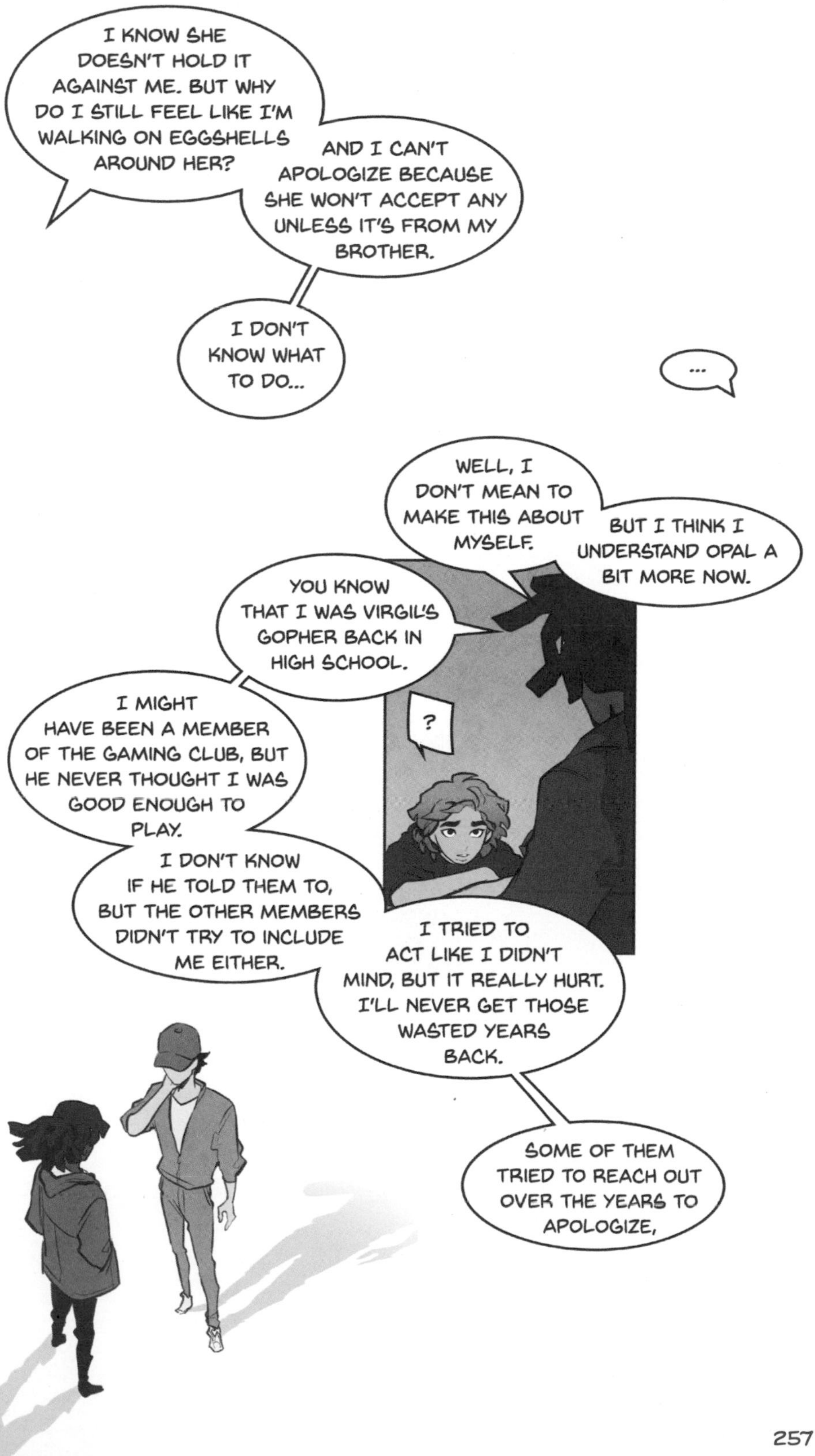
I KNOW SHE DOESN'T HOLD IT AGAINST ME. BUT WHY DO I STILL FEEL LIKE I'M WALKING ON EGGSHELLS AROUND HER?
AND I CAN'T APOLOGIZE BECAUSE SHE WON'T ACCEPT ANY UNLESS IT'S FROM MY BROTHER.
I DON'T KNOW WHAT TO DO...
...
WELL, I DON'T MEAN TO MAKE THIS ABOUT MYSELF.
BUT I THINK I UNDERSTAND OPAL A BIT MORE NOW.
YOU KNOW THAT I WAS VIRGIL'S GOPHER BACK IN HIGH SCHOOL.
?
I MIGHT HAVE BEEN A MEMBER OF THE GAMING CLUB, BUT HE NEVER THOUGHT I WAS GOOD ENOUGH TO PLAY.
I DON'T KNOW IF HE TOLD THEM TO, BUT THE OTHER MEMBERS DIDN'T TRY TO INCLUDE ME EITHER.
I TRIED TO ACT LIKE I DIDN'T MIND, BUT IT REALLY HURT. I'LL NEVER GET THOSE WASTED YEARS BACK.
SOME OF THEM TRIED TO REACH OUT OVER THE YEARS TO APOLOGIZE,

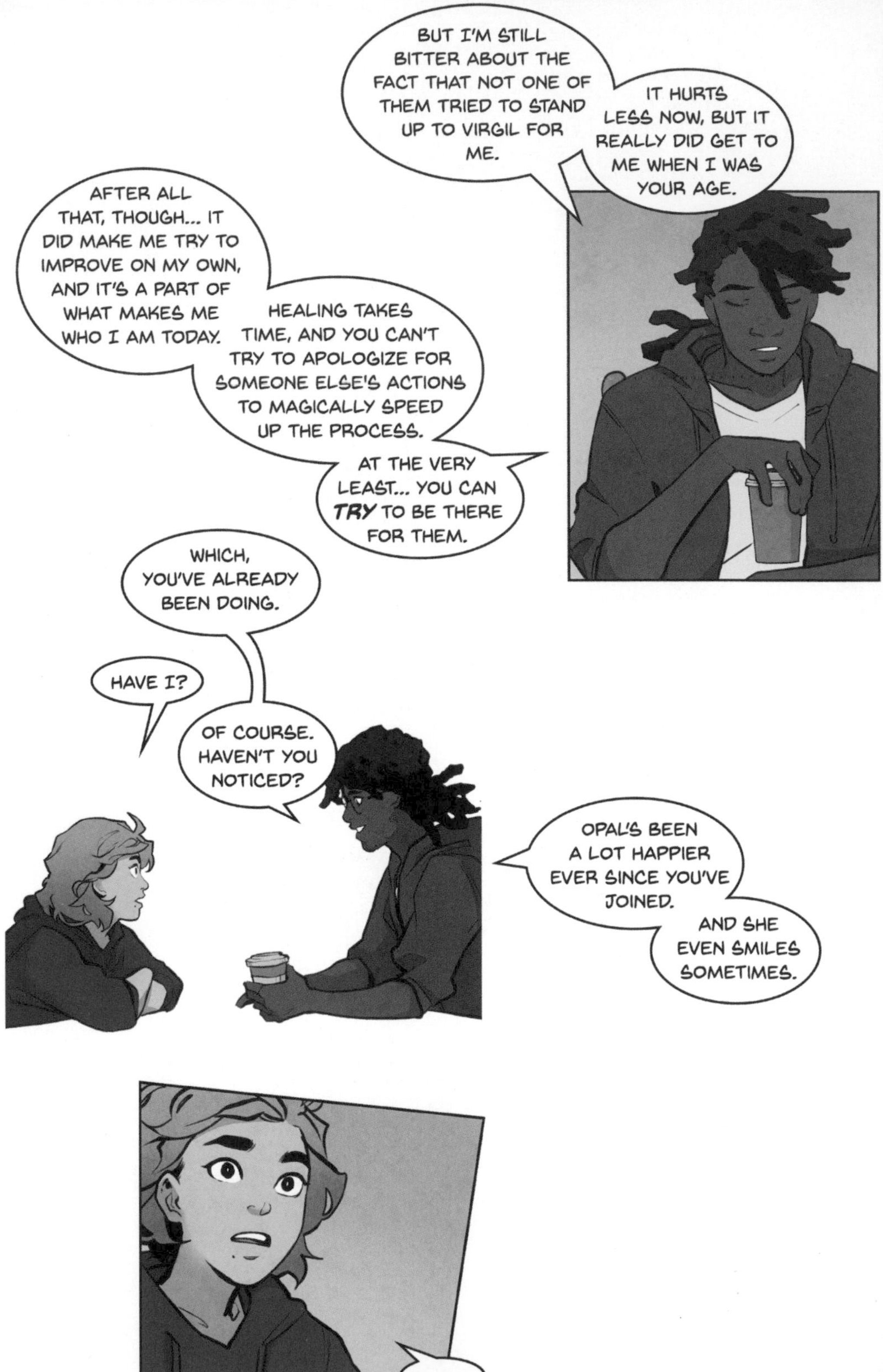
BUT I'M STILL BITTER ABOUT THE FACT THAT NOT ONE OF THEM TRIED TO STAND UP TO VIRGIL FOR ME.
IT HURTS LESS NOW, BUT IT REALLY DID GET TO ME WHEN I WAS YOUR AGE.
AFTER ALL THAT, THOUGH... IT DID MAKE ME TRY TO IMPROVE ON MY OWN, AND IT'S A PART OF WHAT MAKES ME WHO I AM TODAY.
HEALING TAKES TIME, AND YOU CAN'T TRY TO APOLOGIZE FOR SOMEONE ELSE'S ACTIONS TO MAGICALLY SPEED UP THE PROCESS.
AT THE VERY LEAST... YOU CAN ***TRY*** TO BE THERE FOR THEM.
WHICH, YOU'VE ALREADY BEEN DOING.
HAVE I?
OF COURSE. HAVEN'T YOU NOTICED?
OPAL'S BEEN A LOT HAPPIER EVER SINCE YOU'VE JOINED.
AND SHE EVEN SMILES SOMETIMES.
...

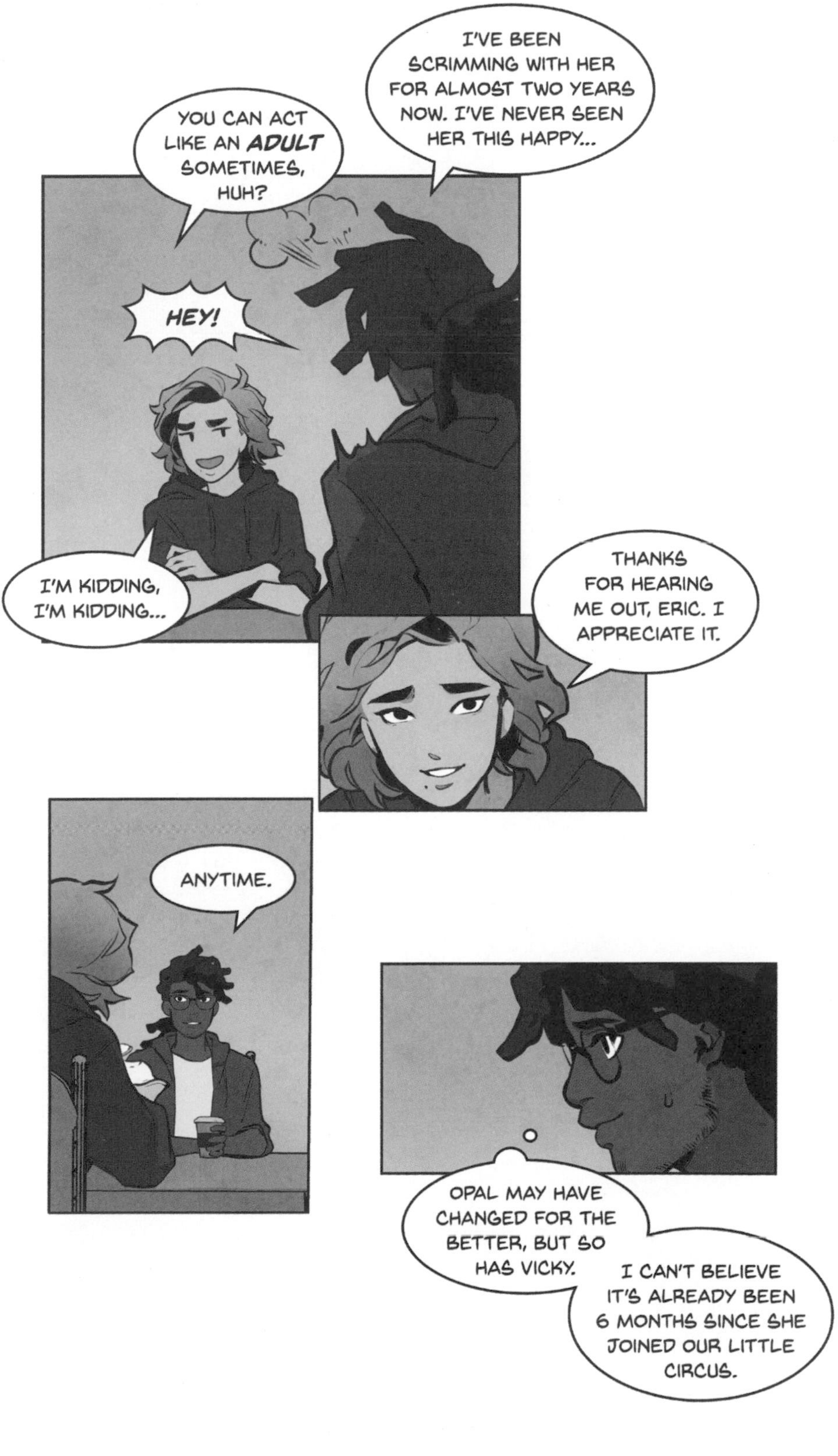
YOU CAN ACT LIKE AN ADULT SOMETIMES, HUH?
I'VE BEEN SCRIMMING WITH HER FOR ALMOST TWO YEARS NOW. I'VE NEVER SEEN HER THIS HAPPY...
HEY!
I'M KIDDING, I'M KIDDING...
THANKS FOR HEARING ME OUT, ERIC. I APPRECIATE IT.
ANYTIME.
OPAL MAY HAVE CHANGED FOR THE BETTER, BUT SO HAS VICKY.
I CAN'T BELIEVE IT'S ALREADY BEEN 6 MONTHS SINCE SHE JOINED OUR LITTLE CIRCUS.

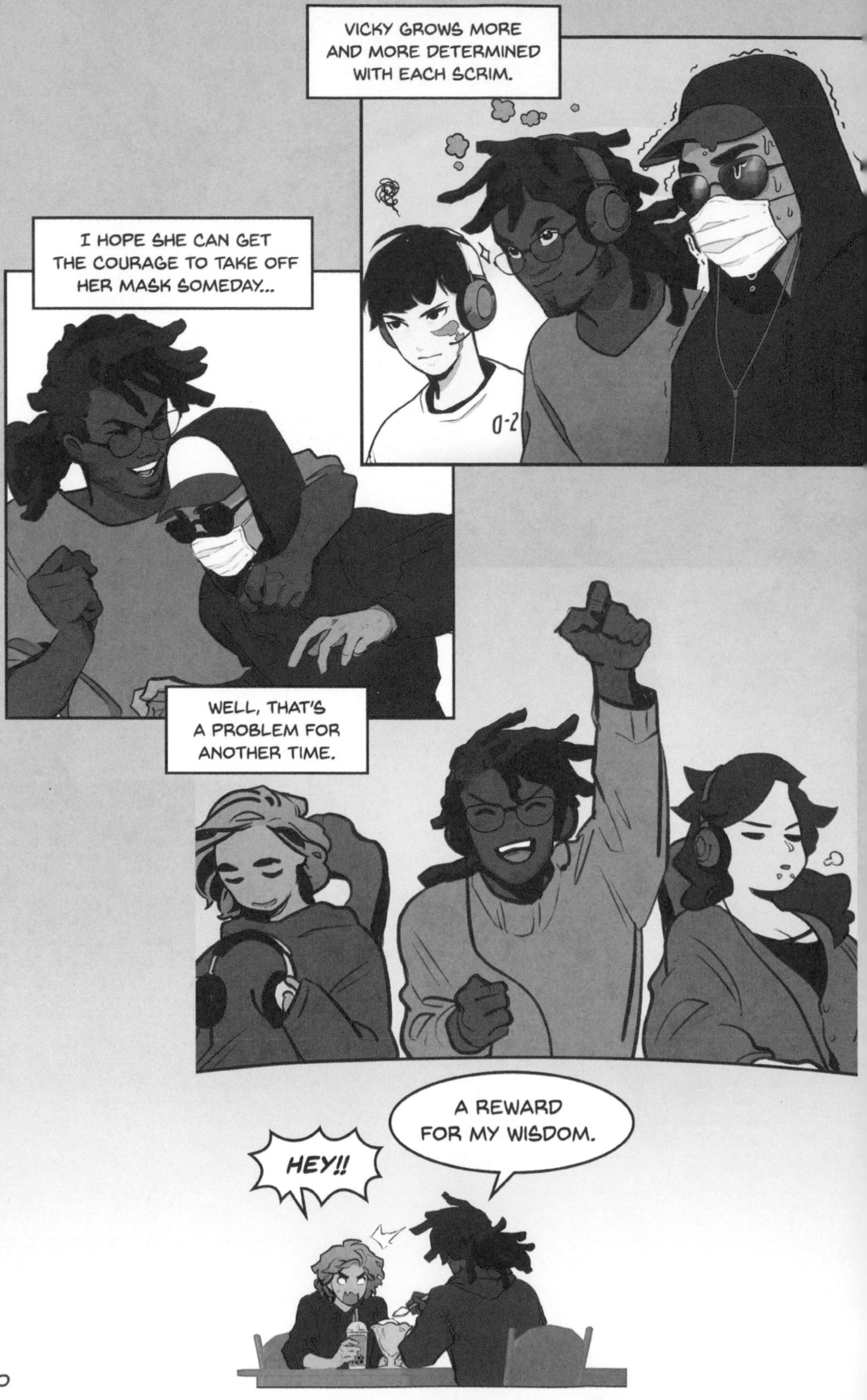
VICKY GROWS MORE AND MORE DETERMINED WITH EACH SCRIM.
0-2
I HOPE SHE CAN GET THE COURAGE TO TAKE OFF HER MASK SOMEDAY...
WELL, THAT'S A PROBLEM FOR ANOTHER TIME.
A REWARD FOR MY WISDOM.
HEY!!

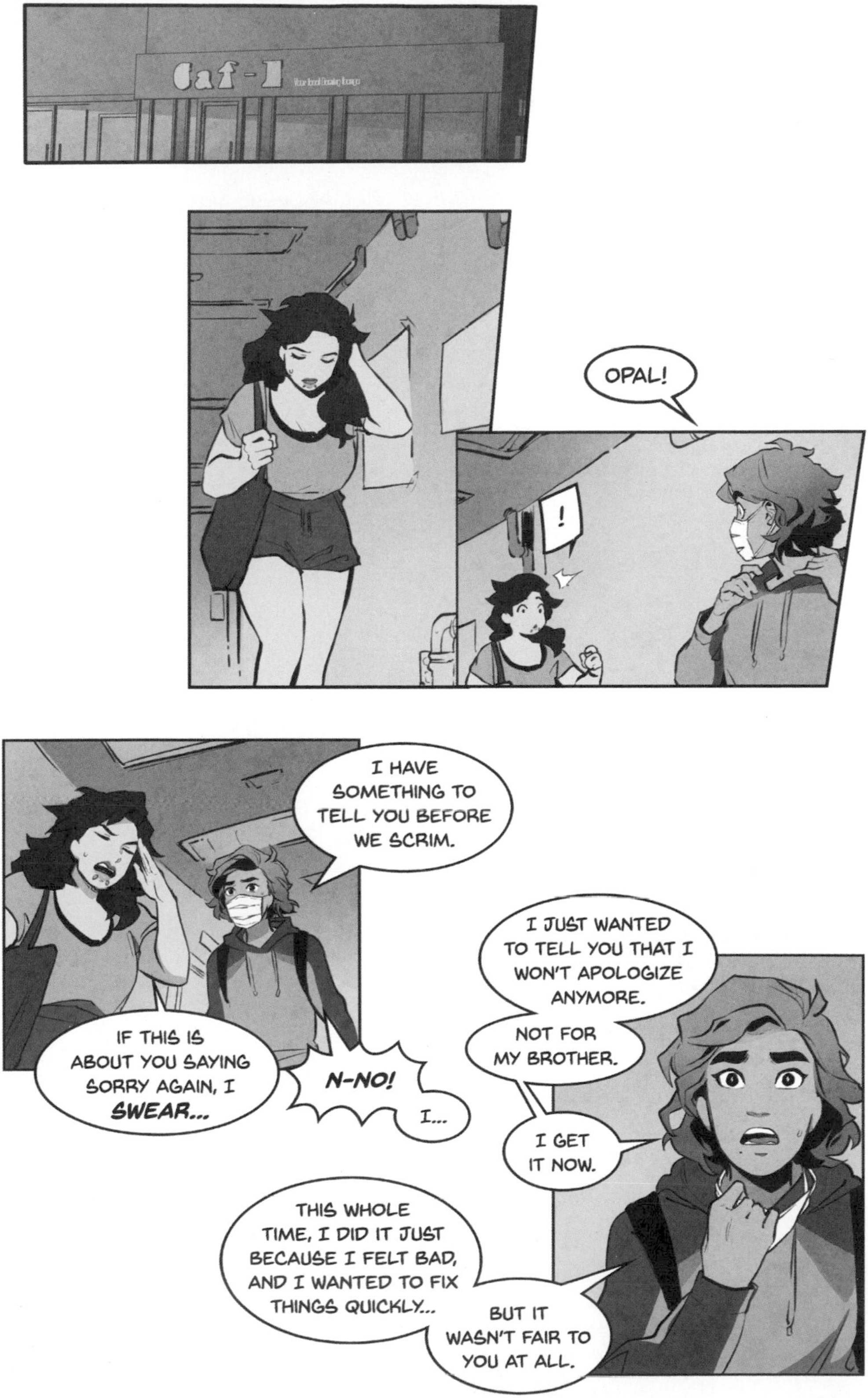
Caf-1
OPAL!
!
I HAVE SOMETHING TO TELL YOU BEFORE WE SCRIM.
IF THIS IS ABOUT YOU SAYING SORRY AGAIN, I **SWEAR...**
N-NO!
I...
I JUST WANTED TO TELL YOU THAT I WON'T APOLOGIZE ANYMORE.
NOT FOR MY BROTHER.
I GET IT NOW.
THIS WHOLE TIME, I DID IT JUST BECAUSE I FELT BAD, AND I WANTED TO FIX THINGS QUICKLY...
BUT IT WASN'T FAIR TO YOU AT ALL.

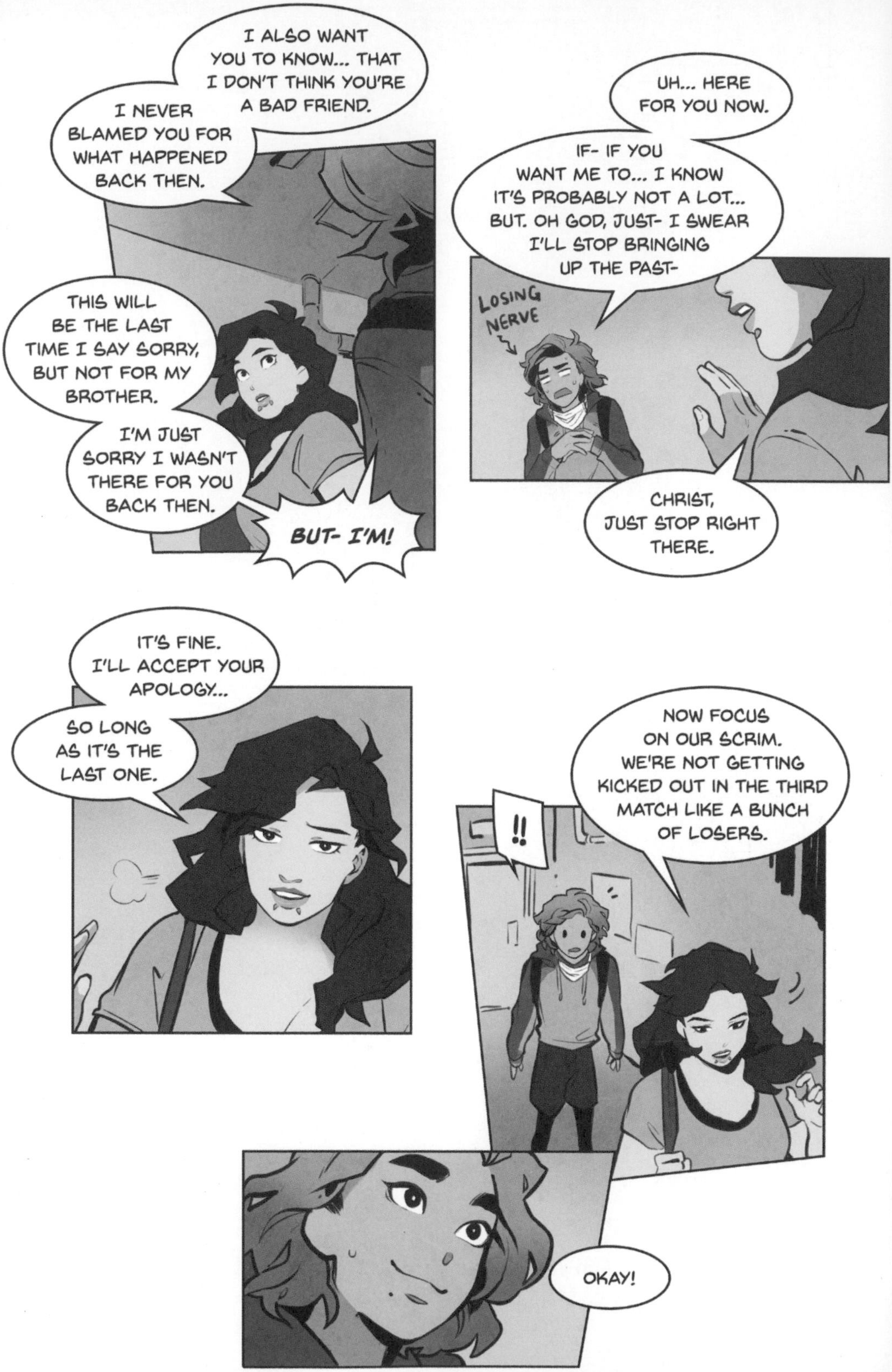
I ALSO WANT YOU TO KNOW... THAT I DON'T THINK YOU'RE A BAD FRIEND.
I NEVER BLAMED YOU FOR WHAT HAPPENED BACK THEN.
THIS WILL BE THE LAST TIME I SAY SORRY, BUT NOT FOR MY BROTHER.
I'M JUST SORRY I WASN'T THERE FOR YOU BACK THEN.
BUT- I'M!
UH... HERE FOR YOU NOW.
IF- IF YOU WANT ME TO... I KNOW IT'S PROBABLY NOT A LOT... BUT. OH GOD, JUST- I SWEAR I'LL STOP BRINGING UP THE PAST-
LOSING NERVE
CHRIST, JUST STOP RIGHT THERE.
IT'S FINE. I'LL ACCEPT YOUR APOLOGY...
SO LONG AS IT'S THE LAST ONE.
!!
NOW FOCUS ON OUR SCRIM. WE'RE NOT GETTING KICKED OUT IN THE THIRD MATCH LIKE A BUNCH OF LOSERS.
OKAY!

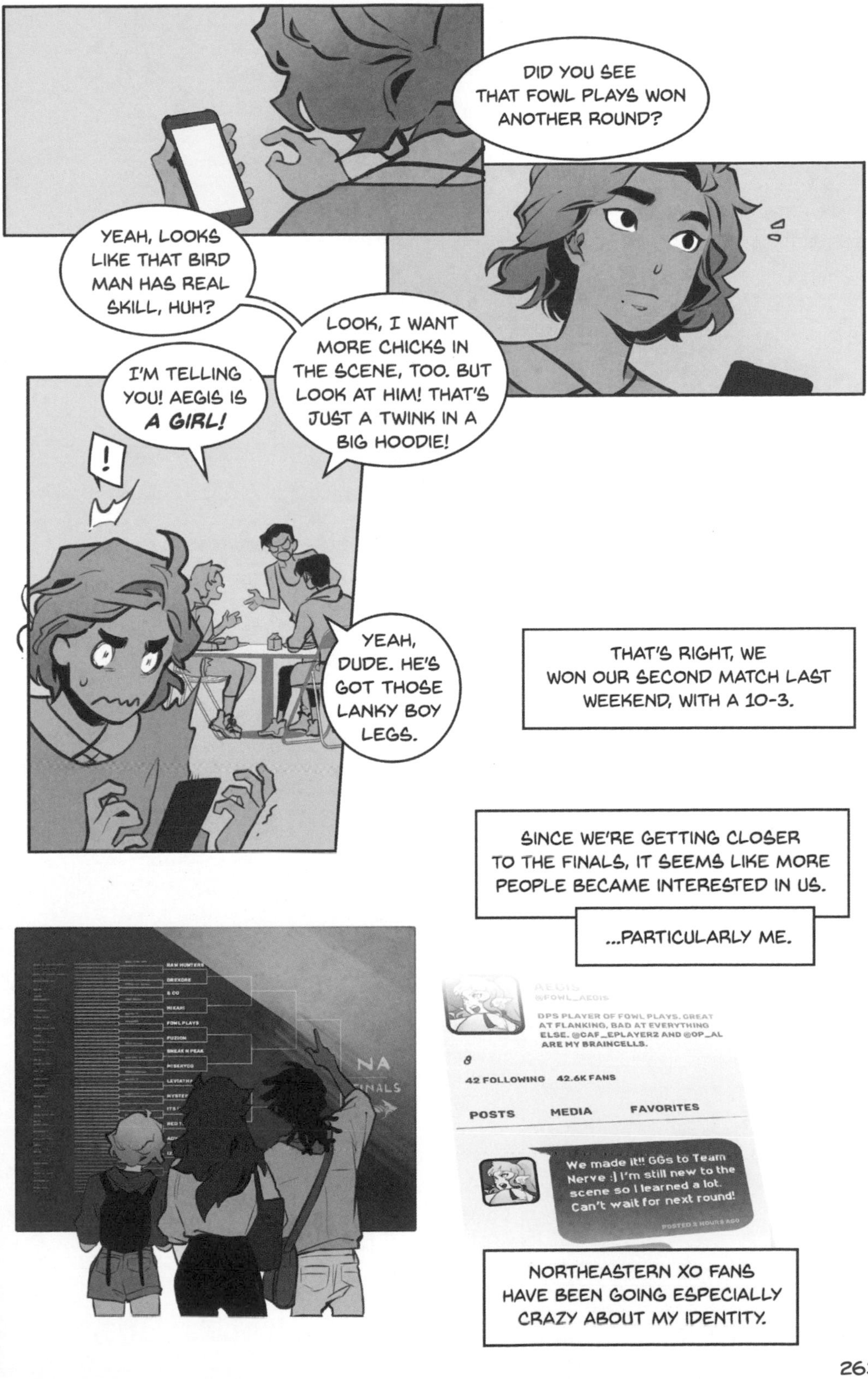
DID YOU SEE THAT FOWL PLAYS WON ANOTHER ROUND?
YEAH, LOOKS LIKE THAT BIRD MAN HAS REAL SKILL, HUH?
I'M TELLING YOU! AEGIS IS ***A GIRL!***
LOOK, I WANT MORE CHICKS IN THE SCENE, TOO. BUT LOOK AT HIM! THAT'S JUST A TWINK IN A BIG HOODIE!
!
YEAH, DUDE. HE'S GOT THOSE LANKY BOY LEGS.
THAT'S RIGHT, WE WON OUR SECOND MATCH LAST WEEKEND, WITH A 10-3.
SINCE WE'RE GETTING CLOSER TO THE FINALS, IT SEEMS LIKE MORE PEOPLE BECAME INTERESTED IN US.
...PARTICULARLY ME.
NA FINALS
AEGIS
@FOWL_AEGIS
DPS PLAYER OF FOWL PLAYS. GREAT AT FLANKING, BAD AT EVERYTHING ELSE. @CAF_EPLAYER2 AND @OP_AL ARE MY BRAINCELLS.
42 FOLLOWING 42.6K FANS
POSTS MEDIA FAVORITES
We made it!! GGs to Team Nerve :] I'm still new to the scene so I learned a lot. Can't wait for next round!
NORTHEASTERN XO FANS HAVE BEEN GOING ESPECIALLY CRAZY ABOUT MY IDENTITY.

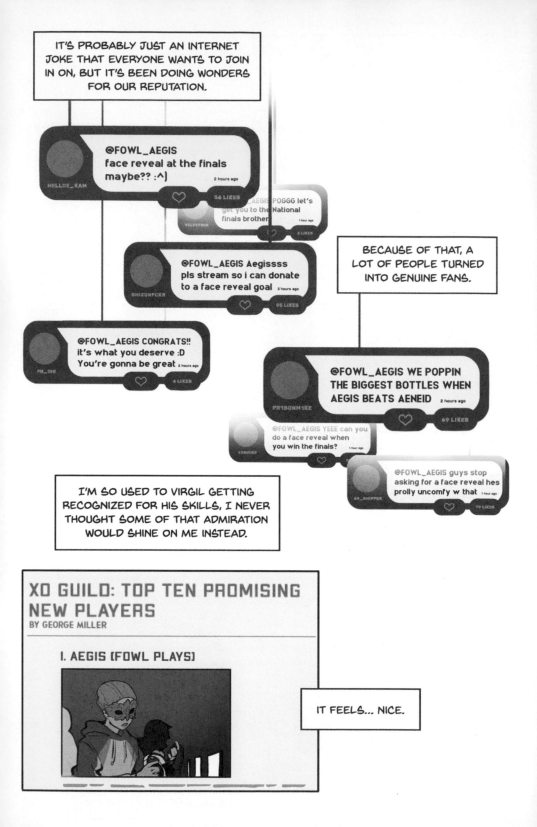

IT'S PROBABLY JUST AN INTERNET JOKE THAT EVERYONE WANTS TO JOIN IN ON, BUT IT'S BEEN DOING WONDERS FOR OUR REPUTATION.

@FOWL_AEGIS face reveal at the finals maybe?? :^]

HELLOE_KAM

56 LIKES

2 hours ago

_AEGIS POGGG let's get you to the National finals brother

VELVETSUN

2 LIKES

1 hour ago

@FOWL_AEGIS Aegissss pls stream so i can donate to a face reveal goal

SHIZUNFCKR

95 LIKES

2 hours ago

BECAUSE OF THAT, A LOT OF PEOPLE TURNED INTO GENUINE FANS.

@FOWL_AEGIS CONGRATS!! it's what you deserve :D You're gonna be great

PB_DIG

4 LIKES

2 hours ago

@FOWL_AEGIS WE POPPIN THE BIGGEST BOTTLES WHEN AEGIS BEATS AENEID

PR1SONM1KE

69 LIKES

2 hours ago

@FOWL_AEGIS YEEE can you do a face reveal when you win the finals?

XORUCES

1 hour ago

I'M SO USED TO VIRGIL GETTING RECOGNIZED FOR HIS SKILLS, I NEVER THOUGHT SOME OF THAT ADMIRATION WOULD SHINE ON ME INSTEAD.

@FOWL_AEGIS guys stop asking for a face reveal hes prolly uncomfy w that

69_SHIPPER

79 LIKES

1 hour ago

XO GUILD: TOP TEN PROMISING NEW PLAYERS
BY GEORGE MILLER

I. AEGIS (FOWL PLAYS)

IT FEELS... NICE.

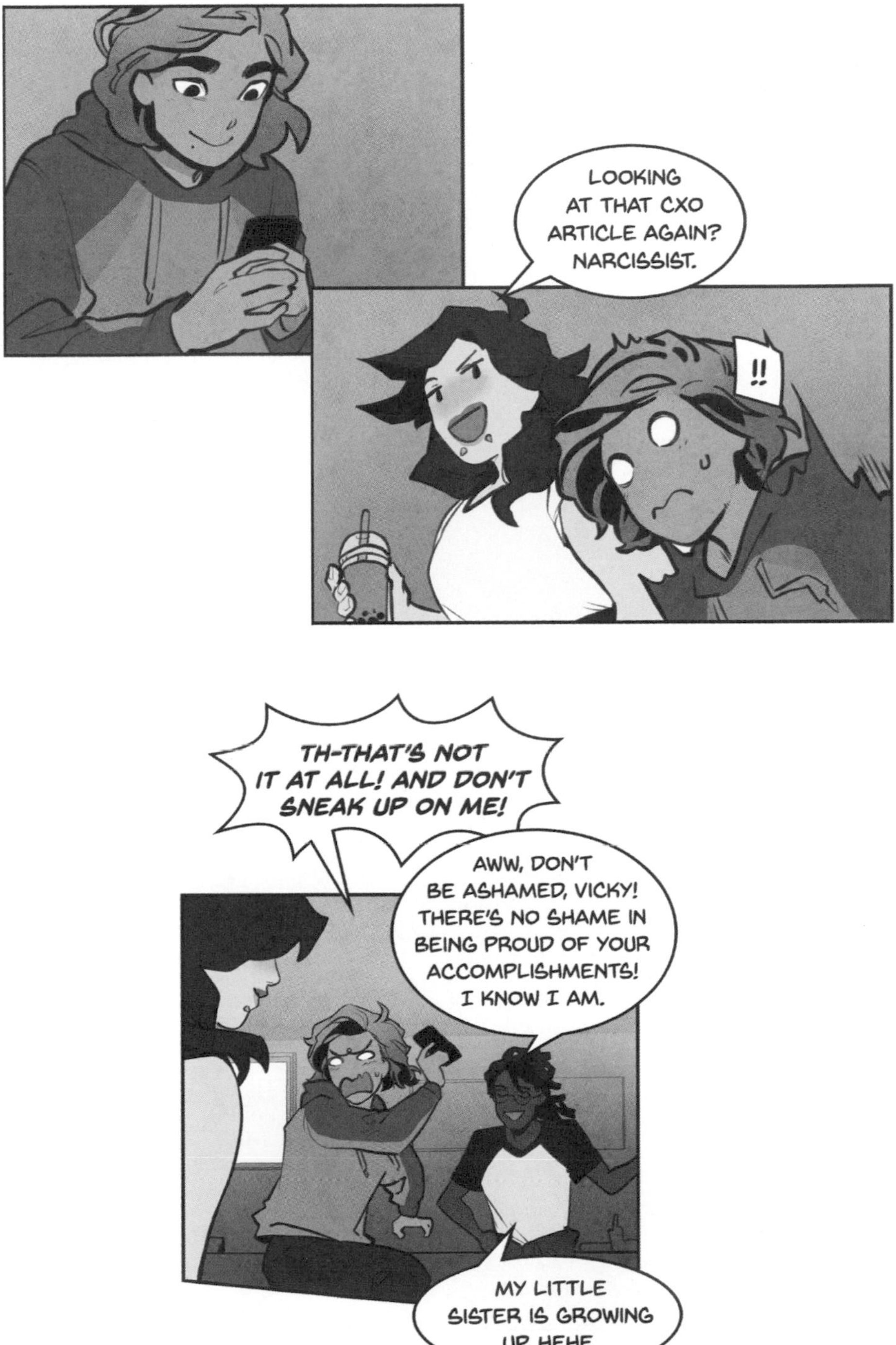
LOOKING AT THAT CXO ARTICLE AGAIN? NARCISSIST.
!!
TH-THAT'S NOT IT AT ALL! AND DON'T SNEAK UP ON ME!
AWW, DON'T BE ASHAMED, VICKY! THERE'S NO SHAME IN BEING PROUD OF YOUR ACCOMPLISHMENTS! I KNOW I AM.
MY LITTLE SISTER IS GROWING UP, HEHE.

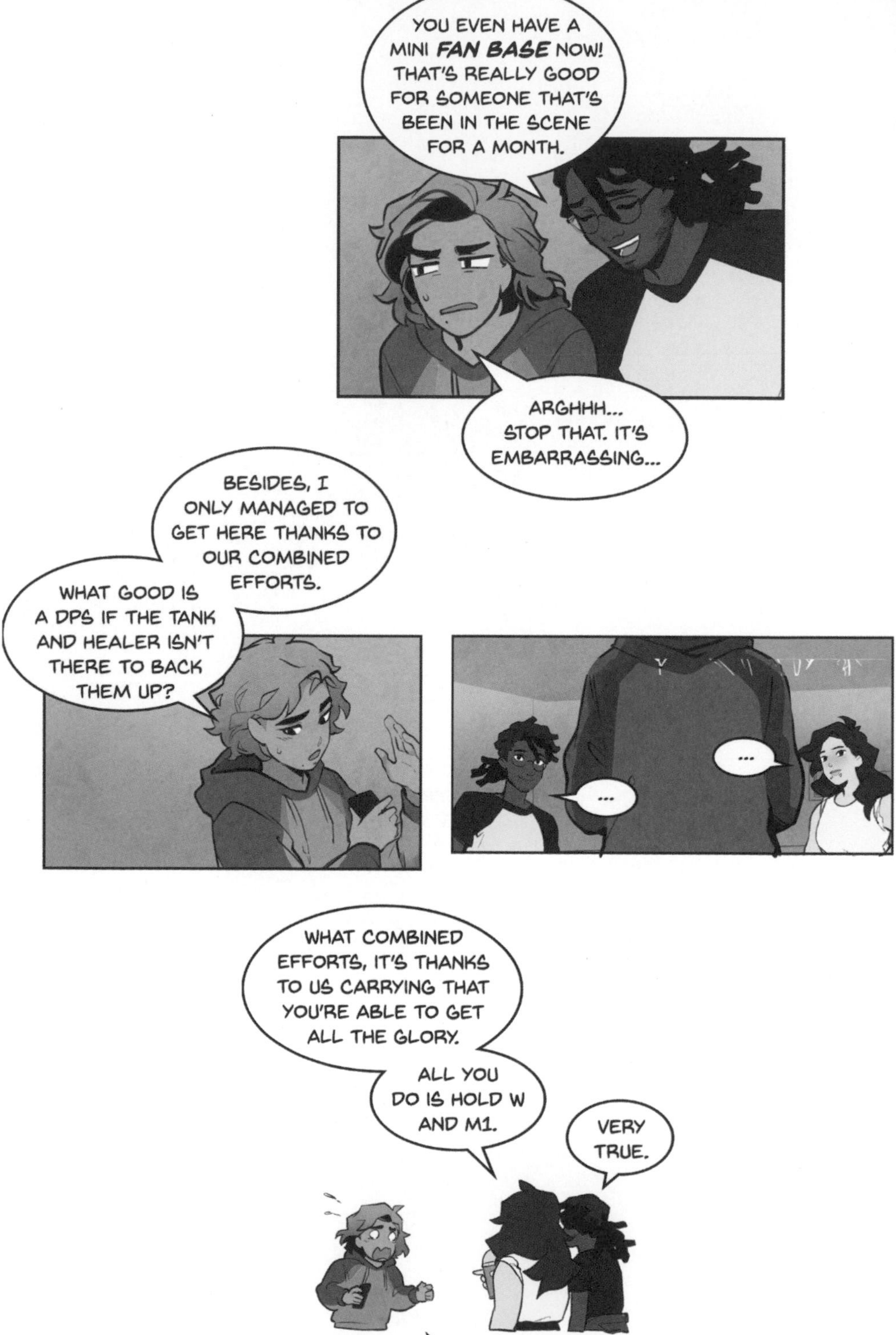
YOU EVEN HAVE A MINI FAN BASE NOW! THAT'S REALLY GOOD FOR SOMEONE THAT'S BEEN IN THE SCENE FOR A MONTH.
ARGHHH... STOP THAT. IT'S EMBARRASSING...
BESIDES, I ONLY MANAGED TO GET HERE THANKS TO OUR COMBINED EFFORTS.
WHAT GOOD IS A DPS IF THE TANK AND HEALER ISN'T THERE TO BACK THEM UP?
...
...
WHAT COMBINED EFFORTS, IT'S THANKS TO US CARRYING THAT YOU'RE ABLE TO GET ALL THE GLORY.
ALL YOU DO IS HOLD W AND M1.
VERY TRUE.
YOU GUYS...!!

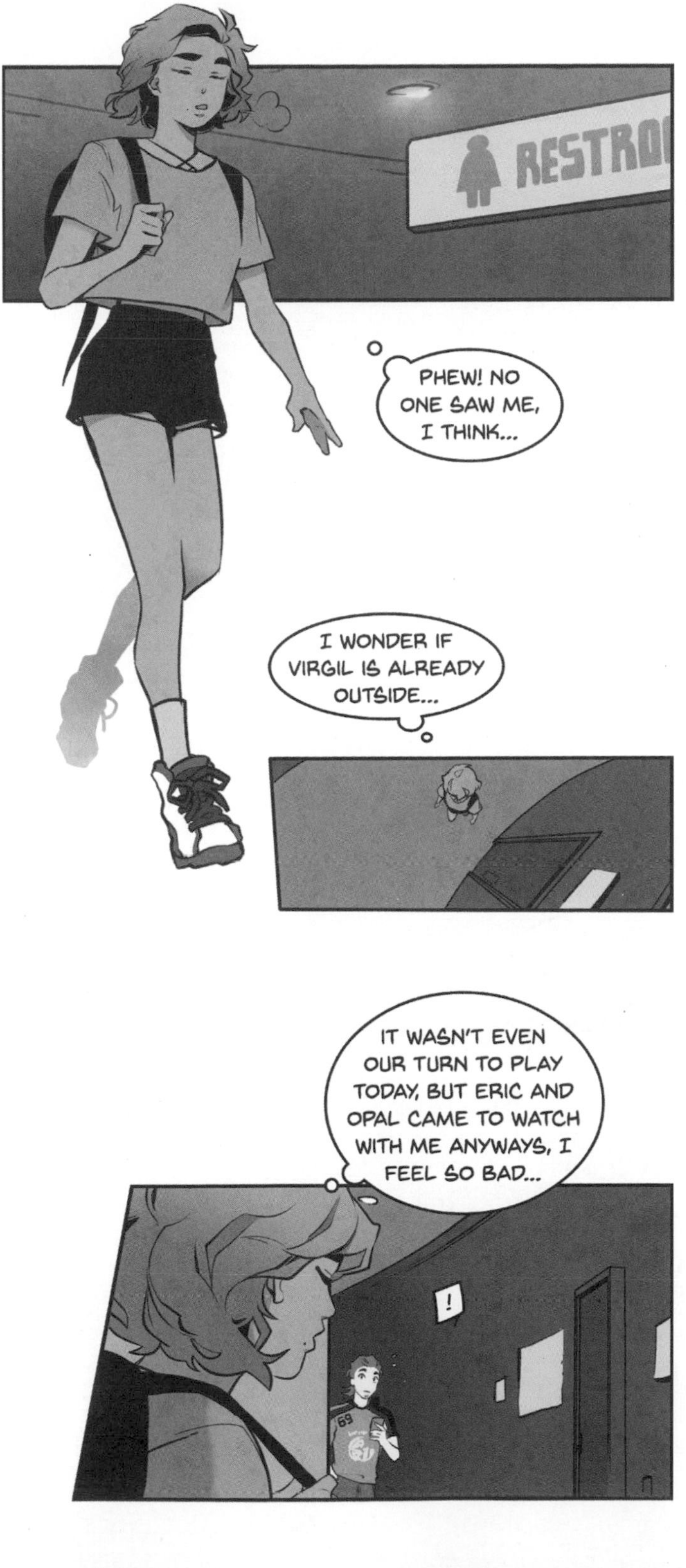
RESTRO
PHEW! NO ONE SAW ME, I THINK...
I WONDER IF VIRGIL IS ALREADY OUTSIDE...
IT WASN'T EVEN OUR TURN TO PLAY TODAY, BUT ERIC AND OPAL CAME TO WATCH WITH ME ANYWAYS, I FEEL SO BAD...
!

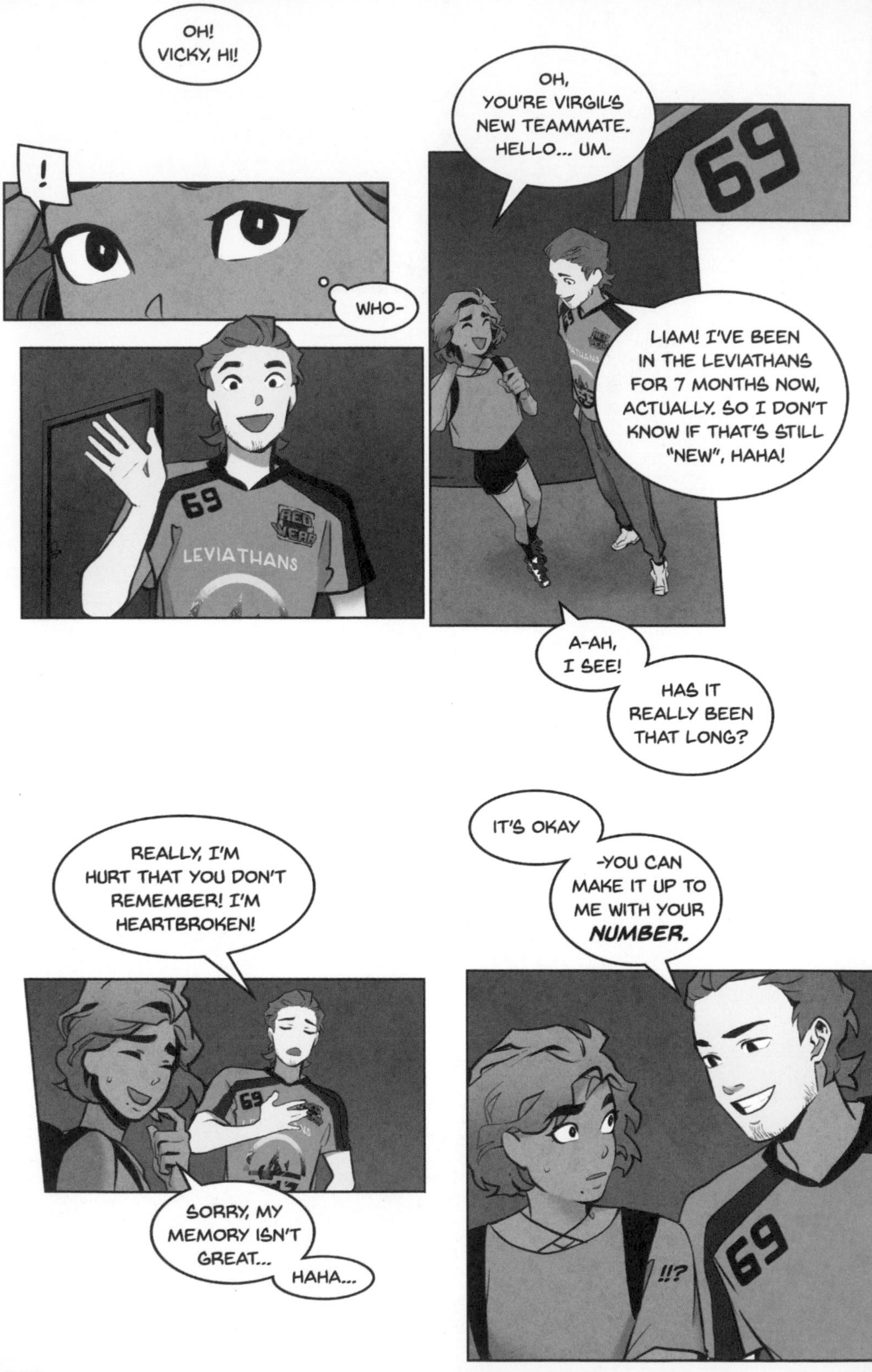

OH! VICKY, HI!
!
WHO-
OH, YOU'RE VIRGIL'S NEW TEAMMATE. HELLO... UM.
LIAM! I'VE BEEN IN THE LEVIATHANS FOR 7 MONTHS NOW, ACTUALLY. SO I DON'T KNOW IF THAT'S STILL "NEW", HAHA!
A-AH, I SEE!
HAS IT REALLY BEEN THAT LONG?
REALLY, I'M HURT THAT YOU DON'T REMEMBER! I'M HEARTBROKEN!
SORRY, MY MEMORY ISN'T GREAT...
HAHA...
IT'S OKAY
-YOU CAN MAKE IT UP TO ME WITH YOUR ***NUMBER.***
!!?

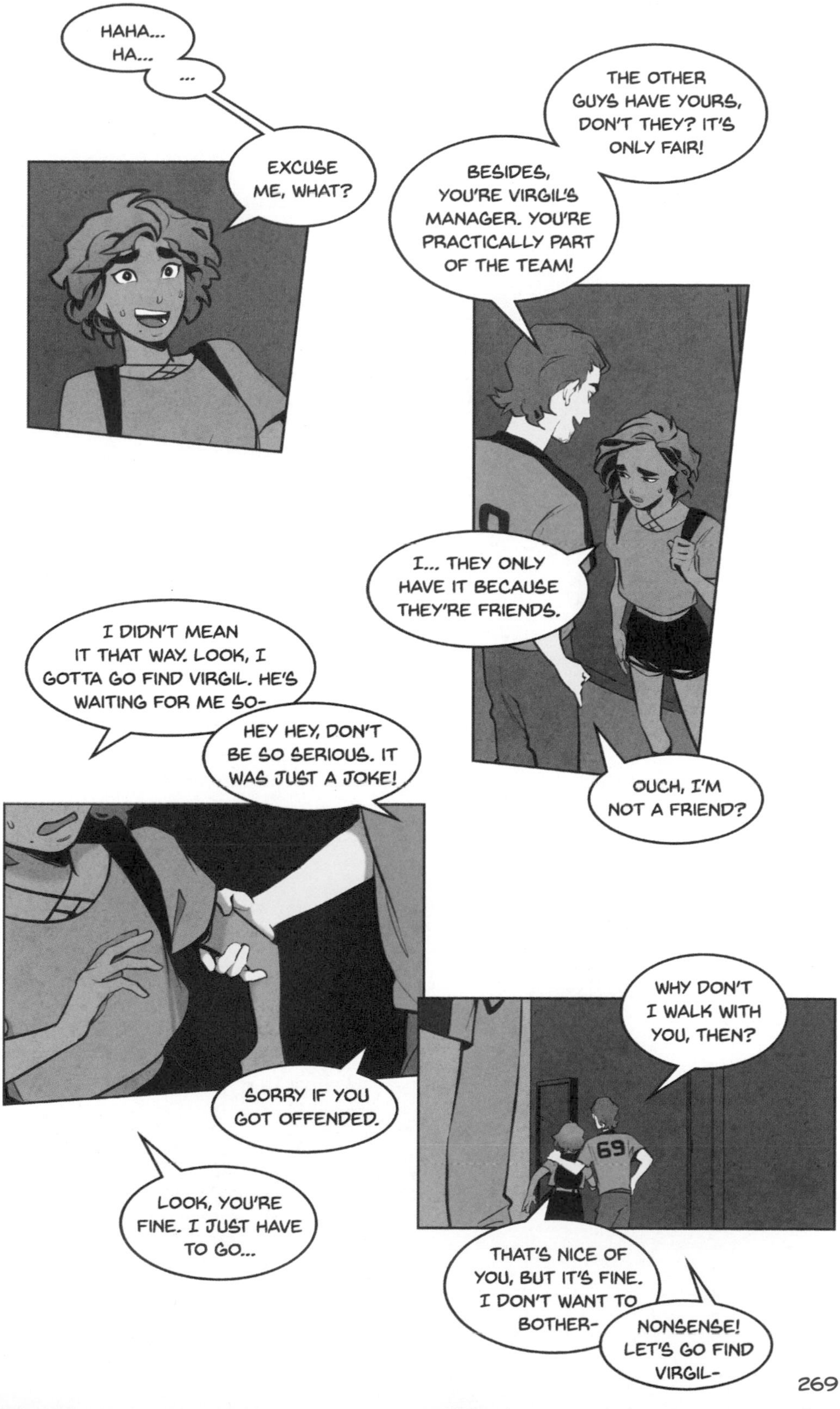
HAHA... HA... ...
EXCUSE ME, WHAT?
THE OTHER GUYS HAVE YOURS, DON'T THEY? IT'S ONLY FAIR!
BESIDES, YOU'RE VIRGIL'S MANAGER. YOU'RE PRACTICALLY PART OF THE TEAM!
I... THEY ONLY HAVE IT BECAUSE THEY'RE FRIENDS.
OUCH, I'M NOT A FRIEND?
I DIDN'T MEAN IT THAT WAY. LOOK, I GOTTA GO FIND VIRGIL. HE'S WAITING FOR ME SO-
HEY HEY, DON'T BE SO SERIOUS. IT WAS JUST A JOKE!
SORRY IF YOU GOT OFFENDED.
LOOK, YOU'RE FINE. I JUST HAVE TO GO...
WHY DON'T I WALK WITH YOU, THEN?
THAT'S NICE OF YOU, BUT IT'S FINE. I DON'T WANT TO BOTHER-
NONSENSE! LET'S GO FIND VIRGIL-

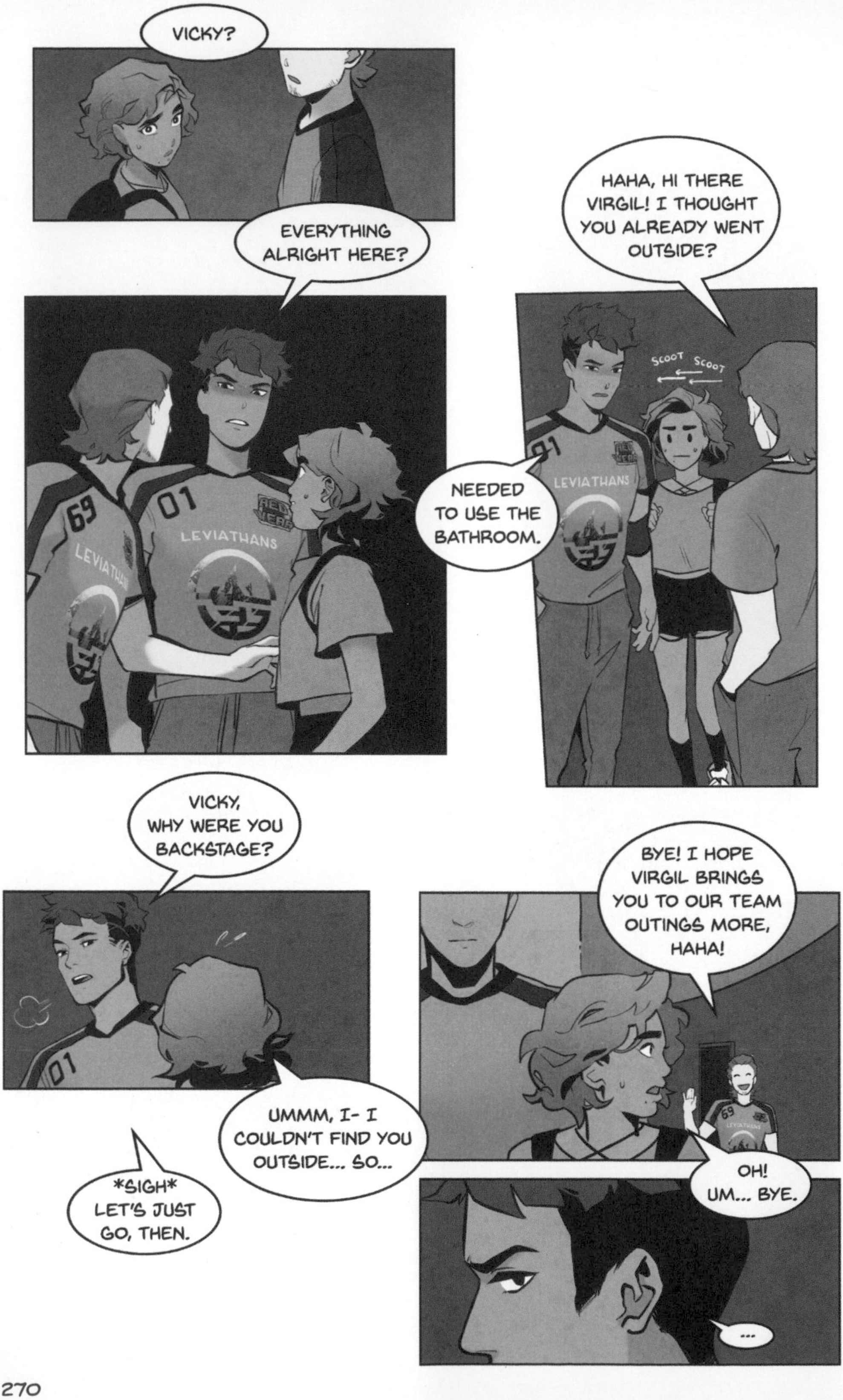
VICKY?
EVERYTHING ALRIGHT HERE?
HAHA, HI THERE VIRGIL! I THOUGHT YOU ALREADY WENT OUTSIDE?
SCOOT SCOOT
NEEDED TO USE THE BATHROOM.
VICKY, WHY WERE YOU BACKSTAGE?
UMMM, I- I COULDN'T FIND YOU OUTSIDE... SO...
SIGH LET'S JUST GO, THEN.
BYE! I HOPE VIRGIL BRINGS YOU TO OUR TEAM OUTINGS MORE, HAHA!
OH! UM... BYE.
...

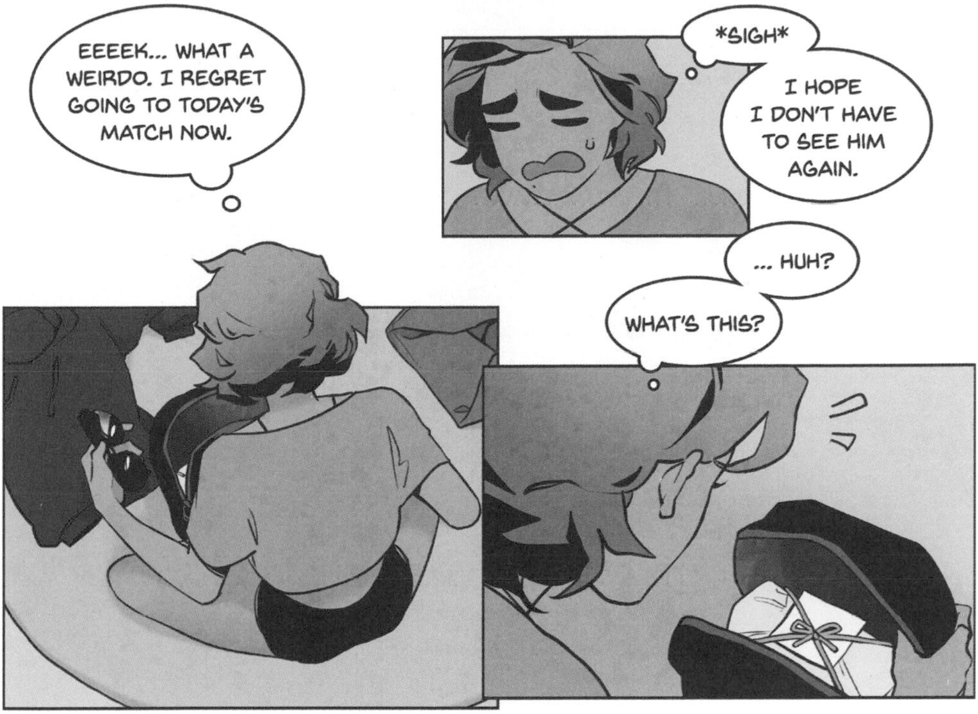
EEEEK... WHAT A WEIRDO. I REGRET GOING TO TODAY'S MATCH NOW.
SIGH
I HOPE I DON'T HAVE TO SEE HIM AGAIN.
... HUH?
WHAT'S THIS?

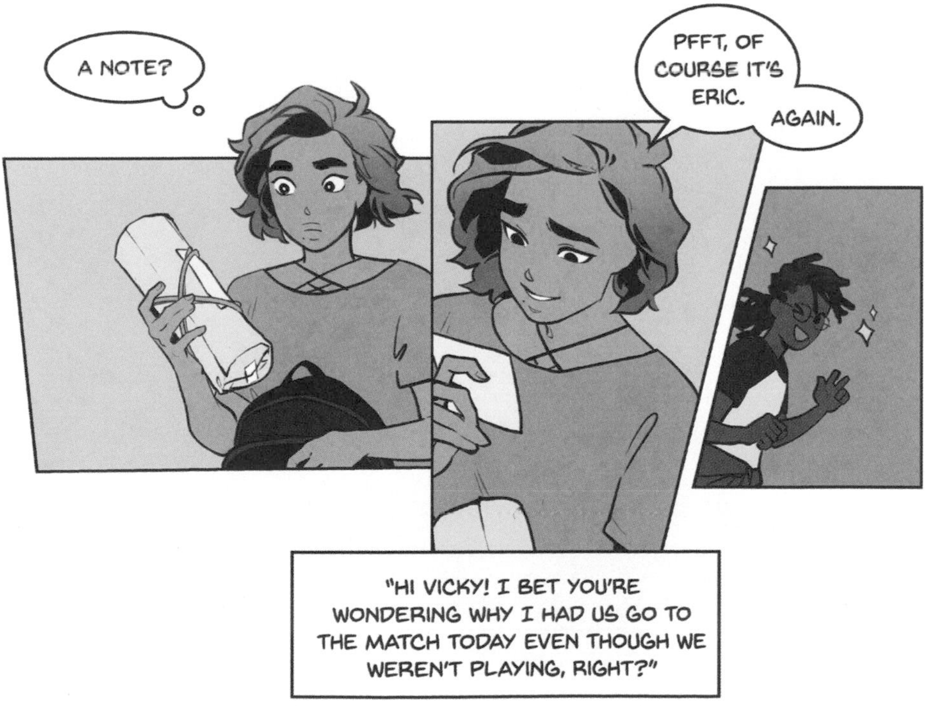
A NOTE?
PFFT, OF COURSE IT'S ERIC.
AGAIN.
"HI VICKY! I BET YOU'RE WONDERING WHY I HAD US GO TO THE MATCH TODAY EVEN THOUGH WE WEREN'T PLAYING, RIGHT?"

"YOU SEE, I WANTED TO SURPRISE YOU GUYS WITH THIS! I WANTED TO SHARE IT NEXT SCRIM, BUT I COULDN'T WAIT ANYMORE."

"IT'S FROM MY BROTHER."

"HE CUSTOM MADE IT FOR US TO CHEER US ON! I HOPE YOU LIKE IT, I REALLY DO!"

"LET'S REPRESENT THE CAF-E PROUDLY!"

"FROM ERIC"

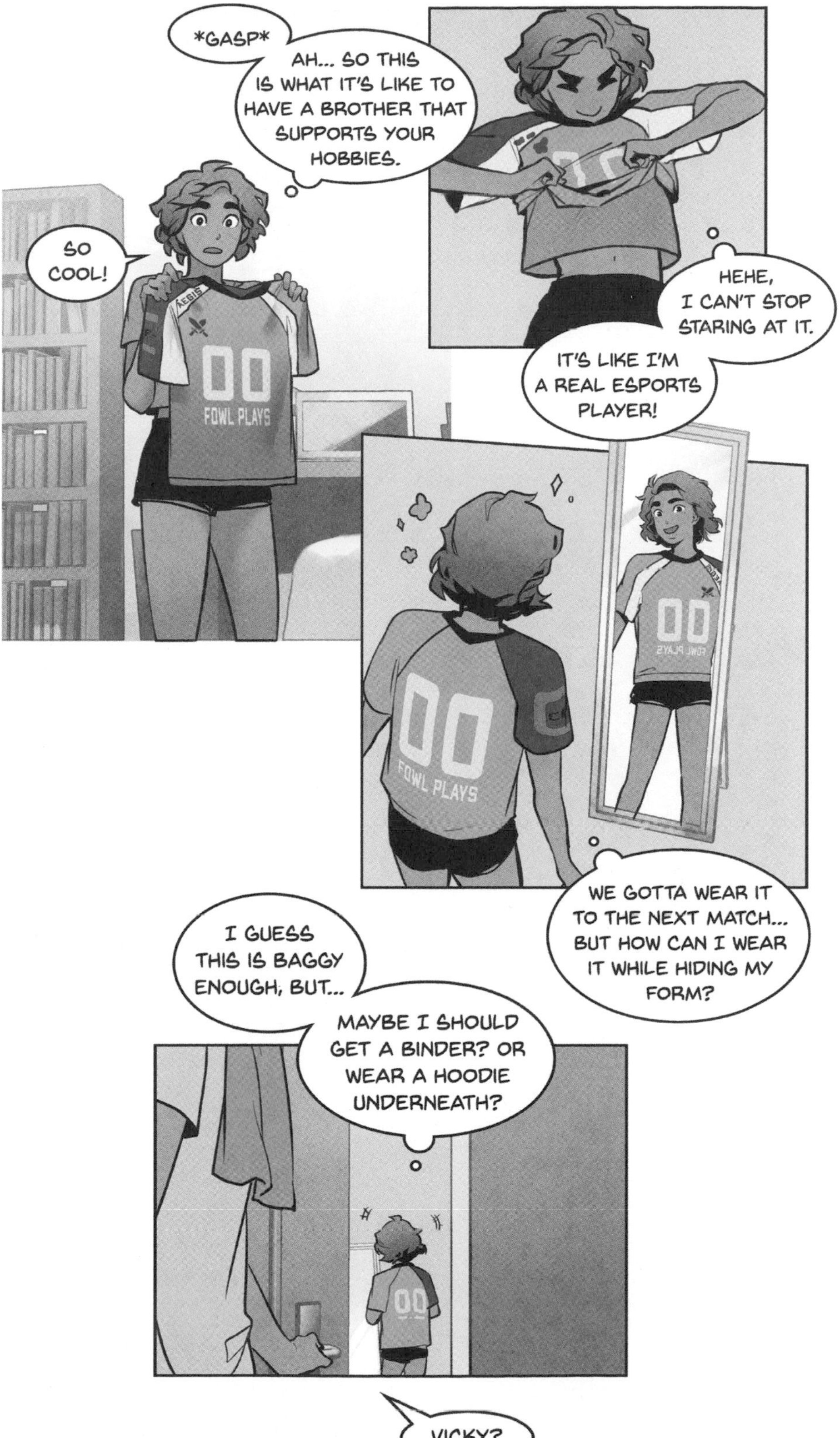
GASP
AH... SO THIS IS WHAT IT'S LIKE TO HAVE A BROTHER THAT SUPPORTS YOUR HOBBIES.
SO COOL!
00
FOWL PLAYS
HEHE, I CAN'T STOP STARING AT IT.
IT'S LIKE I'M A REAL ESPORTS PLAYER!
00
FOWL PLAYS
WE GOTTA WEAR IT TO THE NEXT MATCH... BUT HOW CAN I WEAR IT WHILE HIDING MY FORM?
I GUESS THIS IS BAGGY ENOUGH, BUT...
MAYBE I SHOULD GET A BINDER? OR WEAR A HOODIE UNDERNEATH?
VICKY?

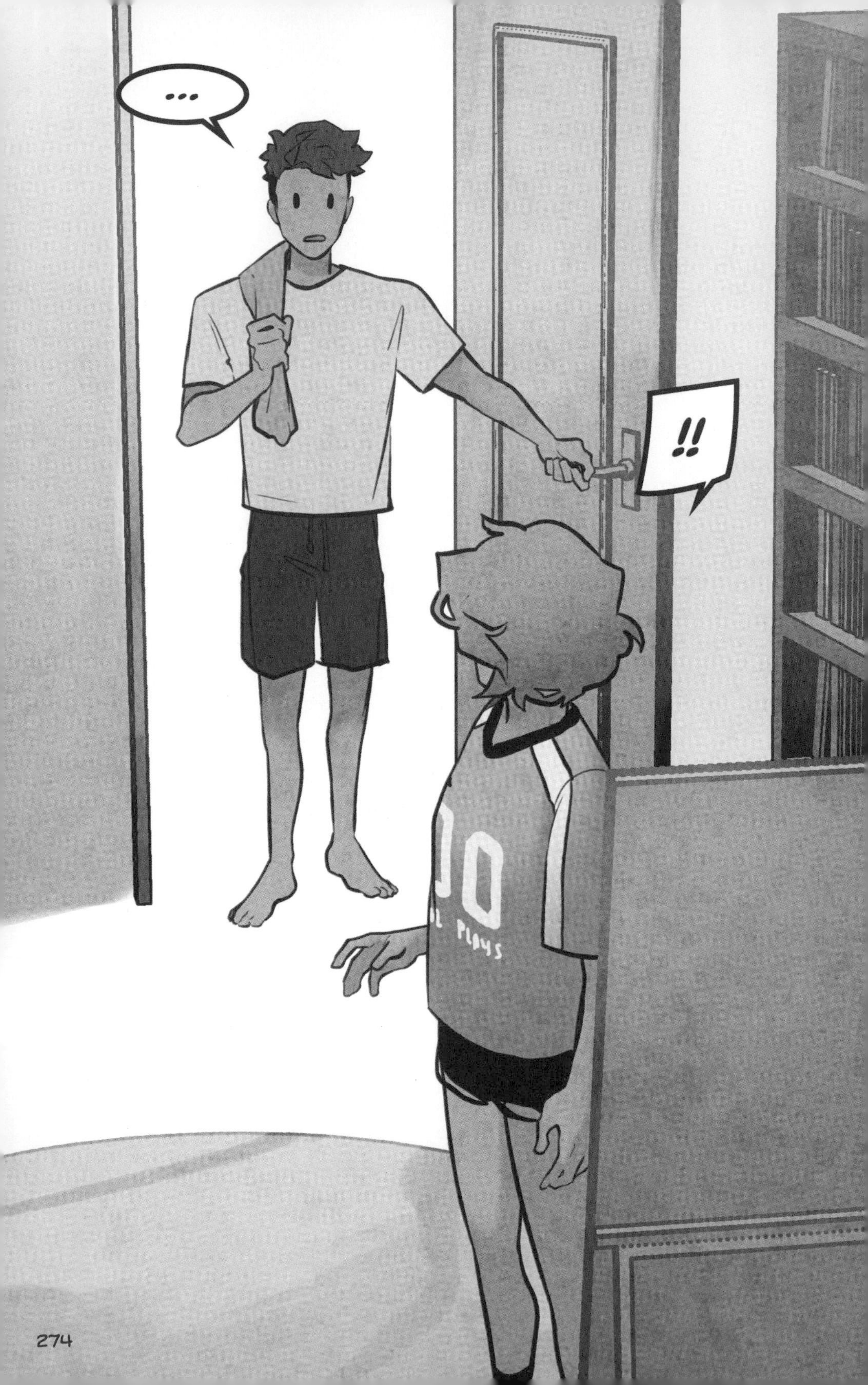
...
!!

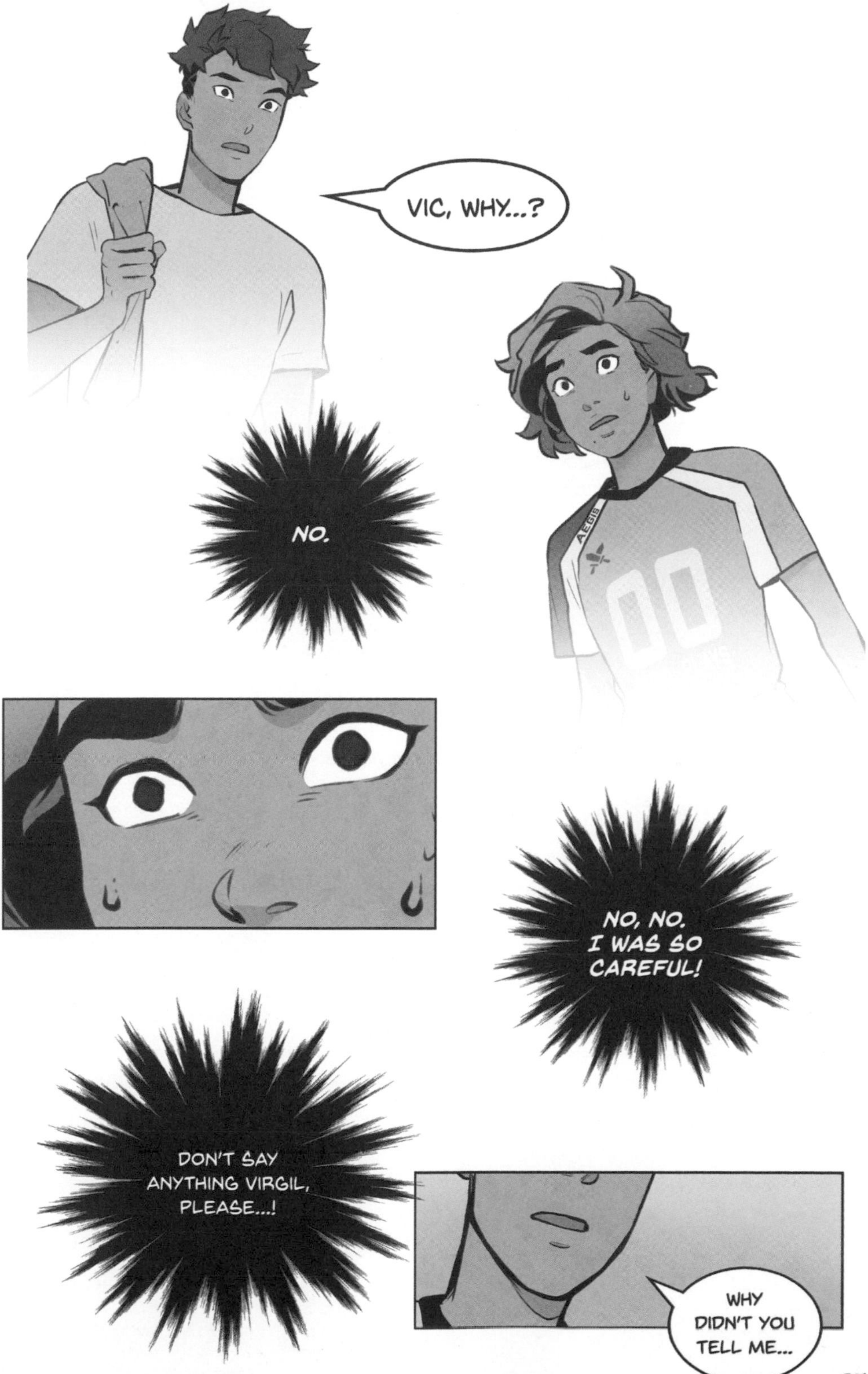

VIC, WHY...?
NO.
NO, NO. I WAS SO CAREFUL!
DON'T SAY ANYTHING VIRGIL, PLEASE...!
WHY DIDN'T YOU TELL ME...

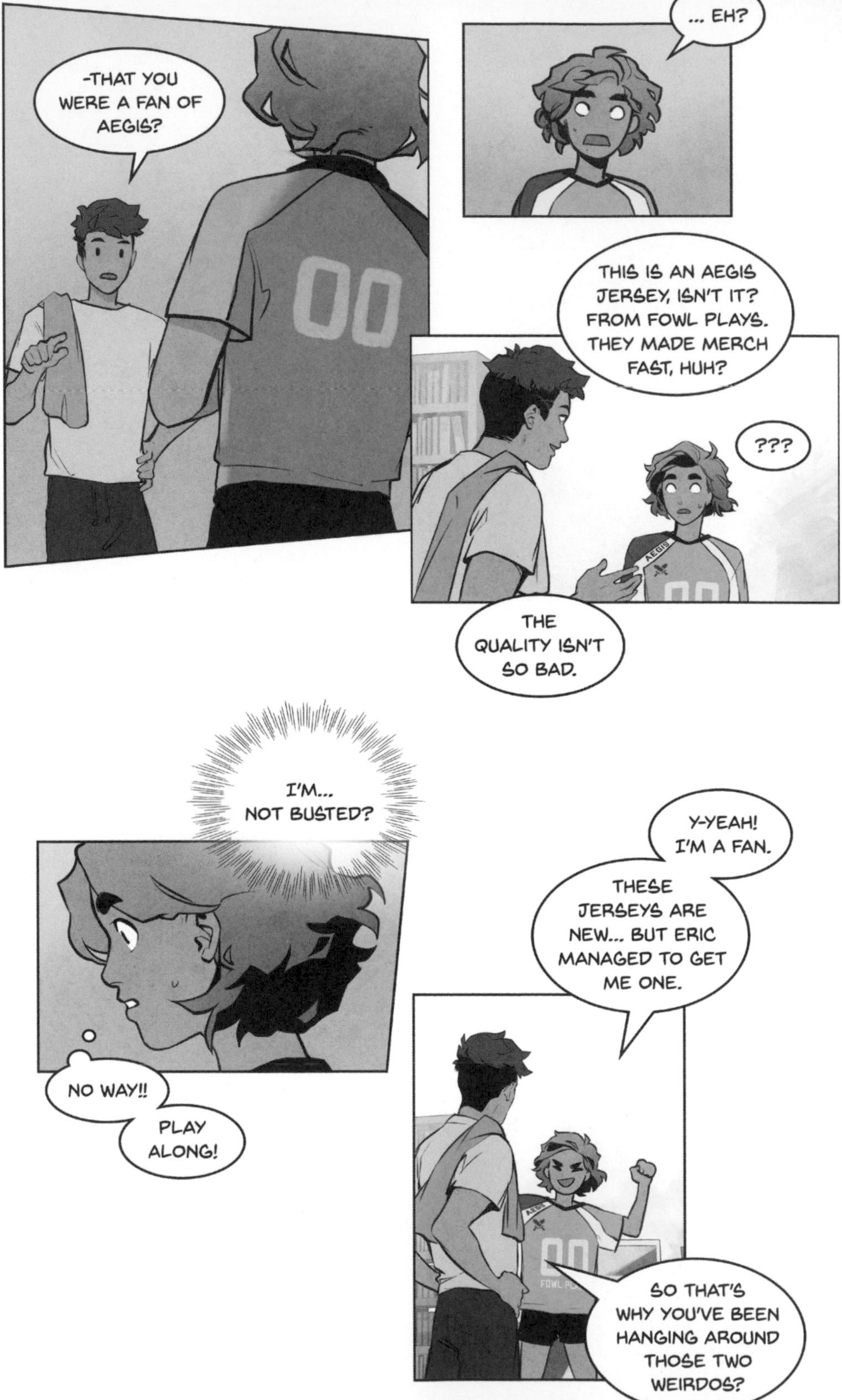
-THAT YOU WERE A FAN OF AEGIS?
... EH?
THIS IS AN AEGIS JERSEY, ISN'T IT? FROM FOWL PLAYS. THEY MADE MERCH FAST, HUH?
???
THE QUALITY ISN'T SO BAD.
I'M... NOT BUSTED?
NO WAY!!
PLAY ALONG!
Y-YEAH! I'M A FAN.
THESE JERSEYS ARE NEW... BUT ERIC MANAGED TO GET ME ONE.
SO THAT'S WHY YOU'VE BEEN HANGING AROUND THOSE TWO WEIRDOS?

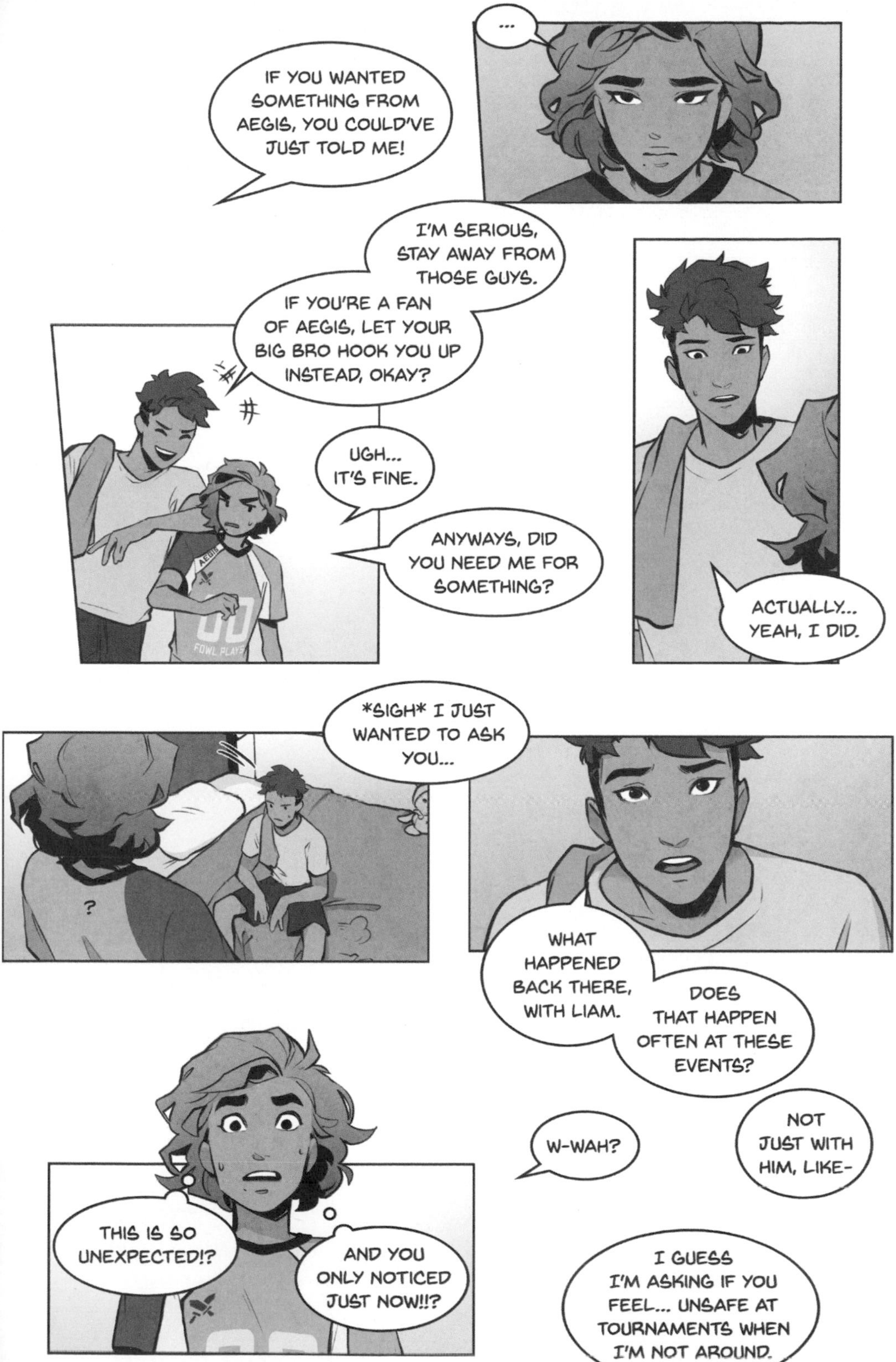
IF YOU WANTED SOMETHING FROM AEGIS, YOU COULD'VE JUST TOLD ME!
...
I'M SERIOUS, STAY AWAY FROM THOSE GUYS.
IF YOU'RE A FAN OF AEGIS, LET YOUR BIG BRO HOOK YOU UP INSTEAD, OKAY?
UGH... IT'S FINE.
ANYWAYS, DID YOU NEED ME FOR SOMETHING?
AEGIS
00
FOWL PLAYS
ACTUALLY... YEAH, I DID.
SIGH I JUST WANTED TO ASK YOU...
?
WHAT HAPPENED BACK THERE, WITH LIAM.
DOES THAT HAPPEN OFTEN AT THESE EVENTS?
THIS IS SO UNEXPECTED!?
AND YOU ONLY NOTICED JUST NOW!!?
W-WAH?
NOT JUST WITH HIM, LIKE-
I GUESS I'M ASKING IF YOU FEEL... UNSAFE AT TOURNAMENTS WHEN I'M NOT AROUND.

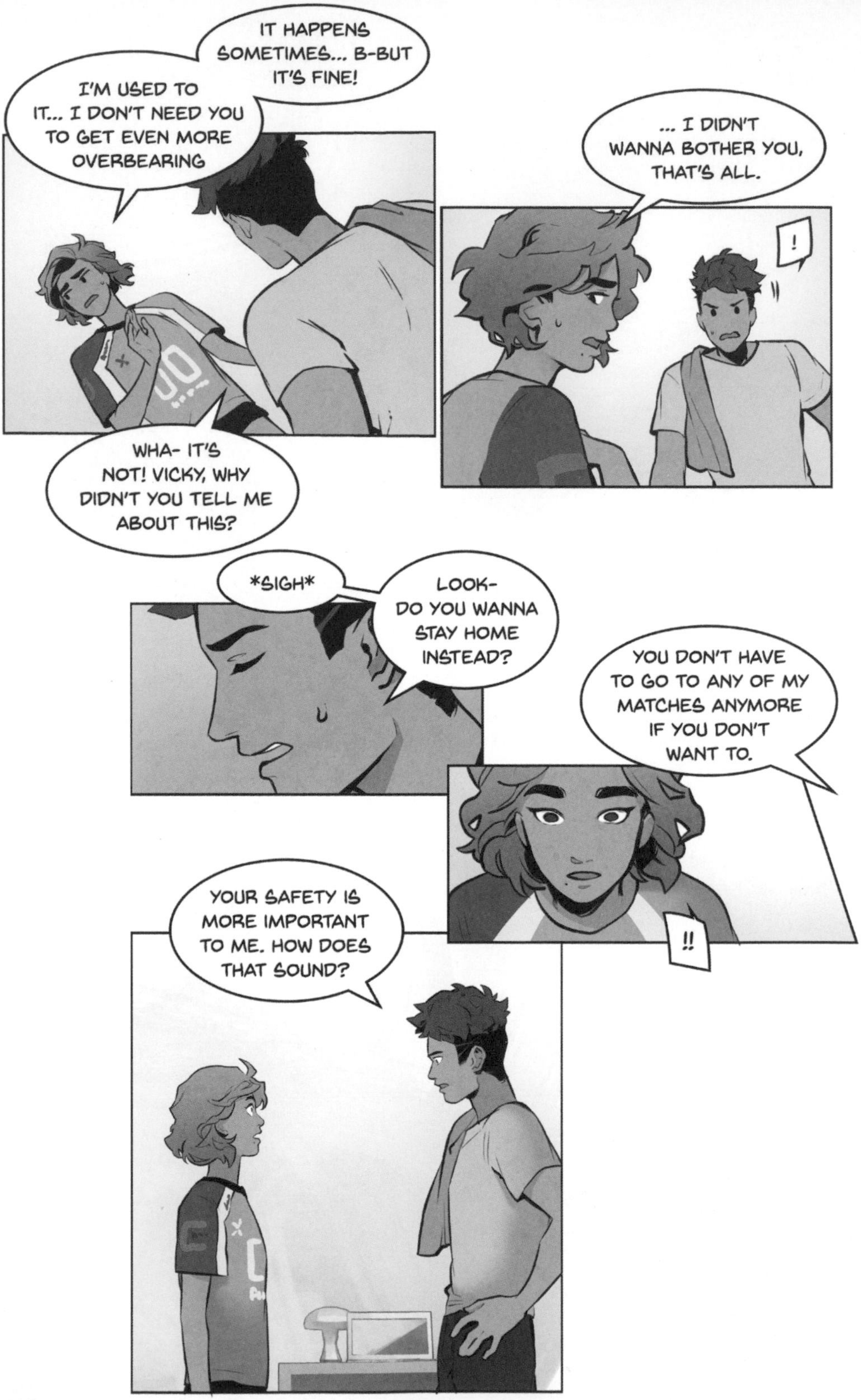
IT HAPPENS SOMETIMES... B-BUT IT'S FINE!
I'M USED TO IT... I DON'T NEED YOU TO GET EVEN MORE OVERBEARING
WHA- IT'S NOT! VICKY, WHY DIDN'T YOU TELL ME ABOUT THIS?
... I DIDN'T WANNA BOTHER YOU, THAT'S ALL.
!
SIGH
LOOK- DO YOU WANNA STAY HOME INSTEAD?
YOU DON'T HAVE TO GO TO ANY OF MY MATCHES ANYMORE IF YOU DON'T WANT TO.
!!
YOUR SAFETY IS MORE IMPORTANT TO ME. HOW DOES THAT SOUND?

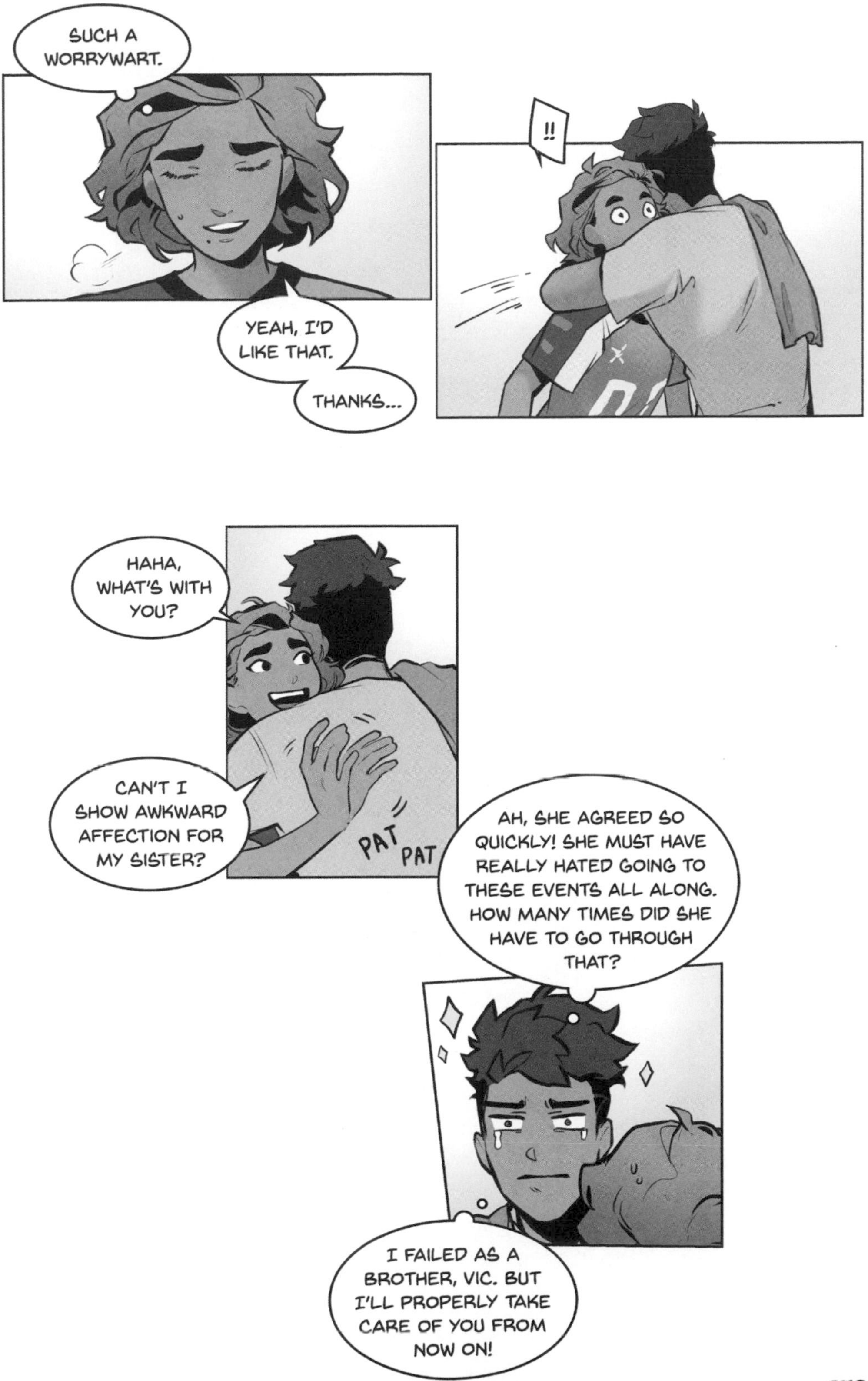
SUCH A WORRYWART.
YEAH, I'D LIKE THAT.
THANKS...
!!
HAHA, WHAT'S WITH YOU?
CAN'T I SHOW AWKWARD AFFECTION FOR MY SISTER?
PAT PAT
AH, SHE AGREED SO QUICKLY! SHE MUST HAVE REALLY HATED GOING TO THESE EVENTS ALL ALONG. HOW MANY TIMES DID SHE HAVE TO GO THROUGH THAT?
I FAILED AS A BROTHER, VIC. BUT I'LL PROPERLY TAKE CARE OF YOU FROM NOW ON!

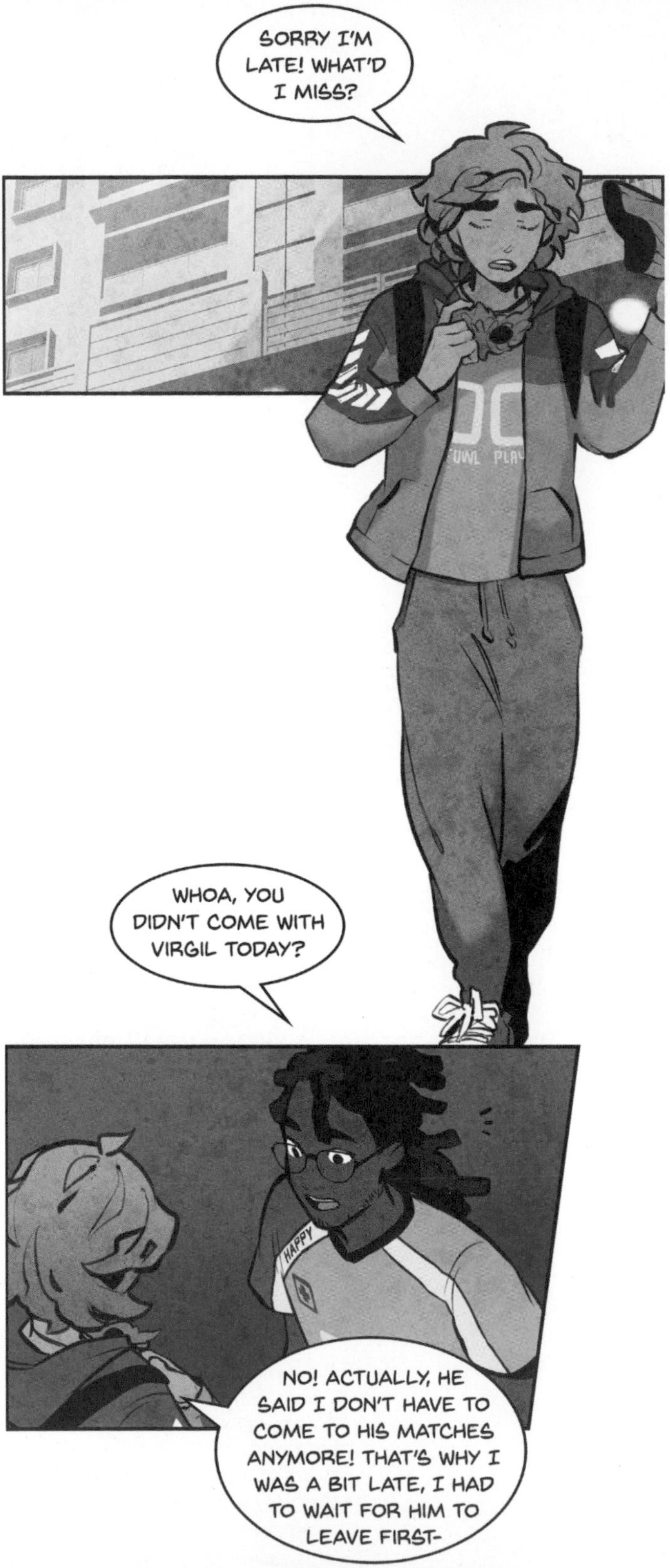
SORRY I'M LATE! WHAT'D I MISS?
FOWL PLAY
WHOA, YOU DIDN'T COME WITH VIRGIL TODAY?
HAPPY
NO! ACTUALLY, HE SAID I DON'T HAVE TO COME TO HIS MATCHES ANYMORE! THAT'S WHY I WAS A BIT LATE, I HAD TO WAIT FOR HIM TO LEAVE FIRST-

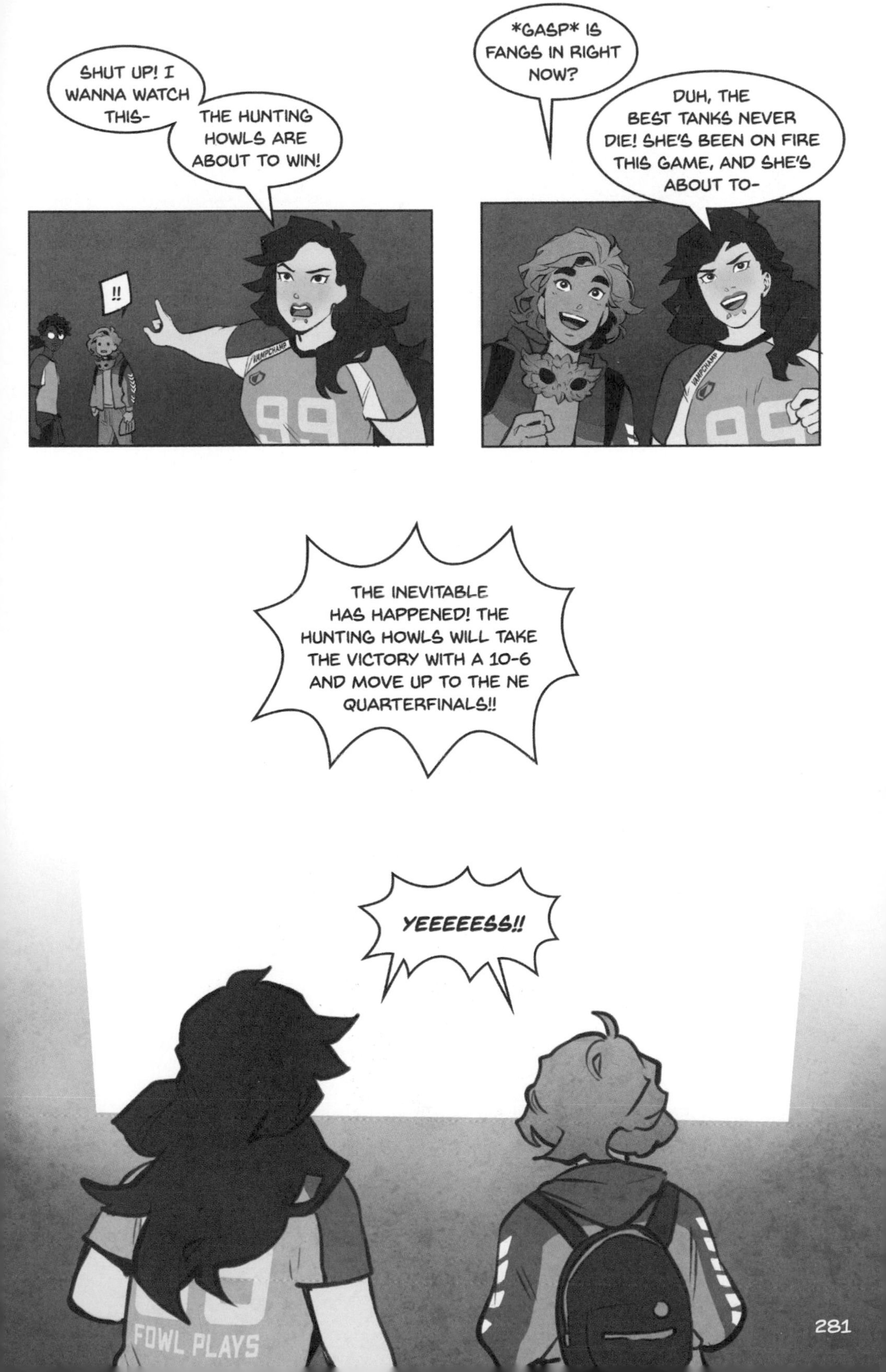
SHUT UP! I WANNA WATCH THIS-
THE HUNTING HOWLS ARE ABOUT TO WIN!
!!
VAMPCHAMP
99
GASP IS FANGS IN RIGHT NOW?
DUH, THE BEST TANKS NEVER DIE! SHE'S BEEN ON FIRE THIS GAME, AND SHE'S ABOUT TO-
VAMPCHAMP
THE INEVITABLE HAS HAPPENED! THE HUNTING HOWLS WILL TAKE THE VICTORY WITH A 10-6 AND MOVE UP TO THE NE QUARTERFINALS!!
YEEEEESS!!
FOWL PLAYS

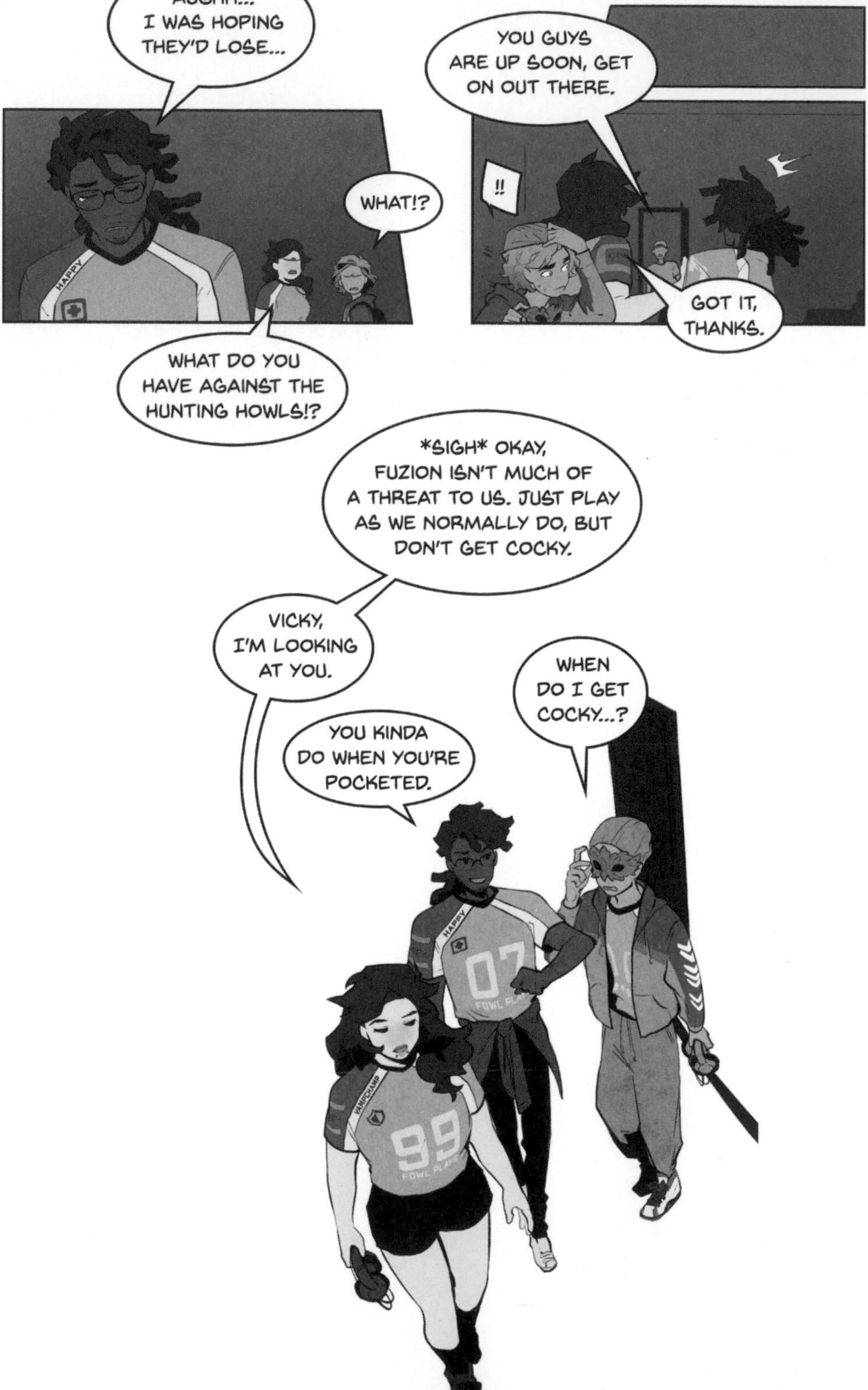
AUGHH... I WAS HOPING THEY'D LOSE...
WHAT!?
WHAT DO YOU HAVE AGAINST THE HUNTING HOWLS!?
YOU GUYS ARE UP SOON, GET ON OUT THERE.
!!
GOT IT, THANKS.
SIGH OKAY, FUZION ISN'T MUCH OF A THREAT TO US. JUST PLAY AS WE NORMALLY DO, BUT DON'T GET COCKY.
VICKY, I'M LOOKING AT YOU.
WHEN DO I GET COCKY...?
YOU KINDA DO WHEN YOU'RE POCKETED.

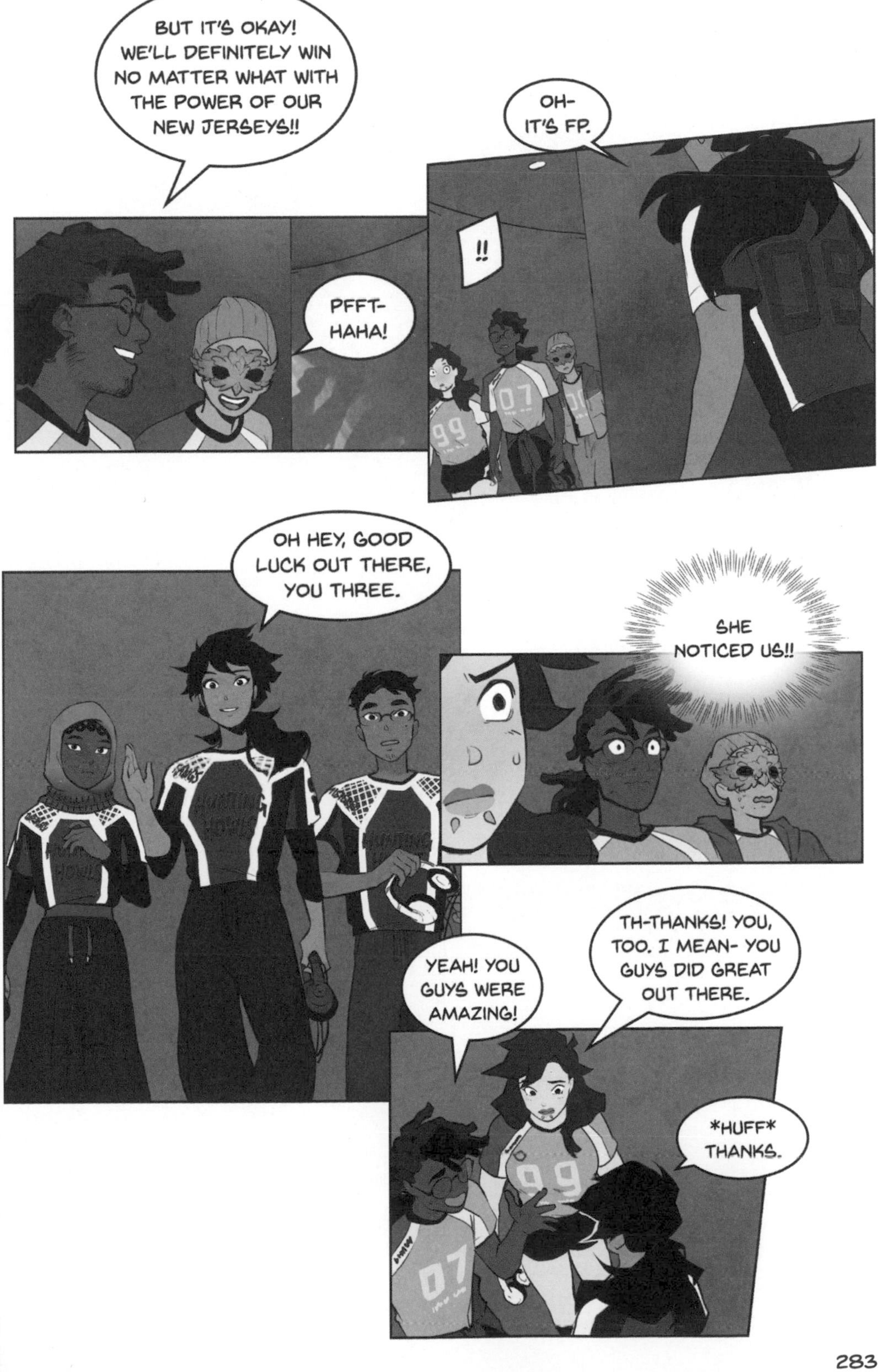
BUT IT'S OKAY! WE'LL DEFINITELY WIN NO MATTER WHAT WITH THE POWER OF OUR NEW JERSEYS!!
PFFT- HAHA!
OH- IT'S FP.
!!
OH HEY, GOOD LUCK OUT THERE, YOU THREE.
SHE NOTICED US!!
YEAH! YOU GUYS WERE AMAZING!
TH-THANKS! YOU, TOO. I MEAN- YOU GUYS DID GREAT OUT THERE.
HUFF THANKS.

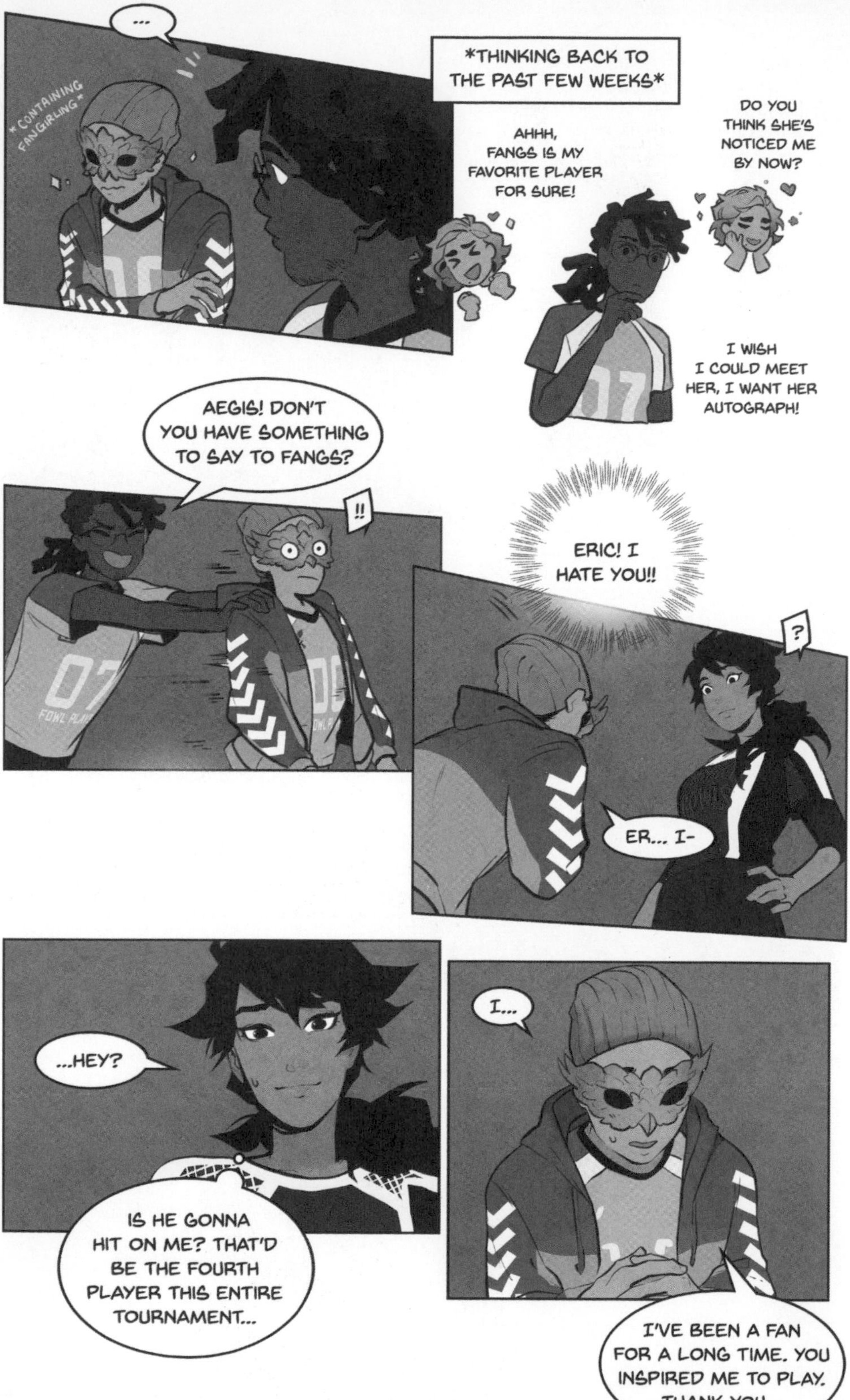
...
CONTAINING FANGIRLING
THINKING BACK TO THE PAST FEW WEEKS
AHHH, FANGS IS MY FAVORITE PLAYER FOR SURE!
DO YOU THINK SHE'S NOTICED ME BY NOW?
I WISH I COULD MEET HER, I WANT HER AUTOGRAPH!
AEGIS! DON'T YOU HAVE SOMETHING TO SAY TO FANGS?
!!
07
FOWL PLAY
ERIC! I HATE YOU!!
?
ER... I-
...HEY?
IS HE GONNA HIT ON ME? THAT'D BE THE FOURTH PLAYER THIS ENTIRE TOURNAMENT...
I...
I'VE BEEN A FAN FOR A LONG TIME. YOU INSPIRED ME TO PLAY. THANK YOU...

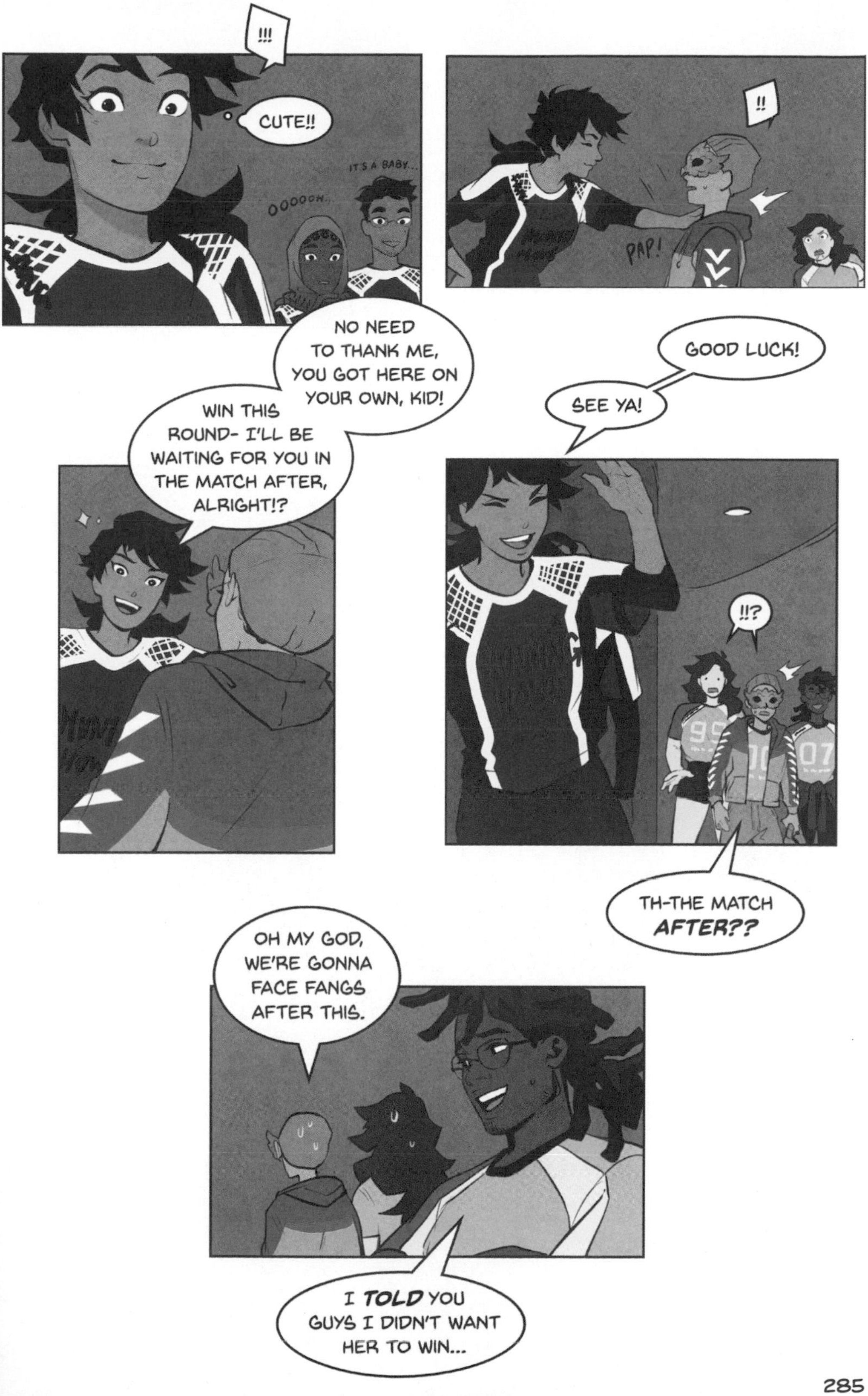
!!!
CUTE!!
OOOOCH...
IT'S A BABY...
!!
PAP!
NO NEED TO THANK ME, YOU GOT HERE ON YOUR OWN, KID!
WIN THIS ROUND- I'LL BE WAITING FOR YOU IN THE MATCH AFTER, ALRIGHT!?
SEE YA!
GOOD LUCK!
!!?
TH-THE MATCH **AFTER??**
OH MY GOD, WE'RE GONNA FACE FANGS AFTER THIS.
I **TOLD** YOU GUYS I DIDN'T WANT HER TO WIN...

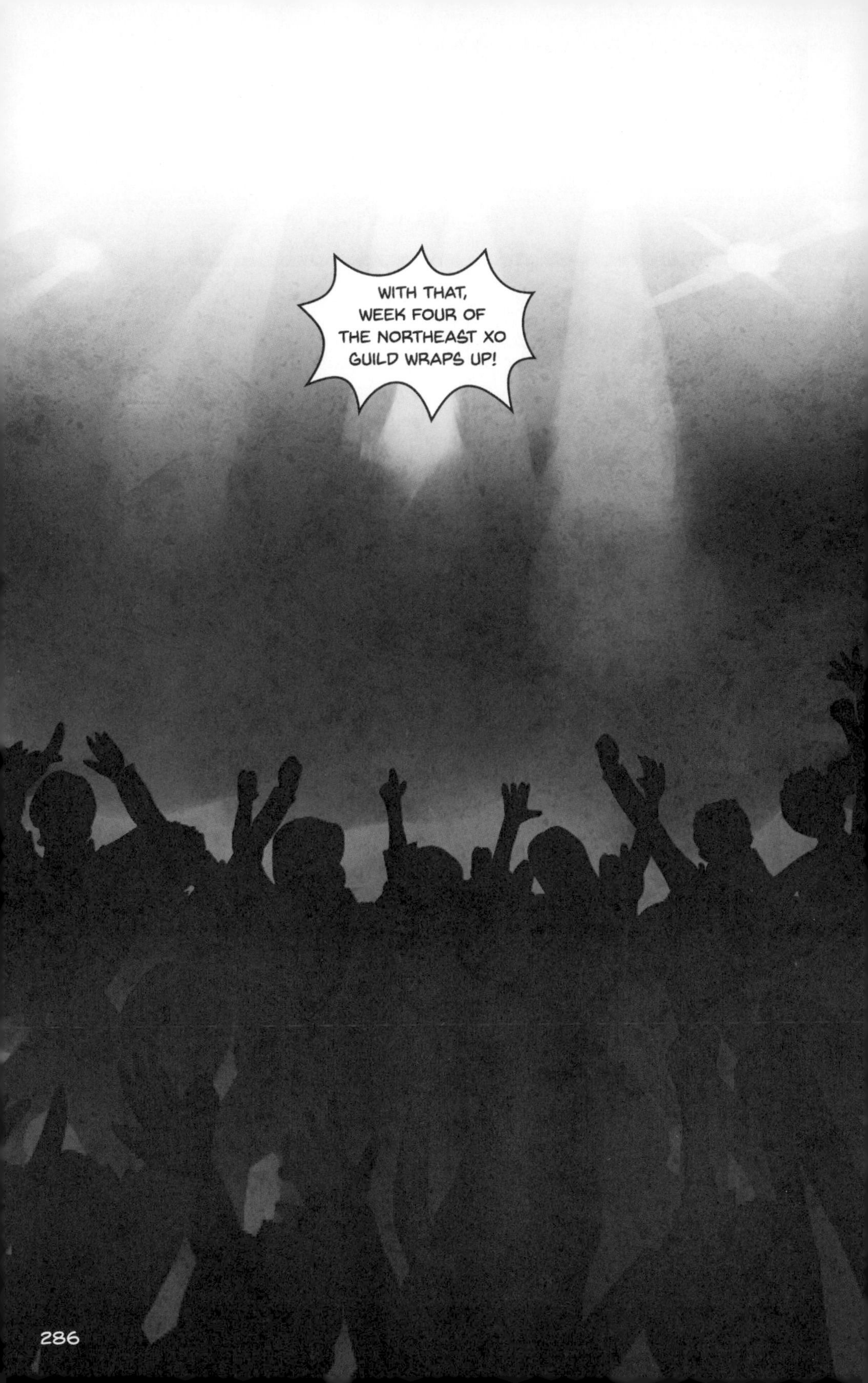
WITH THAT, WEEK FOUR OF THE NORTHEAST XO GUILD WRAPS UP!

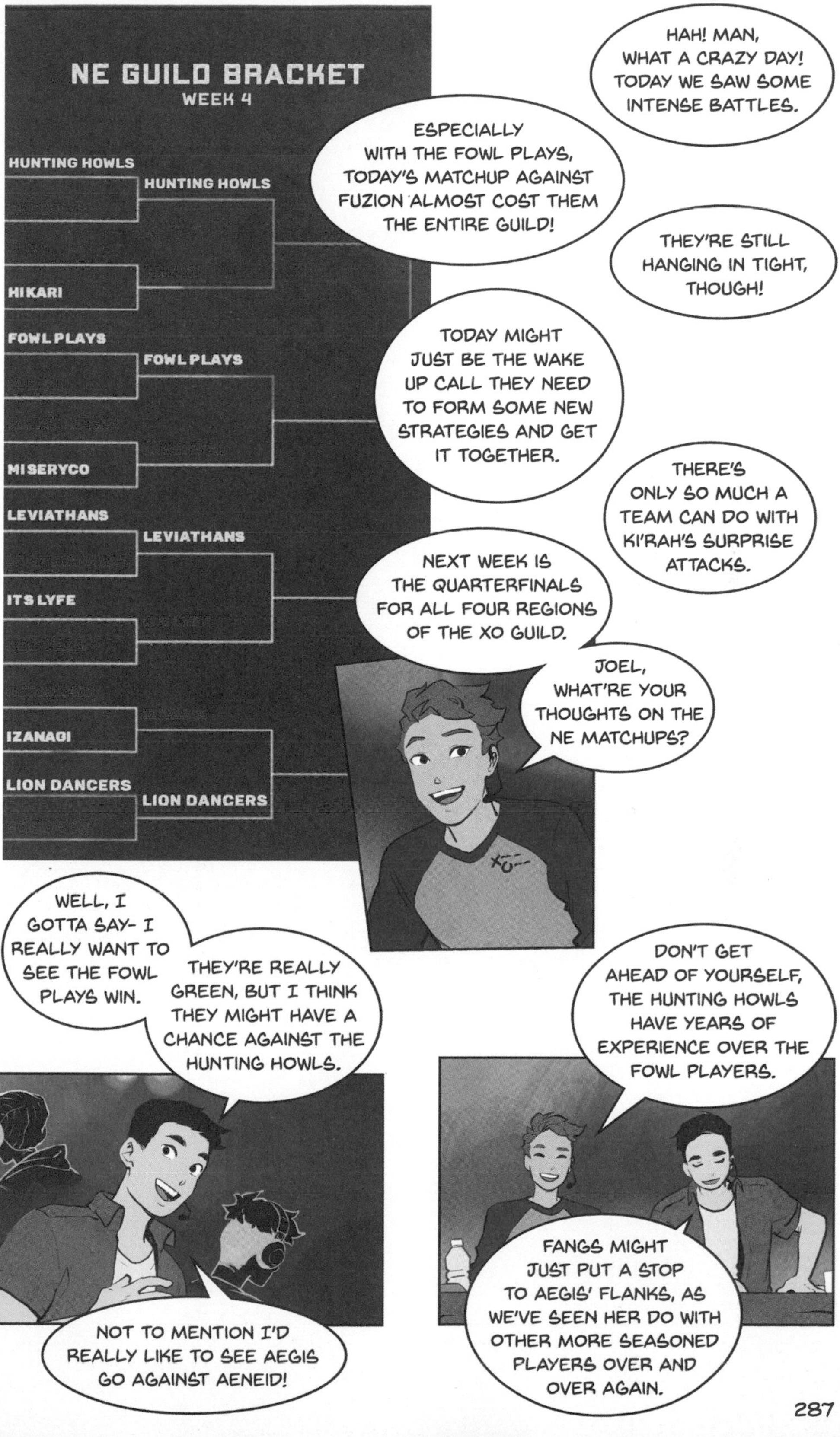
NE GUILD BRACKET
WEEK 4
HUNTING HOWLS
HUNTING HOWLS
HIKARI
FOWL PLAYS
FOWL PLAYS
MISERYCO
LEVIATHANS
LEVIATHANS
ITS LYFE
IZANAGI
LION DANCERS
LION DANCERS
HAH! MAN, WHAT A CRAZY DAY! TODAY WE SAW SOME INTENSE BATTLES.
ESPECIALLY WITH THE FOWL PLAYS, TODAY'S MATCHUP AGAINST FUZION ALMOST COST THEM THE ENTIRE GUILD!
THEY'RE STILL HANGING IN TIGHT, THOUGH!
TODAY MIGHT JUST BE THE WAKE UP CALL THEY NEED TO FORM SOME NEW STRATEGIES AND GET IT TOGETHER.
THERE'S ONLY SO MUCH A TEAM CAN DO WITH KI'RAH'S SURPRISE ATTACKS.
NEXT WEEK IS THE QUARTERFINALS FOR ALL FOUR REGIONS OF THE XO GUILD.
JOEL, WHAT'RE YOUR THOUGHTS ON THE NE MATCHUPS?
XO
WELL, I GOTTA SAY- I REALLY WANT TO SEE THE FOWL PLAYS WIN.
THEY'RE REALLY GREEN, BUT I THINK THEY MIGHT HAVE A CHANCE AGAINST THE HUNTING HOWLS.
NOT TO MENTION I'D REALLY LIKE TO SEE AEGIS GO AGAINST AENEID!
DON'T GET AHEAD OF YOURSELF, THE HUNTING HOWLS HAVE YEARS OF EXPERIENCE OVER THE FOWL PLAYERS.
FANGS MIGHT JUST PUT A STOP TO AEGIS' FLANKS, AS WE'VE SEEN HER DO WITH OTHER MORE SEASONED PLAYERS OVER AND OVER AGAIN.

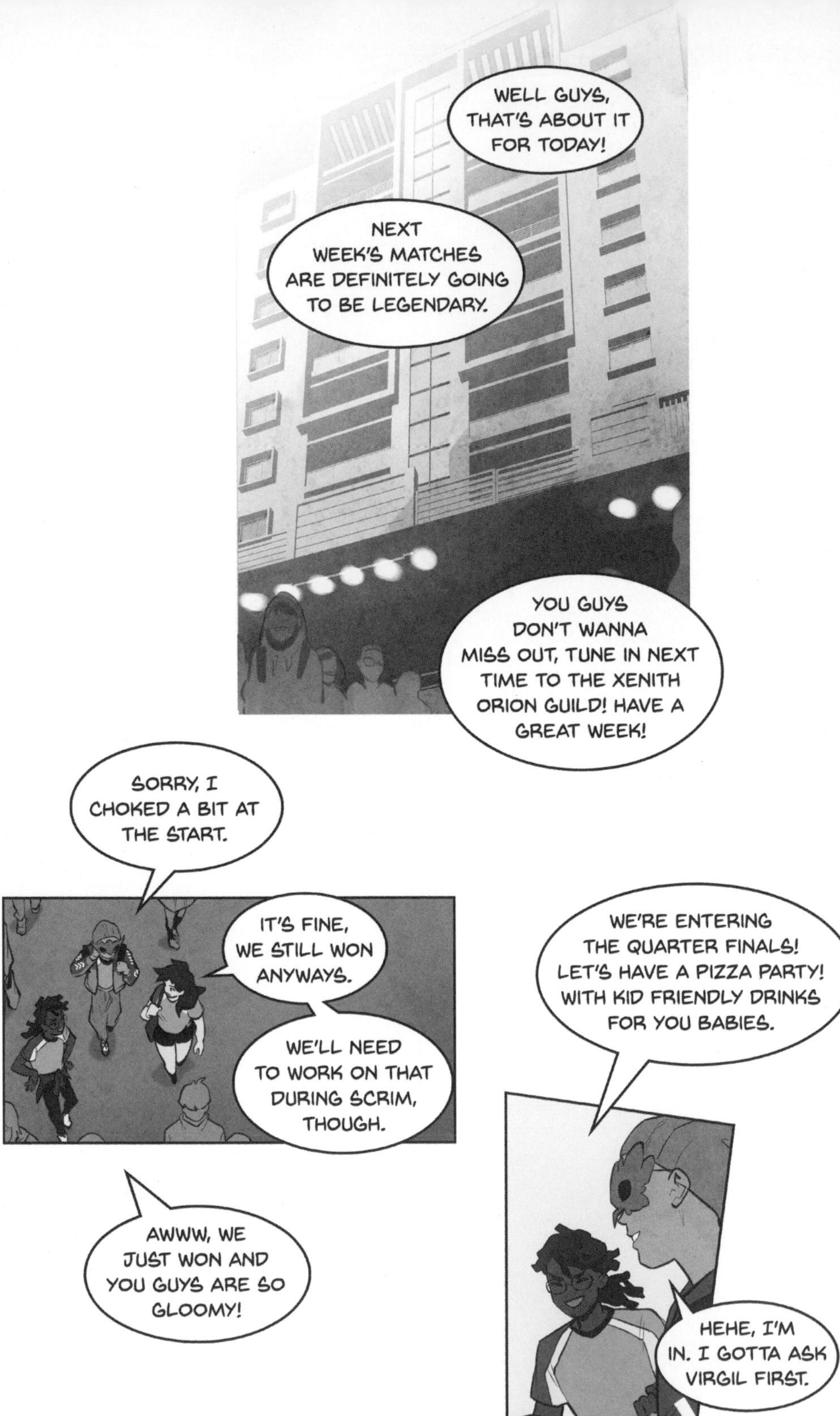
WELL GUYS, THAT'S ABOUT IT FOR TODAY!
NEXT WEEK'S MATCHES ARE DEFINITELY GOING TO BE LEGENDARY.
YOU GUYS DON'T WANNA MISS OUT, TUNE IN NEXT TIME TO THE XENITH ORION GUILD! HAVE A GREAT WEEK!
SORRY, I CHOKED A BIT AT THE START.
IT'S FINE, WE STILL WON ANYWAYS.
WE'LL NEED TO WORK ON THAT DURING SCRIM, THOUGH.
AWWW, WE JUST WON AND YOU GUYS ARE SO GLOOMY!
WE'RE ENTERING THE QUARTER FINALS! LET'S HAVE A PIZZA PARTY! WITH KID FRIENDLY DRINKS FOR YOU BABIES.
HEHE, I'M IN. I GOTTA ASK VIRGIL FIRST.

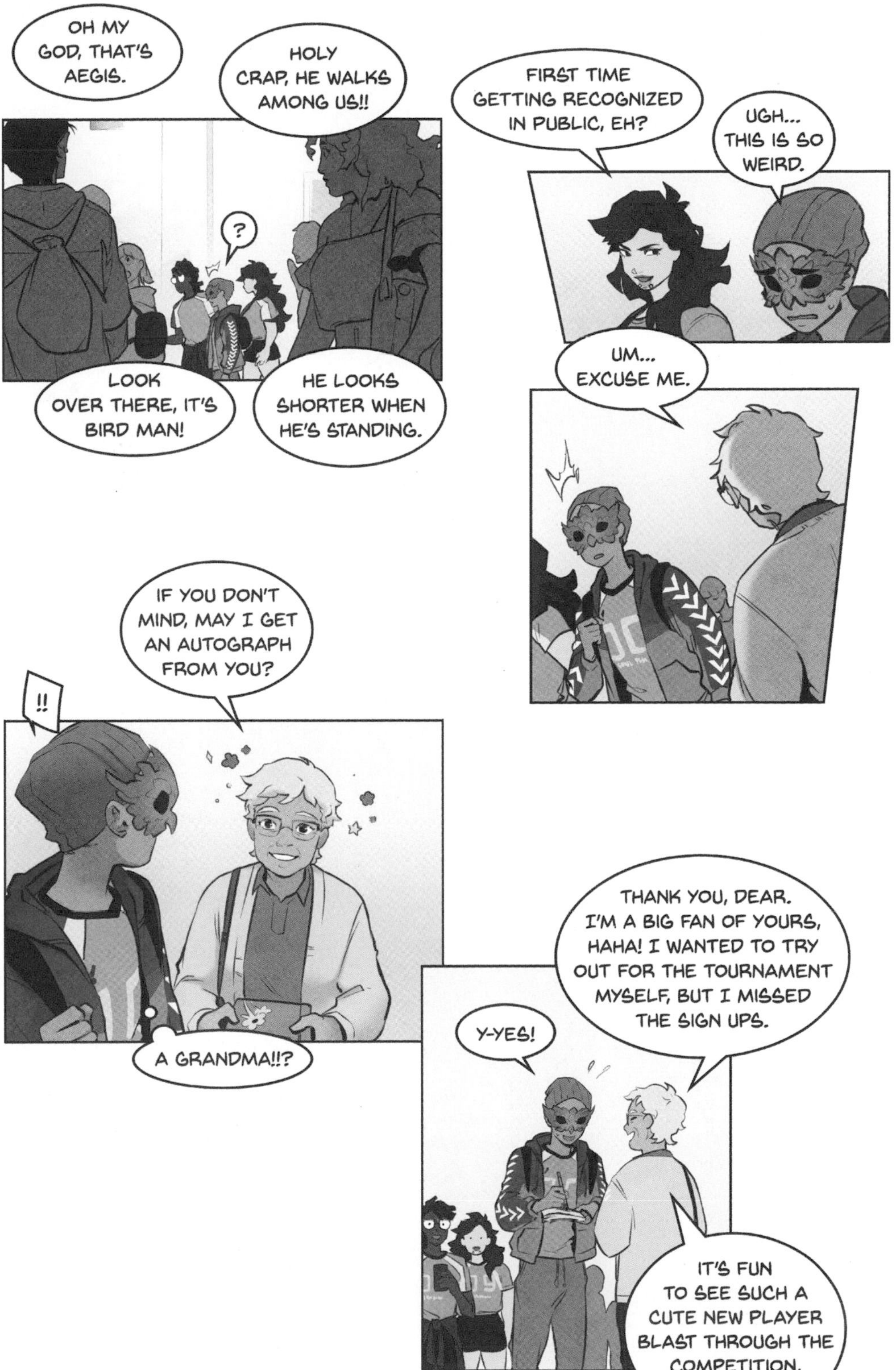
OH MY GOD, THAT'S AEGIS.
HOLY CRAP, HE WALKS AMONG US!!
?
LOOK OVER THERE, IT'S BIRD MAN!
HE LOOKS SHORTER WHEN HE'S STANDING.
FIRST TIME GETTING RECOGNIZED IN PUBLIC, EH?
UGH... THIS IS SO WEIRD.
UM... EXCUSE ME.
IF YOU DON'T MIND, MAY I GET AN AUTOGRAPH FROM YOU?
!!
A GRANDMA!!?
THANK YOU, DEAR. I'M A BIG FAN OF YOURS, HAHA! I WANTED TO TRY OUT FOR THE TOURNAMENT MYSELF, BUT I MISSED THE SIGN UPS.
Y-YES!
IT'S FUN TO SEE SUCH A CUTE NEW PLAYER BLAST THROUGH THE COMPETITION, THOUGH!

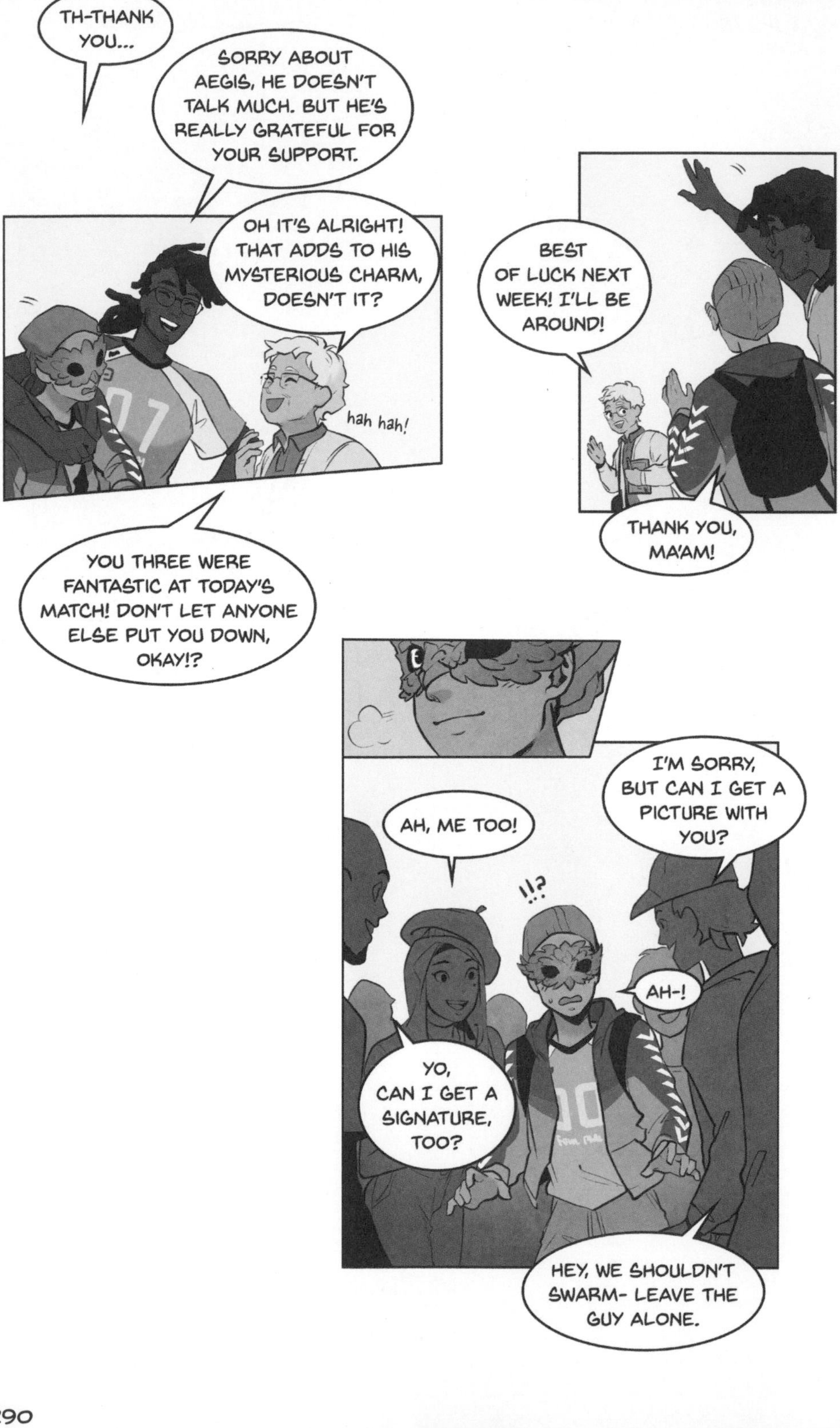
TH-THANK YOU...
SORRY ABOUT AEGIS, HE DOESN'T TALK MUCH. BUT HE'S REALLY GRATEFUL FOR YOUR SUPPORT.
OH IT'S ALRIGHT! THAT ADDS TO HIS MYSTERIOUS CHARM, DOESN'T IT?
hah hah!
YOU THREE WERE FANTASTIC AT TODAY'S MATCH! DON'T LET ANYONE ELSE PUT YOU DOWN, OKAY!?
BEST OF LUCK NEXT WEEK! I'LL BE AROUND!
THANK YOU, MA'AM!
I'M SORRY, BUT CAN I GET A PICTURE WITH YOU?
AH, ME TOO!
!!?
AH-!
YO, CAN I GET A SIGNATURE, TOO?
HEY, WE SHOULDN'T SWARM- LEAVE THE GUY ALONE.

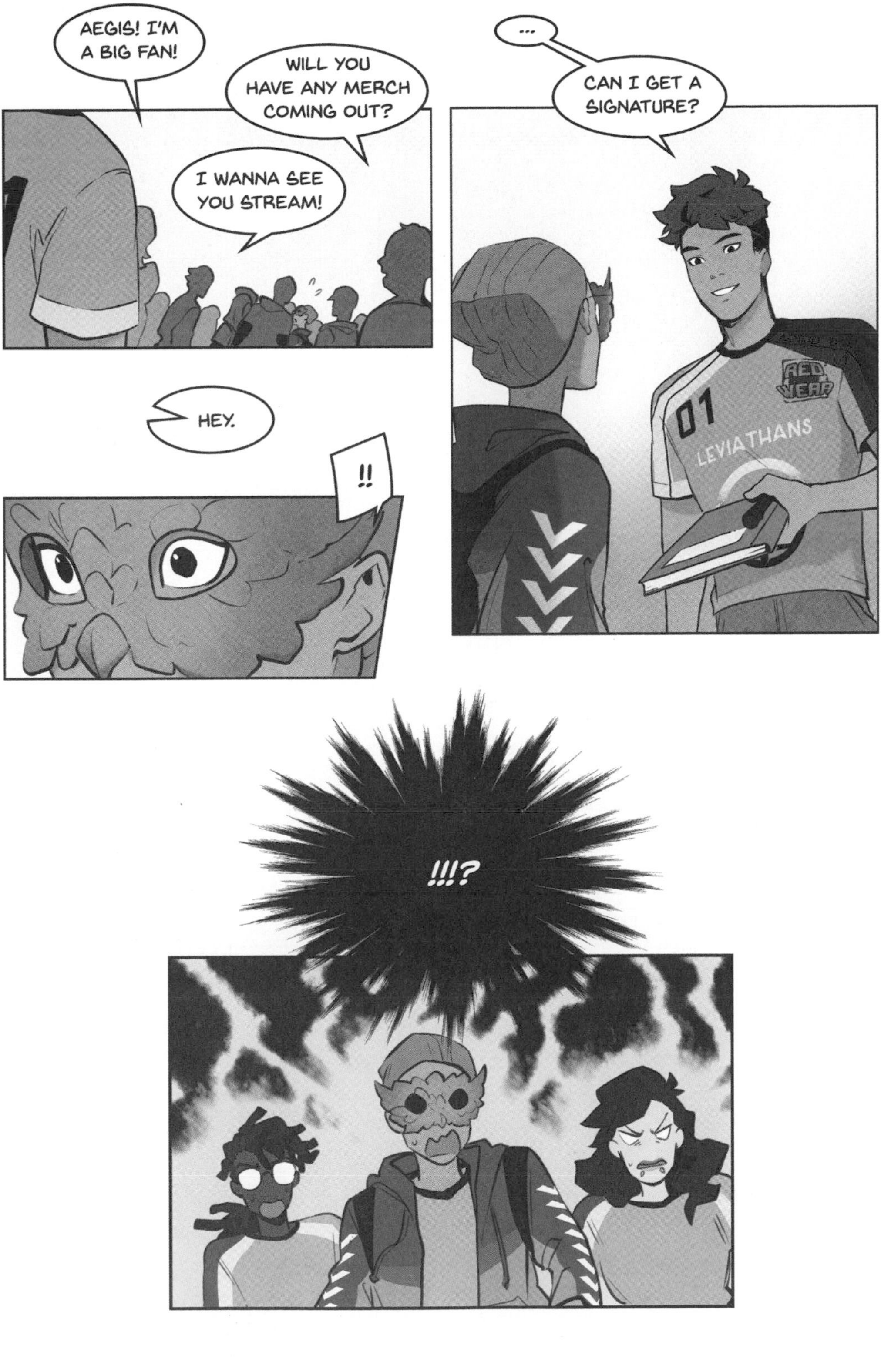
AEGIS! I'M A BIG FAN!
WILL YOU HAVE ANY MERCH COMING OUT?
I WANNA SEE YOU STREAM!
HEY.
!!
...
CAN I GET A SIGNATURE?
RED WEAR
01
LEVIATHANS
!!!?

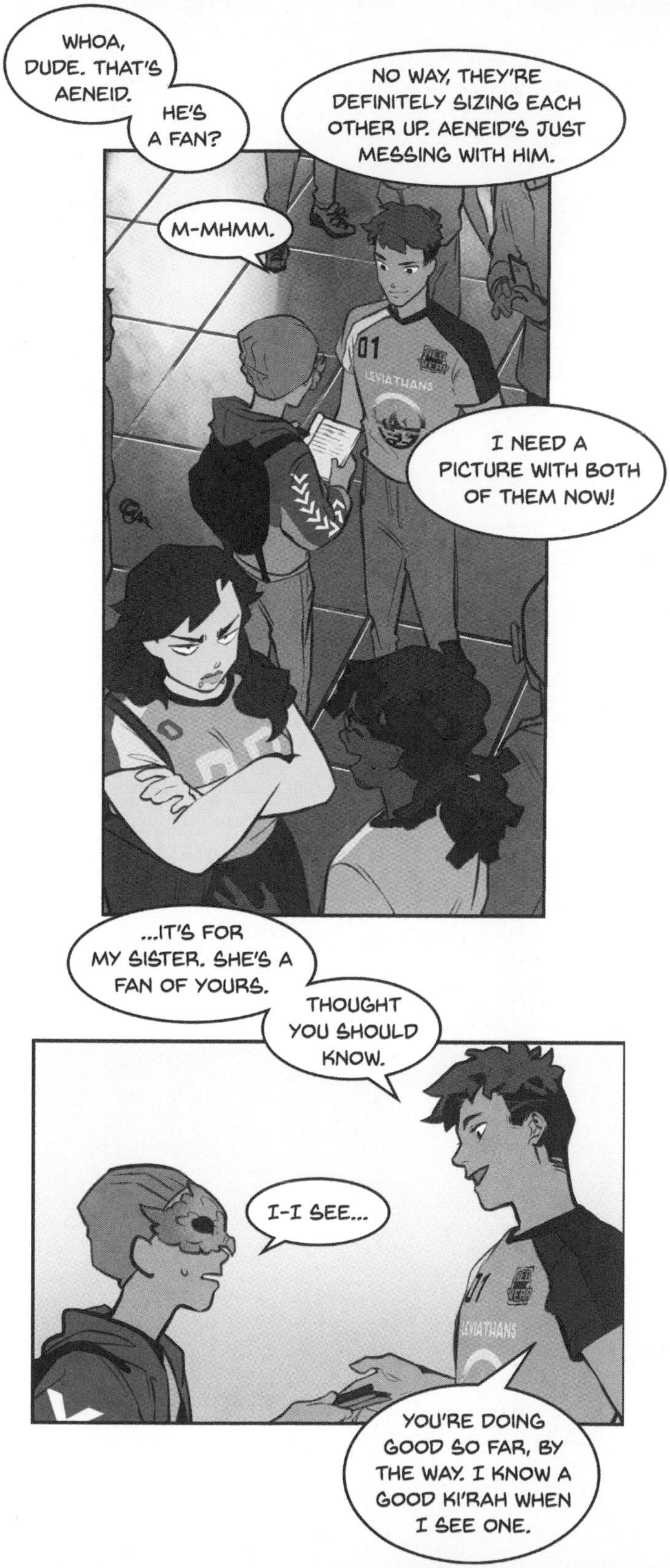
WHOA, DUDE. THAT'S AENEID.
HE'S A FAN?
NO WAY, THEY'RE DEFINITELY SIZING EACH OTHER UP. AENEID'S JUST MESSING WITH HIM.
M-MHMM.
01
LEVIATHANS
I NEED A PICTURE WITH BOTH OF THEM NOW!
...IT'S FOR MY SISTER. SHE'S A FAN OF YOURS.
THOUGHT YOU SHOULD KNOW.
I-I SEE...
LEVIATHANS
YOU'RE DOING GOOD SO FAR, BY THE WAY. I KNOW A GOOD KI'RAH WHEN I SEE ONE.

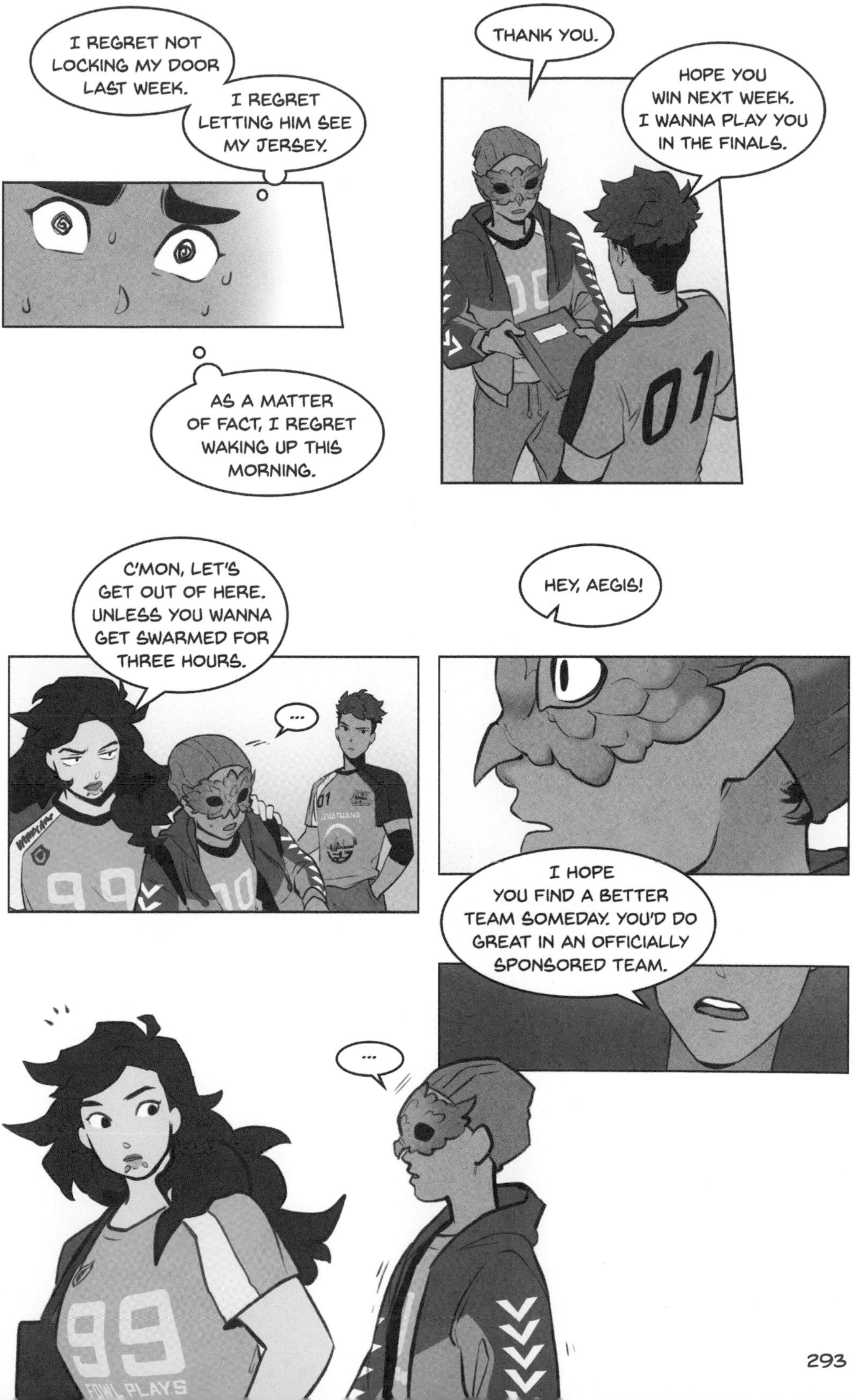

I REGRET NOT LOCKING MY DOOR LAST WEEK.
I REGRET LETTING HIM SEE MY JERSEY.
AS A MATTER OF FACT, I REGRET WAKING UP THIS MORNING.
THANK YOU.
HOPE YOU WIN NEXT WEEK. I WANNA PLAY YOU IN THE FINALS.
C'MON, LET'S GET OUT OF HERE. UNLESS YOU WANNA GET SWARMED FOR THREE HOURS.
...
HEY, AEGIS!
I HOPE YOU FIND A BETTER TEAM SOMEDAY. YOU'D DO GREAT IN AN OFFICIALLY SPONSORED TEAM.
...
FOWL PLAYS

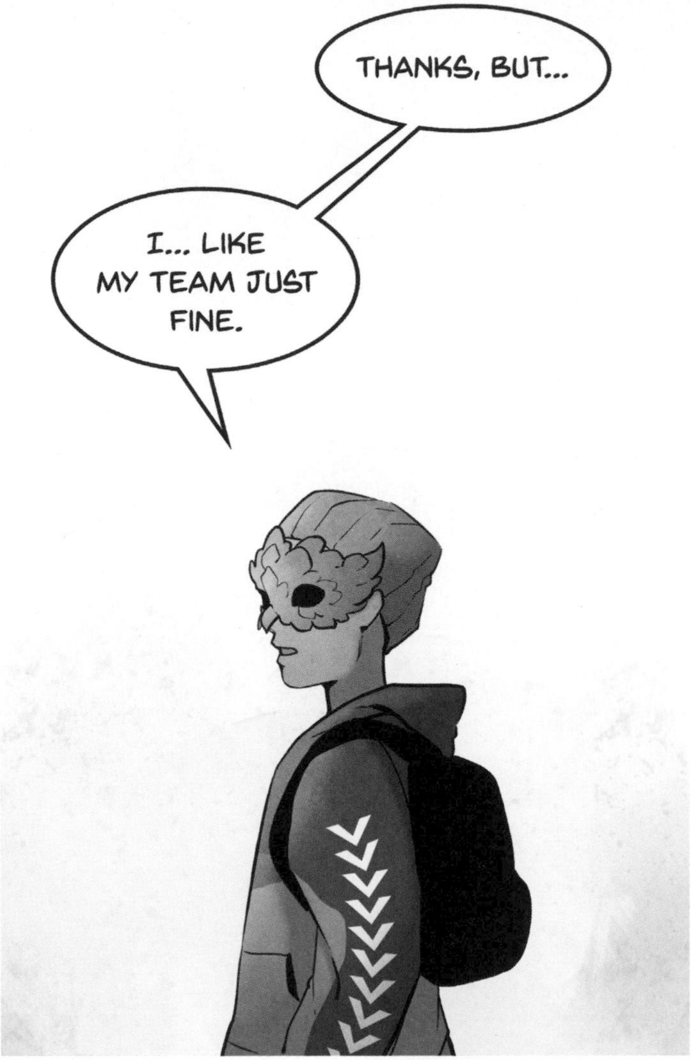
THANKS, BUT...
I... LIKE MY TEAM JUST FINE.

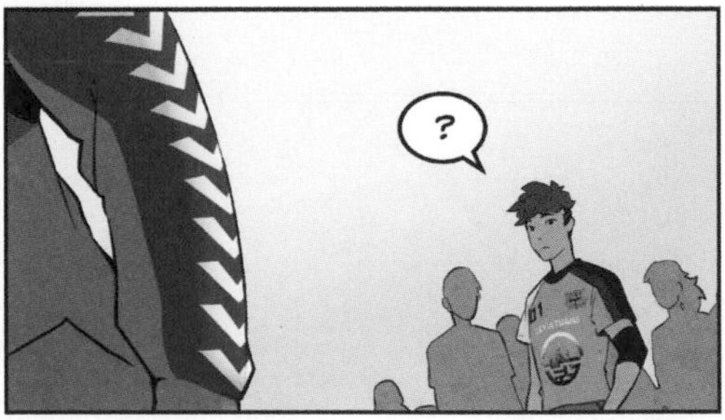
?

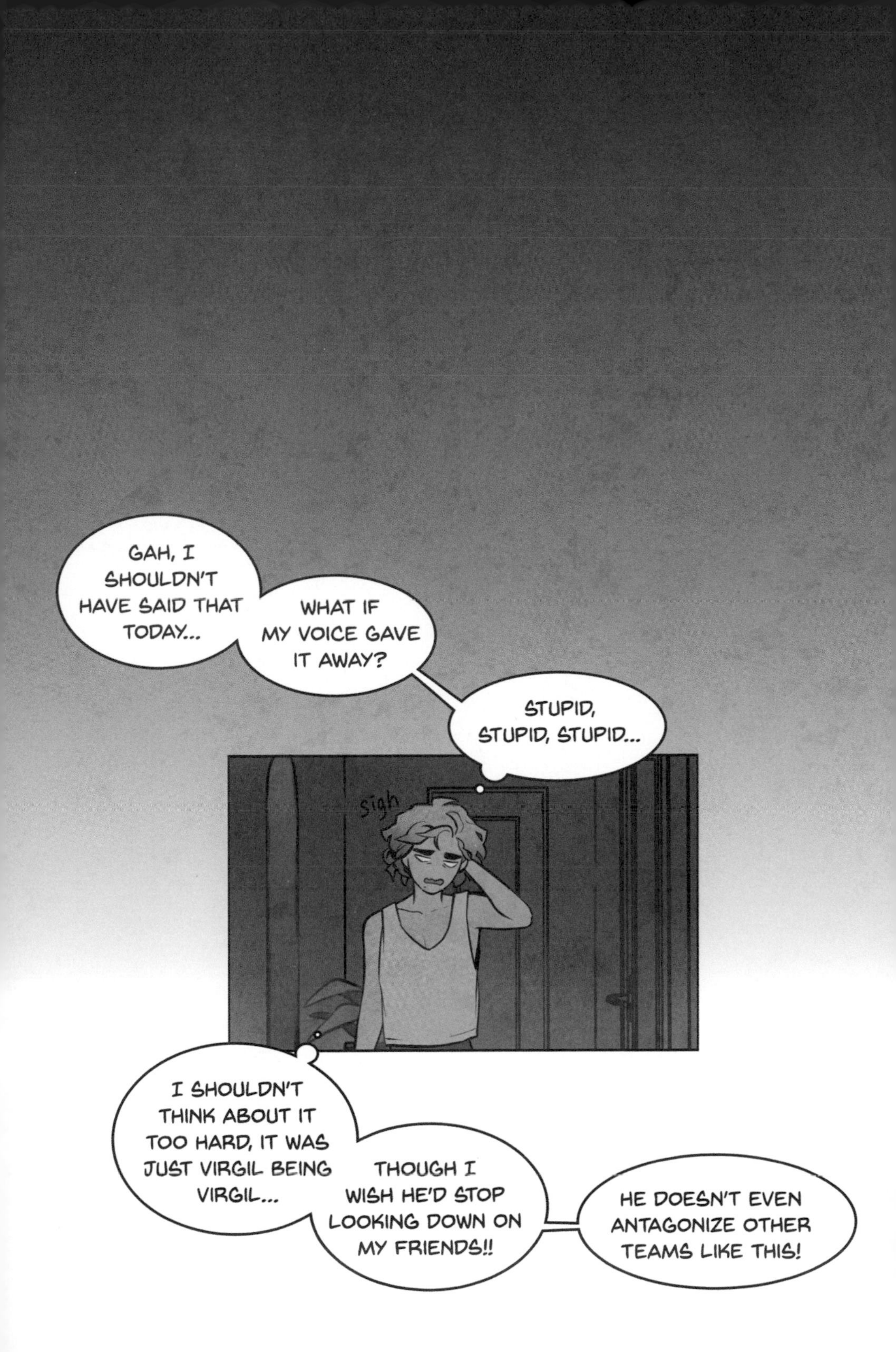
GAH, I SHOULDN'T HAVE SAID THAT TODAY...
WHAT IF MY VOICE GAVE IT AWAY?
STUPID, STUPID, STUPID...
sigh
I SHOULDN'T THINK ABOUT IT TOO HARD, IT WAS JUST VIRGIL BEING VIRGIL...
THOUGH I WISH HE'D STOP LOOKING DOWN ON MY FRIENDS!!
HE DOESN'T EVEN ANTAGONIZE OTHER TEAMS LIKE THIS!

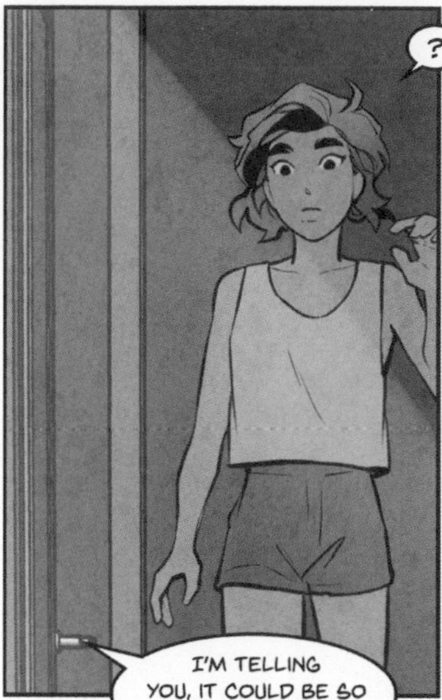
?
I'M TELLING YOU, IT COULD BE SO MUCH BETTER.

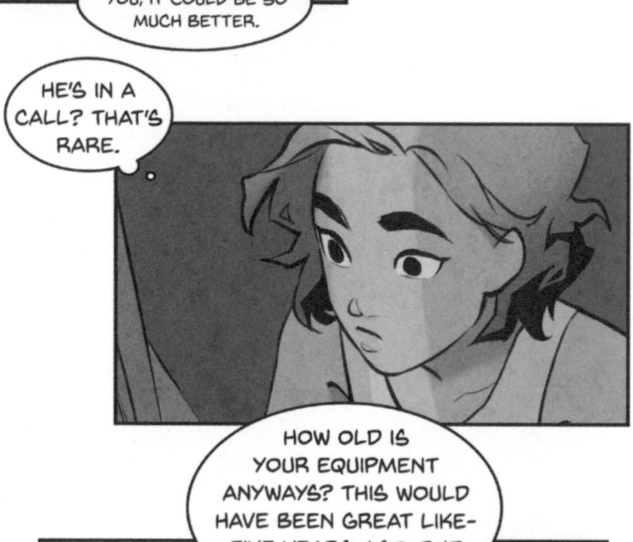
HE'S IN A CALL? THAT'S RARE.

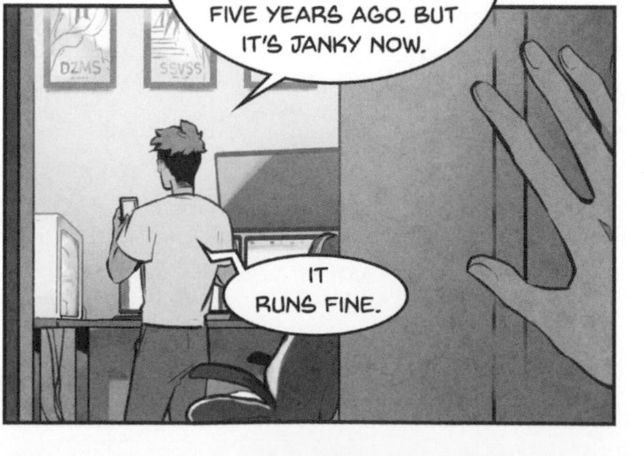
HOW OLD IS YOUR EQUIPMENT ANYWAYS? THIS WOULD HAVE BEEN GREAT LIKE-FIVE YEARS AGO. BUT IT'S JANKY NOW.
IT RUNS FINE.

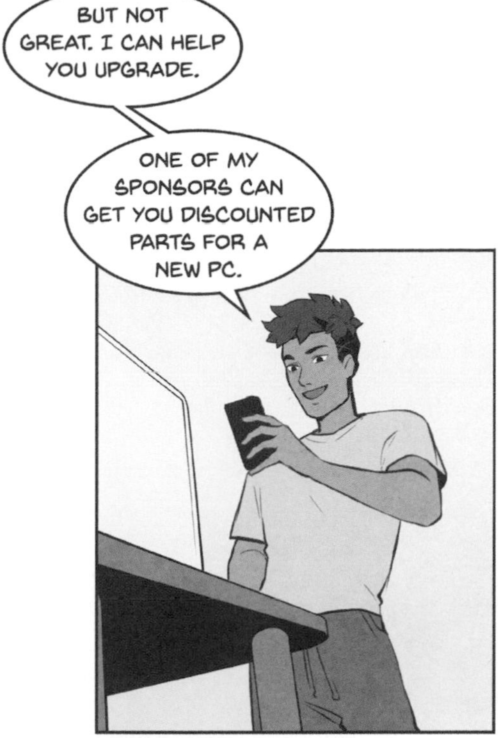
BUT NOT GREAT. I CAN HELP YOU UPGRADE.
ONE OF MY SPONSORS CAN GET YOU DISCOUNTED PARTS FOR A NEW PC.
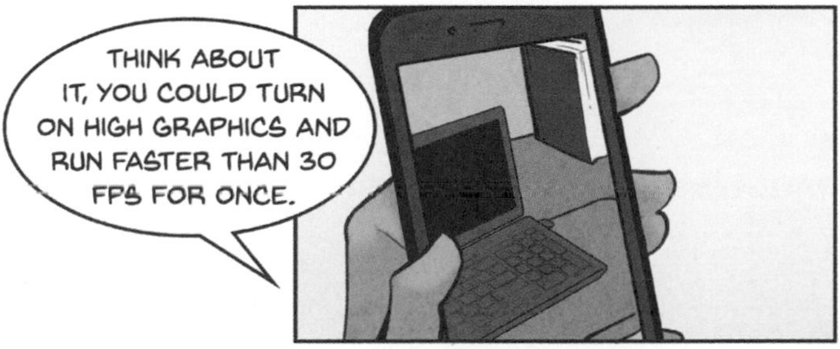
THINK ABOUT IT, YOU COULD TURN ON HIGH GRAPHICS AND RUN FASTER THAN 30 FPS FOR ONCE.
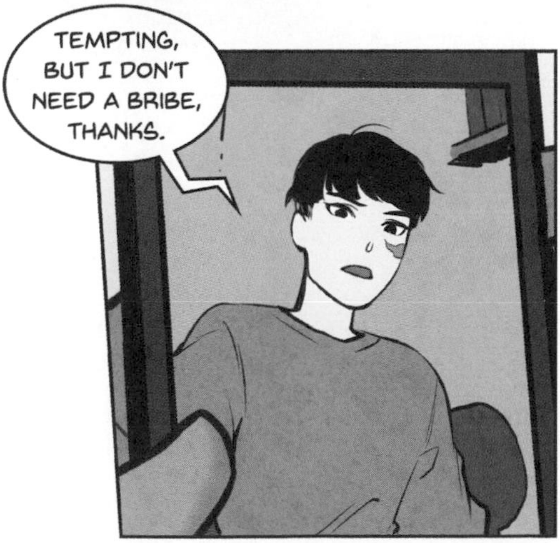
TEMPTING, BUT I DON'T NEED A BRIBE, THANKS.

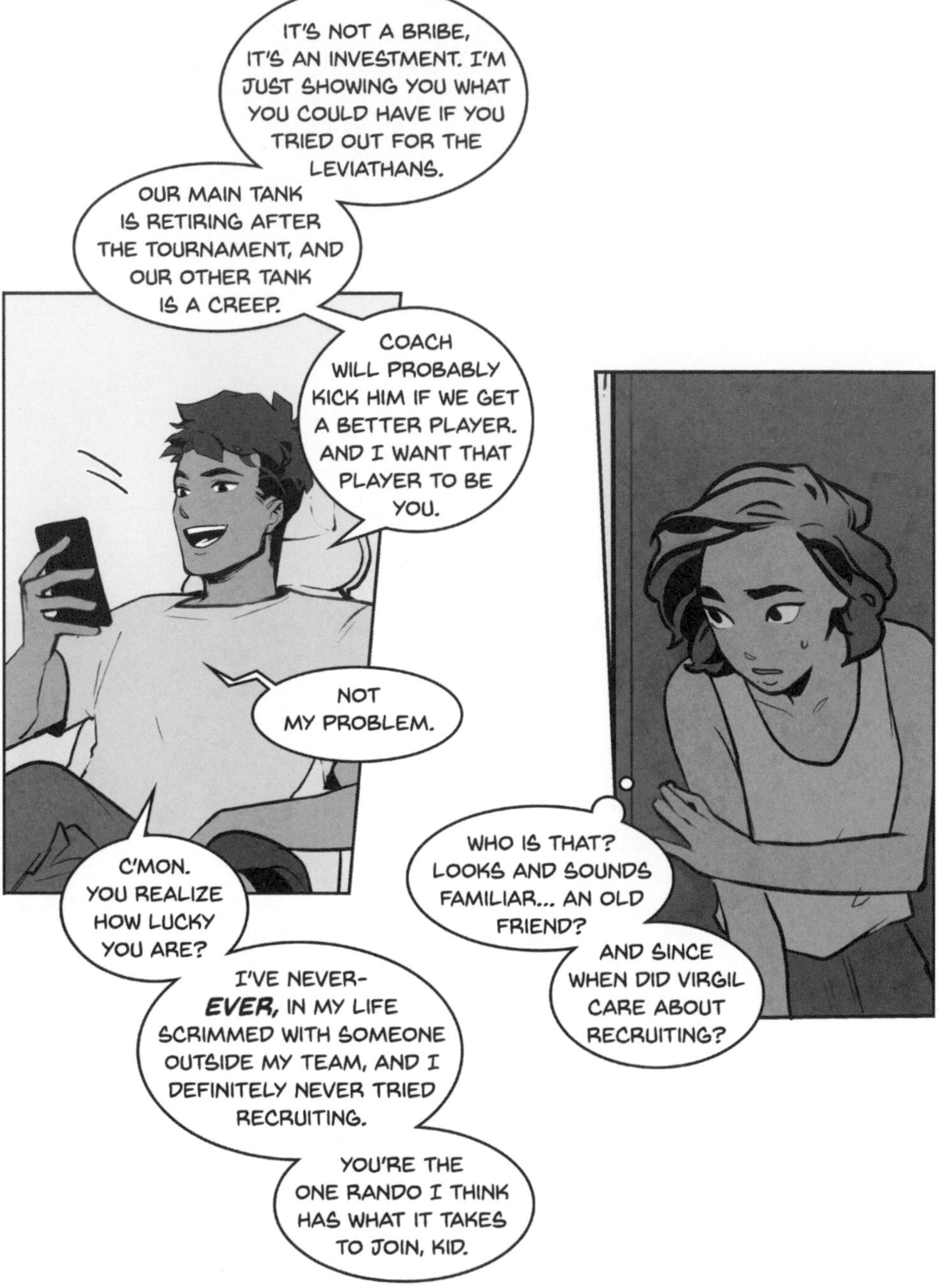
IT'S NOT A BRIBE, IT'S AN INVESTMENT. I'M JUST SHOWING YOU WHAT YOU COULD HAVE IF YOU TRIED OUT FOR THE LEVIATHANS.
OUR MAIN TANK IS RETIRING AFTER THE TOURNAMENT, AND OUR OTHER TANK IS A CREEP.
COACH WILL PROBABLY KICK HIM IF WE GET A BETTER PLAYER. AND I WANT THAT PLAYER TO BE YOU.
NOT MY PROBLEM.
C'MON. YOU REALIZE HOW LUCKY YOU ARE?
I'VE NEVER- ***EVER,*** IN MY LIFE SCRIMMED WITH SOMEONE OUTSIDE MY TEAM, AND I DEFINITELY NEVER TRIED RECRUITING.
YOU'RE THE ONE RANDO I THINK HAS WHAT IT TAKES TO JOIN, KID.
WHO IS THAT? LOOKS AND SOUNDS FAMILIAR... AN OLD FRIEND?
AND SINCE WHEN DID VIRGIL CARE ABOUT RECRUITING?

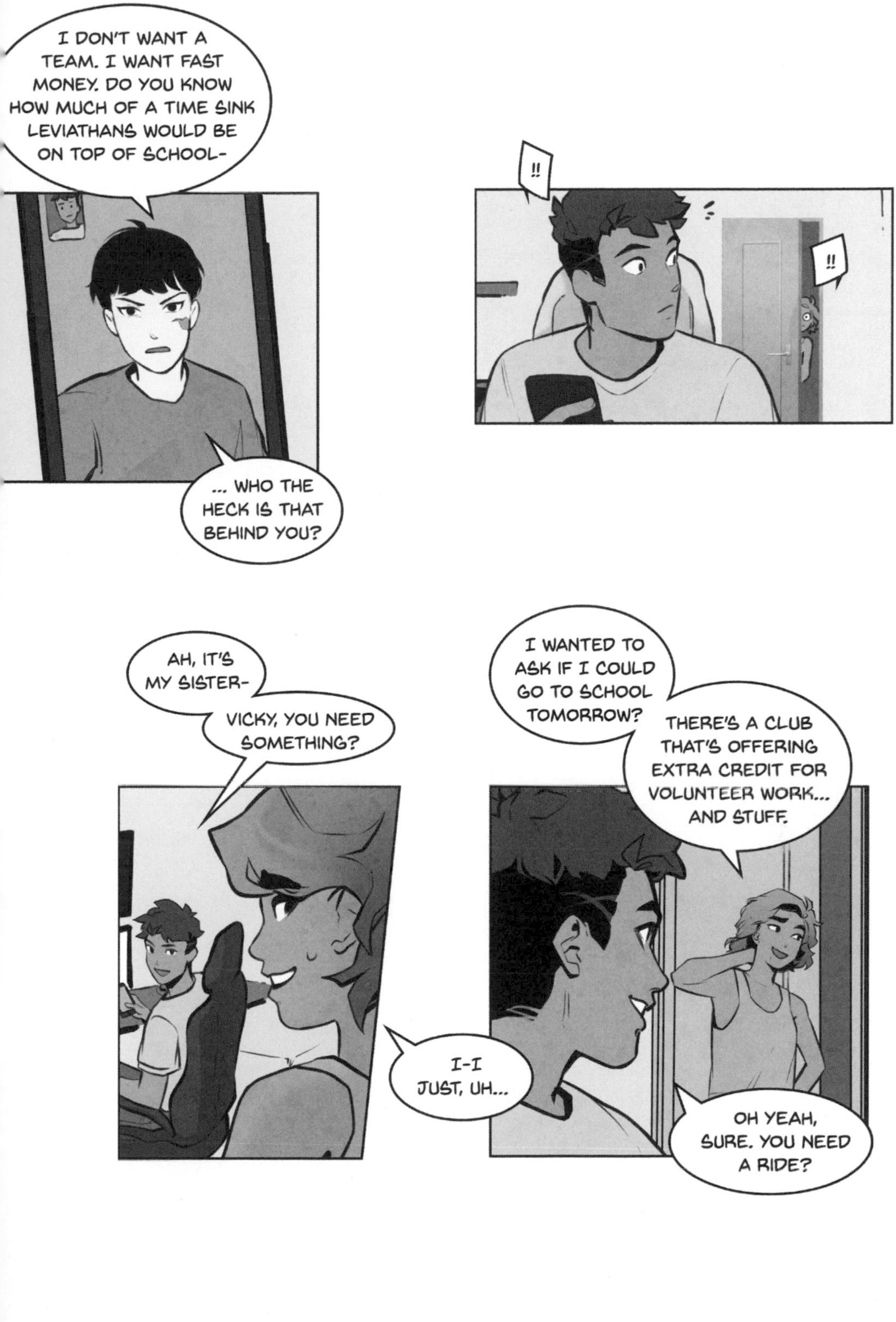
I DON'T WANT A TEAM. I WANT FAST MONEY. DO YOU KNOW HOW MUCH OF A TIME SINK LEVIATHANS WOULD BE ON TOP OF SCHOOL-
... WHO THE HECK IS THAT BEHIND YOU?
!!
!!
AH, IT'S MY SISTER-
VICKY, YOU NEED SOMETHING?
I-I JUST, UH...
I WANTED TO ASK IF I COULD GO TO SCHOOL TOMORROW?
THERE'S A CLUB THAT'S OFFERING EXTRA CREDIT FOR VOLUNTEER WORK... AND STUFF.
OH YEAH, SURE. YOU NEED A RIDE?

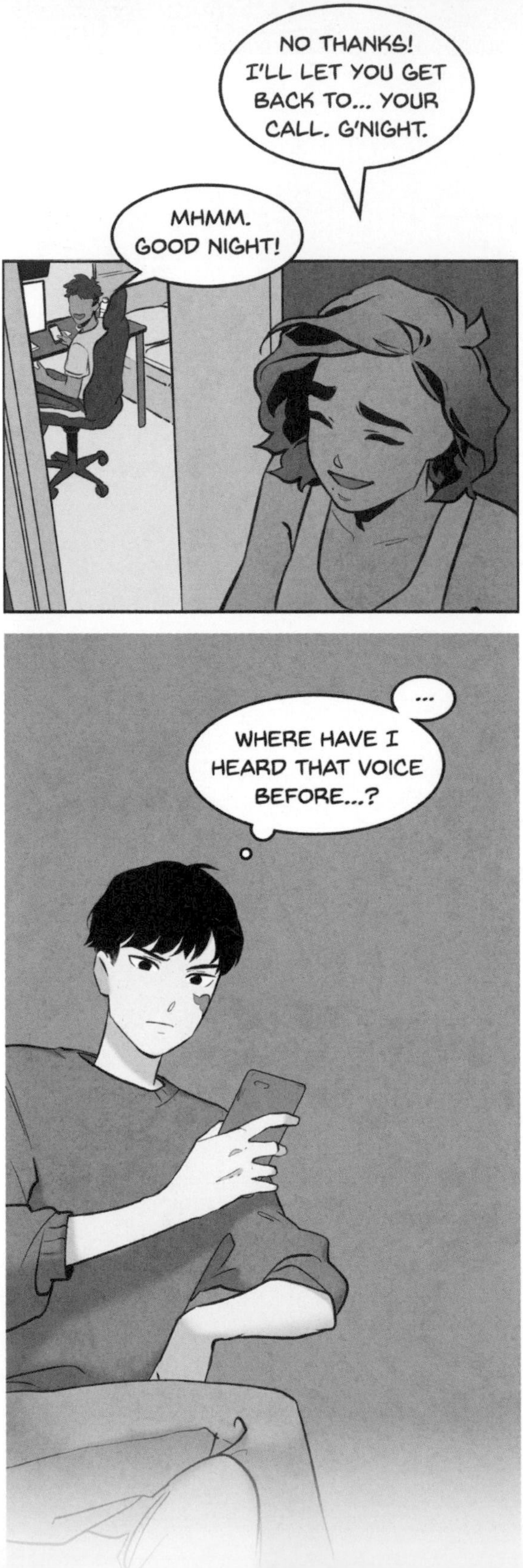
NO THANKS! I'LL LET YOU GET BACK TO... YOUR CALL. G'NIGHT.
MHMM. GOOD NIGHT!
...
WHERE HAVE I HEARD THAT VOICE BEFORE...?

CHAPTER 6: A PROMISE

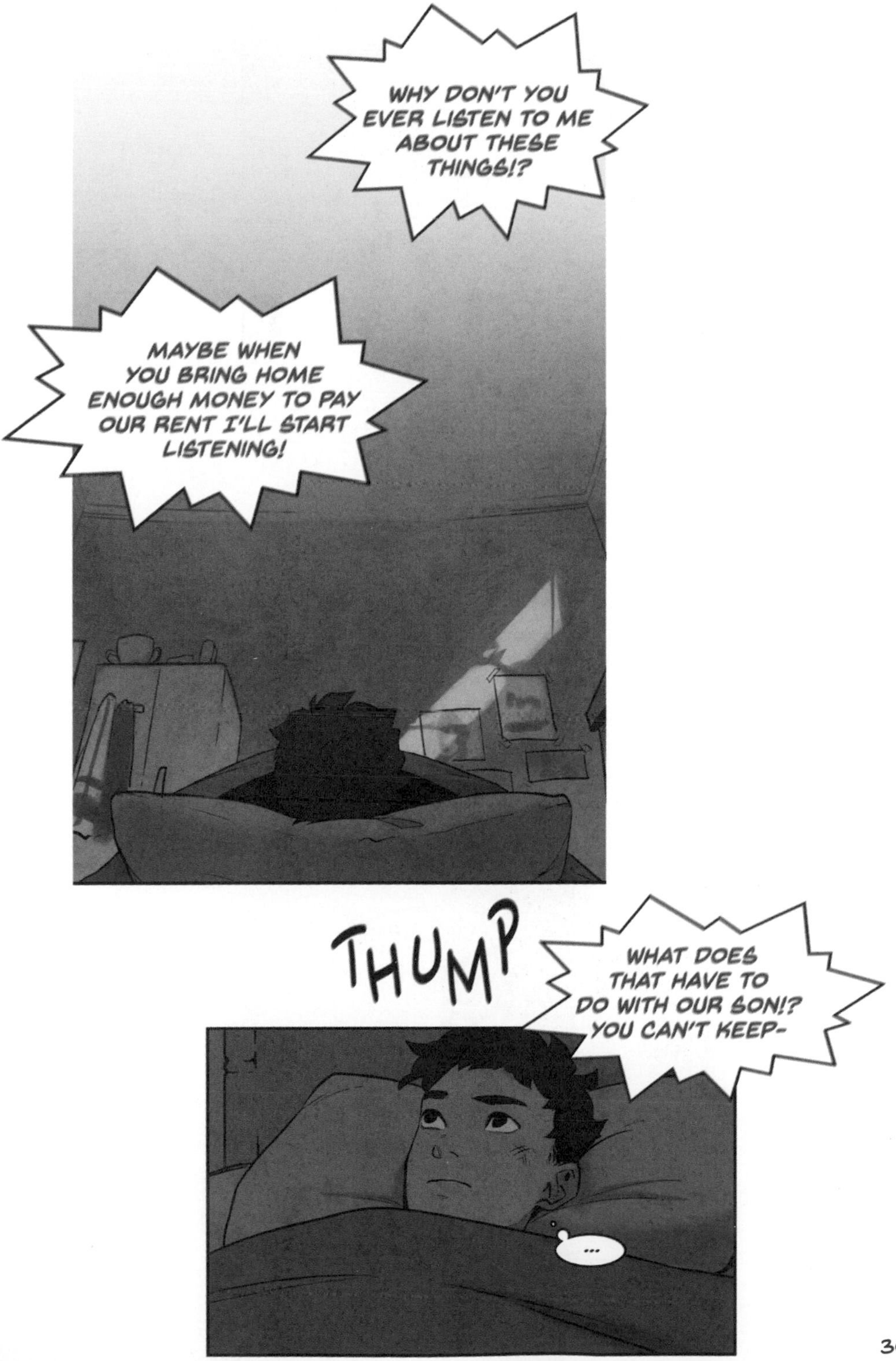
WHY DON'T YOU EVER LISTEN TO ME ABOUT THESE THINGS!?
MAYBE WHEN YOU BRING HOME ENOUGH MONEY TO PAY OUR RENT I'LL START LISTENING!
THUMP
WHAT DOES THAT HAVE TO DO WITH OUR SON!? YOU CAN'T KEEP-
...

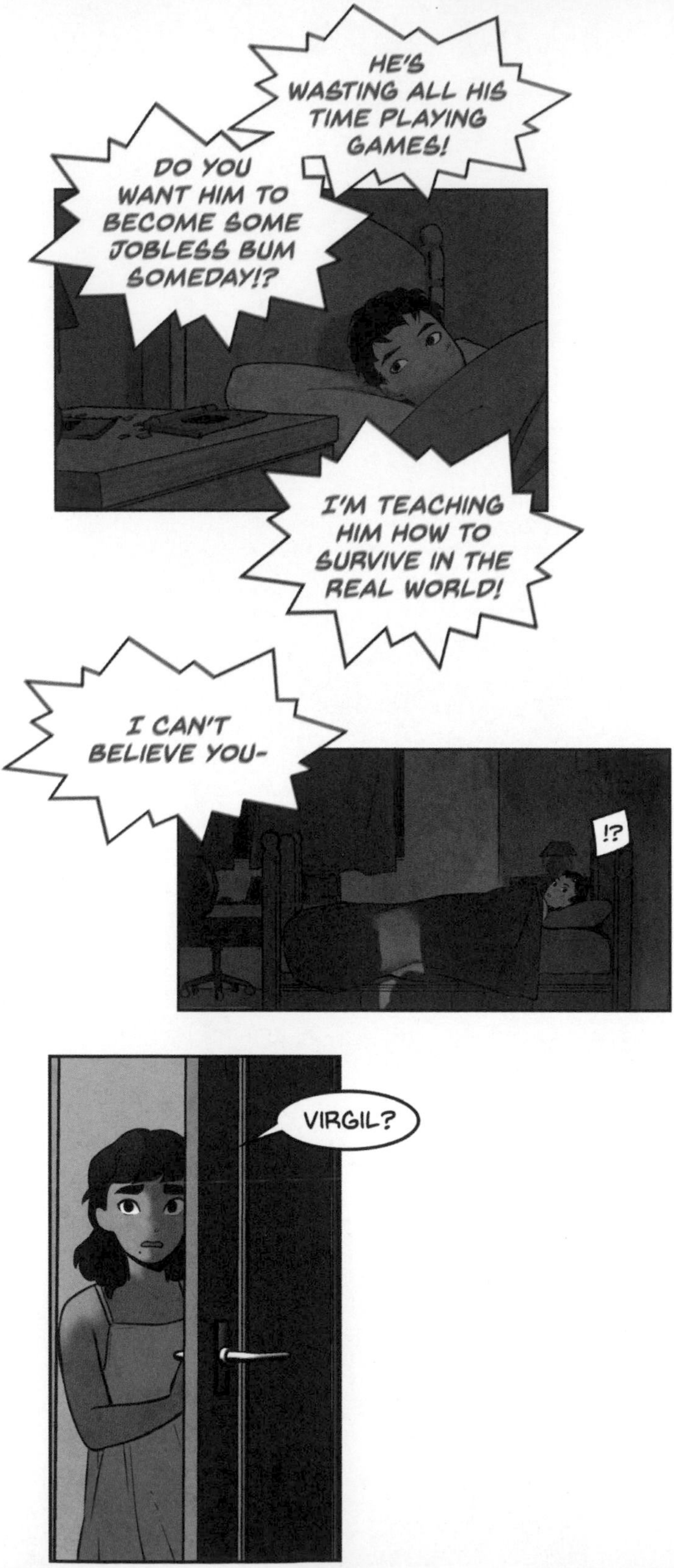
DO YOU WANT HIM TO BECOME SOME JOBLESS BUM SOMEDAY!?
HE'S WASTING ALL HIS TIME PLAYING GAMES!
I'M TEACHING HIM HOW TO SURVIVE IN THE REAL WORLD!
I CAN'T BELIEVE YOU-
!?
VIRGIL?

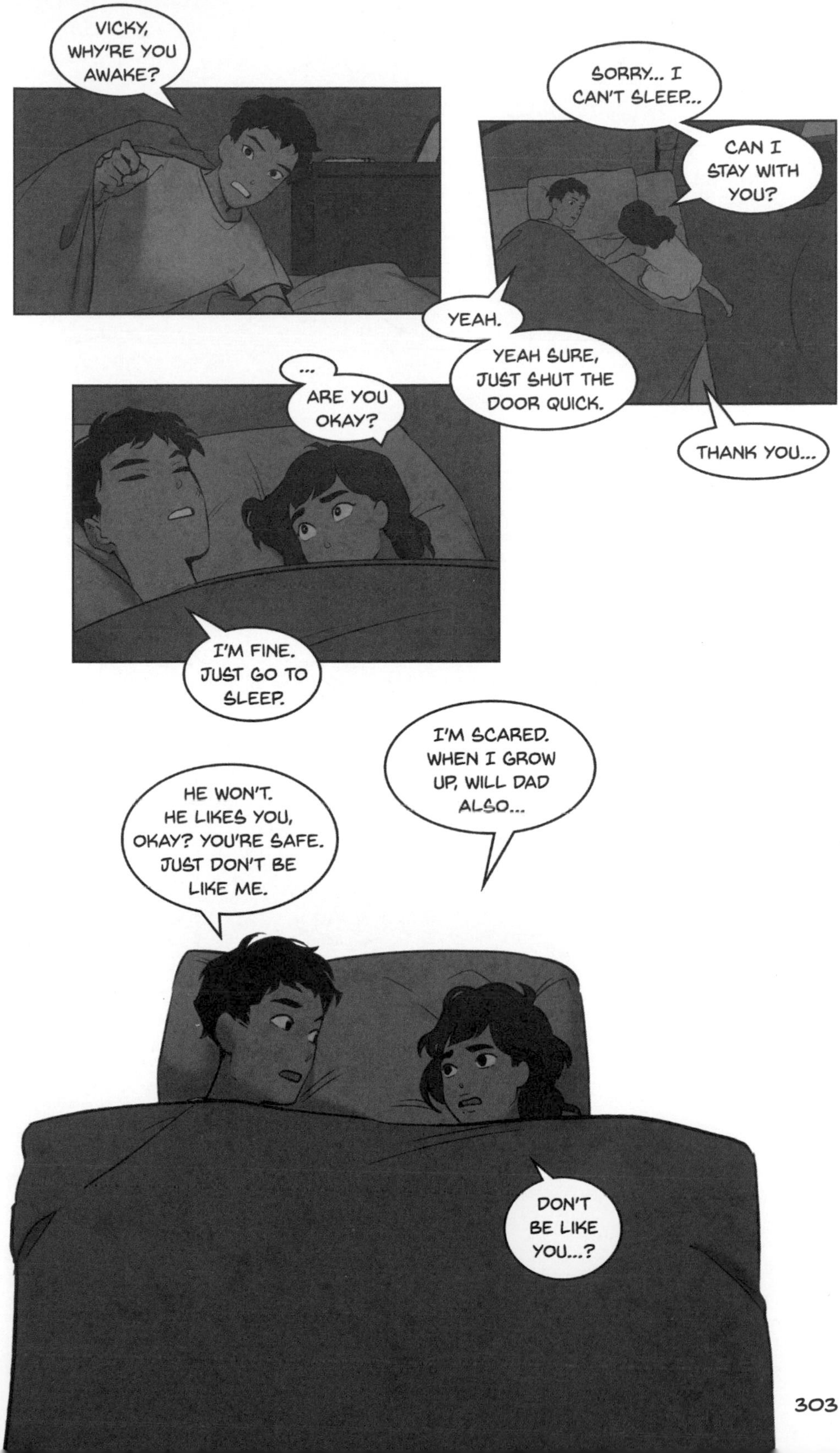
VICKY, WHY'RE YOU AWAKE?
SORRY... I CAN'T SLEEP...
CAN I STAY WITH YOU?
YEAH.
YEAH SURE, JUST SHUT THE DOOR QUICK.
THANK YOU...
...
ARE YOU OKAY?
I'M FINE. JUST GO TO SLEEP.
I'M SCARED. WHEN I GROW UP, WILL DAD ALSO...
HE WON'T. HE LIKES YOU, OKAY? YOU'RE SAFE. JUST DON'T BE LIKE ME.
DON'T BE LIKE YOU...?

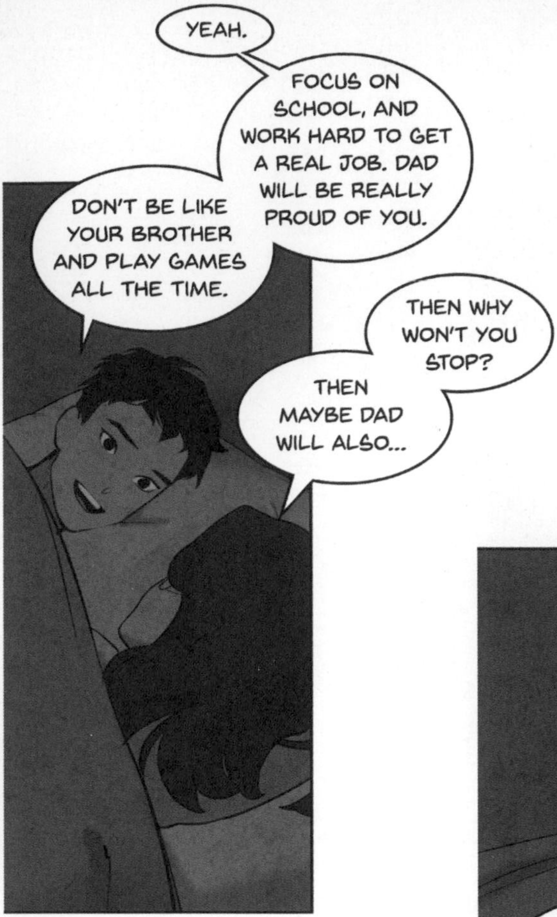
YEAH.
FOCUS ON SCHOOL, AND WORK HARD TO GET A REAL JOB. DAD WILL BE REALLY PROUD OF YOU.
DON'T BE LIKE YOUR BROTHER AND PLAY GAMES ALL THE TIME.
THEN WHY WON'T YOU STOP?
THEN MAYBE DAD WILL ALSO...

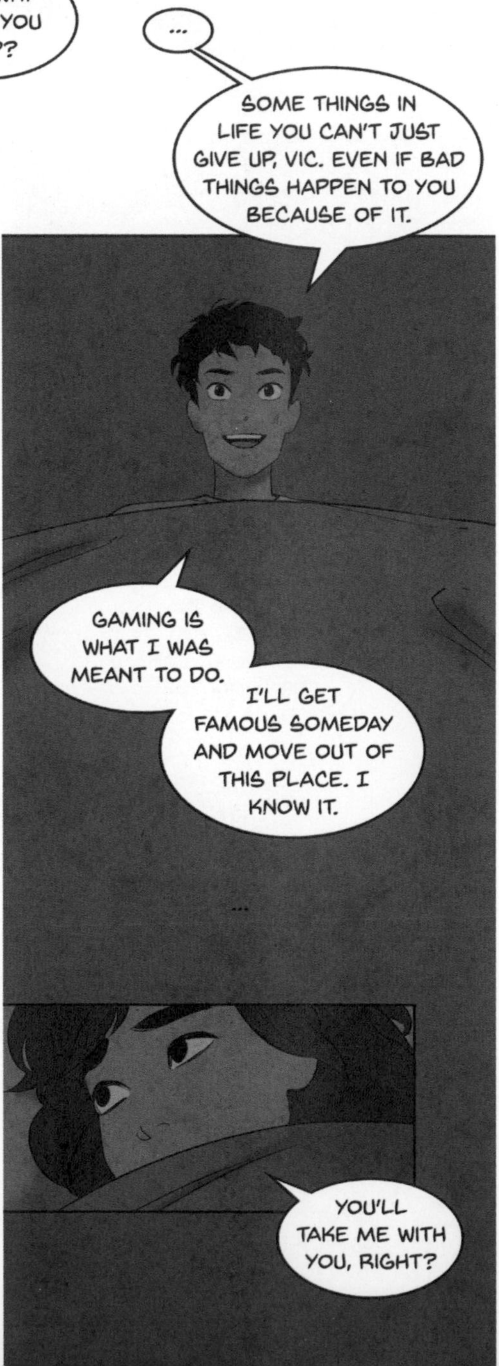
...
SOME THINGS IN LIFE YOU CAN'T JUST GIVE UP, VIC. EVEN IF BAD THINGS HAPPEN TO YOU BECAUSE OF IT.
GAMING IS WHAT I WAS MEANT TO DO.
I'LL GET FAMOUS SOMEDAY AND MOVE OUT OF THIS PLACE. I KNOW IT.
...
YOU'LL TAKE ME WITH YOU, RIGHT?

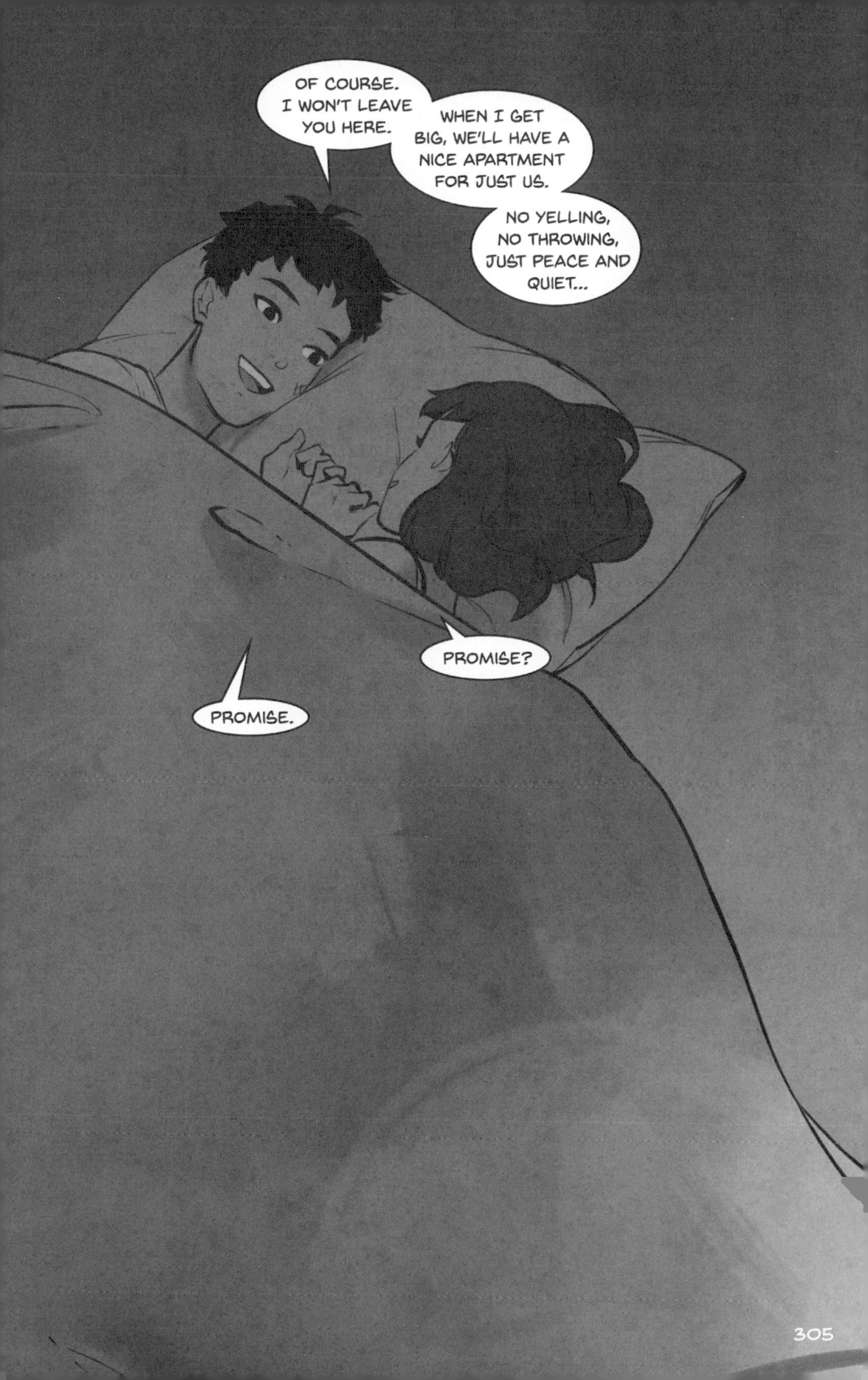
OF COURSE. I WON'T LEAVE YOU HERE.
WHEN I GET BIG, WE'LL HAVE A NICE APARTMENT FOR JUST US.
NO YELLING, NO THROWING, JUST PEACE AND QUIET...
PROMISE?
PROMISE.

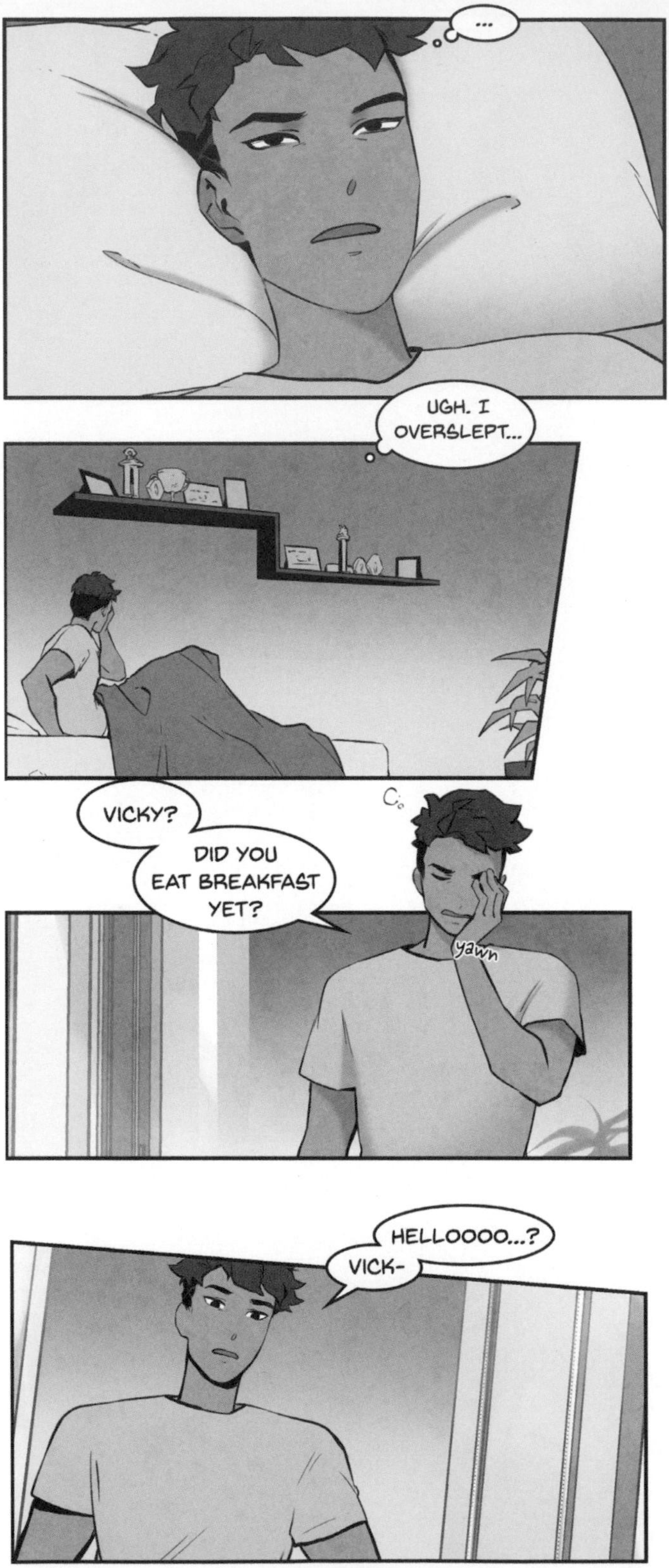
...
UGH. I OVERSLEPT...
VICKY?
DID YOU EAT BREAKFAST YET?
yawn
VICK-
HELLOOOO...?

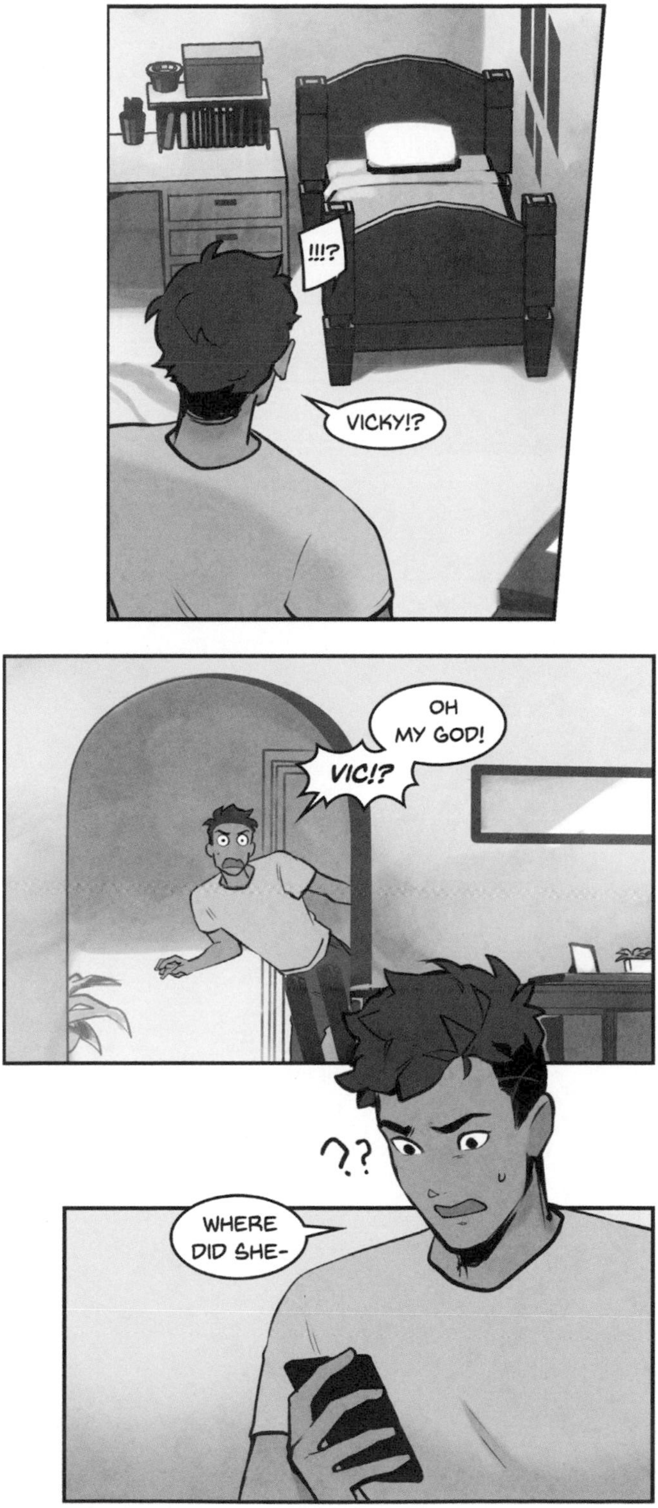
!!!?
VICKY!?
VIC!?
OH MY GOD!
??
WHERE DID SHE-

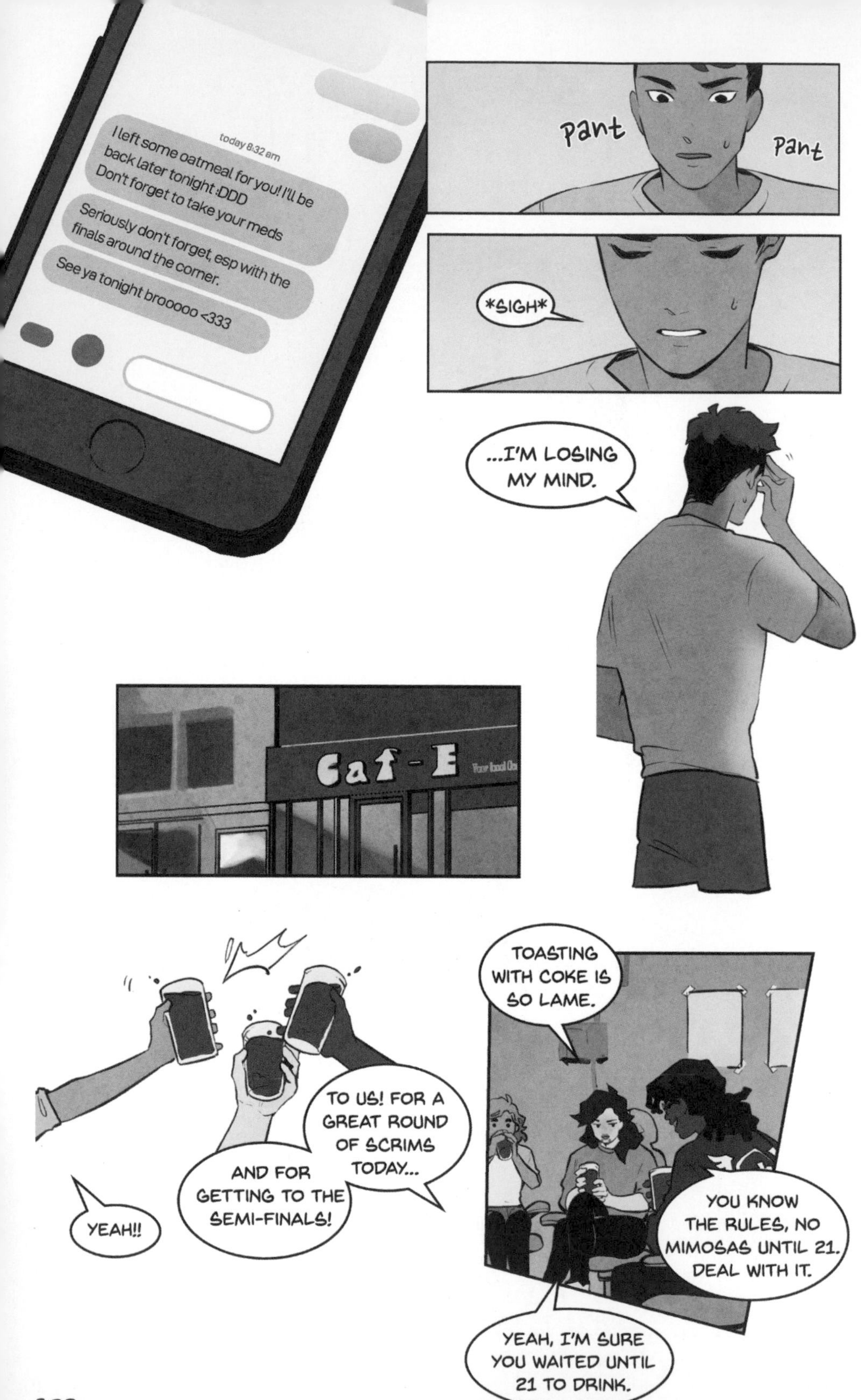
today 8:32 am
I left some oatmeal for you! I'll be back later tonight :DDD
Don't forget to take your meds
Seriously don't forget, esp with the finals around the corner.
See ya tonight brooooo <333
pant
pant
SIGH
...I'M LOSING MY MIND.
Caf-E
TO US! FOR A GREAT ROUND OF SCRIMS TODAY...
AND FOR GETTING TO THE SEMI-FINALS!
YEAH!!
TOASTING WITH COKE IS SO LAME.
YOU KNOW THE RULES, NO MIMOSAS UNTIL 21. DEAL WITH IT.
YEAH, I'M SURE YOU WAITED UNTIL 21 TO DRINK.

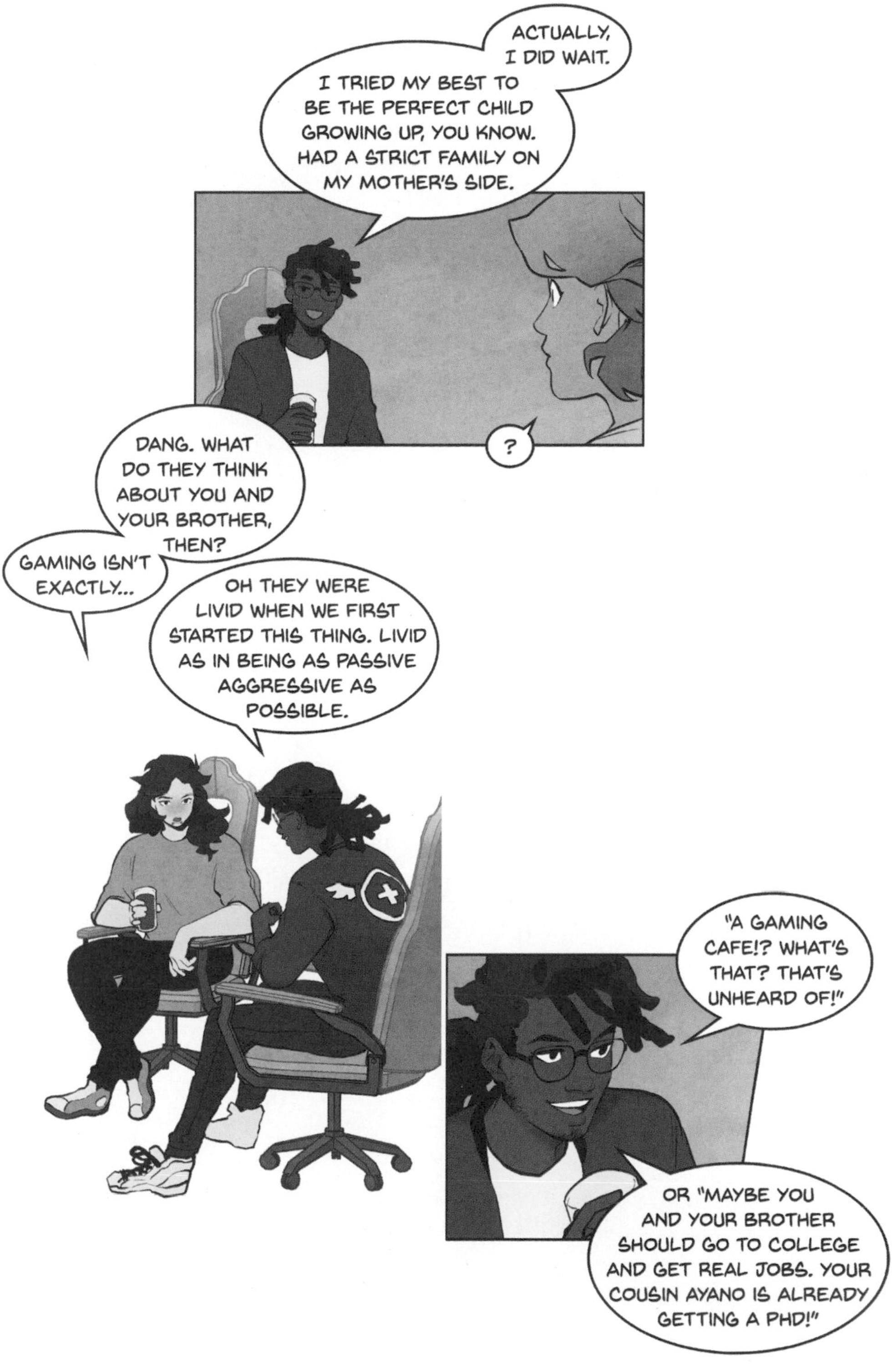
ACTUALLY, I DID WAIT.
I TRIED MY BEST TO BE THE PERFECT CHILD GROWING UP, YOU KNOW. HAD A STRICT FAMILY ON MY MOTHER'S SIDE.
?
DANG. WHAT DO THEY THINK ABOUT YOU AND YOUR BROTHER, THEN?
GAMING ISN'T EXACTLY...
OH THEY WERE LIVID WHEN WE FIRST STARTED THIS THING. LIVID AS IN BEING AS PASSIVE AGGRESSIVE AS POSSIBLE.
"A GAMING CAFE!? WHAT'S THAT? THAT'S UNHEARD OF!"
OR "MAYBE YOU AND YOUR BROTHER SHOULD GO TO COLLEGE AND GET REAL JOBS. YOUR COUSIN AYANO IS ALREADY GETTING A PHD!"

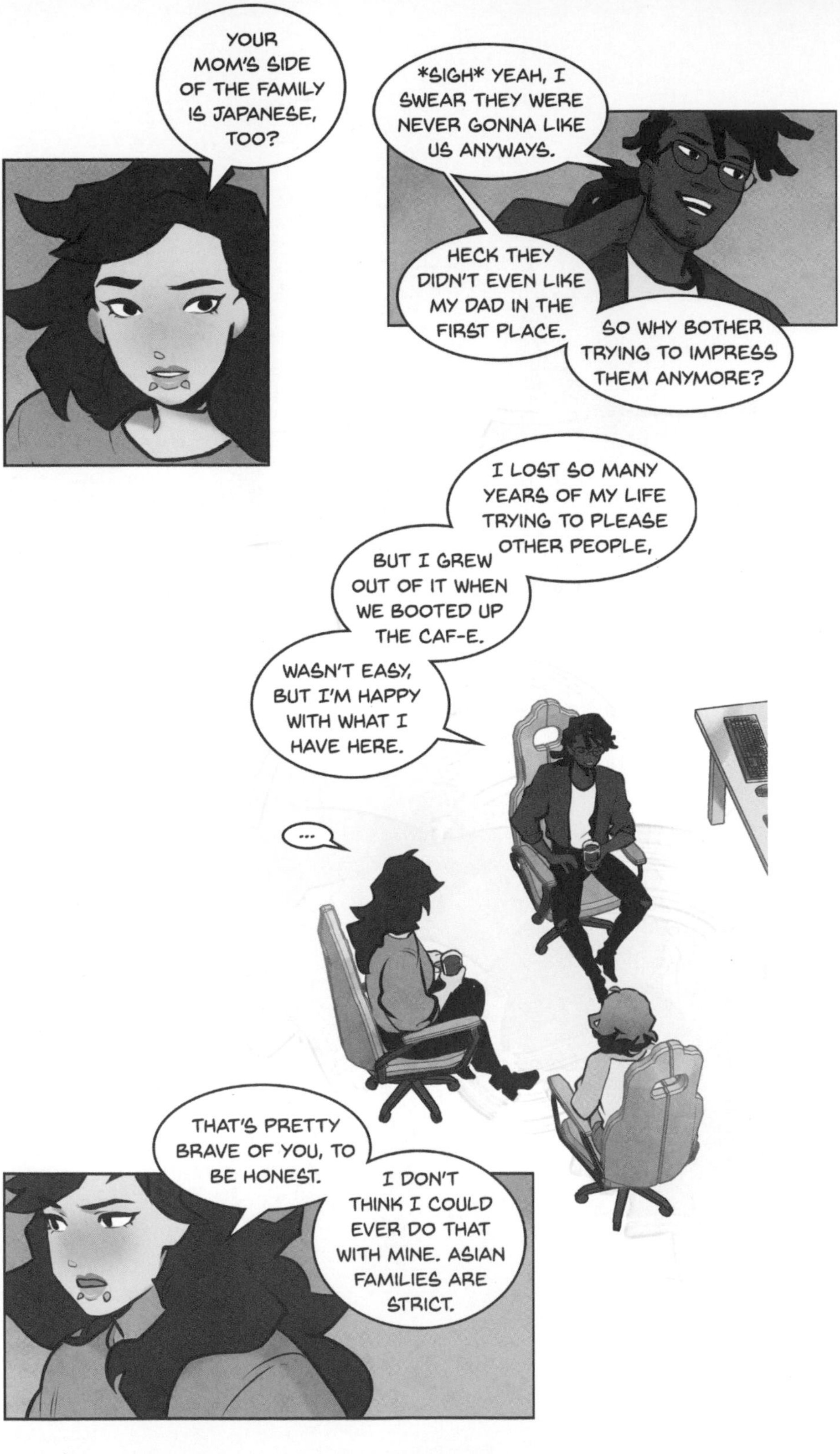
YOUR MOM'S SIDE OF THE FAMILY IS JAPANESE, TOO?
SIGH YEAH, I SWEAR THEY WERE NEVER GONNA LIKE US ANYWAYS.
HECK THEY DIDN'T EVEN LIKE MY DAD IN THE FIRST PLACE.
SO WHY BOTHER TRYING TO IMPRESS THEM ANYMORE?
I LOST SO MANY YEARS OF MY LIFE TRYING TO PLEASE OTHER PEOPLE,
BUT I GREW OUT OF IT WHEN WE BOOTED UP THE CAF-E.
WASN'T EASY, BUT I'M HAPPY WITH WHAT I HAVE HERE.
...
THAT'S PRETTY BRAVE OF YOU, TO BE HONEST.
I DON'T THINK I COULD EVER DO THAT WITH MINE. ASIAN FAMILIES ARE STRICT.

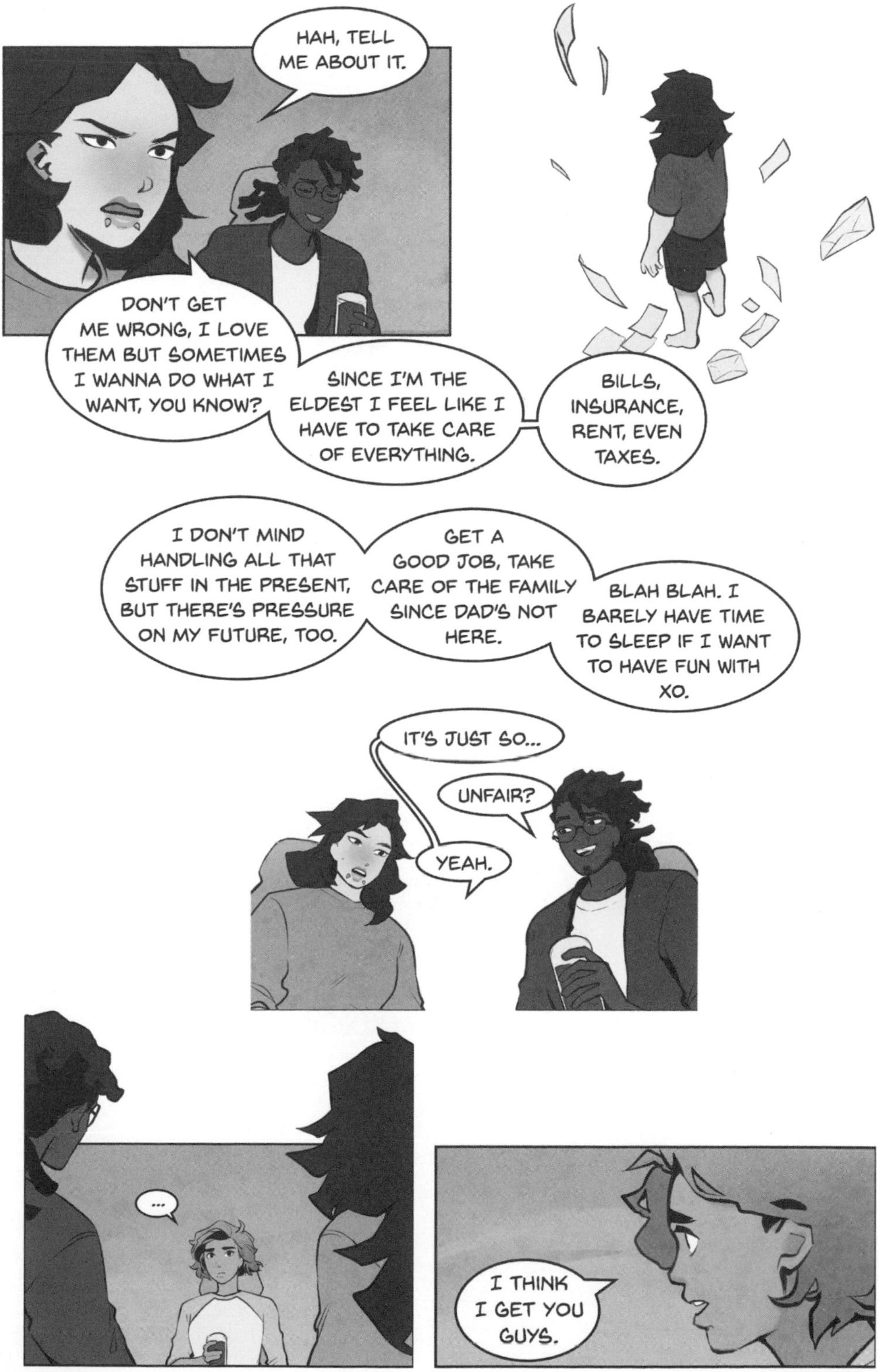
HAH, TELL ME ABOUT IT.
DON'T GET ME WRONG, I LOVE THEM BUT SOMETIMES I WANNA DO WHAT I WANT, YOU KNOW?
SINCE I'M THE ELDEST I FEEL LIKE I HAVE TO TAKE CARE OF EVERYTHING.
BILLS, INSURANCE, RENT, EVEN TAXES.
I DON'T MIND HANDLING ALL THAT STUFF IN THE PRESENT, BUT THERE'S PRESSURE ON MY FUTURE, TOO.
GET A GOOD JOB, TAKE CARE OF THE FAMILY SINCE DAD'S NOT HERE.
BLAH BLAH. I BARELY HAVE TIME TO SLEEP IF I WANT TO HAVE FUN WITH XO.
IT'S JUST SO...
UNFAIR?
YEAH.
...
I THINK I GET YOU GUYS.

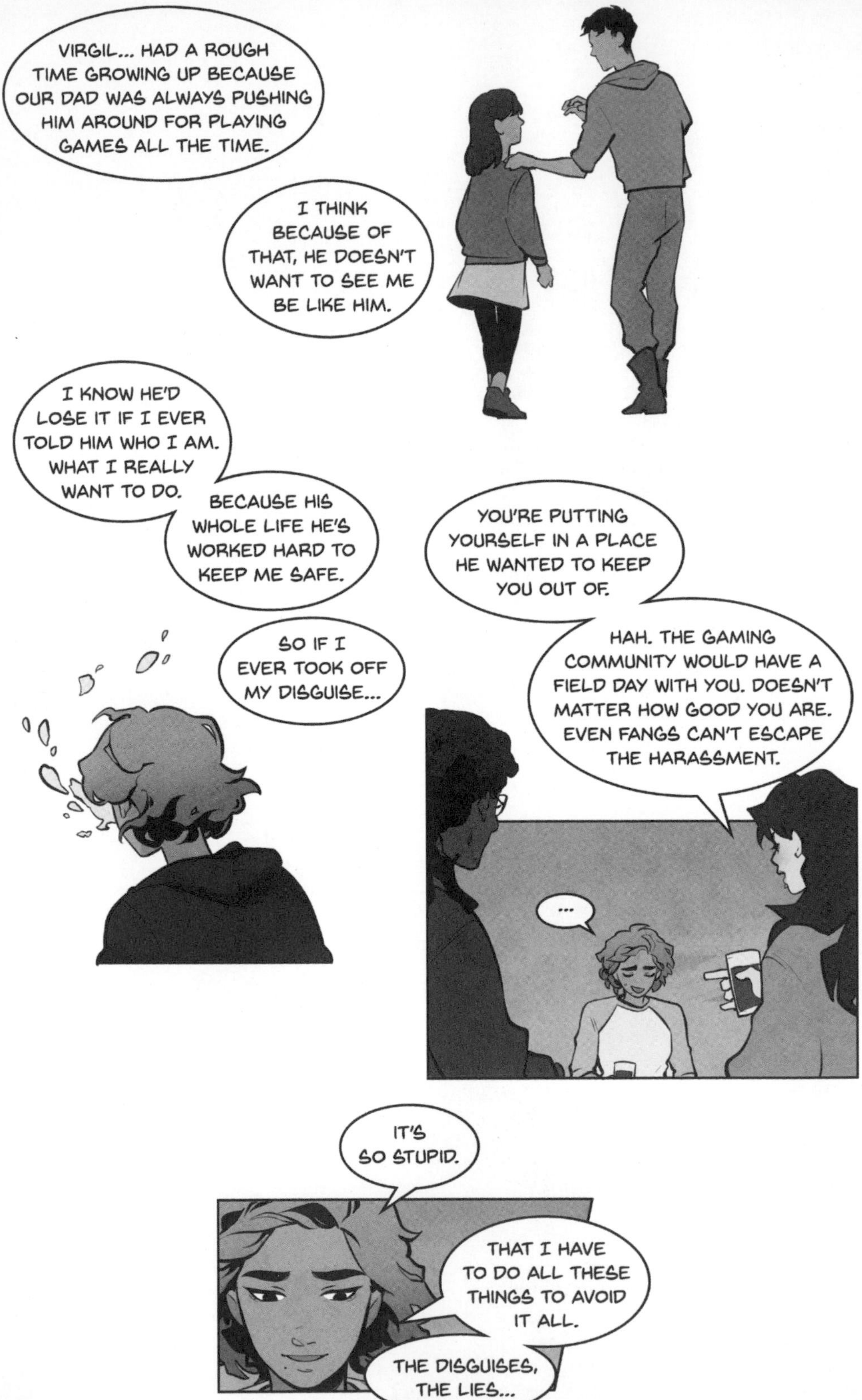
VIRGIL... HAD A ROUGH TIME GROWING UP BECAUSE OUR DAD WAS ALWAYS PUSHING HIM AROUND FOR PLAYING GAMES ALL THE TIME.
I THINK BECAUSE OF THAT, HE DOESN'T WANT TO SEE ME BE LIKE HIM.
I KNOW HE'D LOSE IT IF I EVER TOLD HIM WHO I AM. WHAT I REALLY WANT TO DO.
BECAUSE HIS WHOLE LIFE HE'S WORKED HARD TO KEEP ME SAFE.
SO IF I EVER TOOK OFF MY DISGUISE...
YOU'RE PUTTING YOURSELF IN A PLACE HE WANTED TO KEEP YOU OUT OF.
HAH. THE GAMING COMMUNITY WOULD HAVE A FIELD DAY WITH YOU. DOESN'T MATTER HOW GOOD YOU ARE. EVEN FANGS CAN'T ESCAPE THE HARASSMENT.
...
IT'S SO STUPID.
THAT I HAVE TO DO ALL THESE THINGS TO AVOID IT ALL.
THE DISGUISES, THE LIES...

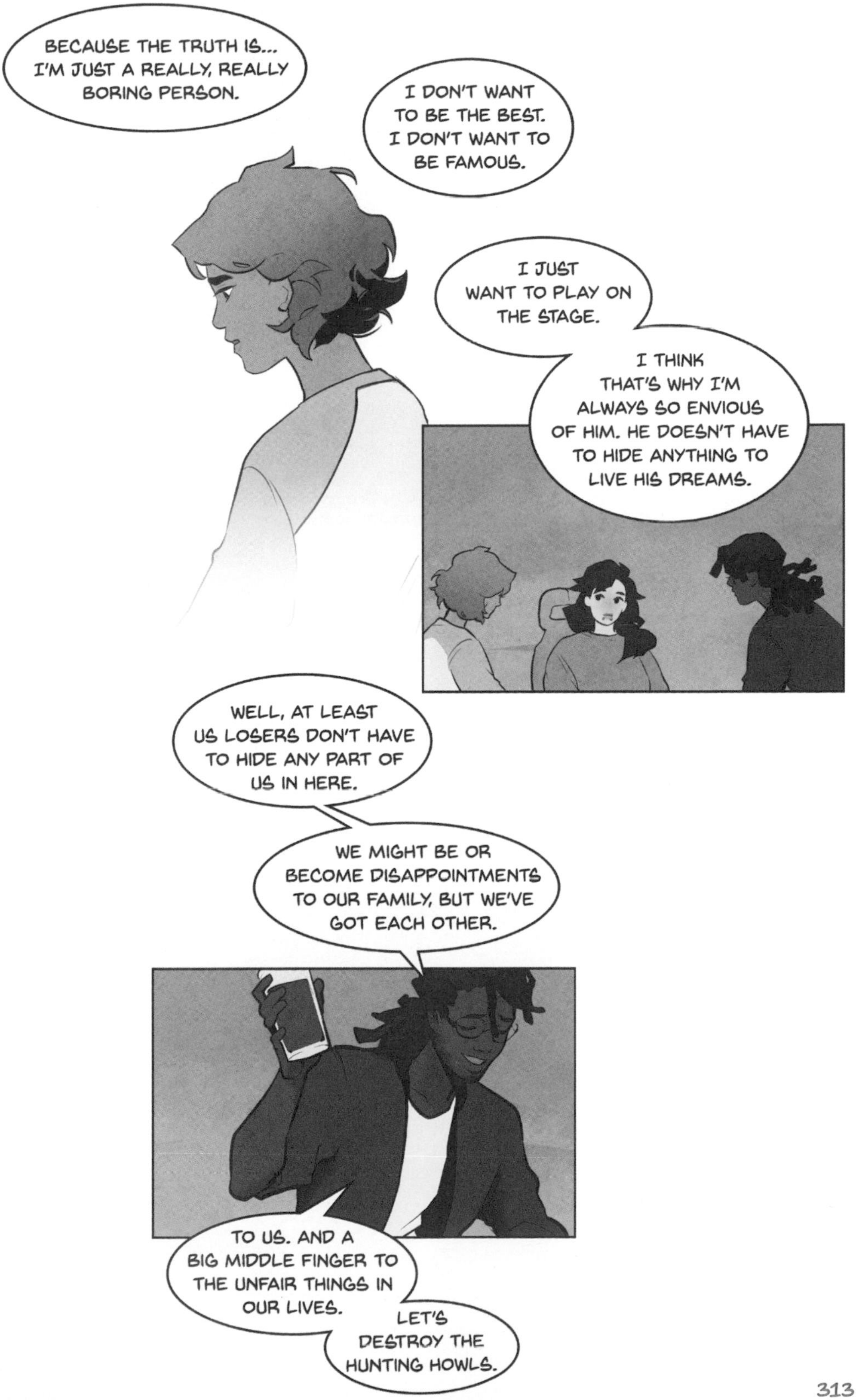
BECAUSE THE TRUTH IS... I'M JUST A REALLY, REALLY BORING PERSON.
I DON'T WANT TO BE THE BEST. I DON'T WANT TO BE FAMOUS.
I JUST WANT TO PLAY ON THE STAGE.
I THINK THAT'S WHY I'M ALWAYS SO ENVIOUS OF HIM. HE DOESN'T HAVE TO HIDE ANYTHING TO LIVE HIS DREAMS.
WELL, AT LEAST US LOSERS DON'T HAVE TO HIDE ANY PART OF US IN HERE.
WE MIGHT BE OR BECOME DISAPPOINTMENTS TO OUR FAMILY, BUT WE'VE GOT EACH OTHER.
TO US. AND A BIG MIDDLE FINGER TO THE UNFAIR THINGS IN OUR LIVES.
LET'S DESTROY THE HUNTING HOWLS.

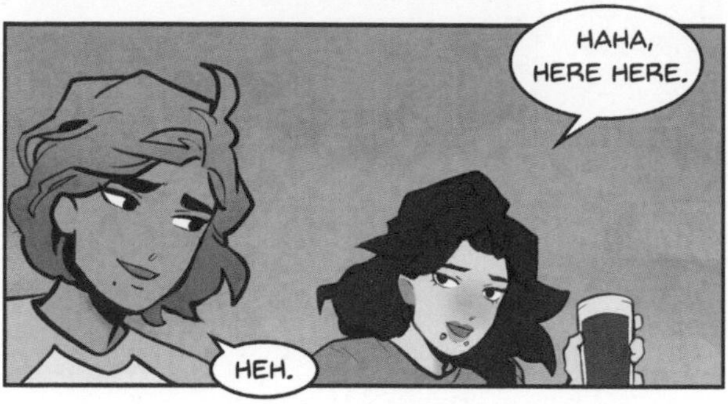
HAHA, HERE HERE.
HEH.

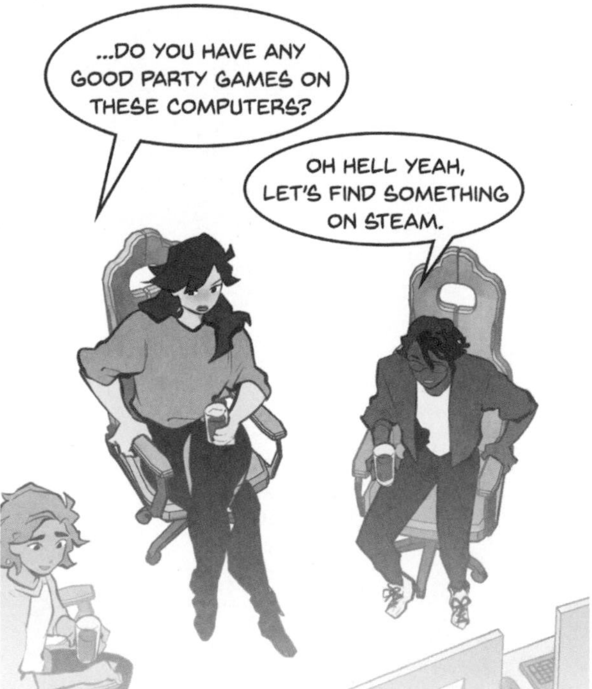
...DO YOU HAVE ANY GOOD PARTY GAMES ON THESE COMPUTERS?
OH HELL YEAH, LET'S FIND SOMETHING ON STEAM.

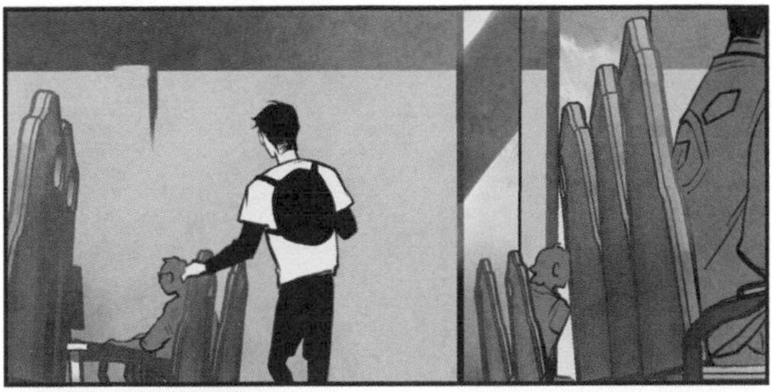

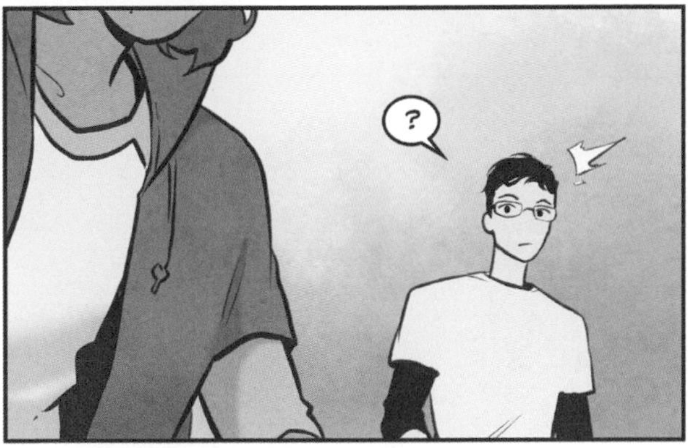
?

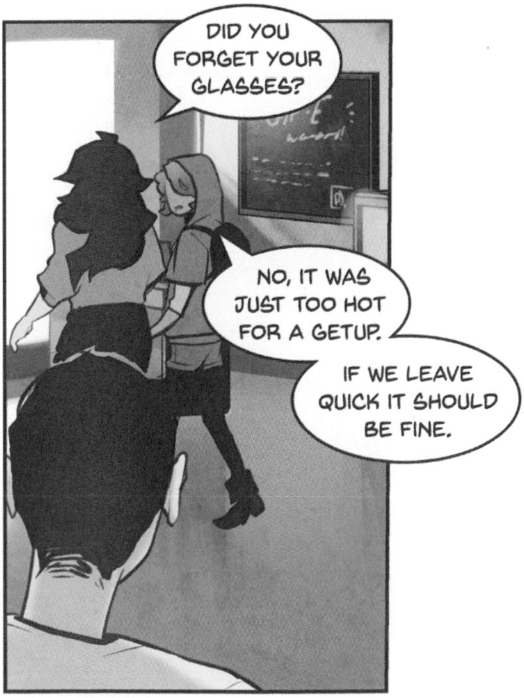
DID YOU FORGET YOUR GLASSES?
NO, IT WAS JUST TOO HOT FOR A GETUP.
IF WE LEAVE QUICK IT SHOULD BE FINE.

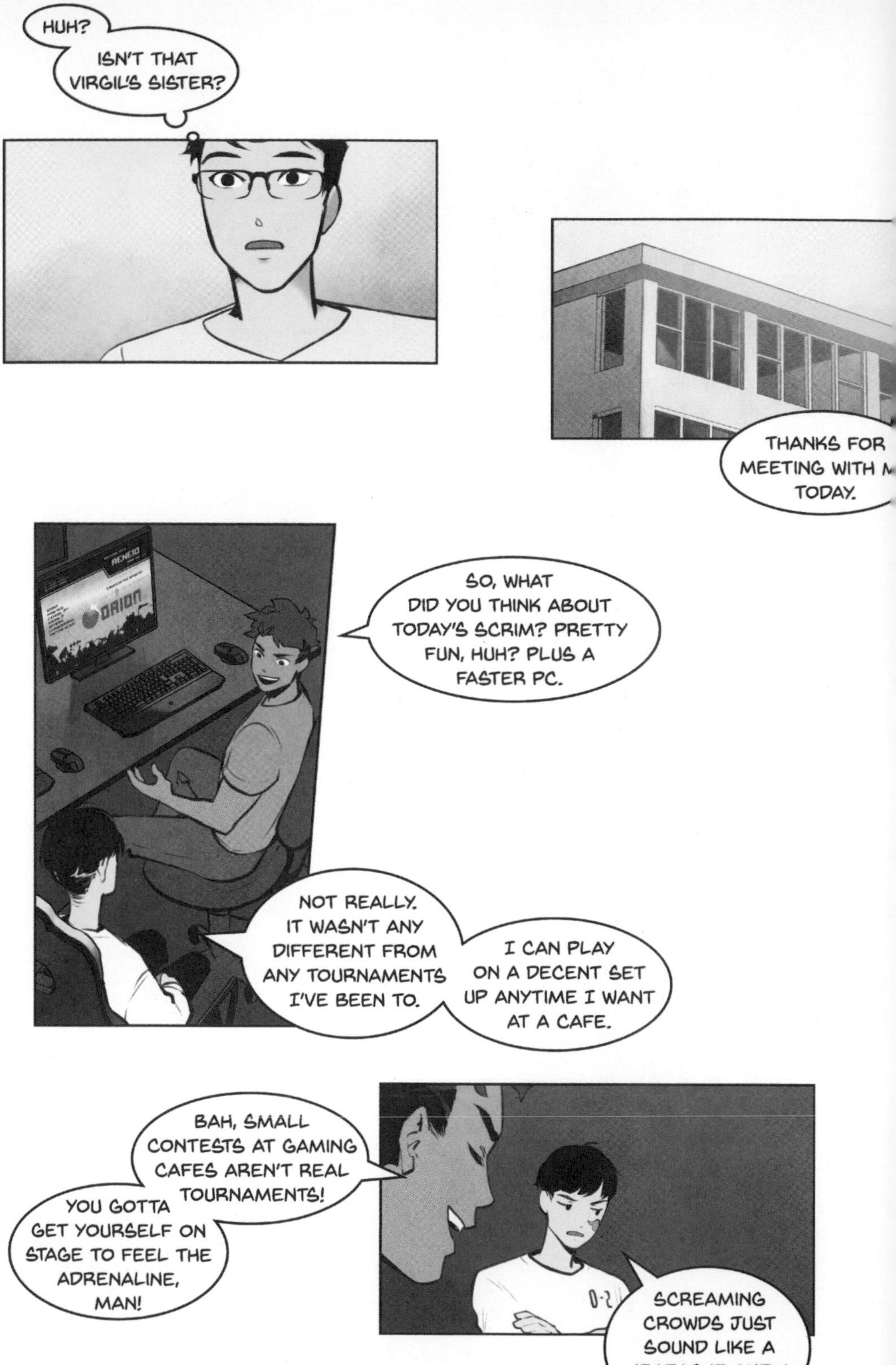
HUH? ISN'T THAT VIRGIL'S SISTER?
THANKS FOR MEETING WITH M
TODAY.
SO, WHAT DID YOU THINK ABOUT TODAY'S SCRIM? PRETTY FUN, HUH? PLUS A FASTER PC.
NOT REALLY. IT WASN'T ANY DIFFERENT FROM ANY TOURNAMENTS I'VE BEEN TO.
I CAN PLAY ON A DECENT SET UP ANYTIME I WANT AT A CAFE.
BAH, SMALL CONTESTS AT GAMING CAFES AREN'T REAL TOURNAMENTS!
YOU GOTTA GET YOURSELF ON STAGE TO FEEL THE ADRENALINE, MAN!
SCREAMING CROWDS JUST SOUND LIKE A HEADACHE AND A DISTRACTION.

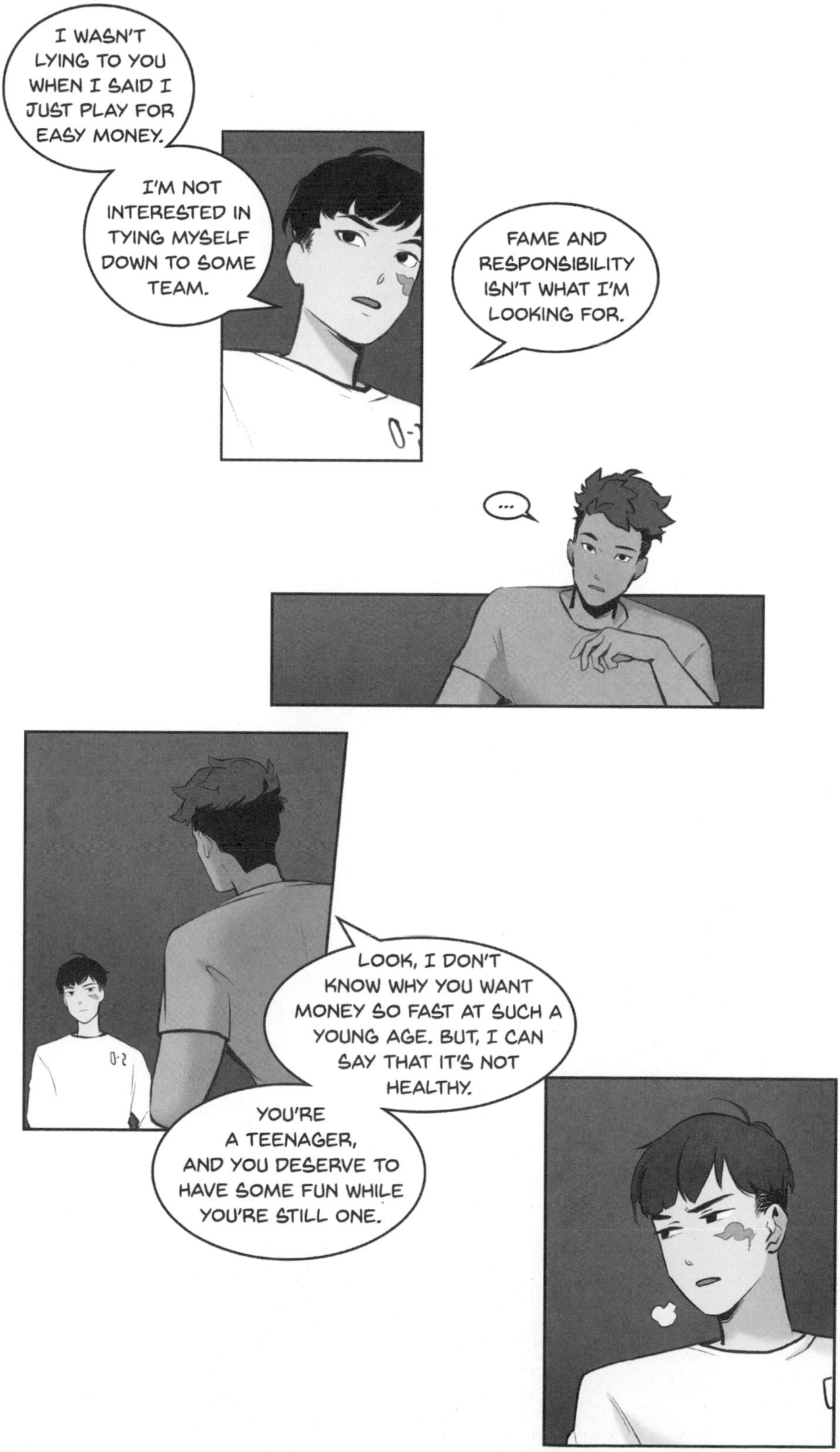
I WASN'T LYING TO YOU WHEN I SAID I JUST PLAY FOR EASY MONEY.
I'M NOT INTERESTED IN TYING MYSELF DOWN TO SOME TEAM.
FAME AND RESPONSIBILITY ISN'T WHAT I'M LOOKING FOR.
...
LOOK, I DON'T KNOW WHY YOU WANT MONEY SO FAST AT SUCH A YOUNG AGE. BUT, I CAN SAY THAT IT'S NOT HEALTHY.
YOU'RE A TEENAGER, AND YOU DESERVE TO HAVE SOME FUN WHILE YOU'RE STILL ONE.

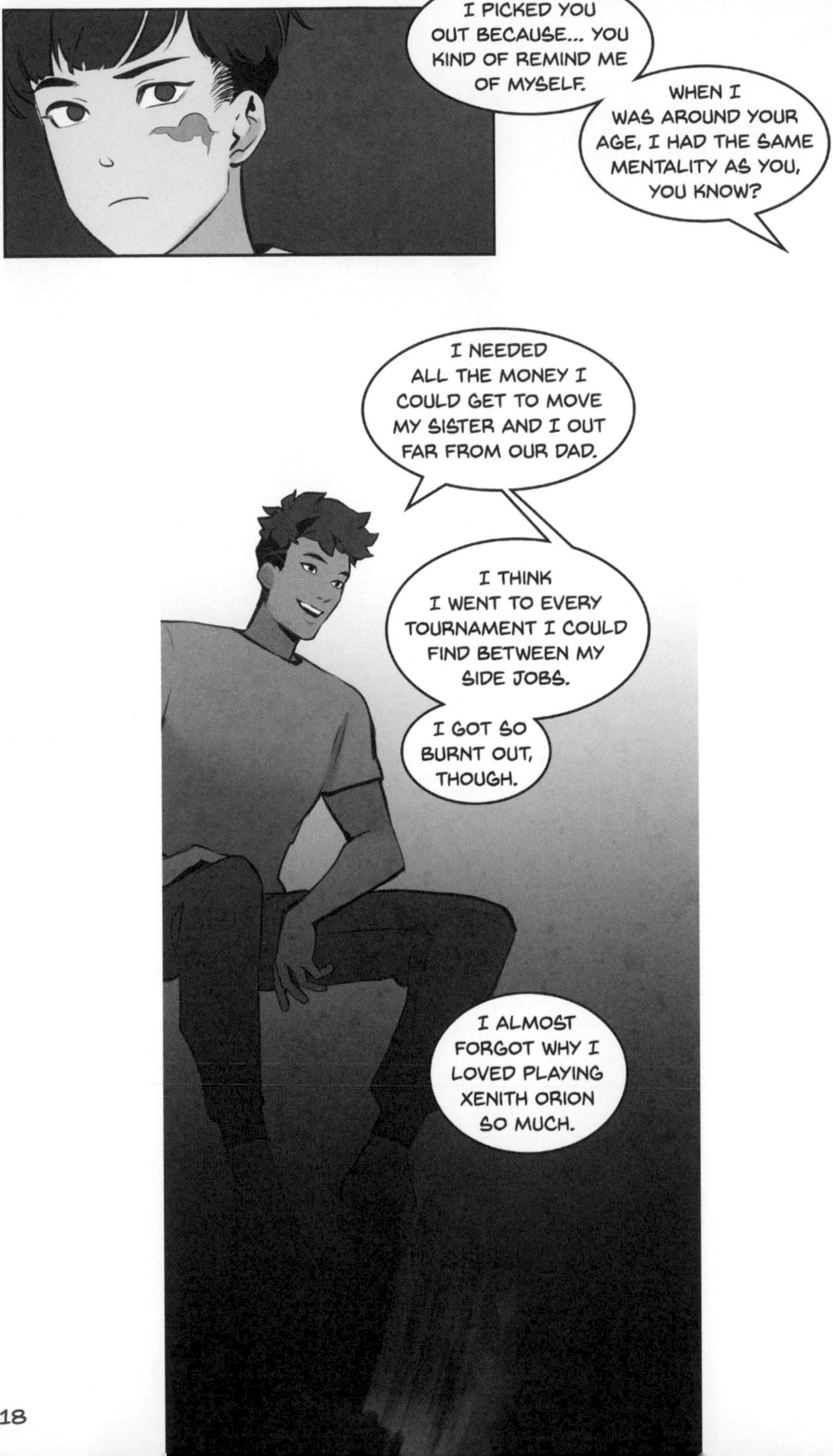
I PICKED YOU OUT BECAUSE... YOU KIND OF REMIND ME OF MYSELF.
WHEN I WAS AROUND YOUR AGE, I HAD THE SAME MENTALITY AS YOU, YOU KNOW?
I NEEDED ALL THE MONEY I COULD GET TO MOVE MY SISTER AND I OUT FAR FROM OUR DAD.
I THINK I WENT TO EVERY TOURNAMENT I COULD FIND BETWEEN MY SIDE JOBS.
I GOT SO BURNT OUT, THOUGH.
I ALMOST FORGOT WHY I LOVED PLAYING XENITH ORION SO MUCH.

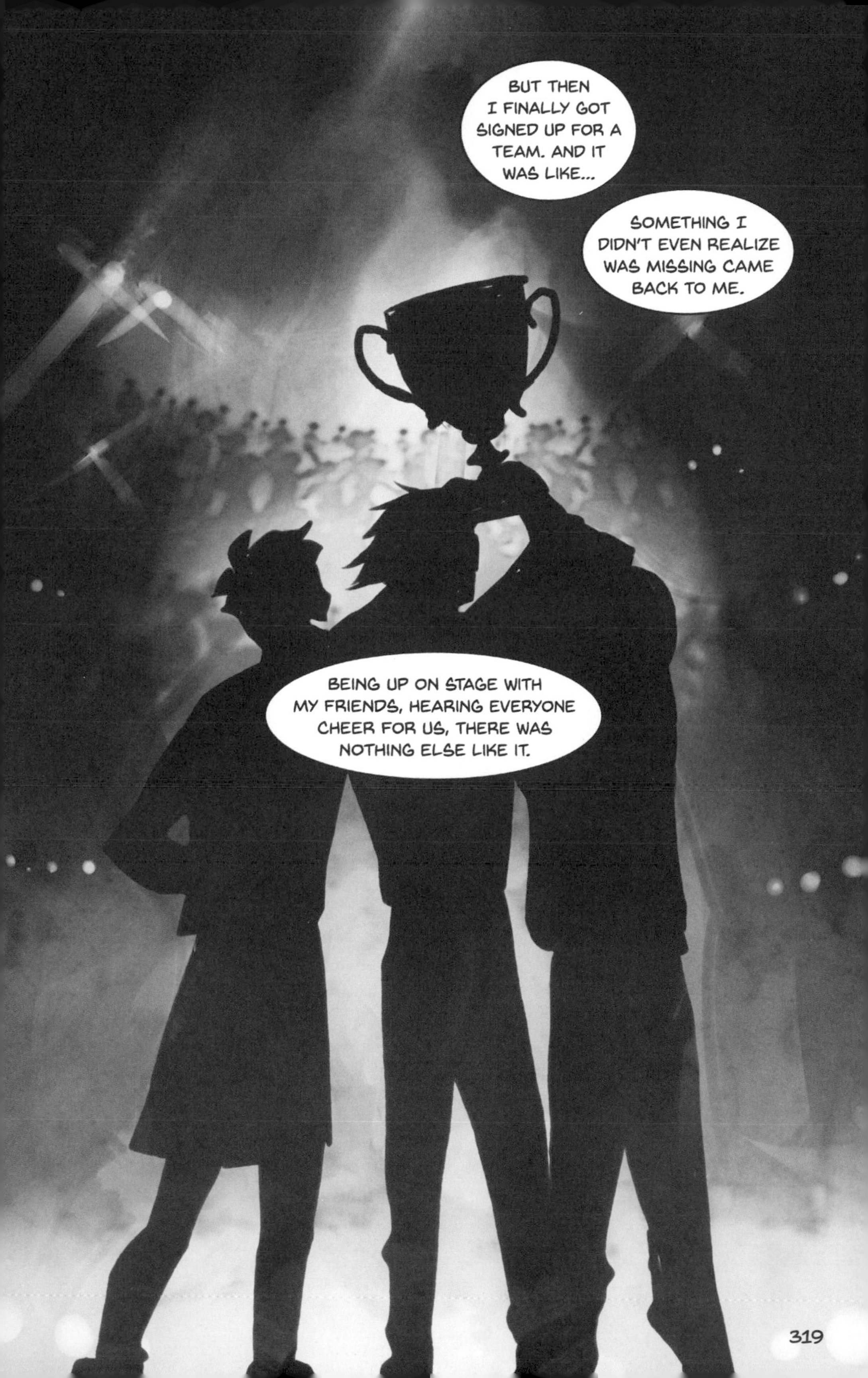
BUT THEN I FINALLY GOT SIGNED UP FOR A TEAM. AND IT WAS LIKE...
SOMETHING I DIDN'T EVEN REALIZE WAS MISSING CAME BACK TO ME.
BEING UP ON STAGE WITH MY FRIENDS, HEARING EVERYONE CHEER FOR US, THERE WAS NOTHING ELSE LIKE IT.

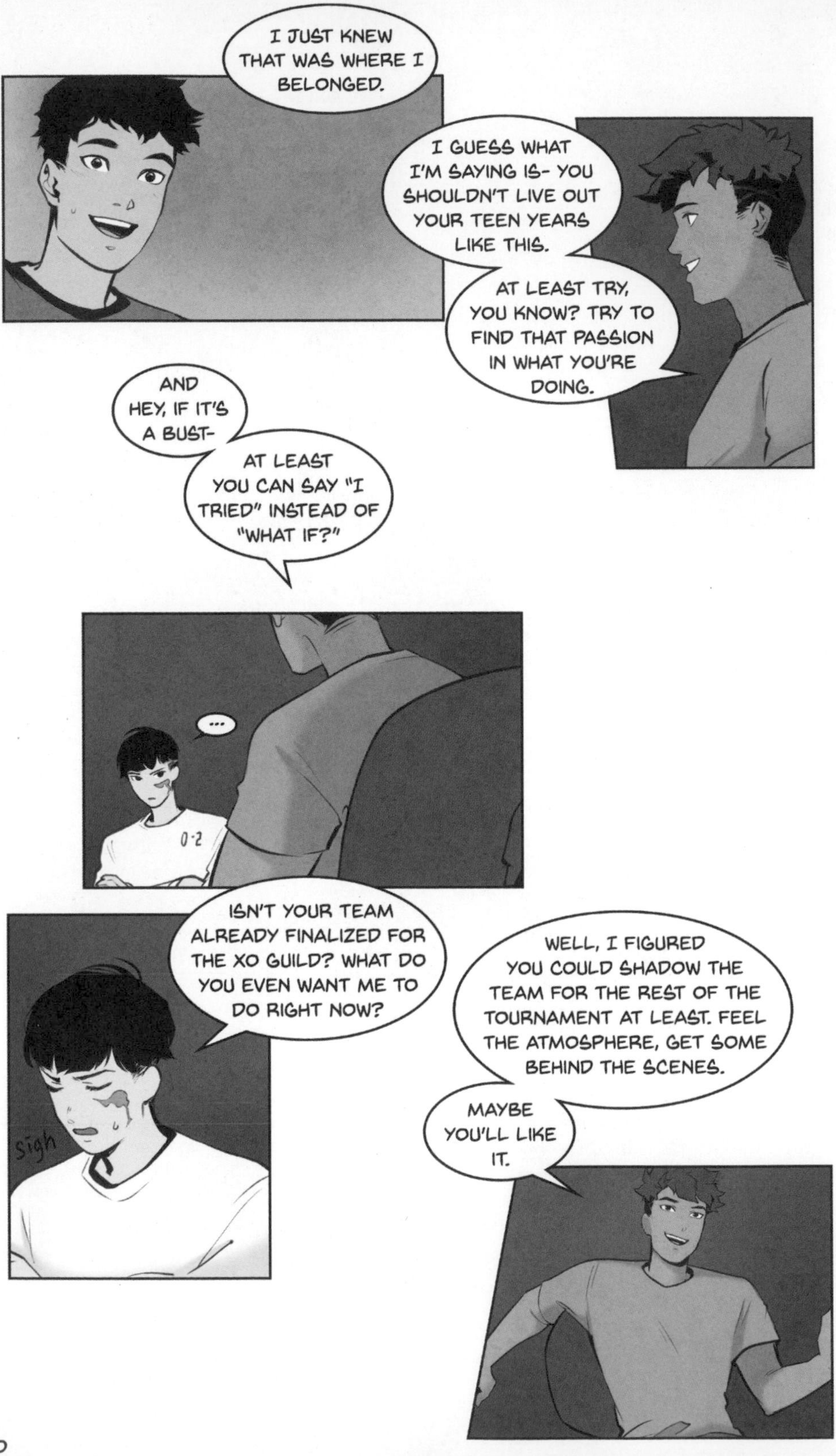
I JUST KNEW THAT WAS WHERE I BELONGED.
I GUESS WHAT I'M SAYING IS- YOU SHOULDN'T LIVE OUT YOUR TEEN YEARS LIKE THIS.
AT LEAST TRY, YOU KNOW? TRY TO FIND THAT PASSION IN WHAT YOU'RE DOING.
AND HEY, IF IT'S A BUST-
AT LEAST YOU CAN SAY "I TRIED" INSTEAD OF "WHAT IF?"
...
0·2
ISN'T YOUR TEAM ALREADY FINALIZED FOR THE XO GUILD? WHAT DO YOU EVEN WANT ME TO DO RIGHT NOW?
sigh
WELL, I FIGURED YOU COULD SHADOW THE TEAM FOR THE REST OF THE TOURNAMENT AT LEAST. FEEL THE ATMOSPHERE, GET SOME BEHIND THE SCENES.
MAYBE YOU'LL LIKE IT.

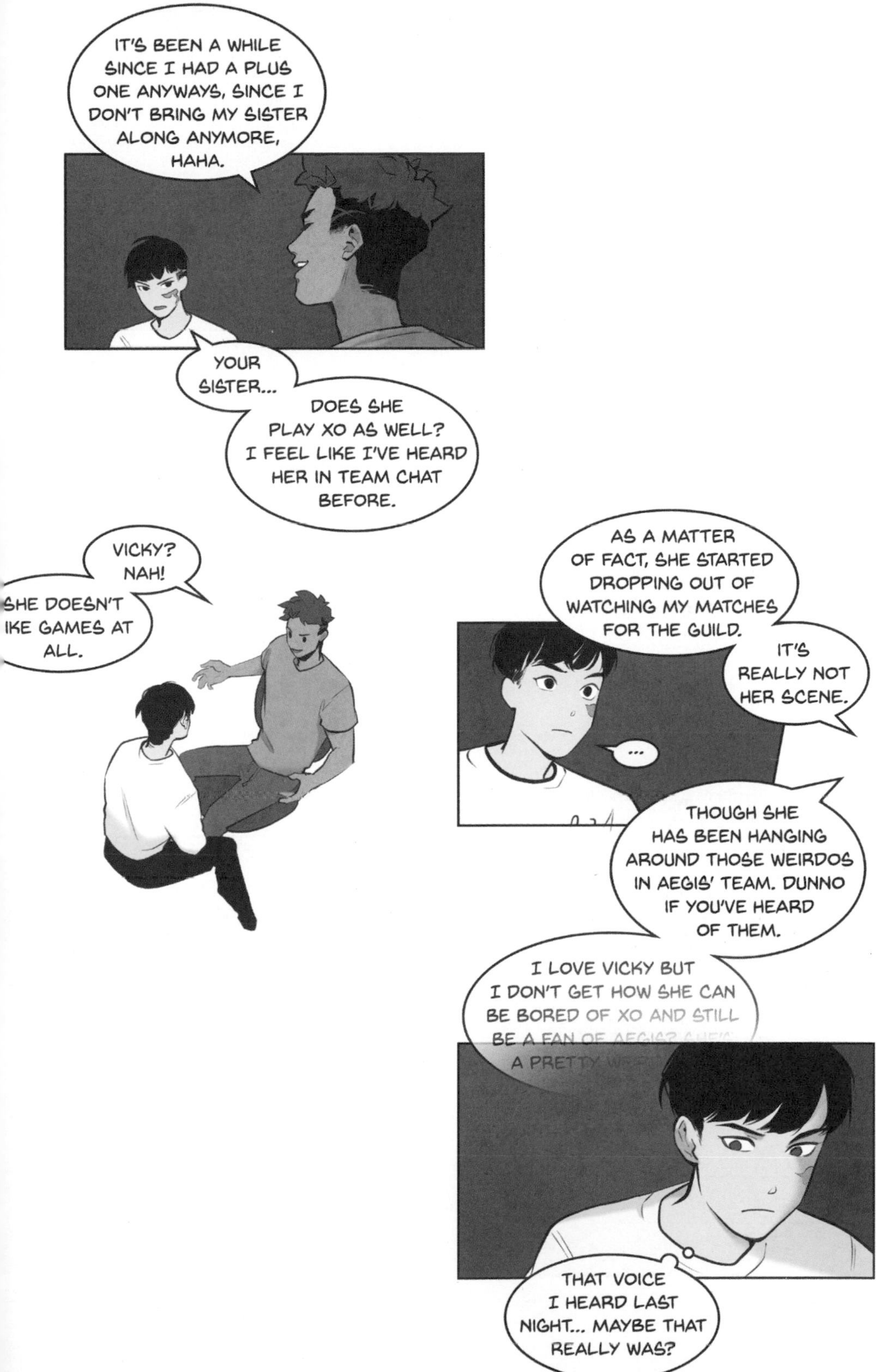
IT'S BEEN A WHILE SINCE I HAD A PLUS ONE ANYWAYS, SINCE I DON'T BRING MY SISTER ALONG ANYMORE, HAHA.
YOUR SISTER...
DOES SHE PLAY XO AS WELL? I FEEL LIKE I'VE HEARD HER IN TEAM CHAT BEFORE.
VICKY? NAH!
SHE DOESN'T IKE GAMES AT ALL.
AS A MATTER OF FACT, SHE STARTED DROPPING OUT OF WATCHING MY MATCHES FOR THE GUILD.
IT'S REALLY NOT HER SCENE.
...
THOUGH SHE HAS BEEN HANGING AROUND THOSE WEIRDOS IN AEGIS' TEAM. DUNNO IF YOU'VE HEARD OF THEM.
I LOVE VICKY BUT I DON'T GET HOW SHE CAN BE BORED OF XO AND STILL BE A FAN OF
THAT VOICE I HEARD LAST NIGHT... MAYBE THAT REALLY WAS?

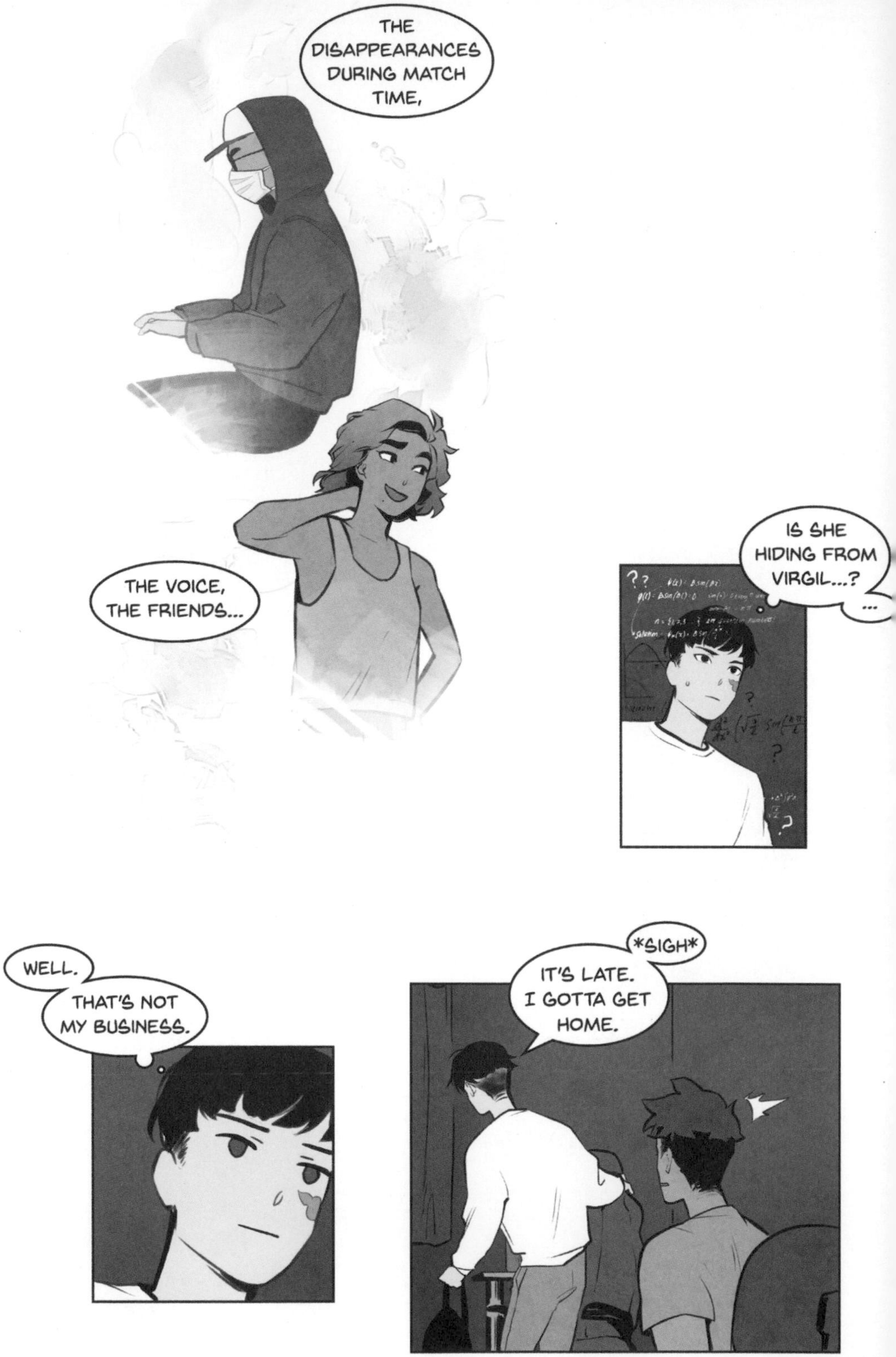
THE DISAPPEARANCES DURING MATCH TIME,
THE VOICE, THE FRIENDS...
IS SHE HIDING FROM VIRGIL...?
...
WELL.
THAT'S NOT MY BUSINESS.
SIGH
IT'S LATE. I GOTTA GET HOME.

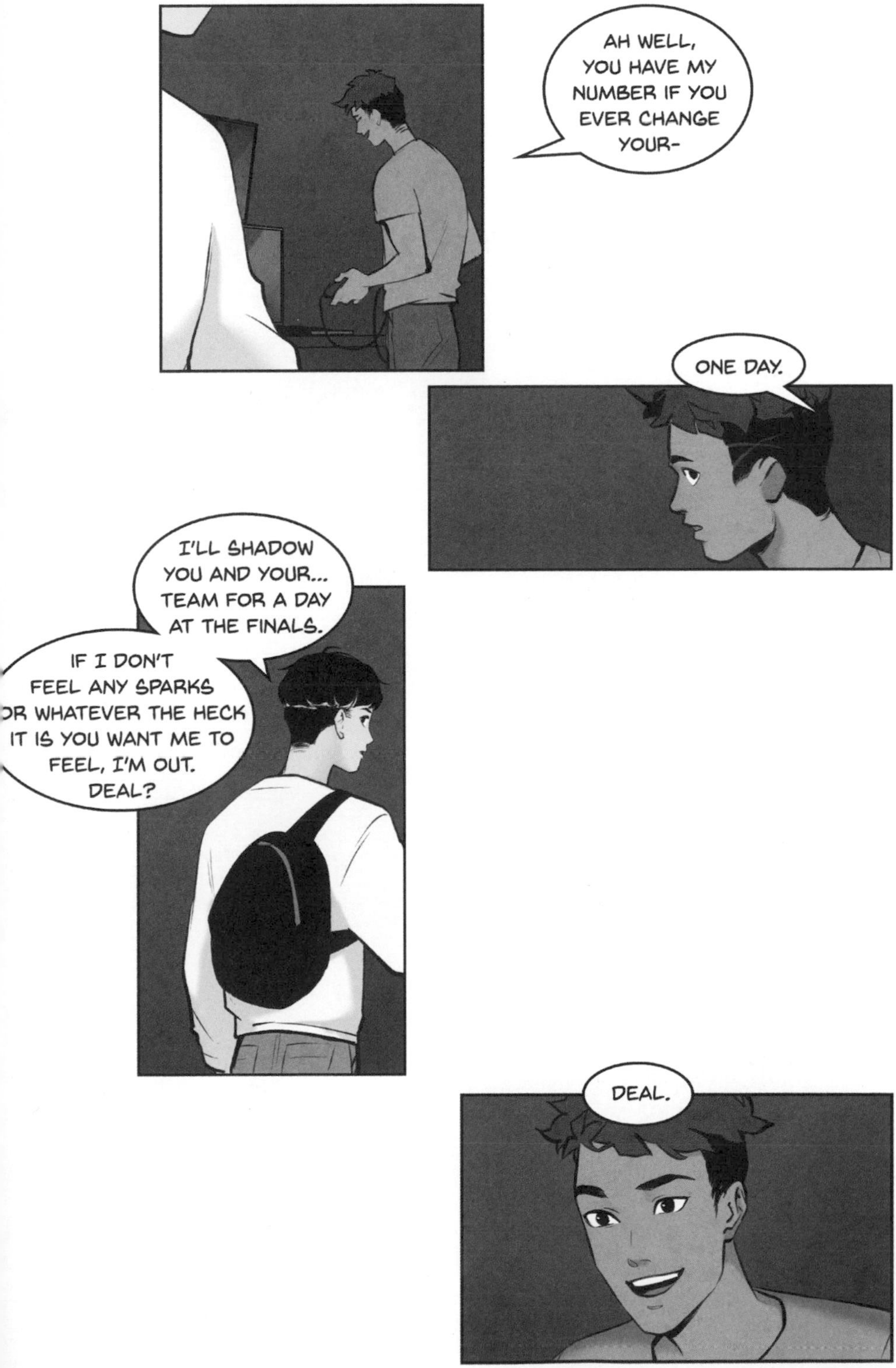
AH WELL, YOU HAVE MY NUMBER IF YOU EVER CHANGE YOUR-
ONE DAY.
I'LL SHADOW YOU AND YOUR... TEAM FOR A DAY AT THE FINALS.
IF I DON'T FEEL ANY SPARKS OR WHATEVER THE HECK IT IS YOU WANT ME TO FEEL, I'M OUT. DEAL?
DEAL.

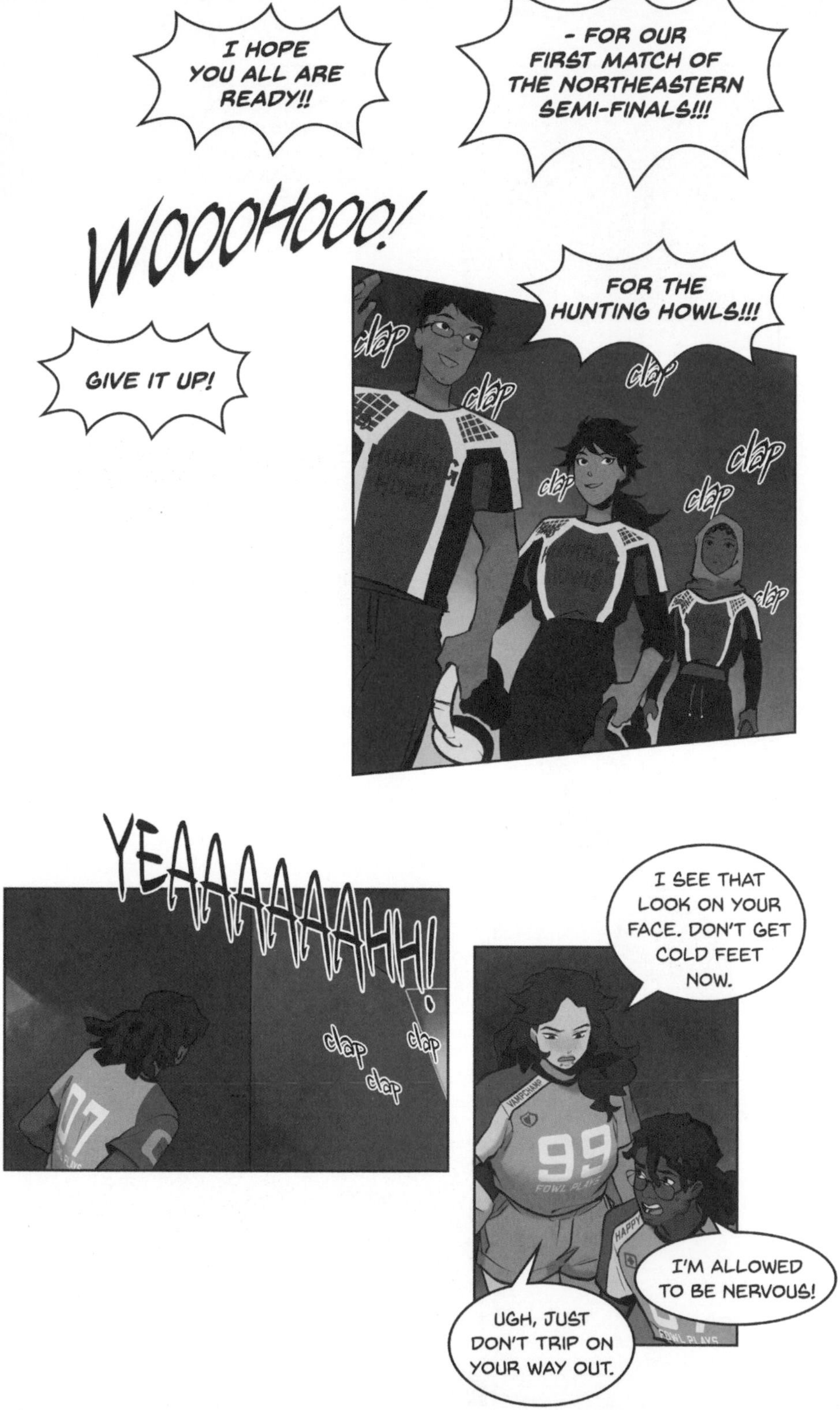
I HOPE YOU ALL ARE READY!!
- FOR OUR FIRST MATCH OF THE NORTHEASTERN SEMI-FINALS!!!
WOOOHOOO!
FOR THE HUNTING HOWLS!!!
GIVE IT UP!
clap
clap
clap
clap
clap
clap
clap
YEAAAAAAAHH!
clap
clap
clap
I SEE THAT LOOK ON YOUR FACE. DON'T GET COLD FEET NOW.
I'M ALLOWED TO BE NERVOUS!
UGH, JUST DON'T TRIP ON YOUR WAY OUT.

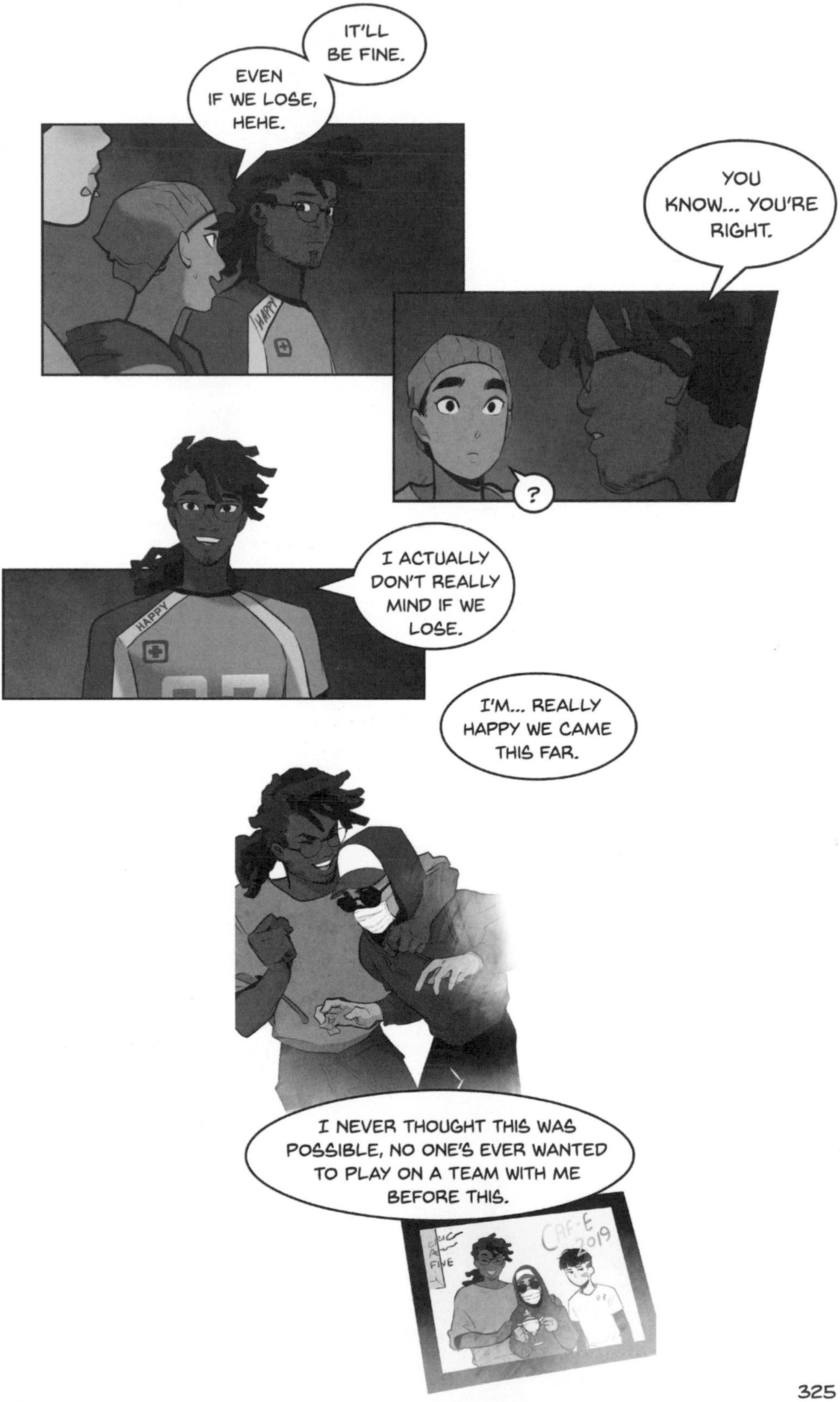
EVEN IF WE LOSE, HEHE.
IT'LL BE FINE.
YOU KNOW... YOU'RE RIGHT.
?
I ACTUALLY DON'T REALLY MIND IF WE LOSE.
I'M... REALLY HAPPY WE CAME THIS FAR.
I NEVER THOUGHT THIS WAS POSSIBLE, NO ONE'S EVER WANTED TO PLAY ON A TEAM WITH ME BEFORE THIS.
CAF-E 2019

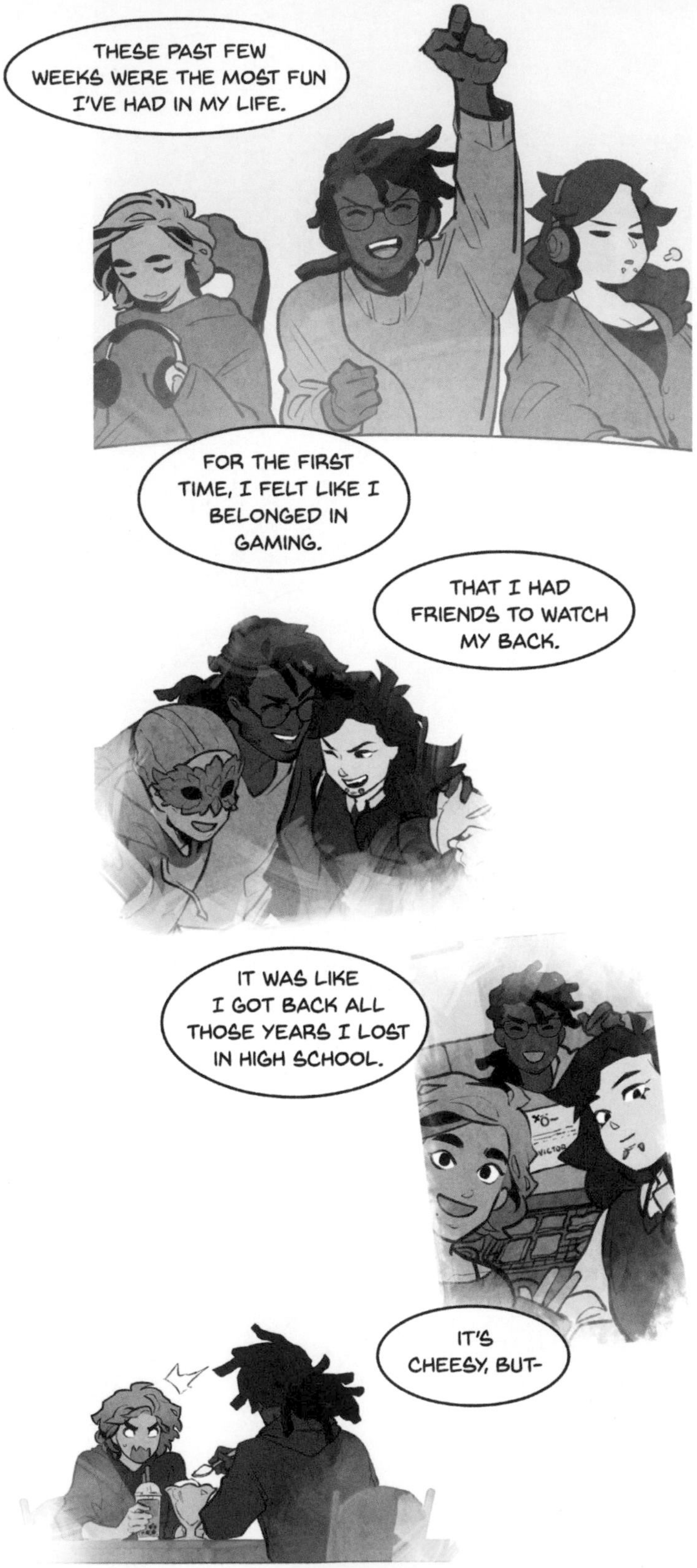
THESE PAST FEW WEEKS WERE THE MOST FUN I'VE HAD IN MY LIFE.
FOR THE FIRST TIME, I FELT LIKE I BELONGED IN GAMING.
THAT I HAD FRIENDS TO WATCH MY BACK.
IT WAS LIKE I GOT BACK ALL THOSE YEARS I LOST IN HIGH SCHOOL.
IT'S CHEESY, BUT-

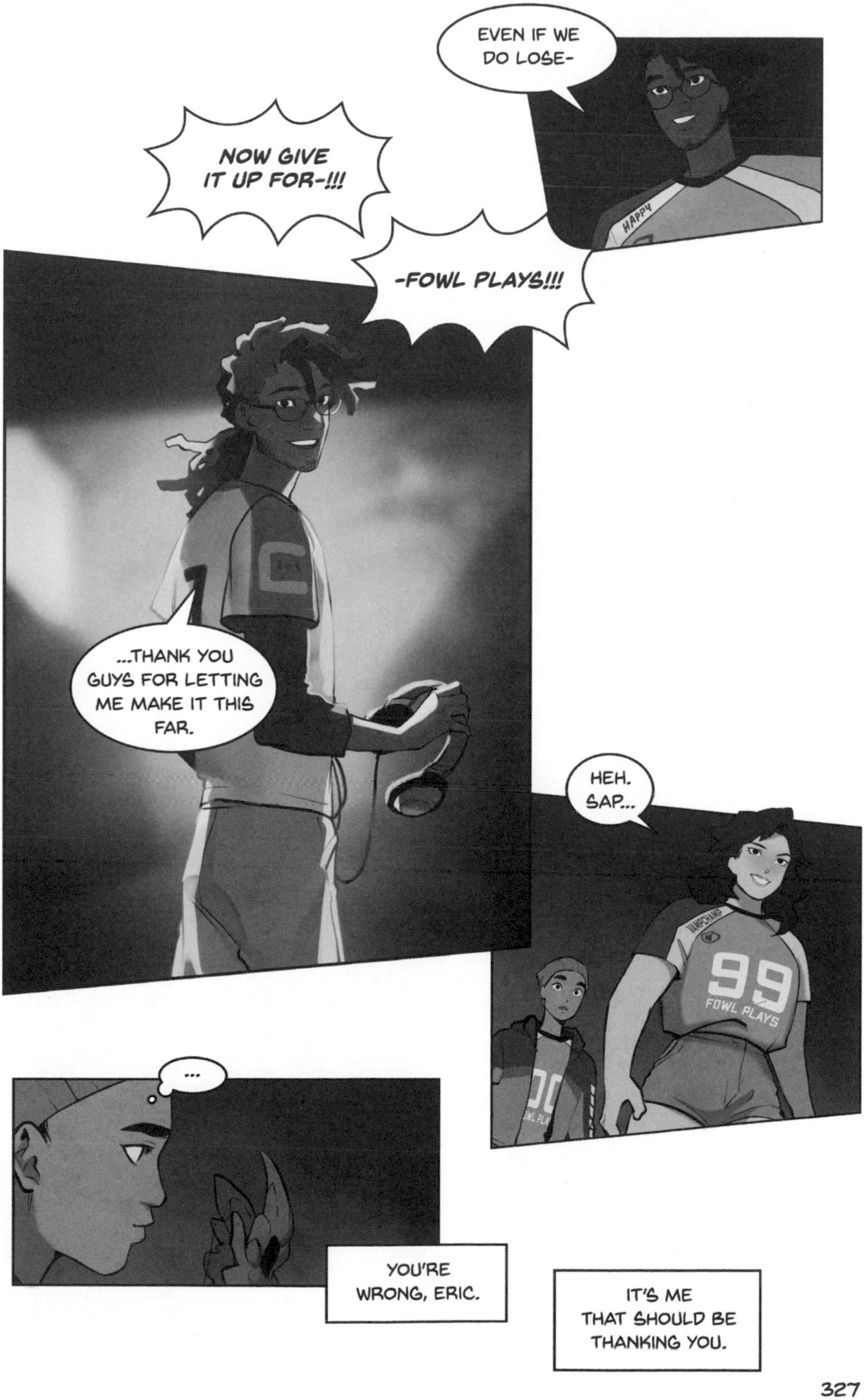
EVEN IF WE DO LOSE-
NOW GIVE IT UP FOR-!!!
-FOWL PLAYS!!!
...THANK YOU GUYS FOR LETTING ME MAKE IT THIS FAR.
HEH. SAP...
99
FOWL PLAYS
...
YOU'RE WRONG, ERIC.
IT'S ME THAT SHOULD BE THANKING YOU.

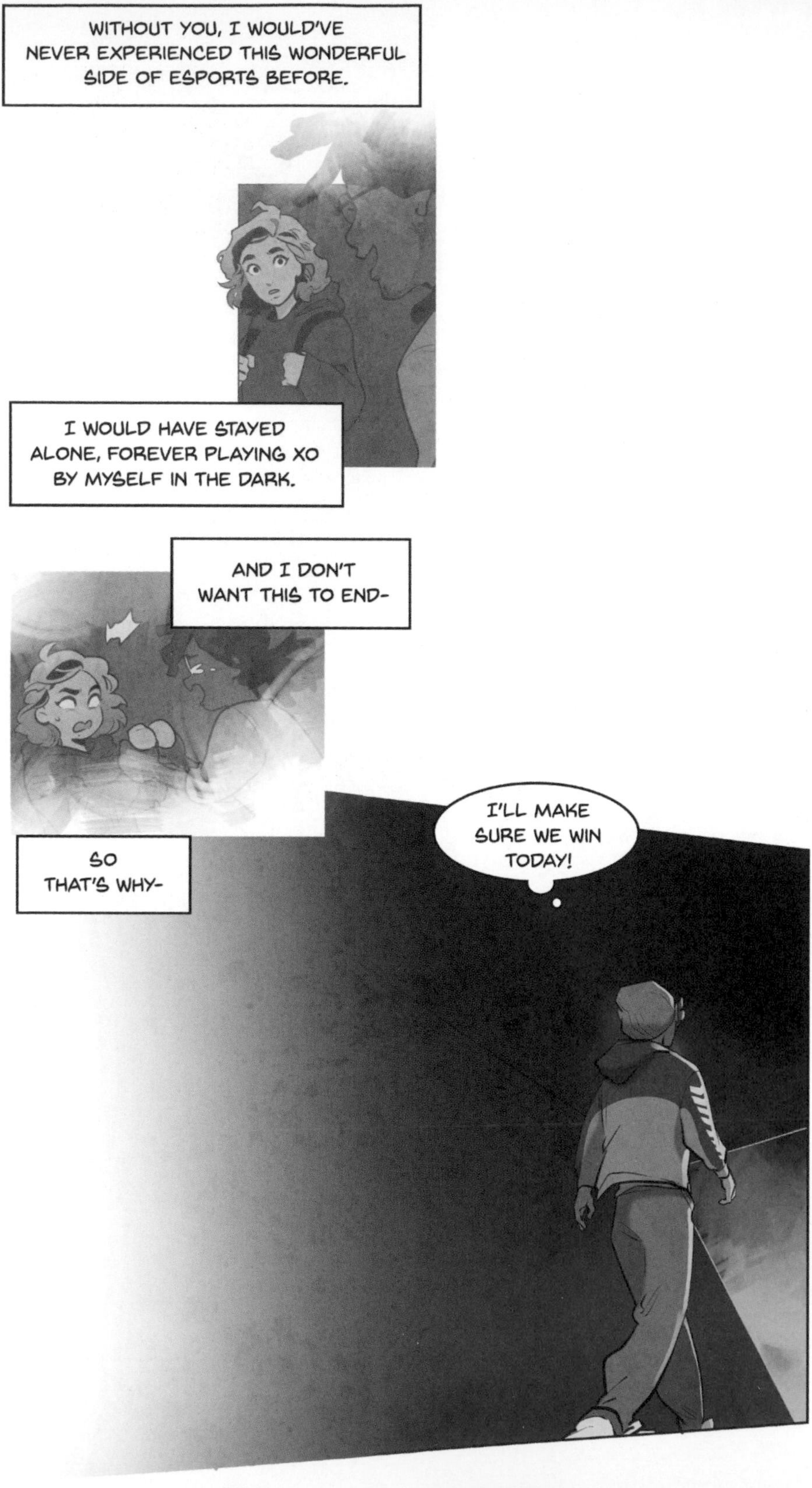
WITHOUT YOU, I WOULD'VE NEVER EXPERIENCED THIS WONDERFUL SIDE OF ESPORTS BEFORE.
I WOULD HAVE STAYED ALONE, FOREVER PLAYING XO BY MYSELF IN THE DARK.
AND I DON'T WANT THIS TO END-
SO THAT'S WHY-
I'LL MAKE SURE WE WIN TODAY!

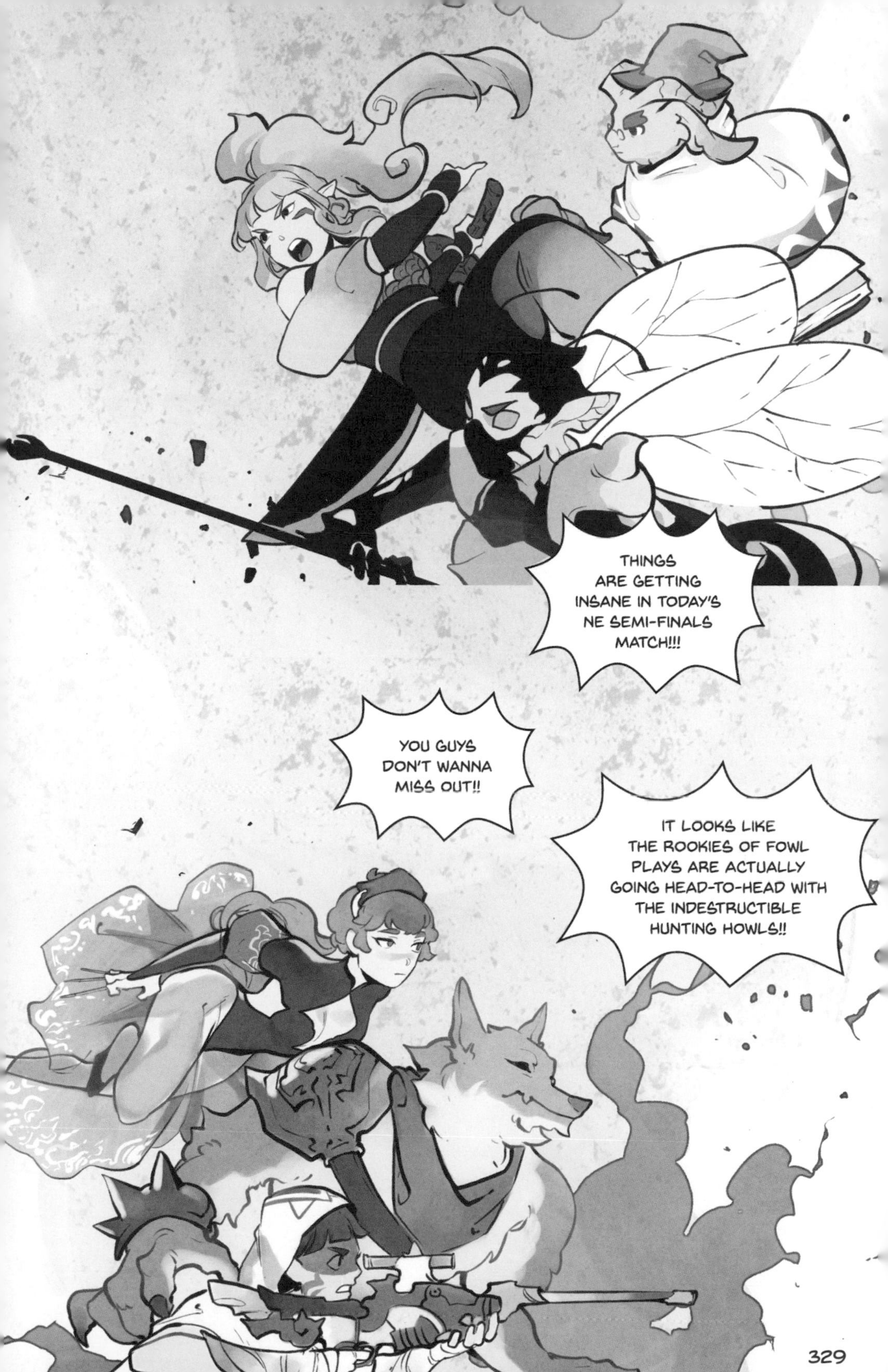
THINGS ARE GETTING INSANE IN TODAY'S NE SEMI-FINALS MATCH!!!
YOU GUYS DON'T WANNA MISS OUT!!
IT LOOKS LIKE THE ROOKIES OF FOWL PLAYS ARE ACTUALLY GOING HEAD-TO-HEAD WITH THE INDESTRUCTIBLE HUNTING HOWLS!!

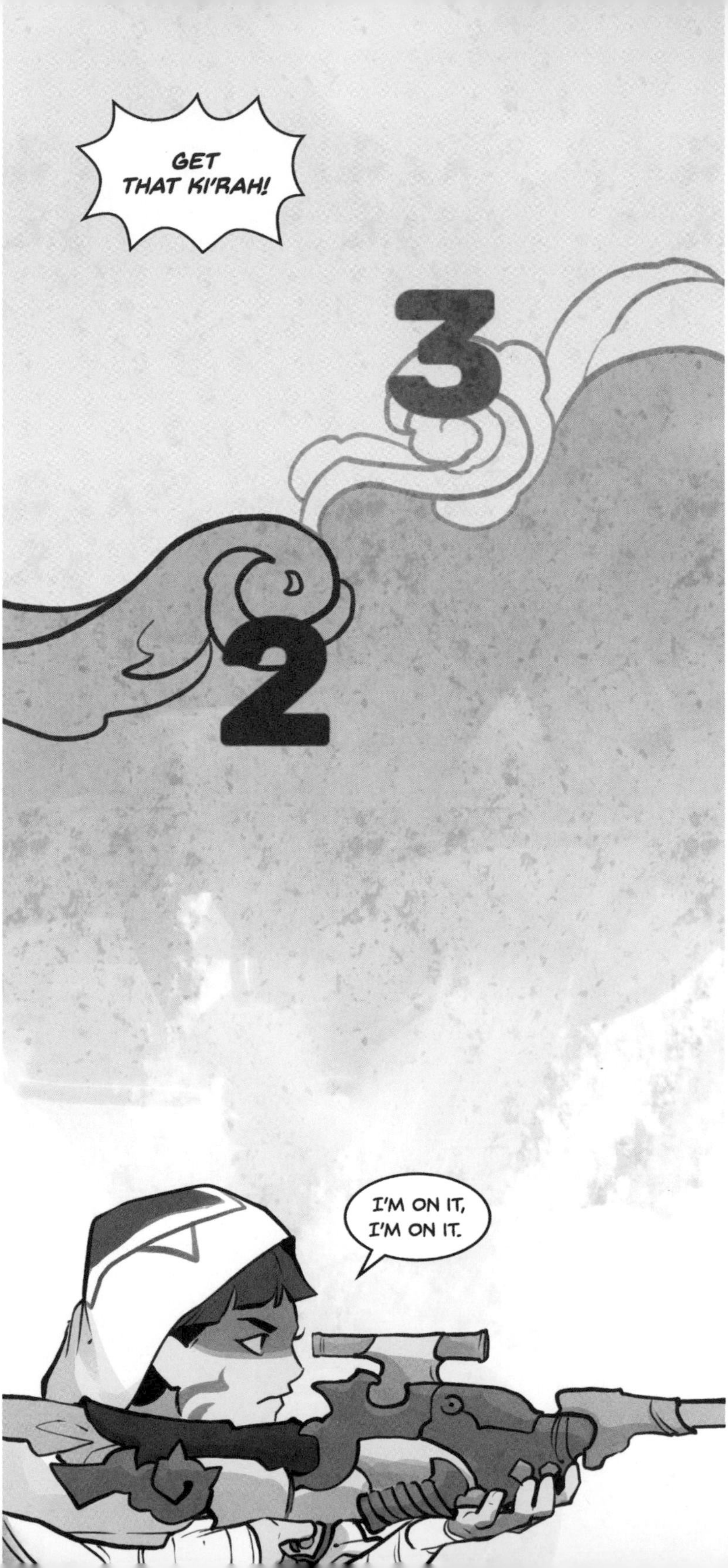
GET THAT KI'RAH!
3
2
I'M ON IT, I'M ON IT.

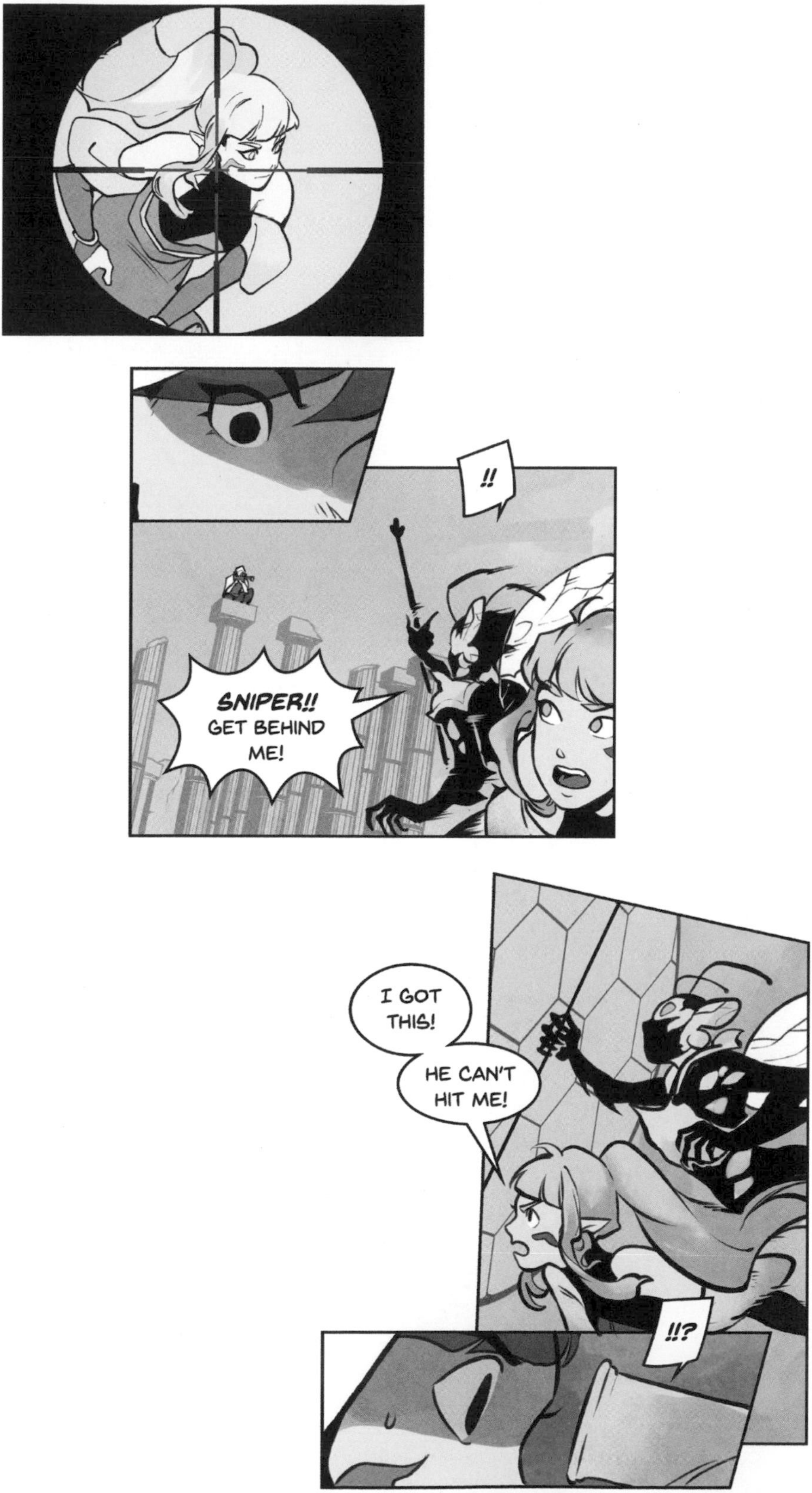
!!
SNIPER!! GET BEHIND ME!
I GOT THIS!
HE CAN'T HIT ME!
!!?

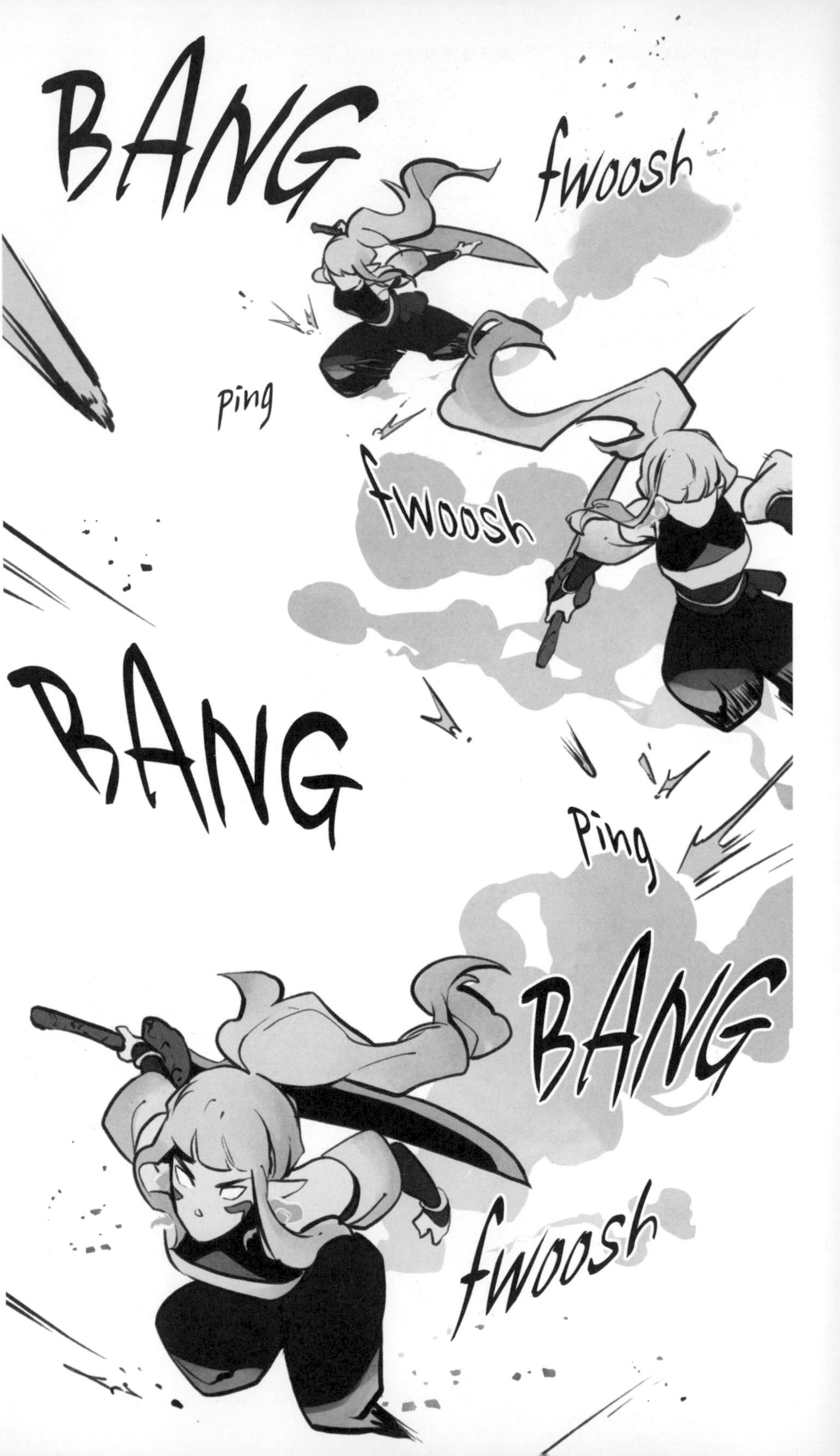
BANG
fwoosh
ping
fwoosh
BANG
Ping
BANG
fwoosh

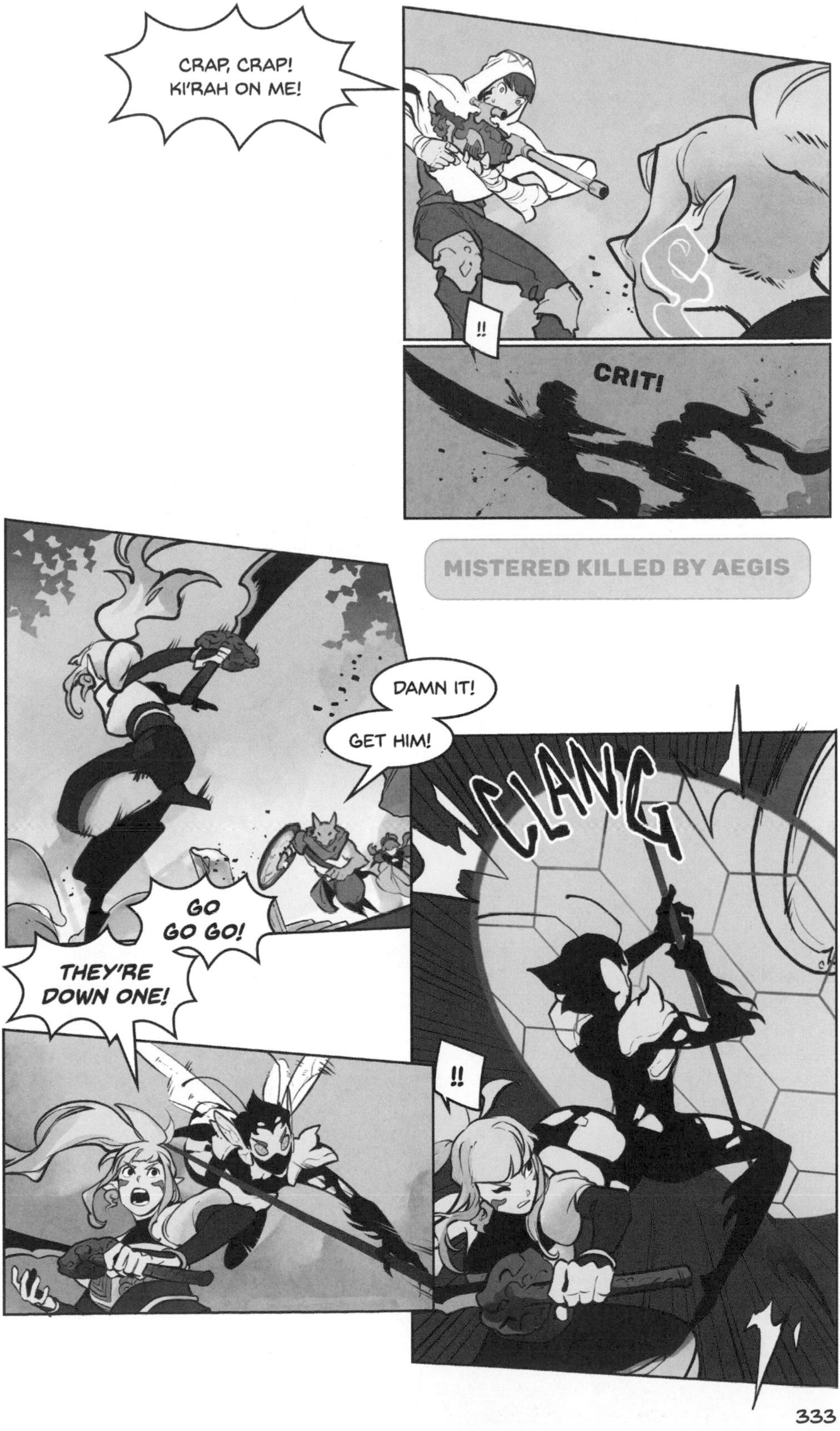
CRAP, CRAP!
KI'RAH ON ME!
!!
CRIT!
MISTERED KILLED BY AEGIS
DAMN IT!
GET HIM!
GO
GO GO!
THEY'RE
DOWN ONE!
CLANG
!!

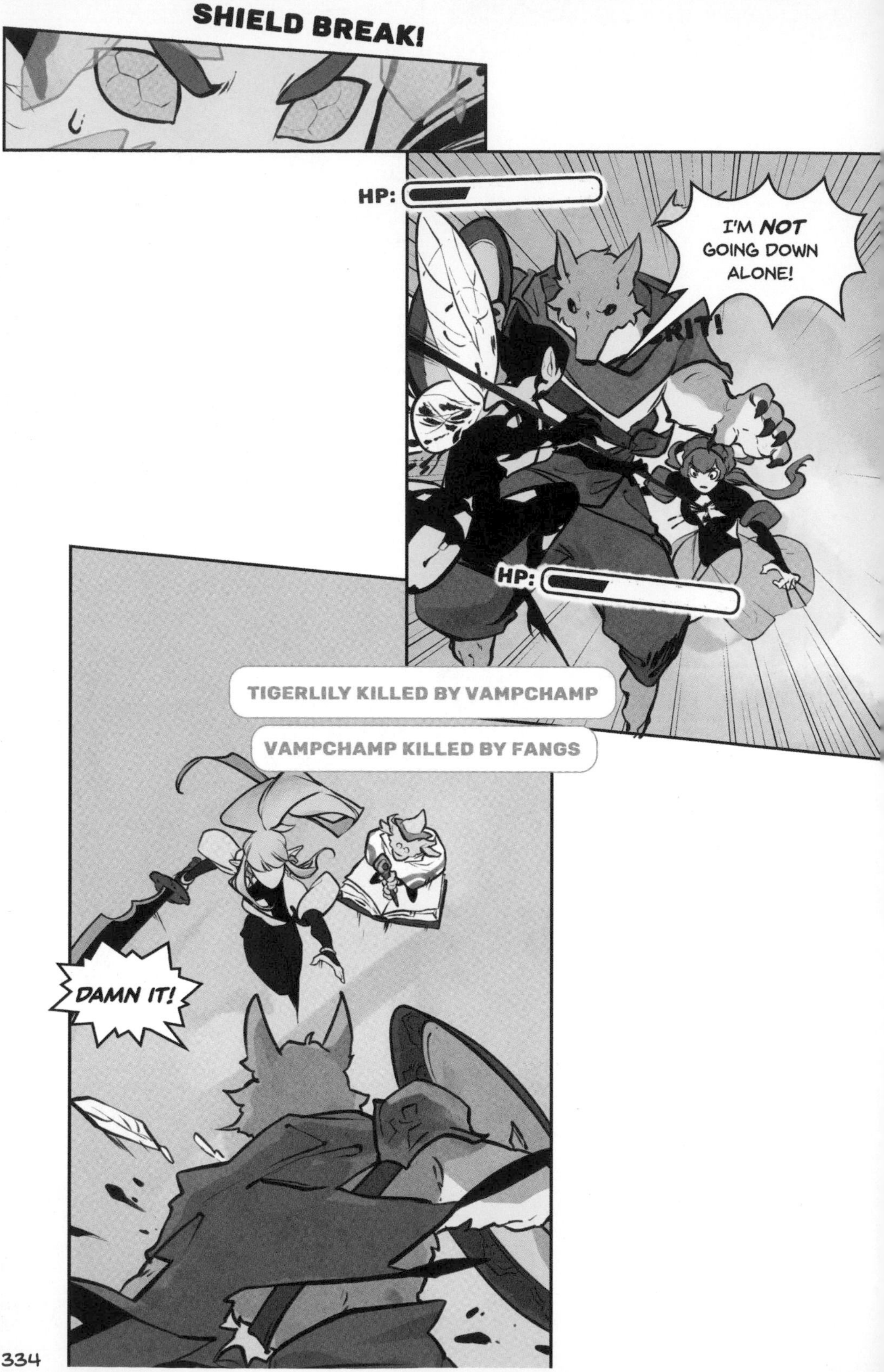
SHIELD BREAK!
HP:
I'M NOT GOING DOWN ALONE!
HP:
TIGERLILY KILLED BY VAMPCHAMP
VAMPCHAMP KILLED BY FANGS
DAMN IT!

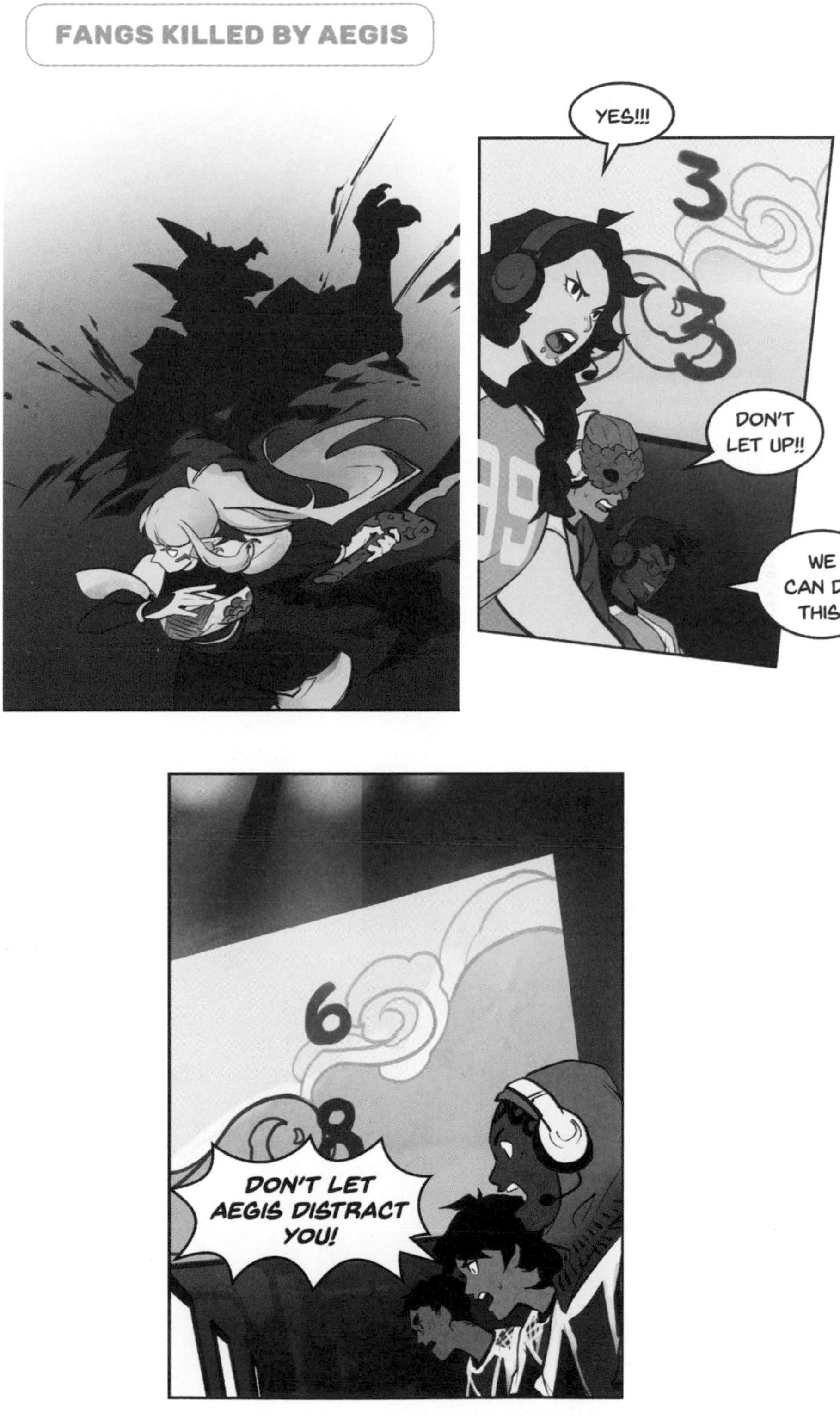
FANGS KILLED BY AEGIS
YES!!!
DON'T LET UP!!
WE CAN DO THIS!
DON'T LET AEGIS DISTRACT YOU!

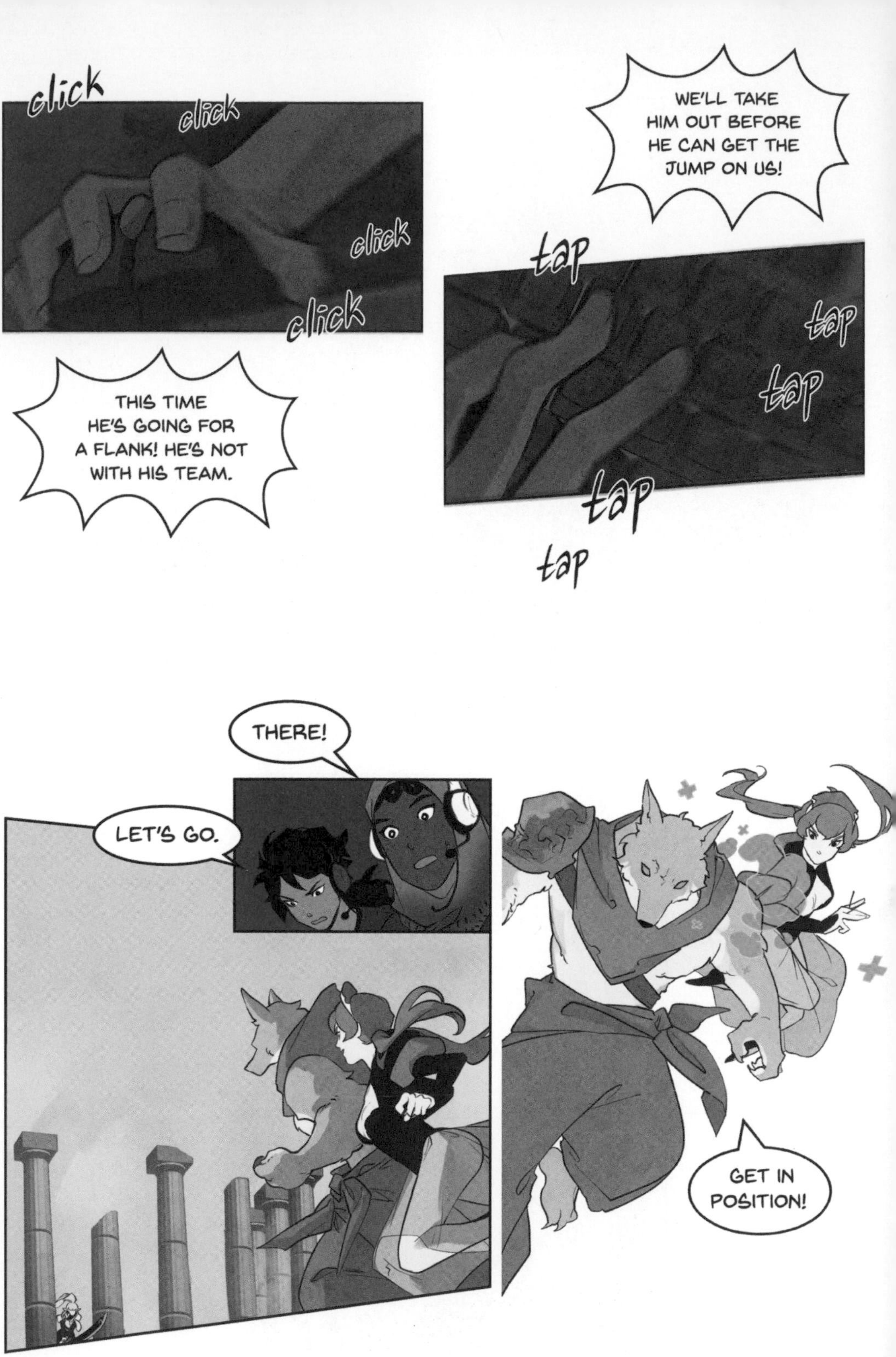
click
click
click
click
WE'LL TAKE HIM OUT BEFORE HE CAN GET THE JUMP ON US!
THIS TIME HE'S GOING FOR A FLANK! HE'S NOT WITH HIS TEAM.
tap
tap
tap
tap
tap
THERE!
LET'S GO.
GET IN POSITION!

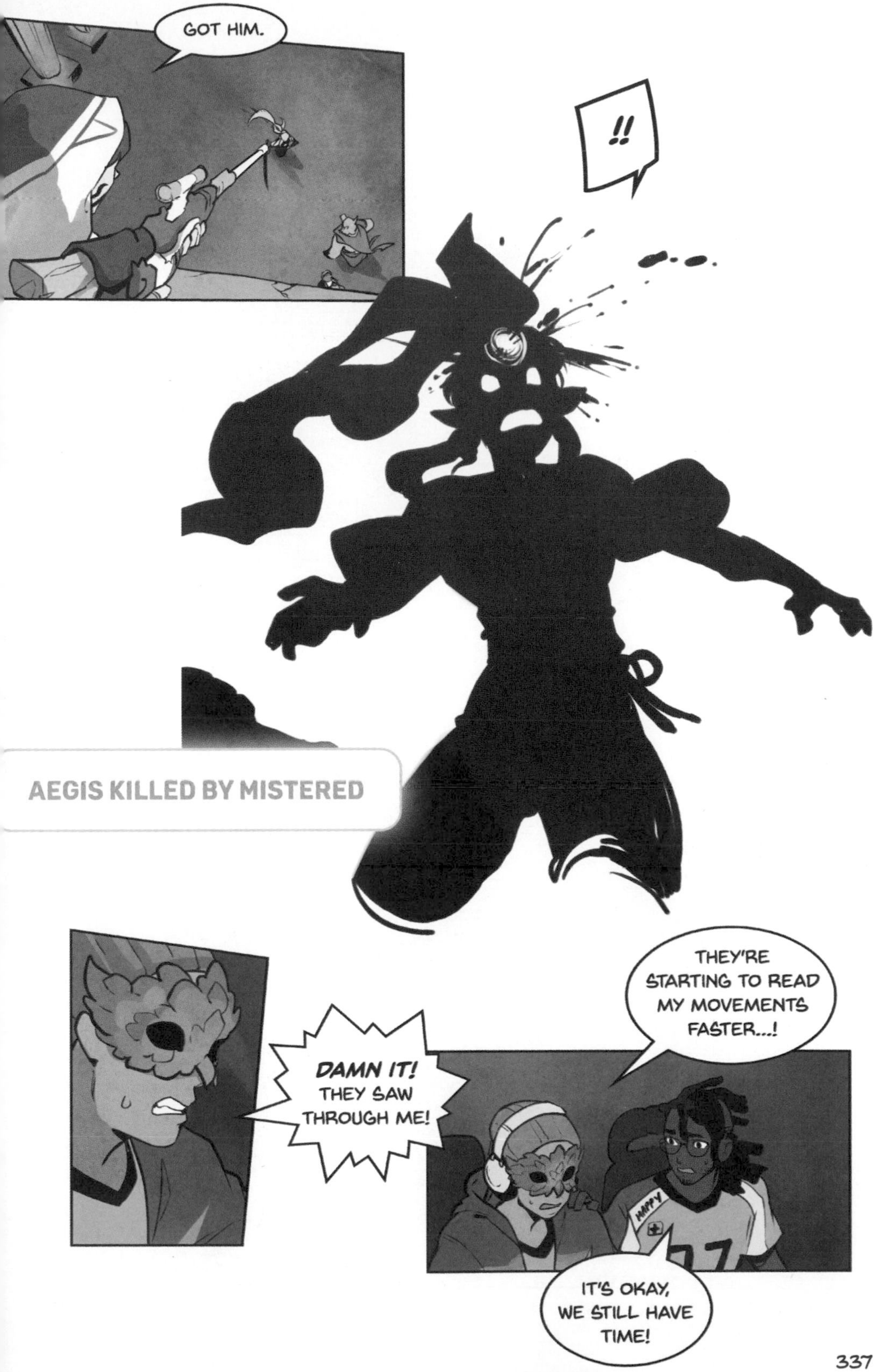

GOT HIM.
!!
AEGIS KILLED BY MISTERED
DAMN IT! THEY SAW THROUGH ME!
THEY'RE STARTING TO READ MY MOVEMENTS FASTER...!
IT'S OKAY, WE STILL HAVE TIME!

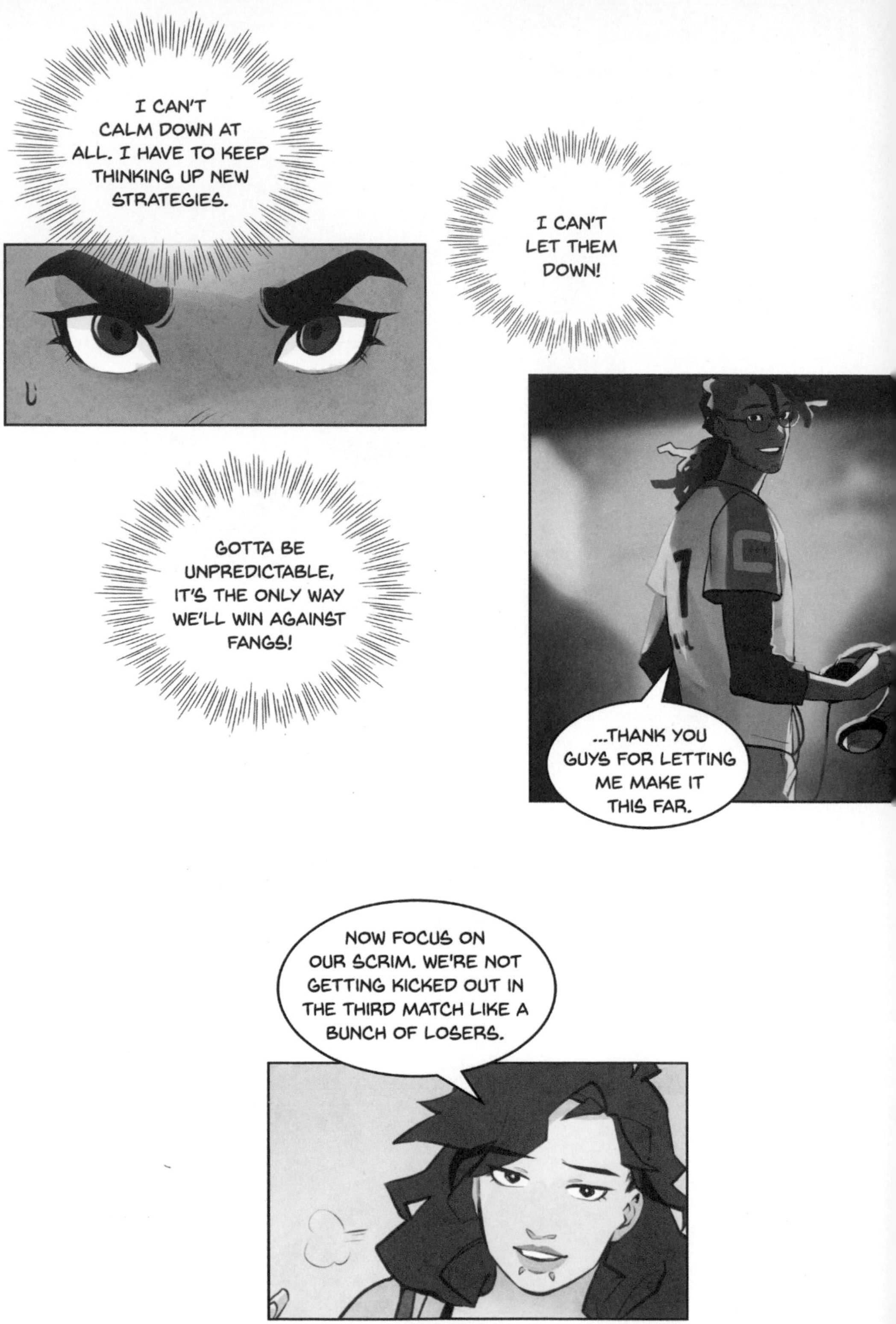
I CAN'T CALM DOWN AT ALL. I HAVE TO KEEP THINKING UP NEW STRATEGIES.
I CAN'T LET THEM DOWN!
GOTTA BE UNPREDICTABLE, IT'S THE ONLY WAY WE'LL WIN AGAINST FANGS!
...THANK YOU GUYS FOR LETTING ME MAKE IT THIS FAR.
NOW FOCUS ON OUR SCRIM. WE'RE NOT GETTING KICKED OUT IN THE THIRD MATCH LIKE A BUNCH OF LOSERS.

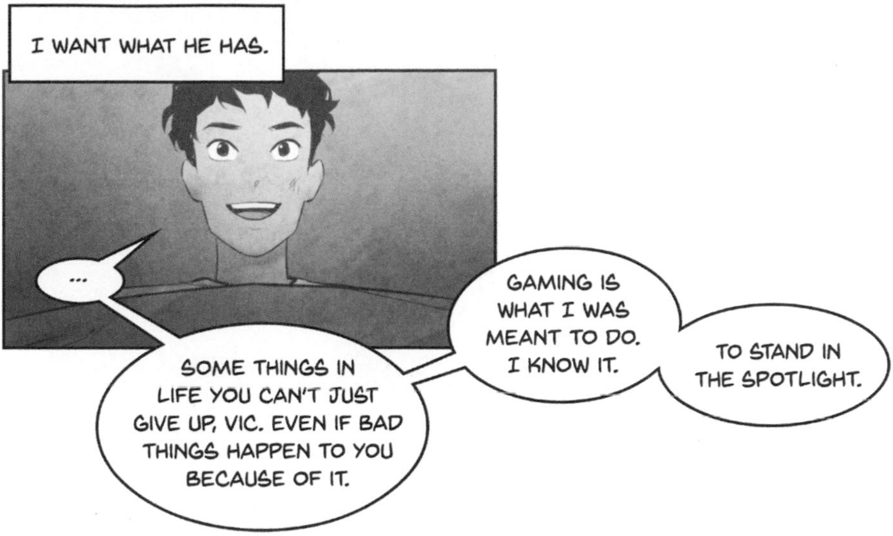
I WANT WHAT HE HAS.
...
SOME THINGS IN LIFE YOU CAN'T JUST GIVE UP, VIC. EVEN IF BAD THINGS HAPPEN TO YOU BECAUSE OF IT.
GAMING IS WHAT I WAS MEANT TO DO. I KNOW IT.
TO STAND IN THE SPOTLIGHT.

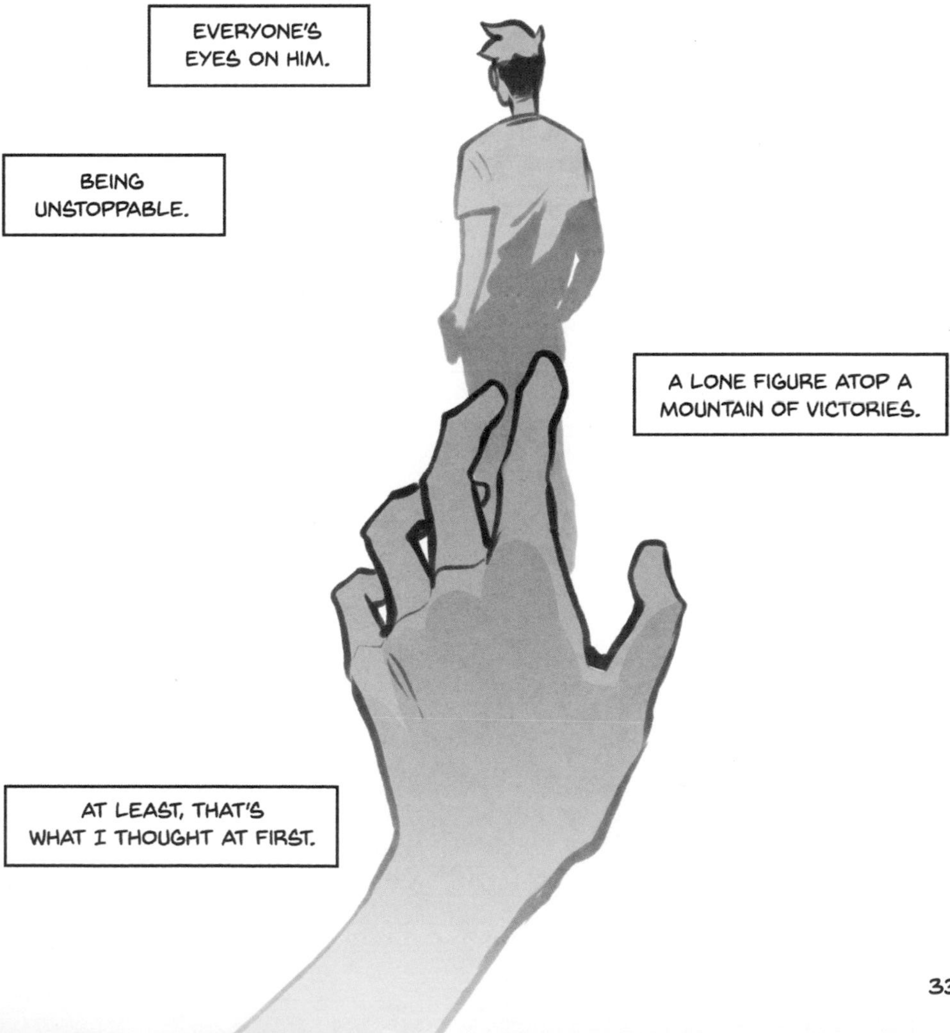
EVERYONE'S EYES ON HIM.
BEING UNSTOPPABLE.
A LONE FIGURE ATOP A MOUNTAIN OF VICTORIES.
AT LEAST, THAT'S WHAT I THOUGHT AT FIRST.

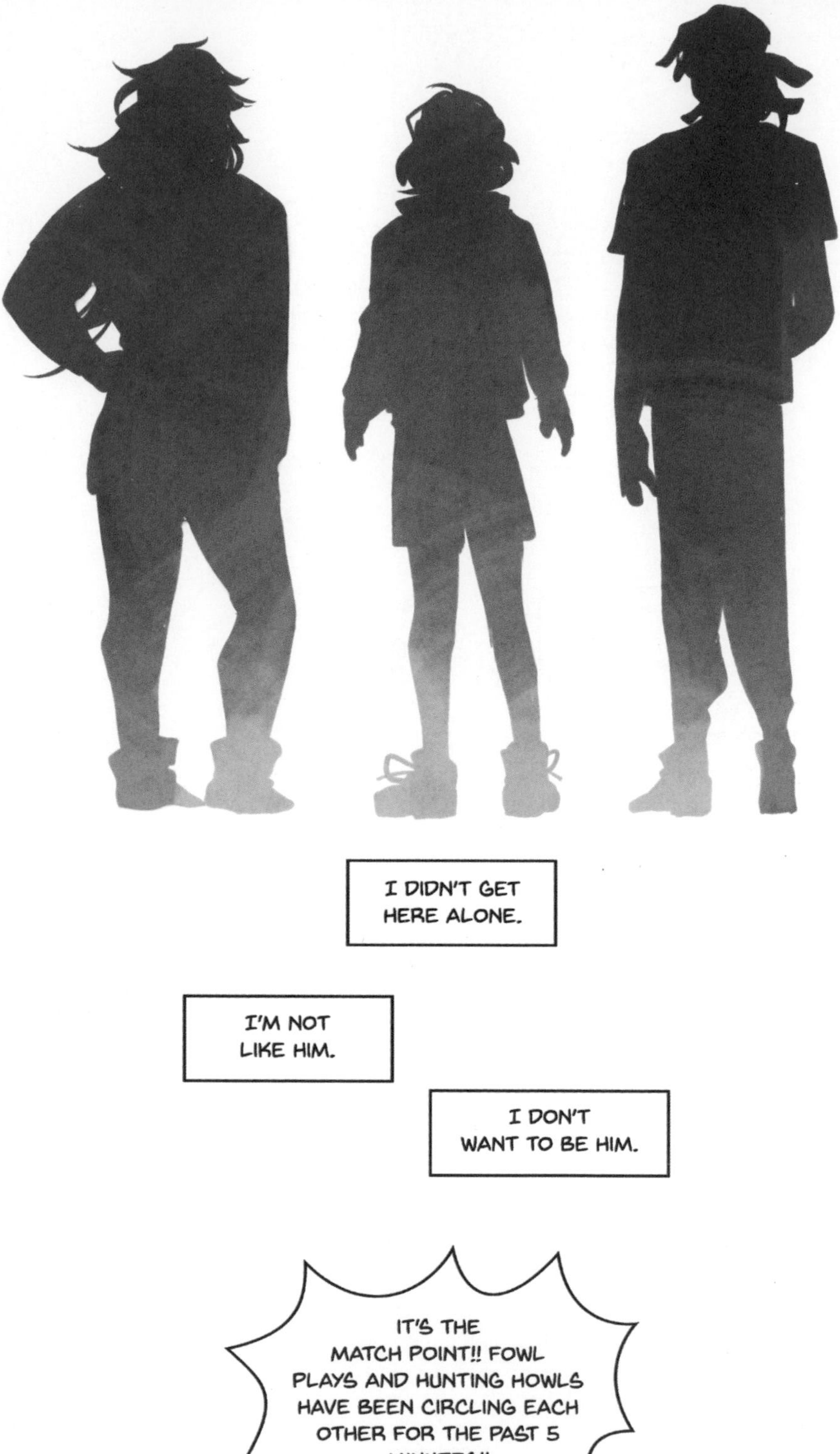
I DIDN'T GET HERE ALONE.
I'M NOT LIKE HIM.
I DON'T WANT TO BE HIM.
IT'S THE MATCH POINT!! FOWL PLAYS AND HUNTING HOWLS HAVE BEEN CIRCLING EACH OTHER FOR THE PAST 5 MINUTES!!

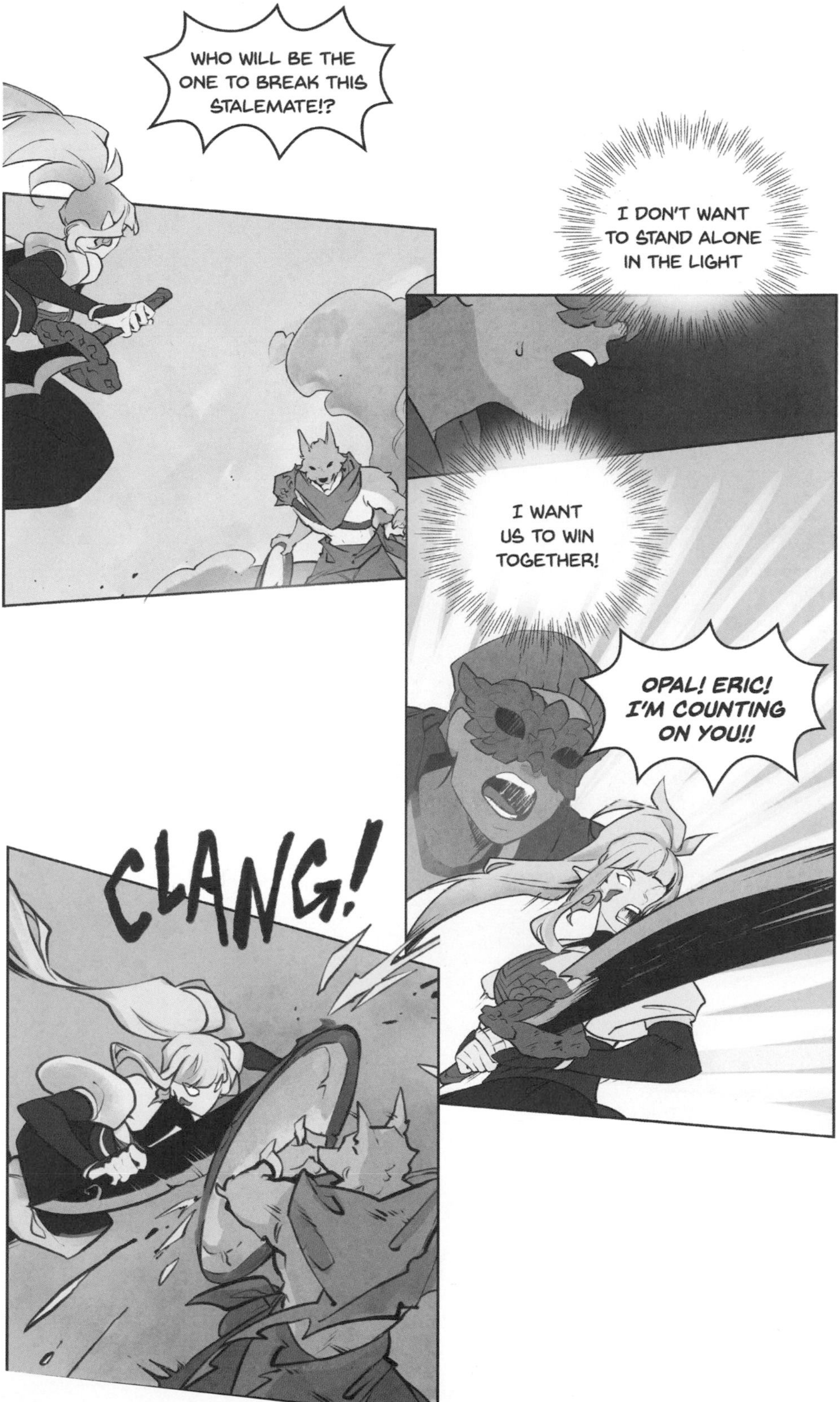
WHO WILL BE THE ONE TO BREAK THIS STALEMATE!?
I DON'T WANT TO STAND ALONE IN THE LIGHT
I WANT US TO WIN TOGETHER!
OPAL! ERIC! I'M COUNTING ON YOU!!
CLANG!

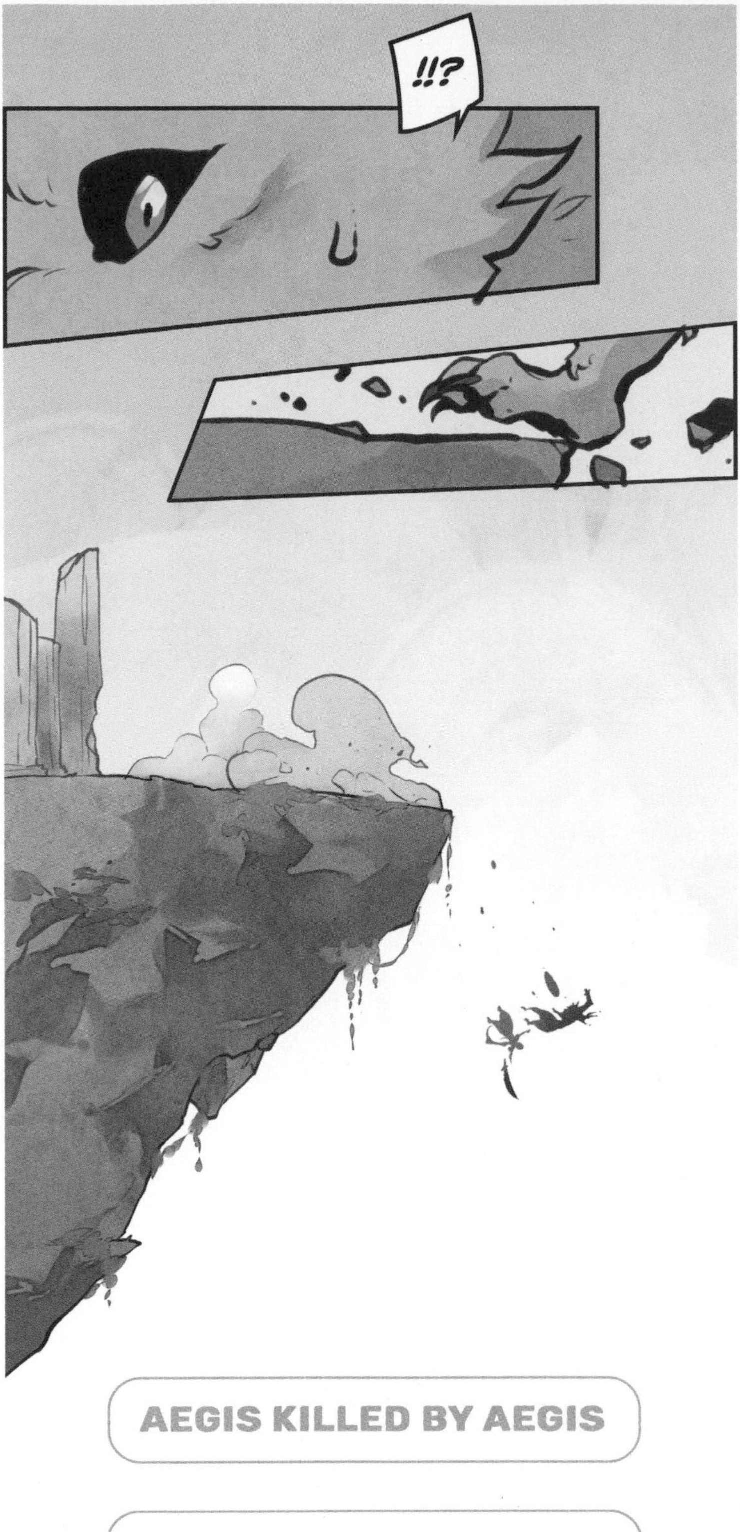
!!?
AEGIS KILLED BY AEGIS
FANGS KILLED BY AEGIS

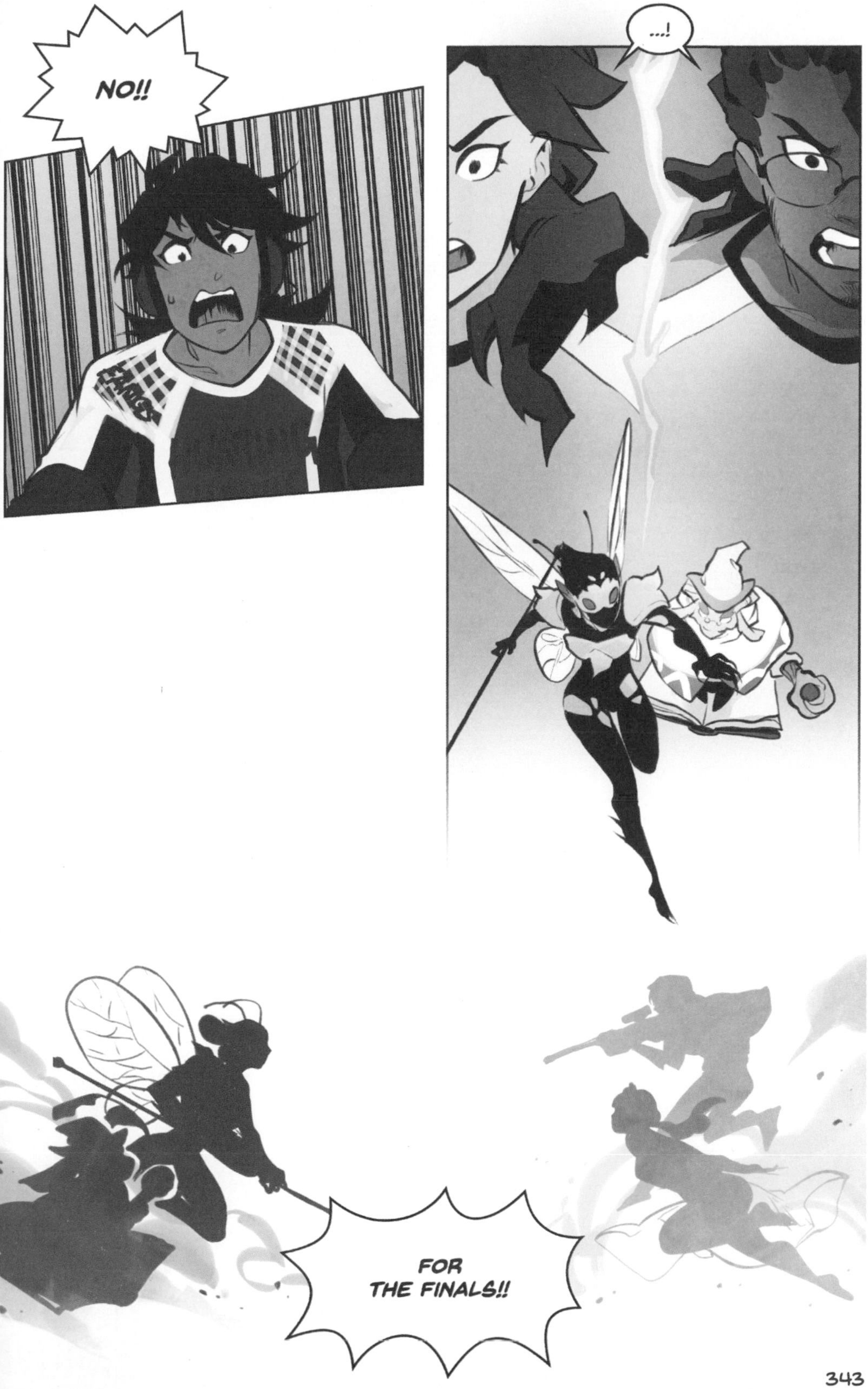
NO!!
...!
FOR THE FINALS!!

CHAPTER 7: LONELY

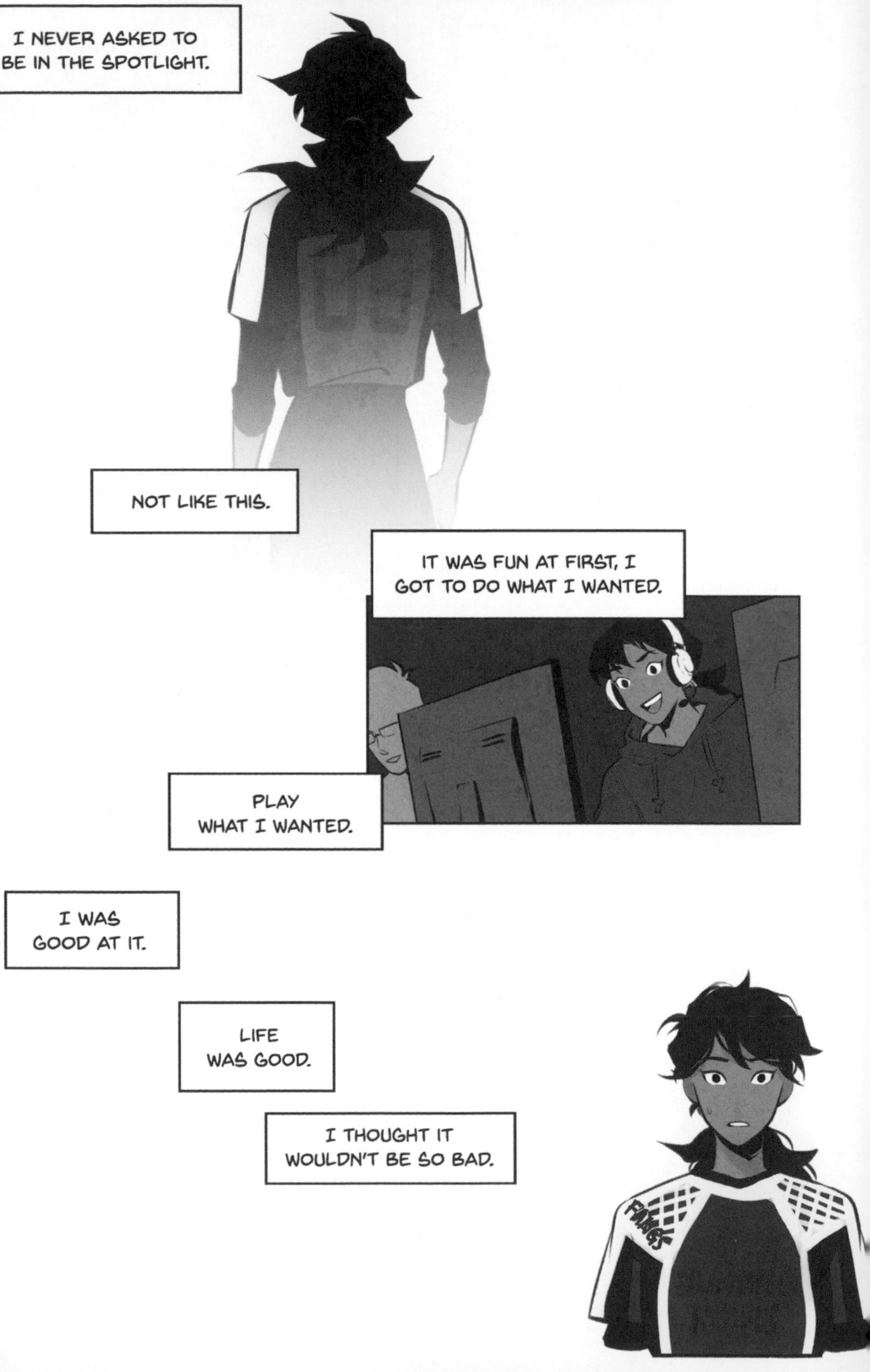
I NEVER ASKED TO BE IN THE SPOTLIGHT.
NOT LIKE THIS.
IT WAS FUN AT FIRST, I GOT TO DO WHAT I WANTED.
PLAY WHAT I WANTED.
I WAS GOOD AT IT.
LIFE WAS GOOD.
I THOUGHT IT WOULDN'T BE SO BAD.

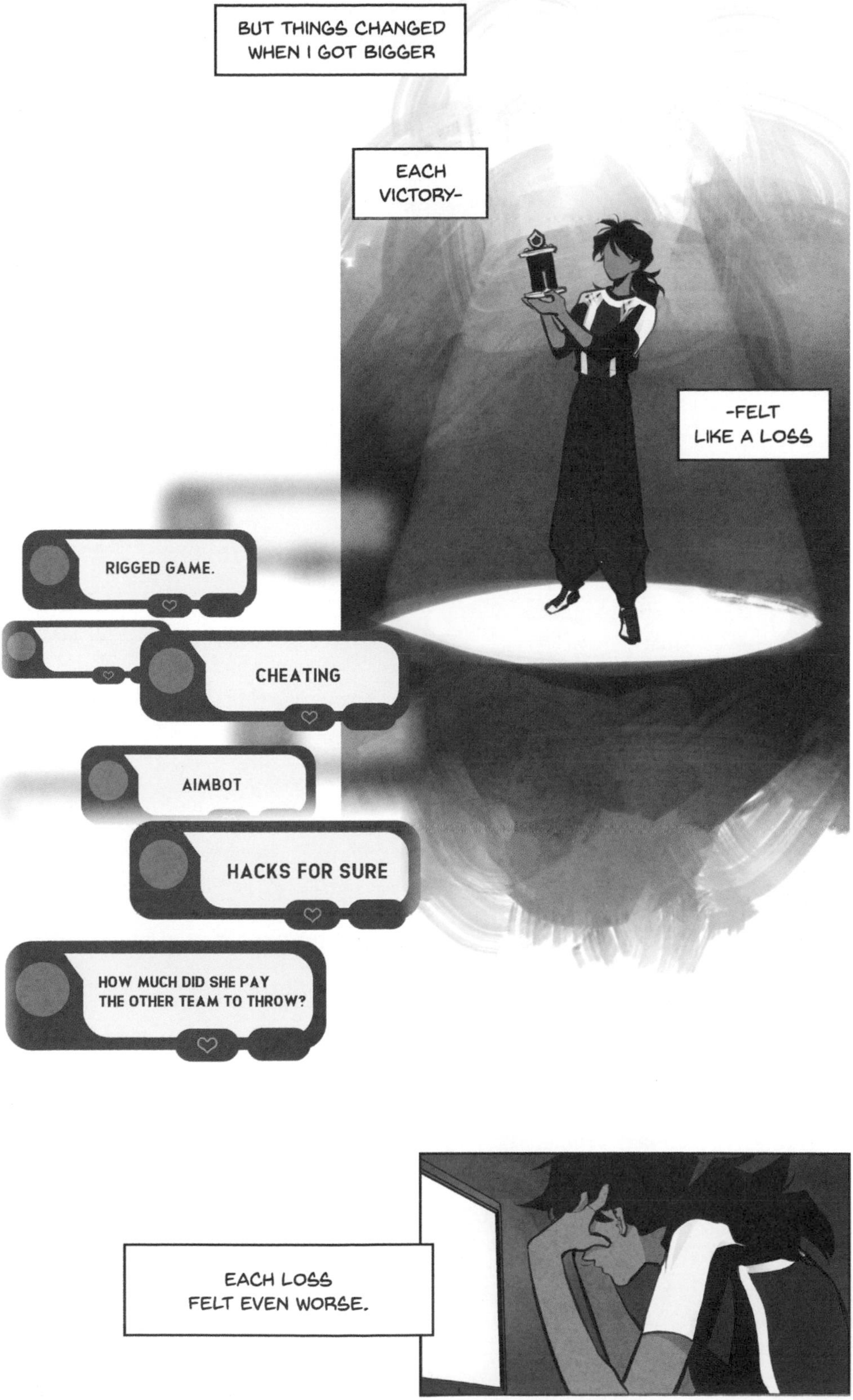
BUT THINGS CHANGED WHEN I GOT BIGGER
EACH VICTORY-
-FELT LIKE A LOSS
RIGGED GAME.
CHEATING
AIMBOT
HACKS FOR SURE
HOW MUCH DID SHE PAY THE OTHER TEAM TO THROW?
EACH LOSS FELT EVEN WORSE.

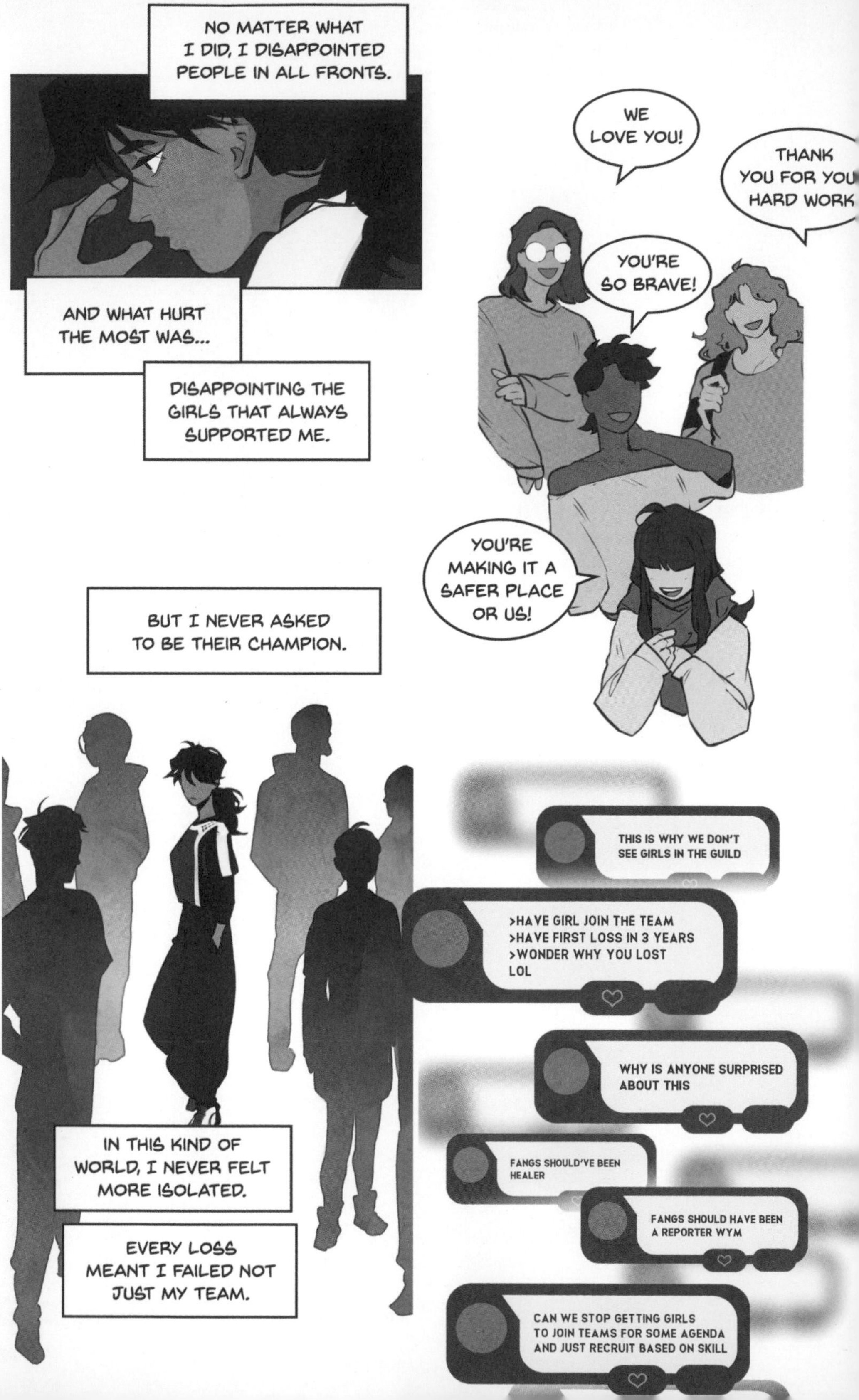
NO MATTER WHAT I DID, I DISAPPOINTED PEOPLE IN ALL FRONTS.
AND WHAT HURT THE MOST WAS...
DISAPPOINTING THE GIRLS THAT ALWAYS SUPPORTED ME.
BUT I NEVER ASKED TO BE THEIR CHAMPION.
WE LOVE YOU!
THANK YOU FOR YOU HARD WORK
YOU'RE SO BRAVE!
YOU'RE MAKING IT A SAFER PLACE OR US!
IN THIS KIND OF WORLD, I NEVER FELT MORE ISOLATED.
EVERY LOSS MEANT I FAILED NOT JUST MY TEAM.
THIS IS WHY WE DON'T SEE GIRLS IN THE GUILD
>HAVE GIRL JOIN THE TEAM
>HAVE FIRST LOSS IN 3 YEARS
>WONDER WHY YOU LOST
LOL
WHY IS ANYONE SURPRISED ABOUT THIS
FANGS SHOULD'VE BEEN HEALER
FANGS SHOULD HAVE BEEN A REPORTER WYM
CAN WE STOP GETTING GIRLS TO JOIN TEAMS FOR SOME AGENDA AND JUST RECRUIT BASED ON SKILL

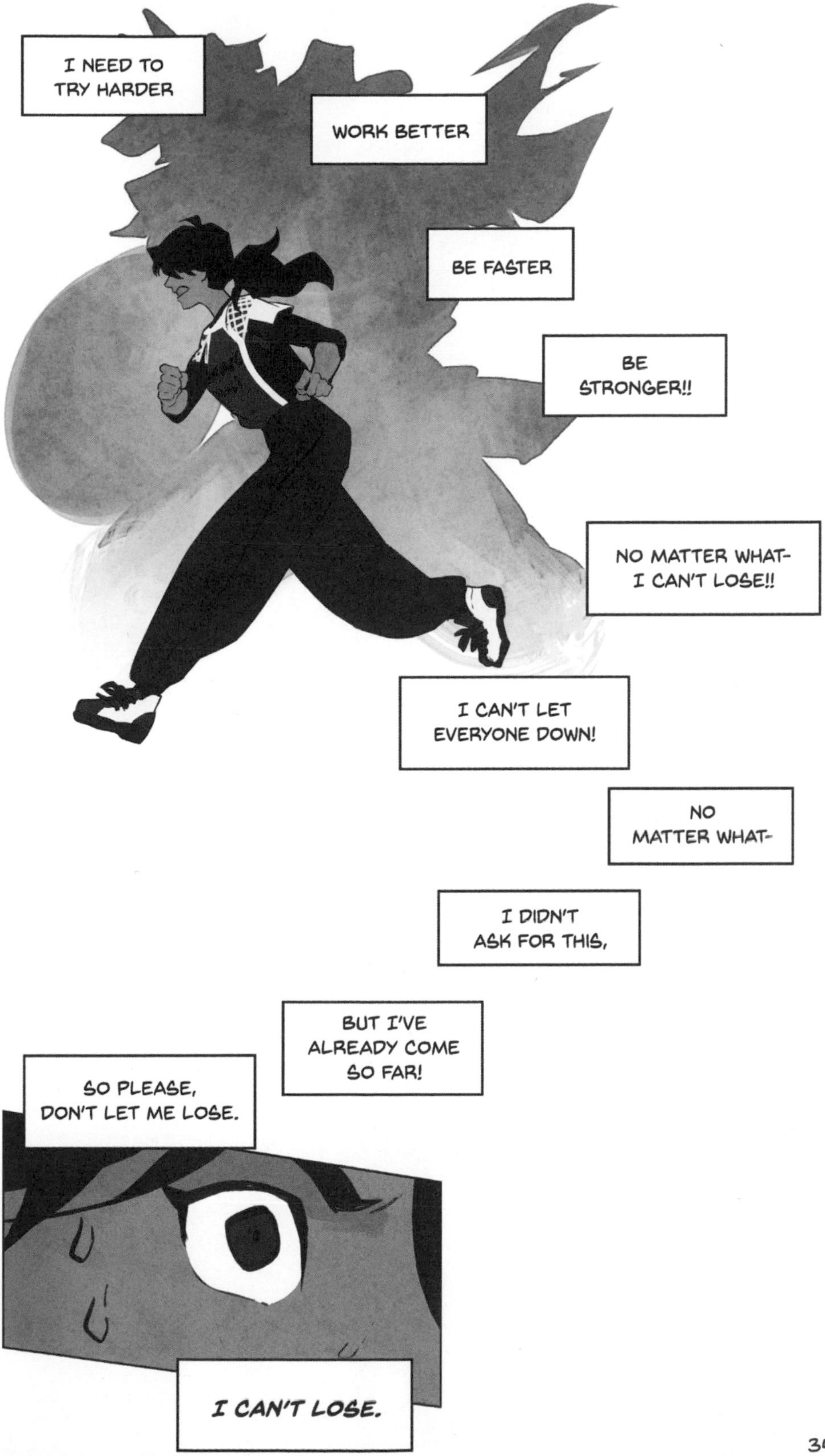
I NEED TO TRY HARDER
WORK BETTER
BE FASTER
BE STRONGER!!
NO MATTER WHAT- I CAN'T LOSE!!
I CAN'T LET EVERYONE DOWN!
NO MATTER WHAT-
I DIDN'T ASK FOR THIS,
BUT I'VE ALREADY COME SO FAR!
SO PLEASE, DON'T LET ME LOSE.
I CAN'T LOSE.

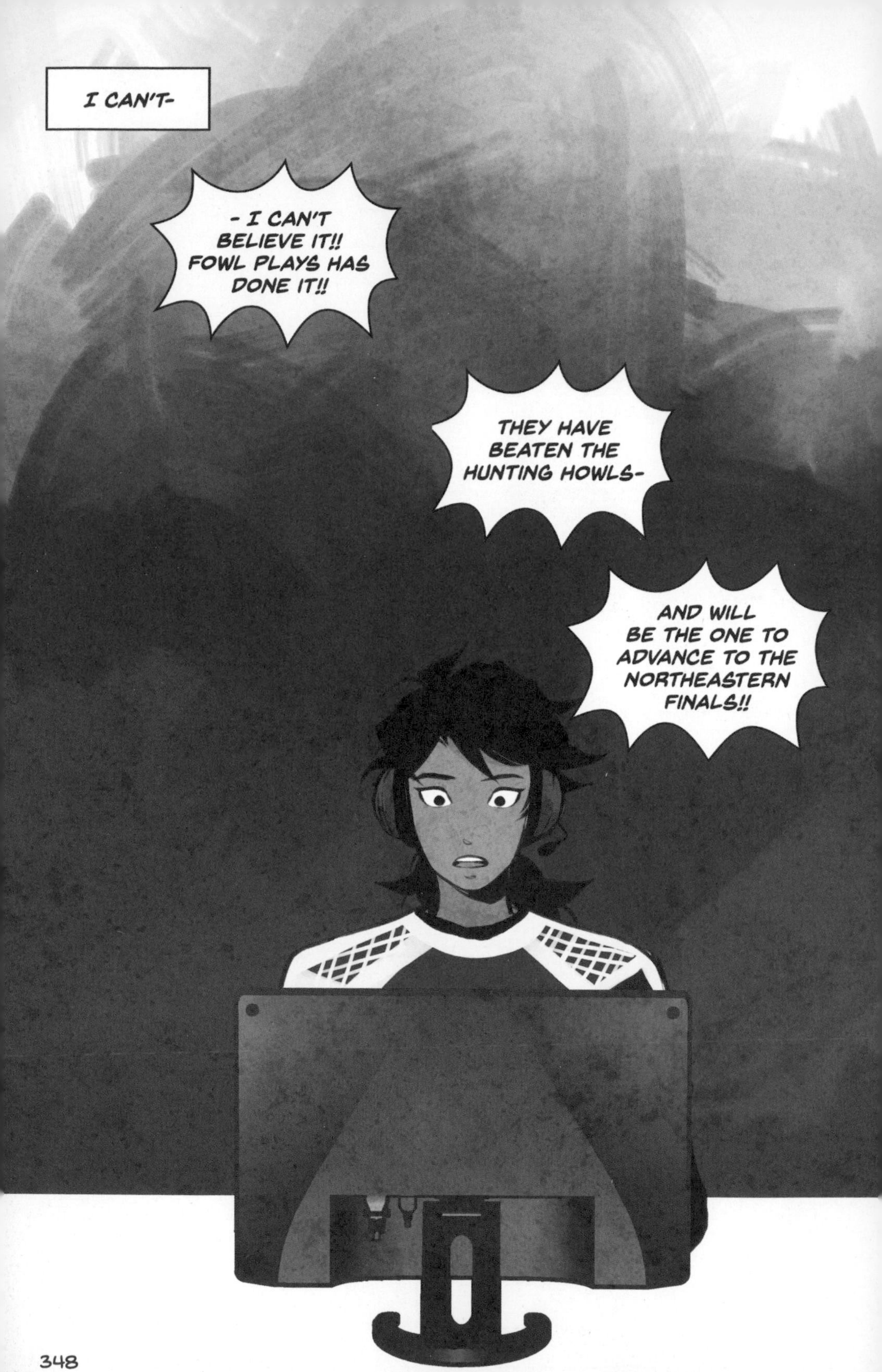
I CAN'T-
- I CAN'T BELIEVE IT!! FOWL PLAYS HAS DONE IT!!
THEY HAVE BEATEN THE HUNTING HOWLS-
AND WILL BE THE ONE TO ADVANCE TO THE NORTHEASTERN FINALS!!

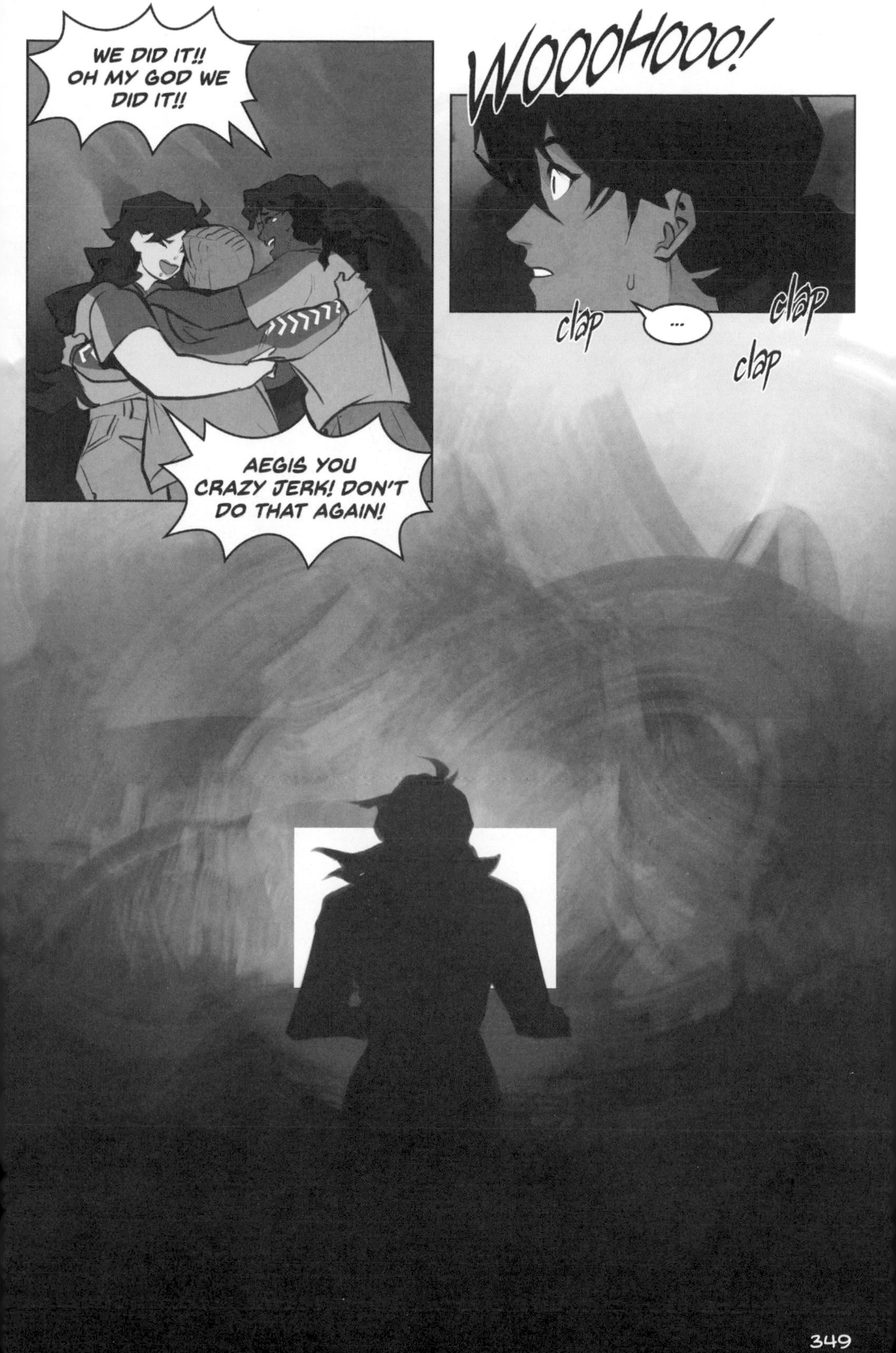
WE DID IT!! OH MY GOD WE DID IT!!
AEGIS YOU CRAZY JERK! DON'T DO THAT AGAIN!
WOOOHOOO!
clap
...
clap
clap

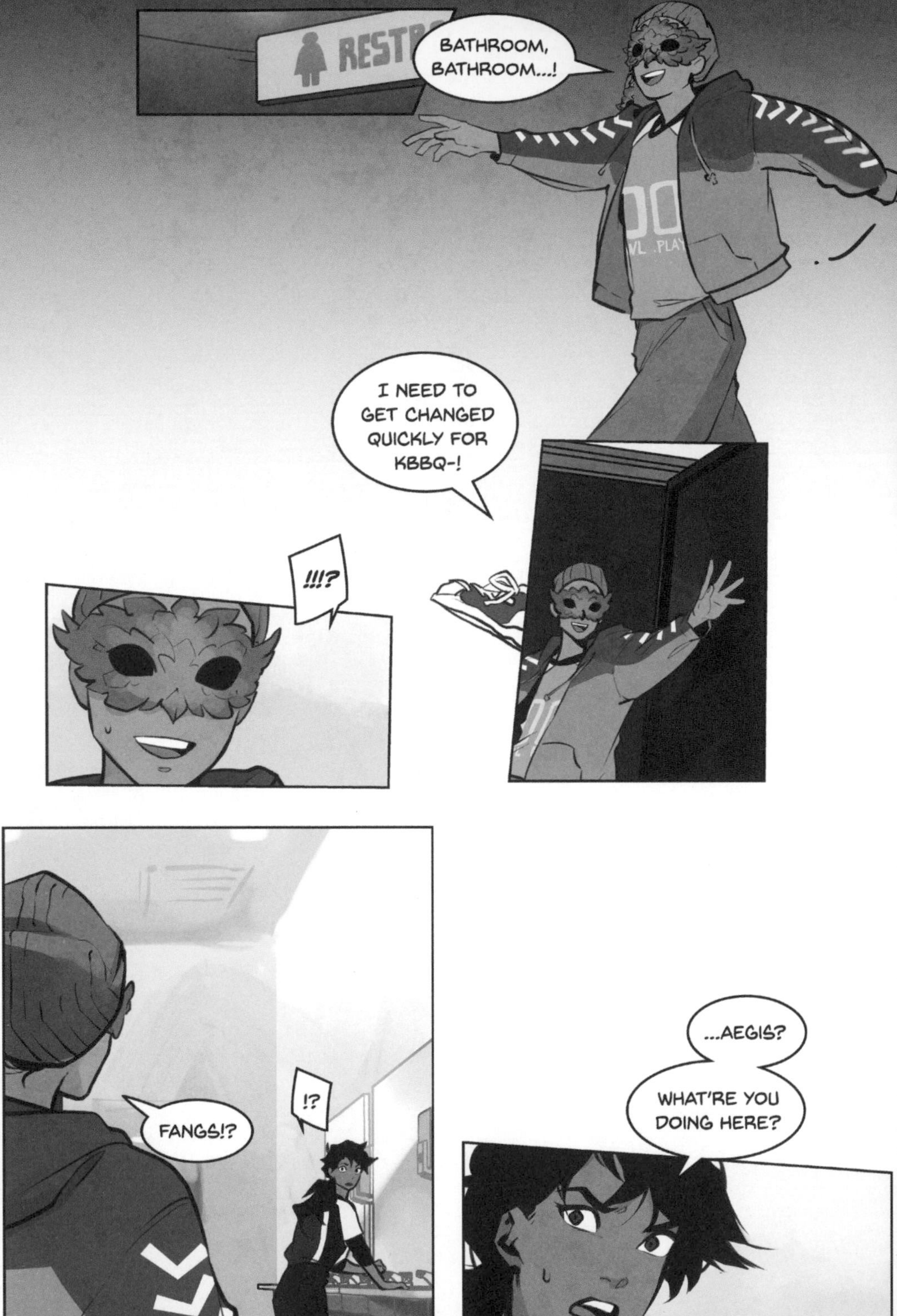
BATHROOM, BATHROOM...!
I NEED TO GET CHANGED QUICKLY FOR KBBQ-!
!!!?
FANGS!?
!?
...AEGIS?
WHAT'RE YOU DOING HERE?

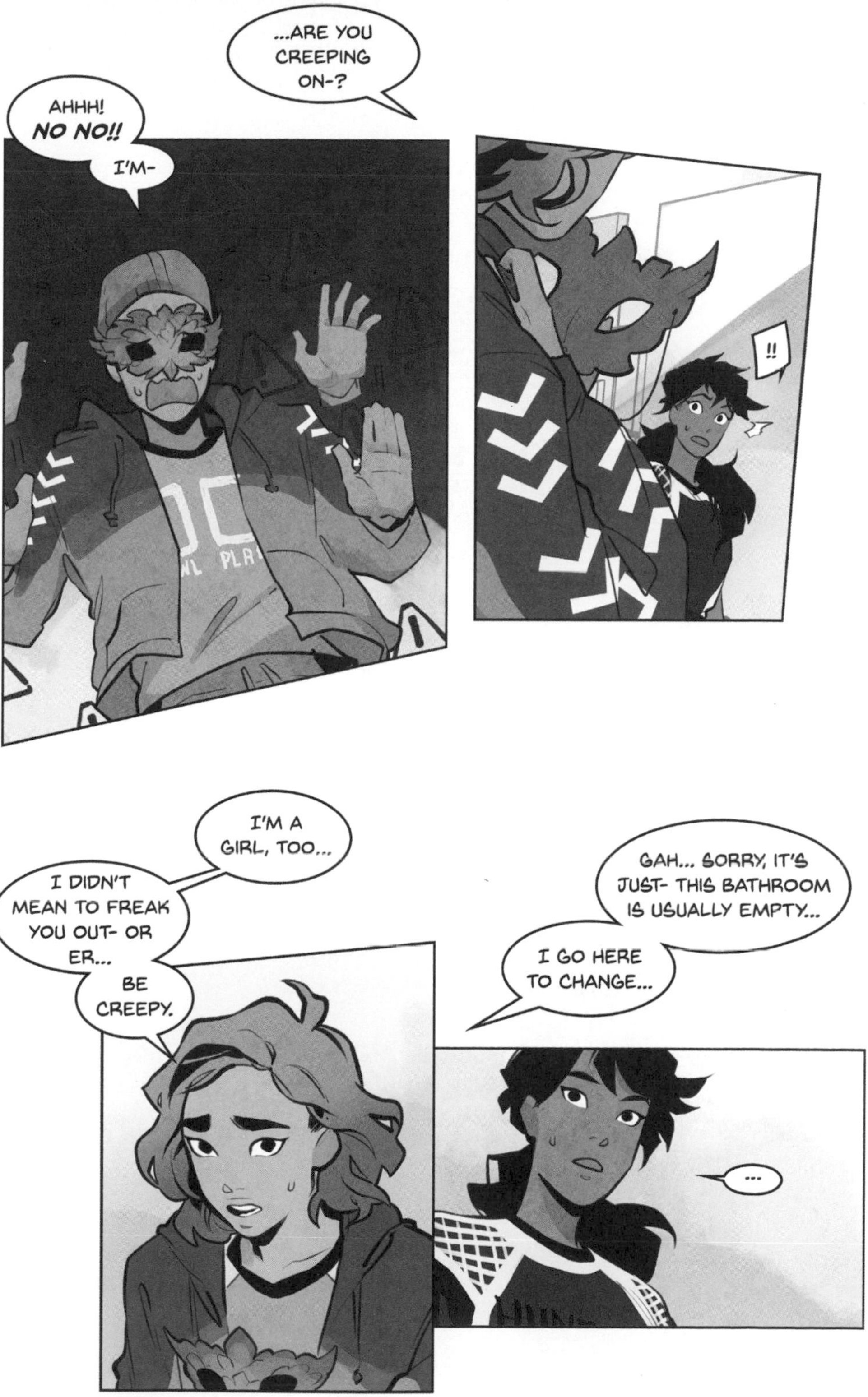
...ARE YOU CREEPING ON-?
AHHH! ***NO NO!!***
I'M-
!!
I'M A GIRL, TOO...
I DIDN'T MEAN TO FREAK YOU OUT- OR ER...
BE CREEPY.
GAH... SORRY, IT'S JUST- THIS BATHROOM IS USUALLY EMPTY...
I GO HERE TO CHANGE...
...

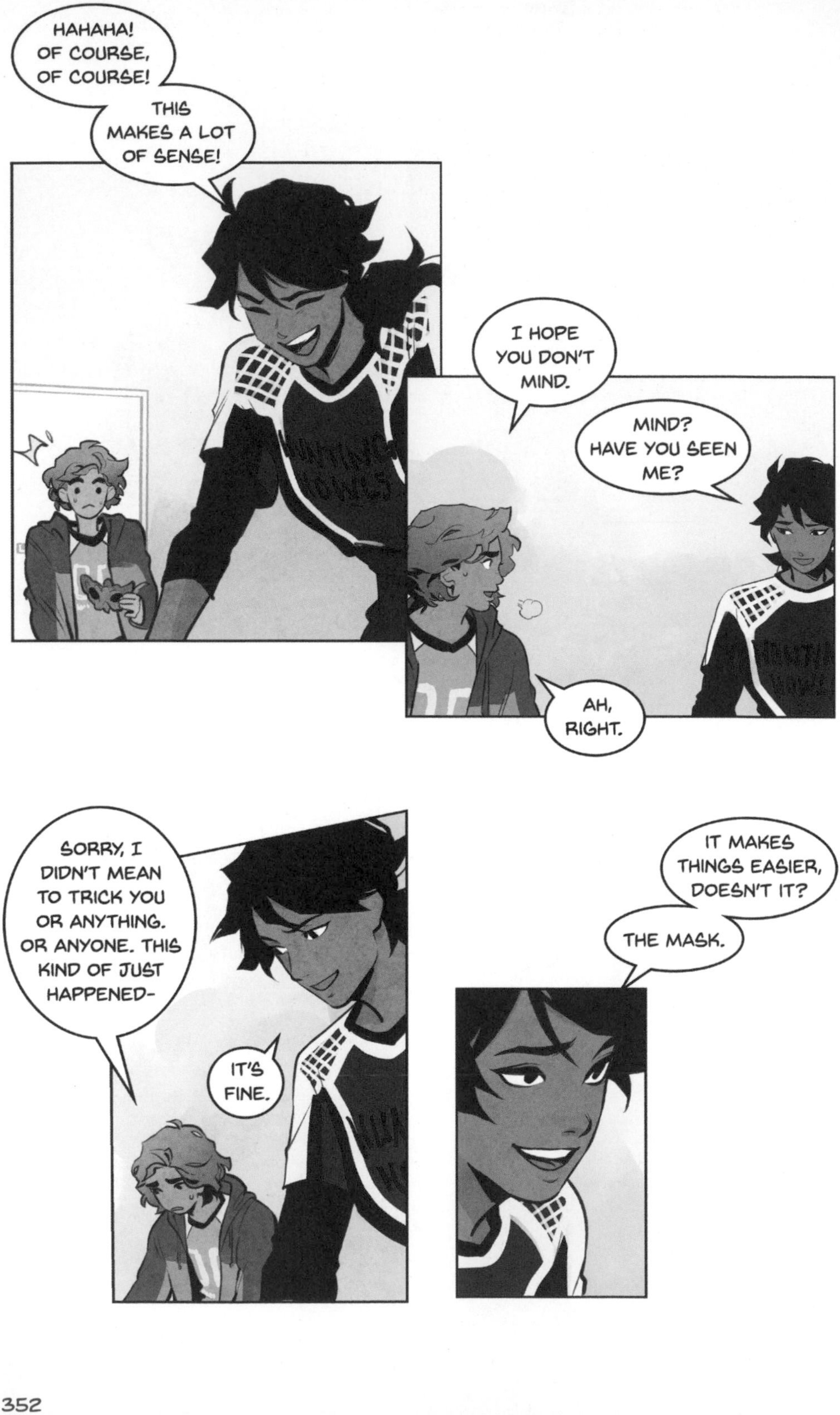
HAHAHA! OF COURSE, OF COURSE!
THIS MAKES A LOT OF SENSE!
I HOPE YOU DON'T MIND.
MIND? HAVE YOU SEEN ME?
AH, RIGHT.
SORRY, I DIDN'T MEAN TO TRICK YOU OR ANYTHING. OR ANYONE. THIS KIND OF JUST HAPPENED-
IT'S FINE.
IT MAKES THINGS EASIER, DOESN'T IT?
THE MASK.

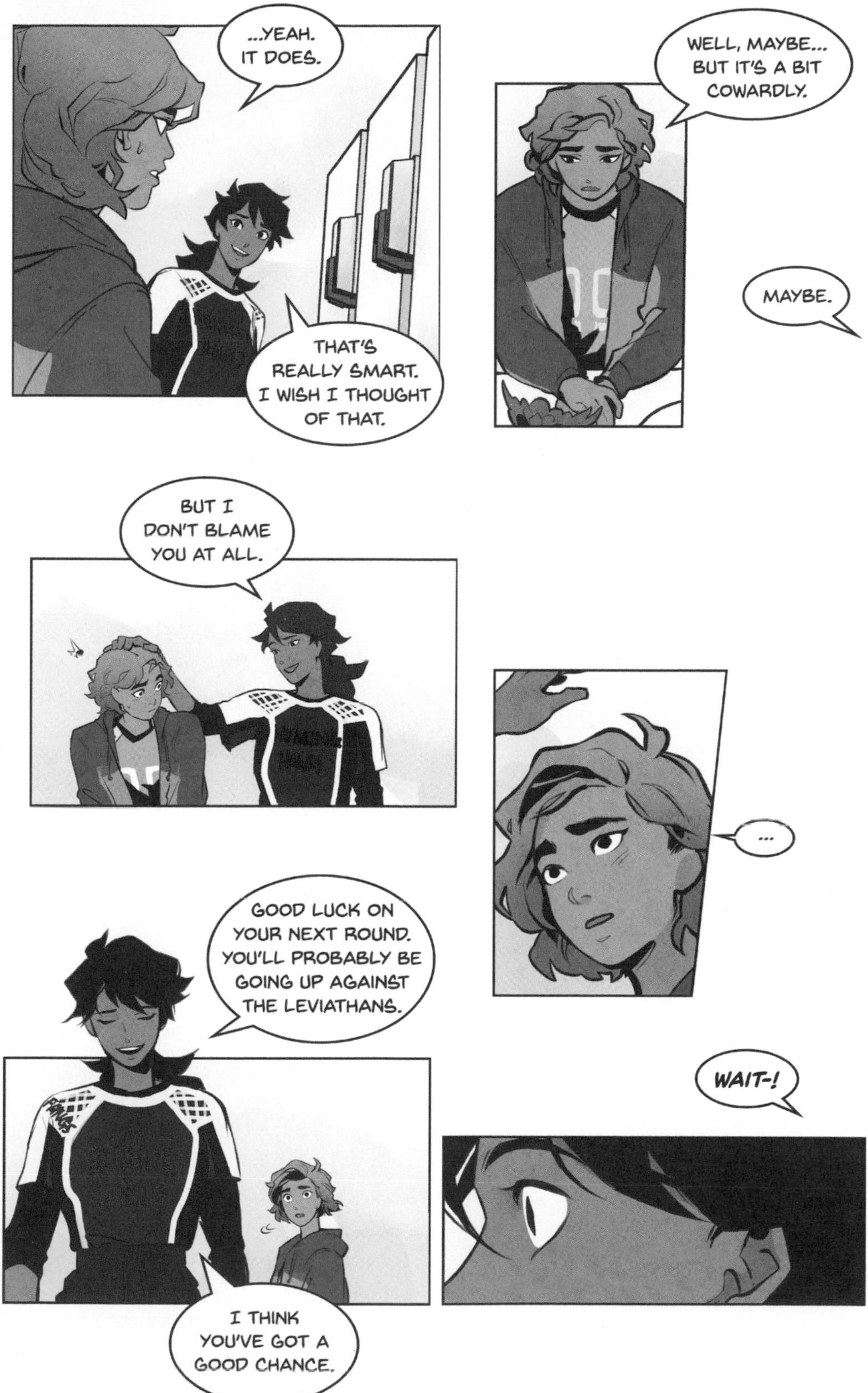
...YEAH. IT DOES.
THAT'S REALLY SMART. I WISH I THOUGHT OF THAT.
WELL, MAYBE... BUT IT'S A BIT COWARDLY.
MAYBE.
BUT I DON'T BLAME YOU AT ALL.
...
GOOD LUCK ON YOUR NEXT ROUND. YOU'LL PROBABLY BE GOING UP AGAINST THE LEVIATHANS.
I THINK YOU'VE GOT A GOOD CHANCE.
WAIT-!

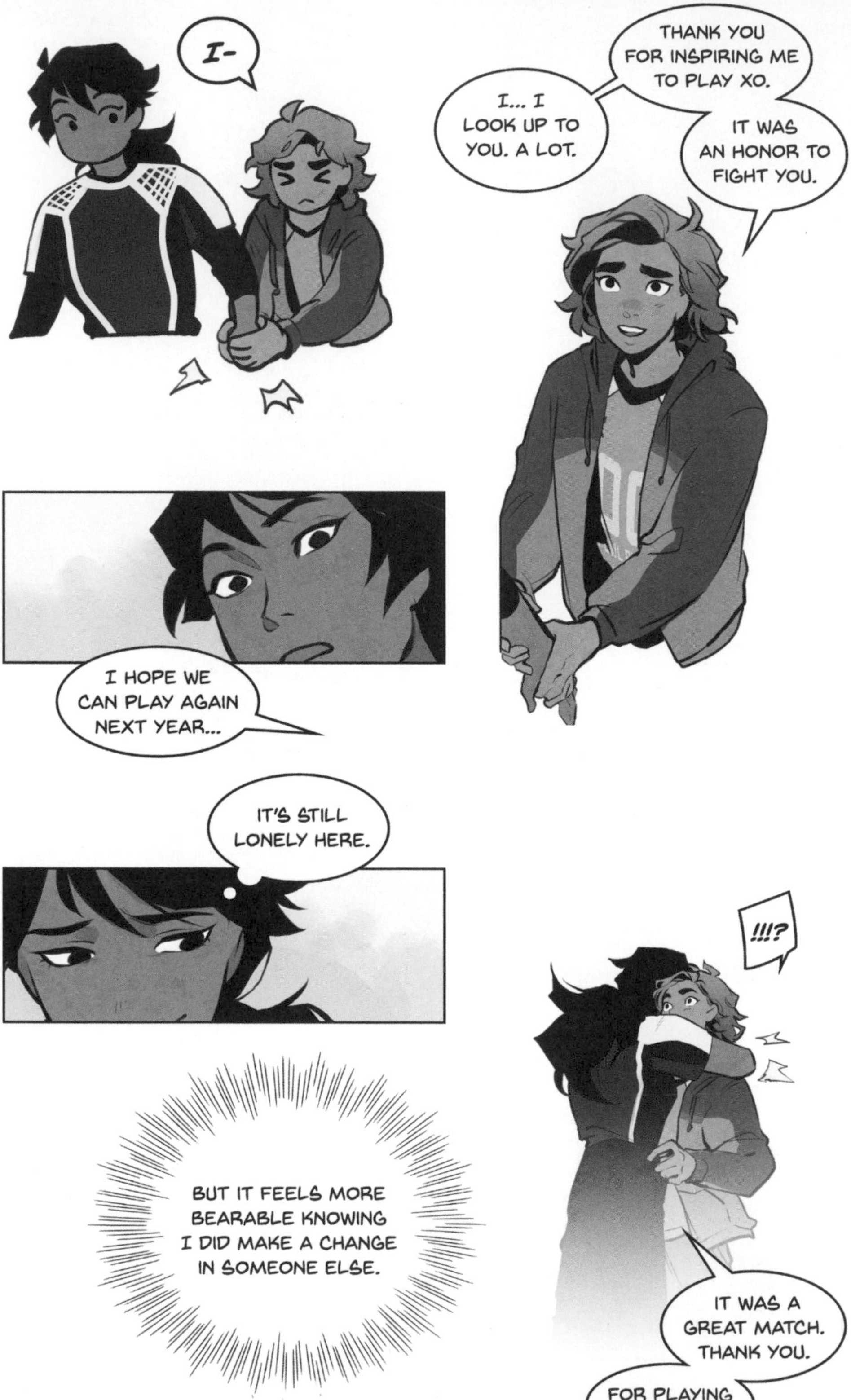
I-
I HOPE WE CAN PLAY AGAIN NEXT YEAR...
I... I LOOK UP TO YOU. A LOT.
THANK YOU FOR INSPIRING ME TO PLAY XO.
IT WAS AN HONOR TO FIGHT YOU.
IT'S STILL LONELY HERE.
BUT IT FEELS MORE BEARABLE KNOWING I DID MAKE A CHANGE IN SOMEONE ELSE.
!!!?
IT WAS A GREAT MATCH. THANK YOU.
FOR PLAYING WITH ME.

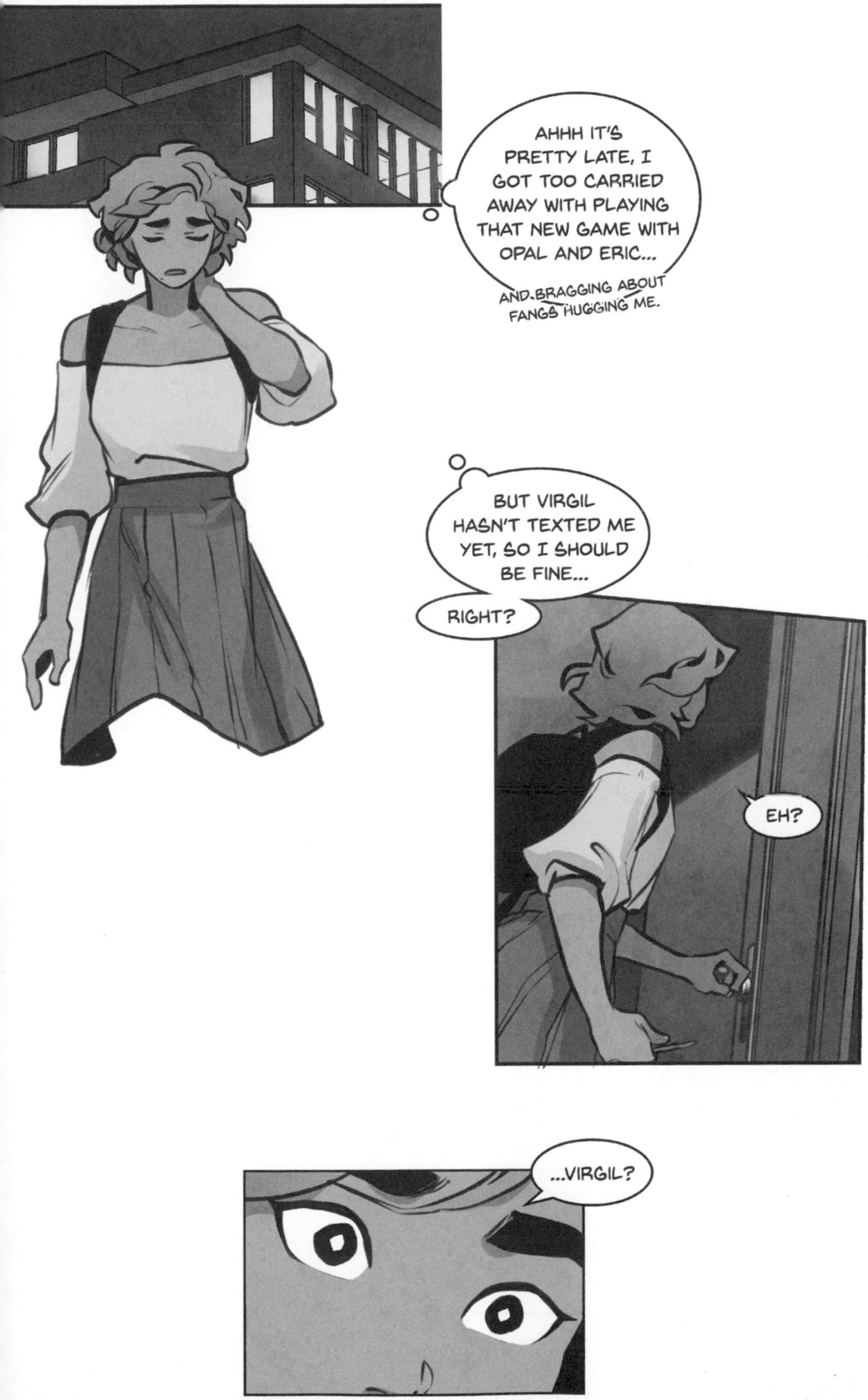
AHHH IT'S PRETTY LATE, I GOT TOO CARRIED AWAY WITH PLAYING THAT NEW GAME WITH OPAL AND ERIC...
AND BRAGGING ABOUT FANGS HUGGING ME.
BUT VIRGIL HASN'T TEXTED ME YET, SO I SHOULD BE FINE...
RIGHT?
EH?
...VIRGIL?

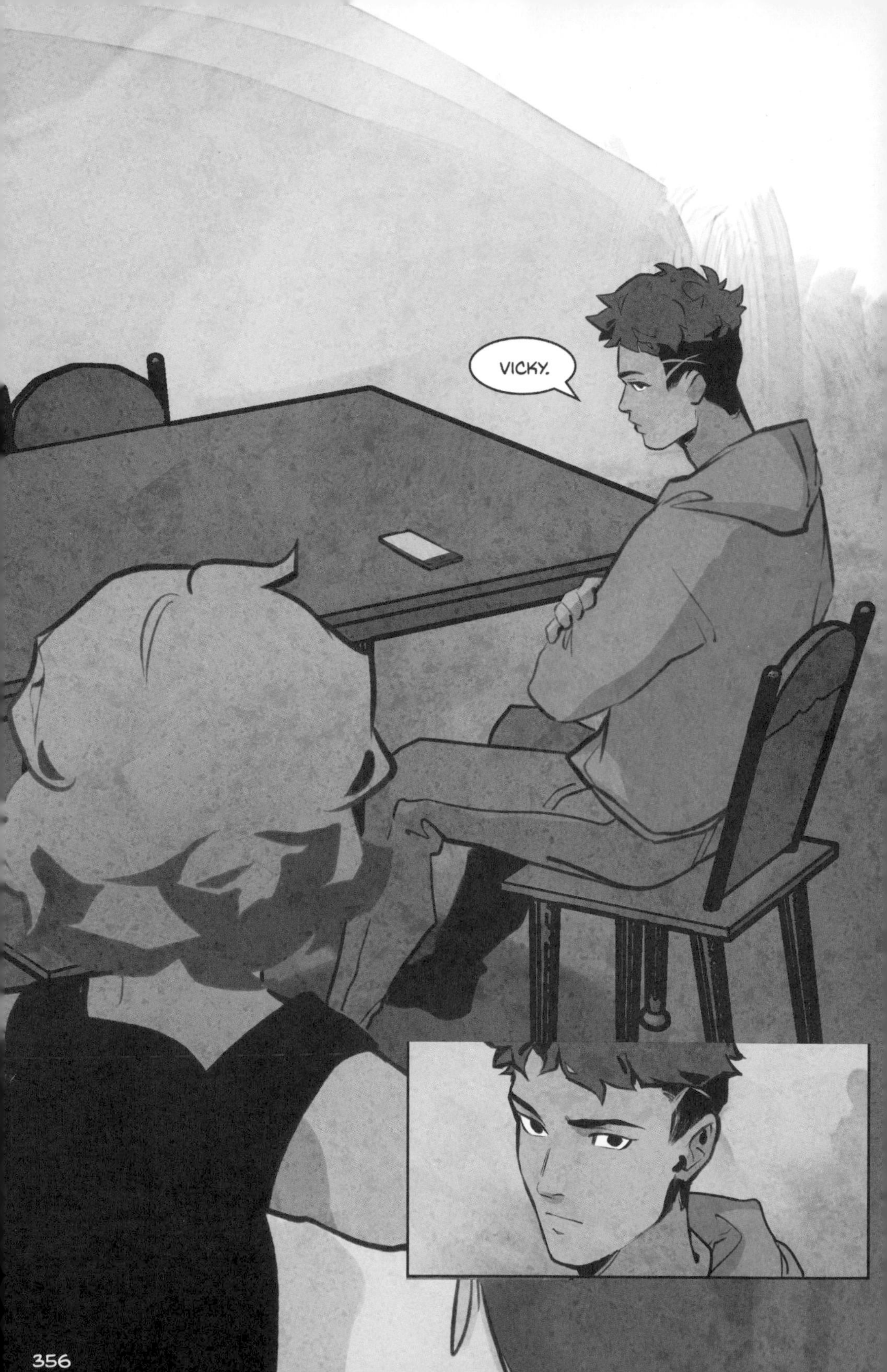
VICKY.

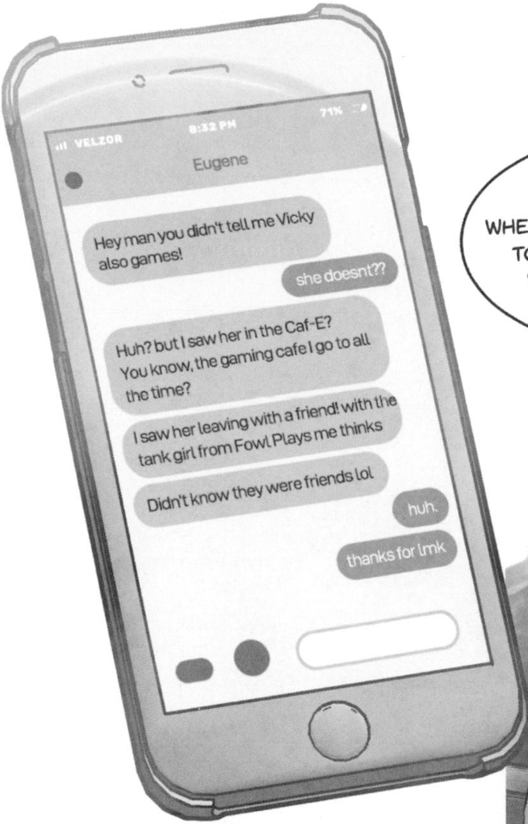
VELZOR
8:32 PM
71%
Eugene
Hey man you didn't tell me Vicky also games!
she doesnt??
Huh? but I saw her in the Caf-E? You know, the gaming cafe I go to all the time?
I saw her leaving with a friend! with the tank girl from Fowl Plays me thinks
Didn't know they were friends lol
huh.
thanks for lmk

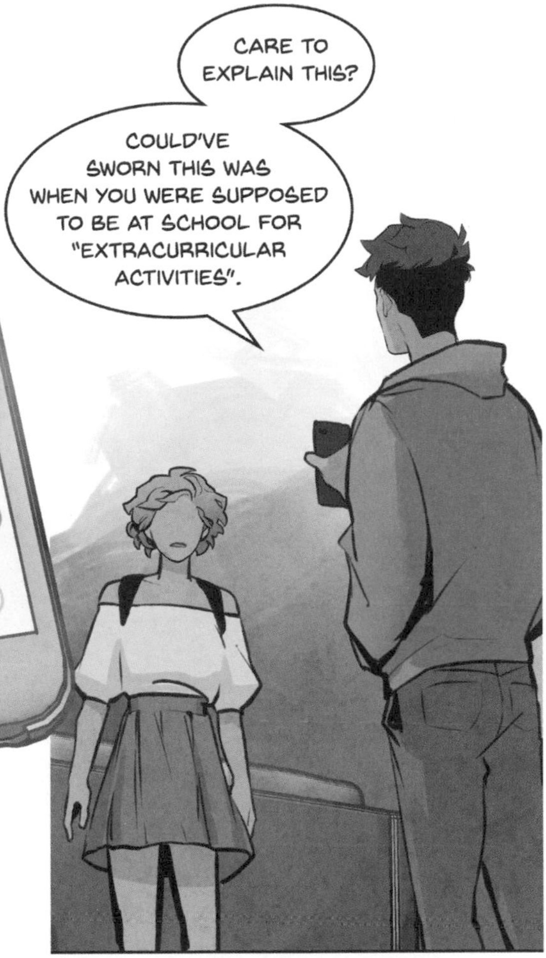
CARE TO EXPLAIN THIS?
COULD'VE SWORN THIS WAS WHEN YOU WERE SUPPOSED TO BE AT SCHOOL FOR "EXTRACURRICULAR ACTIVITIES".

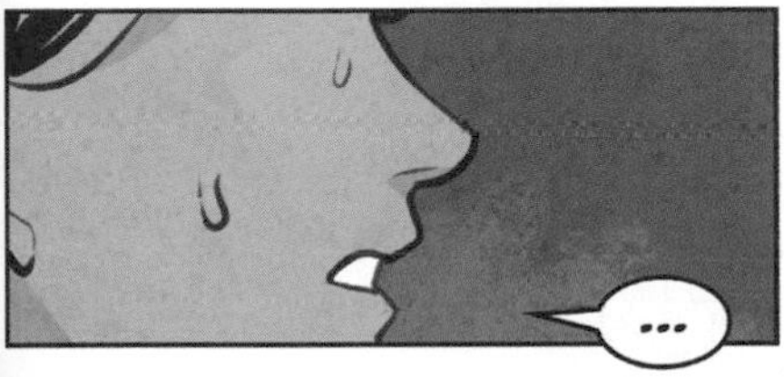
...

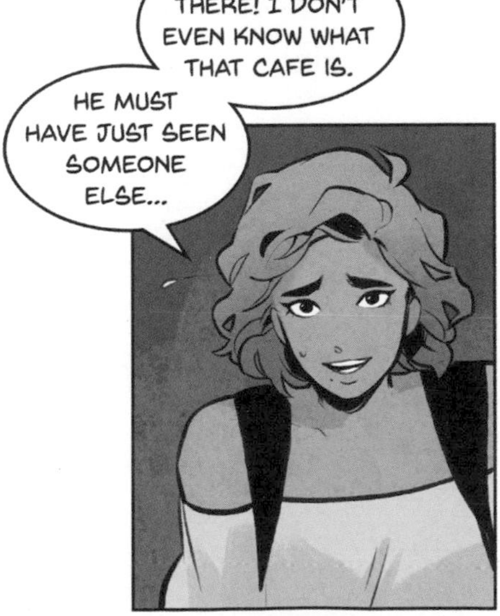
I WASN'T THERE! I DON'T EVEN KNOW WHAT THAT CAFE IS.
HE MUST HAVE JUST SEEN SOMEONE ELSE...

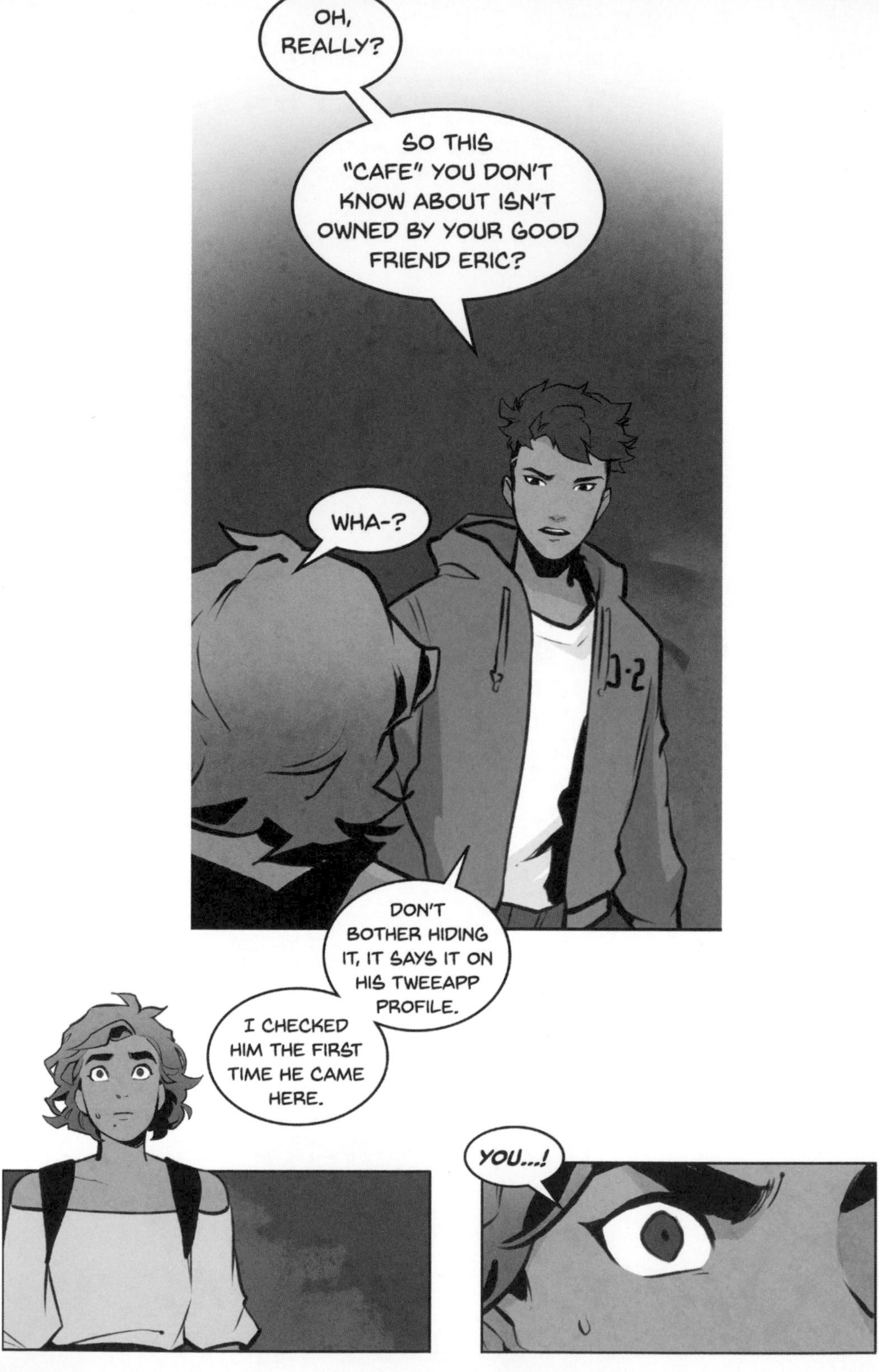
OH, REALLY?
SO THIS "CAFE" YOU DON'T KNOW ABOUT ISN'T OWNED BY YOUR GOOD FRIEND ERIC?
WHA-?
DON'T BOTHER HIDING IT, IT SAYS IT ON HIS TWEEAPP PROFILE.
I CHECKED HIM THE FIRST TIME HE CAME HERE.
YOU...!

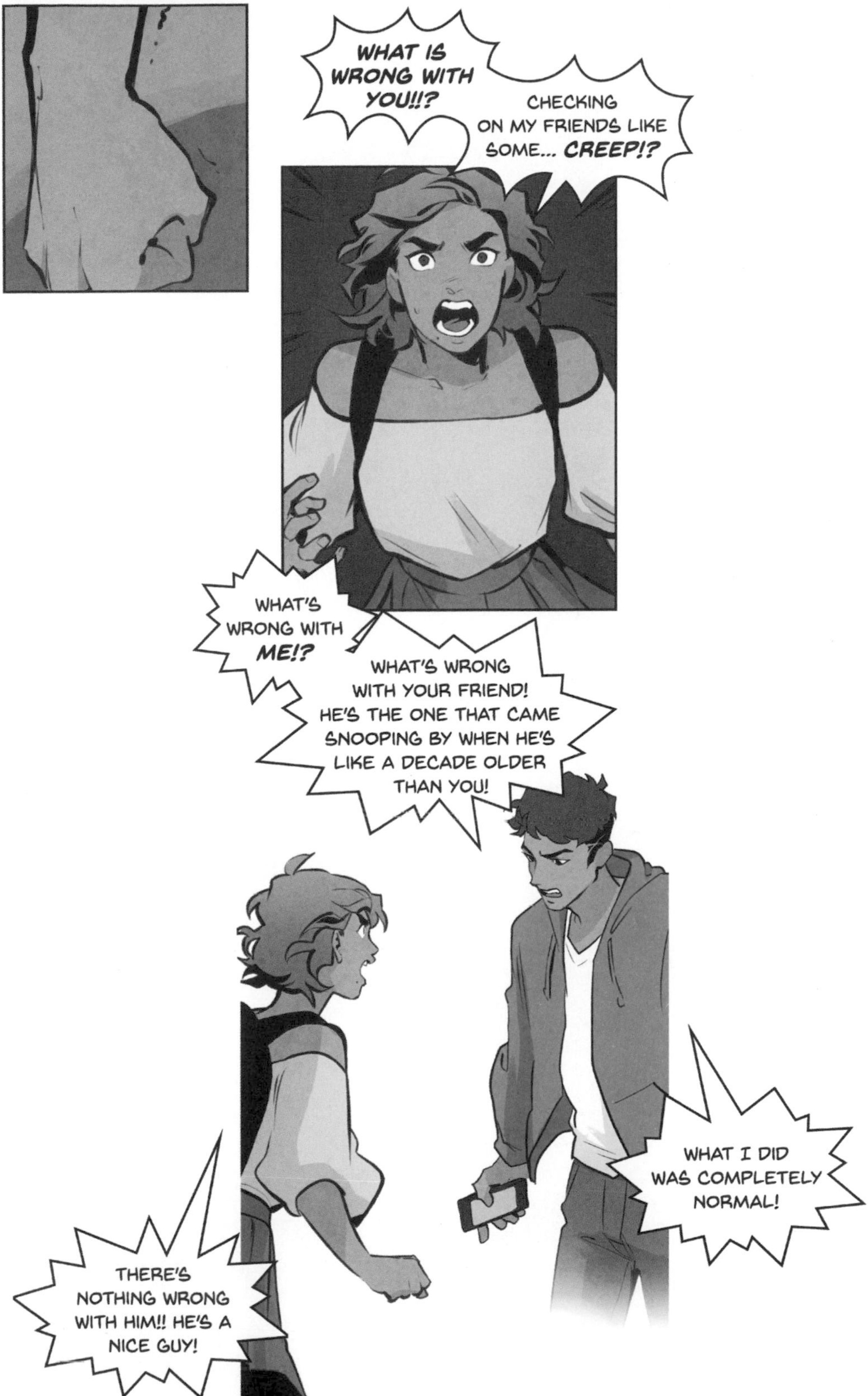
WHAT IS WRONG WITH YOU!!?
CHECKING ON MY FRIENDS LIKE SOME... CREEP!?
WHAT'S WRONG WITH ME!?
WHAT'S WRONG WITH YOUR FRIEND! HE'S THE ONE THAT CAME SNOOPING BY WHEN HE'S LIKE A DECADE OLDER THAN YOU!
THERE'S NOTHING WRONG WITH HIM!! HE'S A NICE GUY!
WHAT I DID WAS COMPLETELY NORMAL!

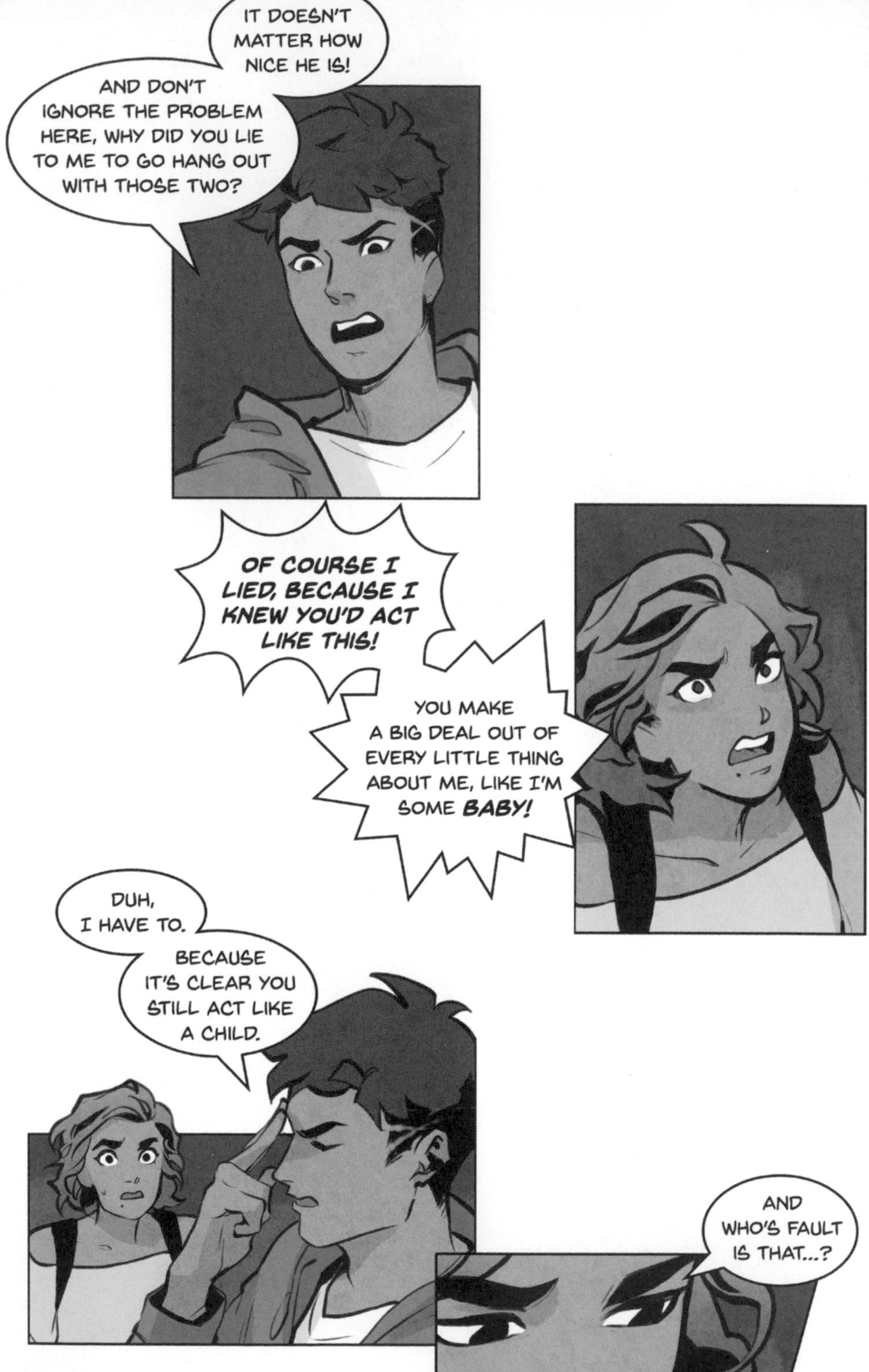
IT DOESN'T MATTER HOW NICE HE IS!
AND DON'T IGNORE THE PROBLEM HERE, WHY DID YOU LIE TO ME TO GO HANG OUT WITH THOSE TWO?
OF COURSE I LIED, BECAUSE I KNEW YOU'D ACT LIKE THIS!
YOU MAKE A BIG DEAL OUT OF EVERY LITTLE THING ABOUT ME, LIKE I'M SOME BABY!
DUH, I HAVE TO.
BECAUSE IT'S CLEAR YOU STILL ACT LIKE A CHILD.
AND WHO'S FAULT IS THAT...?

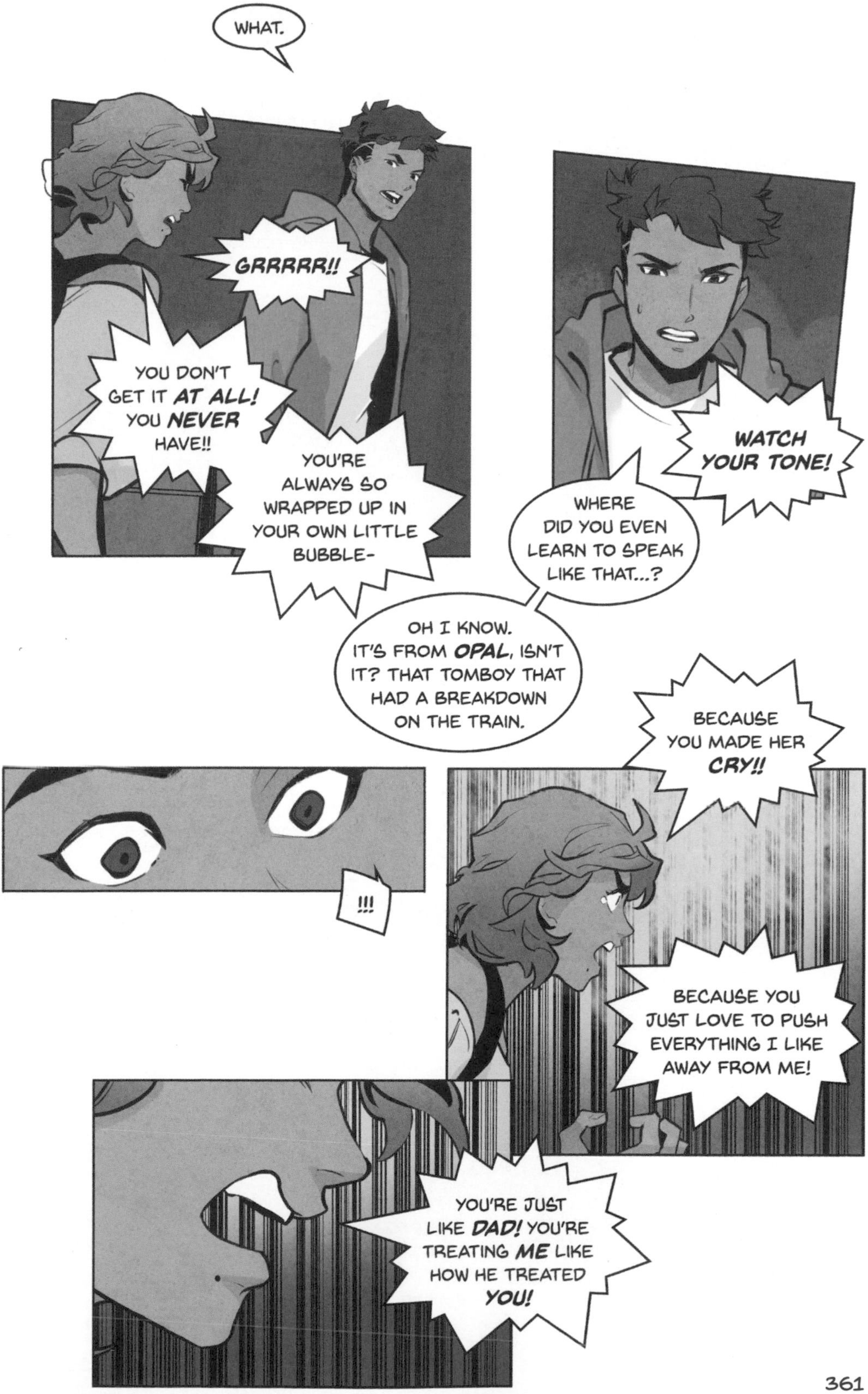
WHAT.
GRRRRR!!
YOU DON'T GET IT AT ALL! YOU NEVER HAVE!!
YOU'RE ALWAYS SO WRAPPED UP IN YOUR OWN LITTLE BUBBLE-
WATCH YOUR TONE!
WHERE DID YOU EVEN LEARN TO SPEAK LIKE THAT...?
OH I KNOW. IT'S FROM OPAL, ISN'T IT? THAT TOMBOY THAT HAD A BREAKDOWN ON THE TRAIN.
!!!
BECAUSE YOU MADE HER CRY!!
BECAUSE YOU JUST LOVE TO PUSH EVERYTHING I LIKE AWAY FROM ME!
YOU'RE JUST LIKE DAD! YOU'RE TREATING ME LIKE HOW HE TREATED YOU!

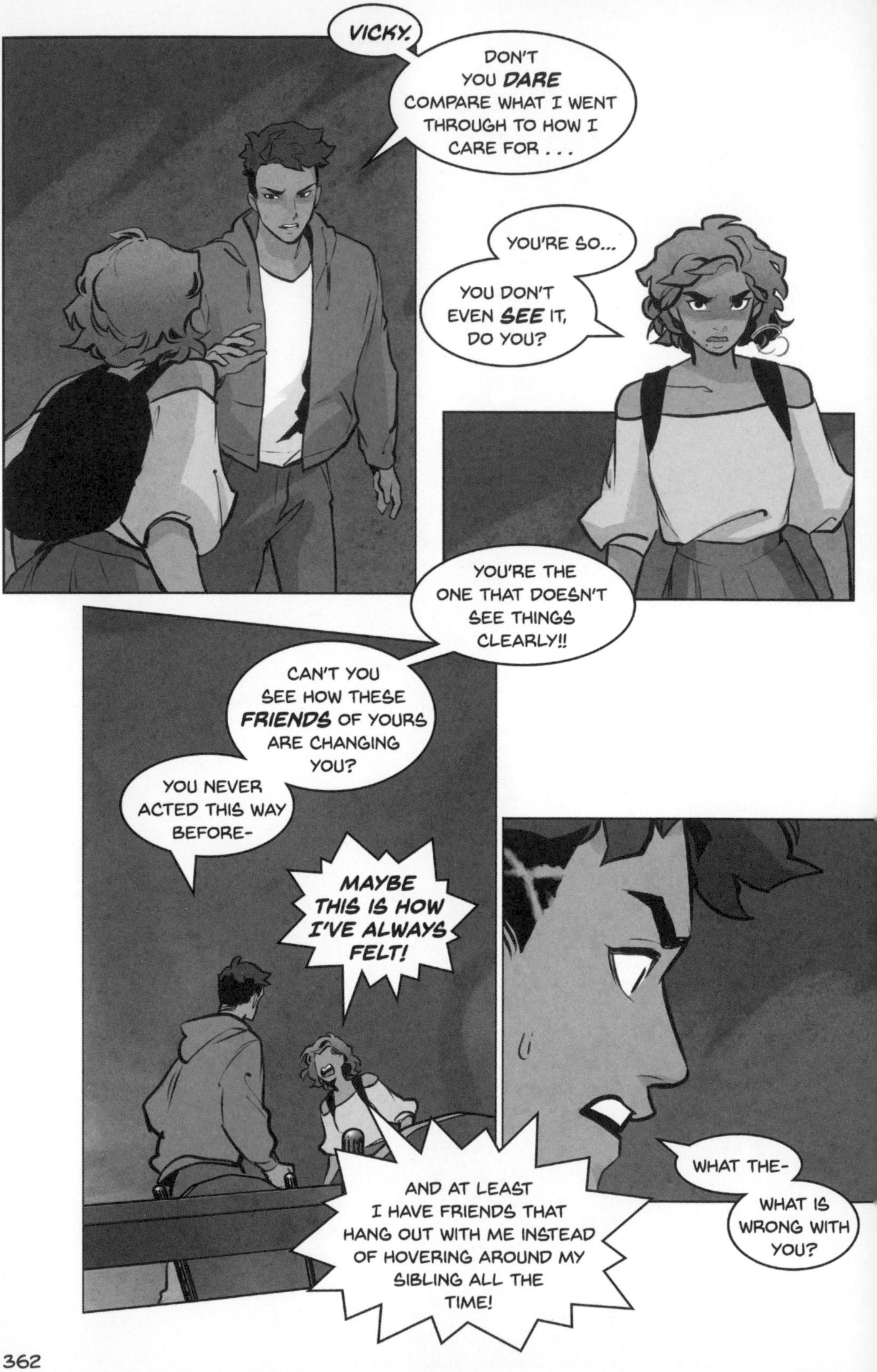

VICKY.
DON'T YOU DARE COMPARE WHAT I WENT THROUGH TO HOW I CARE FOR . . .
YOU'RE SO...
YOU DON'T EVEN SEE IT, DO YOU?
YOU'RE THE ONE THAT DOESN'T SEE THINGS CLEARLY!!
CAN'T YOU SEE HOW THESE FRIENDS OF YOURS ARE CHANGING YOU?
YOU NEVER ACTED THIS WAY BEFORE-
MAYBE THIS IS HOW I'VE ALWAYS FELT!
AND AT LEAST I HAVE FRIENDS THAT HANG OUT WITH ME INSTEAD OF HOVERING AROUND MY SIBLING ALL THE TIME!
WHAT THE-
WHAT IS WRONG WITH YOU?

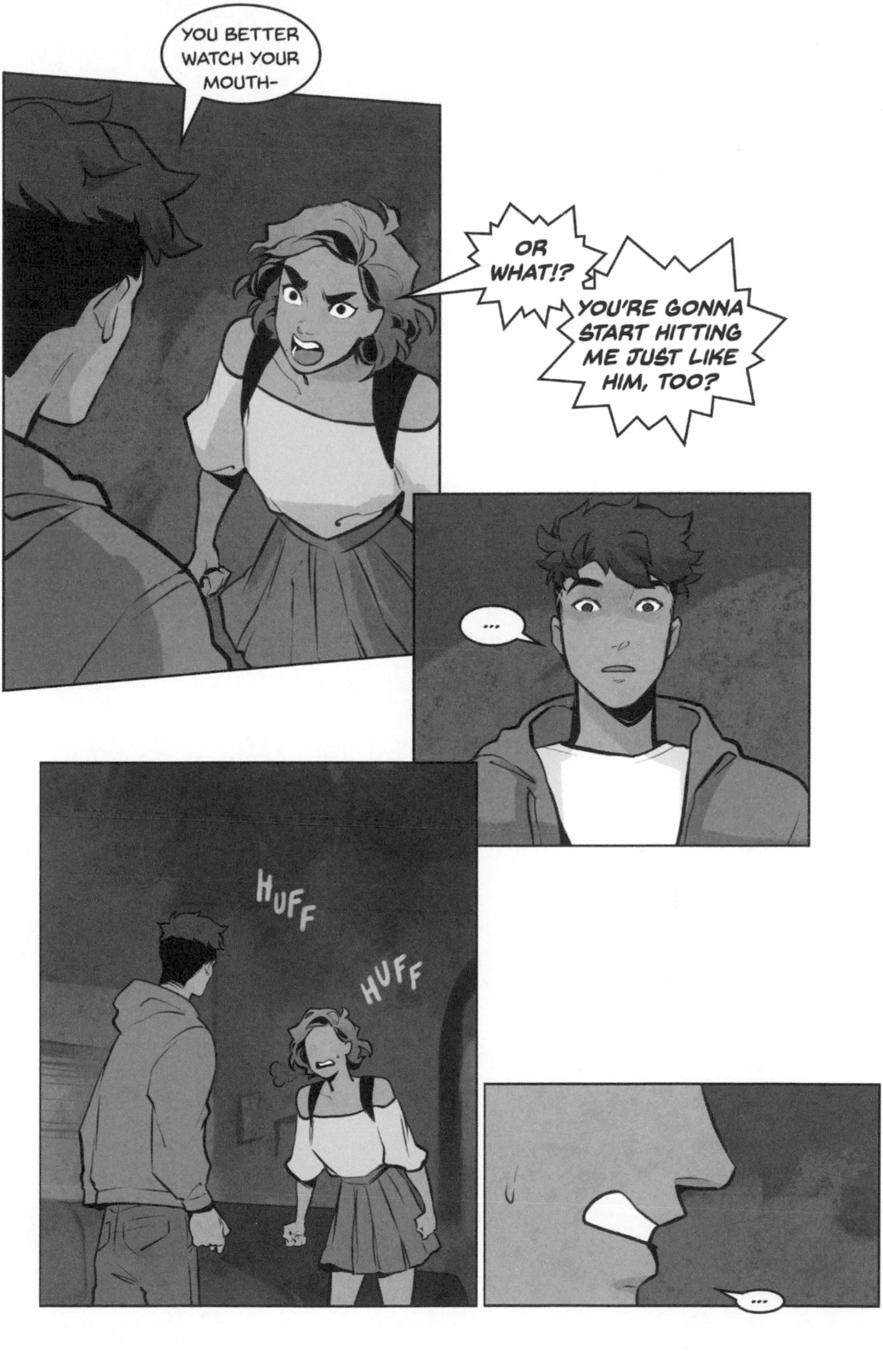

YOU BETTER WATCH YOUR MOUTH-
OR WHAT!?
YOU'RE GONNA START HITTING ME JUST LIKE HIM, TOO?
...
HUFF
HUFF
...

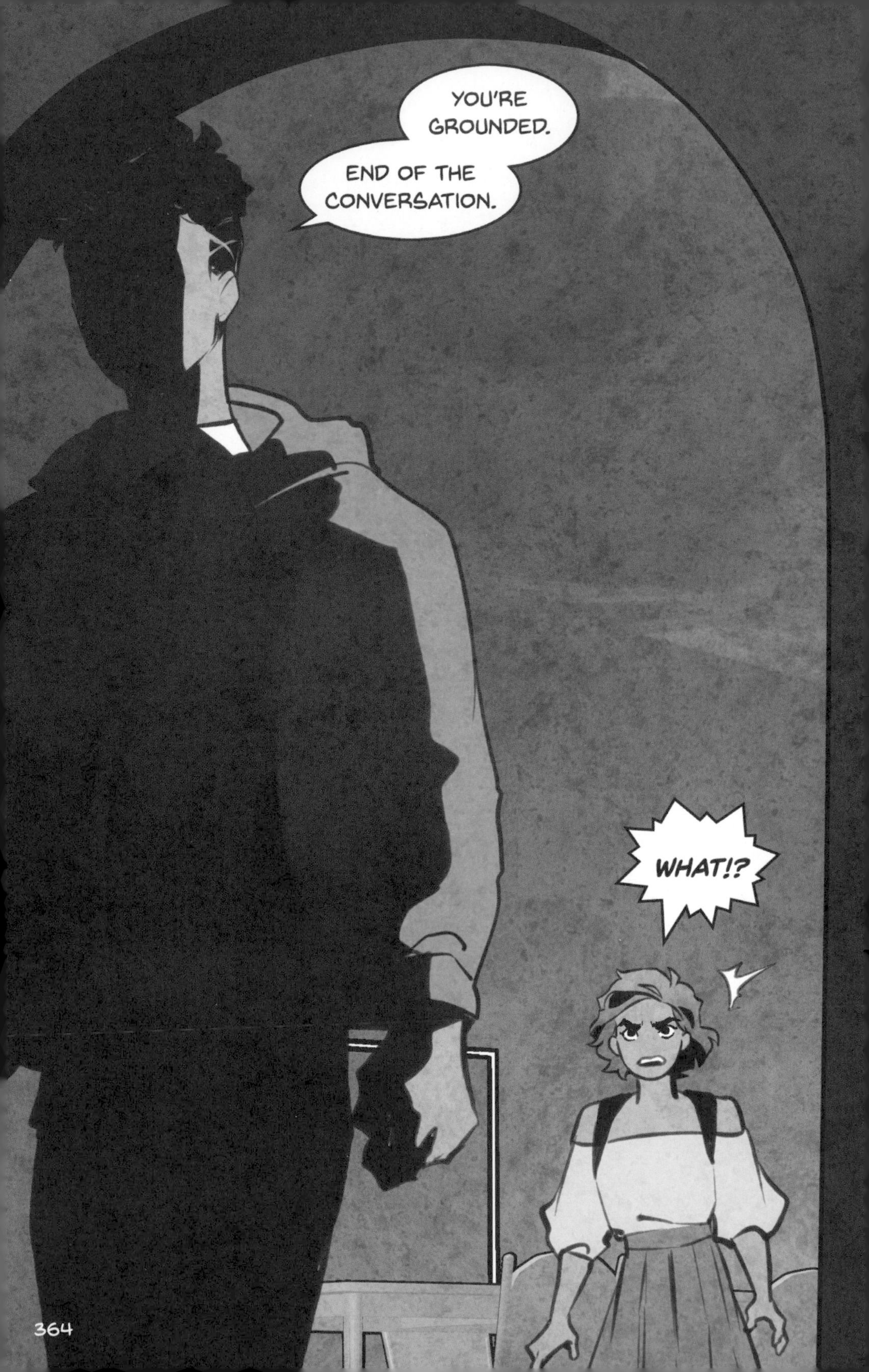
YOU'RE GROUNDED.
END OF THE CONVERSATION.
WHAT!?

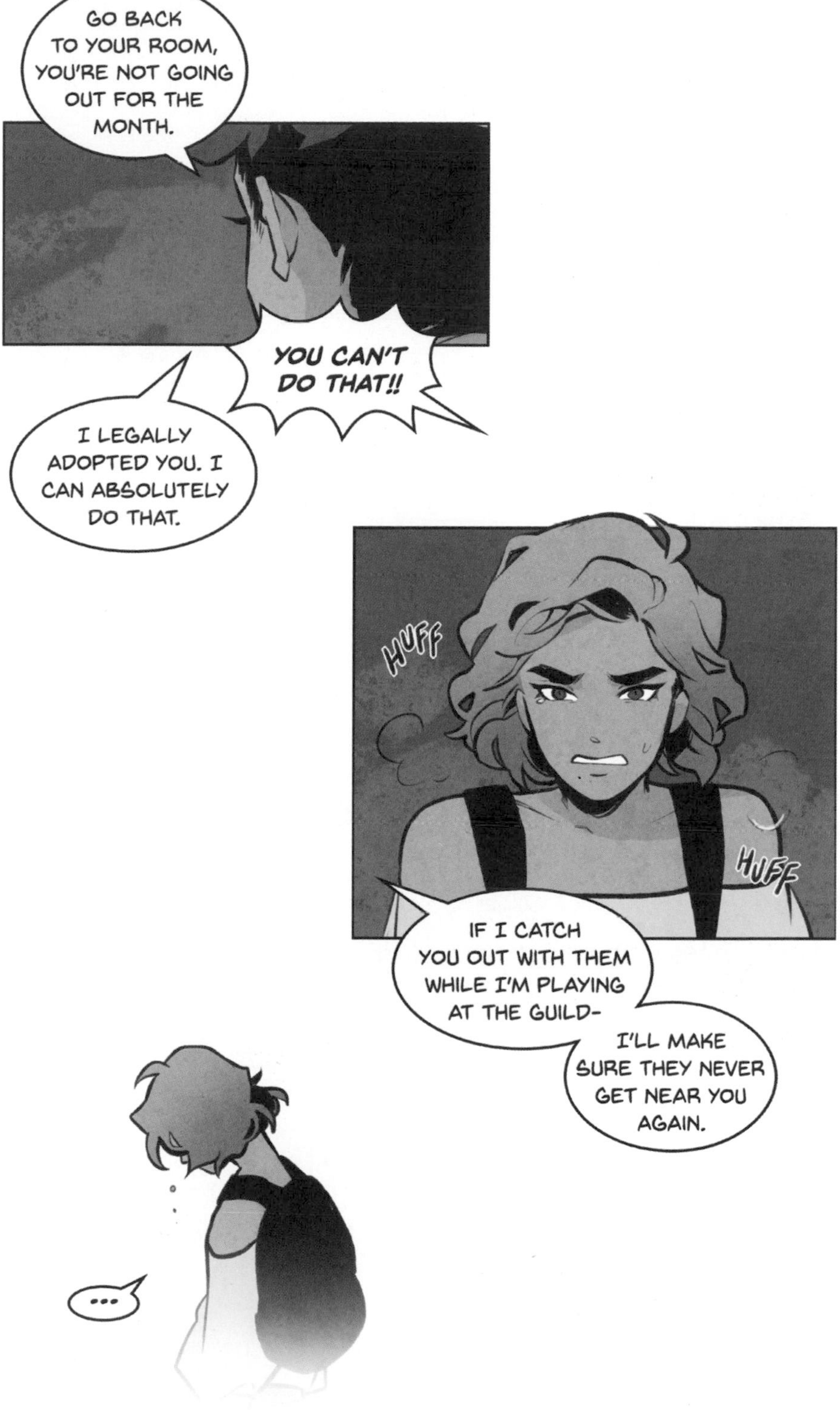
GO BACK TO YOUR ROOM, YOU'RE NOT GOING OUT FOR THE MONTH.
YOU CAN'T DO THAT!!
I LEGALLY ADOPTED YOU. I CAN ABSOLUTELY DO THAT.
HUFF
HUFF
IF I CATCH YOU OUT WITH THEM WHILE I'M PLAYING AT THE GUILD-
I'LL MAKE SURE THEY NEVER GET NEAR YOU AGAIN.
...

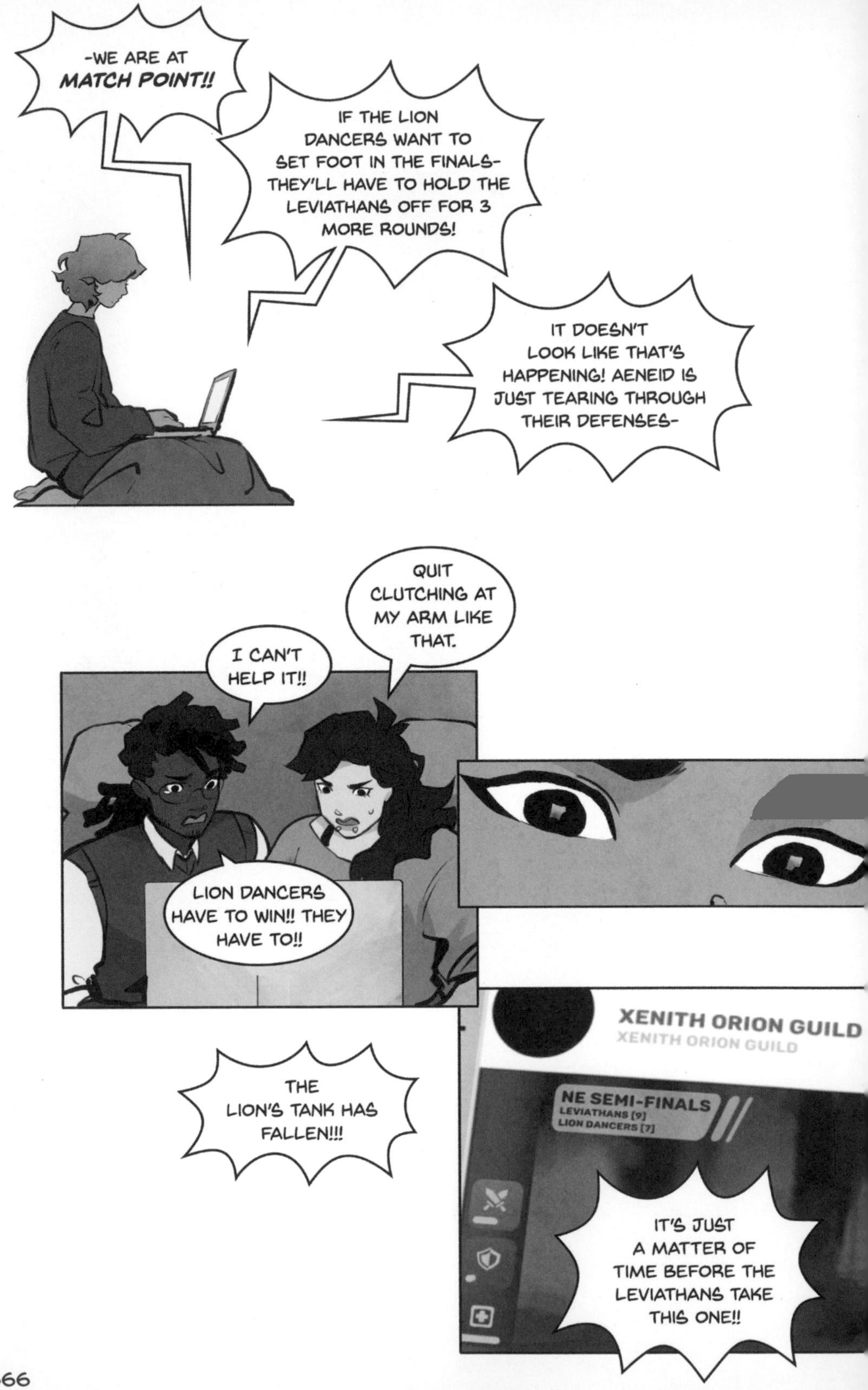

-WE ARE AT MATCH POINT!!
IF THE LION DANCERS WANT TO SET FOOT IN THE FINALS- THEY'LL HAVE TO HOLD THE LEVIATHANS OFF FOR 3 MORE ROUNDS!
IT DOESN'T LOOK LIKE THAT'S HAPPENING! AENEID IS JUST TEARING THROUGH THEIR DEFENSES-
I CAN'T HELP IT!!
QUIT CLUTCHING AT MY ARM LIKE THAT.
LION DANCERS HAVE TO WIN!! THEY HAVE TO!!
THE LION'S TANK HAS FALLEN!!!
XENITH ORION GUILD
XENITH ORION GUILD
NE SEMI-FINALS
LEVIATHANS [9]
LION DANCERS [7]
IT'S JUST A MATTER OF TIME BEFORE THE LEVIATHANS TAKE THIS ONE!!

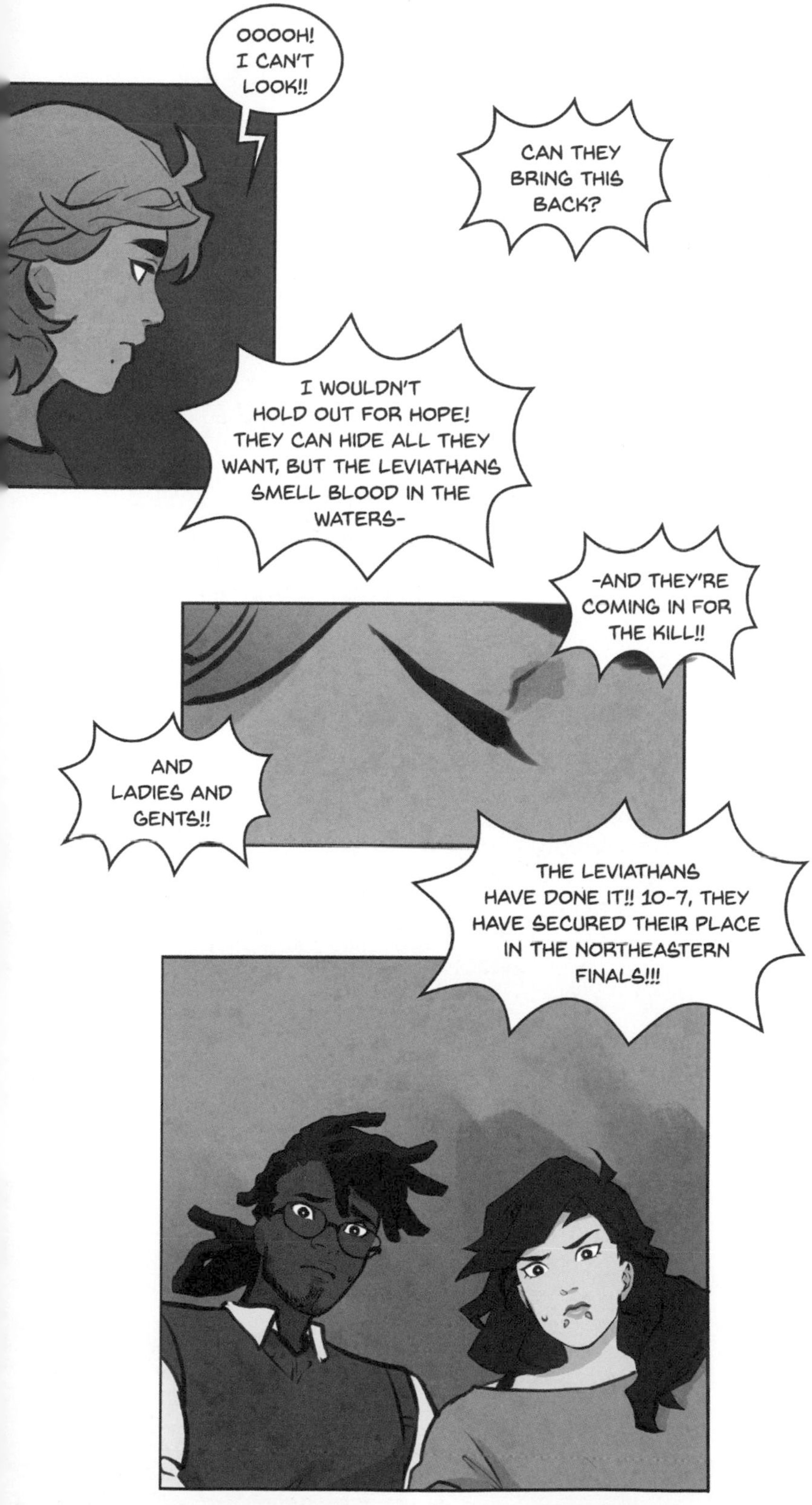
OOOOH! I CAN'T LOOK!!
CAN THEY BRING THIS BACK?
I WOULDN'T HOLD OUT FOR HOPE! THEY CAN HIDE ALL THEY WANT, BUT THE LEVIATHANS SMELL BLOOD IN THE WATERS-
-AND THEY'RE COMING IN FOR THE KILL!!
AND LADIES AND GENTS!!
THE LEVIATHANS HAVE DONE IT!! 10-7, THEY HAVE SECURED THEIR PLACE IN THE NORTHEASTERN FINALS!!!

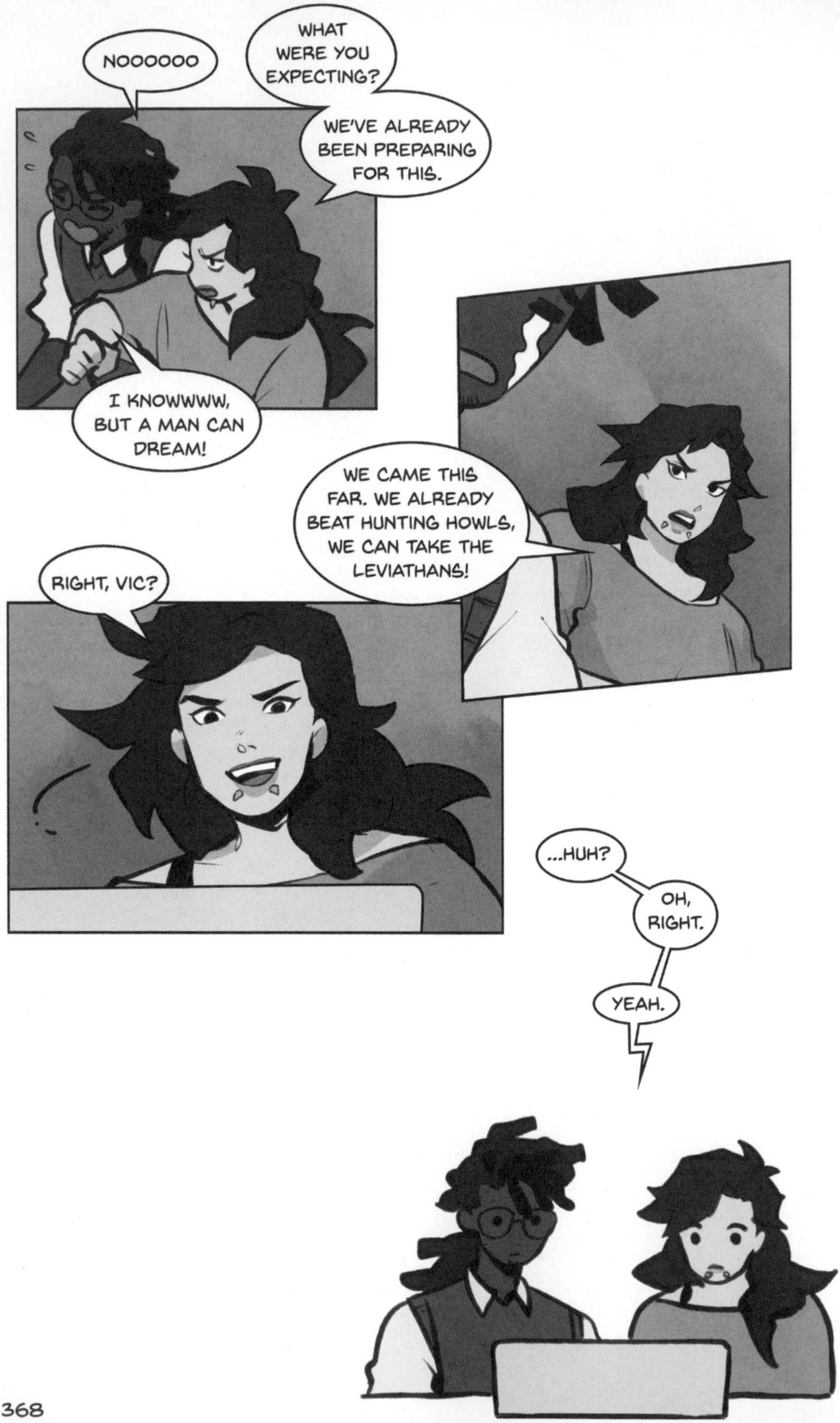
NOOOOOO
WHAT WERE YOU EXPECTING?
WE'VE ALREADY BEEN PREPARING FOR THIS.
I KNOWWWW, BUT A MAN CAN DREAM!
WE CAME THIS FAR. WE ALREADY BEAT HUNTING HOWLS, WE CAN TAKE THE LEVIATHANS!
RIGHT, VIC?
...HUH?
OH, RIGHT.
YEAH.

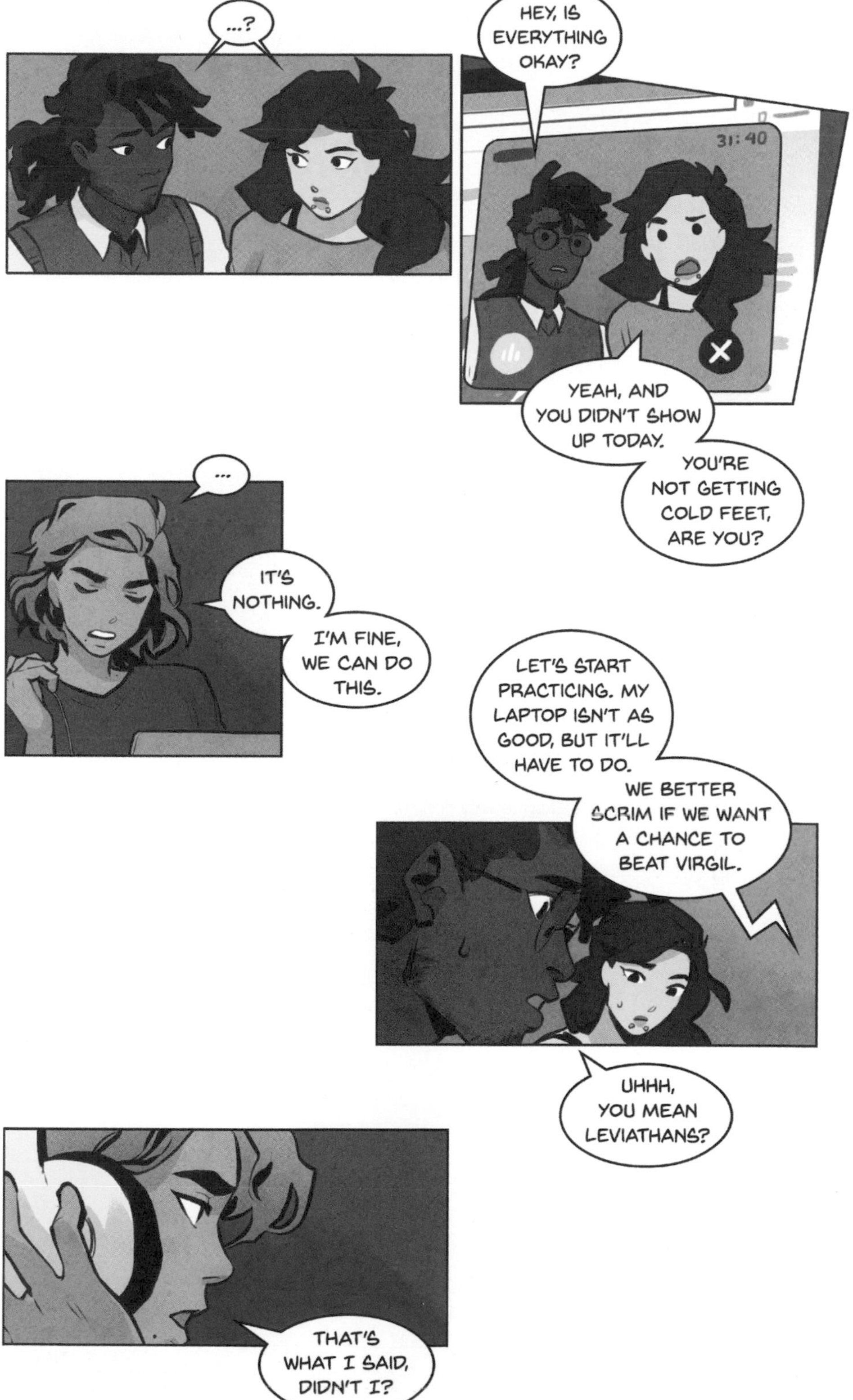
...?
HEY, IS EVERYTHING OKAY?
31:40
YEAH, AND YOU DIDN'T SHOW UP TODAY.
YOU'RE NOT GETTING COLD FEET, ARE YOU?
...
IT'S NOTHING.
I'M FINE, WE CAN DO THIS.
LET'S START PRACTICING. MY LAPTOP ISN'T AS GOOD, BUT IT'LL HAVE TO DO.
WE BETTER SCRIM IF WE WANT A CHANCE TO BEAT VIRGIL.
UHHH, YOU MEAN LEVIATHANS?
THAT'S WHAT I SAID, DIDN'T I?

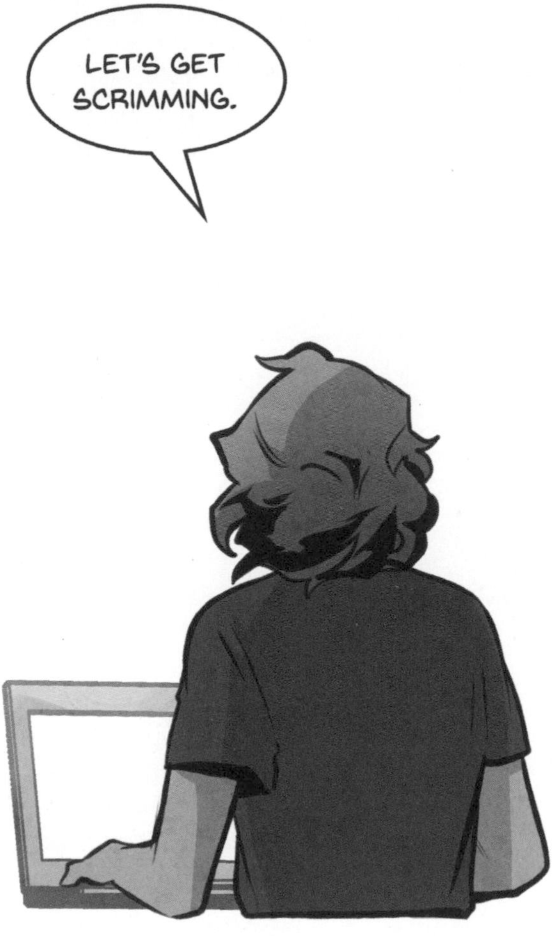
LET'S GET SCRIMMING.

CHAPTER 8: IT'S TIME

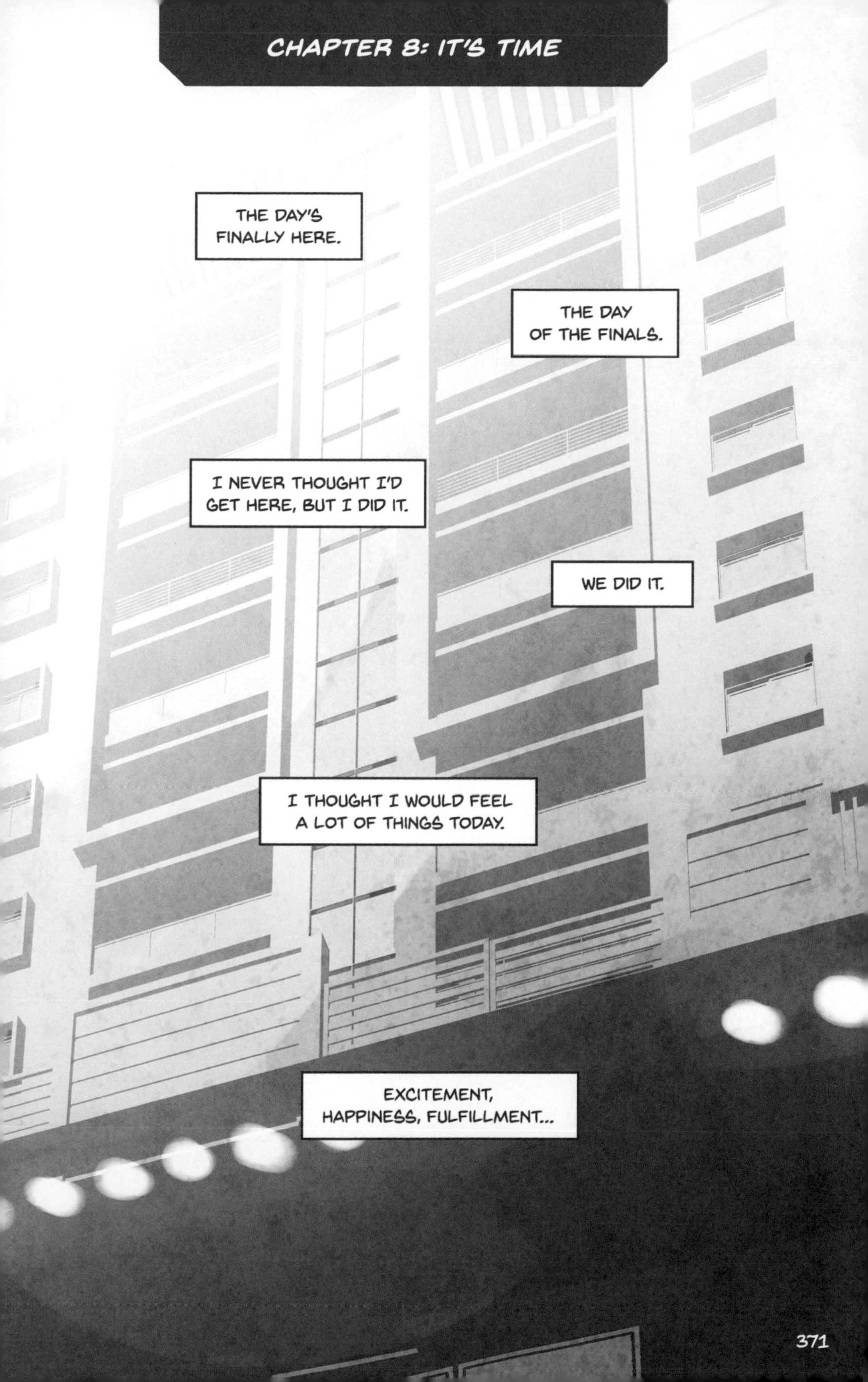
THE DAY'S FINALLY HERE.
THE DAY OF THE FINALS.
I NEVER THOUGHT I'D GET HERE, BUT I DID IT.
WE DID IT.
I THOUGHT I WOULD FEEL A LOT OF THINGS TODAY.
EXCITEMENT, HAPPINESS, FULFILLMENT...

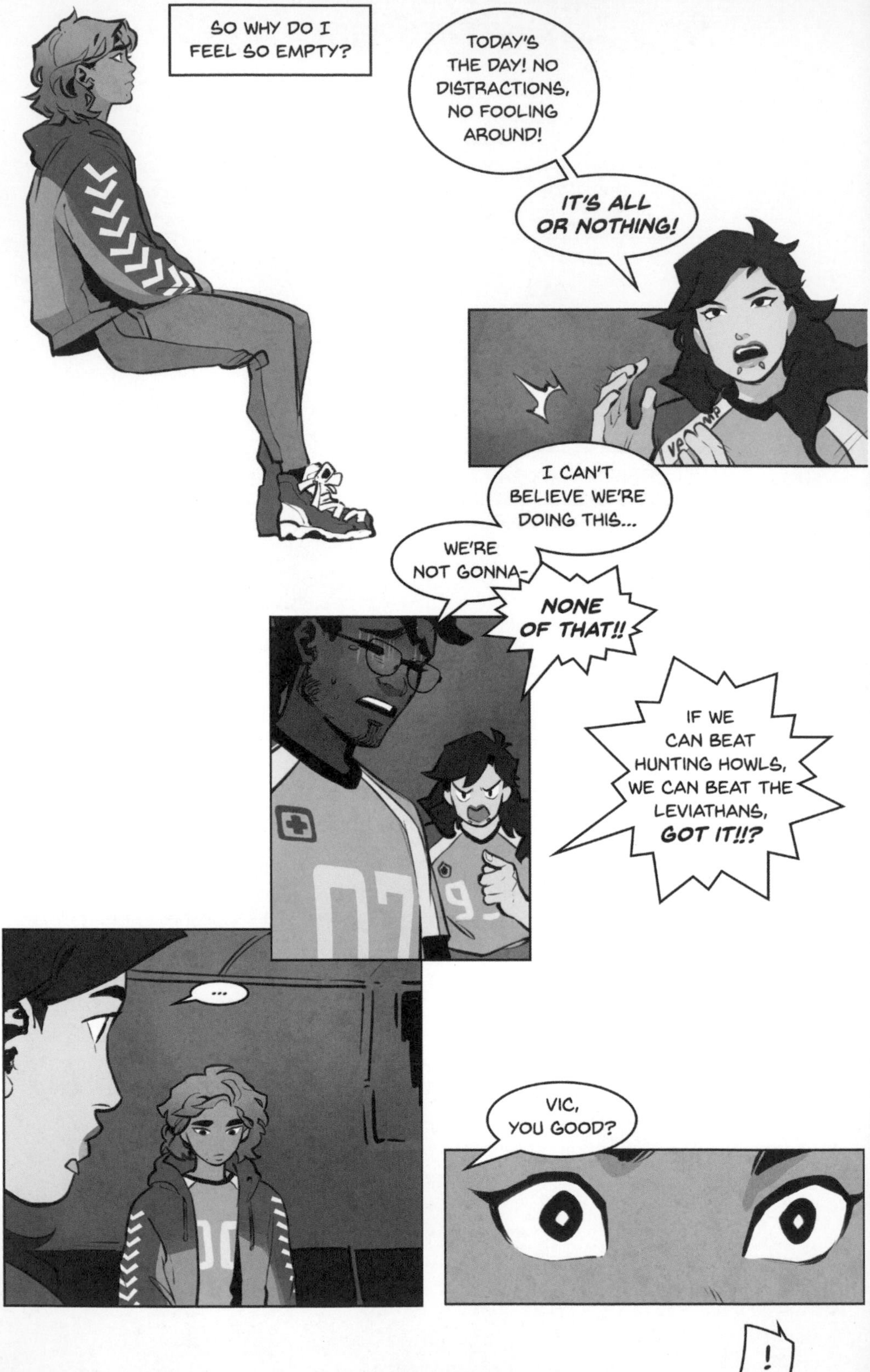
SO WHY DO I FEEL SO EMPTY?
TODAY'S THE DAY! NO DISTRACTIONS, NO FOOLING AROUND!
IT'S ALL OR NOTHING!
I CAN'T BELIEVE WE'RE DOING THIS...
WE'RE NOT GONNA-
NONE OF THAT!!
IF WE CAN BEAT HUNTING HOWLS, WE CAN BEAT THE LEVIATHANS, GOT IT!!?
...
VIC, YOU GOOD?
!

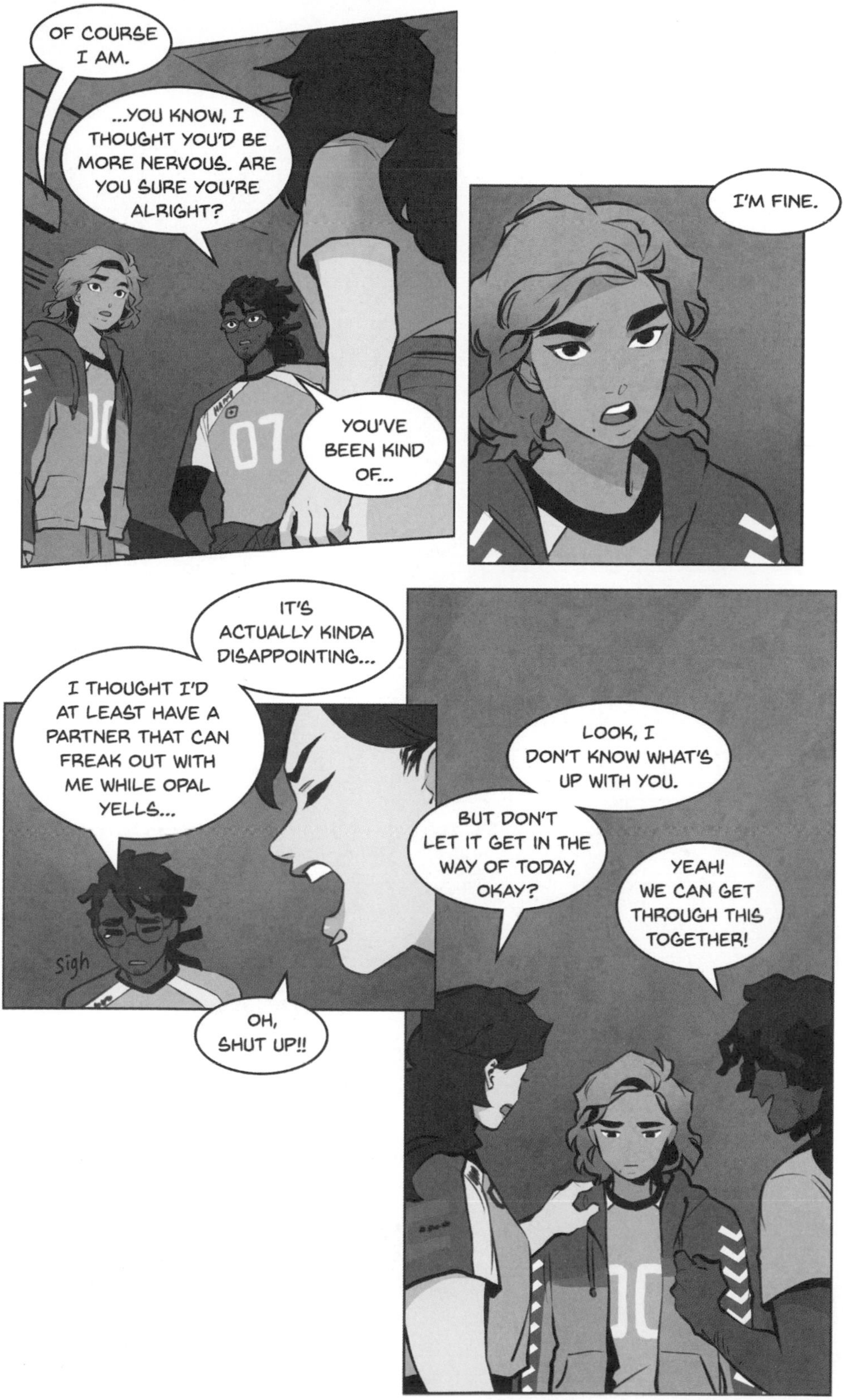
OF COURSE I AM.
...YOU KNOW, I THOUGHT YOU'D BE MORE NERVOUS. ARE YOU SURE YOU'RE ALRIGHT?
YOU'VE BEEN KIND OF...
I'M FINE.
IT'S ACTUALLY KINDA DISAPPOINTING...
I THOUGHT I'D AT LEAST HAVE A PARTNER THAT CAN FREAK OUT WITH ME WHILE OPAL YELLS...
sigh
OH, SHUT UP!!
LOOK, I DON'T KNOW WHAT'S UP WITH YOU.
BUT DON'T LET IT GET IN THE WAY OF TODAY, OKAY?
YEAH! WE CAN GET THROUGH THIS TOGETHER!

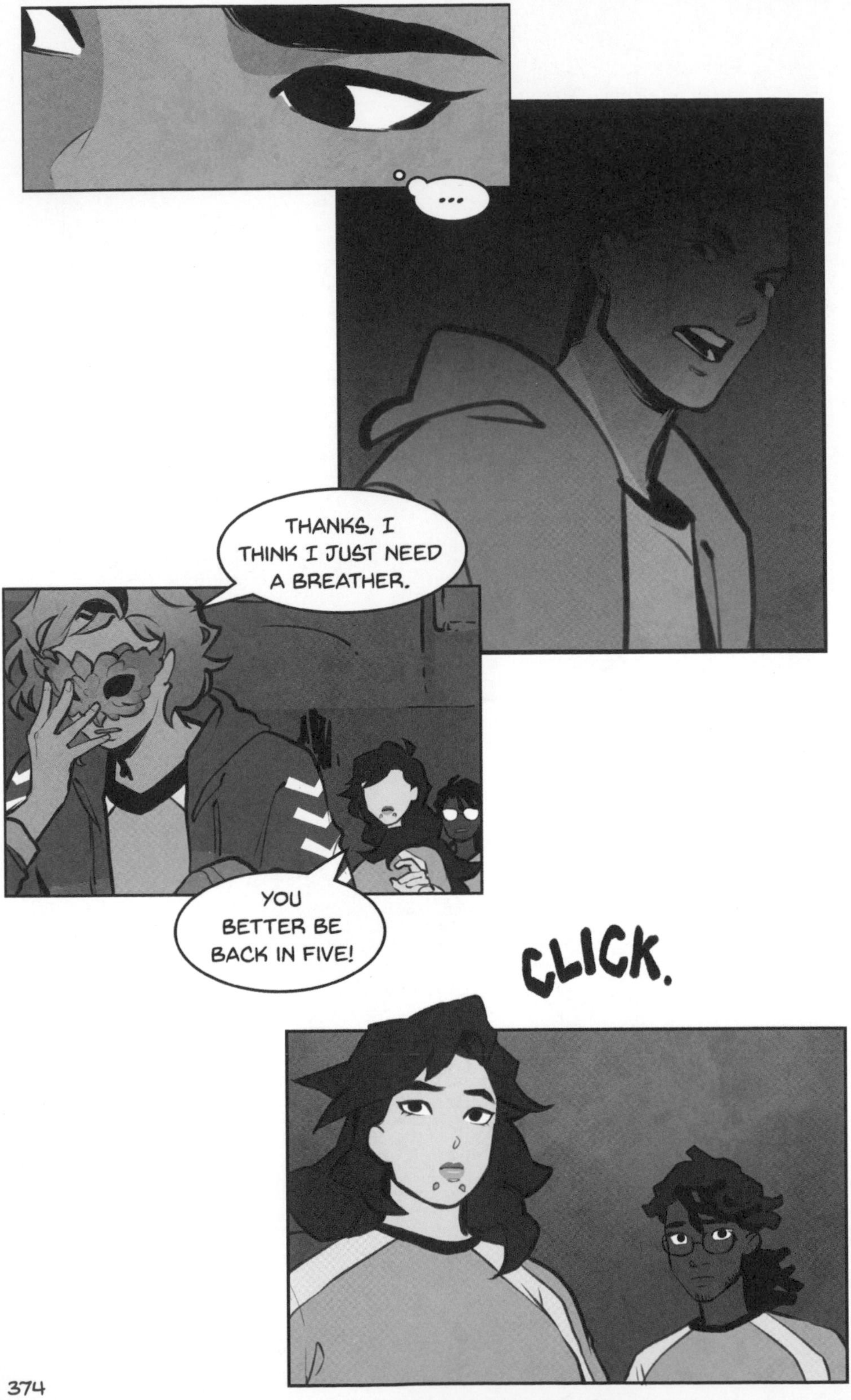
...
THANKS, I THINK I JUST NEED A BREATHER.
YOU BETTER BE BACK IN FIVE!
CLICK.

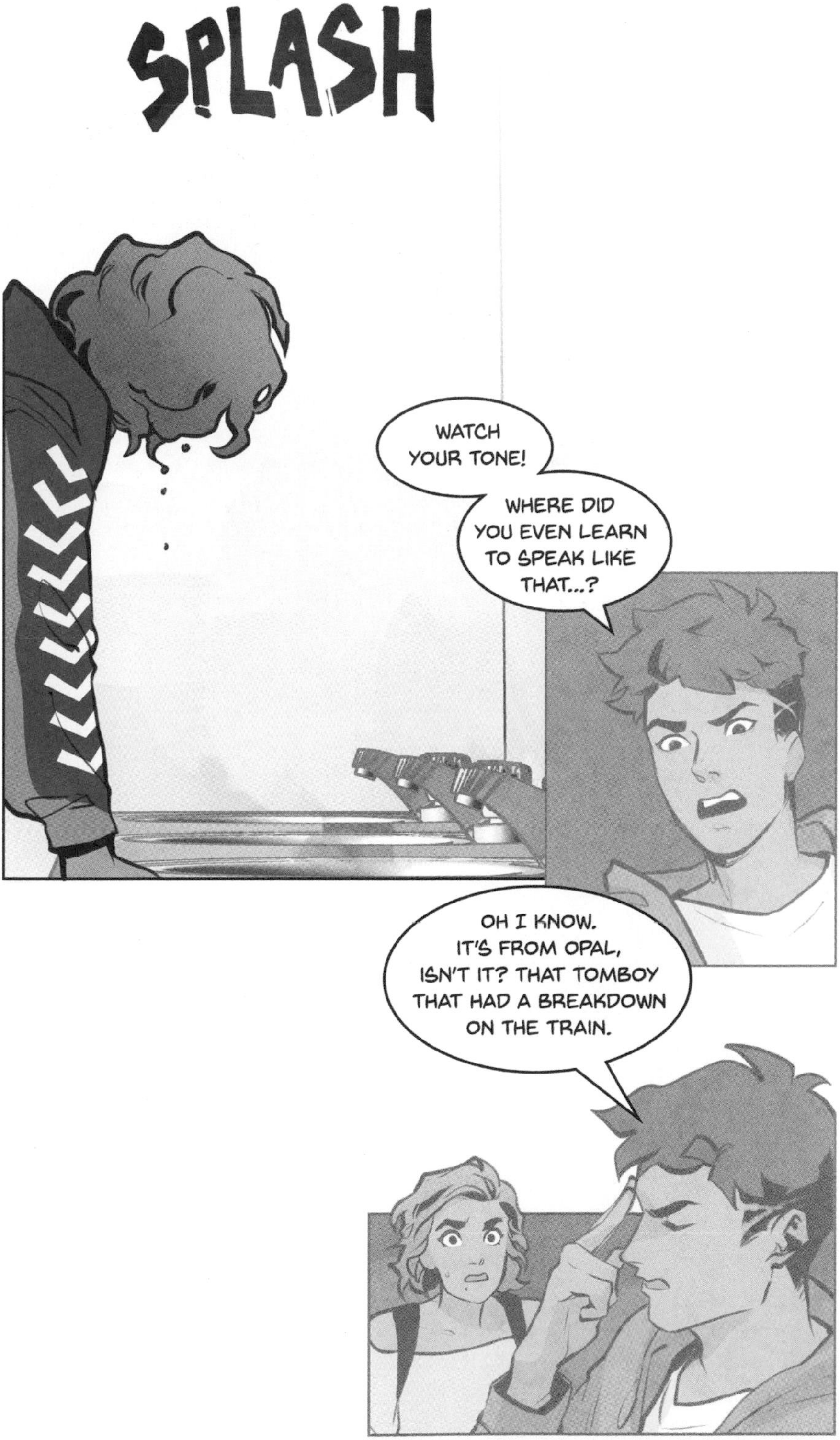
SPLASH
WATCH YOUR TONE!
WHERE DID YOU EVEN LEARN TO SPEAK LIKE THAT...?
OH I KNOW. IT'S FROM OPAL, ISN'T IT? THAT TOMBOY THAT HAD A BREAKDOWN ON THE TRAIN.

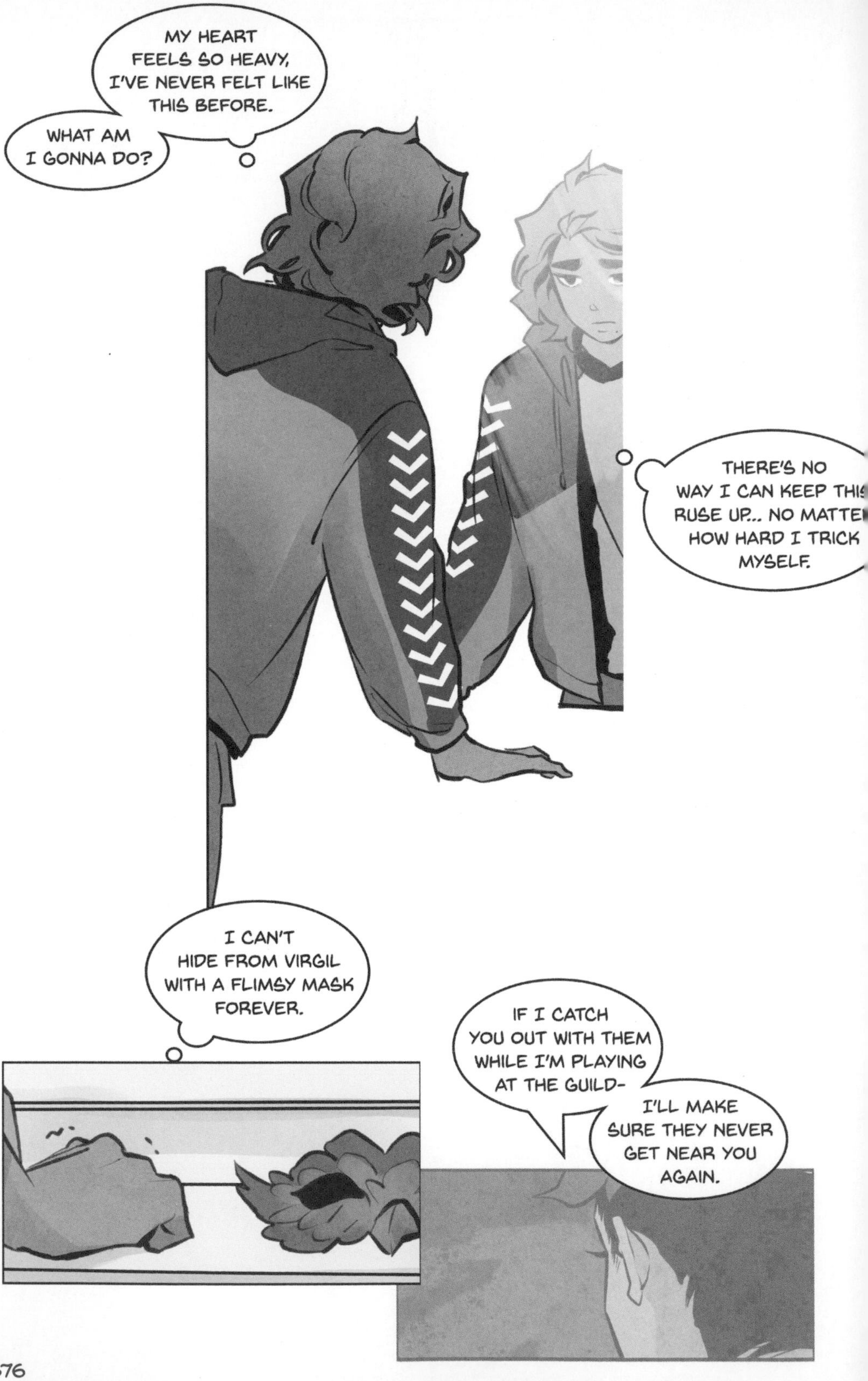
MY HEART FEELS SO HEAVY, I'VE NEVER FELT LIKE THIS BEFORE.
WHAT AM I GONNA DO?
THERE'S NO WAY I CAN KEEP THIS RUSE UP... NO MATTER HOW HARD I TRICK MYSELF.
I CAN'T HIDE FROM VIRGIL WITH A FLIMSY MASK FOREVER.
IF I CATCH YOU OUT WITH THEM WHILE I'M PLAYING AT THE GUILD-
I'LL MAKE SURE THEY NEVER GET NEAR YOU AGAIN.

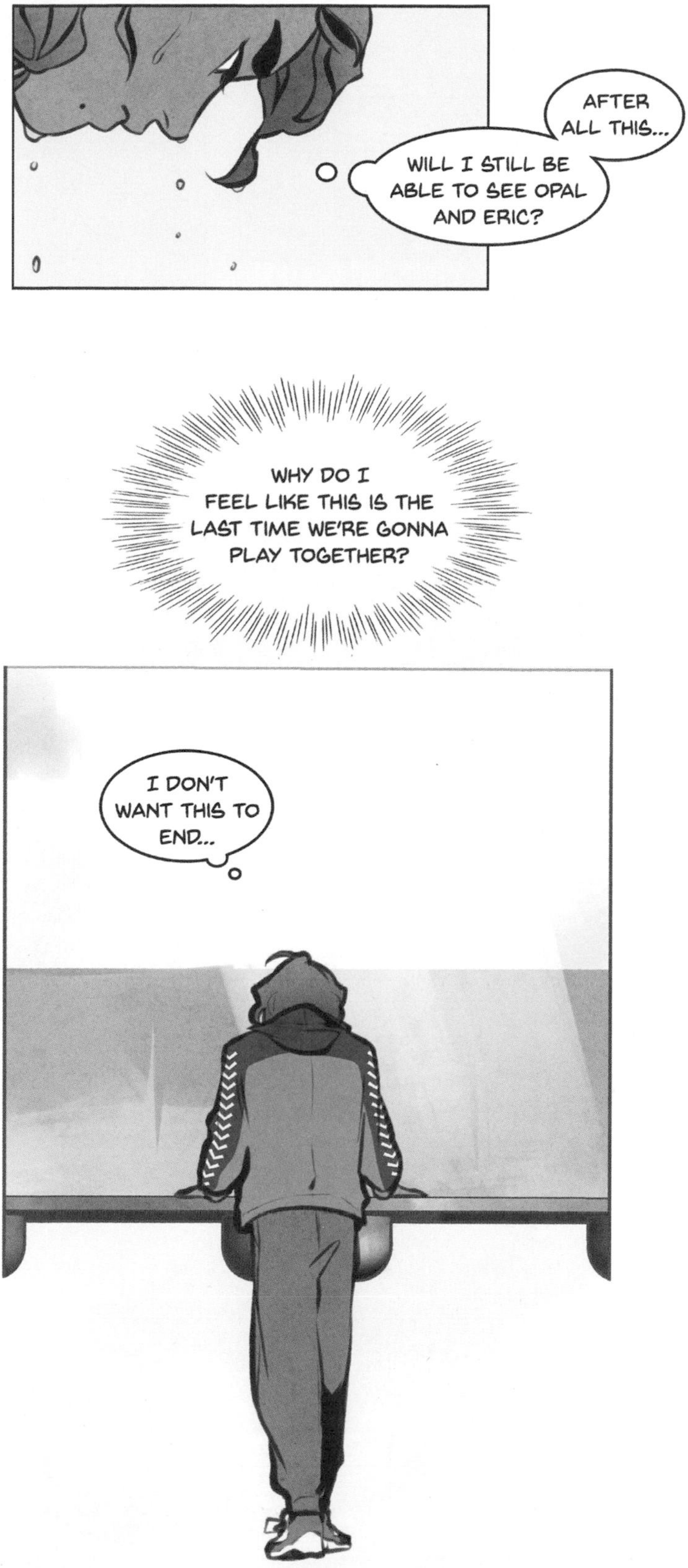
AFTER ALL THIS...
WILL I STILL BE ABLE TO SEE OPAL AND ERIC?
WHY DO I FEEL LIKE THIS IS THE LAST TIME WE'RE GONNA PLAY TOGETHER?
I DON'T WANT THIS TO END...

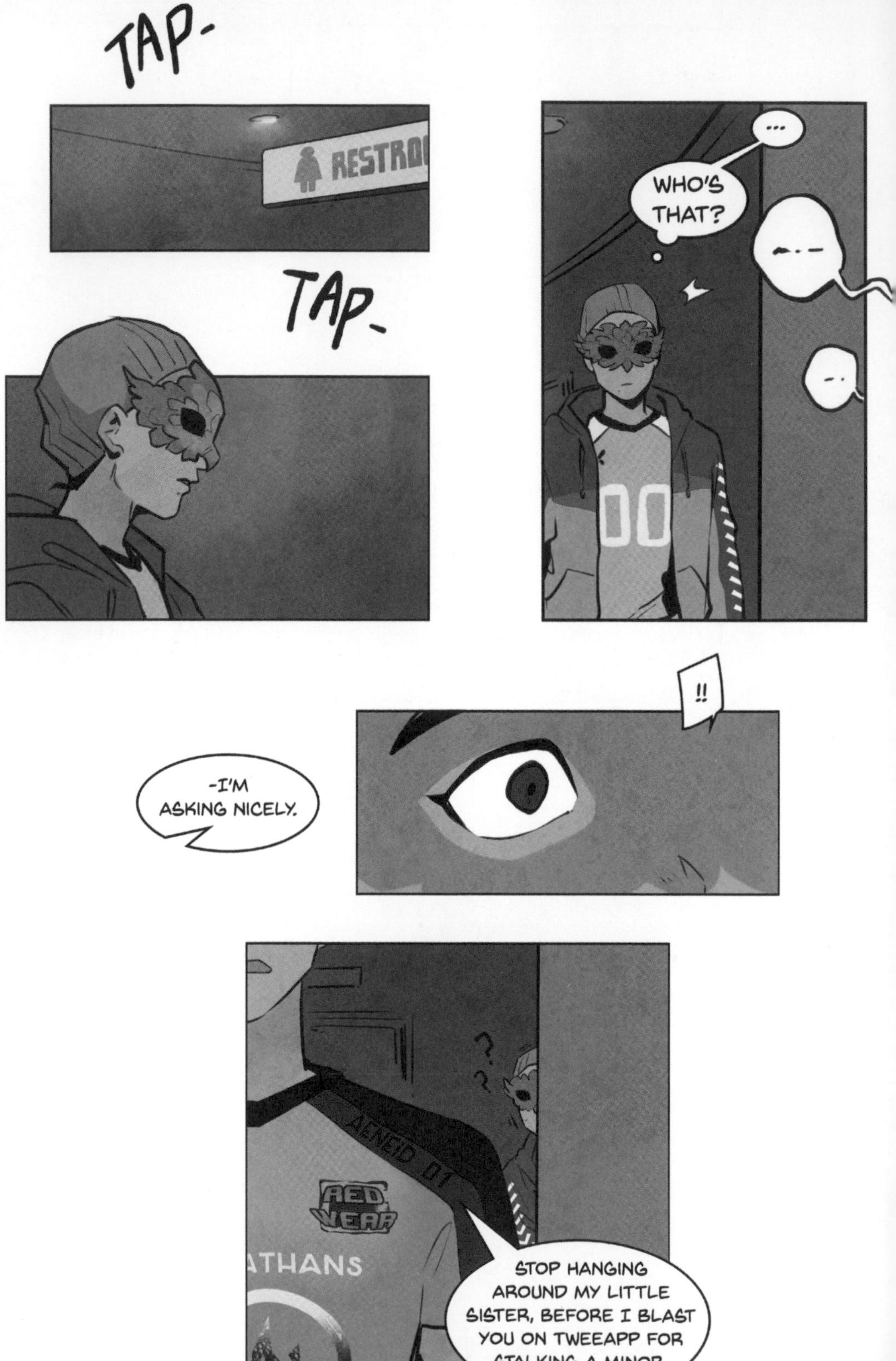
TAP-
RESTRO
TAP-
...
WHO'S THAT?
!!
-I'M ASKING NICELY.
AENEID 01
RED WEAR
ATHANS
STOP HANGING AROUND MY LITTLE SISTER, BEFORE I BLAST YOU ON TWEEAPP FOR STALKING A MINOR.

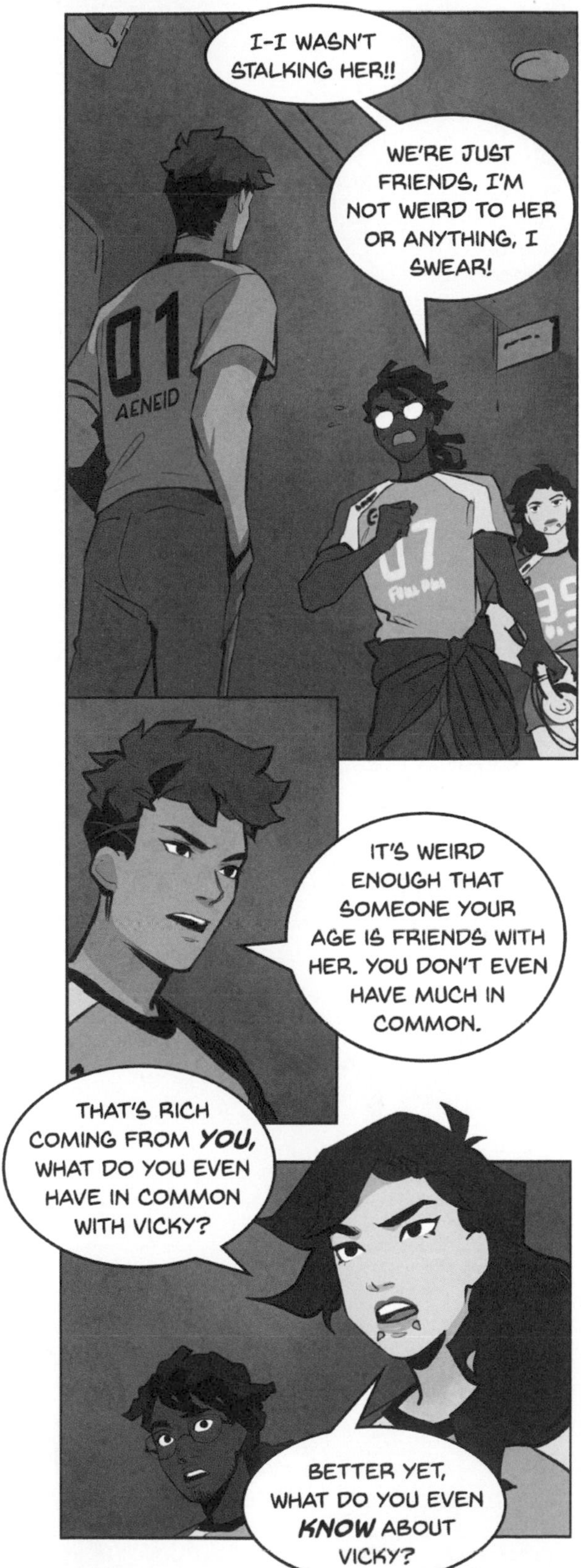
I-I WASN'T STALKING HER!!
WE'RE JUST FRIENDS, I'M NOT WEIRD TO HER OR ANYTHING, I SWEAR!
01
AENEID
07
IT'S WEIRD ENOUGH THAT SOMEONE YOUR AGE IS FRIENDS WITH HER. YOU DON'T EVEN HAVE MUCH IN COMMON.
THAT'S RICH COMING FROM ***YOU,*** WHAT DO YOU EVEN HAVE IN COMMON WITH VICKY?
BETTER YET, WHAT DO YOU EVEN ***KNOW*** ABOUT VICKY?

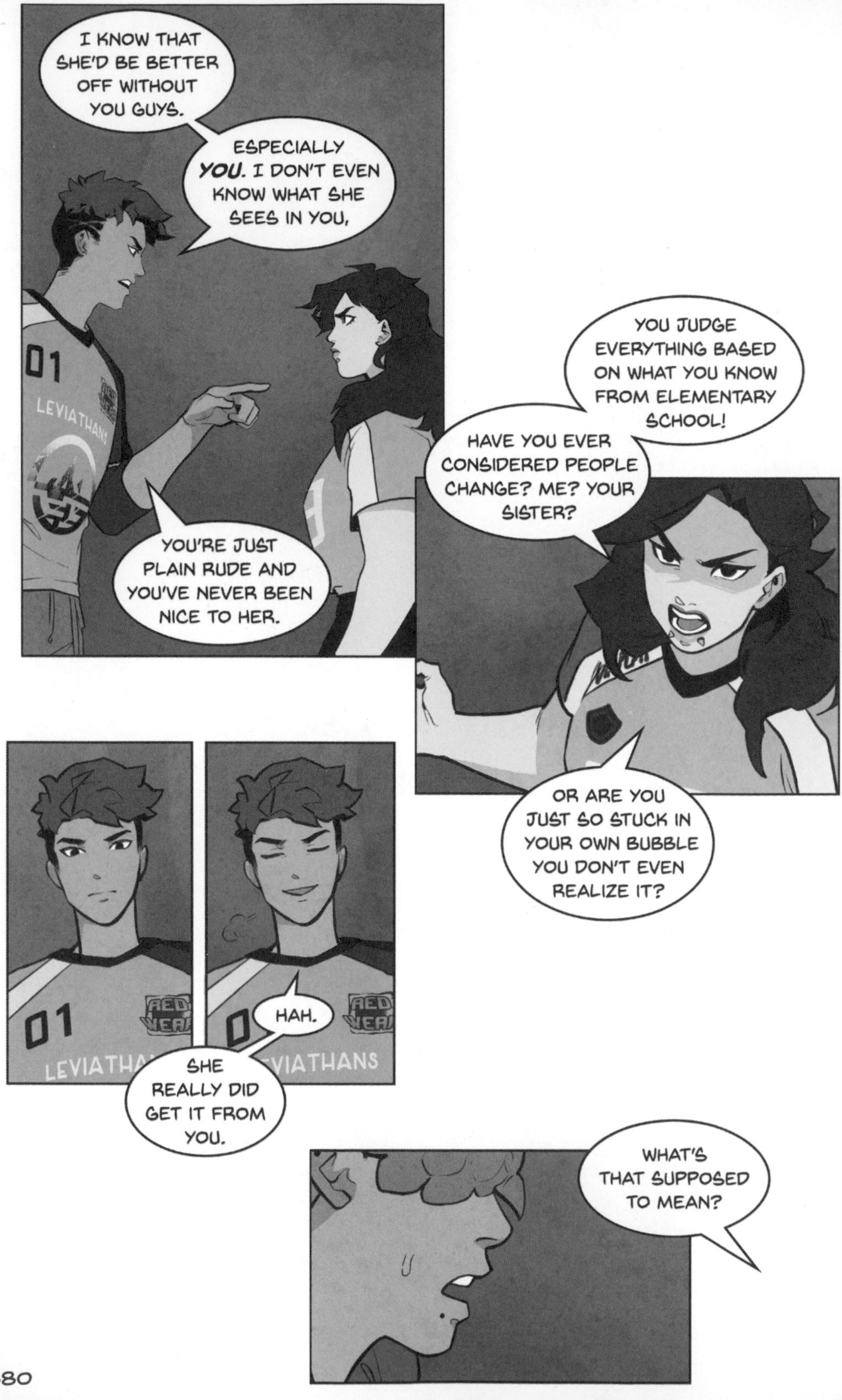
I KNOW THAT SHE'D BE BETTER OFF WITHOUT YOU GUYS.
ESPECIALLY ***YOU***. I DON'T EVEN KNOW WHAT SHE SEES IN YOU,
YOU'RE JUST PLAIN RUDE AND YOU'VE NEVER BEEN NICE TO HER.
YOU JUDGE EVERYTHING BASED ON WHAT YOU KNOW FROM ELEMENTARY SCHOOL!
HAVE YOU EVER CONSIDERED PEOPLE CHANGE? ME? YOUR SISTER?
OR ARE YOU JUST SO STUCK IN YOUR OWN BUBBLE YOU DON'T EVEN REALIZE IT?
HAH.
SHE REALLY DID GET IT FROM YOU.
WHAT'S THAT SUPPOSED TO MEAN?

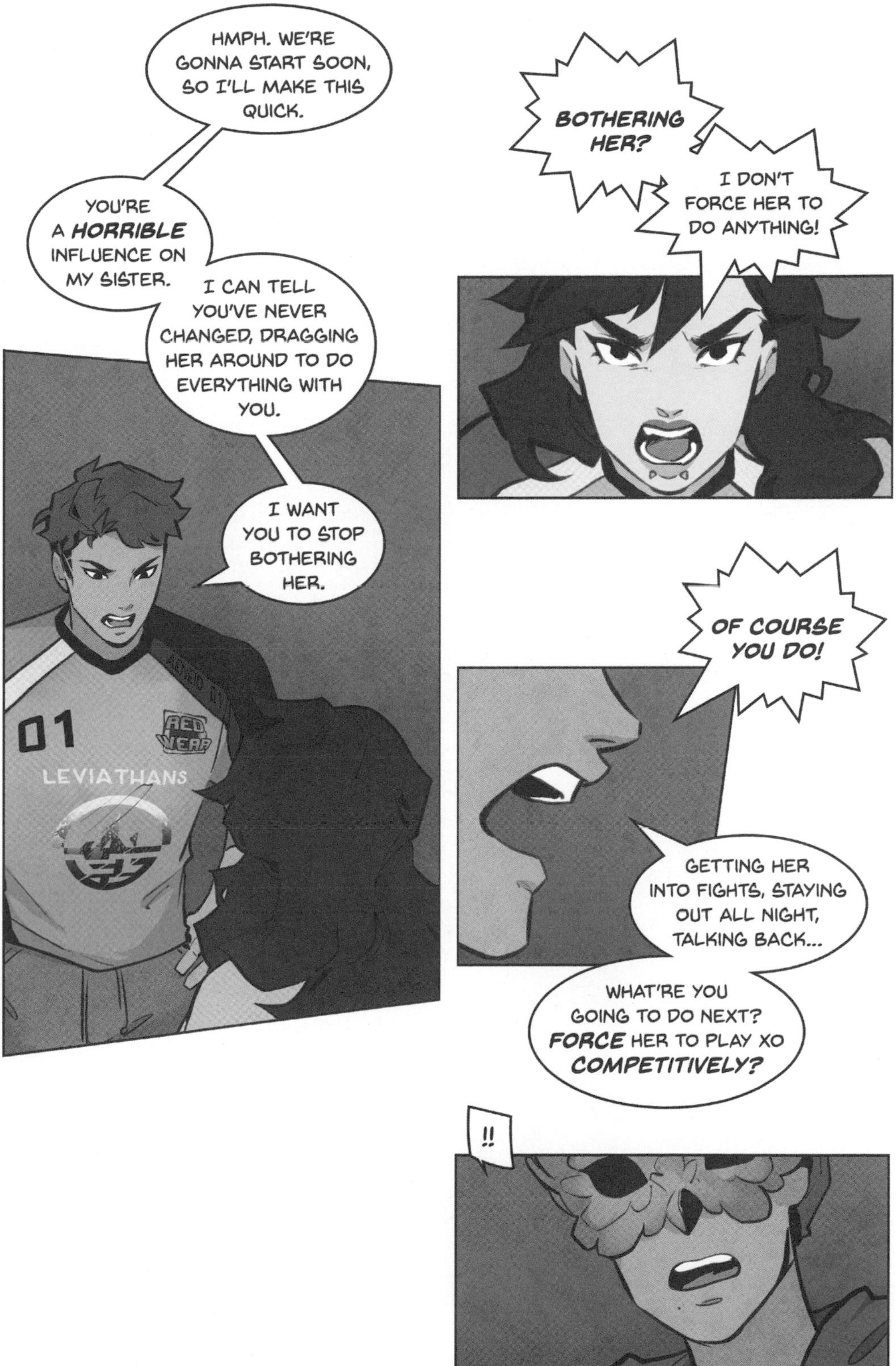
HMPH. WE'RE GONNA START SOON, SO I'LL MAKE THIS QUICK.
YOU'RE A **HORRIBLE** INFLUENCE ON MY SISTER.
I CAN TELL YOU'VE NEVER CHANGED, DRAGGING HER AROUND TO DO EVERYTHING WITH YOU.
I WANT YOU TO STOP BOTHERING HER.
01
LEVIATHANS
BOTHERING HER?
I DON'T FORCE HER TO DO ANYTHING!
OF COURSE YOU DO!
GETTING HER INTO FIGHTS, STAYING OUT ALL NIGHT, TALKING BACK...
WHAT'RE YOU GOING TO DO NEXT? **FORCE** HER TO PLAY XO ***COMPETITIVELY?***
!!

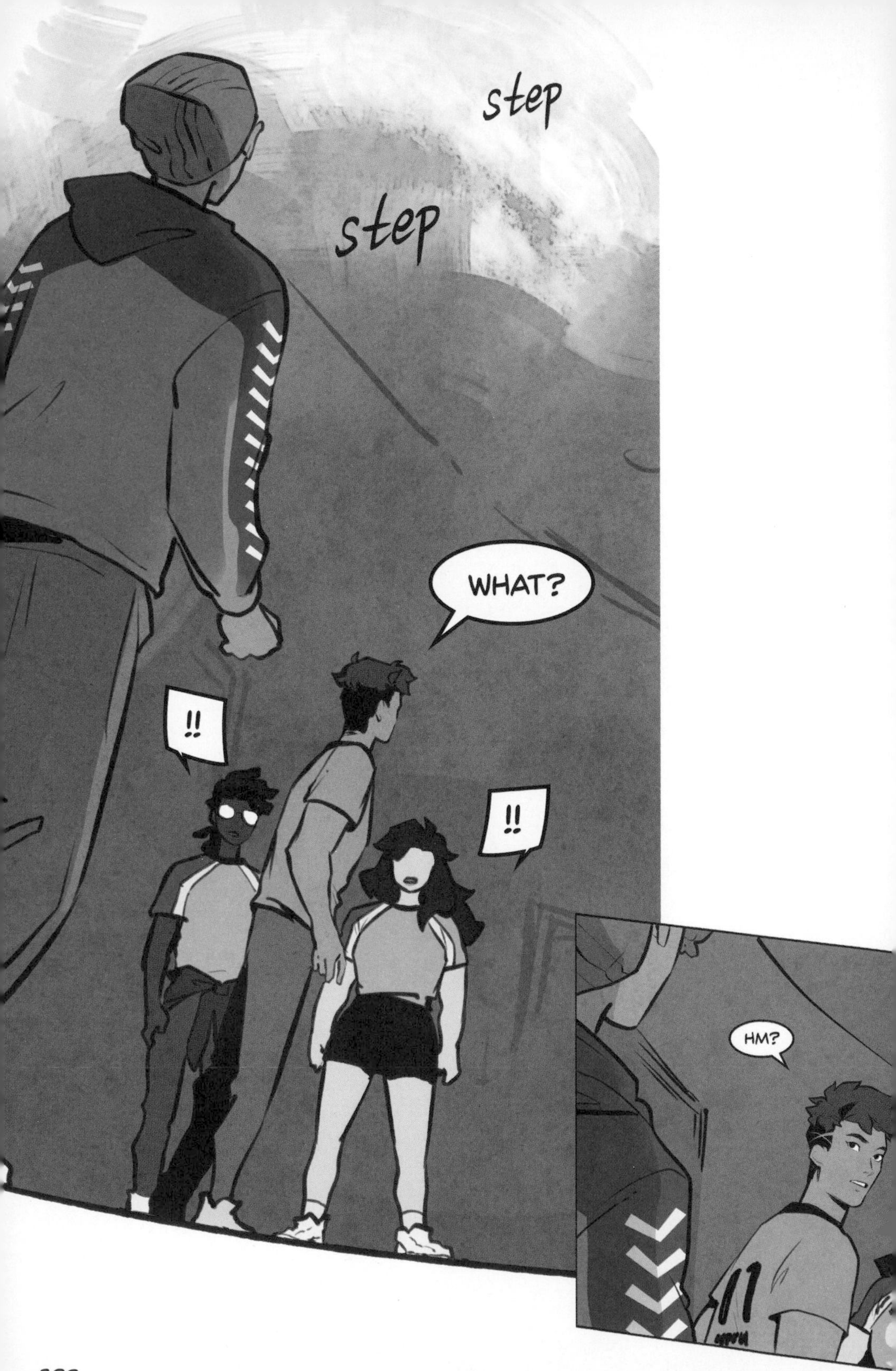
step
step
WHAT?
!!
!!
HM?

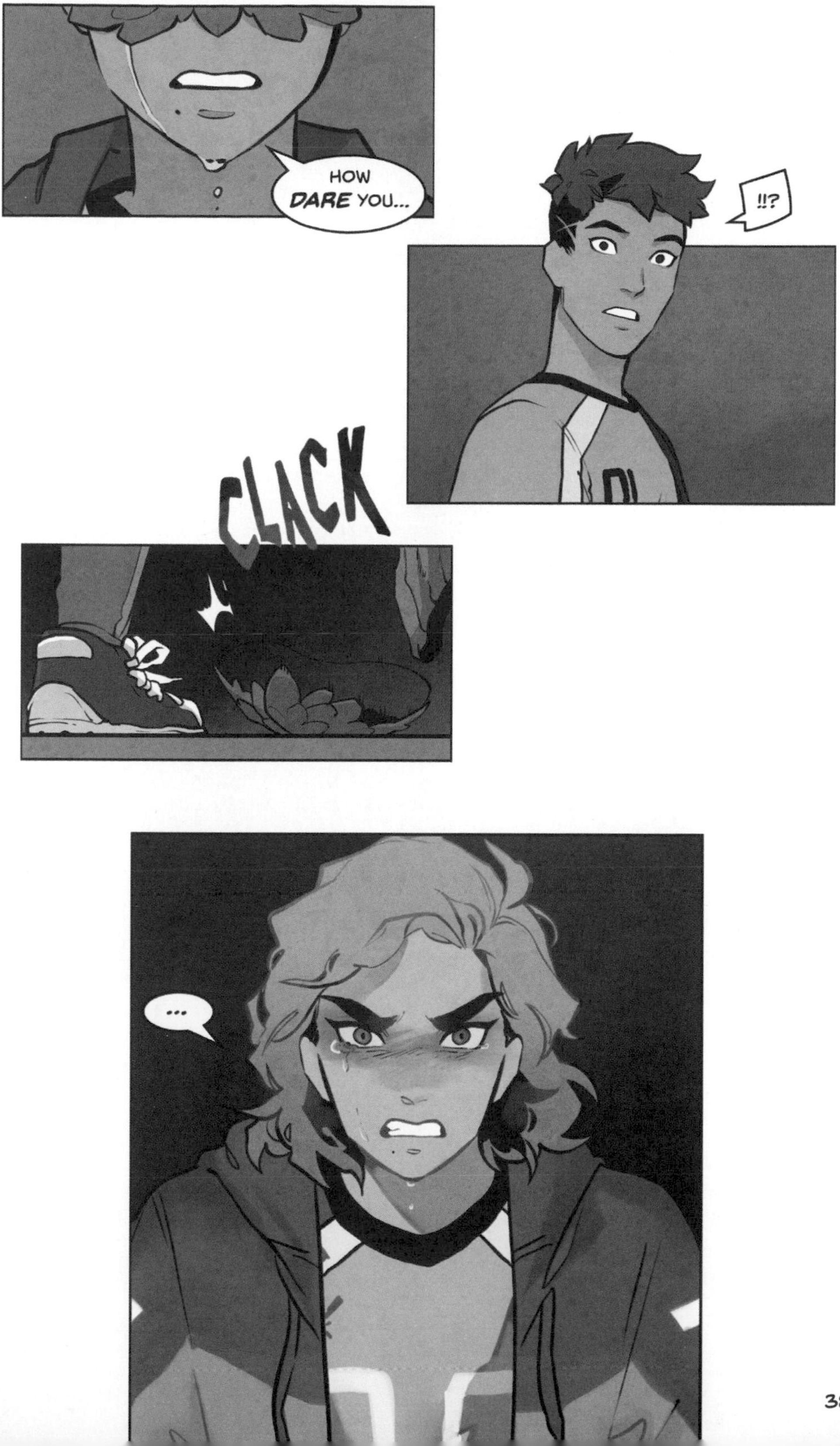
HOW DARE YOU...
!!?
CLACK
...

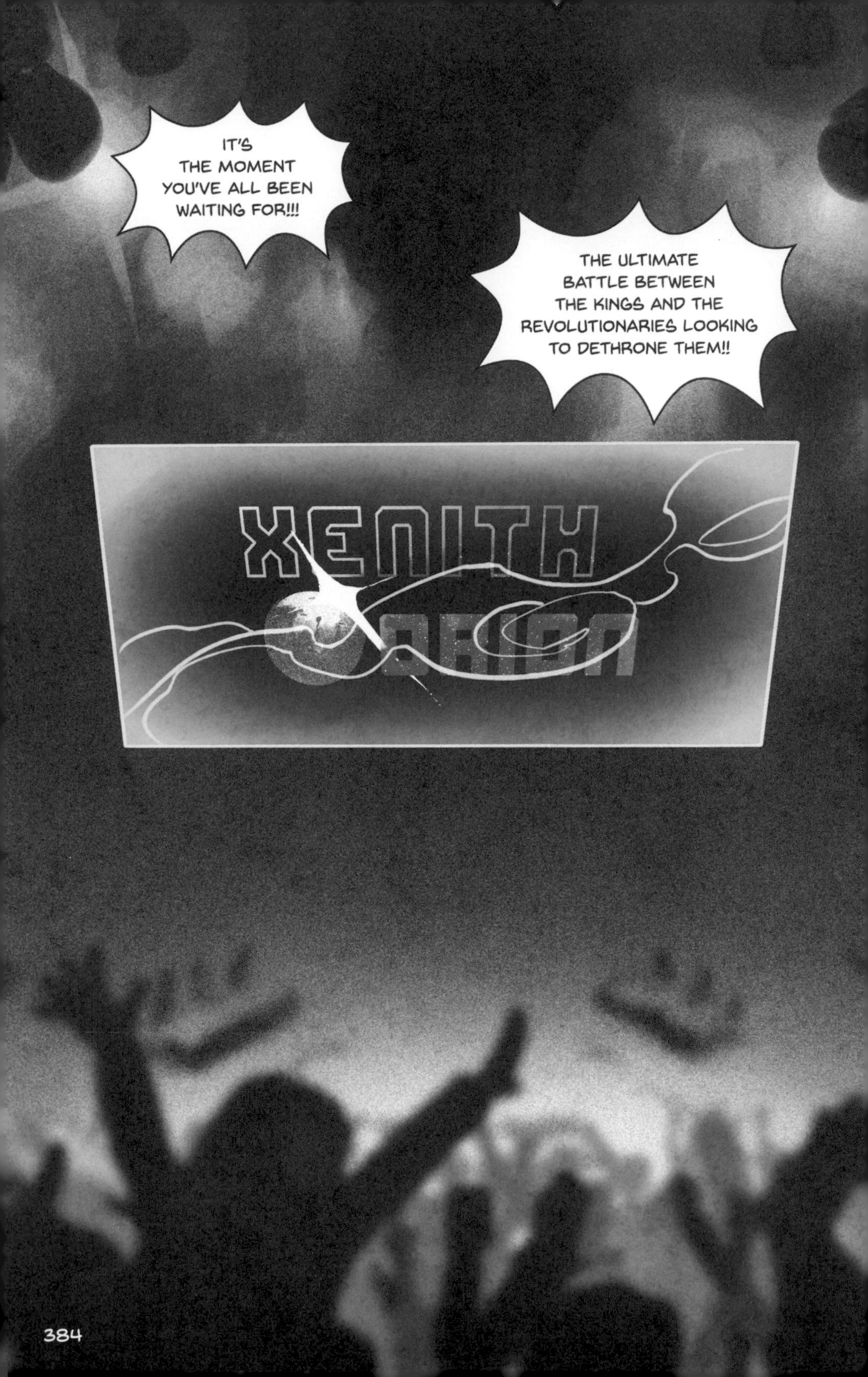
IT'S THE MOMENT YOU'VE ALL BEEN WAITING FOR!!!
THE ULTIMATE BATTLE BETWEEN THE KINGS AND THE REVOLUTIONARIES LOOKING TO DETHRONE THEM!!
XENITH
ORION

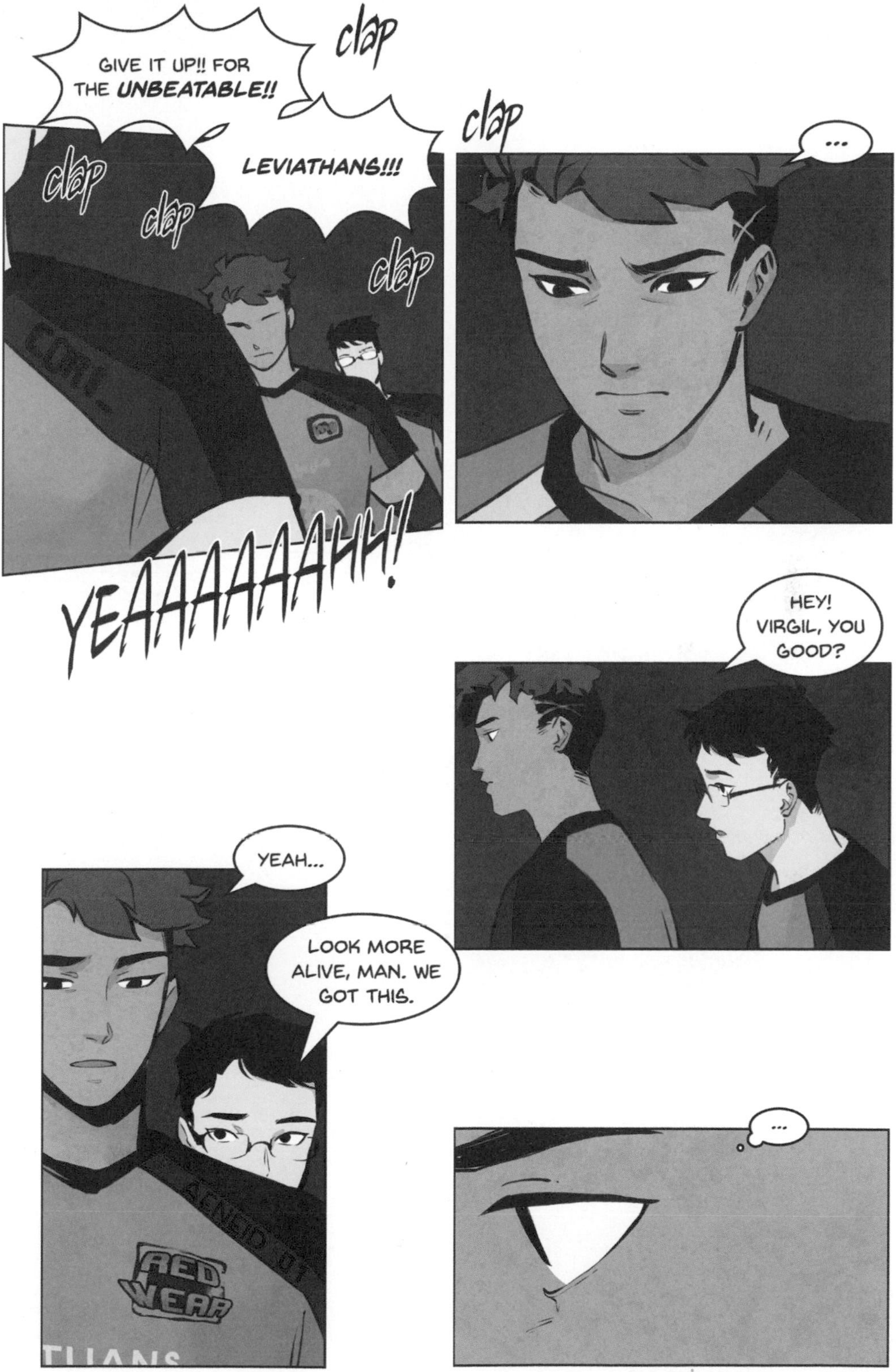
GIVE IT UP!! FOR THE UNBEATABLE!!
clap
clap
LEVIATHANS!!!
clap
clap
clap
YEAAAAAAAHH!
...
HEY! VIRGIL, YOU GOOD?
YEAH...
LOOK MORE ALIVE, MAN. WE GOT THIS.
...

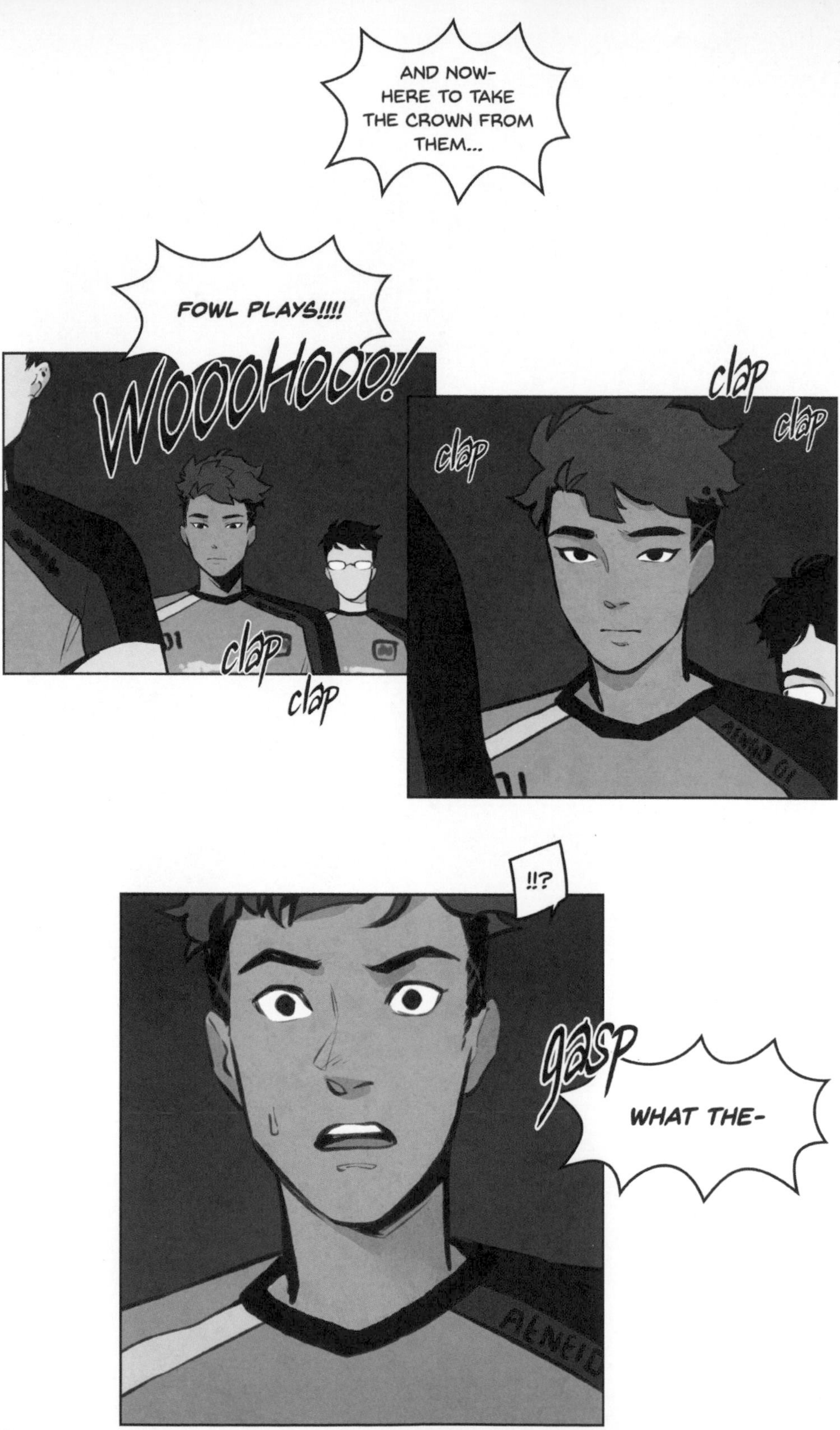
AND NOW- HERE TO TAKE THE CROWN FROM THEM...
FOWL PLAYS!!!!
WOOOHOOO!
clap
clap
clap
clap
clap
!!?
gasp
WHAT THE-

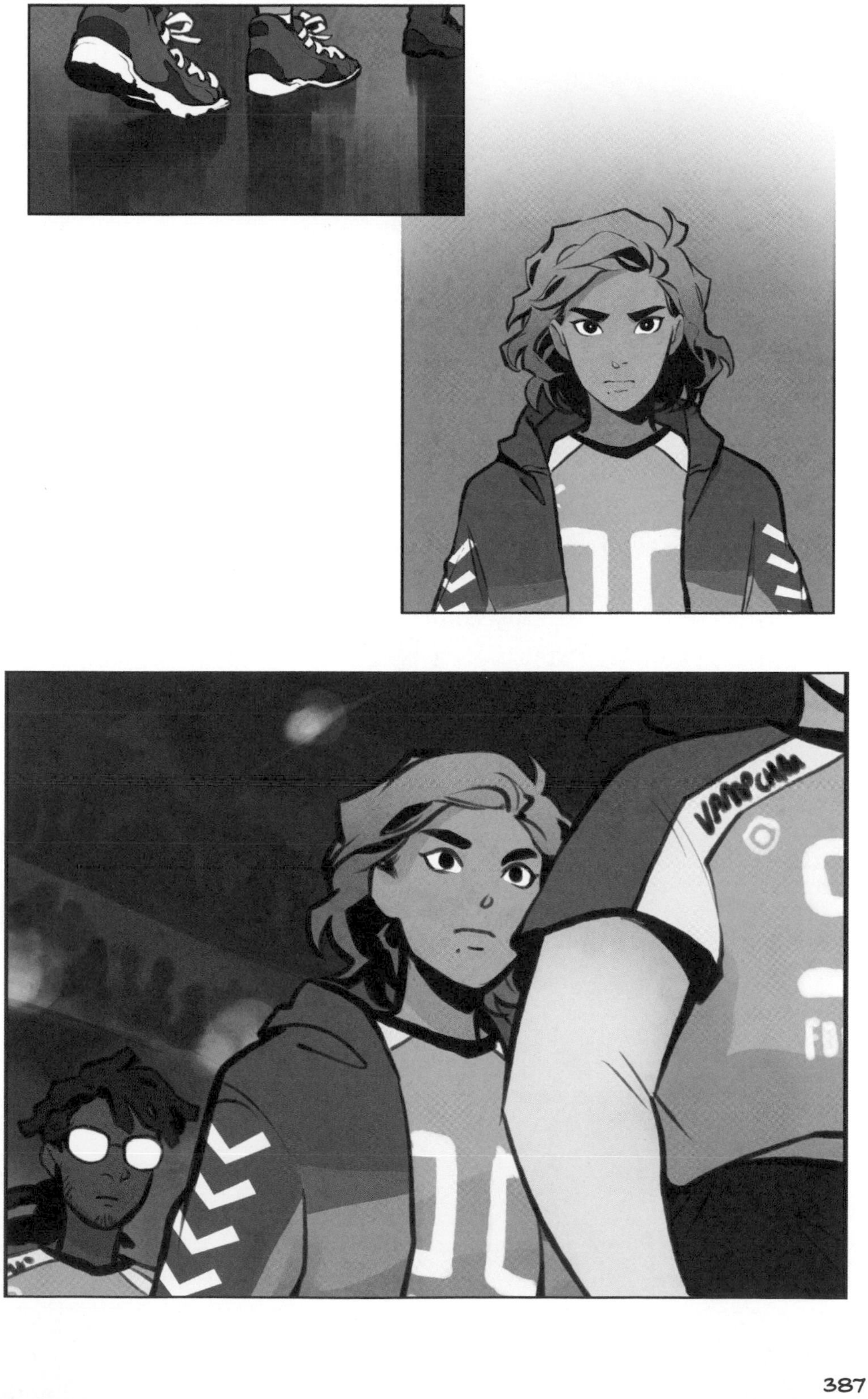

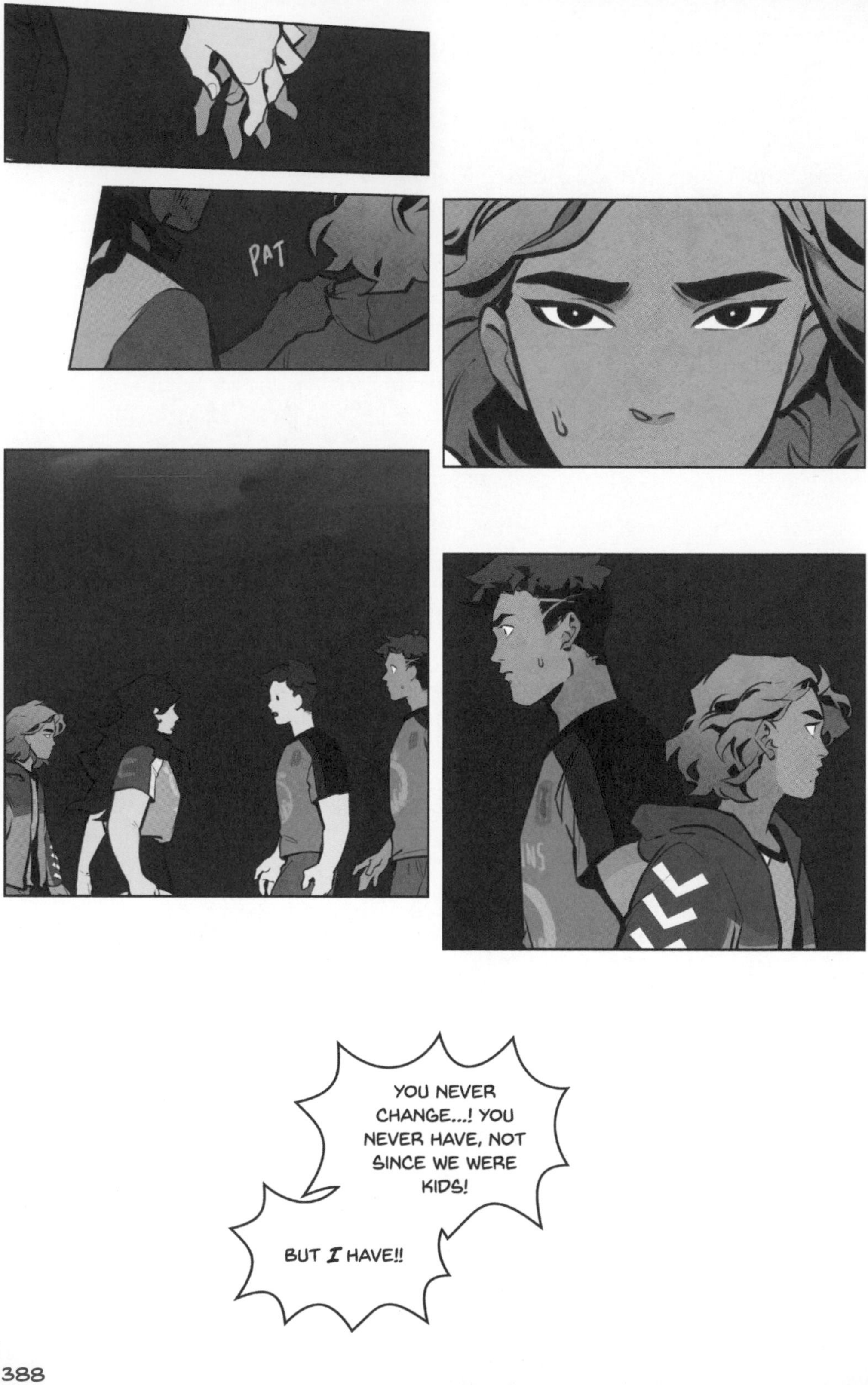
PAT
YOU NEVER CHANGE...! YOU NEVER HAVE, NOT SINCE WE WERE KIDS!
BUT *I* HAVE!!

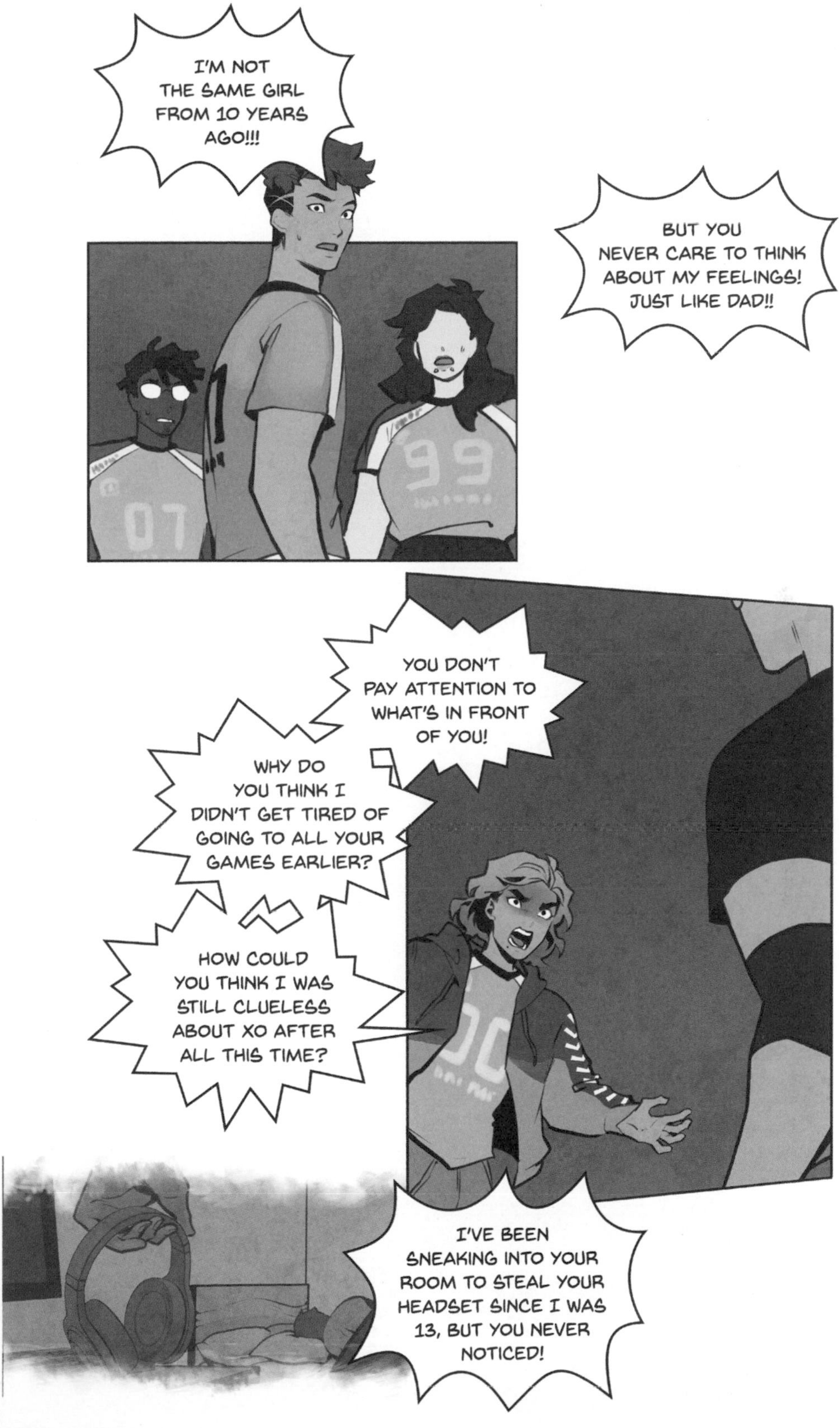
I'M NOT THE SAME GIRL FROM 10 YEARS AGO!!!
BUT YOU NEVER CARE TO THINK ABOUT MY FEELINGS! JUST LIKE DAD!!
YOU DON'T PAY ATTENTION TO WHAT'S IN FRONT OF YOU!
WHY DO YOU THINK I DIDN'T GET TIRED OF GOING TO ALL YOUR GAMES EARLIER?
HOW COULD YOU THINK I WAS STILL CLUELESS ABOUT XO AFTER ALL THIS TIME?
I'VE BEEN SNEAKING INTO YOUR ROOM TO STEAL YOUR HEADSET SINCE I WAS 13, BUT YOU NEVER NOTICED!

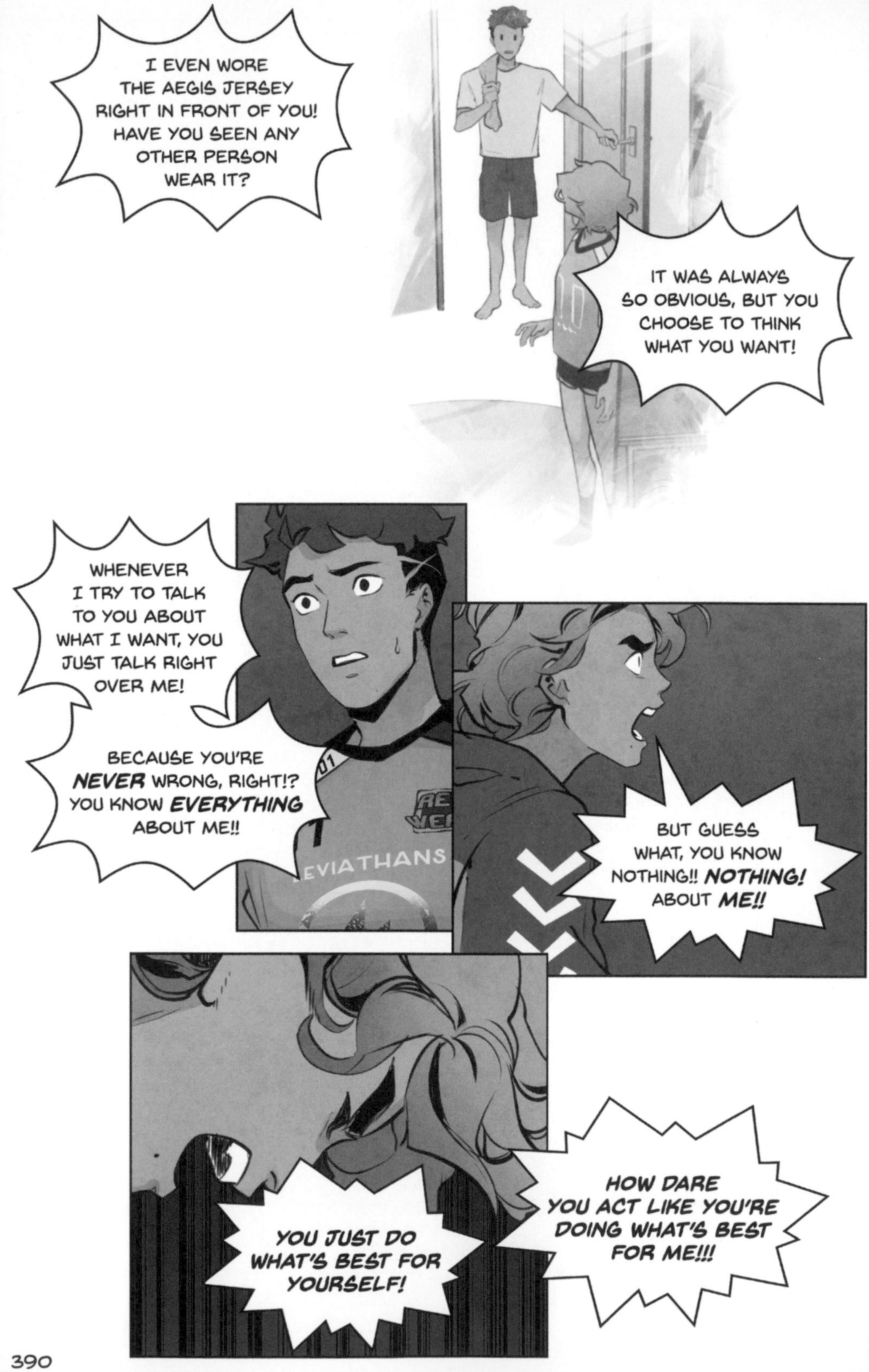
I EVEN WORE THE AEGIS JERSEY RIGHT IN FRONT OF YOU! HAVE YOU SEEN ANY OTHER PERSON WEAR IT?
IT WAS ALWAYS SO OBVIOUS, BUT YOU CHOOSE TO THINK WHAT YOU WANT!
WHENEVER I TRY TO TALK TO YOU ABOUT WHAT I WANT, YOU JUST TALK RIGHT OVER ME!
BECAUSE YOU'RE ***NEVER*** WRONG, RIGHT!? YOU KNOW ***EVERYTHING*** ABOUT ME!!
BUT GUESS WHAT, YOU KNOW NOTHING!! ***NOTHING!*** ABOUT ***ME!!***
YOU JUST DO WHAT'S BEST FOR YOURSELF!
HOW DARE YOU ACT LIKE YOU'RE DOING WHAT'S BEST FOR ME!!!

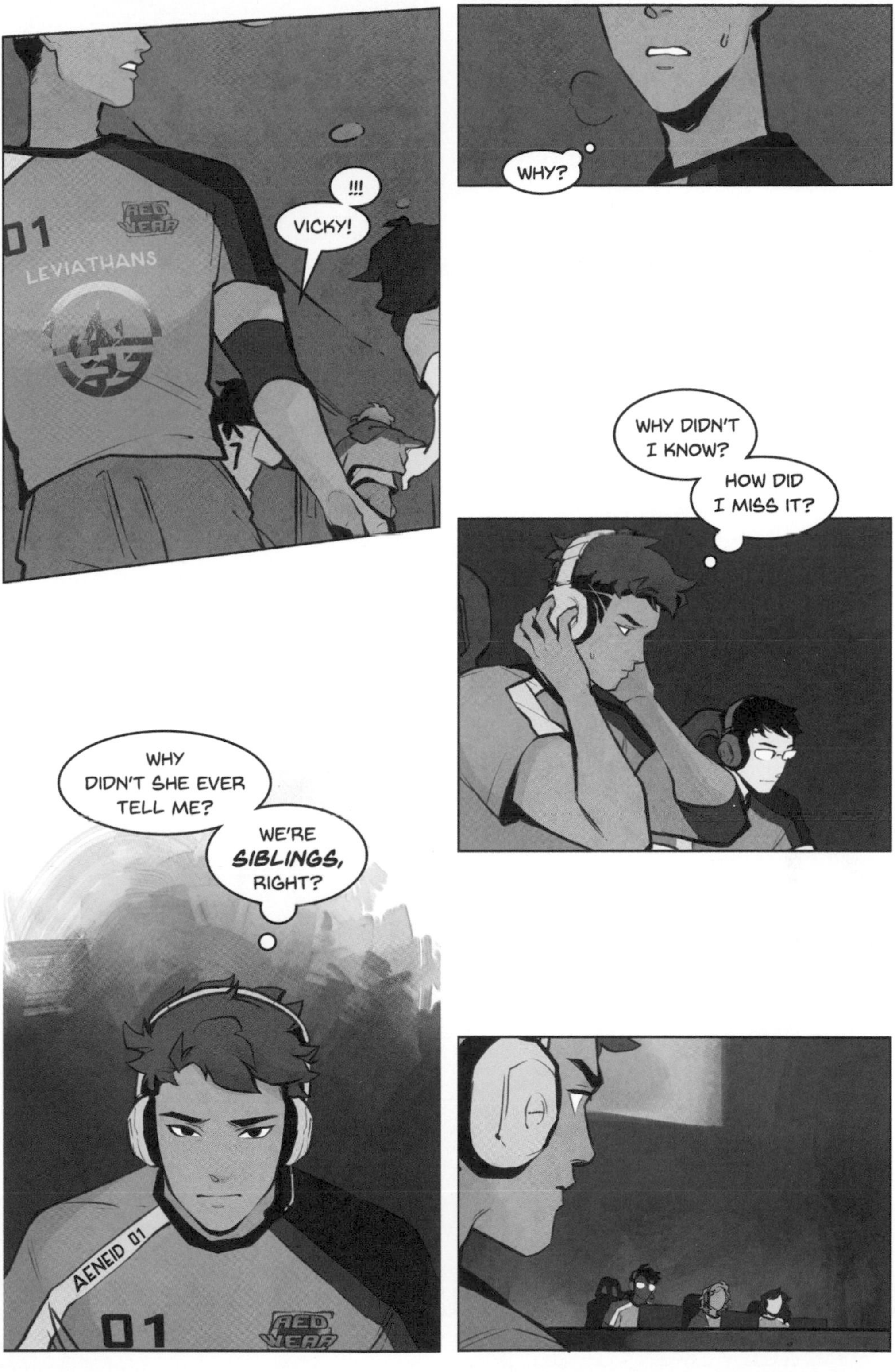
01
LEVIATHANS
!!!
VICKY!
WHY?
WHY DIDN'T I KNOW?
HOW DID I MISS IT?
WHY DIDN'T SHE EVER TELL ME?
WE'RE **SIBLINGS,** RIGHT?
AENEID 01
01

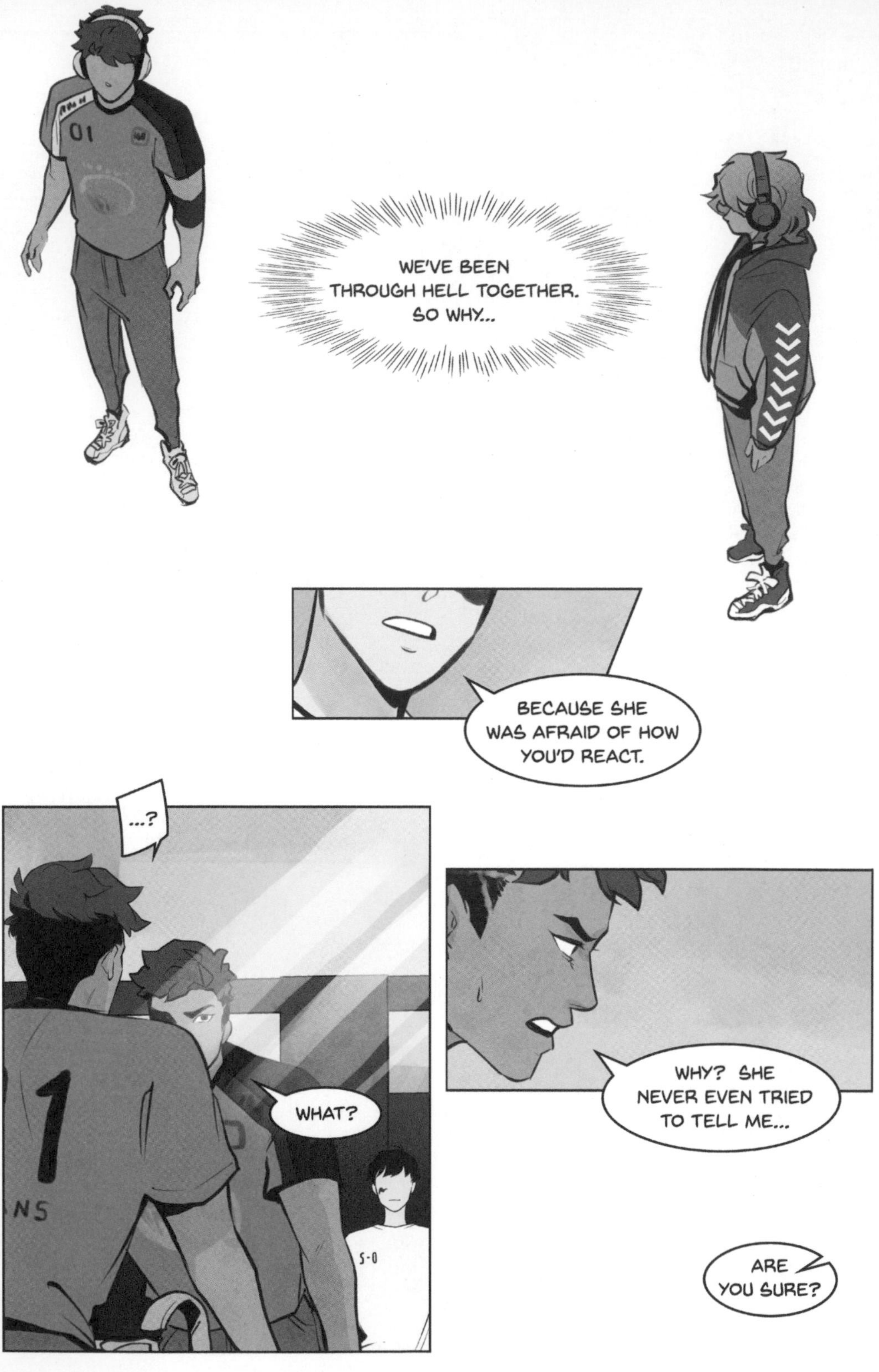
WE'VE BEEN THROUGH HELL TOGETHER. SO WHY...
BECAUSE SHE WAS AFRAID OF HOW YOU'D REACT.
...?
WHAT?
WHY? SHE NEVER EVEN TRIED TO TELL ME...
ARE YOU SURE?

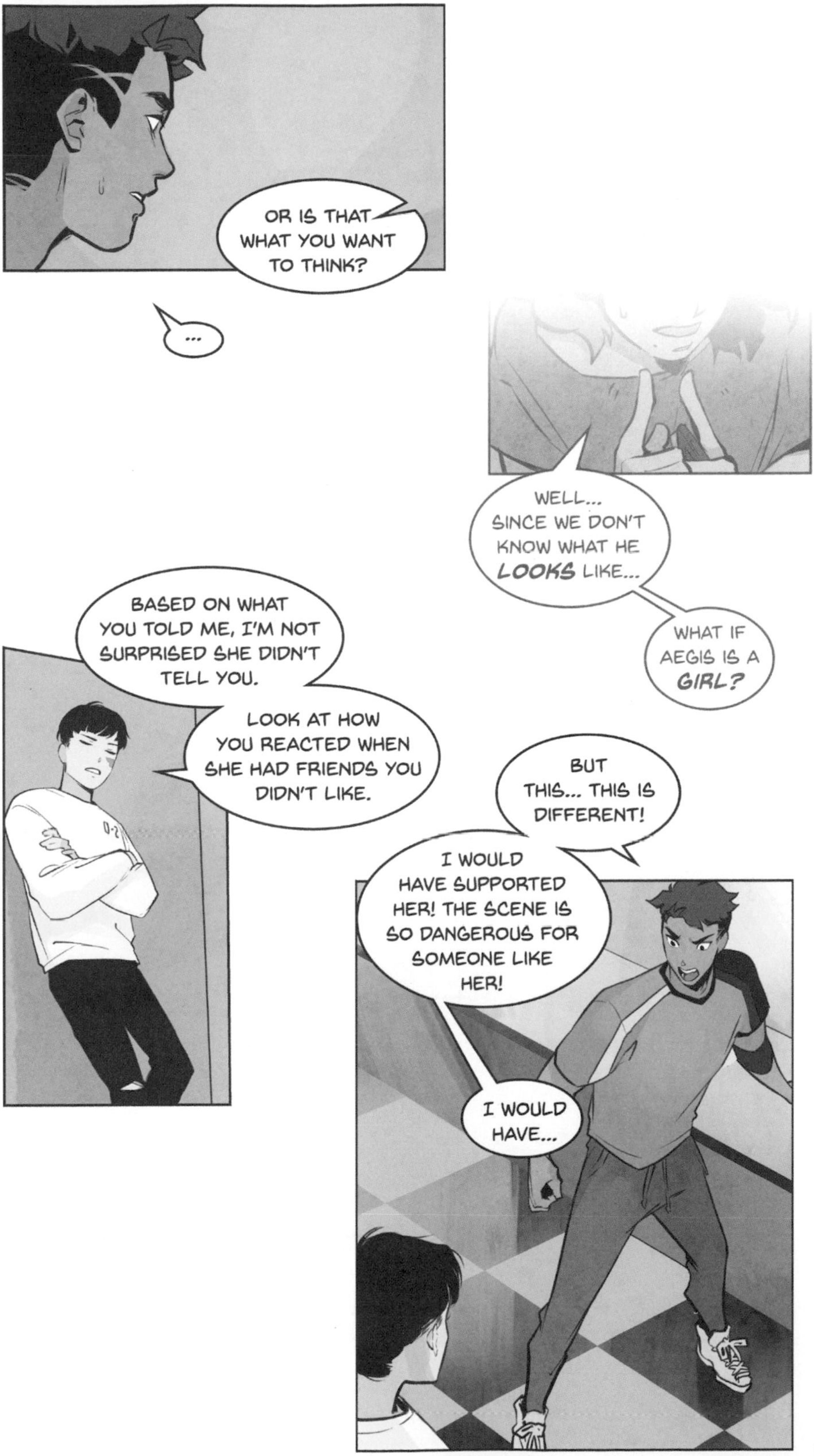
OR IS THAT WHAT YOU WANT TO THINK?
...
WELL... SINCE WE DON'T KNOW WHAT HE LOOKS LIKE...
WHAT IF AEGIS IS A GIRL?
BASED ON WHAT YOU TOLD ME, I'M NOT SURPRISED SHE DIDN'T TELL YOU.
LOOK AT HOW YOU REACTED WHEN SHE HAD FRIENDS YOU DIDN'T LIKE.
BUT THIS... THIS IS DIFFERENT!
I WOULD HAVE SUPPORTED HER! THE SCENE IS SO DANGEROUS FOR SOMEONE LIKE HER!
I WOULD HAVE...

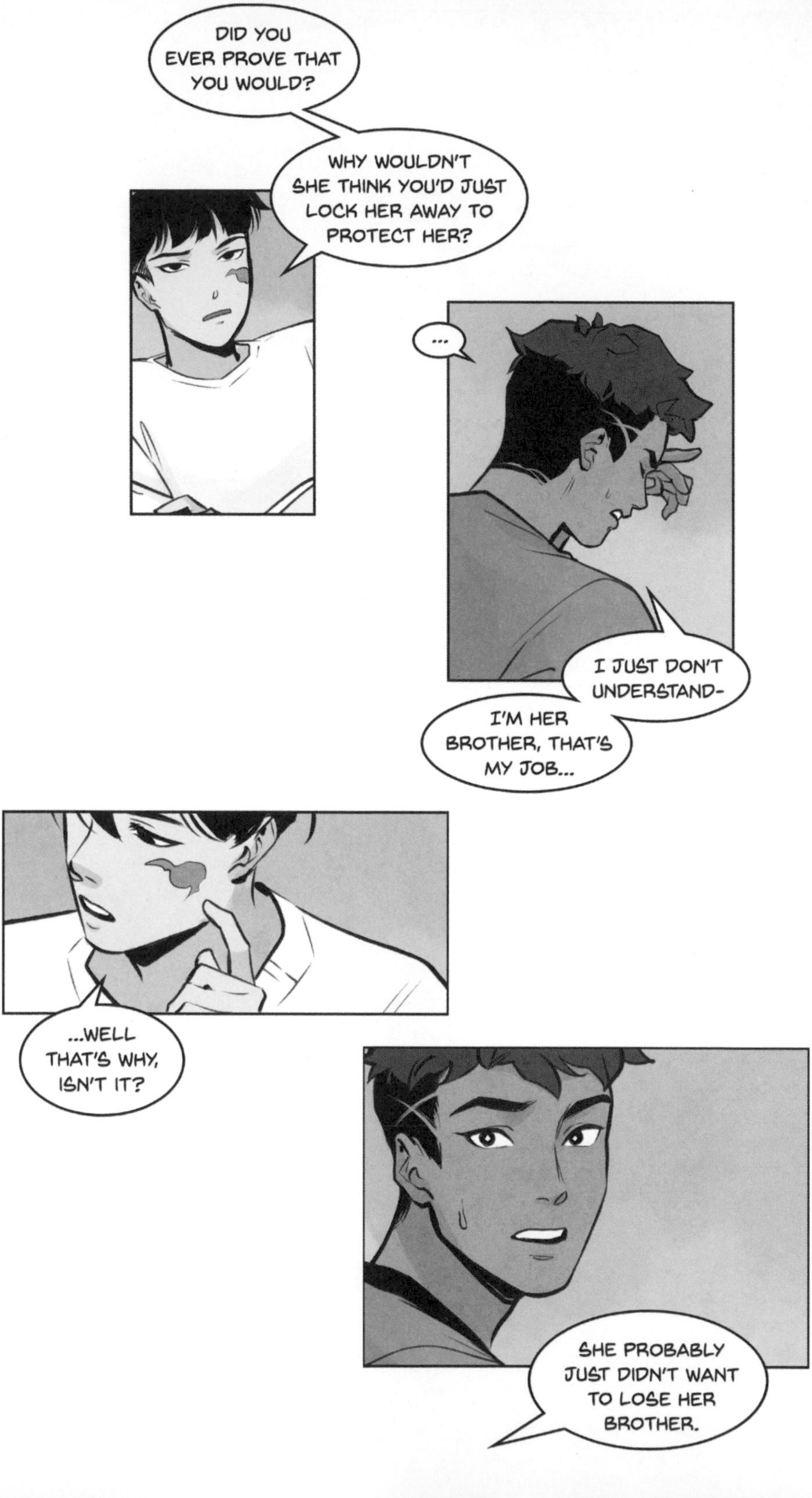
DID YOU EVER PROVE THAT YOU WOULD?
WHY WOULDN'T SHE THINK YOU'D JUST LOCK HER AWAY TO PROTECT HER?
...
I JUST DON'T UNDERSTAND-
I'M HER BROTHER, THAT'S MY JOB...
...WELL THAT'S WHY, ISN'T IT?
SHE PROBABLY JUST DIDN'T WANT TO LOSE HER BROTHER.

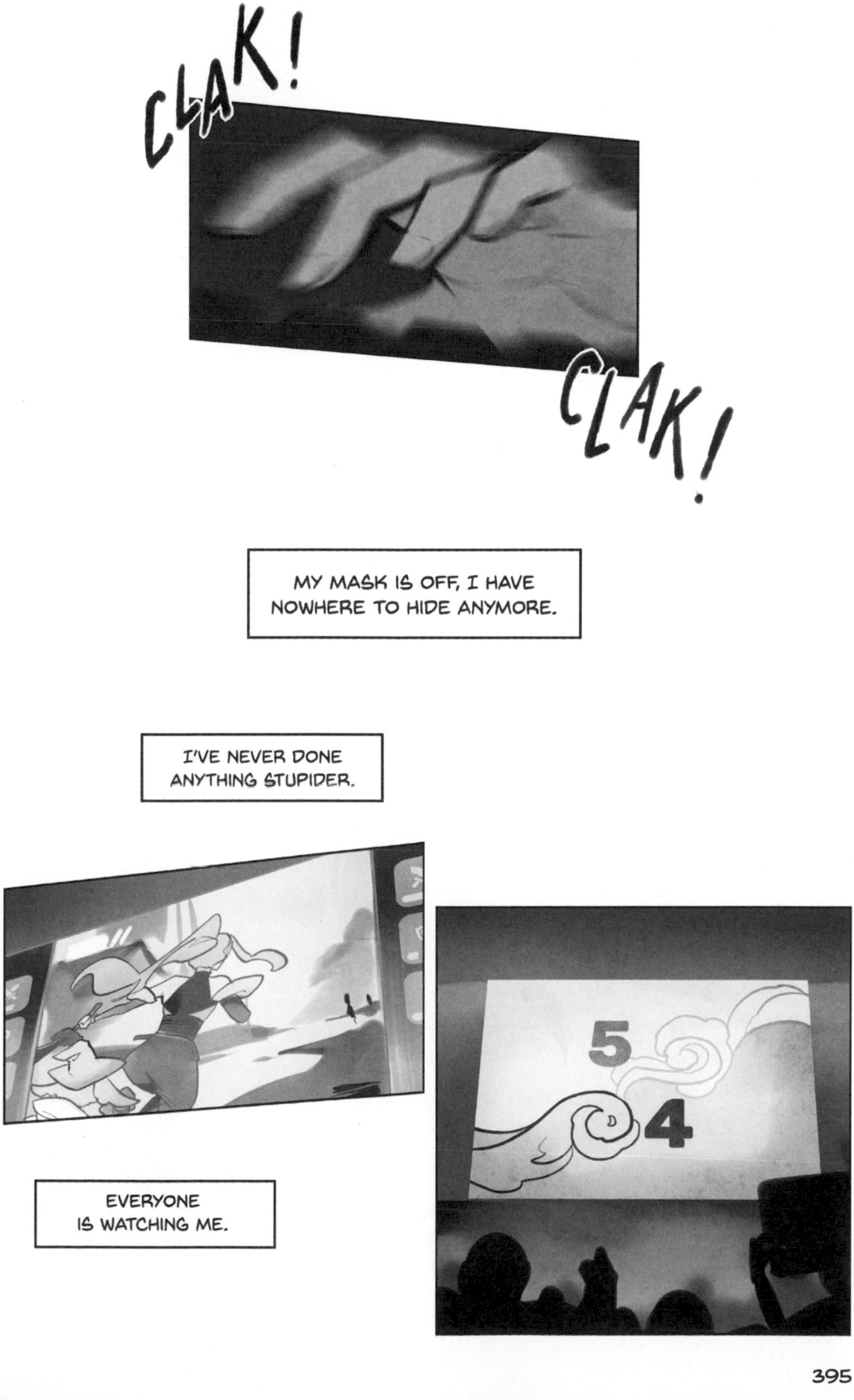
CLAK!
CLAK!
MY MASK IS OFF, I HAVE NOWHERE TO HIDE ANYMORE.
I'VE NEVER DONE ANYTHING STUPIDER.
5
4
EVERYONE IS WATCHING ME.

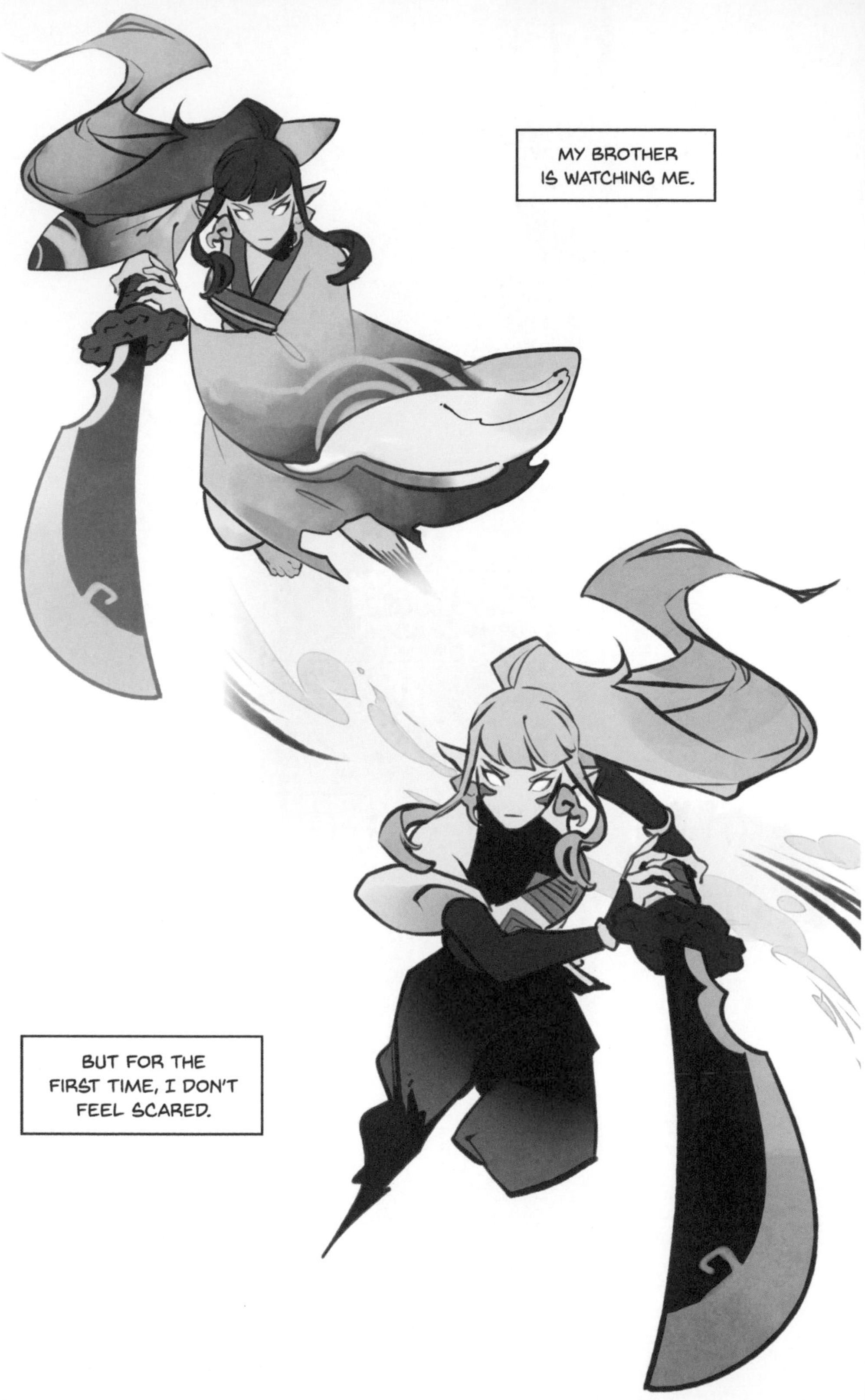
MY BROTHER
IS WATCHING ME.
BUT FOR THE
FIRST TIME, I DON'T
FEEL SCARED.

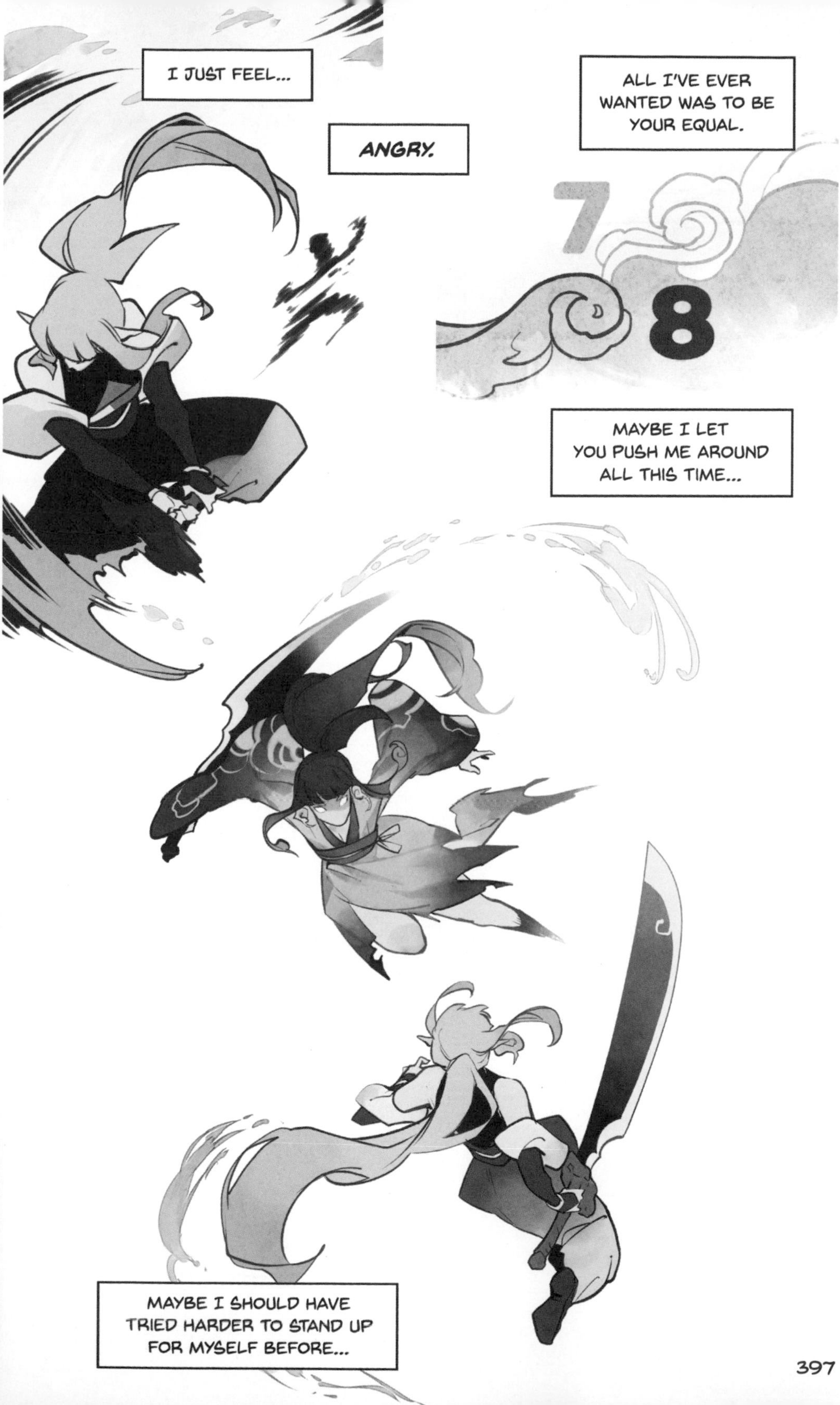
I JUST FEEL...
ANGRY.
ALL I'VE EVER WANTED WAS TO BE YOUR EQUAL.
7
8
MAYBE I LET YOU PUSH ME AROUND ALL THIS TIME...
MAYBE I SHOULD HAVE TRIED HARDER TO STAND UP FOR MYSELF BEFORE...

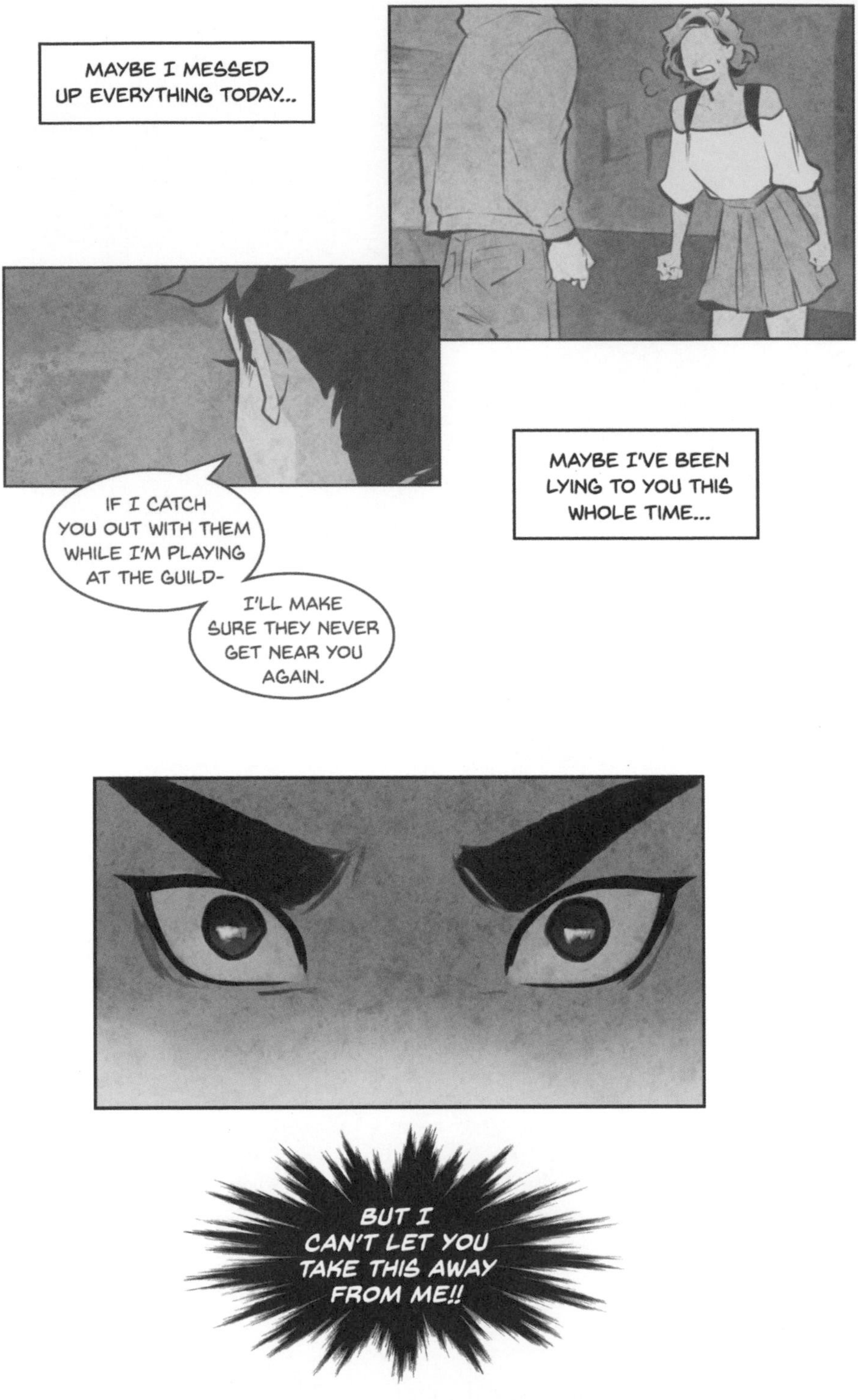
MAYBE I MESSED UP EVERYTHING TODAY...
IF I CATCH YOU OUT WITH THEM WHILE I'M PLAYING AT THE GUILD-
I'LL MAKE SURE THEY NEVER GET NEAR YOU AGAIN.
MAYBE I'VE BEEN LYING TO YOU THIS WHOLE TIME...
BUT I CAN'T LET YOU TAKE THIS AWAY FROM ME!!

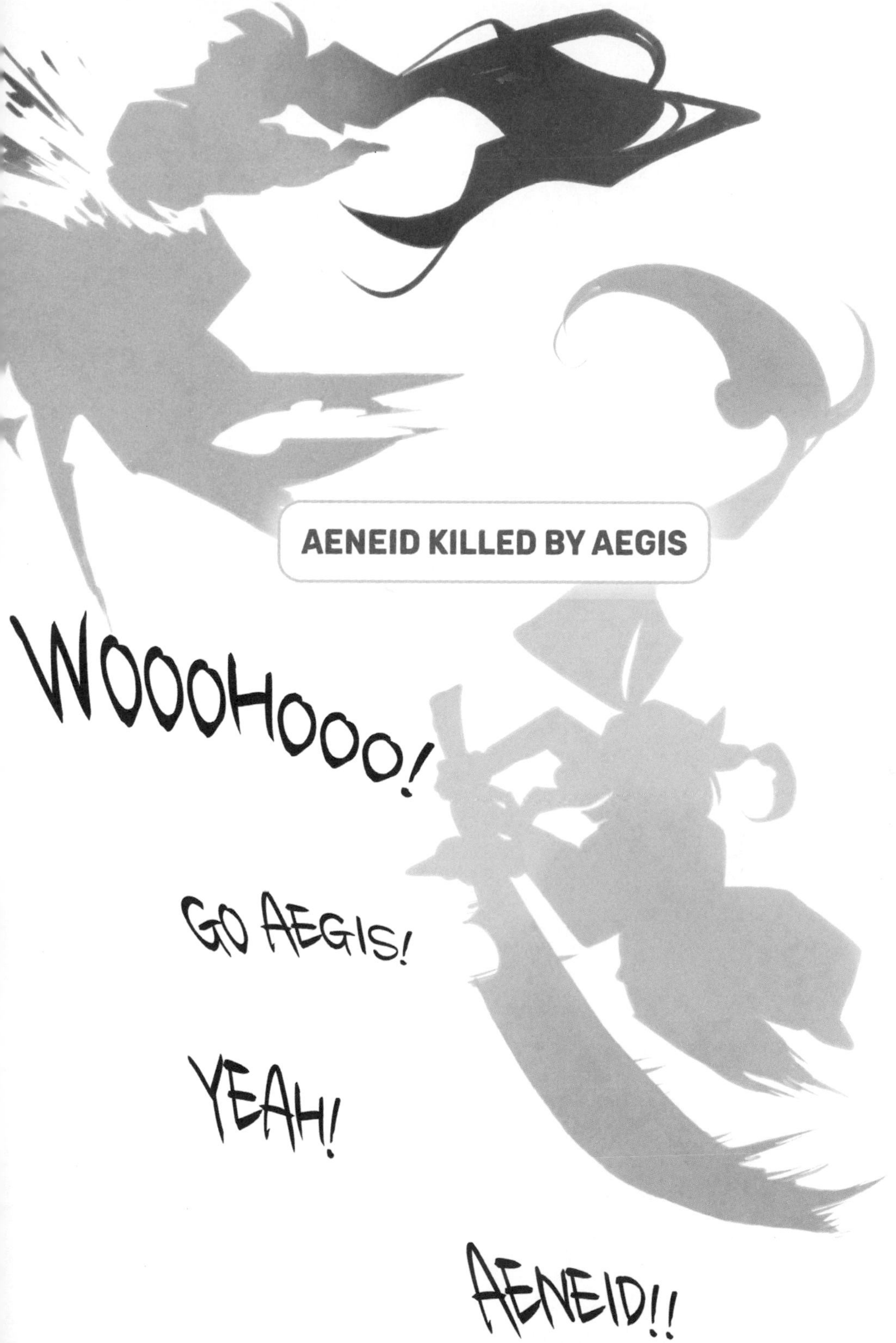
AENEID KILLED BY AEGIS
WOOOHOOO!
GO AEGIS!
YEAH!
AENEID!!

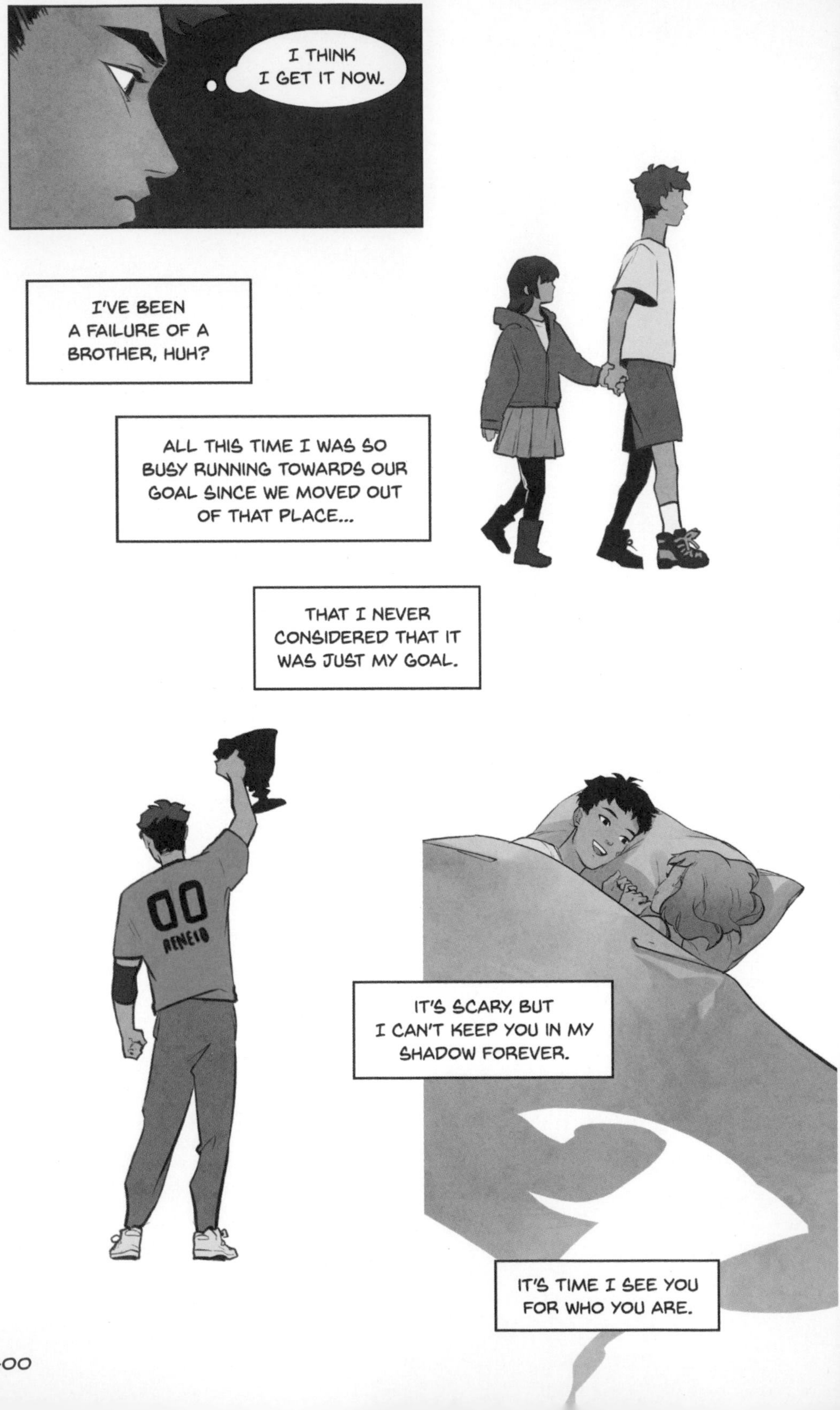
I THINK I GET IT NOW.
I'VE BEEN A FAILURE OF A BROTHER, HUH?
ALL THIS TIME I WAS SO BUSY RUNNING TOWARDS OUR GOAL SINCE WE MOVED OUT OF THAT PLACE...
THAT I NEVER CONSIDERED THAT IT WAS JUST MY GOAL.
IT'S SCARY, BUT I CAN'T KEEP YOU IN MY SHADOW FOREVER.
IT'S TIME I SEE YOU FOR WHO YOU ARE.

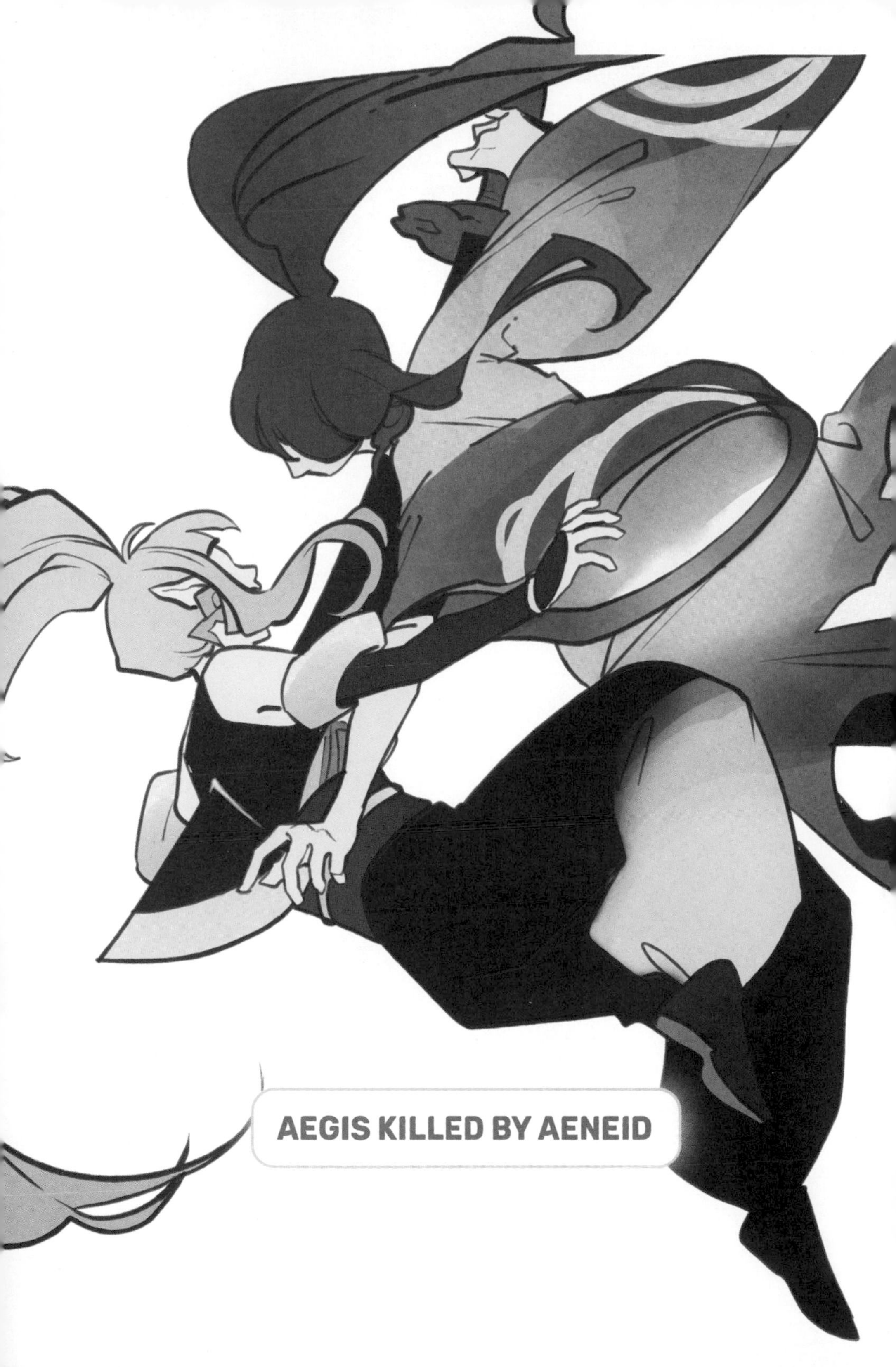
AEGIS KILLED BY AENEID

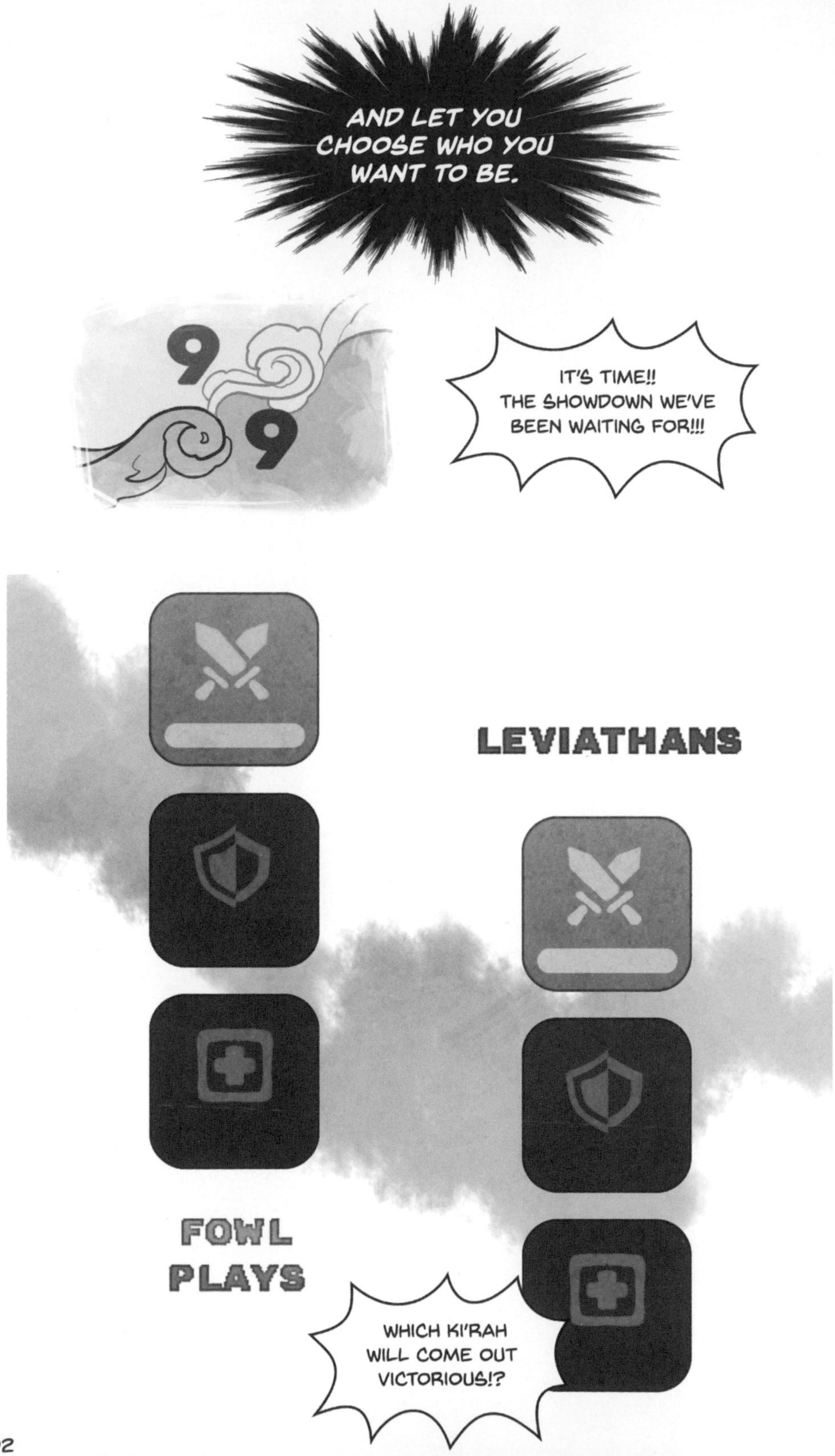
AND LET YOU CHOOSE WHO YOU WANT TO BE.
IT'S TIME!! THE SHOWDOWN WE'VE BEEN WAITING FOR!!!
LEVIATHANS
FOWL PLAYS
WHICH KI'RAH WILL COME OUT VICTORIOUS!?

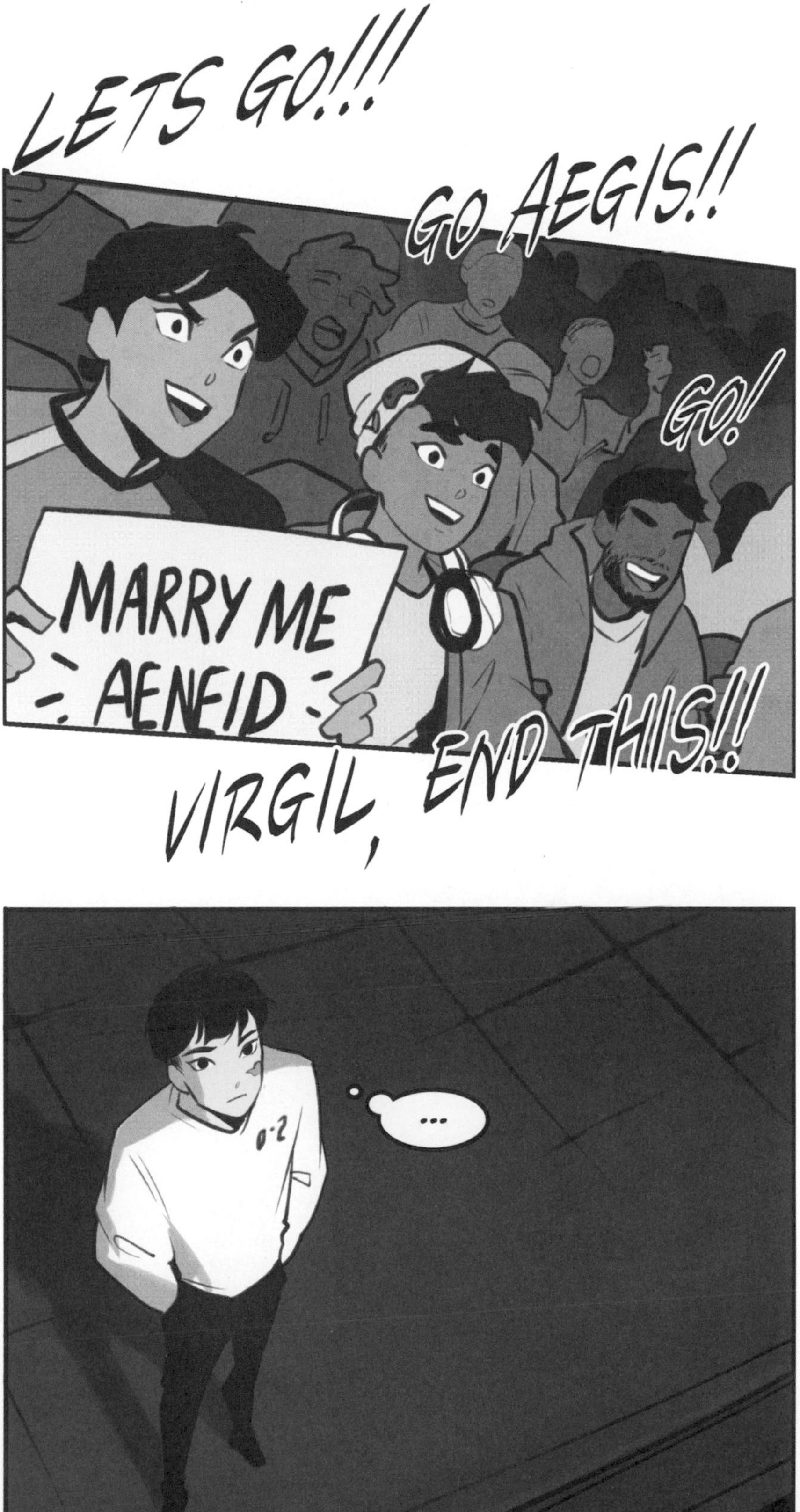
LETS GO!!!
GO AEGIS!!
GO!
MARRY ME AENEID
VIRGIL, END THIS!!
...

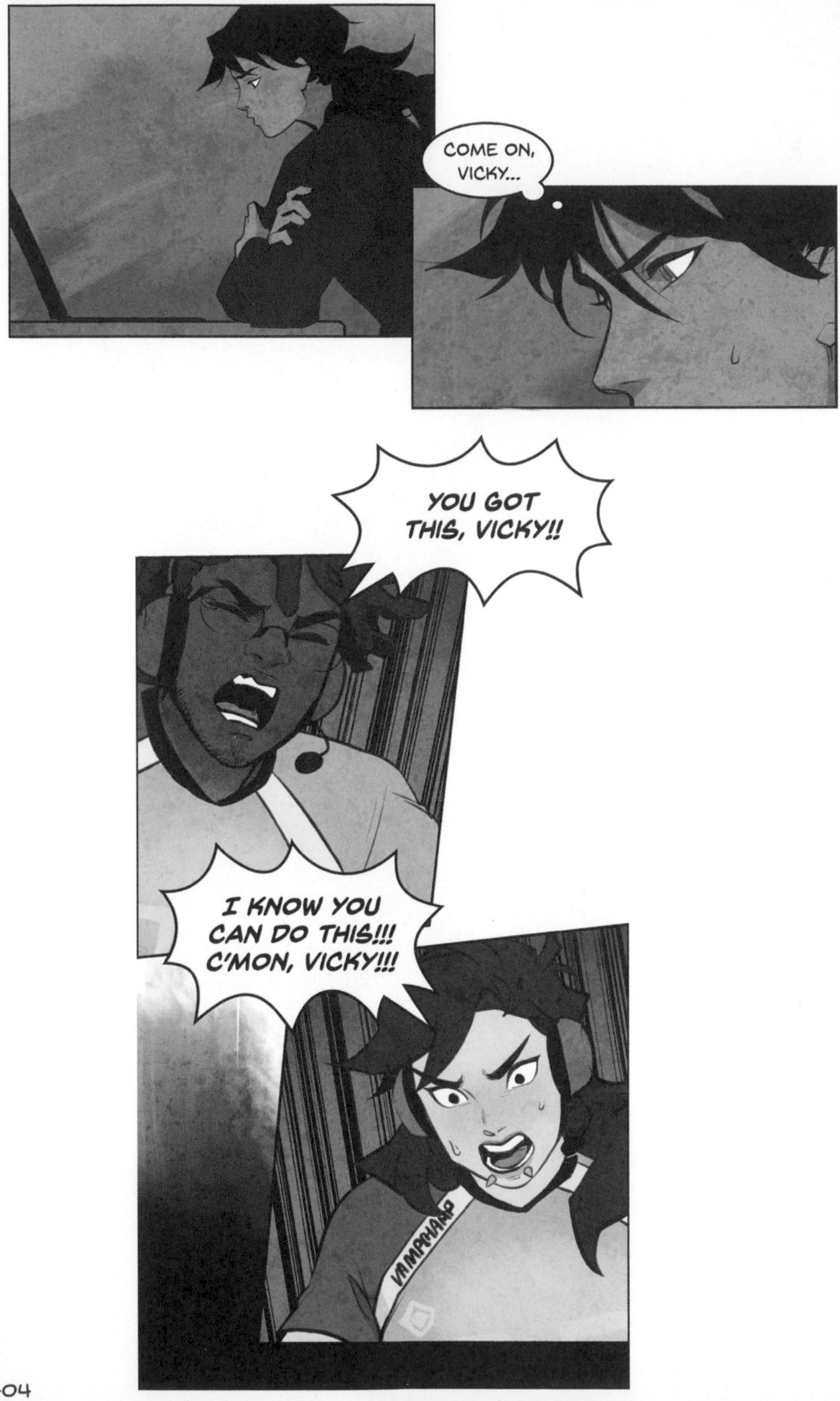
COME ON, VICKY...
YOU GOT THIS, VICKY!!
I KNOW YOU CAN DO THIS!!! C'MON, VICKY!!!

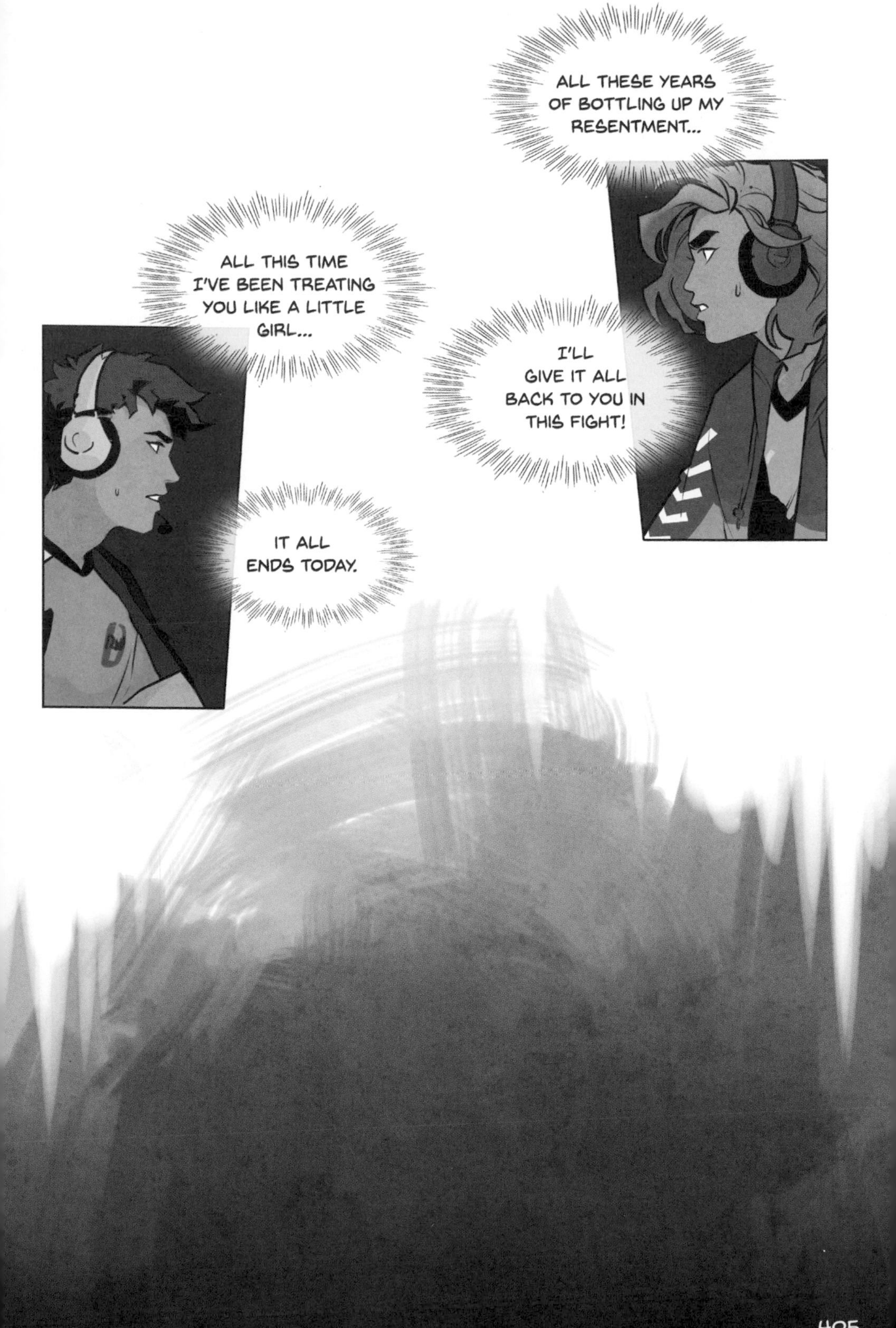
ALL THESE YEARS OF BOTTLING UP MY RESENTMENT...
ALL THIS TIME I'VE BEEN TREATING YOU LIKE A LITTLE GIRL...
I'LL GIVE IT ALL BACK TO YOU IN THIS FIGHT!
IT ALL ENDS TODAY.

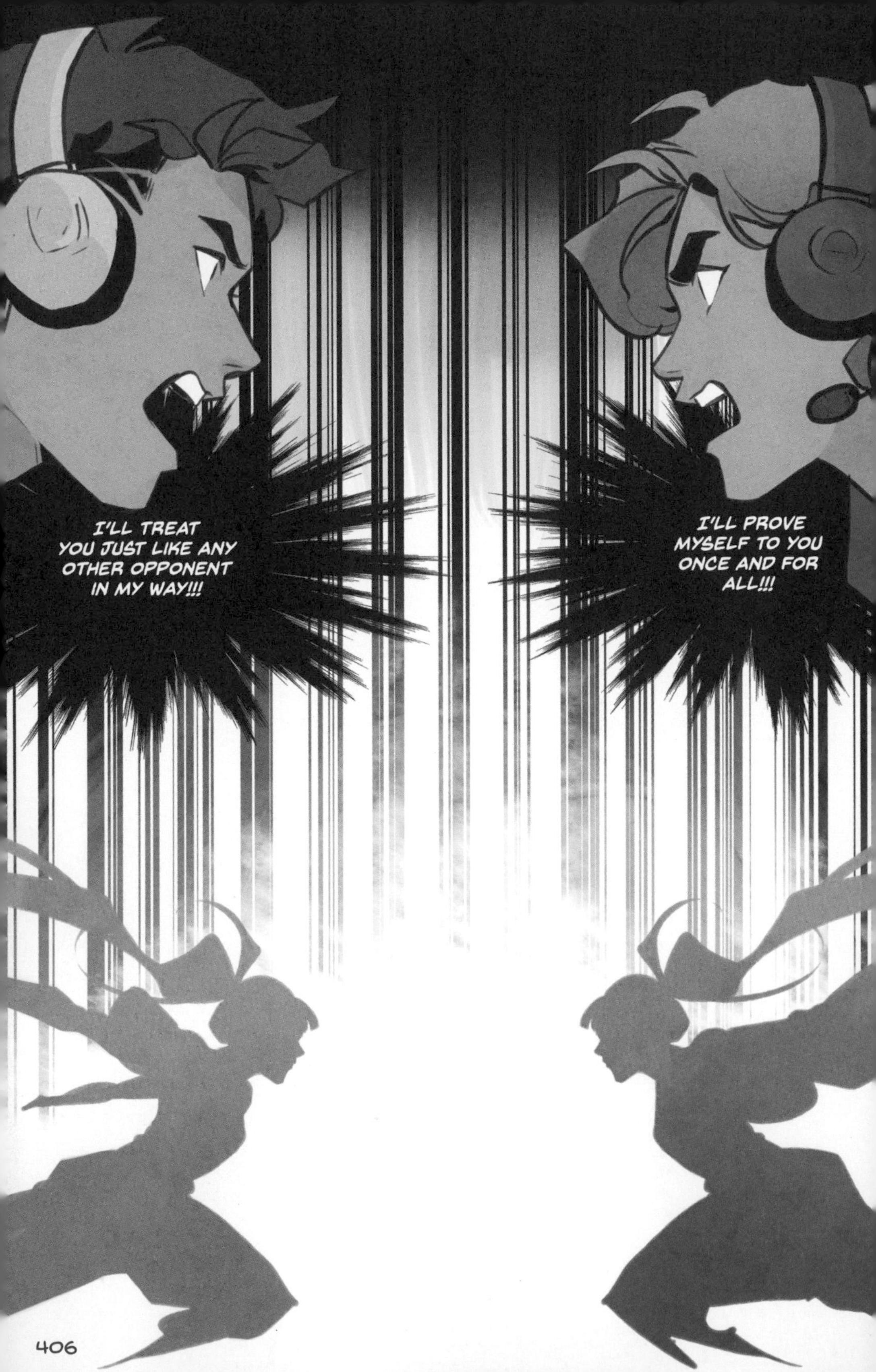
I'LL TREAT YOU JUST LIKE ANY OTHER OPPONENT IN MY WAY!!!
I'LL PROVE MYSELF TO YOU ONCE AND FOR ALL!!!

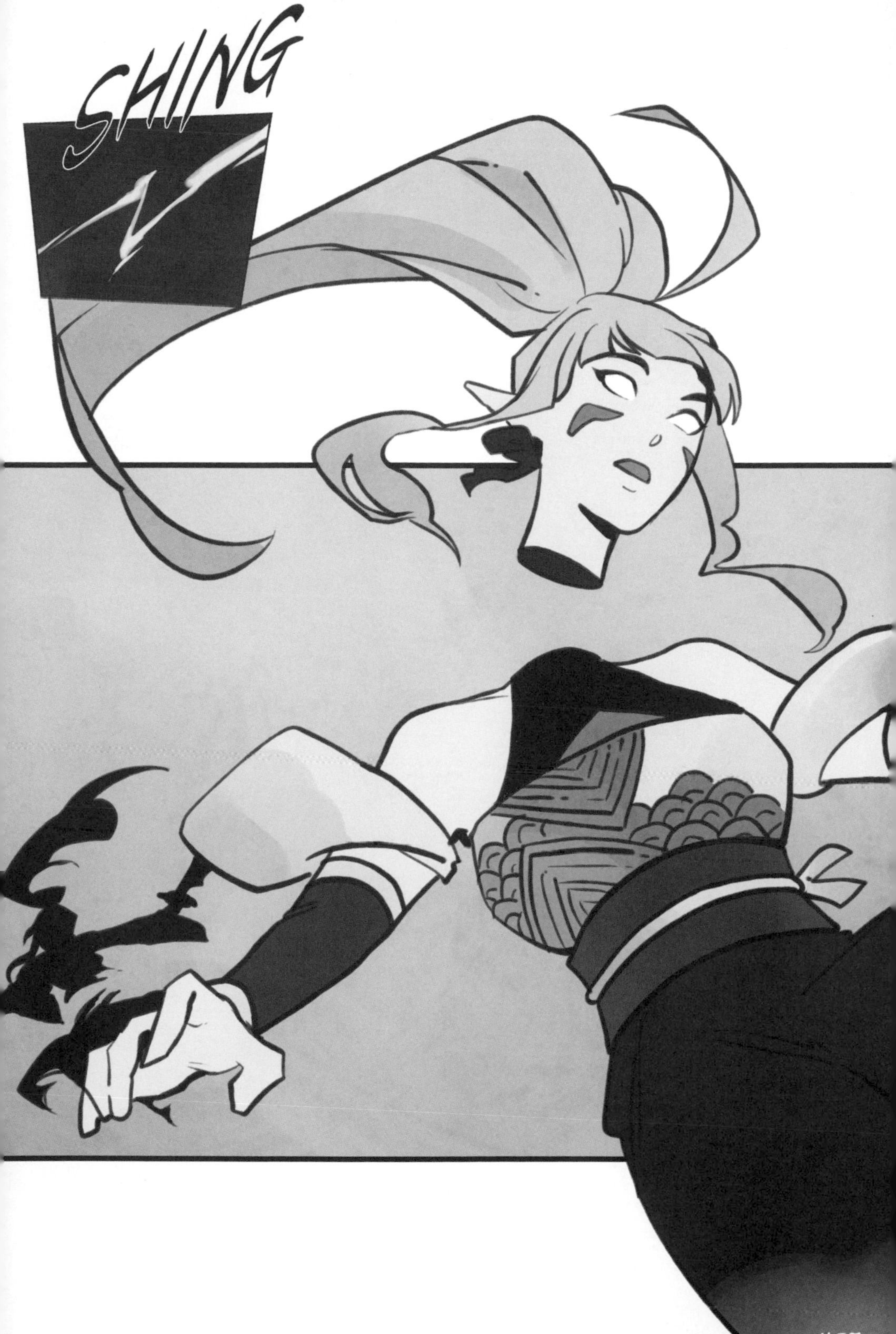
SHING

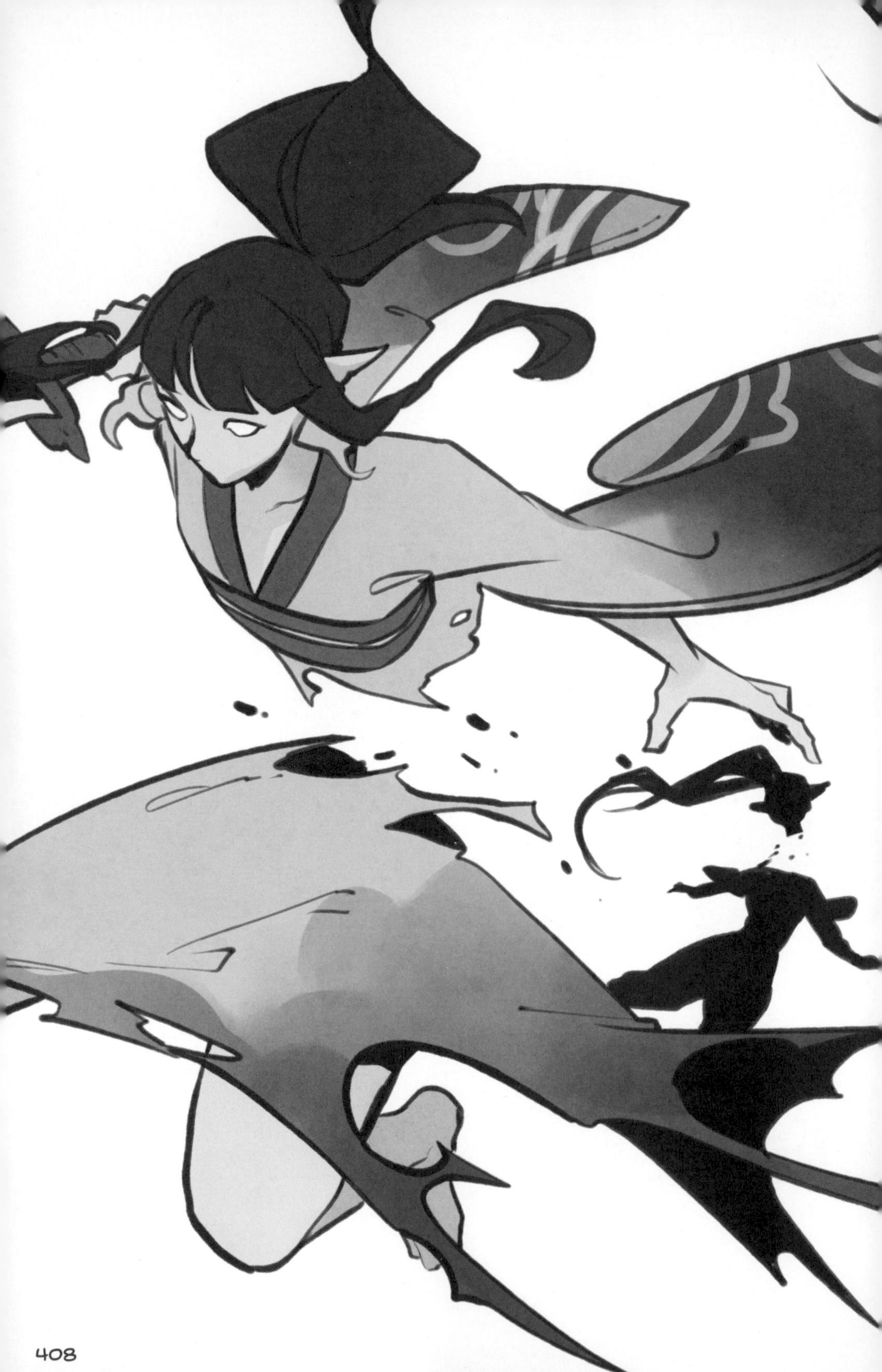

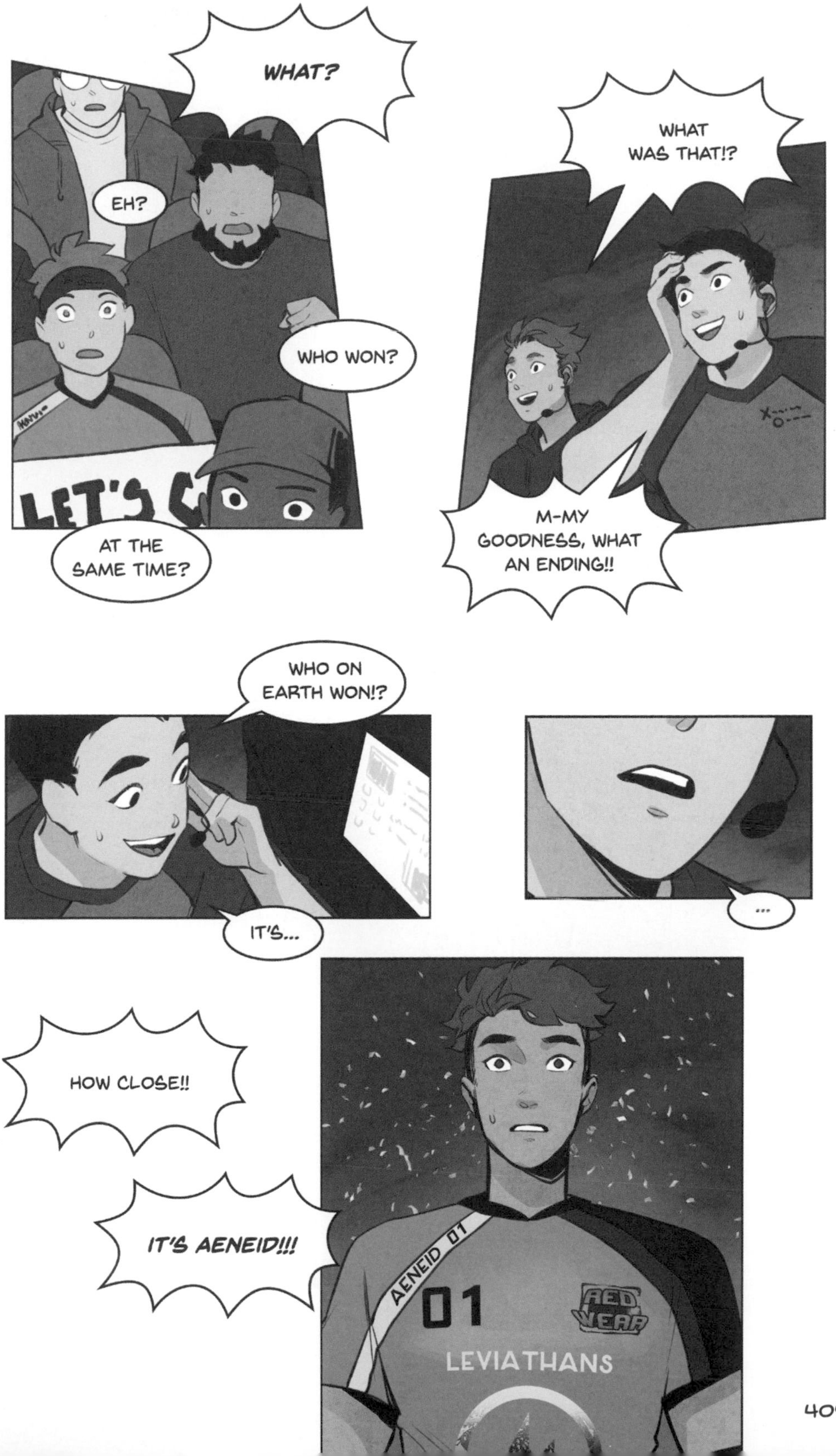
WHAT?
EH?
WHO WON?
AT THE SAME TIME?
WHAT WAS THAT!?
M-MY GOODNESS, WHAT AN ENDING!!
WHO ON EARTH WON!?
IT'S...
...
HOW CLOSE!!
IT'S AENEID!!!
AENEID 01
01
RED WEAR
LEVIATHANS

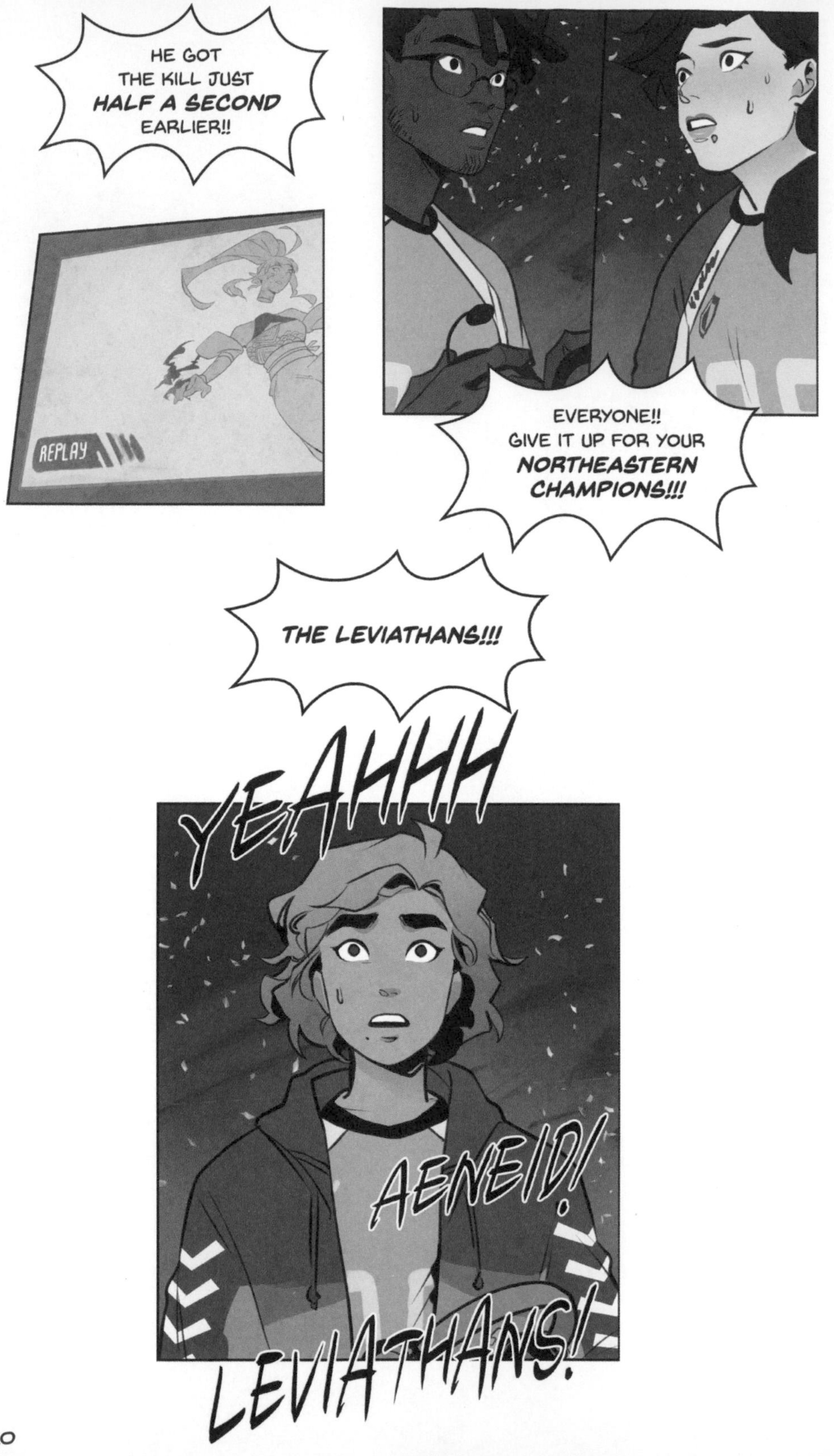
HE GOT THE KILL JUST **HALF A SECOND** EARLIER!!
REPLAY
EVERYONE!! GIVE IT UP FOR YOUR **NORTHEASTERN CHAMPIONS!!!**
THE LEVIATHANS!!!
YEAHHH
AENEID!
LEVIATHANS!

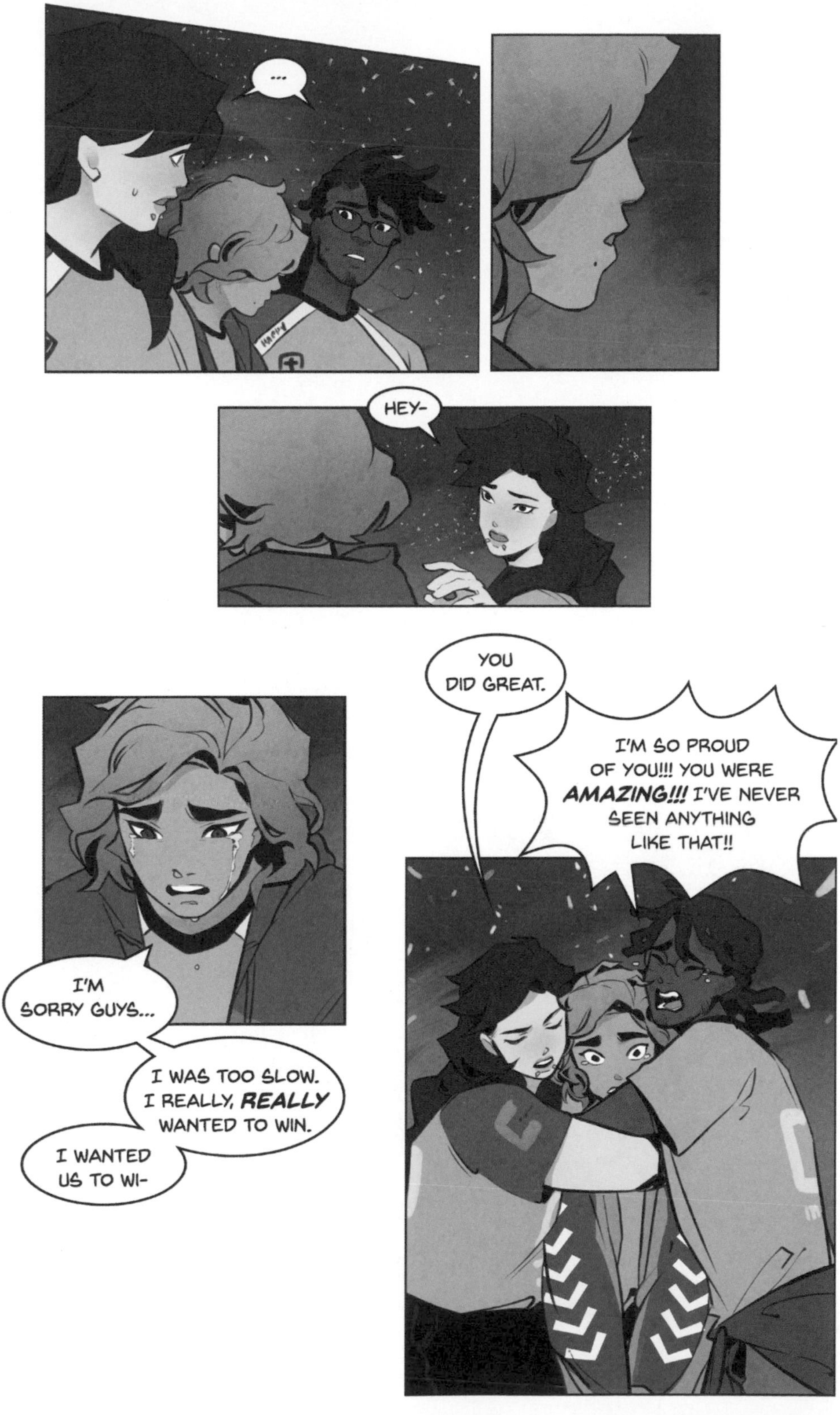
...
HEY-
I'M SORRY GUYS...
I WAS TOO SLOW. I REALLY, ***REALLY*** WANTED TO WIN.
I WANTED US TO WI-
YOU DID GREAT.
I'M SO PROUD OF YOU!!! YOU WERE ***AMAZING!!!*** I'VE NEVER SEEN ANYTHING LIKE THAT!!

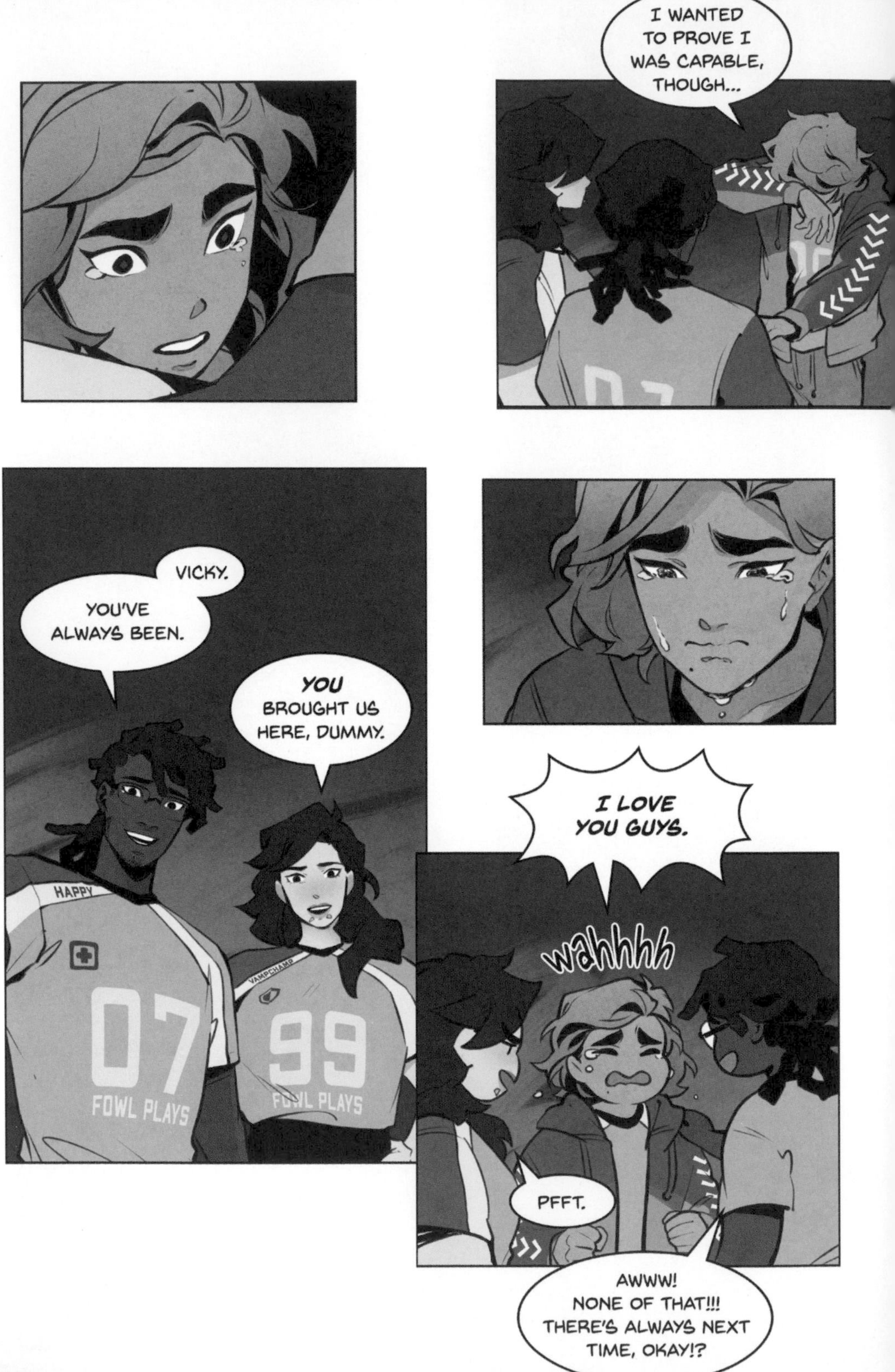
I WANTED TO PROVE I WAS CAPABLE, THOUGH...
VICKY.
YOU'VE ALWAYS BEEN.
YOU BROUGHT US HERE, DUMMY.
I LOVE YOU GUYS.
wahhhh
PFFT.
AWWW! NONE OF THAT!!! THERE'S ALWAYS NEXT TIME, OKAY!?

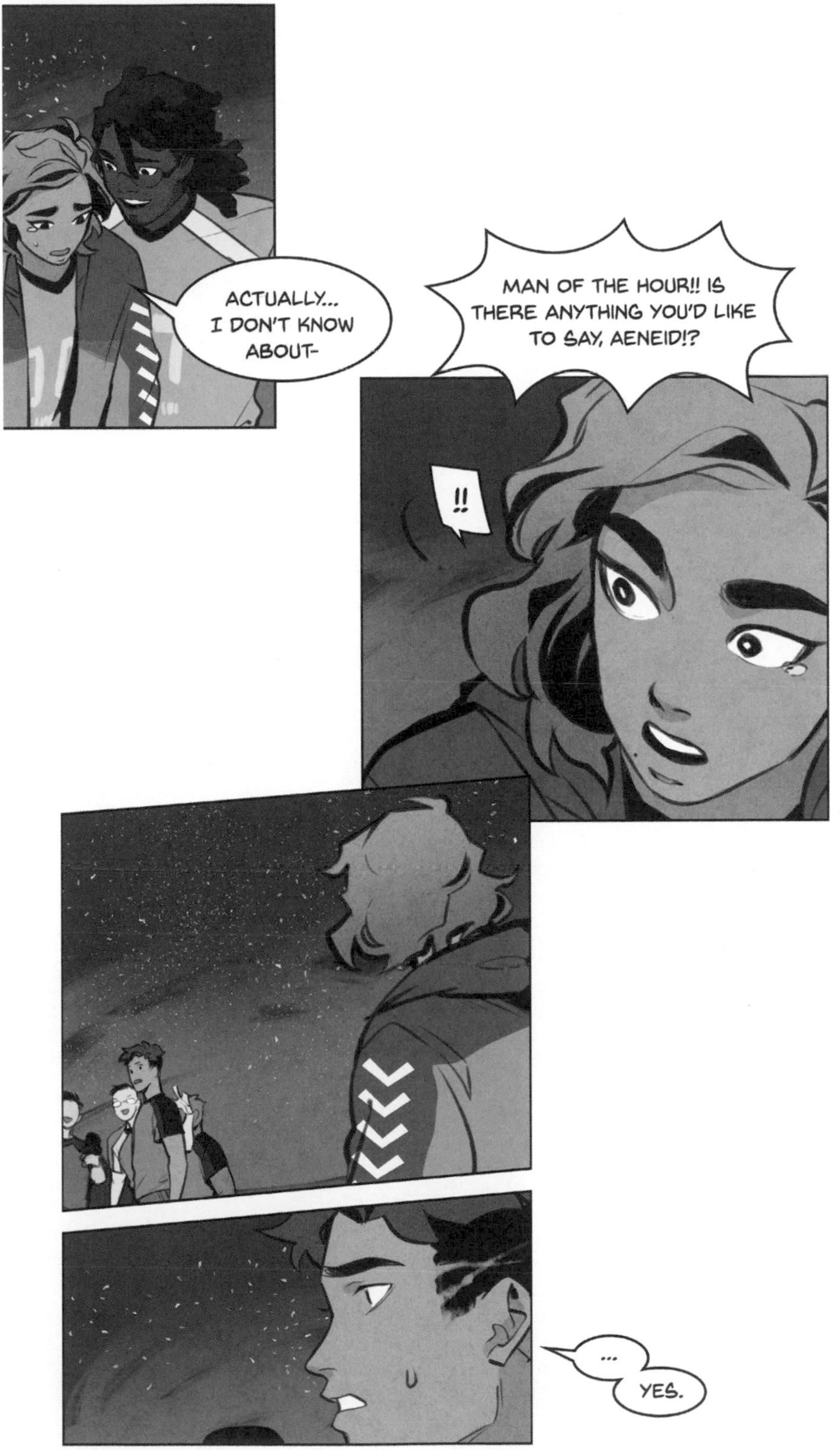
ACTUALLY... I DON'T KNOW ABOUT-
MAN OF THE HOUR!! IS THERE ANYTHING YOU'D LIKE TO SAY, AENEID!?
!!
...
YES.

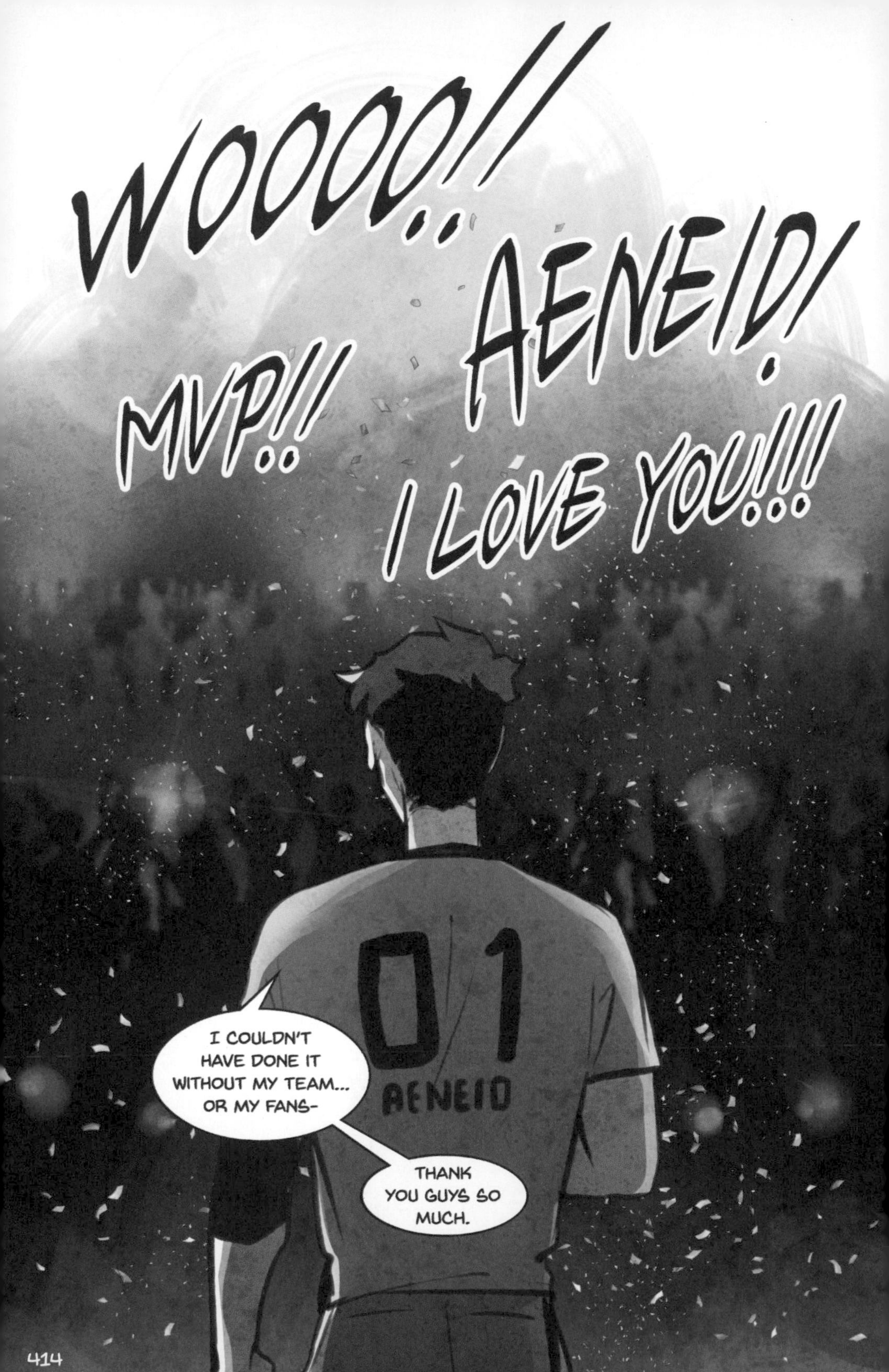
WOOOO!!
MVP!!
AENEID!
I LOVE YOU!!!
01
AENEID
I COULDN'T HAVE DONE IT WITHOUT MY TEAM... OR MY FANS-
THANK YOU GUYS SO MUCH.

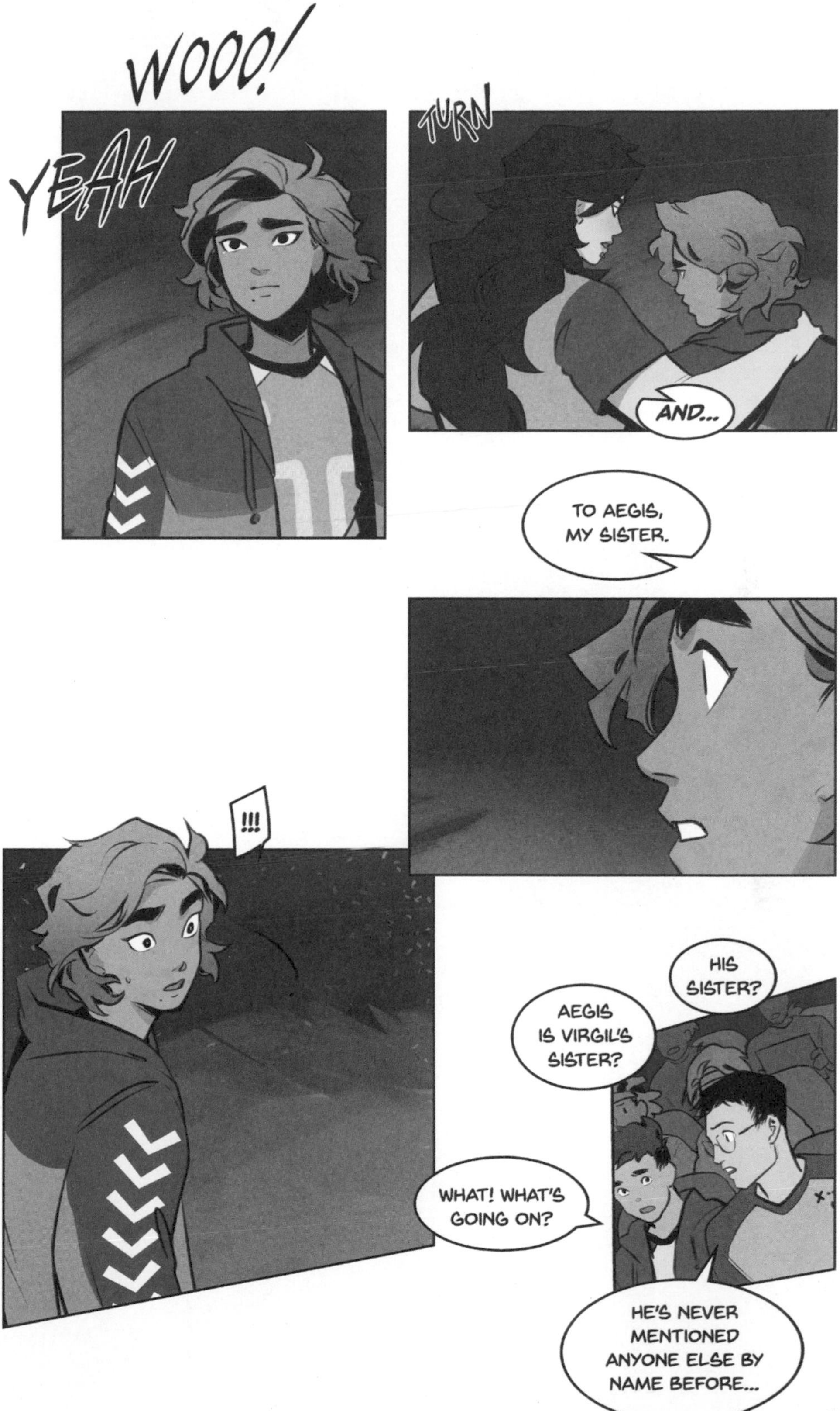
WOOO!
YEAH
TURN
AND...
TO AEGIS, MY SISTER.
!!!
AEGIS IS VIRGIL'S SISTER?
HIS SISTER?
WHAT! WHAT'S GOING ON?
HE'S NEVER MENTIONED ANYONE ELSE BY NAME BEFORE...

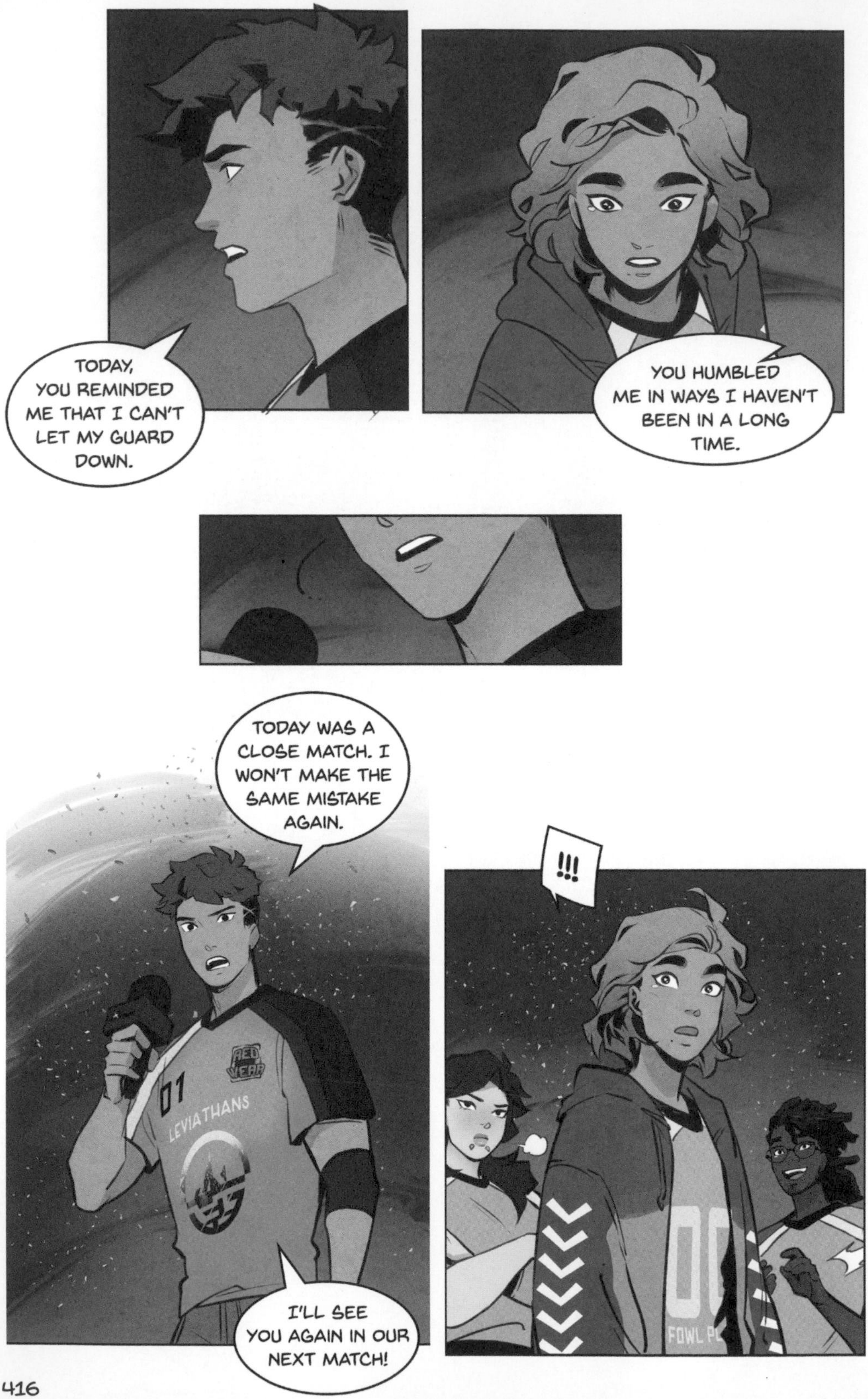
TODAY, YOU REMINDED ME THAT I CAN'T LET MY GUARD DOWN.
YOU HUMBLED ME IN WAYS I HAVEN'T BEEN IN A LONG TIME.
TODAY WAS A CLOSE MATCH. I WON'T MAKE THE SAME MISTAKE AGAIN.
01
LEVIATHANS
I'LL SEE YOU AGAIN IN OUR NEXT MATCH!
!!!

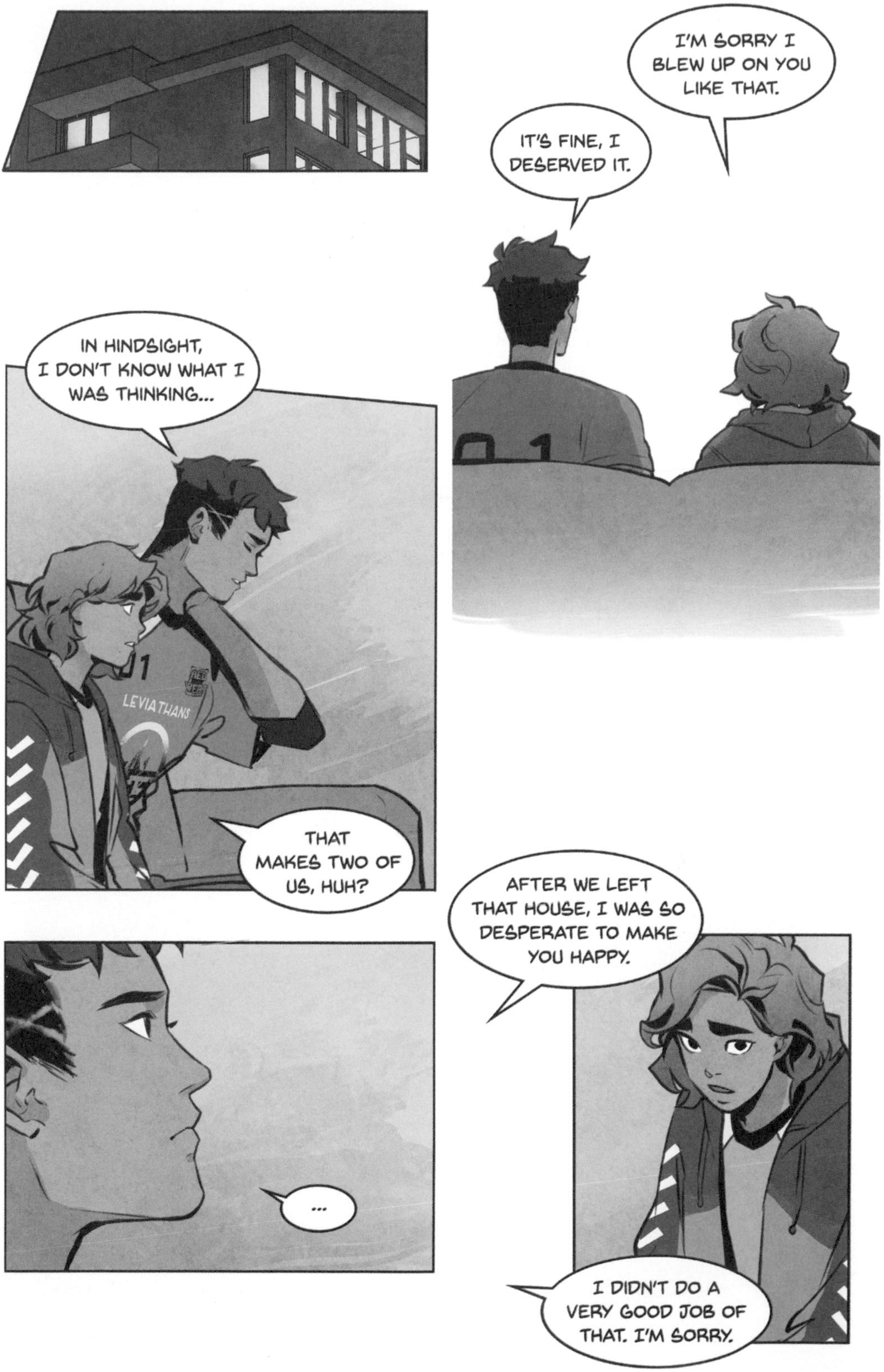
I'M SORRY I BLEW UP ON YOU LIKE THAT.
IT'S FINE, I DESERVED IT.
IN HINDSIGHT, I DON'T KNOW WHAT I WAS THINKING...
LEVIATHANS
THAT MAKES TWO OF US, HUH?
...
AFTER WE LEFT THAT HOUSE, I WAS SO DESPERATE TO MAKE YOU HAPPY.
I DIDN'T DO A VERY GOOD JOB OF THAT. I'M SORRY.

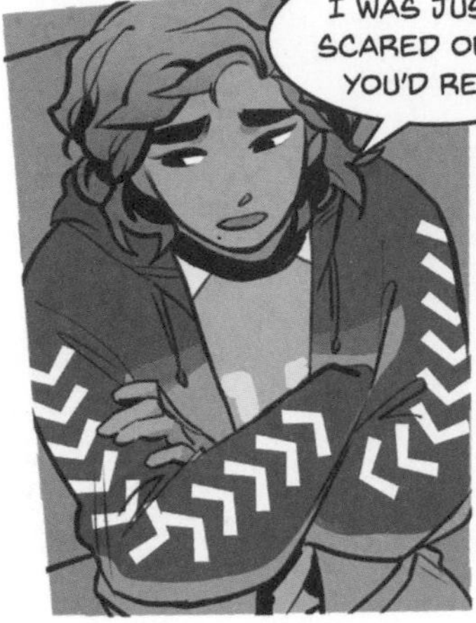
I'M SORRY FOR ALWAYS KEEPING STUFF FROM YOU, TOO.
I WAS JUST SO SCARED OF HOW YOU'D REACT.

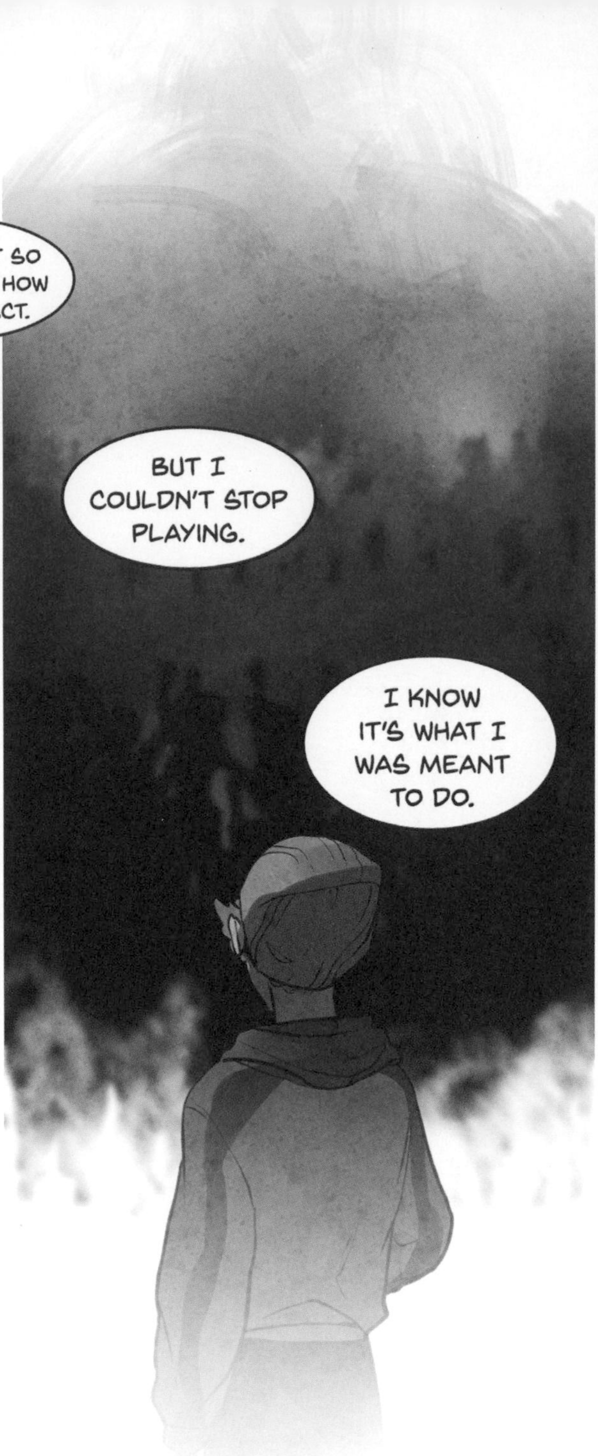
BUT I COULDN'T STOP PLAYING.
I KNOW IT'S WHAT I WAS MEANT TO DO.
NO MATTER WHAT YOU THOUGHT OF ME.

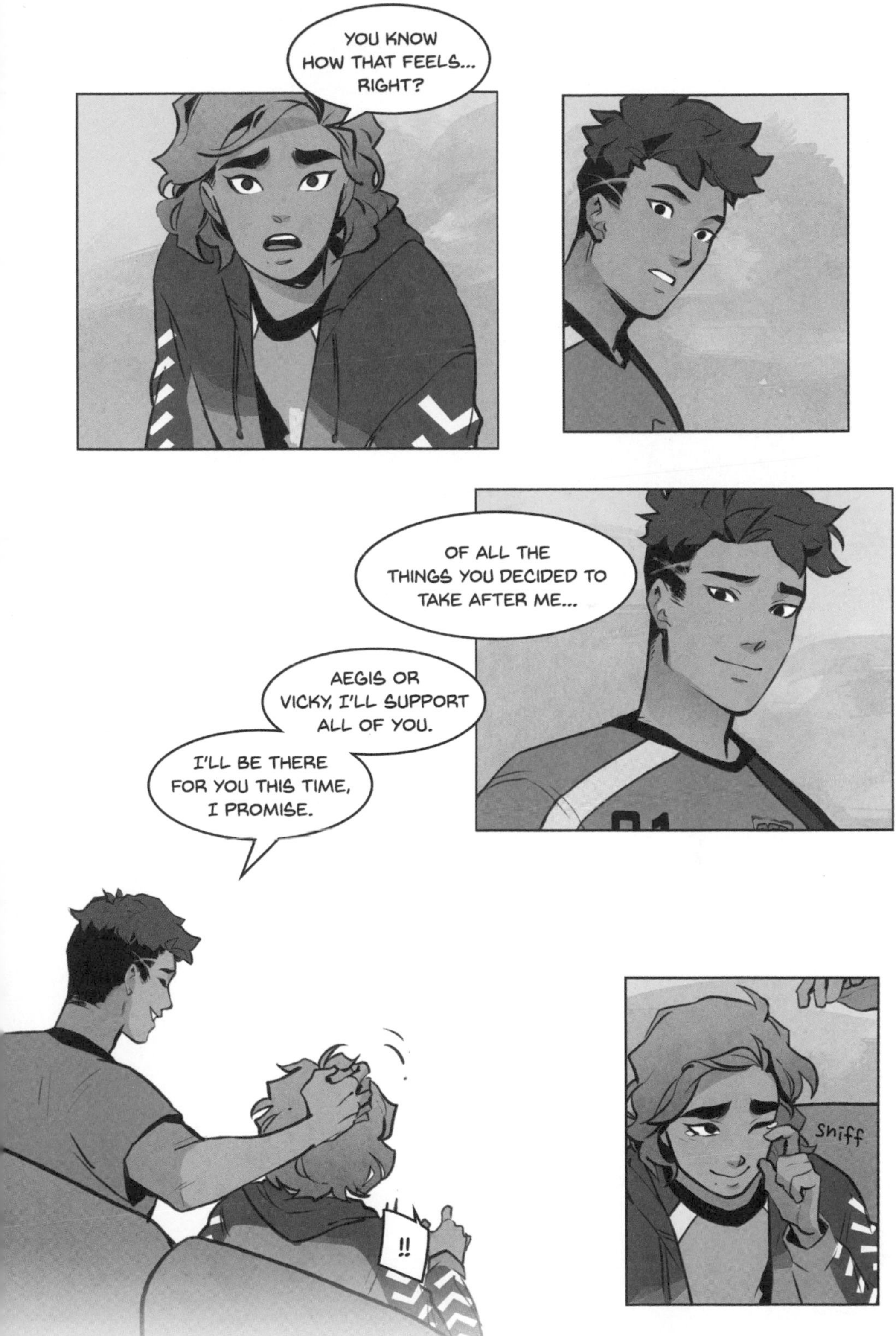
YOU KNOW HOW THAT FEELS... RIGHT?
OF ALL THE THINGS YOU DECIDED TO TAKE AFTER ME...
AEGIS OR VICKY, I'LL SUPPORT ALL OF YOU.
I'LL BE THERE FOR YOU THIS TIME, I PROMISE.
!!
sniff

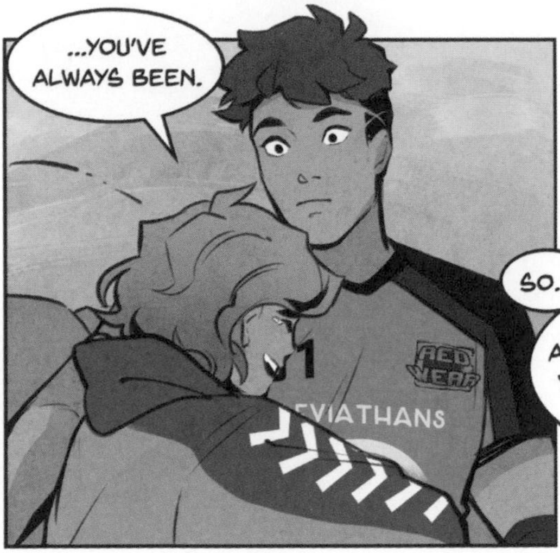
...YOU'VE ALWAYS BEEN.
RED WEAR
LEVIATHANS
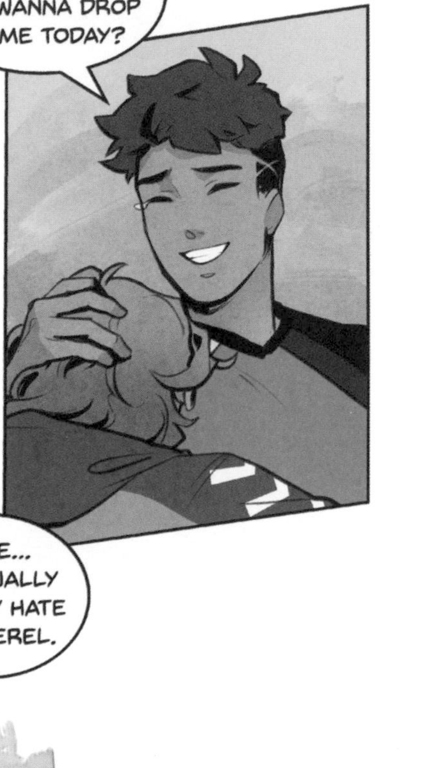
SO...
ARE THERE ANY OTHER BOMBS YOU WANNA DROP ON ME TODAY?
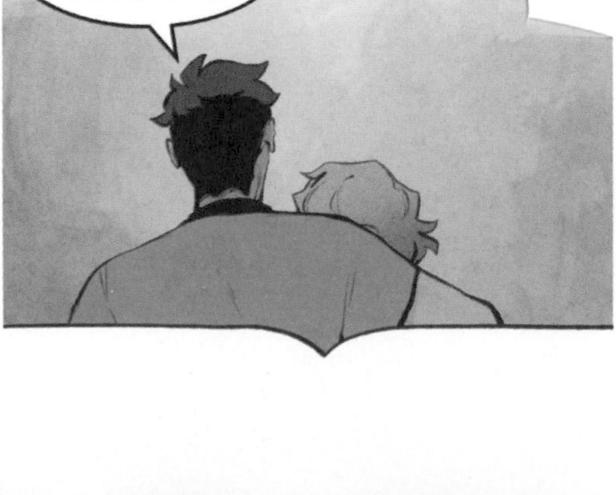
HEHE... I ACTUALLY REALLY HATE MACKEREL.
OH THANK GOD. I CAN'T EAT ANY MORE OF IT.

EARLY CONCEPTS

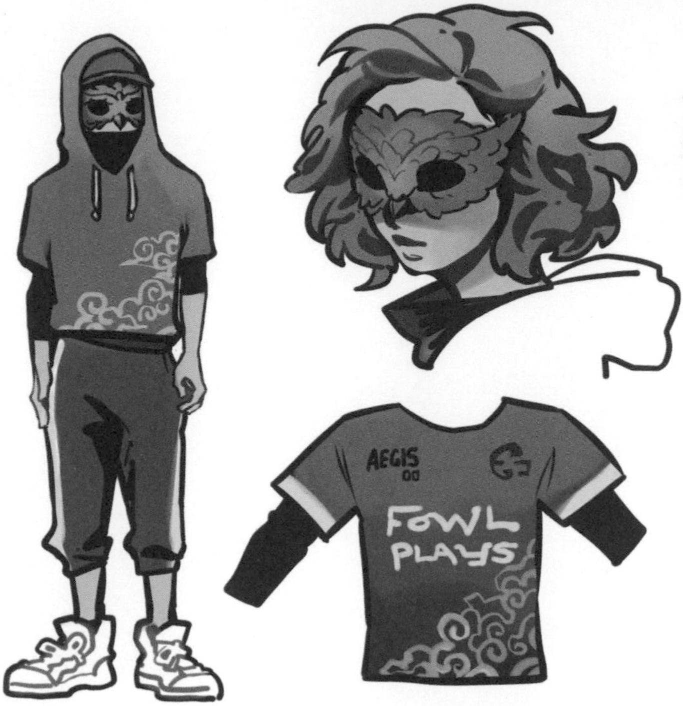
AEGIS
00
FOWL PLAYS

INITIAL JERSEY DESIGNS.
THE CLOUDS WERE KIND OF NEAT BUT MAYBE A TAD BIT TOO PRETENTIOUS FOR A TEAM THAT SPROUTED OUT OF VIRTUALLY NOWHERE.

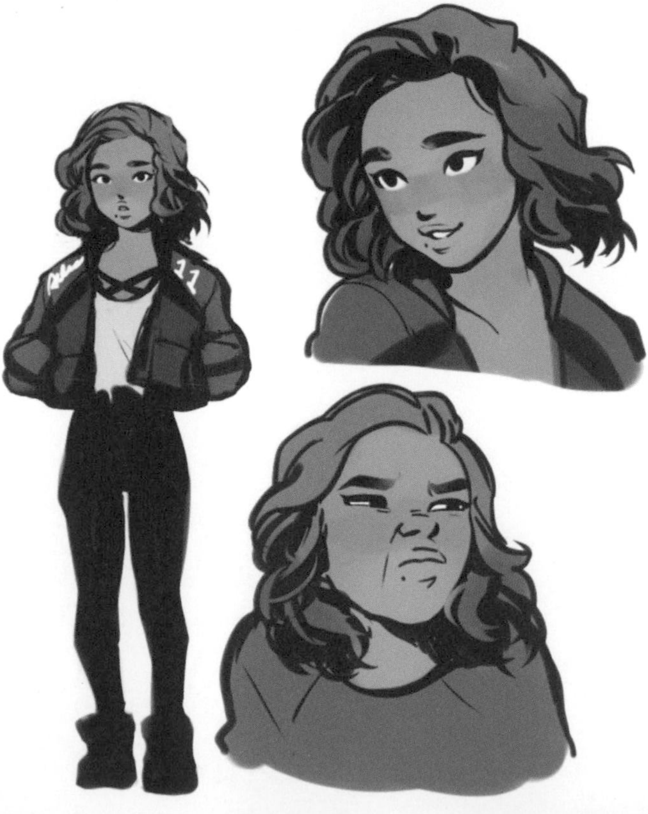
11

EVERYONE'S DESIGNS WERE MORE OR LESS FLESHED OUT, I DIDN'T HAVE TO GO THROUGH MANY CHANGES TO SETTLE ON THEIR FINAL DESIGNS! HOWEVER, THEIR OUTFITS WERE CHALLENGING, SINCE ESPORTS WEAR TENDS TO BE QUITE COLORFUL. VICKY AND VIRGIL'S JERSEYS GAVE ME SO MUCH TROUBLE, AND I ESPECIALLY HAD TROUBLE CHOOSING THE RIGHT FONTS AND COMPOSITION ON THEIR TEAM JERSEYS.

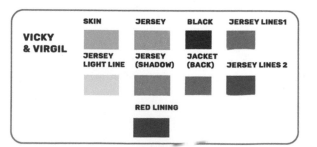

VICKY & VIRGIL

SKIN	JERSEY	BLACK	JERSEY LINES1
JERSEY LIGHT LINE	JERSEY (SHADOW)	JACKET (BACK)	JERSEY LINES 2
	RED LINING		

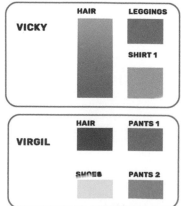

VICKY

| HAIR | LEGGINGS |
| | SHIRT 1 |

VIRGIL

| HAIR | PANTS 1 |
| SHOES | PANTS 2 |

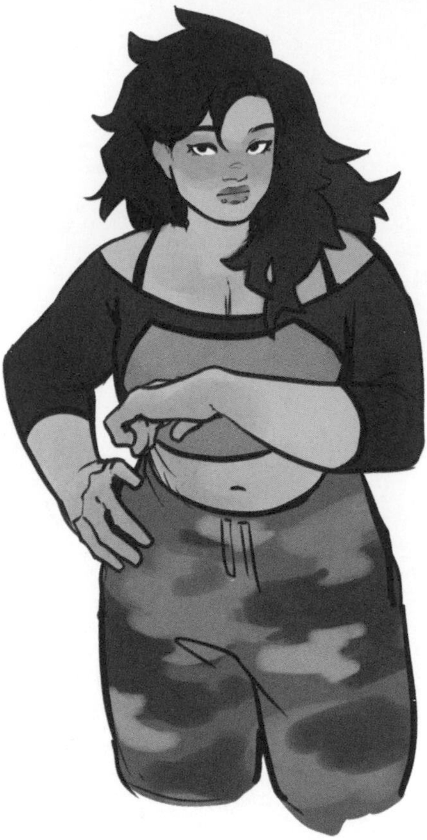

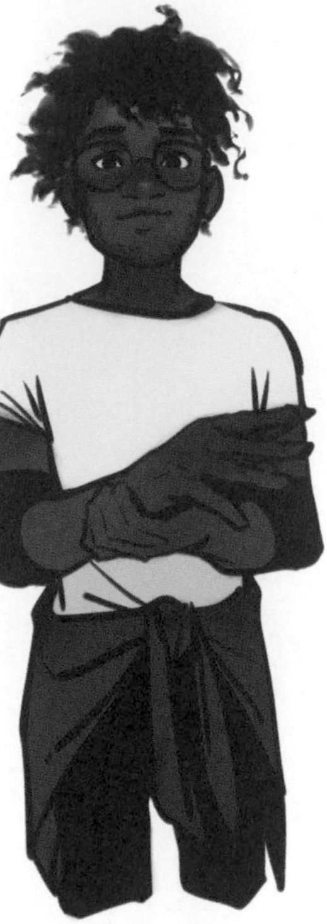

I DIDN'T HAVE TO PLAY AROUND MUCH WITH OPAL'S DESIGN. I ALWAYS PICTURED HER LIKE THIS IN MY MIND! I REALLY WANTED HER TO LOOK LIKE SOMEONE WHO REFUSED TO BE PUSHED AROUND AND SOMEONE YOU COULD RELY ON AS A FRIEND. LIKE A PILLAR! OR A TANK.

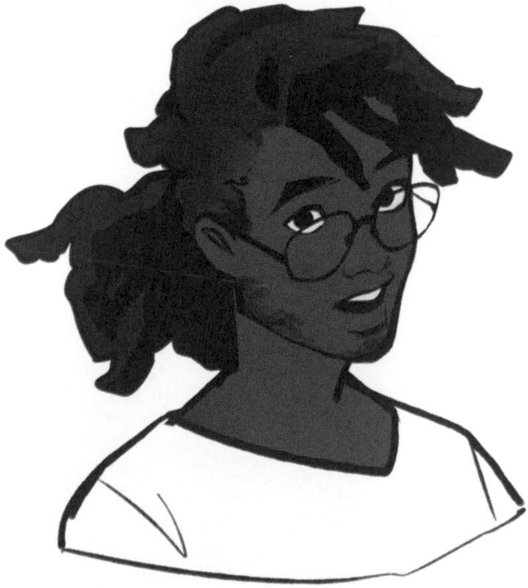

ERIC WAS INITIALLY YOUNGER! HE WAS MEANT TO BE VICKY AND OPAL'S AGE IN EARLY STAGES OF THE STORY, AND FORM AN ESPORTS TEAM AT THEIR HIGH SCHOOL WITH THE TWO. HOWEVER, THE STORY CHANGED AND ERIC BECAME CO-OWNER OF THE CAF-E, MEANING HE'D BE AN ADULT. I LIKE HOW HE LOOKS MUCH MORE NOW, TO BE HONEST.

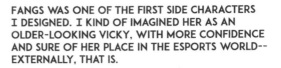

FANGS WAS ONE OF THE FIRST SIDE CHARACTERS I DESIGNED. I KIND OF IMAGINED HER AS AN OLDER-LOOKING VICKY, WITH MORE CONFIDENCE AND SURE OF HER PLACE IN THE ESPORTS WORLD-- EXTERNALLY, THAT IS.

THE RED JERSEY IS SUPPOSED TO BE SHARP AND DEADLY, SOLIDIFYING HER AS A POWERFUL FOE FOR THE FOWL PLAYERS.

FIVE WASN'T DESIGNED LITERALLY FIVE MINUTES BEFORE I BEGAN DRAWING THE EPISODE HE DEBUTED IN. ABSOLUTELY NOT!

ACKNOWLEDGMENTS

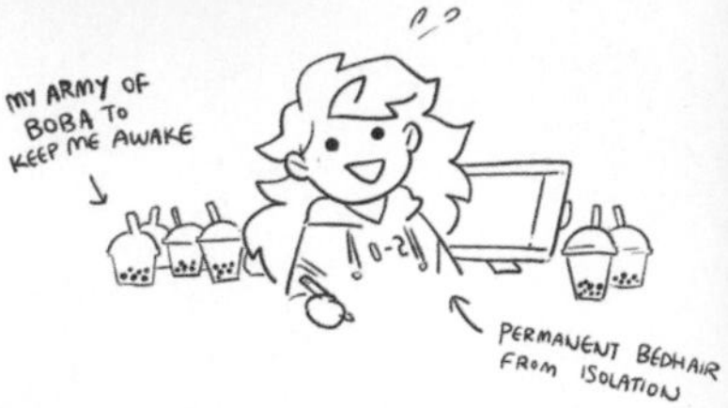
MY ARMY OF BOBA TO KEEP ME AWAKE
PERMANENT BEDHAIR FROM ISOLATION

Thank you to everyone that's read *DPS Only!* I'm so grateful for all the support this comic has gotten. Truly, I'm very grateful. I made a lot of mistakes during the creation of *DPS Only!* but I learned so much more because of them. In some strange way, I feel like I've grown with Vicky.

Massive thank yous to the Tapas team, especially Gabby for editing, Dojo and Serpyra for coloring, Claire for lettering, Hayden for keeping us on track, and Michael for the opportunity! Thank you to Alex and to Andrews McMeel Publishing for bringing this to print. Without you lovely folks, *DPS Only!* would have remained a weird e-sports anime fever dream in my head.

And thank you readers once again for reading, enjoying, and supporting *DPS Only!* It was a pleasure to write a story that resonated with you and kept you entertained for a short while.

Until next time!

–Velinxi

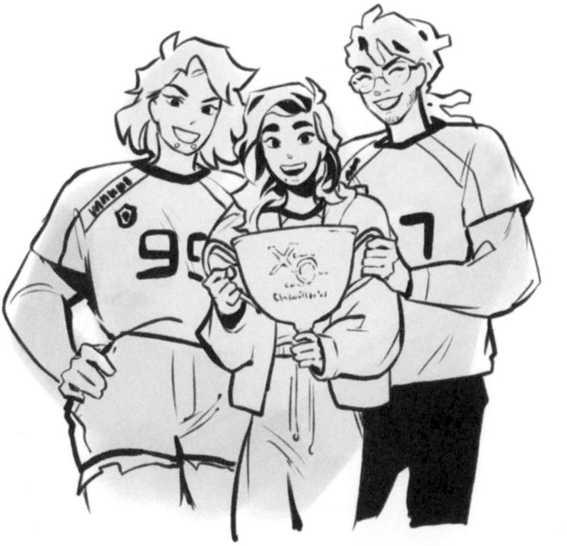

ABOUT THE AUTHOR

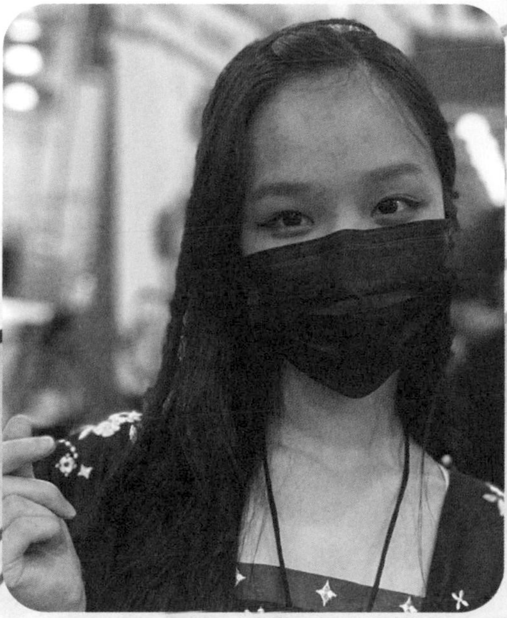

Author photo: Maddie Kong

Xiao Tong "Velinxi" Kong is the creator of *DPS Only!* and the ongoing webcomic *Countdown to Countdown*. Her greatest passion lies in storytelling through illustrations, which she has been doing for the past few years (with varying stages of success). You can find more of her work on Twitter and Instagram @Velinxi, including sneak peeks of her future projects, fan art, and occasional memes.

PICK UP GREAT GRAPHIC NOVELS FROM TAPAS!

Available wherever books are sold.